LES MISÉRABLES

LES MISÉRABLES

VOLUME 2

Victor Hugo

The second part of a novel bound in two volumes

WORDSWORTH CLASSICS

This edition published 1994 by Wordsworth Editions Limited
Cumberland House, Crib Street, Ware, Hertfordshire SG12 9ET

ISBN 1 85326 050 9

Typeset by Antony Gray
Printed and bound in Great Britain by
Mackays of Chatham plc, Chatham, Kent

PART THREE: MARIUS

continued

BOOK 6: THE CONJUNCTION OF TWO STARS *CONTINUED*

5. *Sundry thunderbolts fall upon Ma'am Bougon*

Next day, Ma'am Bougon – thus Courfeyrac designated the old portress-landlady of the Gorbeau tenement – Ma'am Bougon – her name was in reality Madame Bougon, as we have stated, but this terrible fellow Courfeyrac respected nothing – Ma'am Bougon was stupefied with astonishment to see Monsieur Marius go out again with his new coat.

He went again to the Luxembourg, but did not get beyond his seat midway of the walk. He sat down there as on the day previous, gazing from a distance and seeing distinctly the white hat, the black dress, and especially the bluish light. He did not stir from the seat, and did not go home until the gates of the Luxembourg were shut. He did not see Monsieur Leblanc and his daughter retire. He concluded from that that they left the garden by the gate on the Rue de l'Ouest. Later, some weeks afterwards, when he thought of it, he could not remember where he had dined that night.

The next day, for the third time, Ma'am Bougon was thunderstruck. Marius went out with his new suit. 'Three days running!' she exclaimed.

She made an attempt to follow him, but Marius walked briskly and with immense strides; it was a hippopotamus undertaking to catch a chamois. In two minutes she lost sight of him, and came back out of breath, three quarters choked by her asthma, and furious. 'The silly fellow,' she muttered, 'to put on his handsome clothes every day and make people run like that!'

Marius had gone to the Luxembourg.

The young girl was there with Monsieur Leblanc. Marius approached as near as he could, seeming to be reading a book, but he was still very far off, then he returned and sat down on his seat, where he spent four hours watching the artless little sparrows as they hopped along the walk; they seemed to him to be mocking him.

Thus a fortnight rolled away. Marius went to the Luxembourg, no longer to promenade, but to sit down, always in the same place, and without knowing why. Once there he did not stir. Every morning he put on his new suit, not to be conspicuous, and he began again the next morning.

She was indeed of a marvellous beauty. The only remark which could be made, that would resemble a criticism, is that the contradiction between her look, which was sad, and her smile, which was joyous, gave to her countenance something a little wild, which produced this effect, that at certain moments this sweet face became strange without ceasing to be charming.

6. *Taken prisoner*

On one of the last days of the second week, Marius was as usual sitting on his seat, holding in his hand an open book of which he had not turned a leaf for two hours. Suddenly he trembled. A great event was commencing at the end of the walk. Monsieur Leblanc and his daughter had left their seat, the daughter had taken the arm of the father, and they were coming slowly towards the middle of the walk where Marius was. Marius closed his book, then he opened it, then he made an attempt to read. He trembled. The halo was coming straight towards him. 'O dear!' thought he, 'I shall not have time to take an attitude.' However, the man with the white hair and the young girl were advancing. It seemed to him that it would last a century, and that it was only a second. 'What are they coming by here for?' he asked himself. 'What! is she going to pass this place! Are her feet to press this ground in this walk, but a step from me?' He was overwhelmed, he would gladly have been very handsome, he would gladly have worn the cross of the Legion of Honour. He heard the gentle and measured sound of their steps approaching. He imagined that Monsieur Leblanc was hurling angry looks upon him. 'Is he going to speak to me?' thought he. He bowed his head; when he raised it they were quite near him. The young girl passed, and in passing she looked at him. She looked at him steadily, with a sweet and thoughtful look which made Marius tremble from head to foot. It seemed to him that she reproached him for having been so long without coming to her, and that she said: 'It is I who come.' Marius was bewildered by these eyes full of flashing light and fathomless abysses.

He felt as though his brain were on fire. She had come to him, what happiness! And then, how she had looked at him! She seemed more beautiful than she had ever seemed before. Beautiful with a beauty which combined all of the woman with all of the angel, a beauty which would have made Petrarch sing and Dante kneel. He felt as though he was swimming in the deep blue sky. At the same time he was horribly disconcerted, because he had a little dust on his boots.

He felt sure that she had seen his boots in this condition.

He followed her with his eyes till she disappeared, then he began to walk in the Luxembourg like a madman. It is probable that at times he laughed, alone as he was, and spoke aloud. He was so strange and dreamy when near the child's nurses that everyone thought he was in love with her.

He went out of the Luxembourg to find her again in some street.

He met Courfeyrac under the arches of the Odeon and said: 'Come and dine with me.' They went to Rousseau's and spent six francs. Marius ate like an ogre. He gave six sous to the waiter. At dessert he said to Courfeyrac: 'Have you read the paper? What a fine speech Audry de Puyraveau has made!'

He was desperately in love.

After dinner he said to Courfeyrac, 'Come to the theatre with me.' They went to the Porte Saint Martin to see Frederick in *L'Auberge des Adrets*. Marius was hugely amused.

At the same time he became still more strange and incomprehensible. On leaving the theatre, he refused to look at the garter of a little milliner who was crossing a gutter, and when Courfeyrac said: '*I would not object to putting that woman in my collection*,' it almost horrified him.

Courfeyrac invited him to breakfast next morning at the Café Voltaire. Marius went and ate still more than the day before. He was very thoughtful, and yet very gay. One would have said that he seized upon all possible occasions to burst out laughing. To every country-fellow who was introduced to him he gave a tender embrace. A circle of students gathered round the table, and there was talk of the flummery paid for by the government, which was retailed at the Sorbonne; then the conversation fell upon the faults and gaps in the dictionaries and prosodies of Quicherat. Marius interrupted the discussion by exclaiming: 'However, it is a very pleasant thing to have the Cross.'

'He is a comical fellow!' said Courfeyrac, aside to Jean Prouvaire.

'No,' replied Jean Prouvaire, 'he is serious.'

He was serious, indeed. Marius was in this first vehement and fascinating period in which the grand passion commences.

One glance had done all that.

When the mine is loaded, and the match is ready, nothing is simpler. A glance is a spark.

It was all over with him. Marius loved a woman. His destiny was entering upon the unknown.

The glances of women are like certain apparently peaceful but really formidable machines. You pass them every day quietly, with impunity, and without suspicion of danger. There comes a moment when you forget even that they are there. You come and go, you muse, and talk, and laugh. Suddenly you feel that you are seized! it is done. The wheels have caught you, the glance has captured you. It has taken you, no matter how or where, by any portion whatever of your thought which was trailing, through any absence of mind. You are lost. You will be drawn in entirely. A train of mysterious forces has gained possession of you. You struggle in vain. No human succour is possible. You will be drawn down from wheel to wheel, from anguish to anguish, from torture to torture. You, your mind, your fortune, your future, your soul; and you will not escape from the terrible machine, until, according as you are in the power of a malevolent nature, or a noble heart, you shall be disfigured by shame or transfigured by love.

7. *Adventures of the letter U abandoned to conjecture*

ISOLATION, SEPARATION from all things, pride, independence, a taste for nature, lack of everyday material activity, life in oneself, the secret struggles of chastity, and an ecstasy of goodwill towards the whole creation, had prepared Marius for this possession which is called love. His worship for his father had become almost a religion, and, like all religion, had retired into the depths of his heart. He needed something above that. Love came.

A whole month passed during which Marius went every day to the Luxembourg. When the hour came, nothing could keep him away. 'He is out at service,' said Courfeyrac. Marius lived in transports. It is certain that the young girl looked at him.

He finally grew bolder, and approached nearer to the seat. However he passed before it no more, obeying at once the instinct of timidity and the instinct of prudence, peculiar to lovers. He thought it better not to attract the 'attention of the father.' He formed his combinations of stations behind trees and the pedestals of statues with consummate art, so as to be seen as much as possible by the young girl and as little as possible by the old gentleman. Sometimes he would stand for half an hour motionless behind some Leonidas or Spartacus with a book in his hand, over which his eyes, timidly raised, were looking for the young girl, while she, for her part, was turning her charming profile towards him, suffused with a smile. While yet talking in the most natural and quiet way in the world with the white-haired man, she rested upon Marius all the dreams of a maidenly and passionate eye. Ancient and immemorial art which Eve knew from the first day of the world, and which every woman knows from the first day of her life! Her tongue replied to one and her eyes to the other.

We must, however, suppose that M. Leblanc perceived something of this at last, for often when Marius came, he would rise and begin to promenade. He had left their accustomed place, and had taken the seat at the other end of the walk, near the Gladiator, as if to see whether Marius would follow them. Marius did not understand it, and committed that blunder. 'The father' began to be less punctual, and did not bring 'his daughter' every day. Sometimes he came alone. Then Marius did not stay. Another blunder.

Marius took no note of these symptoms. From the phase of timidity he had passed, a natural and inevitable progress, to the phase of blindness. His love grew. He dreamed of her every night. And then there came to him a good fortune for which he had not even hoped, oil upon the fire, double darkness upon his eyes. One night, at dusk, he found on the seat, which 'M. Leblanc and his daughter' had just left, a handkerchief, a plain handkerchief without embroidery, but white, fine, and which appeared to him to exhale ineffable odours. He seized it in transport. This handkerchief was marked with the letters U. F.: Marius knew nothing of this beautiful girl, neither her family, nor her name, nor her dwelling; these two letters were the first thing he had caught of her, adorable initials upon which he began straightway to build his castle. It was evidently her first name. Ursula, thought he, what a sweet name! He kissed the handkerchief, inhaled its perfume, put it over his heart, on his flesh in the day-time, and at night went to sleep with it on his lips.

'I feel her whole soul in it!' he exclaimed.

This handkerchief belonged to the old gentleman, who had simply let it fall from his pocket.

For days and days after this piece of good fortune, he always appeared at the Luxembourg kissing this handkerchief and placing it on his heart. The beautiful child did not understand this at all, and indicated it to him by signs, which he did not perceive.

'Oh, modesty!' said Marius.

8. Even the Invalides may be lucky

Since we have pronounced the word *modesty*, and since we conceal nothing, we must say that once however, through all his ecstasy, 'his Ursula' gave him a very serious pang. It was upon one of the days when she prevailed upon M. Leblanc to leave the seat and to promenade on the walk. A brisk north wind was blowing, which swayed the tops of the plane trees. Father and daughter, arm in arm, had just passed before Marius' seat. Marius had risen behind them and was following them with his eyes, as it was natural that he should in this desperate situation of his heart.

Suddenly a gust of wind, rather more lively than the rest, and probably entrusted with the little affairs of spring, flew down from La Pepinière, rushed upon the walk, enveloped the young girl in a transporting tremor worthy of the nymphs of Virgil and the fauns of Theocritus, and raised her skirt, this skirt more sacred than that of Isis, almost to the height of the garter. A limb of exquisite mould was seen. Marius saw it. He was exasperated and furious.

The young girl had put down her dress with a divinely startled movement, but he was outraged none the less. True, he was alone in the walk. But there might have been somebody there. And if anybody had been there! could one conceive of such a thing ? what she had done was horrible! Alas, the poor child had done nothing; there was but one culprit, the wind; and yet Marius in whom all the Bartholo which there is in Cherubin was confusedly trembling, was determined to be dissatisfied, and was jealous of his shadow. For it is thus that is awakened in the human heart, and imposed upon man, even unjustly, the bitter and strange jealousy of the flesh. Besides, and throwing this jealousy out of consideration, there was nothing that was agreeable to him in the sight of that beautiful limb; the white stocking of the first woman that came along would have given him more pleasure.

When 'his Ursula', reaching the end of the walk, returned with M. Leblanc, and passed before the seat on which Marius had again sat down, Marius threw at her a cross and cruel look. The young girl slightly straightened back, with that elevation of the eyelids, which says: 'Well, what is the matter with him ?'

That was 'their first quarrel'.

Marius had hardly finished this scene with her when somebody came down the walk. It was an Invalide, very much bent, wrinkled and pale with age, in the uniform of Louis XV, with the little oval patch of red cloth with crossed swords on his back, the soldier's Cross of Saint Louis, and decorated also by a coat sleeve in which there was no arm, a silver chin, and a wooden leg. Marius thought he could discern that this man appeared to be very much pleased. It seemed to him even that the old cynic, as he hobbled along by him, had addressed to him a very fraternal and very merry wink, as if by some chance they had been put into communication and had enjoyed some dainty bit of good fortune together. What had he seen to be so pleased, this relic of Mars? What had happened between this leg of wood and the other ? Marius had a paroxysm of jealousy. 'Perhaps he was by!' said he; 'perhaps he saw!' And he would have been glad to exterminate the Invalide.

Time lending his aid, every point is blunted. This anger of Marius against 'Ursula', however just and proper it might be, passed away. He forgave her at last; but it was a great effort; he pouted at her three days.

Meanwhile, in spite of all that, and because of all that, his passion was growing, and was growing mad.

9. An eclipse

WE HAVE SEEN how Marius discovered, or thought he discovered, that Her name was Ursula.

Hunger comes with love. To know that her name was Ursula had been much; it was little. In three or four weeks Marius had devoured this piece of good fortune. He desired another. He wished to know where she lived.

He had committed one blunder in falling into the snare of the seat by the Gladiator. He had committed a second by not remaining at the Luxembourg when Monsieur Leblanc came there alone. He committed a third, a monstrous one. He followed 'Ursula'.

She lived in the Rue de l'Ouest, in the least frequented part of it, in a new three-storey house, of modest appearance.

From that moment Marius added to his happiness in seeing her at the Luxembourg, the happiness of following her home.

His hunger increased. He knew her name, her first name, at least, the charming name, the real name of a woman; he knew where she lived; he desired to know who she was.

One night after he had followed them home, and seen them disappear at the *porte-cochère*, he entered after them, and said boldly to the porter:

'Is it the gentleman on the first floor who has just come in?'

'No,' answered the porter. 'It is the gentleman on the third.'

Another fact. This success made Marius still bolder.

'In front?' he asked.

'Faith!' said the porter, 'the house is only built on the street.'

'And what is this gentleman?'

'He lives on his income, monsieur, A very kind man, who does a great deal of good among the poor, though not rich.'

'What is his name?' continued Marius.

The porter raised his head, and said:

'Is monsieur a detective?'

Marius retired, much abashed, but still in great transports. He was getting on.

'Good,' thought he. 'I know that her name is Ursula, that she is the daughter of a retired gentleman, and that she lives there, in the third storey, in the Rue de l'Ouest.'

Next day Monsieur Leblanc and his daughter made but a short visit to the Luxembourg; they went away while it was yet broad daylight. Marius followed them into the Rue de l'Ouest, as was his custom. On reaching the *porte-cochère*, Monsieur Leblanc passed his daughter in, and then stopped, and before entering himself, turned and looked steadily at Marius. The day after that they did not come to the Luxembourg. Marius waited in vain all day.

At nightfall he went to the Rue de l'Ouest, and saw a light in the windows of the third storey. He walked beneath these windows until the light was put out.

The next day nobody at the Luxembourg. Marius waited all day, and then went to perform his night duty under the windows. That took him till ten o'clock in the evening. His dinner took care of itself. Fever supports the sick man, and love the lover.

He passed a week in this way. Monsieur Leblanc and his daughter appeared at the Luxembourg no more. Marius made melancholy conjectures; he dared not watch the *porte-cochère* during the day. He limited himself to going at night to gaze upon the reddish light of the windows. At times he saw shadows moving, and his heart beat high.

On the eighth day when he reached the house, there was no light in the windows. 'What!' said he, 'the lamp is not yet lighted. But yet it is dark. Or they have gone out?' He waited till ten o'clock. Till midnight. Till one o'clock in the morning. No light appeared in the third storey windows, and nobody entered the house. He went away very gloomy.

On the morrow – for he lived only from morrow to morrow; there was no longer any today, so to speak, to him – on the morrow he found nobody at the Luxembourg, he waited; at dusk he went to the house. No light in the windows; the blinds were closed; the third storey was entirely dark. Marius knocked at the *porte-cochère*; went in and said to the porter:

'The gentleman of the third floor?'

'Moved,' answered the porter.

Marius tottered, and said feebly:

'Since when?'

'Yesterday.'

'Where does he live now ?'

'I don't know anything about it.'

'He has not left his new address, then ?'

'No.'

And the porter, looking up, recognised Marius.

'What! it is you!' said he, but decidedly now, 'you do keep a bright look-out.'

BOOK 7: PATRON MINETTE

1. *The mines and the miners*

EVERY HUMAN SOCIETY has what is called in the theatres a *third sub-stage*. The social soil is mined everywhere, sometimes for good, sometimes for evil. These works are in strata; there are upper mines and lower mines. There is a top and a bottom in this dark sub-soil which sometimes sinks beneath civilisation, and which our indifference and our carelessness trample underfoot. The Encyclopædia, in the last century, was a mine almost on the surface. The dark caverns, these gloomy protectors of primitive Christianity, were awaiting only an opportunity to explode beneath the Cæsars, and to flood the human race with light. For in these sacred shades there is latent light. Volcanoes are full of a blackness, capable of flashing flames. All lava begins as midnight. The catacombs, where the first mass was said, were not merely the cave of Rome; they were the cavern of the world.

There is under the social structure, this complex wonder of a mighty burrow, – of excavations of every kind. There is the religious mine, the philosophic mine, the political mine, the economic mine, the revolutionary mine. This pick with an idea, that pick with a figure, the other pick with a vengeance. They call and they answer from one catacomb to another. Utopias travel under ground in the passages. They branch out in every direction. They sometimes meet there and fraternise. Jean Jacques lends his pick to Diogenes, who lends him his lantern. Sometimes they fight. Calvin takes Socinius by the hair. But nothing checks or interrupts the tension of all these energies towards their object. The vast simultaneous activity, which goes to and fro, and up and down, and up again, in these dusky regions, and which slowly transforms the upper through the lower, and the outer through the inner; vast unknown swarming of workers. Society has hardly a suspicion of this work of undermining which, without touching its surface, changes its substance. So many subterranean degrees, so many differing labours, so many varying excavations. What comes from all this deep delving? The future.

The deeper we sink, the more mysterious are the workers. To a degree which social philosophy can recognise, the work is good; beyond this degree it is doubtful and mixed; below, it becomes terrible. At a certain depth, the excavations become impenetrable to the soul of civilisation, the respirable limit of man is passed; the existence of monsters becomes possible.

The descending ladder is a strange one; each of its rounds corresponds to a step whereupon philosophy can set foot, and where we discover someone of her workers, sometimes divine, sometimes monstrous. Below John Huss is Luther; below Luther is Descartes; below Descartes is Voltaire; below Voltaire is Condorcet; below Condorcet is Robespierre; below Robespierre is Marat; below Marat is Babeuf. And that continues. Lower still, in dusky confusion, at the limit which separates the indistinct from the invisible, glimpses are caught of other men in the gloom, who perhaps no longer exist. Those of yesterday are spectres; those of tomorrow are goblins. The embryonary work of the future is one of the visions of the philosopher.

A fœtus world in limbo, what a wonderful profile!

Saint Simon, Owen, Fourier, are there also, in lateral galleries.

Indeed, although an invisible divine chain links together all these subterranean pioneers, who almost always believe they are alone, yet are not, their labours are very diverse, and the glow of some is in contrast with the flame of others. Some are paradisaic, others are tragic. Nevertheless, be the contrast what it may, all these workers, from the highest to the darkest, from the wisest to the silliest, have one thing in common, and that is disinterestedness. Marat, like Jesus, forgets himself. They throw self aside; they omit self; they do not think of self. They see something other than themselves. They have a light in their eyes, and this light is searching for the absolute. The highest has all heaven in his eyes; the lowest, enigmatical as he may be, has yet beneath his brows the pale glow of the infinite. Venerate him, whatever he may do, who has this sign, the star-eye.

The shadow-eye is the other sign.

With it evil commences. Before him whose eye has no light, reflect and tremble. Social order has its black miners.

There is a point where undermining becomes burial, and where light is extinguished.

Below all these mines which we have pointed out, below all these galleries, below all this immense underground venous system of progress and of utopia, far deeper in the earth, lower than Marat, lower than Babeuf, lower, much lower, and without any connection with the upper galleries, is the last sap. A fear-inspiring place. This is what we have called the third sub-stage. It is the grave of the depths. It is the cave of the blind *Inferi*.

This communicates with the gulfs.

2. *The lowest depth*

THERE DISINTERESTEDNESS vanishes. The demon is dimly rough-hewn; everyone for himself. The eyeless I howls, searches, gropes, and gnaws. The social Ugolino is in this gulf.

The savage outlines which prowl over this grave, half brute, half phantom, have no thought for universal progress, they ignore ideas and words, they have no care but for individual glut. They are almost unconscious, and there is in them a horrible defacement. They have two mothers, both stepmothers, ignorance and misery. They have one guide, want; and their only form of satisfaction is appetite. They are voracious as beasts, that is to say ferocious, not like the tyrant, but like the tiger. From suffering these goblins pass to crime; fated filiation, giddy procreation, the logic of darkness. What crawls in the third sub-stage is no longer the stifled demand for the absolute, it is the protest of matter. Man there becomes dragon. Hunger and thirst are the point of departure; Satan is the point of arrival. From this cave comes Lacenaire.

We have just seen, in the fourth book, one of the compartments of the upper mine, the great political, revolutionary, and philosophic sap. There, as we have said, all is noble, pure, worthy, and honourable. There, it is true, men may be deceived and are deceived, but there error is venerable, so much heroism does it imply. For the sum of all the work which is done there, there is one name: Progress.

The time has come to open other depths, the depths of horror.

There is beneath society, we must insist upon it, and until the day when ignorance shall be no more, there will be, the great cavern of evil.

This cave is beneath all, and is the enemy of all. It is hate universal. This cave knows no philosophers; its poniard has never made a pen. Its blackness has no relation to the sublime blackness of script. Never have the fingers of night, which are clutching beneath this asphyxiating vault, turned the leaves of a book, or unfolded a journal. Babeuf is a speculator to Cartouche; Marat is an aristocrat to Schinderhannes. The object of this cave is the ruin of all things.

Of all things. Including therein the upper saps, which it execrates. It does not undermine, in its hideous crawl, merely the social order of the time; it undermines philosophy, it undermines science, it undermines law, it undermines human thought, it undermines civilisation, it undermines revolution, it undermines progress. It goes by the naked names of theft, prostitution, murder, and assassination. It is darkness, and it desires chaos. It is vaulted in with ignorance.

All the others, those above it, have but one object – to suppress it. To that end philosophy and progress work through all their organs at the same time, through amelioration of the real as well as through contemplation of the absolute. Destroy the cave Ignorance, and you destroy the mole Crime.

We will condense in a few words a portion of what we have just said. The only social peril is darkness.

Humanity is identity. All men are the same clay. No difference, here below at least, in predestination. The same darkness before, the same flesh during, the same ashes after life. But ignorance, mixed with the human composition, blackens it. This incurable ignorance possesses the heart of man, and there becomes Evil.

3. Babet, Gueulemer, Claquesous and Montparnasse

A QUARTETTE of bandits, Claquesous, Gueulemer, Babet and Montparnasse, ruled from 1830 to 1835 over the third sub-stage of Paris.

Gueulemer was a Hercules without a pedestal. His cave was the Arche-Marion sewer. He was six feet high, and had a marble chest, brazen biceps, cavernous lungs, a colossus' body, and a bird's skull. You would think you saw the Farnese Hercules dressed in duck pantaloons and a cotton-velvet waistcoat. Gueulemer, built in this sculptural fashion, could have subdued monsters; he found it easier to become one. Low forehead, large temples, less than forty, the foot of a goose, coarse short hair, a bushy cheek, a wild boar's beard; from this you see the man. His muscles asked for work, his stupidity would have none. This was a huge lazy force. He was an assassin through nonchalance. He was thought to be a creole. Probably there was a little of Marshal Brown in him, he having been a porter at Avignon in 1815. After this he had become a bandit.

The diaphaneity of Babet contrasted with the meatiness of Gueulemer. Babet was thin and shrewd. He was transparent, but impenetrable. You could see the light through his bones, but nothing through his eye. He professed to be a chemist. He had been bar-keeper for Bobèche, and clown for Bobino. He had played vaudeville at Saint Mihiel. He was an affected man, a great talker, who italicised his smiles and quoted his gestures. His business was to sell plaster busts and portraits of the 'head of the Government' in the street. Moreover, he pulled teeth. He had exhibited monstrosities at fairs, and had a booth with a trumpet and this placard: 'Babet, dental artist, member of the Academies, physical experimenter on metals and metalloids, extirpates teeth, removes stumps left by other dentists. Price: one tooth, one franc fifty centimes; two teeth, two francs; three teeth, two francs fifty centimes. Improve your opportunity.' (This 'improve your opportunity', meant: get as many pulled as possible.) He had been married, and had had children. What had become of his wife and children, he did not know. He had lost them as one loses his pocket-handkerchief. A remarkable exception in the obscure world to which he belonged, Babet read the papers. One day, during the time he had his family with him in his travelling booth, he had read in the *Messenger* that a woman had been delivered of a child, likely to live, which had the face of a calf, and he had exclaimed: '*There is a piece of good luck! My wife hasn't the sense to bring me a child like that.*' Since then, he had left everything, 'to take Paris in hand'. His own expression.

What was Claquesous ? He was night. Before showing himself, he waited till the sky was daubed with black. At night he came out of a hole, which he went into again before day. Where was this hole? Nobody knew. In the most perfect obscurity, and to his accomplices, he always turned his back when he spoke. Was his name Claquesous? No. He said: 'My name is Nothing-at-all.' If a candle was brought, he put on a mask. He was a ventriloquist. Babet said: '*Claque-sous is a night-bird with two voices.*' Claquesous was restless, roving, terrible. It was not certain that he had a name, Claquesous being a nickname; it was not certain that he had a voice, his chest speaking oftener than his mouth; it was not certain that he had a face, nobody having ever seen anything but his mask. He disappeared as if he sank into the ground; he came like an apparition.

A mournful sight was Montparnasse. Montparnasse was a child; less than twenty, with a pretty face, lips like cherries, charming black locks, the glow of spring in his eyes; he had all the vices and aspired to all the crimes. The digestion of what was bad gave him an appetite for what was worse. He was the *gamin* turned vagabond, and the vagabond become an assassin. He was genteel, effeminate, graceful, robust, weak, and ferocious. He wore his hat turned upon the left side, to make room for the tuft of hair, according to the fashion of 1829. He lived by robbery. His coat was of the most fashionable cut but threadbare. Montparnasse was a fashion-plate living in distress and committing murders. The cause of all the crimes of this young man was his desire to be well dressed. The first grisette who had said to him: 'You are handsome,' had thrown the stain of darkness into his heart, and had made a Cain of this Abel. Thinking that he was handsome, he had desired to be elegant; now the first of elegances is idleness: idleness for a poor man is crime. Few prowlers were so much feared as Montparnasse. At eighteen, he had already left several corpses on his track. More than one traveller lay in the shadow of this wretch, with extended arms and with his face in a pool of blood. Frizzled, pomaded, with slender waist, hips like a woman, the bust of a Prussian officer, a buzz of admiration about him from the girls of the boulevard, an elaborately-tied cravat, a sling-shot in his pocket, a flower in his button-hole; such was this charmer of the sepulchre.

4. *Composition of the band*

THESE FOUR BANDITS formed a sort of Proteus, winding through the police and endeavouring to escape from the indiscreet glances of Vidocq 'under various form, tree, flame, and fountain', lending each other their name and their tricks, concealing themselves in their own shadow, each a refuge and a hiding-place for the others, throwing off their personalities, as one takes off a false nose at a masked ball, sometimes simplifying themselves till they are but one, sometimes multiplying themselves till Coco Lacour himself took them for a multitude.

These four men were not four men; it was a sort of mysterious robber with four heads preying upon Paris by wholesale; it was the monstrous polyp of evil which inhabits the crypt of society.

By means of their ramifications and the underlying network of their relations, Babet, Gueulemer, Claquesous, and Montparnasse, controlled the general lying-in-wait business of the Department of the Seine. Originators of ideas in this line, men of midnight imagination came to them for the execution. The four villains being furnished with the single draft they took charge of putting it on the stage. They worked upon scenario. They were always in condition to furnish a company proportioned and suitable to any enterprise which stood in need of aid, and was sufficiently lucrative. A crime being in search of arms, they sublet accomplices to it. They had a company of actors of darkness at the disposition of every cavernous tragedy.

They usually met at nightfall, their waking hour, in the waste grounds near La Salpêtrière. There they conferred. They had the twelve dark hours before them; they allotted their employ.

Patron-Minette, such was the name which was given in subterranean society to the association of these four men. In the old, popular, fantastic language, which now is dying out every day, *Patron-Minette* means morning, just as *entre chien et loup* [between dog and wolf], means night. This appellation, Patron-Minette, probably came from the hour at which their work ended, the dawn being the moment for the disappearance of phantoms and the separation of bandits. These four were known by this title. When the Chief Judge of the Assizes visited Lacenaire in prison, he questioned him in relation to some crime which Lacenaire denied. 'Who did do it?' asked the judge. Lacenaire made this reply, enigmatical to the magistrate, but clear to the police: 'Patron-Minette, perhaps.'

Sometimes a play may be imagined from the announcement of the characters: so, too, we may almost understand what a band is from the list of the bandits. We give, for these names are preserved in the documents, the appellations to which the principal subordinates of Patron-Minette responded:

Panchaud, alias Printanier, alias Bigrenaille.

Brujon. (There was a dynasty of Brujons; we shall say something about it hereafter.)

Boulatruelle, the road-mender, already introduced.

Laveuve.

Finistère.

Homer Hogu, a negro.

Mardisoir.

Dépêche.

Fauntleroy, alias Bouquetière.

Glorieux, a liberated convict.

Barrecarrosse, alias Monsieur Dupont.

L'esplanade-du-Sud.

Poussagrive.

Carmagnolet.

Kruideniers, alias Bizarro.

Mangedentelle.

Les-pieds-en-l'air.

Demi-liard, alias Deux-milliards.

Etc., etc.

We pass over some of them, and not the worst. These names have faces. They express not only beings, but species. Each of these names answers to a variety of these shapeless toadstools of the cellars of civilisation.

These beings, by no means free with their faces, were not of those whom we see passing in the streets. During the day, wearied out by their savage nights, they went away to sleep, sometimes in the parget-kilns, sometimes in the abandoned quarries of Montmartre or Montrouge, sometimes in the sewers. They burrowed.

What has become of these men ? They still exist. They have always existed. Horace speaks of them: *Ambubaiarum collegia, pharmacopolæ, mendici, mimæ;* and so long as society shall be what it is, they will be what they are. Under the dark vault of their cave, they are for ever reproduced from the ooze of society. They return, spectres, always the same; but they bear the same name no longer, and they are no longer in the same skins.

The individuals extirpated, the tribe still exists.

They have always the same faculties. From beggar to the prowler the race preserves its purity. They divine purses in pockets, they scent watches in fobs. Gold and silver to them are odorous. There are simple bourgeois of whom you might say that they have a robable appearance. These men follow these bourgeois patiently. When a foreigner or a countryman passes by they have spider thrills.

Such men, when, towards midnight, on a lone boulevard, you meet them or catch a glimpse of them, are terrifying. They seem not men, but forms fashioned of the living dark; you would say that they are generally an integral portion of the darkness, that they are not distinct from it, that they have no other soul than the gloom, and that it is only temporarily and to live for a few minutes a monstrous life, that they are disaggregated from the night.

What is required to exorcise these goblins? Light. Light in floods. No bat resists the dawn. Illuminate the bottom of society.

BOOK 8: THE NOXIOUS POOR

1. Marius, looking for a girl with a hat, meets a man with a cap

Summer passed, then autumn; winter came. Neither M. Leblanc nor the young girl had set foot in the Luxembourg. Marius had now but one thought, to see that sweet, that adorable face again. He searched continually; he searched everywhere: he found nothing. He was no longer Marius the enthusiastic dreamer, the resolute man, ardent yet firm, the bold challenger of destiny, the brain which projected and built future upon future, the young heart full of plans, projects, prides, ideas, and desires; he was a lost dog. He fell into a melancholy. It was all over with him. Work disgusted him, walking fatigued him, solitude wearied him, vast nature, once so full of forms, of illuminations, of voices, of counsels, of perspectives, of horizons, of teachings, was now a void before him. It seemed to him that everything had disappeared.

He was still full of thought, for he could not be otherwise; but he no longer found pleasure in his thoughts. To all which they were silently but incessantly proposing to him, he answered in the gloom: What is the use?

He reproached himself a hundred times. Why did I follow her? I was so happy in seeing her only! She looked upon me; was not that infinite? She had the appearance of loving me. Was not that everything? I desired to have what? There is nothing more after that. I was a fool. It is my fault, etc., etc. Courfeyrac, to whom he confided nothing; that was his nature; but who found out a little of everything; that was his nature also; had begun by felicitating him upon being in love, and wondering at it withal; then seeing Marius fallen into this melancholy, he had at last said to him: 'I see that you have been nothing but an animal. Here, come to the Cabin.'

Once, confiding in a beautiful September sun, Marius allowed himself to be taken to the Bal de Sceaux, by Courfeyrac, Bossuet, and Grantaire, hoping, what a dream! that he might possibly find her there. We need not say that he did not see her whom he sought. 'But yet it is here that all the lost women are to be found,' muttered Grantaire aside. Marius left his friends at the ball, and went back on foot, alone, tired, feverish, with sad and troubled eyes, in the night, overcome by the noise and dust of the joyous coaches full of singing parties who passed by him returning from the festival, while he, discouraged, was breathing in the pungent odour of the walnut trees by the wayside, to restore his brain .

He lived more and more alone, bewildered, overwhelmed, given up to his inward anguish, walking to and fro in his grief like a wolf in a cage, seeking everywhere for the absent, stupefied with love.

At another time, an accidental meeting produced a singular effect upon him. In one of the little streets in the neighbourhood of the Boulevard des Invalides, he saw a man dressed like a labourer, wearing a cap with a long visor, from beneath which escaped a few locks of very white hair. Marius was struck by the beauty of this white hair, and noticed the man who was walking with slow steps and seemed absorbed in painful meditation. Strangely enough, it appeared to him that he recognised M. Leblanc. It was the same hair, the same profile, as far as the cap allowed him to see, the same manner, only sadder. But why these working-man's clothes? what did that mean? what did this disguise signify? Marius was astounded. When he came to himself, his first impulse was to follow the man; who knows but he had at last caught the trace which he was seeking ? At all events, he must see the man again nearer, and clear up the enigma. But this idea occurred to him too late, the man was now gone. He had taken some little side-street, and Marius could not find him again. This adventure occupied his mind for a few days, and then faded away. 'After all,' said he to himself, 'it is probably only a resemblance.'

2. *A waif*

MARIUS STILL LIVED in the Gorbeau tenement. He paid no attention to anybody there.

At this time, it is true, there were no occupants remaining in the house but himself and those Jondrettes whose rent he had once paid, without having ever spoken, however, either to the father, or to the mother, or to the daughters. The other tenants had moved away or died, or had been turned out for not paying their rent.

One day, in the course of this winter, the sun shone a little in the afternoon, but it was the second of February, that ancient Candlemas day whose treacherous sun, the precursor of six weeks of cold, inspired Matthew Laensberg with these two lines, which have deservedly become classic:

Qu'il luise ou qu'il luiserne,
L'ours rentre en sa caverne.*

Marius had just left his; night was falling. It was his dinner hour; for it was still necessary for him to go to dinner, alas! oh, infirmity of the ideal passions.

He had just crossed his door-sill which Ma'am Bougon was sweeping at that very moment, muttering at the same time this memorable monologue:

'What is there that is cheap now? everything is dear. There is nothing but people's trouble that is cheap; that comes for nothing, people's trouble.'

Marius went slowly up the boulevard towards the barrière, on the way to the Rue Saint Jacques. He was walking thoughtfully, with his head down.

Suddenly he felt that he was elbowed in the dusk; he turned, and saw two young girls in rags, one tall and slender, the other a little shorter, passing rapidly by, breathless, frightened, and apparently in flight; they had met him, had not seen him, and had jostled him in passing. Marius could see in the twilight their livid faces, their hair tangled and flying, their frightful bonnets, their tattered skirts, and their naked feet. As they ran they were talking to each other. The taller one said in a very low voice:

'The *cognes* came. They just missed *pincer* me at the *demi-cercle*.'

The other answered: 'I saw them. I *cavalé*, *cavalé*, *cavalé*.'

* Let it gleam or let it glitter,
The bear returns into his cave.

Marius understood, through this dismal argot, that the gendarmes, or the city police, had not succeeded in seizing these two girls, and that the girls had escaped.

They plunged in under the trees of the boulevard behind him, and for a few seconds made a kind of dim whiteness in the obscurity which soon faded out.

Marius stopped for a moment.

He was about to resume his course when he perceived a little greyish packet on the ground at his feet. He stooped down and picked it up. It was a sort of envelope which appeared to contain papers.

'Good,' said he, 'those poor creatures must have dropped this!'

He retraced his steps, he called, he did not find them; he concluded they were already beyond hearing, put the packet in his pocket, and went to dinner.

On his way, in an alley on the Rue Mouffetard, he saw a child's coffin covered with a black cloth, placed upon three chairs and lighted by a candle. The two girls of the twilight returned to his mind.

'Poor mothers,' thought he. 'There is one thing sadder than to see their children die – to see them lead evil lives.'

Then these shadows which had varied his sadness went out from his thoughts, and he fell back into his customary train. He began to think of his six months of love and happiness in the open air and the broad daylight under the beautiful trees of the Luxembourg.

'How dark my life has become!' said he to himself. 'Young girls still pass before me. Only formerly they were angels; now they are ghouls.'

3. *Quadrifrons*

In the evening, as he was undressing to go to bed, he happened to feel in his coat-pocket the packet which he had picked up on the boulevard. He had forgotten it. He thought it might be well to open it, and that the packet might perhaps contain the address of the young girls, if, in reality, it belonged to them, or at all events the information necessary to restore it to the person who had lost it.

He opened the envelope.

It was unsealed and contained four letters, also unsealed.

The addresses were upon them.

All four exhaled an odour of wretched tobacco.

The first letter was addressed: *To Madame, Madame the Marchioness de Grucheray, Square opposite the Chamber of Deputies, No. —.*

Marius said to himself that he should probably find in this letter the information of which he was in search, and that, moreover, as the letter was not sealed, probably it might be read without impropriety.

It was in these words:

> Madame the Marchioness:
>
> The virtue of kindness and piety is that which binds sosiety most closely. Call up your christian sentiment, and cast a look of compassion upon this unfortunate Spanish victim of loyalty and attachment to the sacred cause of legitimacy, which he has paid for with his blood, consecrated his fortune,

wholy, to defend this cause, and today finds himself in the greatest missery. He has no doubt that your honourable self will furnish him assistance to preserve an existence extremely painful for a soldier of education and of honour full of wounds, reckons in advance upon the humanity which animmates you and upon the interest which Madame the Marchioness feels in a nation so unfortunate. Their prayer will not be in vain, and their memory will retain herr charming souvenir.

From my respectful sentiments with which I have the honour to be Madame,

DON ALVERES, Spanish captain of cabalry, royalist refuge in France, who finds himself traveling for his country and ressources fail him to continue his travells.'

No address was added to the signature. Marius hoped to find the address in the second letter the superscription of which ran: *To Madame, Madame the Comtess de Montvernet, Rue Cassette, No. 9.* Marius read as follows:

MADAME THE COMTESS,

It is an unfortunate mothur of a family of six children the last of whom is only eight months old. Me sick since my last lying-in, abandoned by my husband for five months haveing no ressource in the world the most frightful indigance.

In the hope of Madame the Comtesse, she has the honour to be, Madame, with a profound respect,

MOTHER BALIZARD.

Marius passed to the third letter, which was, like the preceding, a begging one; it read:

MONSIEUR PABOURGEOT, elector, wholesale merchant-milliner, Rue Saint Denis, corner of the Rue aux Fers.

I take the liberty to address you this letter to pray you to accord me the pretious favour of your simpathies and to interest you in a man of letters who has just sent a drama to the Théâtre Français. Its subject is historical, and the action takes place in Auvergne in the time of the empire: its style, I believe, is natural, laconic, and perhaps has some merit. There are verses to be sung in four places. The comic, the serious, the unforeseen, mingle themselves with the variety of the characters and with a tint of romance spread lightly over all the plot which advances misteriously, and by striking terns, to a denouement in the midst of several hits of splendid scenes.

My principal object is to satisfie the desire which animates progressively the man of our century, that is to say, fashion, that caprisious and grotesque weathercock which changes almost with every new wind.

In spite of these qualities I have reason to fear that jealousy, the selfishness of the privileged authors, may secure my exclusion from the theatre, for I am not ignorant of the distaste with which newcomers are swallowed.

Monsieur Pabourgeot, your just reputation as an enlightened protector of literary fokes emboldens me to send my daughter to you, who will expose to you our indigant situation, wanting bread and fire in this wynter season. To tell you that I pray you to accept the homage which I desire to offer you in my drama and in all those which I make, is to prove to you how ambicious I am of the honour of sheltering myself under your aegis, and of adorning my writings with your name. If you deign to honour me with the most modest offering, I shall occupy myself immediately in making a piese of verse for you to pay my tribut of recognition. This piese, which I shall endeavour to render as perfect as possible, will be sent to you before being inserted in the beginning of the drama and given upon the stage.

To Monsieur and Madam Pabourgeot,

My most respectful homage,

GENFLOT, man of letters.

P.S. Were it only forty sous.

Excuse me for sending my daughter and for not presenting myself, but sad motives of dress do not permit me, alas! to go out –

Marius finally opened the fourth letter. There was on the address: *To the beneficent gentleman of the church Saint Jaques du Haut Pas.* It contained these few lines:

BENEFICENT MAN,

If you will deign to accompany my daughter, you will see a misserable calamity, and I will show you my certificates.

At the sight of these writings your generous soul will be moved with a sentiment of lively benevolence, for true philosophers always experience vivid emotions.

Agree, compassionate man, that one must experience the most cruel necessity, and that it is very painful, to obtain relief, to have it attested by authority as if we were not free to suffer and to die of inanition while waiting for someone to relieve our missery. The fates are very cruel to some and too lavish or too careful to others.

I await your presence or your offering, if you deign to make it, and I pray you to have the kindness to accept the respectful sentiments with which I am proud to be,

Truly magnanimous man,

Your very humble

And very obedient servant,

P. FABANTOU, dramatic artist.

After reading these four letters, Marius did not find himself much wiser than before.

In the first place none of the signers gave his address.

Then they seemed to come from four different individuals, Don Alvarès, Mother Balizard, the poet Genflot, and the dramatic artist Fabantou; but, strangely enough, these letters were all four written in the same hand.

What was the conclusion from that, unless that they came from the same person ?

Moreover, and this rendered the conjecture still more probable, the paper, coarse and yellow, was the same in all four, the odour of tobacco was the same, and although there was an evident endeavour to vary the style, the same faults of orthography were reproduced with a very quiet certainty, and Genflot, the man of letters, was no more free from them than the Spanish captain.

To endeavour to unriddle this little mystery was a useless labour. If it had not been a waif, it would have had the appearance of a mystification. Marius was too sad to take a joke kindly even from chance, or to lend himself to the game which the street pavement seemed to wish to play with him. It appeared to him that he was like Colin Maillard among the four letters, which were mocking him.

Nothing, however, indicated that these letters belonged to the girls whom Marius had met on the boulevard. After all, they were but waste paper evidently without value.

Marius put them back into the envelope, threw it into a corner, and went to bed.

About seven o'clock in the morning, he had got up and breakfasted, and was trying to set about his work when there was a gentle rap at his door.

As he owned nothing, he never locked his door, except sometimes, and that very rarely, when he was about some pressing piece of work. And, indeed, even when absent, he left his key in the lock. 'You will be robbed,' said Ma'am Bougon. 'Of what?' said Marius. The fact is, however, that one day somebody had stolen an old pair of boots, to the great triumph of Ma'am Bougon.

There was a second rap, very gentle like the first.

'Come in,' said Marius.

The door opened.

'What do you want, Ma'am Bougon?' asked Marius, without raising his eyes from the books and papers which he had on his table.

A voice, which was not Ma'am Bougon's, answered:

'I beg your pardon, Monsieur – '

It was a hollow, cracked, smothered, rasping voice, the voice of an old man, roughened by brandy and by liquors.

Marius turned quickly and saw a young girl.

4. *A rose in misery*

A GIRL WHO WAS QUITE YOUNG, was standing in the half-opened door. The little round window through which the light found its way into the garret was exactly opposite the door, and lit up this form with a pallid light. It was a pale, puny, meagre creature, nothing but a chemise and a skirt covered a shivering and chilly nakedness. A string for a belt, a string for a headdress, sharp shoulders protruding from the chemise, a blonde and lymphatic pallor, dirty shoulder-blades, red hands, the mouth open and sunken, some teeth gone, the eyes dull, bold, and drooping, the form of an unripe young girl and the look of a corrupted old woman; fifty years joined with fifteen; one of those beings who are both feeble and horrible at once, and who make those shudder whom they do not make weep.

Marius arose and gazed with a kind of astonishment upon this being, so much like the shadowy forms which pass across our dreams.

The most touching thing about it was that this young girl had not come into the world to be ugly. In her early childhood, she must have even been pretty. The grace of her youth was still struggling against the hideous old age brought on by debauchery and poverty. A remnant of beauty was dying out upon this face of sixteen, like the pale sun which is extinguished by frightful clouds at the dawn of a winter's day.

The face was not absolutely unknown to Marius. He thought he remembered having seen it somewhere.

'What do you wish, mademoiselle?' asked he.

The young girl answered with her voice like a drunken galley-slave's:

'Here is a letter for you, Monsieur Marius.'

She called Marius by his name; he could not doubt that her business was with him; but what was this girl? how did she know his name?

Without waiting for an invitation, she entered. She entered resolutely, looking at the whole room and the unmade bed with a sort of assurance which chilled the heart. She was barefooted. Great holes in her skirt revealed her long limbs and her sharp knees. She was shivering.

She had really in her hand a letter which she presented to Marius.

Marius, in opening this letter, noticed that the enormously large wafer was still wet. The message could not have come far. He read:

> My amiable neighbour, young man!
>
> I have lerned your kindness towards me, that you have paid my rent six months ago. I bless you, young man. My eldest daughter will tell you that we have been without a morsel of bread for two days, four persons, and my spouse sick. If I am not desseived by my thoughts, I think I may hope that your generous heart will soften at this exposure and that the desire will subjugate you of being propitious to me by deigning to lavish upon me some light gift.
>
> I am with the distinguished consideration which is due to the benefactors of humanity,
>
> Jondrette.
>
> P.S. My daughter will await your orders, dear Monsieur Marius.

This letter, in the midst of the obscure accident which had occupied Marius's thoughts since the previous evening, was a candle in a cave. Everything was suddenly cleared up.

This letter came from the same source as the other four. It was the same writing, the same style, the same orthography, the same paper, the same odour of tobacco.

There were five missives, five stories, five names, five signatures, and a single signer. The Spanish Captain Don Alvarès, the unfortunate mother Balizard, the dramatic poet Genflot, the old comedy writer Fabantou, were all four named Jondrette, if indeed the name of Jondrette himself was Jondrette.

During the now rather long time that Marius had lived in the tenement, he had had, as we have said, but very few opportunities to see, or even catch a glimpse of his very poor neighbours. His mind was elsewhere, and where the mind is, thither the eyes are directed, He must have met the Jondrettes in the passage and on the stairs, more than once, but to him they were only shadows; he had taken so little notice that on the previous evening he had brushed against the Jondrette girls upon the boulevard without recognising them; for it was evidently they; and it was with great difficulty that this girl, who had just come into his room, had awakened in him, beneath his disgust and pity, a vague remembrance of having met with her elsewhere.

Now he saw everything clearly. He understood that the occupation of his neighbour Jondrette in his distress was to work upon the sympathies of benevolent persons; that he procured their addresses, and that he wrote under assumed names letters to people whom he deemed rich and compassionate, which his daughters carried, at their risk and peril; for this father was one who risked his daughters; he was playing a game with destiny, and he put them into the stake. Marius understood, to judge by their flight in the evening, by their breathlessness, by their terror, by those words of argot which he had heard, that probably these unfortunate things were carrying on also some of the secret trades of darkness, and that from all this the result was, in the midst of human society constituted as it is, two miserable beings who were neither children, nor girls, nor women, a species of impure yet innocent monsters produced by misery.

Sad creatures without name, without age, without sex, to whom neither good nor evil were any longer possible, and for whom, on leaving childhood, there is nothing more in this world, neither liberty, nor virtue, nor responsibility. Souls blooming yesterday, faded today, like those flowers which fall in the street and are bespattered by the mud before a wheel crushes them.

Meantime, while Marius fixed upon her an astonished and sorrowful look, the young girl was walking to and fro in the room with the boldness of a spectre. She bustled about regardless of her nakedness. At times, her chemise, unfastened and torn, fell almost to her waist. She moved the chairs, she disarranged the toilet articles on the bureau, she felt of Marius' clothes, she searched over what there was in the corners.

'Ah,' said she, 'you have a mirror!'

And she hummed, as if she had been alone, snatches of songs, light refrains which were made dismal by her harsh and guttural voice. Beneath this boldness could be perceived an indescribable constraint, restlessness, and humility. Effrontery is a shame.

Nothing was more sorrowful than to see her amusing herself, and, so to speak, fluttering about the room with the movements of a bird which is startled by the light, or which has a wing broken. You feel that under other conditions of education and of destiny, the gay and free manner of this young girl might have been something sweet and charming. Never among animals does the creature which is born to be a dove change into an osprey. That is seen only among men.

Marius was reflecting, and let her go on.

She went to the table.

'Ah!' said she, 'books!'

A light flashed through her glassy eye. She resumed, and her tone expressed that happiness of being able to boast of something, to which no human creature is insensible:

'I can read, I can.'

She hastily caught up the book which lay open on the table, and read fluently:

' – General Bauduin received the order to take five battalions of his brigade and carry the chateau of Hougomont, which is in the middle of the plain of Waterloo – '

She stopped:

'Ah, Waterloo! I know that. It is a battle in old times. My father was there; my father served in the armies. We are jolly good Bonapartists at home, that we are. Against English, Waterloo is.'

She put down the book, took up a pen, and exclaimed:

'And I can write, too!'

She dipped the pen in the ink, and turning towards Marius:

'Would you like to see? Here, I am going to write a word to show.'

And before he had had time to answer, she wrote upon a sheet of blank paper which was on the middle of the table: '*The Cognes are here.*'

Then, throwing down the pen:

'There are no mistakes in spelling. You can look. We have received an education, my sister and I. We have not always been what we are. We were not made – '

Here she stopped, fixed her faded eye upon Marius, and burst out laughing, saying in a tone which contained complete anguish stifled by complete cynicism: 'Bah!'

And she began to hum these words, to a lively air:

J'ai faim, mon père.
Pas de fricot.
J'ai froid, ma mère.
Pas de tricot.
Grelotte
Lolotte!
Sariglote,
Jacquot

Hardly had she finished this stanza when she exclaimed:

'Do you ever go to the theatre, Monsieur Marius? I do. I have a little brother who is a friend of some artists, and who gives me tickets sometimes. Now, I do not like the seats in the galleries. You are crowded, you are uncomfortable. There are sometimes coarse people there; there are also people who smell bad.'

Then she looked at Marius, put on a strange manner, and said to him:

'Do you know, Monsieur Marius, that you are a very pretty boy?'

And at the same time the same thought occurred to both of them, which made her smile and made him blush.

She went to him, and laid her hand on his shoulder: 'You pay no attention to me, but I know you, Monsieur Marius. I meet you here on the stairs, and then I see you visiting a man named Father Mabeuf, who lives out by Austerlitz, sometimes, when I am walking that way. That becomes you very well, your tangled hair.'

Her voice tried to be very soft, but succeeded only in being very low. Some of her words were lost in their passage from the larynx to the lips, as upon a keyboard in which some notes are missing.

Marius had drawn back quietly.

'Mademoiselle,' said he, with his cold gravity, 'I have here a packet, which is yours, I think. Permit me to return it to you.'

And he handed her the envelope, which contained the four letters.

She clapped her hands and exclaimed:

'We have looked everywhere!'

Then she snatched the packet, and opened the envelope, saying:

'Lordy, Lordy, haven't we looked, my sister and I? And you have found it! on the boulevard, didn't you? It must have been on the boulevard? You see, this dropped when we ran. It was my brat of a sister who made the stupid blunder. When we got home, we could not find it. As we did not want to be beaten, since that is needless, since that is entirely needless, since that is absolutely needless, we said at home that we had carried the letters to the persons, and that they told us: Nix! Now here they are, these poor letters. And how did you know they were mine? Ah, yes! by the writing! It was you, then, that we knocked against last evening. We did not see you, really! I said to my sister: Is that a gentleman? My sister said – I think it is a gentleman!'

Meanwhile, she had unfolded the petition addressed 'to the beneficent gentleman of the church Saint Jacques du Haut Pas'.

'Here!' said she, 'this is for the old fellow who goes to mass. And this too is the hour. I am going to carry it to him. He will give us something perhaps for breakfast.'

Then she began to laugh, and added:

'Do you know what it will be if we have breakfast today? It will be that we shall have had our breakfast for day before yesterday, our dinner for day before yesterday, our breakfast for yesterday, our dinner for yesterday, all that at one time this morning. Yes! zounds! if you're not satisfied, stuff till you burst, dogs!'

This reminded Marius of what the poor girl had come to his room for.

He felt in his waistcoat, he found nothing there.

The young girl continued, seeming to talk as if she were no longer conscious that Marius was there present.

'Sometimes I go away at night. Sometimes I do not come back. Before coming to this place, the other winter, we lived under the arches of the bridges. We hugged close to each other so as not to freeze. My little sister cried. How chilly the water is! When I thought of drowning myself, I said: No; it is too cold. I go all alone when I want to, I sleep in the ditches sometimes. Do you know, at night, when I walk on the boulevards I see the trees like gibbets, I see all the great black houses like the towers of Notre Dame, I imagine that the white walls are the river, I say to myself: Here, there is water there! The stars are like illumination lamps, one would say that they smoke, and that the wind blows them out, I am confused, as if I had horses breathing in my ear; though it is night, I hear hand-organs and spinning wheels, I don't know what. I think that somebody is throwing stones at me, I run without knowing it, it is all a whirl, all a whirl. When one has not eaten, it is very queer.'

And she looked at him with a wandering eye.

After a thorough exploration of his pockets, Marius had at last got together five francs and sixteen sous. This was at the time all that he had in the world. 'That is enough for my dinner today,' thought he, 'tomorrow we will see.' He took the sixteen sous, and gave the five francs to the young girl.

She took the piece eagerly.

'Good,' said she, 'there is some sunshine!'

And as if the sun had had the effect to loosen an avalanche of argot in her brain, she continued:

'Five francs! a shiner! a monarch! in this *piolle!* it is *chenâtre!* You are a good *mion*. I give you my *palpitant*. Bravo for the *fanandels!* Two days of *pivois!* and of *viande-muche!* and of *fricotmar!* we shall *pitancer chenument!* and *bonne mouise!*'

She drew her chemise up over her shoulders, made a low bow to Marius, then a familiar wave of the hand, and moved towards the door, saying:

'Good morning, monsieur. It is all the same. I am going to find my old man.'

On her way she saw on the bureau a dry crust of bread moulding there in the dust; she sprang upon it, and bit it, muttering:

'That is good! it is hard! it breaks my teeth!'

Then she went out.

5. *The Judas of providence*

FOR FIVE YEARS Marius had lived in poverty, in privation, in distress even, but he perceived that he had never known real misery. Real misery he had just seen. It was this sprite which had just passed before his eyes. In fact, he who has seen the misery of man only has seen nothing, he must see the misery of woman; he who has seen the misery of woman only has seen nothing, he must see the misery of childhood.

When man has reached the last extremity, he comes, at the same time, to the last expedients. Woe to the defenceless beings who surround him! Work, wages, bread, fire, courage, willingness, all fail him at once. The light of day seems to die away without, the moral light dies out within; in this gloom, man meets the weakness of woman and childhood, and puts them by force to ignominious uses.

Then all horrors are possible. Despair is surrounded by fragile walls which all open into vice or crime.

Health, youth, honour, the holy and passionate delicacies of the still tender flesh, the heart, virginity, modesty, that epidermis of the soul, are fatally disposed of by that blind groping which seeks for aid, which meets degradation, and which accommodates itself to it. Fathers, mothers, children, brothers, sisters, men, women, girls, cling together, and almost grow together like a mineral formation, in that dark promiscuity of sexes, of relationships, of ages, of infancy, of innocence. They crouch down, back to back, in a kind of fate-hovel. They glance at one another sorrowfully. Oh, the unfortunate! how pallid they are! how cold they are! It seems as though they were on a planet much further from the sun than we.

This young girl was to Marius a sort of messenger from the night.

She revealed to him an entire and hideous aspect of the darkness.

Marius almost reproached himself with the fact that he had been so absorbed in his reveries and passion that he had not until now cast a glance upon his neighbours. Paying their rent was a mechanical impulse; everybody would have had that impulse; but he, Marius, should have done better. What! a mere wall separated him from these abandoned beings, who lived by groping in the night without the pale of the living; he came in contact with them, he was in some sort the last link of the human race which they touched, he heard them live or rather breathe beside him, and he took no notice of them! every day at every moment, he heard them through the wall, walking, going, coming, talking, and he did not lend his ear! and in these words there were groans, and he did not even listen, his thoughts were elsewhere, upon dreams, upon impossible glimmerings, upon loves in the sky, upon infatuations; and all the while human beings, his brothers in Jesus Christ, his brothers in the people, were suffering death agonies beside him! agonising uselessly; he even caused a portion of their suffering, and aggravated it. For had they had another neighbour, a less chimerical and more observant neighbour, an ordinary and charitable man, it was clear that their poverty would have been noticed, their signals of distress would have been seen, and long ago perhaps they would have been gathered up and saved! Undoubtedly they seemed very depraved, very corrupt, very vile, very hateful, even, but those are rare who fall without becoming degraded; there is a point, moreover, at which the unfortunate and the infamous are associated and confounded in a single word, a fatal word, *Les Misérables*; whose fault is it? And then, is it not when the fall is lowest that charity ought to be greatest?

While he thus preached to himself, for there were times when Marius, like all truly honest hearts, was his own monitor, and scolded himself more than he deserved, he looked at the wall which separated him from the Jondrettes, as if he could send his pitying glance through that partition to warn those unfortunate beings. The wall was a thin layer of plaster, upheld by laths and joists, through which, as we have just seen, voices and words could be distinguished perfectly. None but the dreamer, Marius, would not have perceived this before. There was no paper hung on this wall, either on the side of the Jondrettes, or on Marius' side; its coarse construction was bare to the eye. Almost unconsciously, Marius examined this partition; sometimes reverie examines, observes, and scrutinises, as thought would do. Suddenly he arose, he noticed towards the top, near the ceiling, a triangular hole, where three laths left a space between them. The plaster which should have stopped this hole was gone, and by getting upon the bureau he could see through that hole into the Jondrettes' garret. Pity has and should have its curiosity. This hole was a kind of Judas. It is lawful to look upon misfortune like a betrayer for the sake of relieving it. 'Let us see what these people are,' thought Marius, 'and to what they are reduced.'

He climbed upon the bureau, put his eye to the crevice, and looked.

6. The wild man in his lair

CITIES, like forests, have their dens in which hide all their vilest and most terrible monsters. But in cities, what hides thus is ferocious, unclean, and petty, that is to say, ugly; in forests, what hides is ferocious, savage, and grand, that is to say, beautiful. Den for den, those of beasts are preferable to those of men. Caverns are better than the wretched holes which shelter humanity.

What Marius saw was a hole.

Marius was poor and his room was poorly furnished, but even as his poverty was noble, his garret was clean. The den into which his eyes were at that moment directed, was abject, filthy, fetid, infectious, gloomy, unclean. All the furniture was a straw chair, a rickety table, a few old broken dishes, and in two of the corners two indescribable pallets; all the light came from a dormer window of four panes, curtained with spiders' webs. Just enough light came through that loophole to make a man's face appear like the face of a phantom. The walls had a leprous look, and were covered with seams and scars like a face disfigured by some horrible malady; a putrid moisture oozed from them. Obscene pictures could be discovered upon them coarsely sketched in charcoal.

The room which Marius occupied had a broken brick pavement; this one was neither paved nor floored; the inmates walked immediately upon the old plastering of the ruinous tenement, which had grown black under their feet. Upon this uneven soil where the dust was, as it were, encrusted, and which was virgin soil in respect only of the broom, were grouped at random constellations of socks, old shoes, and hideous rags; however, this room had a fireplace; so it rented for forty francs a year. In the fireplace there was a little of everything, a chafing-dish, a kettle, some broken boards, rags hanging on nails, a birdcage, some ashes, and even a little fire. Two embers were smoking sullenly.

The size of this garret added still more to its horror. It had projections, angles, black holes, recesses under the roof, bays, and promontories. Beyond were hideous, unfathomable corners, which seemed as if they must be full of spiders as big as one's fist, centipedes as large as one's foot, and perhaps even some unknown monsters of humanity.

One of the pallets was near the door, the other near the window. Each had one end next the chimney and both were opposite Marius. In a corner near the opening through which Marius was looking, hanging upon the wall in a black wooden frame, was a coloured engraving at the bottom of which was written in large letters: THE DREAM. It represented a sleeping woman and a sleeping child, the child upon the woman's lap, an eagle in a cloud with a crown in his beak, and the woman putting away the crown from the child's head, but without waking; in the background Napoleon in a halo, leaning against a large blue column with a yellow capital adorned with this inscription:

MARINGO
AUSTERLITS
IENA
WAGRAMME
ELOT

Below this frame a sort of wooden panel longer than it was wide was standing on the floor and leaning at an angle against the wall. It had the appearance of a picture set against the wall, of a frame probably daubed on the other side, of a pier glass taken down from a wall and forgotten to be hung again.

By the table, upon which Marius saw a pen, ink, and paper, was seated a man of about sixty, small, thin, livid, haggard, with a keen, cruel, and restless air; a hideous harpy.

Lavater, if he could have studied this face, would have found in it a mixture of vulture and pettifogger; the bird of prey and the man of tricks rendering each other ugly and complete, the man of tricks making the bird of prey ignoble, the bird of prey making the man of tricks horrible.

This man had a long grey beard. He was dressed in a woman's chemise, which showed his shaggy breast and his naked arms bristling with grey hairs. Below this chemise, were a pair of muddy pantaloons and boots from which the toes stuck out.

He had a pipe in his mouth, and was smoking. There was no more bread in the den, but there was tobacco.

He was writing, probably some such letter as those which Marius had read.

On one corner of the table was an old odd volume with a reddish cover, the size of which, the old duodecimo of series of books, betrayed that it was a novel. On the cover was displayed the following title, printed in huge capitals: GOD, THE KING, HONOUR AND THE LADIES, BY DUCRAY DOMINIL 1814.

As he wrote, the man talked aloud, and Marius heard his words:

'To think that there is no equality even when we are dead! Look at Père Lachaise! The great, those who are rich, are in the upper part, in the avenue of the acacias, which is paved. They can go there in a carriage. The low, the poor, the unfortunate, they are put in the lower part, where there is mud up to the knees, in holes, in the wet. They are put there so that they may rot sooner! You cannot go to see them without sinking into the ground.'

Here he stopped, struck his fist on the table, and added, gnashing his teeth:

'Oh! I could eat the world!'

A big woman, who might have been forty years old or a hundred, was squatting near the fireplace, upon her bare feet.

She also was dressed only in a chemise and a knit skirt patched with pieces of old cloth. A coarse tow apron covered half the skirt. Although this woman was bent and drawn up into herself, it could be seen that she was very tall. She was a kind of giantess by the side of her husband. She had hideous hair, light red sprinkled with grey, that she pushed back from time to time with her huge shining hands which had flat nails.

Lying on the ground, at her side, wide open, was a volume of the same appearance as the other, and probably of the same novel.

Upon one of the pallets Marius could discern a sort of slender little wan girl seated, almost naked, with her feet hanging down, having the appearance neither of listening, nor of seeing, nor of living.

The younger sister, doubtless, of the one who had come to his room.

She appeared to be eleven or twelve years old. On examining her attentively, he saw that she must be fourteen. It was the child who, the evening before, on the boulevard, said: 'I *cavalé, cavalé, cavalé!*'

She was of that sickly species which long remains backward, then pushes forward rapidly, and all at once. These sorry human plants are produced by want. These poor creatures have neither childhood nor youth. At fifteen they appear to be twelve; at sixteen they appear to be twenty. Today a little girl, tomorrow a woman. One would say that they leap through life, to have done with it sooner.

This being now had the appearance of a child.

Nothing, moreover, indicated the performance of any labour in this room; not a loom, not a wheel, not a tool. In one corner a few scraps of iron of an equivocal appearance. It was that gloomy idleness which follows despair, and which precedes the death-agony.

Marius looked for some time into that funereal interior more fearful than the interior of a tomb; for here were felt the movements of a human soul, and the palpitation of life.

The garret, the cellar, the deep ditch, in which some of the wretched crawl at the bottom of the social edifice, are not the sepulchre itself; they are its antechamber; but like those rich men who display their greatest magnificence at the entrance of their palace, death, who is close at hand, seems to display his greatest wretchedness in this vestibule.

The man became silent, the woman did not speak, the girl did not seem to breathe. Marius could hear the pen scratching over the paper.

The man muttered out, without ceasing to write, 'Rabble! rabble! all is rabble!'

This variation upon the ejaculation of Solomon drew a sigh from the woman.

'My darling, be calm,' said she. 'Do not hurt yourself, dear. You are too good to write to all those people, my man.'

In poverty bodies hug close to each other, as in the cold, but hearts grow distant. This woman, according to all appearance, must have loved this man with as much love as was in her; but probably, in the repeated mutual reproaches which grew out of the frightful distress that weighed upon them all, this love had become extinguished. She now felt towards her husband nothing more than the ashes of affection. Still the words of endearment, as often happens, had survived. She said to him: *Dear; my darling; my man*, etc., with her lips, her heart was silent.

The man returned to his writing.

7. *Strategy and tactics*

MARIUS, WITH A HEAVY HEART, was about to get down from the sort of observatory which he had extemporised, when a sound attracted his attention, and induced him to remain in his place.

The door of the garret was hastily opened. The eldest daughter appeared upon the threshold. On her feet she had coarse men's shoes, covered with mud, which had been spattered as high as her red ankles, and she was wrapped in a ragged old gown which Marius had not seen upon her an hour before, but which she had probably left at his door that she might inspire the more pity, and which she must have put on upon going out. She came in, pushed the door to behind her, stopped to take breath, for she was quite breathless, then cried with an expression of joy and triumph:

'He is coming!'

The father turned his eyes, the woman turned her head, the younger sister did not stir.

'Who?' asked the father.

'The gentleman!'

'The philanthropist?'

'Yes.'

'Of the church of Saint Jacques?'

'Yes.'

'That old man?'

'Yes.'

'He is going to come?'

'He is behind me.'

'You are sure?'

'I am sure.'

'There, true, he is coming?'

'He is coming in a fiacre.'

'In a fiacre. It is Rothschild?'

The father arose.

'How are you sure? if he is coming in a fiacre, how is it that you get here before him? you gave him the address, at least? you told him the last door at the end of the hall on the right? provided he does not make a mistake? you found him, at the church then? did he read my letter? what did he say to you?'

'Tut, tut, tut!' said the girl, 'how you run on, goodman! I'll tell you: I went into the church, he was at his usual place, I made a curtsey to him, and I gave him the letter, he read it and said to me: Where do you live, my child? I said: Monsieur, I will show you. He said to me: No, give me your address; my daughter has some purchases to make, I am going to take a carriage and I will get to your house as soon as you do. I gave him the address. When I told him the house, he appeared surprised and hesitated an instant, then he said: It is all the same, I will go. When mass was over, I saw him leave the church with his daughter. I saw them get into a fiacre. And I told him plainly the last door at the end of the hall on the right.'

'And how do you know that he will come?'

'I just saw the fiacre coming into the Rue du Petit Banquier. That is what made me run.'

'How do you know it is the same fiacre?'

'Because I had noticed the number.'

'What is the number?'

'Four hundred and forty.'

'Good, you are a clever girl.'

The girl looked resolutely at her father, and showing the shoes which she had on, said:

'A clever girl, that may be, but I tell you that I shall never put on these shoes again, and that I will not do it, for health first, and then for decency's sake. I know nothing more provoking than soles that squeak and go ghee, ghee, ghee, all along the street. I would rather go barefoot.'

'You are right,' answered the father, in a mild tone which contrasted with the rudeness of the young girl, 'but they would not let you go into the churches; the poor must have shoes. People do not go to God's house barefooted,' added he bitterly. Then returning to the subject which occupied his thoughts:

'And you are sure, then, sure that he is coming?'

'He is at my heels,' said she.

The man sprang up. There was a sort of illumination on his face.

'Wife!' cried he, 'you hear. Here is the philanthropist. Put out the fire.'

The astounded woman did not stir.

The father, with the agility of a mountebank, caught a broken pot which stood on the mantel, and threw some water upon the embers.

Then turning to his elder daughter:

'You! unbottom the chair!'

His daughter did not understand him at all.

He seized the chair, and with a kick he ruined the seat. His leg went through it.

As he drew out his leg, he asked his daughter:

'Is it cold?'

'Very cold. It snows.'

The father turned towards the younger girl, who was on the pallet near the window, and cried in a thundering voice:

'Quick! off the bed, good-for-nothing! will you never do anything? break a pane of glass!'

The little girl sprang off the bed trembling.

'Break a pane of glass!' said he again.

The child was speechless.

'Do you hear me?' repeated the father, 'I tell you to break a pane!'

The child, with a sort of terrified obedience, rose upon tiptoe, and struck her fist into a pane. The glass broke and fell with a crash.

'Good,' said the father.

He was serious, yet rapid. His eye ran hastily over all the nooks and corners of the garret.

You would have said he was a general, making his final preparations at the moment when the battle was about to begin.

The mother, who had not yet said a word, got up and asked in a slow, muffled tone, her words seeming to come out as if curdled:

'Dear, what is it you want to do?'

'Get into bed,' answered the man.

His tone admitted of no deliberation. The mother obeyed, and threw herself heavily upon one of the pallets.

Meanwhile a sob was heard in a corner.

'What is that?' cried the father.

The younger daughter, without coming out of the darkness into which she had shrunk, showed her bleeding fist. In breaking the glass she had cut herself; she had gone to her mother's bed, and she was weeping in silence.

It was the mother's turn to rise and cry out.

'You see now! what stupid things you are doing? breaking your glass, she has cut herself!'

'So much the better!' said the man. 'I knew she would.'

'How! so much the better?' resumed the woman.

'Silence!' replied the father. 'I suppress the liberty of the press.'

Then tearing the chemise which he had on, he made a bandage with which he hastily wrapped up the little girl's bleeding wrist.

That done, his eye fell upon the torn chemise with satisfaction.

'And the chemise too,' said he, 'all this has a good appearance.'

An icy wind whistled at the window and came into the room. The mist from without entered and spread about like a whitish wadding picked apart by invisible fingers. Through the broken pane the falling snow was seen. The cold promised the day before by the Candlemas sun had come indeed.

The father cast a glance about him as if to assure himself that he had forgotten nothing. He took an old shovel and spread ashes over the moistened embers in such a way as to hide them completely.

Then rising and standing with his back to the chimney:

'Now,' said he, 'we can receive the philanthropist.'

8. The sunbeam in the hole

THE LARGE GIRL went to her father and laid her hand on his.

'Feel how cold I am,' said she.

'Pshaw!' answered the father. 'I am a good deal colder than that.'

The mother cried impetuously:

'You always have everything better than the rest, even pain.'

'Down!' said the man.

The mother, after a peculiar look from the man, held her peace.

There was a moment of silence in the den. The eldest daughter was scraping the mud off the bottom of her dress with a careless air, the young sister continued to sob; the mother had taken her head in both hands and was covering her with kisses, saying to her in a low tone:

'My treasure, I beg of you, it will be nothing, do not cry, you will make your father angry.'

'No!' cried the father, 'on the contrary! sob! sob! that does finely.'

Then turning to the eldest:

'Ah! but he does not come! if he was not coming, I shall have put out my fire, knocked the bottom out of my chair, torn my chemise, and broken my window for nothing.'

'And cut the little girl!' murmured the mother.

'Do you know,' resumed the father, 'that it is as cold as a dog in this devilish garret? If this man should not come! Oh! that is it! he makes us wait for him! he says: Well! they will wait for me! that is what they are for! – Oh! how I hate them, and how I would strangle them with joy and rejoicing, enthusiasm and satisfaction, these rich men! all the rich! these professed charitable men, who make their plums, who go to mass, who follow the priesthood, preachy, preachy, who give in to the cowls, and who think themselves above us, and who come to humiliate us, and to bring us clothes! as they call them! rags which are not worth four sous, and bread! that is not what I want of the rabble! I want money! But money, never! because they say that we would go and drink it, and that we are drunkards and do-nothings! And what then are they, and what have they been in their time? Thieves! they would not have got rich without that! Oh! somebody ought to take society by the four corners of the sheet and toss it all into the air! Everything would be crushed, it is likely, but at least nobody would have anything, there would be so much gained! But what now is he doing, your mug of a benevolent gentleman? is he coming? The brute may have forgotten the address! I will bet that the old fool – '

Just then there was a light rap at the door, the man rushed forward and opened it, exclaiming with many low bows and smiles of adoration:

'Come in, monsieur! deign to come in, my noble benefactor, as well as your charming young lady.'

A man of mature age and a young girl appeared at the door of the garret.

Marius had not left his place. What he felt at that moment escapes human language.

It was She.

Whoever has loved, knows all the radiant meaning contained in the three letters of this word: She.

It was indeed she. Marius could hardly discern her through the luminous vapour which suddenly spread over his eyes. It was that sweet absent being, that star which had been his light, for six months, it was that eye, that brow, that mouth, that beautiful vanished face which had produced night when it went away. The vision had been in an eclipse, it was reappearing.

She appeared again in this gloom, in this garret, in this shapeless den, in this horror!

Marius shuddered desperately. What! it was she! the beating of his heart disturbed his sight. He felt ready to melt into tears. What! at last he saw her again after having sought for her so long! it seemed to him that he had just lost his soul and that he had just found it again.

She was still the same, a little paler only; her delicate face was set in a violet velvet hat, her form was hidden under a black satin pelisse, below her long dress he caught a glimpse of her little foot squeezed into a silk buskin.

She was still accompanied by Monsieur Leblanc.

She stepped into the room and laid a large package on the table.

The elder Jondrette girl had retreated behind the door and was looking upon that velvet hat, that silk dress, and that charming happy face, with an evil eye.

9. Jondrette weeps almost

THE DEN was so dark that people who came from outdoors felt as if they were entering a cellar on coming in. The two newcomers stepped forward, therefore, with some hesitation, hardly discerning the dim forms about them, while they were seen and examined with perfect ease by the tenants of the garret, whose eyes were accustomed to this twilight.

Monsieur Leblanc approached with his kind and compassionate look, and said to the father:

'Monsieur, you will find in this package some new clothes, some stockings, and some new coverlets.'

'Our angelic benefactor overwhelms us,' said Jondrette, bowing down to the floor. Then, stooping to his eldest daughter's ear, while the two visitors were examining this lamentable abode, he added rapidly in a whisper:

'Well! what did I tell you? rags? no money. They are all alike! Tell me, how was the letter to this old blubber-lip signed?'

'Fabantou,' answered the daughter.

'The dramatic artist, good!'

This was lucky for Jondrette, for at that very moment Monsieur Leblanc turned towards him and said to him, with the appearance of one who is trying to recollect a name:

'I see that you are indeed to be pitied, Monsieur – '

'Fabantou,' said Jondrette quickly.

'Monsieur Fabantou, yes, that is it. I remember.'

'Dramatic artist, monsieur, and who has had his successes.'

Here Jondrette evidently thought the moment come to make an impression upon the 'philanthropist'. He exclaimed in a tone of voice which belongs to the braggadocio of the juggler at a fair, and, at the same time, to the humility of a beggar on the highway: 'Pupil of Talma! Monsieur! I am a pupil of Talma! Fortune once smiled on me. Alas! now it is the turn of misfortune. Look, my benefactor, no bread, no fire. My poor darlings have no fire! My only chair unseated! A broken window! in such weather as is this! My spouse in bed! sick!'

'Poor woman!' said Monsieur Leblanc.

'My child injured!' added Jondrette.

The child, whose attention had been diverted by the arrival of the strangers, was staring at 'the young lady', and had ceased her sobbing.

'Why don't you cry? why don't you scream?' said Jondrette to her in a whisper.

At the same time he pinched her injured hand. All this with the skill of a juggler.

The little one uttered loud cries.

The adorable young girl whom Marius in his heart called 'his Ursula' went quickly to her:

'Poor, dear child!' said she.

'Look, my beautiful young lady,' pursued Jondrette, 'her bleeding wrist! It is an accident which happened in working at a machine by which she earned six sous a day. It may be necessary to cut off her arm.'

'Indeed!' said the old gentleman alarmed.

The little girl, taking this seriously, began to sob again beautifully.

'Alas, yes, my benefactor!' answered the father.

For some moments, Jondrette had been looking at 'the philanthropist' in a strange manner. Even while speaking, he seemed to scrutinise him closely as if he were trying to recall some reminiscence. Suddenly, taking advantage of a moment when the newcomers were anxiously questioning the smaller girl about her mutilated hand, he passed over to his wife who was lying in her bed, appearing to be overwhelmed and stupid, and said to her quickly and in a very low tone:

'Notice that man!'

Then turning towards M. Leblanc, and continuing his lamentation:

'You see, monsieur! my whole dress is nothing but a chemise of my wife's! and that all torn! in the heart of winter. I cannot go out, for lack of a coat. If I had a sign of a coat, I should go to see Mademoiselle Mars, who knows me, and of whom I am a great favourite. She is still living in the Rue de la Tour des Dames, is not she? You know, monsieur, we have played together in the provinces. I shared her laurels. Celimène would come to my relief, monsieur! Elmira would give alms to Belisarius! But no, nothing! And not a sou in the house! My wife sick, not a sou! My daughter dangerously injured, not a sou! My spouse has choking fits. It is her time of life, and then the nervous system has something to do with it. She needs aid, and my daughter also! But the doctor! but the druggist! how can I pay them! not a penny! I would fall on my knees before a penny, monsieur! You see how the arts are fallen! And do you know, my charming young lady, and you, my generous patron, do you know, you who breathe virtue and goodness, and who perfume that church where my daughter, in going to say her prayers, sees you every day? For I bring up my daughters religiously, monsieur. I have not allowed them to take to the theatre. Ah! the rogues! that I should see them tripping! I do not jest! I fortify them with sermons about honour, about morals, about virtue! Ask them! They must walk straight. They have a father. They are none of those unfortunates, who begin by having no family, and who end by marrying the public. They are Mamselle Nobody, and become Madame Everybody. Thank heaven! none of that in the Fabantou family! I mean to educate them virtuously, and that they may be honest, and that they may be genteel, and that they may believe in God's sacred name! Well, monsieur, my worthy monsieur, do you know what is going to happen tomorrow? Tomorrow is the 4th of February, the fatal day, the last delay that my landlord will give me; if I do not pay him this evening, tomorrow my eldest daughter, myself, my spouse with her fever, my child with her wound, we shall all four be turned out of doors, and driven off into the street, upon the boulevard, without shelter, into the rain, upon the snow. You see, monsieur, I owe four quarters, a year! that is sixty francs.'

Jondrette lied. Four quarters would have made but forty francs, and he could not have owed for four, since it was not six months since Marius had paid for two.

M. Leblanc took five francs from his pocket and threw them on the table.

Jondrette had time to mutter into the ear of his elder daughter:

'The whelp! what does he think I am going to do with his five francs? That will not pay for my chair and my window! I must make my expenses!'

Meantime, M. Leblanc had taken off a large brown overcoat, which he wore over his blue surtout, and hung it over the back of the chair.

'Monsieur Fabantou,' said he, 'I have only these five francs with me; but I am going to take my daughter home, and I will return this evening; is it not this evening that you have to pay?'

Jondrette's face lighted up with a strange expression. He answered quickly:

'Yes, my noble monsieur. At eight o'clock, I must be at my landlord's.'

'I will be here at six o'clock, and I will bring you the sixty francs.'

'My benefactor!' cried Jondrette, distractedly.

And he added in an undertone:

'Take a good look at him, wife!'

M. Leblanc took the arm of the beautiful young girl, arid turned towards the door:

'Till this evening, my friends,' said he.

'Six o'clock,' said Jondrette.

'Six o'clock precisely.'

Just then the overcoat on the chair caught the eye of the elder daughter.

'Monsieur,' said she, 'you forget your coat.'

Jondrette threw a crushing glance at his daughter, accompanied by a terrible shrug of the shoulders.

M. Leblanc turned and answered with a smile:

'I do not forget it, I leave it.'

'O my patron,' said Jondrette, 'my noble benefactor, I am melting into tears! Allow me to conduct you to your carriage.'

'If you go out,' replied M. Leblanc, 'put on this overcoat. It is really very cold.'

Jondrette did not make him say it twice. He put on the brown overcoat very quickly.

And they went out all three, Jondrette preceding the two strangers.

10. *Price of public cabriolets: two francs an hour*

MARIUS HAD LOST nothing of all this scene, and yet in reality he had seen nothing of it. His eyes had remained fixed upon the young girl, his heart had, so to speak, seized upon her and enveloped her entirely, from her first step into the garret. During the whole time she had been there, he had lived that life of ecstasy which suspends material perceptions and precipitates the whole soul upon a single point. He contemplated, not that girl, but that light in a satin pelisse and a velvet hat. Had the star Sirius entered the room he would not have been more dazzled.

While the young girl was opening the bundle, unfolding the clothes and the coverlets, questioning the sick mother kindly and the little injured girl tenderly, he watched all her motions, he endeavoured to hear her words. He knew her eyes, her forehead, her beauty, her stature, her gait, he did not know the sound of her voice. He thought he had caught a few words of it once at the Luxembourg, but he was not absolutely sure. He would have given ten years of his life to hear it, to be able to carry a little of that music in his soul. But all was lost in the wretched displays and trumpet blasts of Jondrette. This added a real anger to the transport of Marius. He brooded her with his eyes. He could not imagine that it really was that divine creature which he saw in the midst of the misshapen beings of this monstrous den. He seemed to see a humming-bird among toads.

When he went out, he had but one thought, to follow her, not to give up her track, not to leave her without knowing where she lived, not to lose her again, at least, after having so miraculously found her! He leaped down from the bureau and took his hat. As he was putting his hand on the bolt, and was just going out, he reflected and stopped. The hall was long, the stairs steep, Jondrette a great talker, M. Leblanc doubtless had not yet got into his carriage; if he should turn round in the passage, or on the stairs, or on the doorstep, and perceive him, Marius, in that house, he would certainly be alarmed and would find means to escape him anew, and it would be all over at once. What was to be done? wait a little? but during the delay the carriage might go. Marius was perplexed. At last he took the risk and went out of his room.

There was nobody in the hall. He ran to the stairs. There was nobody on the stairs. He hurried down, and reached the boulevard in time to see a fiacre turn the corner of the Rue du Petit Banquier and return into the city.

Marius rushed in that direction. When he reached the corner of the boulevard, he saw the fiacre again going rapidly down the Rue Mouffetard; the fiacre was already at a long distance, there was no means of reaching it; what should he do? run after it? impossible; and then from the carriage they would certainly notice a man running at full speed in pursuit of them, and the father would recognise him. Just at this moment, marvellous and unheard-of good fortune, Marius saw a public cab passing along the boulevard, empty. There was but one course to take, to get into this cab, and follow the fiacre. That was sure, effectual, and without danger.

Marius made a sign to the driver to stop, and cried to him:

'Right away!'

Marius had no cravat, he had on his old working coat, some of the buttons of which were missing, and his shirt was torn in one of the plaits of the bosom.

The driver stopped, winked, and reached his left hand towards Marius, rubbing his forefinger gently with his thumb.

'What?' said Marius.

'Pay in advance,' said the driver.

Marius remembered that he had only sixteen sous with him.

'How much?' he asked.

'Forty sous.'

'I will pay when I get back.'

The driver made no reply, but to whistle an air from La Palisse and whip up his horse.

Marius saw the cab move away with a bewildered air. For the want of twenty-four sous he was losing his joy, his happiness, his love! he was falling back into night! he had seen, and he was again becoming blind. He thought bitterly, and it must indeed be said, with deep regret, of the five francs he had given that very morning to that miserable girl. Had he had those five francs he would have been saved, he would have been born again, he would have come out of limbo and darkness, he would have come out of his isolation, his spleen, his bereavement; he would have again knotted the black thread of his destiny with that beautiful golden thread which had just floated before his eyes and broken off once more! He returned to the old tenement in despair.

He might have thought that M. Leblanc had promised to return in the evening, and that he had only to take better care to follow him then; but in his wrapt contemplation he had hardly understood it.

Just as he went up the stairs, he noticed on the other side of the boulevard, beside the deserted wall of the Rue de la Barrière des Gobelins, Jondrette in the 'philanthropist's' overcoat, talking to one of those men of dangerous appearance, who, by common consent, are called *prowlers of the barrières*; men of equivocal faces, suspicious speech, who have an appearance of evil intentions, and who usually sleep by day, which leads us to suppose that they work by night.

These two men quietly talking while the snow was whirling about them in its fall made a picture which a policeman certainly would have observed, but which Marius hardly noticed.

Nevertheless, however mournful was the subject of his reflections, he could not help saying to himself that this prowler of the barrières with whom Jondrette was talking, resembled a certain Panchaud, alias Printanier, alias Bigrenaille, whom Courfeyrac had once pointed out to him, and who passed in the quarter for a very dangerous night-wanderer. We have seen this man's name in the preceding book. This Panchaud, alias Printanier, alias Bigrenaille, figured afterwards in several criminal trials, and has since become a celebrated scoundrel. He was still at that time only a notorious scoundrel. He is now a matter of tradition among bandits and assassins. He was the head of a school near the close of the last reign. And in the evening, at nightfall, at the hour when crowds gather and speak low, he was talked about at the La Force in La Fosse aux Lions. You might even, in that prison, just at the spot where that privy sewer, which served for the astonishing escape of thirty prisoners in broad day in 1843, passes under the encircling passage-way; you might, above the flagging of that sewer, read his name, PANCHAUD, audaciously cut by himself upon the outer wall in one of his attempts to escape. In 1832 the police already had him under their eye, but he had not yet really made his début.

11. Offers of service by misery to grief

Marius mounted the stairs of the old tenement with slow steps; just as he was going into his cell, he perceived in the hall behind him the elder Jondrette girl, who was following him. This girl was odious to his sight; it was she who had his five francs, it was too late to ask her for them, the cab was there no longer, the fiacre was far away. Moreover she would not give them back to him. As to questioning her about the address of the people who had just come, that was useless; it was plain that she did not know, since the letter signed Fabantou was addressed *to the beneficent gentleman of the Church Saint Jacques du Haut Pas.*

Marius went into his room and pushed to his door behind him. It did not close; he turned and saw a hand holding the door partly open.

'What is it?' he asked; 'who is there?'

It was the Jondrette girl.

'Is it you?' said Marius almost harshly, 'you again? What do you want of me?'

She seemed thoughtful and did not look at him. She had lost the assurance which she had had in the morning. She did not come in, but stopped in the dusky hall, where Marius perceived her through the half-open door.

'Come now, will you answer?' said Marius. 'What is it you want of me?'

She raised her mournful eyes, in which a sort of confused light seemed to shine dimly, and said to him:

'Monsieur Marius, you look sad. What is the matter with you?'

'With me?'

'Yes, you.'

'There is nothing the matter with me.'

'Yes!'

'No.'

'I tell you there is!'

'Let me be quiet!'

Marius pushed the door anew, she still held it back.

'Stop,' said she, 'you are wrong. Though you may not be rich, you were good this morning. Be so again now. You gave me something to eat, tell me now what ails you. You are troubled at something, that is plain. I do not want you to be troubled. What must be done for that? Can I serve you in anything? Let me. I do not ask your secrets, you need not tell them to me, but yet I may be useful. I can certainly help you, since I help my father. When it is necessary to carry letters, go into houses, inquire from door to door, find out an address, follow somebody, I do it. Now, you can certainly tell me what is the matter with you, I will go and speak to the persons; sometimes for somebody to speak to the persons is enough to understand things, and it is all arranged. Make use of me.'

An idea came into Marius' mind. What straw do we despise when we feel that we are sinking?

He approached the girl.

'Listen,' said he to her, kindly.

She interrupted him with a flash of joy in her eyes.

'Oh! yes, talk softly to me! I like that better.'

'Well,' resumed he, 'you brought this old gentleman here with his daughter.'

'Yes.'

'Do you know their address?'

'No.'

'Find it for me.'

The girl's eyes, which had been gloomy, had become joyful; they now became dark.

'Is that what you want?' she asked.

'Yes.'

'Do you know them?'

'No.'

'That is to say,' said she hastily, 'you do not know her, but you want to know her.'

This *them* which had become *her* had an indescribable significance and bitterness.

'Well, can you do it?' said Marius.

'You shall have the beautiful young lady's address.'

There was again, in these words 'the beautiful young lady', an expression which made Marius uneasy. He continued:

'Well, no matter! the address of the father and daughter. Their address, yes!'

She looked steadily at him.

'What will you give me?'

'Anything you wish!'

'Anything I wish?'

'Yes.'

'You shall have the address.'

She looked down, and then with a hasty movement closed the door.

Marius was alone.

He dropped into a chair, with his head and both elbows on the bed, swallowed up in thoughts which he could not grasp, and as if he were in a fit of vertigo. All that had taken place since morning, the appearance of the angel, her disappearance, what this poor creature had just said to him, a gleam of hope floating in an ocean of despair – all this was confusedly crowding his brain.

Suddenly he was violently awakened from his reverie.

He heard the loud, harsh voice of Jondrette pronounce these words for him, full of the strangest interest:

'I tell you that I am sure of it, and that I recognised him!'

Of whom was Jondrette talking? he had recognised whom? M. Leblanc? the father of 'his Ursula'? What! did Jondrette know him? was Marius just about to get in this sudden and unexpected way all the information the lack of which made his life obscure to himself? was he at last to know whom he loved, who that young girl was? who her father was? was the thick shadow which enveloped them to be rolled away? was the veil to be rent? Oh! heavens!

He sprang, rather than mounted, upon the bureau, and resumed his place near the little aperture in the partition.

He again saw the interior of the Jondrette den.

12. Use of M. Leblanc's five-franc piece

NOTHING had changed in the appearance of the family, except that the wife and daughters had opened the package, and put on the woollen stockings and underclothes. Two new coverlets were thrown over the two beds.

Jondrette had evidently just come in. He had not yet recovered his regular breathing. His daughters were sitting on the floor near the fireplace, the elder binding up the hand of the younger. His wife lay as if exhausted upon the pallet near the fireplace, with an astonished countenance. Jondrette was walking up and down the garret with rapid strides. His eyes had an extraordinary look.

The woman, who seemed timid and stricken with stupor before her husband, ventured to say to him:

'What, really? you are sure?'

'Sure! It was eight years ago! but I recognise him! Ah! I recognise him! I recognised him immediately. What! it did not strike you?'

'No.'

'And yet I told you to pay attention. But it is the same height, the same face, hardly any older; there are some men who do not grow old; I don't know how they do it; it is the same tone of voice. He is better dressed, that is all! Ah! mysterious old devil, I have got you, all right!'

He checked himself, and said to his daughters:

'You go out! It is queer that it did not strike your eye.'

They got up to obey.

The mother stammered out:

'With her sore hand?'

'The air will do her good,' said Jondrette. 'Go along.'

It was clear that this man was one of those to whom there is no reply. The two girls went out.

Just as they were passing the door, the father caught the elder by the arm, and said with a peculiar tone:

'You will be here at five o'clock precisely. Both of you. I shall need you.'

Marius redoubled his attention.

Alone with his wife, Jondrette began to walk the room again, and took two or three turns in his silence. Then he spent a few minutes in tucking the bottom of the woman's chemise which he wore into the waist of his trousers.

Suddenly he turned towards the woman, folded his arms, and exclaimed:

'And do you want I should tell you one thing? the young lady – '

'Well, what?' said the woman, 'the young lady?'

Marius could doubt no longer, it was indeed of her that they were talking. He listened with an intense anxiety. His whole life was concentrated in his ears.

But Jondrette stooped down, and whispered to his wife. Then he straightened up and finished aloud:

'It is she!'

'That girl?' said the wife.

'That girl!' said the husband.

No words could express what there was in the *that girl* of the mother. It was surprise, rage, hatred, anger, mingled and combined in a monstrous intonation.

The few words that had been spoken, some name, doubtless, which her husband had whispered in her ear, had been enough to rouse this huge drowsy woman and to change her repulsiveness to hideousness.

'Impossible!' she exclaimed, 'when I think that my daughters go barefoot and have not a dress to put on! What! a satin pelisse, a velvet hat, buskins, and all! more than two hundred francs worth! one would think she was a lady! no, you are mistaken! why, in the first place she was horrid, this one is not bad! she is really not bad! it cannot be she!'

'I tell you it is she. You will see.'

At this absolute affirmation, the woman raised her big red and blonde face and looked at the ceiling with a hideous expression. At that moment she appeared to Marius still more terrible than her husband. She was a swine with the look of a tigress.

'What!' she resumed, 'this horrible beautiful young lady who looked at my girls with an appearance of pity, can she be that beggar! Oh, I would like to stamp her heart out!'

She sprang off the bed, and remained a moment standing, her hair flying, her nostrils distended, her mouth half open, her fists clenched and drawn back. Then she fell back upon the pallet. The man still walked back and forth, paying no attention to his female.

After a few moments of silence, he approached her and stopped before her, with folded arms, as before.

'And do you want I should tell you one thing?'

'What?' she asked.

He answered in a quick and low voice:

'My fortune is made.'

The woman stared at him with that look which means: Has the man who is talking to me gone crazy?

He continued:

'Thunder! it is a good long time now that I have been a parishioner of the die-of-hunger-if-you-have-any-fire-and-die-of-cold-if-you-have-any-bread parish! I have had misery enough! my yoke and the yoke of other people! I jest no longer, I find it comic no longer, enough of puns, good God! No more farces, Father Eternal! I want food for my hunger, I want drink for my thirst! to stuff! to sleep! to do nothing! I want to have my turn, I do! before I burst! I want to be a bit of a millionaire!'

He took a turn about the garret and added:

'Like other people.'

'What do you mean?' asked the woman.

He shook his head, winked and lifted his voice like a street doctor about to make a demonstration:

'What do I mean? listen!'

'Hist!' muttered the woman, 'not so loud! if it means business nobody must hear.'

'Pshaw! who is there to hear? our neighbour? I saw him go out just now. Besides, does he hear, the great stupid? and then I tell you that I saw him go out.'

Nevertheless, by a sort of instinct, Jondrette lowered his voice, not enough, however, for his words to escape Marius. A favourable circumstance, and one which enabled Marius to lose nothing of this conversation, was that the fallen snow deafened the sound of the carriages on the boulevard.

Marius heard this:

'Listen attentively. He is caught, the Crœsus! it is all right. It is already done. Everything is arranged. I have seen the men. He will come this evening at six o'clock. To bring his sixty francs, the rascal! did you see how I got that out, my sixty francs, my landlord, my 4th of February! it is not even a quarter! was that stupid! He will come then at six o'clock! our neighbour is gone to dinner then. Mother Bougon is washing dishes in the city. There is nobody in the house. Our neighbour never comes back before eleven o'clock. The girls will stand watch. You shall help us. He will be his own executor.'

'And if he should not be his own executor,' asked the wife.

Jondrette made a sinister gesture and said:

'We will execute him.'

And he burst into a laugh.

It was the first time that Marius had seen him laugh. This laugh was cold and feeble, and made him shudder.

Jondrette opened a closet near the chimney, took out an old cap and put it on his head after brushing it with his sleeve.

'Now,' said he, 'I am going out. I have still some men to see. Some good ones. You will see how it is going to work. I shall be back as soon as possible, it is a great hand to play, look out for the house.'

And with his two fists in the two pockets of his trousers, he stood a moment in thought, then exclaimed:

'Do you know that it is very lucky indeed that he did not recognise me? If he had been the one to recognise me he would not have come back. He would escape us! It is my beard that saved me! my romantic beard! my pretty little romantic beard!'

And he began to laugh again.

He went to the window. The snow was still falling, and blotted out the grey sky.

'What villainous weather!' said he.

Then folding his coat.

'The skin is too large. It is all the same,' added he, 'he did devilish well to leave it for me, the old scoundrel! Without this I should not have been able to go out and the whole thing would have been spoiled! But on what do things hang!'

And pulling his cap over his eyes, he went out.

Hardly had he had time to take a few steps in the hall, when the door opened and his tawny and cunning face again appeared.

'I forgot,' said he. 'You will have a charcoal fire.'

And he threw into his wife's apron the five-franc piece which the 'philanthropist' had left him.

'A charcoal fire?' asked the woman.

'Yes.'

'How many bushels?'

'Two good ones.'

'That will be thirty sous. With the rest, I will buy something for dinner.'

'The devil, no.'

'Why?'

'The piece of a hundred sous is not to be spent.'

'Why?'

'Because I shall have something to buy.'

'What?'

'Something.'

'How much will you need?'

'Where is there a tool store near here?'

'Rue Mouffetard.'

'Oh! yes, at the corner of some street; I see the shop.'

'But tell me now how much you will need for what you have to buy?'

'Fifty sous or three francs.'

'There won't be much left for dinner.'

'Don't bother about eating today. There is better business.'

'That is enough, my jewel.'

At this word from his wife, Jondrette closed the door, and Marius heard his steps recede along the hall and go rapidly down the stairs.

Just then the clock of Saint Médard struck one.

13. Solus cum solo, in loco remoto, non cogitabantur orare pater noster

MARIUS, ALL DREAMER as he was, was, as we have said, of a firm and energetic nature. His habits of solitary meditation, while developing sympathy and compassion in him, had perhaps diminished his liability to become irritated, but left intact the faculty of indignation; he had the benevolence of a brahmin and the severity of a judge; he would have pitied a toad, but he would have crushed a viper. Now, it was into a viper's hole that he had just been looking; it was a nest of monsters that he had before his eyes.

'I must put my foot on these wretches,' said he.

None of the enigmas which he hoped to see unriddled were yet cleared up; on the contrary, all had perhaps become still darker; he knew nothing more of the beautiful child of the Luxembourg or of the man whom he called M. Leblanc, except that Jondrette knew them. Across the dark words which had been uttered, he saw distinctly but one thing, that an ambuscade was preparing, an ambuscade obscure, but terrible; that they were both running a great risk, she probably, her father certainly; that he must foil the hideous combinations of the Jondrettes and break the web of these spiders.

He looked for a moment at the female Jondrette. She had pulled an old sheet-iron furnace out of a corner and she was fumbling among the old iron.

He got down from the bureau as quietly as he could, taking care to make no noise.

In the midst of his dread at what was in preparation, and the horror with which the Jondrettes had inspired him, he felt a sort of joy at the idea that it would perhaps be given to him to render so great a service to her whom he loved.

But what was he to do? warn the persons threatened? where should he find them? He did not know their address. They had reappeared to his eyes for an instant, then they had again plunged into the boundless depths of Paris. Wait at the door for M. Leblanc at six o'clock in the evening, the time when he would arrive, and warn him of the plot? But Jondrette and his men would see him watching, the place was solitary, they would be stronger than he, they would find means to seize him or get him out of the way, and he whom Marius wished to save would be lost. One o'clock had just struck, the ambuscade was to be carried out at six. Marius had five hours before him.

There was but one thing to be done.

He put on his presentable coat, tied a cravat about his neck, took his hat, and went out, without making any more noise than if he had been walking barefooted upon moss.

Besides the Jondrette woman was still fumbling over her old iron.

Once out of the house, he went to the Rue du Petit Banquier.

He was about midway of that street near a very low wall; which he could have stepped over in some places and which bordered a broad field, he was walking slowly, absorbed in his thoughts as he was, and the snow deafened his steps; all at once he heard voices talking very near him. He turned his head, the street was empty, there was nobody in it, it was broad daylight, and yet he heard voices distinctly.

It occurred to him to look over this wall.

There were in fact two men there with their backs to the wall, seated in the snow, and talking in a low tone.

These two forms were unknown to him, one was a bearded man in a blouse, and the other a long-haired man in tatters. The bearded man had on a Greek cap, the other was bareheaded, and there was snow in his hair.

By bending his head over above them, Marius could hear.

The long-haired one jogged the other with his elbow, and said:

'With Patron-Minette, it can't fail.'

'Do you think so?' said the bearded one; and the long-haired one replied:

'It will be a *fafiot* of five hundred *balles* for each of us, and the worst that can happen: five years, six years, ten years at most!'

The other answered hesitatingly, shivering under his Greek cap:

'Yes, it is a real thing. We can't go against such things.'

'I tell you that the affair can't fail,' replied the long-haired one. 'Father What's-his-name's *maringotte* will be harnessed.'

Then they began to talk about a melodrama which they had seen the evening before at La Gaîté.

Marius went on his way.

It seemed to him that the obscure words of these men, so strangely hidden behind that wall, and crouching down in the snow, were not perhaps without some connection with Jondrette's terrible projects. That must be *the affair*.

He went towards the Faubourg Saint Marceau, and asked at the first shop in his way where he could find a commissary of police.

Number 14, Rue de Pontoise, was pointed out to him.

Marius went thither.

Passing a baker's shop, he bought a two-sou loaf and ate it, foreseeing that he would have no dinner.

On his way he rendered to Providence its due. He thought that if he had not given his five francs to the Jondrette girl in the morning, he would have followed M. Leblanc's fiacre, and consequently known nothing of this, so that there would have been no obstacle to the ambuscade of the Jondrettes, and M. Leblanc would have been lost, and doubtless his daughter with him.

14. In which a police officer gives a lawyer two fisticuffs

ON REACHING Number 14, Rue de Pontoise, he went upstairs and asked for the commissary of police.

'The commissary of police is not in,' said one of the office boys; 'but there is an inspector who answers for him. Would you like to speak to him? is it urgent?'

'Yes,' said Marius.

The office boy introduced him into the commissary's private room. A man of tall stature was standing there, behind a railing, in front of a stove, and holding up with both hands the flaps of a huge overcoat with three capes. He had a square face, a thin and firm mouth, very fierce, bushy, greyish whiskers, and an eye that would turn your pockets inside out. You might have said of this eye, not that it penetrated, but that it ransacked.

This man's appearance was not much less ferocious or formidable than Jondrette's; it is sometimes no less startling to meet the dog than the wolf.

'What do you wish?' said he to Marius, without adding monsieur.

'The commissary of police?'

'He is absent. I answer for him.'

'It is a very secret affair.'

'Speak, then.'

'And very urgent.'

'Then speak quickly.'

This man, calm and abrupt, was at the same time alarming and reassuring. He inspired fear and confidence. Marius related his adventure. – That a person whom he only knew by sight was to be drawn into an ambuscade that very evening; that occupying the room next the place, he, Marius Pontmercy, attorney, had heard the whole plot through the partition; that the scoundrel who had contrived the plot was named Jondrette; that he had accomplices, probably prowlers of the barrières, among others a certain Panchaud, alias Printanier, alias Bigrenaille; that Jondrette's daughters would stand watch; that there was no means of warning the threatened man, as not even his name was known; and finally, that all this was to be done at six o'clock that evening, at the most desolate spot on the Boulevard de l'Hôpital, in the house numbered 50–52.

At that number the inspector raised his head, and said coolly:

'It is then in the room at the end of the hall?'

'Exactly,' said Marius, and he added, 'Do you know that house?'

The inspector remained silent a moment, then answered, warming the heel of his boot at the door of the stove:

'It seems so.'

He continued between his teeth, speaking less to Marius than to his cravat.

'There ought to be a dash of Patron-Minette in this.'

That word struck Marius.

'Patron-Minette,' said he. 'Indeed, I heard that word pronounced.'

And he related to the inspector the dialogue between the long-haired man and the bearded man in the snow behind the wall on the Rue du Petit Banquier.

The inspector muttered:

'The long-haired one must be Brujon, and the bearded one must be Demi-

Liard, alias Deux-Milliards.'

He had dropped his eyes again, and was considering.

'As to the Father What's-his-name, I have a suspicion of who he is. There, I have burnt my coat. They always make too much fire in these cursed stoves. Number 50–52. Old Gorbeau property.'

Then he looked at Marius:

'You have seen only this bearded man and this long-haired man?'

'And Panchaud.'

'You did not see a sort of little devilish rat prowling about there?'

'No.'

'Nor a great, big, clumsy heap, like the elephant in the Jardin des Plantes?'

'No.'

'Nor a villain who has the appearance of an old red cue?'

'No.'

'As to the fourth, nobody sees him, not even his helpers, clerks, and agents. It is not very surprising that you did not see him.'

'No. What are all these beings?' inquired Marius.

The inspector answered:

'And then it is not their hour.'

He relapsed into silence, then resumed:

'No. 50–52. I know the shanty. Impossible to hide ourselves in the interior without the artists perceiving us, then they would leave and break up the play. They are so modest! the public annoys them. None of that, none of that. I want to hear them sing, and make them dance.'

This monologue finished, he turned towards Marius and asked him, looking steadily at him:

'Will you be afraid?'

'Of what?' said Marius.

'Of these men?'

'No more than of you!' replied Marius rudely, who began to notice that this police spy had not yet called him monsieur.

The inspector looked at Marius still more steadily, and continued with a sententious solemnity:

'You speak now like a brave man and an honest man. Courage does not fear crime, and honesty does not fear authority.'

Marius interrupted him:

'That is well enough; but what are you going to do?'

The inspector merely answered:

'The lodgers in that house have latch-keys to get in with at night. You must have one?'

'Yes,' said Marius.

'Have you it with you?'

'Yes.'

'Give it to me,' said the inspector.

Marius took his key from his waistcoat, handed it to the inspector, and added: 'If you trust me, you will come in force.'

The inspector threw a glance upon Marius such as Voltaire would have thrown upon a provincial academician who had proposed a rhyme to him; with a single movement he plunged both his hands, which were enormous, into the two immense pockets of his overcoat, and took out two small steel pistols, of the kind called fisticuffs. He presented them to Marius, saying hastily and abruptly:

'Take these. Go back home. Hide yourself in your room; let them think you have gone out. They are loaded. Each with two balls. You will watch; there is a hole in the wall, as you have told me. The men will come. Let them go on a little. When you deem the affair at a point, and when it is time to stop it, you will fire off a pistol. Not too soon. The rest is my affair. A pistol shot in the air, into the ceiling, no matter where. Above all, not too soon. Wait till the consummation is commenced; you are a lawyer, you know what that is.'

Marius took the pistols and put them in the side pocket of his coat.

'They make a bunch that way, they show,' said the inspector. 'Put them in your fobs rather.'

Marius hid the pistols in his fobs.

'Now,' pursued the inspector, 'there is not a minute to be lost by anybody. What time is it? Half-past two. It is at seven?

'Six o'clock,' said Marius.

'I have time enough,' continued the inspector, 'but I have only enough. Forget nothing of what I have told you. Bang. A pistol shot.'

'Be assured,' answered Marius.

And as Marius placed his hand on the latch of the door to go out, the inspector called to him:

'By the way, if you need me between now and then, come or send here. You will ask for Inspector Javert.'

15. Jondrette makes his purchase

A FEW MOMENTS AFTERWARDS, towards three o'clock, Courfeyrac happened to pass along the Rue Mouffetard in company with Bossuet. The snow was falling still faster, and filled the air. Bossuet was just saying to Courfeyrac:

'To see all these snowflakes falling, one would say that there is a swarm of white butterflies in the sky.' All at once Bossuet perceived Marius, who was going up the street towards the barrière with a very peculiar appearance.

'Hold on, Marius,' said Bossuet.

'I saw him,' said Courfeyrac. 'Don't speak to him.'

'Why?'

'He is busy.'

'At what?'

'Don't you see how he looks?'

'What look?'

'He has the appearance of a man who is following somebody.'

'That is true,' said Bossuet.

'And see what eyes he is making!' added Courfeyrac.

'But who the devil is he following?'

'Some deary-sweety-flowery-bonnet! he is in love.'

'But,' observed Bossuet, 'I do not see any deary, nor any sweety, nor any flowery bonnet in the street. There is no woman.'

Courfeyrac looked, and exclaimed:

'He is following a man!'

In fact a man, with a cap on his head, and whose grey beard they distinguished although only his back could be seen, was walking some twenty paces in advance of Marius.

This man was dressed in a new overcoat, which was too large for him, and a horrid pair of pantaloons in tatters and black with mud.

Bossuet burst out laughing.

'Who is that man?'

'He?' replied Courfeyrac, 'he is a poet. Poets are fond of wearing the trousers of a rabbit-skin pedlar, and the coat of a peer of France.'

'Let us see where Marius is going,' said Bossuet, 'let us see where this man is going, let us follow them, eh?'

'Bossuet!' exclaimed Courfeyrac, 'Eagle of Meaux! you are a prodigious fool. Follow a man who is following a man!'

They went on their way.

Marius had in fact seen Jondrette passing along the Rue Mouffetard and was watching him.

Jondrette went straight on without suspecting that there was now an eye fixed upon him.

He left the Rue Mouffetard, and Marius saw him go into one of the most wretched places on the Rue Gracieuse; he stayed there about a quarter of an hour, and then returned to the Rue Mouffetard. He stopped at a hardware store, which there was in those times at the corner of the Rue Pierre Lombard, and, a few minutes afterwards, Marius saw him come out of the shop, holding in his hand a large cold chisel with a white wooden handle which he concealed under his coat. At the upper end of the Rue de Petit Gentilly, he turned to the left and walked rapidly to the Rue du Petit Banquier. Night was falling; the snow which had ceased to fall for a moment was beginning again; Marius hid just at the corner of the Rue du Petit Banquier, which was solitary, as usual, and did not follow Jondrette further. It was fortunate that he did, for, on reaching the low wall where Marius had heard the long-haired man and the bearded man talking, Jondrette turned around, made sure that nobody was following him or saw him, then stepped over the wall, and disappeared.

The grounds which this wall bounded communicated with the rear court of an old livery stable-keeper of bad repute, who had failed, but who had still a few old vehicles under his sheds.

Marius thought it best to take advantage of Jondrette's absence to get home; besides it was getting late; every evening, Ma'am Burgon, on going out to wash her dishes in the city, was in the habit of closing the house door, which was always locked at dusk; Marius had given his key to the inspector of police; it was important, therefore, that he should make haste.

Evening had come; night had almost closed in; there was now but one spot in the horizon or in the whole sky which was lighted by the sun: that was the moon.

She was rising red behind the low dome of La Salpêtrière.

Marius returned to No. 50–52 with rapid strides. The door was still open, when he arrived. He ascended the stairs on tiptoe, and glided along the wall of the hall as far as his room. This hall, it will be remembered, was lined on both sides by garrets, which were all at that time empty and to let. Ma'am Burgon usually left the doors open. As he passed by one of these doors, Marius thought he perceived in the unoccupied cell four motionless heads, which were made dimly visible by a remnant of daylight falling through the little window. Marius, not wishing to be seen, did not endeavour to see. He succeeded in getting into his room without being perceived and without any noise. It was time. A moment afterwards, he heard Ma'am Burgon going out and closing the door of the house.

16. In which will be found the song to an English air in fashion in 1832

MARIUS SAT DOWN on his bed. It might have been half-past five o'clock. A half-hour only separated him from what was to come. He heard his arteries beat as one hears the ticking of a watch in the dark. He thought of this double march that was going on that moment in the darkness, crime advancing on the one hand, justice coming on the other. He was not afraid, but he could not think without a sort of shudder of the things which were so soon to take place. To him, as to all those whom some surprising adventure has suddenly befallen, this whole day seemed but a dream; and, to assure himself that he was not the prey of a nightmare, he had to feel the chill of the two steel pistols in his fob-pockets.

It was not now snowing; the moon, growing brighter and brighter, was getting clear of the haze, and its light, mingled with the white reflection from the fallen snow, gave the room a twilight appearance.

There was a light in the Jondrette den. Marius saw the hole in the partition shine with a red gleam which appeared to him bloody.

He was sure that this gleam could hardly be produced by a candle. However, there was no movement in their room, nobody was stirring there, nobody spoke, not a breath, the stillness was icy and deep, and save for that light he could have believed that he was beside a sepulchre.

Marius took his boots off softly, and pushed them under his bed.

Some minutes passed. Marius heard the lower door turn on its hinges; a heavy and rapid step ascended the stairs and passed along the corridor, the latch of the garret was noisily lifted; Jondrette came in.

Several voices were heard immediately. The whole family was in the garret. Only they kept silence in the absence of the master, like the cubs in the absence of the wolf.

'It is me,' said he.

'Good evening, *pèremuche*,' squeaked the daughters.

'Well!' said the mother.

'All goes to a charm,' answered Jondrette, 'but my feet are as cold as a dog's. Good, that is right, you are dressed up. You must be able to inspire confidence.'

'All ready to go out.'

'You will forget nothing of what I told you! you will do the whole of it?'

'Rest assured about that.'

'Because – ' said Jondrette. And he did not finish his sentence.

Marius heard him put something heavy on the table, probably the chisel which he had bought.

'Ah, ha!' said Jondrette, 'have you been eating here?'

'Yes,' said the mother, 'I have had three big potatoes and some salt. I took advantage of the fire to cook them.'

'Well,' replied Jondrette, 'tomorrow I will take you to dine with me. There will be a duck and the accompaniments. You shall dine like Charles X; everything is going well?'

Then he added, lowering his voice:

'The mouse-trap is open. The cats are ready.'

He lowered his voice still more and said:

'Put that into the fire.'

Marius heard a sound of charcoal, as if somebody was striking it with pincers or some iron tool, and Jondrette continued:

'Have you greased the hinges of the door, so that they shall not make any noise?'

'Yes,' answered the mother.

'What time is it?'

'Six o'clock, almost. The half has just struck on Saint Médard.'

'The devil!' said Jondrette, 'the girls must go and stand watch. Come here, you children, and listen to me.'

There was a whispering.

Jondrette's voice rose again:

'Has Burgon gone out?'

'Yes,' said the mother.

'Are you sure there is nobody at home in our neighbour's room?'

'He has not been back today, and you know that it is his dinner time.'

'You are sure?'

'Sure.'

'It is all the same,' replied Jondrette; 'there is no harm in going to see whether he is at home. Daughter, take the candle and go.'

Marius dropped on his hands and knees, and crept noiselessly under the bed.

Hardly had he concealed himself, when he perceived a light through the cracks of his door.

'P'pa,' cried a voice, 'he has gone out.'

He recognised the voice of the elder girl.

'Have you gone in?' asked the father.

'No,' answered the girl, 'but as his key is in his door, he has gone out.'

The father cried:

'Go in just the same.'

The door opened, and Marius saw the tall girl come in with a candle. She had the same appearance as in the morning, except that she was still more horrible in this light.

She walked straight towards the bed. Marius had a moment of inexpressible anxiety, but there was a mirror nailed on the wall near the bed; it was to that she was going. She stretched up on tiptoe and looked at herself in it. A sound of old iron rattling was heard in the next room.

She smoothed her hair with the palm of her hand, and smiled at the mirror, singing the while in her broken sepulchral voice:

Nos amours ont duré tout une semaine,
Mais que du bonheur les instants sont courts!
S'adorer huit jours, c'était bien la peine!
Le temps des amours devrait durer toujours!
Devrait durer toujours! devrait durer toujours!

Meanwhile Marius was trembling. It seemed impossible to him that she should not hear his breathing.

She went to the window and looked out, speaking aloud in her half-crazy way.

'How ugly Paris is when he puts a white shirt on!' said she.

She returned to the mirror and renewed her grimaces, taking alternately front and three-quarter views of herself.

'Well,' cried her father, 'what are you doing now?'

'I am looking under the bed and the furniture,' answered she, continuing to arrange her hair; 'there is nobody here.'

'Booby!' howled the father. 'Here immediately, and let us lose no time.'

'I am coming! I am coming!' said she. 'One has no time for anything in this shanty.'

She hummed:

> Vous me quittez pour aller à la gloire,
> Mon triste coeur suivra partout vos pas.

She cast a last glance at the mirror, and went out, shutting the door after her.

A moment afterwards, Marius heard the sound of the bare feet of the two young girls in the passage, and the voice of Jondrette crying to them.

'Pay attention, now! one towards the barrière, the other at the corner of the Rue du Petit Banquier. Don't lose sight of the house door a minute, and if you see the least thing, here immediately! tumble along! You have a key to come in with.'

The elder daughter muttered:

'To stand sentry barefoot in the snow!'

'Tomorrow you shall have boots of beetle colour silk!' said the father.

They went down the stairs, and, a few seconds afterwards, the sound of the lower door shutting announced that they had gone out.

There were now in the house only Marius and the Jondrettes, and probably also the mysterious beings of whom Marius had caught a glimpse in the twilight behind the door of the untenanted garret.

17. *Use of Marius' five-franc piece*

MARIUS judged that the time had come to resume his place at his observatory. In a twinkling, and with the agility of his age, he was at the hole in the partition.

He looked in.

The interior of the Jondrette apartment presented a singular appearance, and Marius found the explanation of the strange light which he had noticed. A candle was burning in a verdigrised candlestick, but it was not that which really lighted the room. The entire den was, as it were, illuminated by the reflection of a large sheet iron furnace in the fireplace, which was filled with lighted charcoal. The fire which the female Jondrette had made ready in the daytime. The charcoal was burning and the furnace was red hot, a blue flame danced over it and helped to show the form of the chisel bought by Jondrette in the Rue Pierre Lombard, which was growing ruddy among the coals. In a corner near the door, and arranged as if for anticipated use, were two heaps which appeared to be, one a heap of old iron, the other a heap of ropes. All this would have made one, who had known nothing of what was going forward, waver between a very sinister idea and a very simple idea. The room thus lighted up seemed rather a smithy than a mouth of hell; but Jondrette, in that glare, had rather the appearance of a demon than of a blacksmith.

The heat of the glowing coals was such that the candle upon the table melted on the side towards the furnace and was burning fastest on that side. An old copper dark lantern, worthy of Diogenes turned Cartouche, stood upon the mantel.

The furnace, which was set into the fireplace, beside the almost extinguished embers, sent its smoke into the flue of the chimney and exhaled no odour.

The moon, shining through the four panes of the window, threw its whiteness into the ruddy and flaming garret; and to Marius' poetic mind, a dreamer even in the moment of action, it was like a thought of heaven mingled with the shapeless nightmares of earth.

A breath of air, coming through the broken square, helped to dissipate the charcoal odour and to conceal the furnace.

The Jondrette lair was, if the reader remembers what we have said of the Gorbeau house, admirably chosen for the theatre of a deed of darkness and violence, and for the concealment of a crime. It was the most retired room of the most isolated house of the most solitary boulevard in Paris. If ambuscade had not existed, it would have been invented there.

The whole depth of a house and a multitude of untenanted rooms separated this hole from the boulevard, and its only window opened upon waste fields enclosed with walls and palisade fences.

Jondrette had lighted his pipe, sat down on the dismantled chair, and was smoking. His wife was speaking to him in a low tone.

If Marius had been Courfeyrac, that is to say, one of those men who laugh at every opportunity in life, he would have burst with laughter when his eye fell upon this woman. She had on a black hat with plumes somewhat similar to the hats of the heralds-at-arms at the consecration of Charles X, an immense tartan shawl over her knit skirt, and the man's shoes which her daughter had disdained in the morning. It was this toilet which had drawn from Jondrette the exclamation: *Good! you are dressed up! you have done well! You must be able to inspire confidence!*

As to Jondrette, he had not taken off the new surtout, too large for him, which M. Leblanc had given him, and his costume continued to offer that contrast between the coat and pantaloons which constituted in Courfeyrac's eyes the ideal of a poet.

Suddenly Jondrette raised his voice:

'By the way, now, I think of it. In such weather as this he will come in a fiacre. Light the lantern, take it, and go down. You will stay there behind the lower door. The moment you hear the carriage stop, you will open immediately, he will come up, you will light him up the stairs and above the hall, and when he comes in here, you will go down again immediately, pay the driver, and send the fiacre away.'

'And the money?' asked the woman.

Jondrette fumbled in his trousers, and handed her five francs.

'What is that?' she exclaimed.

Jondrette answered with dignity:

'It is the monarch which our neighbour gave this morning.'

And he added:

'Do you know? we must have two chairs here.'

'What for?'

'To sit in.'

Marius felt a shiver run down his back on hearing the woman make this quiet reply:

'Pardieu! I will get our neighbour's.'

And with rapid movement she opened the door of the den, and went out into the hall.

Marius physically had not the time to get down from the bureau, and go and hide himself under the bed.

'Take the candle,' cried Jondrette.

'No,' said she, 'that would bother me; I have two chairs to bring. It is moonlight.'

Marius heard the heavy hand of mother Jondrette groping after his key in the dark. The door opened. He stood nailed to his place by apprehension and stupor.

The woman came in.

The gable window let in a ray of moonlight, between two great sheets of shadow. One of these sheets of shadow entirely covered the wall against which Marius was leaning, so as to conceal him.

The mother Jondrette raised her eyes, did not see Marius, took the two chairs, the only chairs which Marius had, and went out, slamming the door noisily behind her.

She went back into the den.

'Here are the two chairs.'

'And here is the lantern,' said the husband. 'Go down quick.'

She hastily obeyed, and Jondrette was left alone.

He arranged the two chairs on the two sides of the table, turned the chisel over in the fire, put an old screen in front of the fireplace, which concealed the furnace, then went to the corner where the heap of ropes was, and stooped down, as if to examine something. Marius then perceived that what he had taken for a shapeless heap, was a rope ladder, very well made, with wooden rounds, and two large hooks to hang it by.

This ladder and a few big tools, actual masses of iron, which were thrown upon the pile of old iron heaped up behind the door, were not in the Jondrette den in the morning, and had evidently been brought there in the afternoon, during Marius' absence.

'Those are smith's tools,' thought Marius.

Had Marius been a little better informed in this line, he would have recognised, in what he took for smith's tools, certain instruments capable of picking a lock or forcing a door, and others capable of cutting or hacking, – the two families of sinister tools, which thieves call *cadets* and *fauchants*.

The fireplace and the table, with the two chairs, were exactly opposite Marius. The furnace was hidden; the room was now lighted only by the candle; the least thing upon the table or the mantel made a great shadow. A broken water-pitcher masked the half of one wall. There was in the room a calm which was inexpressibly hideous and threatening. The approach of some appalling thing could be felt.

Jondrette had let his pipe go out – a sure sign that he was intensely absorbed – and had come back and sat down. The candle made the savage ends and corners of his face stand out prominently. There were contractions of his brows, and abrupt openings of his right hand, as if he were replying to the last counsels of a dark interior monologue. In one of these obscure replies which he was making to himself, he drew the table drawer out quickly towards him, took out a long carving knife which was hidden there, and tried its edge on his nail. This done, he put the knife back into the drawer, and shut it.

Marius, for his part, grasped the pistol which was in his right fob pocket, took it out, and cocked it.

The pistol in cocking gave a little clear, sharp sound.

Jondrette started, and half rose from his chair.

'Who is there?' cried he.

Marius held his breath; Jondrette listened a moment, then began to laugh, saying:

'What a fool I am? It is the partition cracking.'

Marius kept the pistol in his hand.

18. Marius' two chairs face each other

Just then the distant and melancholy vibration of a bell shook the windows. Six o'clock struck on Saint Médard.

Jondrette marked each stroke with a nod of his head. At the sixth stroke, he snuffed the candle with his fingers.

Then he began to walk about the room, listened in the hall, walked, listened again: 'Provided he comes!' muttered he; then he returned to his chair.

He had hardly sat down when the door opened.

The mother Jondrette had opened it, and stood in the hall making a horrible, amiable grimace, which was lighted up from beneath by one of the holes of the dark lantern.

'Walk in,' said she.

'Walk in, my benefactor,' repeated Jondrette, rising precipitately.

Monsieur Leblanc appeared.

He had an air of serenity which made him singularly venerable.

He laid four louis upon the table.

'Monsieur Fabantou,' said he, 'that is for your rent and your pressing wants. We will see about the rest.'

'God reward you, my generous benefactor!' said Jondrette, and rapidly approaching his wife:

'Send away the fiacre!'

She slipped away, while her husband was lavishing bows and offering a chair to Monsieur Leblanc. A moment afterwards she came back and whispered in his ear:

'It is done.'

The snow which had been falling ever since morning, was so deep that they had not heard the fiacre arrive, and did not hear it go away.

Meanwhile Monsieur Leblanc had taken a seat.

Jondrette had taken possession of the other chair opposite Monsieur Leblanc.

Now, to form an idea of the scene which follows, let the reader call to mind the chilly night, the solitudes of La Salpêtrière covered with snow, and white in the moonlight, like immense shrouds, the flickering light of the street lamps here and there reddening these tragic boulevards and the long rows of black elms, not a passer perhaps within a mile around, the Gorbeau tenement at its deepest degree of silence, horror, and night, in that tenement, in the midst of these solitudes, in the midst of this darkness, the vast Jondrette garret lighted by a candle, and in this den two men seated at a table, Monsieur Leblanc tranquil, Jondrette smiling and terrible, his wife, the wolf dam, in a corner, and, behind the partition, Marius, invisible, alert, losing no word, losing no movement, his eye on the watch, the pistol in his grasp.

Marius, moreover, was experiencing nothing but an emotion of horror, no fear. He clasped the butt of the pistol, and felt reassured. 'I shall stop this wretch when I please,' thought he.

He felt that the police was somewhere near by in ambush, awaiting the signal agreed upon, and all ready to stretch out its arm.

He hoped, moreover, that from this terrible meeting between Jondrette and Monsieur Leblanc some light would be thrown upon all that he was interested to know.

19. The distractions of dark corners

No sooner was Monsieur Leblanc seated than he turned his eyes towards the empty pallets.

'How does the poor little injured girl do?' he inquired.

'Badly,' answered Jondrette with a doleful yet grateful smile, 'very badly, my worthy monsieur. Her elder sister has taken her to the Bourbe to have her arm dressed. You will see them, they will be back directly.'

'Madame Fabantou appears to me much better?' resumed Monsieur Leblanc, casting his eyes upon the grotesque accoutrement of the female Jondrette, who, standing between him and the door, as if she were already guarding the exit, was looking at him in a threatening and almost a defiant posture.

'She is dying,' said Jondrette. 'But you see, monsieur! she has so much courage, that woman! She is not a woman, she is an ox.'

The woman, touched by the compliment, retorted with the smirk of a flattered monster:

'You are always too kind to me, Monsieur Jondrette.'

'Jondrette!' said M. Leblanc, 'I thought that your name was Fabantou?'

'Fabantou or Jondrette!' replied the husband hastily. 'Sobriquet as an artist!'

And, directing a shrug of the shoulders towards his wife, which M. Leblanc did not see, he continued with an emphatic and caressing tone of voice:

'Ah! how well we have always got along together, this poor dear and I! What would be left to us, if it were not for that? We are so unfortunate, my respected monsieur! We have arms, no labour! We have courage, no work! I do not know how the government arranges it, but, upon my word of honour, I am no Jacobin, monsieur, I am no brawler, I wish them no harm, but if I were the ministers, upon my most sacred word, it would go differently. Now, for example, I wanted to have my girls learn the trade of making card boxes. You will say: What! a trade? Yes! a trade! a simple trade! a living! What a fall, my benefactor! What a degradation, when one has been what we were! Alas! we have nothing left from our days of prosperity! Nothing but one single thing, a painting, to which I cling, but yet which I shall have to part with, for we must live! item, we must live!'

While Jondrette was talking, with an apparent disorder which detracted nothing from the crafty and cunning expression of his physiognomy, Marius raised his eyes, and perceived at the back of the room somebody whom he had not before seen. A man had come in so noiselessly that nobody had heard the door turn on its hinges. This man had a knit woollen waistcoat of violet colour, old, worn-out, stained, cut, and showing gaps at all its folds, full trousers of cotton velvet, socks on his feet, no shirt, his neck bare, his arms bare and tattooed, and his face stained black. He sat down in silence and with folded arms on the nearest bed, and as he kept behind the woman, he was distinguished only with difficulty.

That kind of magnetic instinct which warns the eye made M. Leblanc turn almost at the same time with Marius. He could not help a movement of surprise, which did not escape Jondrette:

'Ah! I see!' exclaimed Jondrette, buttoning up his coat with a complacent air, 'you are looking at your overcoat. It's a fit! my faith, it's a fit!'

'Who is that man?' said M. Leblanc.

'That man?' said Jondrette, 'that is a neighbour. Pay no attention to him.'

The neighbour had a singular appearance. However, factories of chemical products abound in the Faubourg Saint Marceau. Many machinists might have their faces blacked. The whole person of M. Leblanc, moreover, breathed a candid and intrepid confidence. He resumed:

'Pardon me; what were you saying to me, Monsieur Fabantou?'

'I was telling you, monsieur and dear patron,' replied Jondrette, leaning his elbows on the table, and gazing at M. Leblanc with fixed and tender eyes, similar to the eyes of a boa constrictor, 'I was telling you that I had a picture to sell.'

A slight noise was made at the door. A second man entered, and sat down on the bed behind the female Jondrette. He had his arms bare like the first, and a mask of ink or of soot.

Although this man had, literally, slipped into the room, he could not prevent M. Leblanc from perceiving him.

'Do not mind them,' said Jondrette, 'They are people of the house. I was telling you, then, that I have a valuable painting left. Here, monsieur, look.'

He got up, went to the wall, at the foot of which stood the panel of which we have spoken, and turned it round, still leaving it resting against the wall. It was something, in fact, that resembled a picture, and which the candle scarcely revealed. Marius could make nothing out of it, Jondrette being between him and the picture; he merely caught a glimpse of a coarse daub, with a sort of principal personage, coloured in the crude and glaring style of strolling panoramas and paintings upon screens.

'What is that?' asked M. Leblanc.

Jondrette exclaimed:

'A painting by a master; a picture of great price, my benefactor! I cling to it as to my two daughters, it calls up memories to me! but I have told you, and I cannot unsay it, I am so unfortunate that I would part with it.'

Whether by chance, or whether there was some beginning of distrust, while examining the picture, M. Leblanc glanced towards the back of the room. There were now four men there, three seated on the bed, one standing near the door-casing; all four bare-armed, motionless, and with blackened faces. One of those who were on the bed was leaning against the wall, with his eyes closed, and one would have said he was asleep. This one was old; his white hair over his black face was horrible. The two others appeared young; one was bearded, the other had long hair. None of them had shoes on; those who did not have socks were barefooted.

Jondrette noticed that M. Leblanc's eye was fixed upon these men.

'They are friends. They live near by,' said he. 'They are dark because they work in charcoal. They are chimney doctors. Do not occupy your mind with them, my benefactor, but buy my picture. Take pity on my misery. I shall not sell it to you at a high price. How much do you estimate it worth?'

'But,' said M. Leblanc, looking Jondrette full in the face and like a man who puts himself on his guard, 'this is some tavern sign, it is worth about three francs.'

Jondrette answered calmly:

'Have you your pocket-book here? I will be satisfied with a thousand crowns.'

M. Leblanc rose to his feet, placed his back to the wall, and ran his eye rapidly over the room. He had Jondrette at his left on the side towards the window, and his wife and the four men at his right on the side towards the door. The four men did not stir, and had not even the appearance of seeing him; Jondrette had begun again to talk in a plaintive key, with his eye so wild and his tones so mournful, that M. Leblanc might have thought that he had before his eyes nothing more nor less than a man gone crazy from misery.

'If you do not buy my picture, dear benefactor,' said Jondrette, 'I am without resources, I have only to throw myself into the river. When I think that I wanted to have my two girls learn to work on cardboard demi-fine, cardboard work for gift-boxes. Well! they must have a table with a board at the bottom so that the glasses shall not fall on the ground, they must have a furnace made on purpose, a pot with three compartments for the different degrees of strength which the paste must have according to whether it is used for wood, for paper, or for cloth, a knife to cut the pasteboard, a gauge to adjust it, a hammer for the stamps, pincers, the devil, how do I know what else? and all this to earn four sous a day! and work fourteen hours! and every box passes through the girl's hands thirteen times! and wetting the paper! and to stain nothing! and to keep the paste warm! the devil! I tell you! four sous a day! how do you think one can live?'

While speaking Jondrette did not look at M. Leblanc, who was watching him. M. Leblanc's eye was fixed upon Jondrette, and Jondrette's eye upon the door. Marius' breathless attention went from one to the other. M. Leblanc appeared to ask himself, 'Is this an idiot?' Jondrette repeated two or three times with all sorts of varied inflections in the drawling and begging style: 'I can only throw myself into the river! I went down three steps for that the other day by the side of the bridge of Austerlitz!'

Suddenly his dull eye lighted up with a hideous glare, this little man straightened up and became horrifying, he took a step towards M. Leblanc and cried to him in a voice of thunder:

'But all that is not the question! do you know me?'

20. *The ambuscade*

THE DOOR of the garret had been suddenly flung open, disclosing three men in blue blouses with black paper masks. The first was spare and had a long iron-bound cudgel; the second, who was a sort of colossus, held by the middle of the handle, with the axe down, a butcher's pole-axe. The third, a broad-shouldered man, not so thin as the first, nor so heavy as the second, held in his clenched fist an enormous key stolen from some prison door.

It appeared that it was the arrival of these men for which Jondrette was waiting. A rapid dialogue commenced between him and the man with the cudgel, the spare man.

'Is everything ready?' said Jondrette.

'Yes,' answered the spare man.

'Where is Montparnasse then?'

'The young primate stopped to chat with your daughter.'

'Which one?'

'The elder.'

'Is there a fiacre below?'

'Yes.'

'The *maringotte* is ready?'

'Ready.'

'With two good horses?'

'Excellent.'

'It is waiting where I said it should wait?'

'Yes.'

'Good,' said Jondrette.

M. Leblanc was very pale. He looked over everything in the room about him like a man who understands into what he has fallen, and his head, directed in turn towards all the heads which surrounded him, moved on his neck with an attentive and astonished slowness, but there was nothing in his manner which resembled fear. He had made an extemporised entrenchment of the table; and this man who, the moment before, had the appearance only of a good old man, had suddenly become a sort of athlete, and placed his powerful fist upon the back of his chair with a surprising and formidable gesture.

This old man, so firm and so brave before so great a peril, seemed to be one of those natures who are courageous as they are good, simply and naturally. The father of a woman that we love is never a stranger to us. Marius felt proud of this unknown man.

Three of the men of whom Jondrette had said: they are *chimney doctors*, had taken from the heap of old iron, one a large pair of shears, another a steelyard bar, the third a hammer, and placed themselves before the door without saying a word. The old man was still on the bed, and had merely opened his eyes. The woman Jondrette was sitting beside him.

Marius thought that in a few seconds more the time would come to interfere, and he raised his right hand towards the ceiling, in the direction of the hall, ready to let off his pistol-shot.

Jondrette, after his colloquy with the man who had the cudgel, turned again towards M. Leblanc and repeated his question, accompanying it with that low, smothered, and terrible laugh of his:

'You do not recognise me, then?'

M. Leblanc looked him in the face, and answered:

'No.'

Then Jondrette came up to the table. He leaned forward over the candle, folding his arms, and pushing his angular and ferocious jaws up towards the calm face of M. Leblanc, as nearly as he could without forcing him to draw back, and in that posture, like a wild beast just about to bite, he cried:

'My name is not Fabantou, my name is not Jondrette, my name is Thénardier! I am the innkeeper of Montfermeil! do you understand me? Thénardier! now do you know me?'

An imperceptible flush passed over M. Leblanc's forehead and he answered without tremor or elevation of voice, and with his usual placidness:

'No more than before.'

Marius did not hear this answer. Could anybody have seen him at that moment in that darkness, he would have seen that he was haggard, astounded, and thunderstruck. When Jondrette had said: *My name is Thénadier*, Marius had trembled in every limb, and supported himself against the wall as if he had felt the chill of a sword-blade through his heart. Then his right arm, which was just ready to fire the signal shot, dropped slowly down, and at the moment that Jondrette had repeated: *Do you understand me, Thénardier*? Marius' nerveless fingers had almost dropped the pistol. Jondrette, in unveiling who he was, had not moved M. Leblanc, but he had completely unnerved Marius. That name of Thénardier, which M. Leblanc did not seem to know, Marius knew. Remember what that name was to him! that name he had worn on his heart, written in his father's will! he carried it in the innermost place of his thoughts, in the holiest spot of his memory, in that sacred command: 'A man named Thénardier saved my life. If my son should meet him, he will do him all the good he can.' That name, we remember, was one of the devotions of his soul; he mingled it with the name of his father in his worship. What! here was Thénardier, here was that Thénardier, here was that innkeeper of Montfermeil, for whom he had so long and so vainly sought! He had found him at last, and how? this saviour of his father was a bandit! this man, to whom he, Marius, burned to devote himself, was a monster! this deliverer of Colonel Pontmercy was in the actual commission of a crime, the shape of which Marius did not yet see very distinctly, but which looked like an assassination! and upon whom, Great God! what a fatality! what a bitter mockery of Fate! His father from the depths of his coffin commanded him to do all the good he could to Thénardier; for four years Marius had had no other thought than to acquit this debt of his father, and the moment that he was about to cause a brigand to be seized by justice, in the midst of a crime, destiny called to him: that is Thénardier! his father's life, saved in a storm of grape upon the heroic field of Waterloo, he was at last about to reward this man for, and to reward him with the scaffold! He had resolved, if ever he found this Thénardier, to accost him in no other wise than by throwing himself at his feet, and now he found him indeed, but to deliver him to the executioner! his father said to him: Aid Thénardier! and he was answering that adored and holy voice by crushing Thénardier! presenting as a spectacle to his father in his tomb, the man who had snatched him from death at the peril of his life, executed in the Place St Jaques by the act of his son, this Marius to whom he had bequeathed this man! And what a mockery to have worn so long upon his breast the last wishes of his father, written by his hand, only to act so frightfully contrary to them! but on the other hand, to see this ambuscade and not prevent it! to condemn the victim and spare the assassin, could he be bound to any gratitude towards such a wretch? all the ideas which Marius had had for the last four years were, as it were, pierced through and through by this unexpected blow. He shuddered. Everything depended upon him. He held in his hand, they all unconscious, these beings who were moving there before his eyes. If he fired the pistol, M. Leblanc was saved and Thénardier was lost; if he did not, M. Leblanc was sacrificed, and, perhaps, Thénardier escaped. To hurl down the one, or to let the other fall! remorse on either hand. What was to be done? which should he choose? be wanting to his most imperious memories, to so many deep resolutions, to his most sacred duty, to that most venerated paper! be wanting to his father's will, or suffer a crime to be accomplished? He seemed on the one hand to hear 'his Ursula' entreating him for her father, and on the other the colonel commending Thénardier to him. He felt that he was mad. His knees gave way beneath him; and he had not even time to deliberate, with such fury was the scene which he had before his eyes rushing forward. It was like a whirlwind, which he had thought himself master of, and which was carrying him away. He was on the point of fainting.

Meanwhile Thénardier, we will call him by no other name henceforth, was walking to and fro before the table in a sort of bewilderment and frenzied triumph.

He clutched the candle and put it on the mantel with such a shock that the flame was almost extinguished and the tallow was spattered upon the wall.

Then he turned towards M. Leblanc, and with a frightful look, spat out this:

'Singed! smoked! basted! spitted!'

And he began to walk again, in full explosion.

'Ha!' cried he, 'I have found you again at last, monsieur philanthropist! monsieur threadbare millionaire! monsieur giver of dolls! old marrow-bones! ha! you do not know me? no, it was not you who came to Montfermeil, to my inn, eight years ago, the night of Christmas 1823! it was not you who took away Fantine's child from my house! the Lark! it was not you who had a yellow coat! no! and a package of clothes in your hand just as you came here this morning! say now, wife! it is his mania it appears, to carry packages of woollen stockings into houses! old benevolence, get out! Are you a hosier, monsieur millionaire? you give the poor your shop sweepings, holy man! what a charlatan! Ha! you do not know me? Well, I knew you! I knew you immediately as soon as you stuck your nose in here. Ah! you are going to find out at last that it is not all roses to go into people's houses like that, under pretext of their being inns, with worn-out clothes, with the appearance of a pauper, to whom anybody would have given a sou, to deceive persons, to act the generous, take their help away, and threaten them in the woods, and that you do not get quit of it by bringing back afterward, when people are ruined, an overcoat that is too large and two paltry hospital coverlets, old beggar, child-stealer!'

He stopped, and appeared to be talking to himself for a moment. One would have said that his fury dropped like the Rhone into some hole; then, as if he were finishing aloud something that he had been saying to himself, he struck his fist on the table and cried:

'With his honest look!'

And apostrophising M. Leblanc:

'Zounds! you made a mock of me once! You are the cause of all my misfortunes! For fifteen hundred francs you got a girl that I had, and who certainly belonged to rich people, and who had already brought me in a good deal of money, and from whom I ought to have got enough to live on all my life! A girl who would have made up all that I lost in that abominable chop-house where they had such royal sprees and where I devoured my all like a fool! Oh! I wish that all the wine that was drunk in my house had been poison to those who drank it! But no matter! Say, now! you must have thought me green when you went away with the Lark? you had your club in the woods! you were the strongest! Revenge! The trumps are in my hand today. You are skunked, my good man! Oh! but don't I laugh! Indeed, I do! Didn't he fall into the trap? I told him that I was an actor, that my name was Fabantou, that I had played comedy with Mamselle Mars, with Mamselle Muche, that my landlord must be paid tomorrow the 4th of February, and he did not even think that the 8th of January is quarter day and not the 4th of February! The ridiculous fool! And these four paltry philippes that he brings me! Rascal! He had not even heart enough to go up to a hundred francs! And how he swallowed my platitudes! The fellow amused me. I said to myself: Blubber-lips! Go on, I have got you, lick your paws this morning! I will gnaw your heart tonight!'

Thénardier stopped. He was out of breath. His little narrow chest was blowing like a blacksmith's bellows. His eye was full of the base delight of a feeble, cruel, and cowardly animal, which can finally prostrate that of which it has stood in awe, and insult what it has flattered, the joy of a dwarf putting his heel upon the head of Goliath, the joy of a jackal beginning to tear a sick bull, dead enough not to be able to defend himself, alive enough yet to suffer.

M. Leblanc did not interrupt him but said when he stopped:

'I do not know what you mean. You are mistaken. I am a very poor man and anything but a millionaire. I do not know you; you mistake me for another.'

'Ha!' screamed Thénardier, 'good mountebank! You stick to that joke yet! You are in the fog, my old boy! Ah! you do not remember! You do not see who I am!'

'Pardon me, monsieur,' answered M. Leblanc, with a tone of politeness which, at such a moment, had a peculiarly strange and powerful effect, 'I see that you are a bandit.'

Who has not noticed it, hateful beings have their tender points; monsters are easily annoyed. At this word bandit, the Thénardiess sprang off the bed. Thénardier seized his chair as if he were going to crush it in his hands: 'Don't you stir,' cried he to his wife, and turning towards M. Leblanc:

'Bandit! Yes, I know that you call us so, you rich people! Yes! it is true I have failed; I am in concealment, I have no bread; I have not a sou, I am a bandit! Here are three days that I have eaten nothing, I am a bandit! Ah! you warm your feet; you have Sacoski pumps, you have wadded overcoats like archbishops, you live on the first floor in houses with a porter, you eat truffles, you eat forty-franc bunches of asparagus in the month of January, and green peas, you stuff yourselves, and when you want to know if it is cold you look in the newspaper to see at what degree the thermometer of the inventor, Chevalier, stands. But we are our own thermometers! We have no need to go to the quay at the corner of the Tour de l'Horloge, to see how many degrees below zero it is; we feel the blood stiffen in our veins and the ice reach our hearts, and we say: 'There is no God!' And you come into our caverns, yes, into our caverns, and call us bandits. But we will eat you! but we will devour you, poor little things! Monsieur Millionaire! know this: I have been a man established in business, I have been licensed, I have been an elector, I am a citizen, I am! And you, perhaps, are not one?'

Here Thénardier took a step towards the men who were before the door, and added with a shudder:

'When I think that he dares to come and talk to me, as if I were a cobbler!'

Then addressing M. Leblanc with a fresh burst of frenzy:

'And know this, too, monsieur philanthropist! I am no doubtful man. I am not a man whose name nobody knows, and who comes into houses to carry off children. I am an old French soldier; I ought to be decorated. I was at Waterloo, I was, and in that battle I saved a general, named the Comte de Pontmercy. This picture which you see, and which was painted by David at Bruqueselles, do you know who it represents? It represents me. David desired to immortalise that feat of arms. I have General Pontmercy on my back, and I am carrying him through the storm of grape. That is history. He has never done anything at all for me, this general; he is no better than other people. But, nevertheless, I saved his life at the risk of my own, and I have my pockets full of certificates. I am a soldier of Waterloo – name of a thousand names! And now that I have had the goodness to tell you all this, let us make an end of it; I must have some money; I must have a good deal of money, I must have an immense deal of money, or I will exterminate you, by the thunder of God!'

Marius had regained some control over his distress, and was listening. The last possibility of doubt had now vanished. It was indeed the Thénardier of the will. Marius shuddered at that reproach of ingratitude flung at his father, and which he was on the point of justifying so fatally. His perplexities were redoubled. Moreover, there was in all these words of Thénardier, in his tone, in his gestures, in his look which flashed out flames at every word, there was in this explosion of an evil nature exposing its entire self, in this mixture of braggadocio and abjectness, of pride and pettiness, of rage and folly in this chaos of real grievances and false sentiments, in this shamelessness of a wicked man tasting the sweetness of violence, in this brazen nakedness of a deformed soul, in this conflagration of every suffering combined with every hatred, something which was as hideous as evil and as sharp and bitter as the truth.

The picture by a master, the painting by David, the purchase of which he had proposed to M. Leblanc, was, the reader has guessed, nothing more than the sign of his chop-house, painted, as will be remembered, by himself, the only relic which he had saved from his shipwreck at Montfermeil.

As he had ceased to intercept Marius' line of vision, Marius could now look at the thing, and in this daub he really made out a battle, a background of smoke, and one man carrying off another. It was the group of Thénardier and Pontmercy; the saviour sergeant, the colonel saved. Marius was as it were intoxicated; this picture in some sort restored his father to life; it was not now the sign of the Montfermeil inn, it was a resurrection; in it a tomb half opened, from it a phantom arose. Marius heard his heart ring in his temples, he had the cannon of Waterloo sounding in his ears; his bleeding father dimly painted upon this dusky panel startled him, and it seemed to him that that shapeless shadow was gazing steadily upon him.

When Thénardier had taken breath he fixed his bloodshot eyes upon Monsieur Leblanc, and said in a low and abrupt tone:

'What have you to say before we begin to dance with you?'

Monsieur Leblanc said nothing. In the midst of this silence a hoarse voice threw in this ghastly sarcasm from the hall:

'If there is any wood to split, I am on hand!'

It was the man with the pole-axe who was making merry.

At the same time a huge face, bristly and dirty, appeared in the doorway, with a hideous laugh, which showed not teeth, but fangs.

It was the face of the man with the pole-axe.

'What have you taken off your mask for?' cried Thénardier, furiously.

'To laugh,' replied the man.

For some moments, Monsieur Leblanc had seemed to follow and to watch all the movements of Thénardier, who, blinded and bewildered by his own rage, was walking to and fro in the den with the confidence inspired by the feeling that the door was guarded, having armed possession of a disarmed man, and being nine to one, even if the Thénardiess should count for but one man. In his apostrophe to the man with the pole-axe, he turned his back to Monsieur Leblanc.

Monsieur Leblanc seized this opportunity, pushed the chair away with his foot, the table with his hand, and at one bound, with a marvellous agility, before Thénardier had had time to turn around, he was at the window. To open it, get up and step through it, was the work of a second. He was half outside when six strong hands seized him, and drew him forcibly back into the room. The three 'chimney doctors' had thrown themselves upon him. At the same time the Thénardiess had clutched him by the hair.

At the disturbance which this made, the other bandits ran in from the hall. The old man, who was on the bed, and who seemed overwhelmed with wine, got off the pallet, and came tottering along with a road-mender's hammer in his hand.

One of the 'chimney doctors,' whose blackened face was lighted up by the candle, and in whom Marius, in spite of this colouring, recognised Panchaud, alias Printanier, alias Bigrenaille, raised a sort of loaded club made of a bar of iron with a knob of lead at each end, over Monsieur Leblanc's head.

Marius could not endure this sight. 'Father,' thought he, 'pardon me!' And his finger sought the trigger of the pistol. The shot was just about to be fired, when Thénardier's voice cried:

'Do him no harm!'

This desperate attempt of the victim, far from exasperating Thénardier, had calmed him. There were two men in him, the ferocious man and the crafty man. Up to this moment, in the first flush of triumph, before his prey stricken down and motionless, the ferocious man had been predominant; when the victim resisted, and seemed to desire a struggle, the crafty man reappeared and resumed control.

'Do him no harm!' he repeated, and without suspecting it, the first result of this was to stop the pistol which was just ready to go off, and paralyse Marius, to whom the urgency seemed to disappear, and who, in view of this new phase of affairs, saw no impropriety in waiting longer. Who knows but some chance may arise which will save him from the fearful alternative of letting the father of Ursula perish, or destroying the saviour of the colonel!

A herculean struggle had commenced. With one blow full in the chest M. Leblanc had sent the old man sprawling into the middle of the room, then with two back strokes had knocked down two other assailants, whom he held one under each knee; the wretches screamed under the pressure as if they had been under a granite millstone; but the four others had seized the formidable old man by the arms and the back, and held him down over the two prostrate 'chimney doctors.' Thus, master of the latter and mastered by the former, crushing those below him and suffocating under those above him, vainly endeavouring to shake off all the violence and blows which were heaped upon him, M. Leblanc disappeared under the horrible group of the bandits, like a wild boar under a howling pack of hounds and mastiffs.

They succeeded in throwing him over upon the bed nearest to the window, and held him there in awe. The Thénardiess had not let go of his hair.

'Here,' said Thénardier, 'let it alone. You will tear your shawl.'

The Thénardiess obeyed, as the she-wolf obeys her mate, with a growl.

'Now, the rest of you,' continued Thénardier, 'search him.'

M. Leblanc seemed to have given up all resistance. They searched him. There was nothing upon him but a leather purse which contained six francs, and his handkerchief.

Thénardier put the handkerchief in his pocket.

'What! no pocket-book?' he asked.

'Nor any watch,' answered one of the 'chimney doctors'.

'It is all the same,' muttered, with the voice of a ventriloquist, the masked man who had the big key, 'he is an old rough.'

Thénardier went to the corner by the door and took a bundle of ropes which he threw to them.

'Tie him to the foot of the bed,' said he, and perceiving the old fellow who lay motionless, when he was stretched across the room by the blow of M. Leblanc's fist:

'Is Boulatruelle dead?' asked he.

'No,' answered Bigrenaille, 'he is drunk.'

'Sweep him into a corner,' said Thénardier.

Two of the 'chimney doctors' pushed the drunkard up to the heap of old iron with their feet.

'Babet, what did you bring so many for?' said Thénardier in a low tone to the man with the cudgel, 'it was needless.'

'What would you have?' replied the man with the cudgel, 'they all wanted to be in. The season is bad. There is nothing doing.'

The pallet upon which M. Leblanc had been thrown was a sort of hospital bed supported by four big roughly squared wooden posts. M. Leblanc made no resistance. The brigands bound him firmly, standing, with his feet to the floor, by the bedpost furthest from the window and nearest to the chimney.

When the last knot was tied, Thénardier took a chair and came and sat down nearly in front of M. Leblanc. Thénardier looked no longer like himself, in a few seconds the expression of his face had passed from unbridled violence to tranquil and crafty mildness. Marius hardly recognised in that polite, clerkly smile, the almost beastly mouth which was foaming a moment before; he looked with astonishment upon this fantastic and alarming metamorphosis, and he experienced what a man would feel who should see a tiger change itself into an attorney.

'Monsieur,' said Thénardier.

And with a gesture dismissing the brigands who still had their hands upon M. Leblanc:

'Move off a little, and let me talk with monsieur.'

They all retired towards the door. He resumed:

'Monsieur, you were wrong in trying to jump out the window. You might have broken your leg. Now, if you please, we will talk quietly. In the first place I must inform you of a circumstance I have noticed, which is that you have not yet made the least outcry.'

Thénardier was right; this incident was true, although it had escaped Marius in his anxiety. M. Leblanc had only uttered a few words without raising his voice, and, even in his struggle by the window with the six bandits, he had preserved the most profound and the most remarkable silence. Thénardier continued:

'Indeed! you might have cried thief a little, for I should not have found it inconvenient. Murder! that is said upon occasion, and, as far as I am concerned, I should not have taken it in bad part. It is very natural that one should make a little noise when he finds himself with persons who do not inspire him with as much confidence as they might; you might have done it, and we should not have disturbed you. We would not even have gagged you. And I will tell you why. It is because this room is very deaf. That is all I can say for it, but I can say that. It is a cave. We could fire a bomb here, and at the nearest guardhouse it would sound like a drunkard's snore. Here a cannon would go boom, and thunder would go puff. It is a convenient apartment. But, in short, you did not cry out, that was better, I make you my compliments for it, and I will tell you what I conclude from it: my dear monsieur, when a man cries out, who is it that comes? The police. And after the police? Justice. Well! you did not cry out; because you were no more anxious than we to see justice and the police come. It is because, – I suspected as much long ago, – you have some interest in concealing something. For our part we have the same interest. Now we can come to an understanding.'

While speaking thus, it seemed as though Thénardier, with his gaze fixed upon Monsieur Leblanc, was endeavouring to thrust the daggers which he looked, into the very conscience of his prisoner. His language, moreover, marked by a sort of subdued and sullen insolence, was reserved and almost select, and in this wretch who was just before nothing but a brigand, one could now perceive the man who studied to be a priest.

The silence which the prisoner had preserved, this precaution which he had carried even to the extent of endangering his life, this resistance to the first impulse of nature, which is to utter a cry, all this, it must be said, since it had been remarked, was annoying to Marius, and painfully astonished him.

The observation of Thénardier, well founded as it was, added in Marius' eyes still more to the obscurity of the mysterious cloud that enveloped this strange and serious face to which Courfeyrac had given the nickname of Monsieur Leblanc. But whatever he might be, bound with ropes, surrounded by assassins, half buried, so to speak, in a grave which was deepening beneath him every moment, before the fury as well as before the mildness of Thénardier, this man remained impassible; and Marius could not repress at such a moment his admiration for that superbly melancholy face.

Here was evidently a soul inaccessible to fear, and ignorant of dismay. Here was one of those men who are superior to astonishment in desperate situations. However extreme the crisis, however inevitable the catastrophe, there was nothing there of the agony of the drowning man, staring with horrified eyes as he sinks to the bottom.

Thénardier quietly got up, went to the fireplace, took away the screen which he leaned against the nearest pallet, and thus revealed the furnace full of glowing coals in which the prisoner could plainly see the chisel at a white heat, spotted here and there with little scarlet stars.

Then Thénardier came back and sat down by Monsieur Leblanc.

'I continue,' said he. 'Now we can come to an understanding. Let us arrange this amicably. I was wrong to fly into a passion just now. I do not know where my wits were, I went much too far, I talked extravagantly. For instance, because you are a millionaire, I told you that I wanted money, a good deal of money, an immense deal of money. That would not be reasonable. My God, rich as you may be, you have your expenses; who does not have them? I do not want to ruin you, I am not a catch-poll, after all. I am not one of those people who, because they have the advantage in position, use it to be ridiculous. Here, I am willing to go half way and make some sacrifice on my part, I need only two hundred thousand francs.'

Monsieur Leblanc did not breathe a word. Thénardier went on:

'You see that I water my wine pretty well. I do not know the state of your fortune, but I know that you do not care much for money, and a benevolent man like you can certainly give two hundred thousand francs to a father of a family who is unfortunate. Certainly you are reasonable also, you do not imagine that I would take the trouble I have today, and that I would organise the affair of this evening, which is a very fine piece of work, in the opinion of these gentlemen, to end off by asking you for enough to go and drink fifteen sou red wine and eat veal at Desnoyers'. Two hundred thousand francs, it is worth it. That trifle once out of your pocket, I assure you that all is said, and that you need not fear a snap of the finger. You will say: but I have not two hundred thousand francs with me. Oh! I am not exacting. I do not require that. I only ask one thing. Have the goodness to write what I shall dictate.'

Here Thénardier paused, then he added, emphasising each word and casting a smile towards the furnace:

'I give you notice that I shall not admit that you cannot write.'

A grand inquisitor might have envied that smile.

Thénardier pushed the table close up to Monsieur Leblanc, and took the inkstand, a pen, and a sheet of paper from the drawer, which he left partly open, and from which gleamed the long blade of the knife.

He laid the sheet of paper before Monsieur Leblanc.

'Write,' said he.

The prisoner spoke at last:

'How do you expect me to write? I am tied.'

'That is true, pardon me!' said Thénardier, 'you are quite right.'

And turning towards Bigrenaille:

'Untie monsieur's right arm.'

Panchaud, alias Printanier, alias Bigrenaille, executed Thénardier's order. When the prisoner's right hand was free, Thénardier dipped the pen into the ink, and presented it to him.

'Remember, monsieur, that you are in our power, at our discretion, that no human power can take you away from here, and that we should be really grieved to be obliged to proceed to unpleasant extremities. I know neither your name nor your address, but I give you notice that you will remain tied until the person whose duty it will be to carry the letter which you are about to write, has returned. Have the kindness now to write.'

'What?' asked the prisoner.

'I will dictate.'

M. Leblanc took the pen.

Thénardier began to dictate:

'My daughter – '

The prisoner shuddered and lifted his eyes to Thénardier.

'Put "my dear daughter",' said Thénardier. M. Leblanc obeyed. Thénardier continued:

'Come immediately – '

He stopped.

'You call her daughter, do you not?'

'Who?' asked M. Leblanc.

'Zounds!' said Thénardier, 'the little girl, the Lark.'

M. Leblanc answered without the least apparent emotion:

'I do not know what you mean.'

'Well, go on,' said Thénardier, and he began to dictate again. 'Come immediately, I have imperative need of you. The person who will give you this note is directed to bring you to me. I am waiting for you. Come with confidence.'

M. Leblanc had written the whole. Thénardier added:

'Ah! strike out *come with confidence*, that might lead her to suppose that the thing is not quite clear and that distrust is possible.'

M. Leblanc erased the three words.

'Now,' continued Thénardier, 'sign it. What is your name?'

The prisoner laid down the pen and asked:

'For whom is this letter?'

'You know very well,' answered Thénardier, 'for the little girl, I have just told you.'

It was evident that Thénardier avoided naming the young girl in question. He said 'the Lark', he said 'the little girl', but he did not pronounce the name. The precaution of a shrewd man preserving his own secret before his accomplices. To speak the name would have been to give up the whole 'affair' to them, and to tell them more than they needed to know.

He resumed:

'Sign it. What is your name?'

'Urbain Fabre,' said the prisoner.

Thénardier, with the movement of a cat, thrust his hand into his pocket and pulled out the handkerchief taken from M. Leblanc. He looked for the mark upon it and held it up to the candle.

'U. F. That is it. Urbain Fabre. Well, sign U. F.'

The prisoner signed.

'As it takes two hands to fold the letter, give it to me, I will fold it.'

This done, Thénardier resumed:

'Put on the address, *Mademoiselle Fabre*, at your house. I know that you live not very far from here, in the neighbourhood of Saint Jacques du Haut Pas, since you go there to mass every day, but I do not know in what street. I see that you understand your situation. As you have not lied about your name, you will not lie about your address. Put it on yourself.'

The prisoner remained thoughtful for a moment, then he took the pen and wrote:

'Mademoiselle Fabre, at Monsieur Urbain Fabre's, Rue Saint Dominique d'Enfer, No. 17.'

Thénardier seized the letter with a sort of feverish convulsive movement.

'Wife!' cried he.

The Thénardiess sprang forward.

'Here is the letter. You know what you have to do. There is a fiacre below. Go right away, and come back ditto.'

And addressing the man with the pole-axe:

'Here, since you have taken off your hide-your-nose, go with the woman. You will get up behind the fiacre. You know where you left the *maringotte*.'

'Yes,' said the man.

And, laying down his pole-axe in a corner, he followed the Thénardiess.

As they were going away, Thénardier put his head through the half-open door and screamed into the hall:

'Above all things do not lose the letter! remember that you have two hundred thousand francs with you.'

The harsh voice of the Thénardiess answered:

'Rest assured, I have put it in my bosom.'

A minute had not passed when the snapping of a whip was heard, which grew fainter and rapidly died away.

'Good!' muttered Thénardier. 'They are going good speed. At that speed the bourgeoise will be back in three quarters of an hour.'

He drew a chair near the fireplace and sat down, folding his arms and holding his muddy boots up to the furnace.

'My feet are cold,' said he.

There were now but five bandits left in the den with Thénardier and the prisoner. These men, through the masks or the black varnish which covered their faces and made of them, as fear might suggest, charcoal men, negroes, or demons, had a heavy and dismal appearance, and one felt that they would execute a crime as they would any drudgery, quietly, without anger and without mercy, with a sort of irksomeness. They were heaped together in a corner like brutes, and were silent. Thénardier was warming his feet. The prisoner had relapsed into his taciturnity. A gloomy stillness had succeeded the savage tumult which filled the garret a few moments before.

The candle, in which a large thief had formed, hardly lighted up the enormous den, the fire had grown dull, and all their monstrous heads made huge shadows on the walls and on the ceiling.

No sound could be heard save the quiet breathing of the drunken old man, who was asleep.

Marius was waiting in an anxiety which everything increased. The riddle was more impenetrable than ever. Who was this 'little girl', whom Thénardier had also called the Lark? was it his 'Ursula?' The prisoner had not seemed to be moved by this word, the Lark, and answered in the most natural way in the world: I do not know what you mean. On the other hand, the two letters U. F. were explained; it was Urbain Fabre, and Ursula's name was no longer Ursula. This Marius saw most clearly. A sort of hideous fascination held him spellbound to the place from which he observed and commanded this whole scene. There he was, almost incapable of reflection and motion, as if annihilated by such horrible things in so close proximity. He was waiting, hoping for some movement, no matter what, unable to collect his ideas and not knowing what course to take.

'At all events,' said he, 'if the Lark is she, I shall certainly see her, for the Thénardiess is going to bring her here. Then all will be plain. I will give my blood and my life if need be, but I will deliver her. Nothing shall stop me.'

Nearly half an hour passed thus. Thénardier appeared absorbed in a dark meditation, the prisoner did not stir. Nevertheless Marius thought he had heard at intervals and for some moments a little dull noise from the direction of the prisoner.

Suddenly Thénardier addressed the prisoner:

'Monsieur Fabre, here, so much let me tell you at once.'

These few words seemed to promise a clearing up. Marius listened closely. Thénardier continued:

'My spouse is coming back, do not be impatient. I think the Lark is really your daughter, and I find it quite natural that you should keep her. But listen a moment; with your letter, my wife is going to find her. I told my wife to dress up, as you saw, so that your young lady would follow her without hesitation. They will both get into the fiacre with my comrade behind. There is somewhere outside one of the barriers a *maringotte* with two very good horses harnessed. They will take your young lady there. She will get out of the carriage. My comrade will get into the *maringotte* with her, and my wife will come back here to tell us: "It is done." As to your young lady, no harm will be done her; the *maringotte* will take her to a place where she will be quiet, and as soon as you have given me the little two hundred thousand francs, she will be sent back to you. If you have me arrested, my comrade will give the Lark a pinch, that is all.'

The prisoner did not utter a word. After a pause, Thénardier continued:

'It is very simple, as you see. There will be no harm done unless you wish there should be. That is the whole story. I tell you in advance so that you may know.'

He stopped; the prisoner did not break the silence, and Thénardier resumed:

'As soon as my spouse has got back and said: "The Lark is on her way," we will release you, and you will be free to go home to bed. You see that we have no bad intentions.'

Appalling images passed before Marius' mind. What! this young girl whom they were kidnapping, they were not going to bring her here? One of those monsters was going to carry her off into the gloom? where? – And if it were she! And it was clear that it was she. Marius felt his heart cease to beat. What was he to do? Fire off the pistol? put all these wretches into the hands of justice? But the hideous man of the pole-axe would none the less be out of all reach with the young girl, and Marius remembered these words of Thénardier, the bloody signification of which he divined: *If you have me arrested, my comrade will give the Lark a pinch.*

Now it was not by the colonel's will alone, it was by his love itself, by the peril of her whom he loved, that he felt himself held back.

This fearful situation, which had lasted now for more than an hour, changed its aspect at every moment. Marius had the strength to pass in review successively all the most heart-rending conjectures, seeking some hope and finding more. The tumult of his thoughts strangely contrasted with the deathly silence of the den.

In the midst of this silence they heard the sound of the door of the stairway which opened, then closed.

The prisoner made a movement in his bonds.

'Here is the bourgeoise,' said Thénardier.

He had hardly said this, when in fact the Thénardiess burst into the room, red, breathless, panting, with glaring eyes, and cried, striking her big hands upon her hips both at the same time:

'False address!'

The bandit whom she had taken with her, came in behind her and picked up his pole-axe again:

'False address?' repeated Thénardier.

She continued:

'Nobody! Rue Saint Dominique, number seventeen, no Monsieur Urbain Fabre! They do not know who he is!'

She stopped for lack of breath, then continued:

'Monsieur Thénardier! this old fellow has cheated you! you are too good, do you see! I would have cut up the *Margoulette* for you in quarters, to begin with! and if he had been ugly, I would have cooked him alive! Then he would have had to talk, and had to tell where the girl is, and had to tell where the rhino is! That is how I would have fixed it! No wonder that they say men are stupider than women! Nobody! number seventeen! It is a large *porte-cochère*! No Monsieur Fabre! Rue Saint Dominique, full gallop, and drink-money to the driver, and all! I spoke to the porter and the portress, who is a fine stout woman, they did not know the fellow.'

Marius breathed. She, Ursula or the Lark, she whom he no longer knew what to call, was safe.

While his exasperated wife was vociferating, Thénardier had seated himself on the table; he sat a few seconds without saying a word, swinging his right leg, which was hanging down, and gazing upon the furnace with a look of savage reverie.

At last he said to the prisoner with a slow and singularly ferocious inflexion:

'A false address! what did you hope for by that?'

'To gain time!' cried the prisoner with a ringing voice.

And at the same moment he shook off his bonds; they were cut. The prisoner was no longer fastened to the bed save by one leg.

Before the seven men had had time to recover themselves and to spring upon him, he had bent over to the fireplace, reached his hand towards the furnace, then rose up, and now Thénardier, the Thénardiess, and the bandits, thrown by the shock into the back part of the room, beheld him with stupefaction, holding above his head the glowing chisel, from which fell an ominous light, almost free and in a formidable attitude.

At the judicial inquest, to which the ambuscade in the Gorbeau tenement gave rise in the sequel, it appeared that a big sou, cut and worked in a peculiar fashion, was found in the garret, when the police made a descent upon it; this big sou was one of those marvels of labour which the patience of the galleys produces in the darkness and for the darkness, marvels which are nothing else but instruments of escape. These hideous and delicate products of a wonderful art are to jewellery what the metaphors of argot are to poetry. There are Benvenuto Cellinis in the galleys, even as there are Villons in language. The unhappy man who aspires to deliverance, finds the means, sometimes without tools, with a folding knife, with an old case knife, to split a sou into two thin plates, to hollow out these two plates without touching the stamp of the mint, and to cut a screw-thread upon the edge of the sou, so as to make the plates adhere anew. This screws and unscrews at will; it is a box. In this box, they conceal a watch-spring, and this watch-spring, well handled, cuts off rings of some size and bars of iron. The unfortunate convict is supposed to possess only a sou; no, he possesses liberty. A big sou of this kind, on subsequent examination by the police, was found open and in two pieces in the room under the pallet near the window. There was also discovered a little saw of blue steel which could be concealed in the big sou. It is probable that when the bandits were searching the prisoner's pockets, he had this big sou upon him and succeeded in hiding it in his hand; and that afterwards, having his right hand free, he unscrewed it and used the saw to cut the ropes by which he was fastened, which would explain the slight noise and the imperceptible movements which Marius had noticed.

Being unable to stoop down for fear of betraying himself, he had not cut the cords on his left leg.

The bandits had recovered their first surprise.

'Be easy,' said Bigrenaille to Thénardier. 'He holds yet by one leg, and he will not go off, I answer for it. I tied that shank for him.'

The prisoner now raised his voice:

'You are pitiable, but my life is not worth the trouble of so long a defence. As to your imagining that you could make me speak, that you could make me write what I do not wish to write, that you could make me say what I do not wish to say – '

He pulled up the sleeve of his left arm, and added:

'Here.'

At the same time he extended his arm, and laid upon the naked flesh the glowing chisel, which he held in his right hand, by the wooden handle.

They heard the hissing of the burning flesh; the odour peculiar to chambers of torture spread through the den. Marius staggered, lost in horror; the brigands themselves felt a shudder; the face of the wonderful old man hardly contracted, and while the red iron was sinking into the smoking, impassible, and almost august wound, he turned upon Thénardier his fine face, in which there was no hatred, and in which suffering was swallowed up in a serene majesty.

With great and lofty natures the revolt of the flesh and the senses against the assaults of physical pain, brings out the soul, and makes it appear on the countenance, in the same way as mutinies of the soldiery force the captain to show himself.

'Wretches,' said he, 'have no more fear for me than I have of you.'

And drawing the chisel out of the wound, he threw it through the window, which was still open; the horrible glowing tool disappeared, whirling into the night, and fell in the distance, and was quenched in the snow.

The prisoner resumed:

'Do with me what you will.'

He was disarmed.

'Lay hold of him,' said Thénardier.

Two of the brigands laid their hands upon his shoulders, and the masked man with the ventriloquist's voice placed himself in front of him, ready to knock out his brains with a blow of the key, at the least motion.

At the same time Marius heard beneath him, at the foot of the partition, but so near that he could not see those who were talking, this colloquy, exchanged in a low voice:

'There is only one thing more to do.'

'To kill him!'

'That is it.'

It was the husband and wife who were holding counsel.

Thénardier walked with slow steps towards the table, opened the drawer, and took out the knife.

Marius was tormenting the trigger of his pistol. Unparalleled perplexity! For an hour there had been two voices in his conscience, one telling him to respect the will of his father, the other crying to him to succour the prisoner. These two voices, without interruption, continued their struggle, which threw him into agony. He had vaguely hoped up to that moment to find some means of reconciling these two duties, but no possible way had arisen. The peril was now urgent, the last limit of hope was passed; at a few steps from the prisoner, Thénardier was reflecting, with the knife in his hand.

Marius cast his eyes wildly about him; the last mechanical resource of despair.

Suddenly he started.

At his feet, on the table, a clear ray of the full moon illuminated, and seemed to point out to him a sheet of paper. Upon that sheet he read this line, written in large letters that very morning by the elder of the Thénardier girls:

'THE COGNES ARE HERE.'

An idea, a flash crossed Marius' mind; that was the means which he sought; the solution of this dreadful problem which was torturing him, to spare the assassin and to save the victim. He knelt down upon his bureau, reached out his arm, caught up the sheet of paper, quietly detached a bit of plaster from the partition, wrapped it in the paper, and threw the whole through the crevice into the middle of the den.

It was time. Thénardier had conquered his last fears, or his last scruples, and was moving towards the prisoner.

'Something fell!' cried the Thénardiess.

'What is it?' said the husband.

The woman had sprung forward, and picked up the piece of plaster wrapped in the paper. She handed it to her husband.

'How did this come in?' asked Thénardier.

'Egad!' said the woman, 'how do you suppose it got in? It came through the window.'

'I saw it pass,' said Bigrenaille.

Thénardier hurriedly unfolded the paper, and held it up to the candle.

'It is Eponine's writing. The devil!'

He made a sign to his wife, who approached quickly, and he showed her the line written on the sheet of paper; then he added in a hollow voice:

'Quick! the ladder! leave the meat in the trap, and clear the camp!'

'Without cutting the man's throat?' asked the Thénardiess.

'We have not the time.'

'Which way?' inquired Bigrenaille.

'Through the window,' answered Thénardier. 'Eponine threw the stone through the window, that shows that the house is not watched on that side.'

The mask with the ventriloquist's voice laid down his big key, lifted both arms into the air, and opened and shut his hands rapidly three times, without saying a word. This was like the signal to clear the decks in a fleet. The brigands, who were holding the prisoner, let go of him; in the twinkling of an eye, the rope ladder was unrolled out of the window, and firmly fixed to the casing by the two iron hooks.

The prisoner paid no attention to what was passing about him. He seemed to be dreaming or praying.

As soon as the ladder was fixed, Thénardier cried:

'Come, bourgeoise!'

And he rushed towards the window.

But as he was stepping out, Bigrenaille seized him roughly by the collar.

'No; say now, old joker! after us.'

'After us!' howled the bandits.

'You are children,' said Thénardier. 'We are losing time. The *railles* are at our heels.'

'Well,' said one of the bandits, 'let us draw lots who shall go out first.'

Thénardier exclaimed:

'Are you fools? are you cracked? You are a mess of *jobards!* Losing time, isn't it? drawing lots, isn't it? with a wet finger! for the short straw! write our names! put them in a cap!'

'Would you like my hat?' cried a voice from the door.

They all turned round. It was Javert.

He had his hat in his hand, and was holding it out smiling.

21. *The victims should always be arrested first*

JAVERT, AT NIGHTFALL, had posted his men and hid himself behind the trees on the Rue de la Barrière des Gobelins, which fronts the Gorbeau tenement on the other side of the boulevard. He commenced by opening 'his pocket,' to put into it the two young girls, who were charged with watching the approaches to the den. But he only 'bagged' Azelma. As for Eponine, she was not at her post; she had disappeared, and he could not take her. Then Javert put himself in rest, and listened for the signal agreed upon. The going and coming of the fiacre fretted him greatly. At last, he became impatient, and, *sure that there was a nest there*, sure of being '*in good luck*', having recognised several of the bandits who had gone in, he finally decided to go up without waiting for the pistol shot.

It will be remembered that he had Marius' pass-key.

He had come at the right time.

The frightened bandits rushed for the arms which they had thrown down anywhere when they had attempted to escape. In less than a second, these seven men, terrible to look upon, were grouped in a posture of defence; one with his pole-axe, another with his key, a third with his club, the others with the shears, the pincers, and the hammers, Thénardier grasping his knife. The Thénardiess seized a huge paving-stone which was in the corner of the window, and which served her daughters for a cricket.

Javert put on his hat again, and stepped into the room, his arms folded, his cane under his arm, his sword in its sheath.

'Halt there,' said he. 'You will not pass out through the window, you will pass out through the door. It is less unwholesome. There are seven of you, fifteen of us. Don't let us collar you like Auvergnats. Be genteel.'

Bigrenaille took a pistol which he had concealed under his blouse, and put it into Thénardier's hand, whispering in his ear:

'It is Javert. I dare not fire at that man. Dare you?'

'*Parbleu!*' answered Thénardier.

'Well, fire.'

Thénardier took the pistol, and aimed at Javert.

Javert, who was within three paces, looked at him steadily, and contented himself with saying:

'Don't fire, now! It will flash in the pan.'

Thénardier pulled the trigger. The pistol flashed in the pan. 'I told you so!' said Javert.

Bigrenaille threw his tomahawk at Javert's feet.

'You are the emperor of the devils! I surrender.'

'And you?' asked Javert of the other bandits.

They answered:

'We, too.'

Javert replied calmly:

'That is it, that is well, I said so, you are genteel.'

'I only ask one thing,' said Bigrenaille, 'that is, that I shan't be refused tobacco while I am in solitary.'

'Granted,' said Javert.

And turning round and calling behind him:

'Come in now!'

A squad of *sergents de ville* with drawn swords, and officers armed with axes and clubs, rushed in at Javert's call. They bound the bandits. This crowd of men, dimly lighted by a candle, filled the den with shadow.

'Handcuffs on all!' cried Javert.

'Come on, then!' cried a voice which was not a man's voice, but of which nobody could have said: 'It is the voice of a woman.'

The Thénardiess had entrenched herself in one of the corners of the window, and it was she who had just uttered this roar.

The *sergents de ville* and officers fell back.

She had thrown off her shawl, but kept on her hat; her husband, crouched down behind her, was almost hidden beneath the fallen shawl, and she covered him with her body, holding the paving stone with both hands above her head with the poise of a giantess who is going to hurl a rock.

'Take care!' she cried.

They all crowded back towards the hall. A wide space was left in the middle of the garret.

The Thénardiess cast a glance at the bandits who had allowed themselves to be tied, and muttered in a harsh and guttural tone:

'The cowards!'

Javert smiled, and advanced into the open space which the Thénardiess was watching with all her eyes.

'Don't come near! get out,' cried she, 'or I will crush you!'

'What a grenadier!' said Javert; 'mother, you have a beard like a man, but I have claws like a woman.'

And he continued to advance.

The Thénardiess, her hair flying wildly and terrible, braced her legs, bent backwards, and threw the paving stone wildly at Javert's head. Javert stooped, the stone passed over him, hit the wall behind, from which it knocked down a large piece of the plastering, and returned, bounding from corner to corner across the room, luckily almost empty, finally stopping at Javert's heels.

At that moment Javert reached the Thénardier couple. One of his huge hands fell upon the shoulder of the woman, and the other upon her husband's head.

'The handcuffs!' cried he.

The police officers returned in a body, and in a few seconds Javert's order was executed.

The Thénardiess, completely crushed, looked at her manacled hands and those of her husband, dropped to the floor and exclaimed, with tears in her eyes:

'My daughters!'

'They are provided for,' said Javert.

Meanwhile the officers had found the drunken fellow who was asleep behind the door, and shook him. He awoke stammering.

'Is it over, Jondrette?'

'Yes,' answered Javert.

The six manacled bandits were standing; however, they still retained their spectral appearance, three blackened, three masked.

'Keep on your masks,' said Javert.

And, passing them in review with the eye of a Frederic II at parade at Potsdam, he said to the three 'chimney doctors':

'Good day, Bigrenaille. Good day, Brujon. Good day, Deux Milliards.'

Then, turning towards the three masks, he said to the man of the pole-axe:

'Good day, Gueulemer.'

And to the man of the cudgel:

'Good day, Babet.'

And to the ventriloquist:

'Your health, Claquesous.'

Just then he perceived the prisoner of the bandits, who, since the entrance of the police, had not uttered a word, and had held his head down.

'Untie monsieur!' said Javert, 'and let nobody go out.'

This said, he sat down with authority before the table, on which the candle and the writing materials still were, drew a stamped sheet from his pocket, and commenced his procès-verbal.

When he had written the first lines, a part of the formula, which is always the same, he raised his eyes:

'Bring forward the gentleman whom these gentlemen had bound.'

The officers looked about them.

'Well,' asked Javert, 'where is he now?'

The prisoner of the bandits, M. Leblanc, M. Urbain Fabre, the father of Ursula, or the Lark, had disappeared.

The door was guarded, but the window was not. As soon as he saw that he was unbound, and while Javert was writing, he had taken advantage of the disturbance, the tumult, the confusion, the obscurity, and a moment when their attention was not fixed upon him, to leap out of the window.

An officer ran to the window, and looked out; nobody could be seen outside.

The rope ladder was still trembling.

'The devil!' said Javert, between his teeth, 'that must have been the best one.'

22. *The little boy who cried in the first volume*

THE DAY following that in which these events took place in the house on the Boulevard de l'Hôpital, a child, who seemed to come from somewhere near the bridge of Austerlitz, went up by the cross alley on the right in the direction of the Barrière de Fontainebleau. Night had closed in. This child was pale, thin, dressed in rags, with tow trousers in the month of February, and was singing with all his might.

At the corner of the Rue du Petit Banquier, an old crone was fumbling in a manure-heap by the light of a street lamp; the child knocked against her as he passed, then drew back, exclaiming:

'Why! I took that for an enormous, enormous dog!'

He pronounced the word enormous the second time with a pompous and sneering voice which capitals would express very well: an enormous, ENORMOUS dog!

The old woman rose up furious.

'Jail-bird!' muttered she. 'If I had not been stooping over, I know where I would have planted my foot!'

The child was now at a little distance.

'K'sss! k'sss!' said he. 'After all, perhaps I was not mistaken.'

The old woman, choking with indignation, sprang up immediately, and the red glare of the lantern fully illuminating her livid face, all hollowed out with angles and wrinkles, with crows' feet at the corners of her mouth. Her body was lost in the shadow, and only her head could be seen. One would have said it was the mask of Decrepitude shrivelled by a flash in the night. The child looked at her.

'Madame,' said he, 'has not the style of beauty that suits me.'

He went on his way and began to sing again:

Le roi Coupdesabot
S'en allait à la chasse,
A la chasse aux corbeaux –

At the end of these three lines he stopped. He had reached No. 50–52, and finding the door locked, had begun to batter it with kicks, heroic and re-echoing kicks, that revealed rather the men's shoes which he wore, than the child's feet which he had.

Meantime, this same old woman, whom he had met with at the corner of the Rue du Petit Banquier, was running after him with much clamour and many crazy gestures. What's the matter? what's the matter? Good God! They are staving the door down! They are breaking into the house!

The kicks continued.

The old woman exhausted her lungs.

'Is that the way they use houses nowadays?'

Suddenly she stopped. She had recognised the *gamin*.

'What! it is that Satan!'

'Hullo, it is the old woman,' said the child. 'Good day, Burgonmuche. I have come to see my ancestors.'

The old woman responded, with a composite grimace, an admirable extemporisation of hatred making the most of decay and ugliness, which was unfortunately lost in the obscurity:

'There is nobody there, nosey.'

'Pshaw!' said the child, 'where is my father, then?'

'At La Force.'

'Heigho! and my mother?'

'At Saint Lazare.'

'Well! and my sisters?'

'At Les Madelonnettes.'

The child scratched the back of his ear, looked at Ma'am Burgon and said:

'Ah!'

Then he turned on his heel, and a moment afterwards, the old woman, who stopped on the doorstep, heard him sing with his clear, fresh voice, as he disappeared under the black elms shivering in the wintry winds:

Le roi Coupdesabot
S'en allait à la chasse,
A la chasse aux corbeaux
Monté sur deux échasses.
Quand on passait dessous,
On lui payait deux sous.

PART FOUR: SAINT DENIS AND IDYL OF THE RUE PLUMET

PART FOUR [illegible]

[illegible]

[illegible] principle.

At the same time [illegible] demand [illegible] guarantees. [illegible] the same thing [illegible]

This is what [illegible] demanded [illegible]

[illegible]

BOOK I: A FEW PAGES OF HISTORY

1. Well cut

THE YEARS 1831 and 1832, the two years immediately connected with the Revolution of July, are one of the most peculiar and most striking periods in history. These two years, among those which precede and those which follow them, are like two mountains. They have the revolutionary grandeur. In them we discern precipices. In them the social masses, the very strata of civilisation, the consolidated group of superimposed and cohering interests, the venerable profile of the old French formation, appear and disappear at every instant through the stormy clouds of systems, passions, and theories. These appearances and disappearances have been named resistance and movement. At intervals we see truth gleaming forth, that daylight of the human soul.

This remarkable period is short enough, and is beginning to be far enough from us, so that it is henceforth possible to catch its principal outlines.

We will make the endeavour.

The Restoration had been one of those intermediate phases, difficult of definition, in which there are fatigue, buzzings, murmurs, slumber, tumult, and which are nothing more nor less than the arrival of a great nation at a halting-place. These periods are peculiar, and deceive the politicians who would take advantage of them. At first, the nation asks only for repose; men have but one thirst, for peace; they have but one ambition, to be little. That is a translation of being quiet. Great events, great fortunes, great ventures, great men, thank God, they have seen enough of them; they have been overhead in them. They would exchange Cæsar for Prusias, and Napoleon for the king of Yvetot. 'What a good little king he was!' They have walked since daybreak, it is the evening of a long and rough day; they made the first relay with Mirabeau, the second with Robespierre, the third with Bonaparte, they are thoroughly exhausted. Every one of them asks for a bed.

Devotions wearied out, heroisms grown old, ambitions full-fed, fortunes made, all seek, demand, implore, solicit, what? A place to lie down? They have it. They take possession of peace, quietness, and leisure; they are content. At the same time, however, certain facts arise, compel recognition, and knock at the door on their side, also. These facts have sprung from revolutions and wars; they exist, they live, they have a right to install themselves in society, and they do install themselves; and the most of the time the facts are pioneers and quartermasters that merely prepare the ground for principles.

Then, that is what appears to the political philosopher.

At the same time that weary men demand repose, accomplished facts demand guarantees. Guarantees to facts are the same thing as repose to men.

This is what England demanded of the Stuarts after the Protector; this is what France demanded of the Bourbons after the empire.

These guarantees are a necessity of the times. They must be accorded. The princes 'grant' them, but in reality it is the force of circumstances which gives them. A profound truth, and a piece of useful knowledge, of which the Stuarts had no suspicion in 1662, and of which the Bourbons had not even a glimpse in 1814.

The predestined family which returned to France when Napoleon fell, had the fatal simplicity to believe that it was it that gave, and that what it had given it could take back; that the house of Bourbon possessed Divine Right, that France possessed nothing; and that the political rights conceded in the Charter of Louis XVIII were only a branch of the divine right, detached by the House of Bourbon, and graciously given to the people until such day as it should please the king to take it back again. Still, by the regret which the gift cost them, the Bourbons should have felt that it did not come from them.

They were surly with the nineteenth century. They made a sour face at every development of the nation. To adopt a trivial word, that is to say, a popular and a true one, they looked glum. The people saw it.

They believed that they were strong, because the empire had been swept away before them like a scene at a theatre. They did not perceive that they themselves had been brought in in the same way. They did not see that they also were in that hand which had taken off Napoleon.

They believed that they were rooted because they were the past. They were mistaken; they were a portion of the past, but the whole past was France. The roots of French society were not in the Bourbons but in the nation. These obscure and undying roots did not constitute the right of a family, but the history of a people. They were everywhere except under the throne.

The house of Bourbon was to France the illustrious and blood-stained knot of her history, but it was not the principal element of her destiny, or the essential basis of her politics. She could do without the Bourbons; she had done without them for twenty-two years; there had been a solution of continuity; they did not suspect it. And how should they suspect it, they who imagined that Louis XVII reigned on the 9th Thermidor, and that Louis XVIII reigned on the day of Marengo. Never, since the beginning of history, have princes been so blind in the presence of facts, and of the portion of divine authority which facts contain and promulgate. Never had that earthly pretension which is called the right of kings, denied the divine right to such an extent.

A capital error which led that family to lay its hand upon the guarantees 'granted' in 1814, upon the concessions, as it called them. Sad thing! what they called their concessions were our conquests; what they called our encroachments were our rights.

When its hour seemed come, the Restoration, supposing itself victorious over Bonaparte, and rooted in the country, that is to say, thinking itself strong and thinking itself deep, took its resolution abruptly and risked its throw. One morning it rose in the face of France, and, lifting up its voice, it denied the collective title and the individual title, sovereignty to the nation, liberty to the citizen. In other words, it denied to the nation what made it a nation, and to the citizen what made him a citizen.

This is the essence of those famous acts which are called the ordinances of July.

The Restoration fell.

It fell justly. We must say, however, that it had not been absolutely hostile to all forms of progress. Some grand things were done in its presence.

Under the Restoration the nation became accustomed to discussion with calmness, which was wanting in the republic; and to grandeur in peace, which was wanting in the empire. France, free and strong, had been an encouraging spectacle to the other peoples of Europe. The Revolution had had its say under Robespierre; the cannon had had its say under Bonaparte; under Louis XVIII and Charles X intelligence in its turn found speech. The wind ceased, the torch was relighted. The pure light of mind was seen trembling upon the serene summits. A magnificent spectacle, full of use and charm. For fifteen years there were seen at work, in complete peace, and openly in public places, these great principles, so old to the thinker, so new to the statesman: equality before the law, freedom of conscience, freedom of speech, freedom of the press, the accessibility of every function to every aptitude. This went on thus until 1830. The Bourbons were an instrument of civilisation, which broke in the hands of Providence.

The fall of the Bourbons was full of grandeur, not on their part, but on the part of the nation. They left the throne with gravity, but without authority; their descent into the night was not one of those solemn disappearances which leave a dark emotion to history; it was neither the spectral calmness of Charles I, nor the eagle cry of Napoleon. They went away, that is all. They laid off the crown, and did not keep the halo. They were worthy, but they were not august. They fell short, to some extent, of the majesty of their misfortune. Charles X, during the voyage from Cherbourg, having a round table cut into a square table, appeared more solicitous of imperilled etiquette than of the falling monarchy. This pettiness saddened the devoted men who loved them, and the serious men who honoured their race. The people, for its part, was wonderfully noble. The nation, attacked one morning by force and arms, by a sort of royal insurrection, felt so strong that it had no anger. It defended itself, restrained itself, put things into their places, the government into the hands of the law, the Bourbons into exile, alas! and stopped. It took the old king, Charles X, from under that dais which had sheltered Louis XIV, and placed him gently on the ground. It touched the royal personages sadly and with precaution. It was not a man, it was not a few men, it was France, all France, France victorious and intoxicated with her victory, seeming to remember herself, and putting in practice before the eyes of the whole world these grave words of Guillaume du Vair after the day of the barricades: 'It is easy for those who are accustomed to gather the favours of the great, and to leap, like a bird, from branch to branch, from a grievous to a flourishing fortune, to show themselves bold towards their prince in his adversity; but to me the fortune of my kings will always be venerable, and principally when they are in grief.'

The Bourbons carried with them respect, but not regret. As we have said, their misfortune was greater than they. They faded away in the horizon.

The Revolution of July immediately found friends and enemies throughout the world. The former rushed towards it with enthusiasm and joy, the latter turned away; each according to his own nature. The princes of Europe, at the first moment, owls in this dawn, closed their eyes, shocked and stupefied, and opened them only to threaten. A fright which can be understood, an anger which can be excused. This strange revolution had hardly been a shock; it did not even do vanquished royalty the honour of treating it as an enemy and shedding its blood. In the eyes of the despotic governments, always interested that liberty should calumniate herself, the Revolution of July had the fault of being formidable and yet being mild. Nothing, however, was attempted, or plotted against it. The most dissatisfied, the most irritated, the most horrified, bowed to it; whatever may be our selfishness and our prejudices, a mysterious respect springs from events in which we feel the intervention of a hand higher than that of man.

The Revolution of July is the triumph of the Right prostrating the Fact. A thing full of splendour.

The right prostrating the fact. Thence the glory of the Revolution of 1830, thence its mildness also. The right, when it triumphs, has no need to be violent.

The right is the just and the true.

The peculiarity of the right is that it is always beautiful and pure. The fact, even that which is most necessary in appearance, even that most accepted by its contemporaries, if it exist only as fact, and if it contain too little of the right, or none at all, is destined infallibly to become, in the lapse of time, deformed, unclean, perhaps even monstrous. If you would ascertain at once what degree of ugliness the fact may reach seen in the distance of the centuries, look at Machiavel. Machiavel is not an evil genius, nor a demon, nor a cowardly and miserable writer; he is nothing but the fact. And he is not merely the Italian fact, he is the European fact, the fact of the sixteenth century. He seems hideous, and he is so, in presence of the moral idea of the nineteenth.

This conflict of the right and the fact endures from the origin of society. To bring the duel to an end, to amalgamate the pure ideal with the human reality, to make the right peacefully interpenetrate the fact, and the fact the right, this is the work of the wise.

2. *Badly sewed*

BUT THE WORK of the wise is one thing, the work of the able another.

The Revolution of 1830 soon grounded.

As soon as a revolution strikes the shore, the able carve up the wreck.

The able, in our age, have decreed to themselves the title for statesmen, so that this word, statesman, has come to be, in some sort, a word of argot. Indeed, let no one forget, wherever there is ability only, there is necessarily pettiness. To say 'the able', amounts to saying, 'mediocrity'.

Just as saying, 'statesmen,' is sometimes equivalent to saying 'traitors.'

According to the able, therefore, revolutions such as the Revolution of July, are arteries cut; a prompt ligature is needed. The right, too grandly proclaimed, is disquieting. So, the right once affirmed, the state must be reaffirmed. Liberty being assured, we must take thought for power.

Thus far the wise do not separate from the able, but they begin to distrust. Power, very well. But, first, what is power? Secondly, whence comes it?

The able seem not to hear the murmurs of objection, and they continue their work.

According to these politicians, ingenious in putting a mask of necessity upon profitable fictions, the first need of a people after a revolution, if this people forms part of a monarchical continent, is to procure a dynasty. In this way, say they, it can have peace after its revolution, that is to say, time to staunch its wounds and to repair its house. The dynasty hides the scaffolding and covers the ambulance.

Now, it is not always easy to procure a dynasty.

In case of necessity, the first man of genius, or even the first adventurer you meet, suffices for a king. You have in the first place Bonaparte, and in the second Iturbide.

But the first family you meet with does not suffice to make a dynasty. There must be a certain amount of antiquity in a race, and the wrinkles of centuries are not extemporised.

If we place ourselves at the statesmen's point of view, of course with every reservation, after a revolution, what are the qualities of the king who springs from it? He may be, and it is well that he should be, revolutionary, that is to say, a participant in his own person in this revolution, that he should have taken part in it, that he should be compromised in it, or made illustrious, that he should have touched the axe or handled the sword.

What are the qualities of a dynasty? It should be national; that is to say, revolutionary at a distance, not by acts performed, but by ideas accepted. It should be composed of the past and be historic, of the future and be sympathetic.

All this explains why the first revolutions content themselves with finding a man, Cromwell or Napoleon; and why the second absolutely insist on finding a family, the house of Brunswick or the house of Orleans.

Royal houses resemble those banyan trees of India, each branch of which, by bending to the ground, takes root there and becomes a banyan. Each branch may become a dynasty. On the sole condition that it bend to the people.

Such is the theory of the able.

This, then, is the great art, to give a success something of the sound of a catastrophe, in order that those who profit by it may tremble also, to moderate a step in advance with fear, to enlarge the curve of transition to the extent of retarding progress, to tame down this work, to denounce and restrain the ardencies of enthusiasm, to cut off the corners and the claws, to clog triumph, to swaddle the right, to wrap up the people-giant in flannel and hurry him to bed, to impose a diet upon this excess of health, to put Hercules under convalescent treatment, to hold back the event within the expedient, to offer to minds thirsting for the ideal this nectar extended from barley-water, to take precautions against too much success, to furnish the revolution with a skylight.

The year 1830 carried out this theory, already applied to England by 1688.

The year 1830 is a revolution arrested in mid career. Half progress, quasi right. Now logic ignores the Almost, just as the sun ignores the candle.

Who stops revolutions half-way? The bourgeoisie.

Why?

Because the bourgeoisie is the interest which has attained to satisfaction. Yesterday it was appetite, today it is fulness, tomorrow it will be satiety.

The phenomenon of 1814 after Napoleon, was reproduced in 1830 after Charles X.

There has been an attempt, an erroneous one, to make a special class of the bourgeoisie. The bourgeoisie is simply the contented portion of the people. The bourgeois is the man who has now time to sit down. A chair is not a caste.

But, by wishing to sit down, we may stop the progress even of the human race. That has often been the fault of the bourgeois.

The commission of a fault does not constitute a class. Egotism is not one of the divisions of the social order.

Moreover, we must be just even towards egotism. The state to which, after the shock of 1830, that part of the nation which is called the bourgeoisie aspired, was not inertia, which is a complication of indifference and idleness, and which contains something of shame; it was not slumber, which supposes a momentary forgetfulness accessible to dreams; it was a halt.

Halt is a word formed with a singular and almost contradictory double meaning: a troop on the march, that is to say, movement; a stopping, that is to say, repose.

Halt is the regaining of strength, it is armed and watchful repose; it is the accomplished fact which plants sentinels and keeps itself upon its guard. Halt supposes battle yesterday and battle tomorrow.

This is the interval between 1830 and 1848.

What we here call battle may also be called progress.

The bourgeoisie, then, as well as the statesmen, felt the need of a man who should express this word: Halt! An Although Because. A composite individuality, signifying revolution and signifying stability; in other words, assuring the present through the evident compatibility of the past with the future.

This man was 'found at hand'. His name was Louis Philippe d'Orleans.

The 221 made Louis Philippe king. Lafayette undertook the coronation. He called it *the best of republics.* The Hôtel de Ville of Paris replaced the Cathedral of Rheims.

This substitution of a demi-throne for the complete throne was 'the work of 1830.'

When the able had finished their work, the immense viciousness of their solution became apparent. All this was done without reference to absolute right. The absolute right cried 'I protest!' then, a fearful thing, it went back into the obscurity.

3. Louis Philippe

REVOLUTIONS HAVE a terrible arm and a fortunate hand; they strike hard and choose well. Even when incomplete, even degenerate and abused, and reduced to the condition of revolution junior, like the Revolution of 1830, they almost always retain enough of the light of providence to prevent a fatal fall. Their eclipse is never an abdication.

Still, let us not boast too loudly; revolutions, even, are deceived, and disclose grave mistakes.

Let us return to 1830. The year 1830 was fortunate in its deviation. In the establishment which called itself order after the Revolution was cut short, the king was better than the royalty. Louis Philippe was a rare man.

Son of a father to whom history will certainly allow attenuating circumstances, but as worthy of esteem as that father had been worthy of blame; having all private virtues and many public virtues; careful of his health, his fortune, his person, his business, knowing the value of a minute, though not always the value of a year; sober, serene, peaceful, patient; good man and good prince; sleeping with his wife and having lackeys in his palace whose business it was to exhibit the conjugal bed to the bourgeois, an ostentation of domestic regularity which had its use after the former illegitimate displays of the elder branch; knowing all the languages of Europe, and, what is rarer, all the languages of all interests, and speaking them; admirable representative of 'the middle class', but surpassing it, and in every way greater than it; having the excellent sense, even while appreciating the blood from which he sprang, to estimate himself above all at his own intrinsic worth, and, about the question of his race even, very particular, declaring himself Orleans and not Bourbon; really first Prince of the Blood, while he had only been Most Serene Highness, but a frank bourgeois the day he was Majesty; diffuse in public, concise in private; a declared, but not proven, miser; in reality one of those economical persons who are prodigal in matters of fancy or their duty; well read, but not very appreciative of letters; a gentleman, but not chivalrous; simple, calm, and strong; worshipped by his family and by his house; a seductive talker, an undeceived statesman, interiorly cold, ruled by the present interest, governing always by the nearest convenience, incapable of malice or of gratitude, pitilessly wearing out superiorities upon mediocrities, able in opposing through parliamentary majorities those mysterious unanimities which mutter almost inaudibly beneath thrones; expansive, sometimes imprudent in his expansion, but with marvellous address in that imprudence; fertile in expedients, in faces, in masks; making France afraid of Europe and Europe of France; loving his country incontestably, but preferring his family; prizing domination more than authority, and authority more than dignity; a disposition which is to this extent fatal, that, turning everything towards success, it admits of ruse, and does not absolutely repudiate baseness; but which is profitable to this extent, that it preserves politics from violent shocks, the state from fractures, and society from catastrophes; minute, correct, vigilant, attentive, sagacious, indefatigable; contradicting himself sometimes, and giving himself the lie; bold against Austria at Ancona, obstinate against England in Spain, bombarding Antwerp and paying Pritchard; singing the Marseillaise with conviction; inaccessible to depression, to weariness, to the taste for the beautiful and the ideal, to foolhardy generosity, to Utopia, to chimæras, to anger, to vanity, to fear; having every form of personal bravery; general at Valmy, soldier at Jemappes, his life attempted eight times by regicides, yet always smiling; brave as a grenadier, courageous as a thinker; anxious merely before the chances of a European disturbance, and unfit for great political adventures; always ready to risk his life, never his work; disguising his pleasure in the form of influence that he might be obeyed rather as an intelligence than as a king; endowed with observation and not with divination, paying little attention to minds, but able to read the character of men, that is to say, needing to see in order to judge; prompt and penetrating good sense, practical wisdom, ready speech, prodigious memory; digging incessantly into that memory, his only point of resemblance with Cæsar, Alexander, and Napoleon; knowing facts, details, dates, proper names, ignorant of tendencies, passions, the diverse genii of the multitude, interior aspirations, the hidden and obscure uprisings of souls, in one word, all that might be called the invisible currents of conscience; accepted by the surface, but little in accord with the under-France; making his way by craft; governing too much and not reigning enough; his own prime minister; excelling in making of the pettiness of realities an obstacle to the immensity of ideas; adding to a true creative faculty for civilisation, order, and organisation, an indescribable spirit of routine and chicanery, founder and attorney of a dynasty; possessing something of Charlemagne and something of a lawyer; to sum up, a lofty and original figure, a prince who knew how to gain powers in spite of the restlessness of France, and power in spite of the jealousy of Europe. Louis Philippe will be classed among the eminent men of his century, and would be ranked among the most illustrious rulers of history if he had had a little love of glory, and had appreciated what is great to the same extent that he appreciated what is useful.

Louis Philippe had been handsome, and, when old, was still fine looking; not always agreeable to the nation, he always was to the multitude; he pleased. He had this gift, a charm. Majesty he lacked; he neither wore the crown, though king, nor white hair, though an old man. His manners were of the old régime, and his habits of the new, a mixture of the noble and the bourgeois which was befitting to 1830; Louis Philippe was regnant transition; he had preserved the ancient pronunciation and the ancient orthography which he put into the service of modern opinions; he loved Poland and Hungary, but he wrote *les polonois* and pronounced *les hongrais.* He wore the dress of the National Guard like Charles X, and the cordon of the Legion of Honour like Napoleon.

He went rarely to chapel, not at all to the chase, never to the opera. Incorruptible by priests, dog-keepers, and danseuses; this entered into his popularity with the bourgeoisie. He had no court. He went out with his umbrella under his arm, and this umbrella for a long time was a portion of his glory. He was something of a mason, something of a gardener, and something of a doctor; he bled a postilion who fell from his horse; Louis Philippe no more went without his lancet than Henry III without his poniard. The royalists laughed at this ridiculous king, the first who had spilled blood to save.

In the complaints of history against Louis Philippe, there is a deduction to be made, there is what is to be charged to the royalty, what is to be charged to the reign, and what is to be charged to the king; three columns, each of which gives a different total. The right of democracy confiscated, progress made the second interest, the protests of the street violently repressed, the military execution of insurrections, *émeutes* passed over by arms, the Rue Transnonain, the councils of war, the absorption of the real country by the legal country, the theory of the government but half carried out, with three hundred thousand privileged persons, are the acts of the royalty; Belgium refused, Algeria too harshly conquered, and, like India by the English, with more of barbarism than civilisation, the breach of faith with Abd-el-Kader, Blaye, Deutz purchased, Pritchard paid, are the acts of the reign; the policy, which looked rather to the family than to the nation, is the act of the king.

As we see, when the deduction is made, the charge against the king is diminished.

His great fault was this: He was modest in the name of France.

Whence comes this fault?

We must tell.

Louis Philippe was a too fatherly king; this incubation of a family which is to be hatched into a dynasty is afraid of everything, and cannot bear disturbance; hence excessive timidity, annoying to a people who have the 14th of July in their civil traditions, and Austerlitz in their military traditions.

Moreover, if we throw aside public duties, which first demand to be fulfilled, this deep tenderness of Louis Philippe for his family, the family deserved. This domestic group was wonderful. Their virtues emulated their talents. One of Louis Philippe's daughters, Maria d'Orleans, put the name of her race among artists as Charles d'Orleans had put it among poets. Out of her soul she made a statue which she called Jeanne d'Arc. Two of Louis Philippe's sons drew from Metternich this eulogy of a demagogue: *They are young men such as we rarely see, and princes such as we never see.*

This is, without keeping anything back, but also without aggravating anything, the truth about Louis Philippe.

To be Prince Equality, to bear within himself the contradiction of the Restoration and the Revolution, to have this threatening aspect of the revolutionist which becomes reassuring in the ruler, such was the fortune of Louis Philippe in 1830; never was there a more complete adaptation of a man to an event; the one entered into the other, and there was an incarnation. Louis Philippe is 1830 made man. Moreover, he had in his favour that grand designation for the throne, exile. He had been proscribed, a wanderer, poor. He had lived by his labour. In Switzerland, this heir to the richest princely domains in France had sold an old horse, to procure food. At Reichenau he had given lessons in mathematics, while his sister Adelaide did sewing and embroidery. These memories associated with a king, rendered the bourgeoisie enthusiastic. He had with his own hands demolished the last iron cage of Mont Saint Michel, built by Louis XI and used by Louis XV. He was the companion of Dumouriez, he was the friend of Lafayette; he had belonged to the Jacobin Club; Mirabeau had slapped him on the shoulder; Danton had said to him, 'Young man!' At twenty-four years of age, in '93, being M. de Chartres, from the back of an obscure bench in the convention, he had been present at the trial of Louis XVI, so well named *that poor tyrant*. The blind clairvoyance of the Revolution, crushing royalty in the king, and the king with the royalty, almost without noticing the man in the savage overthrow of the idea, the vast storm of the tribunal-assembly, the public wrath questioning, Capet not knowing what to answer, the fearful stupefied vacillation of this royal head under that terrible blow, the relative innocence of all in that catastrophe, of those who condemned as well as of him who was condemned; he had seen these things, he had looked upon this mad whirl; he had seen the centuries appear at the bar of the Convention; he had seen behind Louis XVI, that hapless, responsible by-passer, rising up in the darkness, the fear-inspiring criminal, the monarchy; and there was still in his soul a respectful fear before this limitless justice of the people, almost as impersonal as the justice of God.

The effect which the Revolution produced upon him was tremendous. His memory was like a living impression of those grand years, minute by minute. One day, before a witness whom it is impossible for us to doubt, he corrected from memory the whole letter A of the alphabetic list of the constituent assembly.

Louis Philippe was a king in broad day. While he reigned the press was free, the tribune was free, conscience and speech were free. The laws of September are clear and open. Knowing well the corroding power of light on privileges, he left his throne exposed to the light. History will acknowledge this loyalty.

Louis Philippe, like all historic men who have left the scene, is now to be put upon his trial by the human conscience. He is as yet only before the grand jury.

The hour in which history speaks with its free and venerable accent, has not yet struck for him; the time has not come to pronounce final judgement upon this king; that austere and illustrious historian, Louis Blanc, has himself recently modified his first verdict: Louis Philippe was the elect of those two almosts which are called the 221 and 1830, that is to say, of a demi-parliament and a demi-revolution; and at all events, from the superior point of view in which philosophy ought to place herself, we could judge him here, as we have before intimated, only under certain reservations in the name of the absolute democratic principle; in the eyes of the absolute, beyond these rights: the rights of man first, the rights of the people afterwards, all is usurpation; but we can say at present, having made these reservations, that, to sum up, and in whatever way he is considered, Louis Philippe, taken by himself, and from the point of view of human goodness, will remain, to use the old language of ancient history, one of the best princes that ever sat upon a throne.

What is there against him? That throne. Take from Louis Philippe the king, there remains the man. And the man is good. He is sometimes so good as to be admirable. Often, in the midst of the gravest cares, after a day of struggle against the whole diplomacy of the continent, he retired at evening into his apartment, and there, exhausted with fatigue, bowed down with sleep, what did he do? He took a bundle of documents, and passed the night in reviewing a criminal prosecution, feeling that it was something to make head against Europe, but that it was a much grander thing still to save a man from the executioner. He was obstinate against his keeper of the seals; he disputed inch by inch the ground of the guillotine with the attorney-generals, *those babblers of the law*, as he called them. Sometimes the heaped-up documents covered his table; he examined them all; it was anguish to him to give up those wretched condemned heads. One day he said to the same witness whom we have just now referred to: *Last night I saved seven.* During the early years of his reign, the death penalty was abolished, and the re-erected scaffold was a severe blow to the king. La Grève having disappeared with the elder branch, a bourgeois Grève was instituted under the name of Barrière Saint Jacques; 'practical men' felt the need of a quasi-legitimate guillotine; and this was one of the victories of Casimir Perier, who represented the more conservative portions of the bourgeoisie, over Louis Philippe, who represented its more liberal portions. Louis Philippe annotated Beccaria with his own hand. After the Fieschi machine, he exclaimed: *What a pity that I was not wounded! I could have pardoned him.* At another time, alluding to the resistance of his ministers, he wrote concerning a political convict, who is one of the noblest figures of our times: *His pardon is granted, it only remains for me to obtain it.* Louis Philippe was as gentle as Louis IX, and as good as Henry IV.

Now, to us, in history where goodness is the pearl of great price, he who has been good stands almost above him who has been great.

Louis Philippe having been estimated with severity by some, harshly, perhaps, by others, it is very natural that a man, now himself a phantom, who knew this king, should come forward to testify for him before history; this testimony, whatever it may be, is evidently and above all disinterested; an epitaph written by a dead man is sincere; one shade may console another shade; the sharing of the same darkness gives the right to praise; and there is little fear that it will ever be said of two tombs in exile: This one flattered the other.

4. Crevices under the foundation

AT THE MOMENT the drama which we are relating is about to penetrate into the depths of one of the tragic clouds which cover the first years of the reign of Louis Philippe, we could not be ambiguous, and it was necessary that this book should be explicit in regard to this king.

Louis Philippe entered into the royal authority without violence, without direct action on his part, by the action of a revolutionary transfer, evidently very distinct from the real aim of the revolution, but in which he, the Duke d'Orleans, had no personal initiative. He was a born prince, and believed himself elected king. He had not given himself this command; he had not taken it; it had been offered to him and he had accepted it; convinced, wrongly in our opinion, but convinced, that the offer was consistent with right, and that the acceptance was consistent with duty. Hence a possession in good faith. Now, we say it in all conscience, Louis Philippe being in good faith in his possession, and the democracy being in good faith in their attack, the terror which arises from social struggles is chargeable neither to the king nor to the democracy. A shock of principles resembles a shock of the elements. The ocean defends the water, the hurricane defends the air; the king defends royalty, the democracy defends the people; the relative, which is the monarchy, resists the absolute, which is the republic; society bleeds under this struggle, but what is its suffering today will be its safety hereafter; and, at all events, there is no censure due to those who struggle; one of the two parties is evidently mistaken; right is not like the colossus of Rhodes, upon two shores at once, one foot in the republic, one foot in royalty; it is indivisible, and all on one side; but those who are mistaken are sincerely mistaken; a blind man is no more a criminal than a Vendéen is a brigand. Let us, then, impute these terrible collisions only to the fatality of things. Whatever these tempests may be, human responsibility is not mingled with them.

Let us complete this exposition.

The government of 1830 had from the first a hard life. Born yesterday, it was obliged to fight today.

It was hardly installed when it began to feel on all sides vague movements directed against the machinery of July, still so newly set up, and so far from secure.

Resistance was born on the morrow, perhaps even it was born on the eve.

From month to month the hostility increased, and from dumb it became outspoken.

The Revolution of July, tardily accepted, as we have said, outside of France by the kings, had been diversely interpreted in France.

God makes visible to men his will in events, an obscure text written in a mysterious language. Men make their translations of it forthwith; nasty translations, incorrect, full of faults, omissions, and misreadings. Very few minds comprehend the divine tongue. The most sagacious, the most calm, the most profound, decipher slowly, and, when they arrive with their text, the need has long gone by; there are already twenty translations in the public square. From each translation a party is born, and from each misreading a faction; and each party believes it has the only true text, and each faction believes that it possesses the light.

Often the government itself is a faction.

There are in revolutions some swimmers against the stream, these are the old parties.

To the old parties, who are attached to hereditary right by the grace of God, revolutions having arisen from the right of revolt, there is a right of revolt against them. An error. For in revolutions the revolted party is not the people, it is the king. Revolution is precisely the opposite of revolt. Every revolution, being a normal accomplishment, contains in itself its own legitimacy, which false revolutionists sometimes dishonour, but which persists, even when sullied, which survives, even when stained with blood. Revolutions spring, not from an accident, but from necessity. A revolution is a return from the factitious to the real. It is, because it must be.

The old legitimist parties none the less assailed the Revolution of 1830 with all the violence which springs from false reasoning. Errors are excellent projectiles. They struck it skilfully just where it was vulnerable, at the defect in its cuirass, its want of logic; they attacked this revolution in its royalty. They cried to it: Revolution, why this king? Factions are blind men who aim straight.

This cry was uttered also by the republicans. But, coming from them, this cry was logical. What was blindness with the legitimists was clearsightedness with the democrats. The year 1830 had become bankrupt with the people. The democracy indignantly reproached it with its failure.

Between the attack of the past and the attack of the future, the establishment of July was struggling. It represented the moment, in conflict on the one hand with the monarchical centuries, on the other hand with the eternal right.

Moreover, externally, being no longer the revolution, and becoming the monarchy, 1830 was obliged to keep step with Europe. To preserve peace, an increase of complication. A harmony required in the wrong way is often more onerous than a war. From this sullen conflict, always muzzled but always muttering, is born armed peace, that ruinous expedient of civilisation suspected by herself. The royalty of July reared, in spite of the lash, in the harness of the European cabinets. Metternich would have been glad to put it in kicking-straps. Pushed upon in France by progress, it pushed upon the monarchies in Europe, those tardigrades. Towed, it towed.

Meanwhile, within the country, pauperism, proletariat, wages, education, punishment, prostitution, the lot of woman, riches, misery, production, consumption, distribution, exchange, money, credit, rights of capital, rights of labour, all these questions multiplied over society; a terrible steep.

Outside of the political parties properly speaking, another movement manifested itself. To the democratic fermentation, the philosophic fermentation responded. The elite felt disturbed as well as the multitude; otherwise, but as much.

Thinkers were meditating, while the soil, that is to say, the people, traversed by the revolutionary currents, trembled beneath them with mysterious epileptic shocks. These thinkers, some isolated, others gathered into families and almost into communion, were turning over social questions, peacefully, but profoundly; impassible miners, who were quietly pushing their galleries into the depths of a volcano, scarcely disturbed by the sullen commotions and the half-seen glow of the lava.

This tranquillity was not the least beautiful spectacle of that agitated period.

These men left to political parties the question of rights, they busied themselves with the question of happiness.

The well-being of man was what they wished to extract from society.

They raised the material questions, questions of agriculture, of industry, of commerce, almost to the dignity of a religion. In civilisation such as it is constituted to small extent by God, to great by man, interests are combined, aggregated, and amalgamated in such a manner as to form actual hard rock, according to a dynamic law patiently studied by the economists, those geologists of politics.

These men who grouped themselves under different appellations, but who may all be designated by the generic title of socialists, endeavoured to pierce this rock and to make the living waters of human felicity gush forth from it.

From the question of the scaffold to the question of war, their labours embraced everything. To the rights of man, proclaimed by the French Revolution, they added the rights of woman and the rights of childhood.

No one will be astonished that, for various reasons, we do not here treat fundamentally, from the theoretic point of view, the questions raised by socialism. We limit ourselves to indicating them.

All the problems which the socialists propounded, aside from the cosmogonic visions, dreams, and mysticism, may be reduced to two principal problems.

First problem:

To produce wealth.

Second problem:

To distribute it.

The first problem contains the question of labour.

The second contains the question of wages.

In the first problem the question is of the employment of force.

In the second of the distribution of enjoyment.

From the good employment of force results public power.

From the good distribution of enjoyment results individual happiness.

By good distribution, we must understand not equal distribution, but equitable distribution. The highest equality is equity.

From these two things combined, public power without, individual happiness within, results social prosperity.

Social prosperity means, man happy, the citizen free, the nation great.

England solves the first of these two problems. She creates wealth wonderfully; she distributes it badly. This solution, which is complete only on one side, leads her inevitably to these two extremes: monstrous opulence, monstrous misery. All the enjoyment to a few, all the privation to the rest, that is to say, to the people; privilege, exception, monopoly, feudality, springing from labour itself; a false and dangerous situation which founds public power upon private misery, which plants the grandeur of the state in the suffering of the individual. A grandeur ill constituted, in which all the material elements are combined, and into which no moral element enters.

Communism and agrarian law think they have solved the second problem. They are mistaken. Their distribution kills production. Equal partition abolishes emulation. And consequently labour. It is a distribution made by the butcher, who kills what he divides. It is therefore impossible to stop at these professed solutions. To kill wealth is not to distribute it.

The two problems must be solved together to be well solved. The two solutions must be combined and form but one.

Solve the first only of the two problems, you will be Venice, you will be England. You will have like Venice an artificial power, or like England a material power; you will be the evil rich man, you will perish by violence, as Venice died, or by bankruptcy, as England will fall, and the world will let you die and fall, because the world lets everything fall and die which is nothing but selfishness, everything which does not represent a virtue or an idea for the human race.

It is of course understood that by these words, Venice, England, we designate not the people, but the social constructions; the oligarchies superimposed upon the nations, and not the nations themselves. The nations always have our respect and our sympathy. Venice, the people, will be reborn; England, the aristocracy, will fall, but England, the nation, is immortal. This said, we proceed.

Solve the two problems, encourage the rich, and protect the poor, suppress misery, put an end to the unjust speculation upon the weak by the strong, put a bridle upon the iniquitous jealousy of him who is on the road, against him who has reached his end, adjust mathematically and fraternally wages to labour, join gratuitous and obligatory instruction to the growth of childhood, and make science the basis of manhood, develop the intelligence while you occupy the arm, be at once a powerful people and a family of happy men, democratise property, not by abolishing it, but by universalising it, in such a way that every citizen without exception may be a proprietor, an easier thing than it is believed to be; in two words, learn to produce wealth and learn to distribute it, and you shall have material grandeur and moral grandeur combined; and you shall be worthy to call yourselves France.

This, above and beyond a few sects which ran wild, is what socialism said; that is what it sought to realise; this is what it outlined in men's minds.

Admirable efforts! sacred attempts!

These doctrines, these theories, these resistances, the unforeseen necessity for the statesman to consult with the philosopher, confused evidences half seen, a new politics to create, accordant with the old world, and yet not too discordant with the ideal of the revolution; a state of affairs in which Lafayette must be used to oppose Polignac, the intuition of progress transparent in the *émeute*, the chambers, and the street, competitions to balance about him, his faith in the revolution, perhaps some uncertain eventual resignation arising from the vague acceptance of a definitive superior right, his desire to remain in his race, his family pride, his sincere respect for the people, his own honesty, preoccupied Louis Philippe almost painfully, and at moments, strong and as courageous as he was, overwhelmed him under the difficulties of being king.

He felt beneath his feet a terrible disaggregation which was not, however, a crumbling into dust – France being more France than ever.

Dark drifts covered the horizon. A strange shadow approaching nearer and nearer, was spreading little by little over men, over things, over ideas; a shadow which came from indignations and from systems. All that had been hurriedly stifled was stirring and fermenting. Sometimes the conscience of the honest man caught its breath, there was so much confusion in that air in which sophisms were mingled with truths. Minds trembled in the social anxiety like leaves at the approach of the storm. The electric tension was so great that at certain moments any chance-comer, though unknown, flashed out. Then the twilight obscurity fell again. At intervals, deep and sullen mutterings enabled men to judge of the amount of lightning in the cloud.

Twenty months had hardly rolled away since the revolution of July, the year 1832 had opened with an imminent and menacing aspect. The distress of the people; labourers without bread; the last Prince de Condé lost in the darkness; Brussels driving away the Nassaus, as Paris had driven away the Bourbons; Belgium offering herself to a French prince, and given to an English prince; the Russian hatred of Nicholas; in our rear two demons of the south, Ferdinand in Spain, Miguel in Portugal; the earth quaking in Italy; Metternich extending his hand over Bologna; France bluntly opposing Austria at Ancona; in the north a mysterious ill-omened sound of a hammer nailing Poland again into its coffin; throughout Europe angry looks keeping watch over France; England a suspicious ally, ready to push over whoever might bend, and to throw herself upon whoever might fall; the peerage sheltering itself behind Beccaria, to refuse four heads to the law; the fleur-de-lis erased from the king's carriage; the cross torn down from Notre Dame; Lafayette in decay; Lafitte ruined; Benjamin Constant dead in poverty; Casimir Perier dead from loss of power; the political disease and the social disease breaking out in the two capitals of the realm, one the city of thought, the other the city of labour; at Paris civil war, at Lyons servile war; in the two cities the same furnace glare; the flush of the crater on the forehead of the people; the South fanatical, the West disturbed; the Duchess of Berry in la Vendée; plots, conspiracies, uprisings, the cholera, added to the dismal tumult of ideas, the dismal uproar of events.

5. Facts from which history springs, and which history ignores

TOWARDS the end of April everything was worse. The fermentation became a boiling. Since 1830 there had been here and there some little partial *émeutes*, quickly repressed, but again breaking out, signs of a vast underlying conflagration. Something terrible was brooding. Glimpses were caught of the lineaments, still indistinct and scarcely visible, of a possible revolution. France looked to Paris; Paris looked to the Faubourg Saint Antoine.

The Faubourg Saint Antoine sullenly warmed up, was beginning to boil.

The wine-shops of the Rue de Charonne, although the junction of the two epithets seems singular, applied to wine-shops, were serious and stormy.

In them the simple existence of the government was brought in question. The men there publicly discussed whether it were *the thing to fight or to remain quiet*. There were back shops where an oath was administered to working-men, that they would be in the streets at the first cry of alarm, and 'that they would fight without counting the number of the enemy'. The engagement once taken, a man seated in a corner of the wine-shop 'made a sonorous voice', and said: 'You *understand it! you have sworn it!*' Sometimes they went upstairs into a closed room, and there scenes occurred which were almost masonic. Oaths were administered to the initiated *to render service to them as they would to their own fathers*. That was the formula.

In the lower rooms they read 'subversive' pamphlets. *They pelted the government*, says a secret report of the times.

Such words as these were heard. – '*I don't know the names of the chiefs. As for us, we shall only know the day two hours beforehand.*' A working-man said: '*There are three hundred of us, let us put in ten sous each, that will make a hundred and fifty francs to manufacture powder and ball.*' Another said: '*I don't ask six months, I don't ask two. In less than a fortnight we shall meet the government face to face. With twenty-five thousand men we can make a stand.*' Another said: '*I don't go to bed, because I am making cartridges all night.*' From time to time, men 'like bourgeois, and in fine coats' came, 'causing embarrassment,' and having the air 'of command,' gave a grip of the hand *to the most important*, and went away. They never stayed more than ten minutes. Significant words were exchanged in a low voice: '*The plot is ripe, the thing is complete.*' 'This was buzzed by all who were there,' to borrow the very expression of one of the participants. The exaltation was such, that one day, in a public wine-shop, a working-man exclaimed: *We have no arms!* One of his comrades answered: *The soldiers have!* thus parodying, without suspecting it, Bonaparte's proclamation to the army of Italy. 'When they have anything more secret,' adds a report, 'they do not communicate it in those places.' One can hardly comprehend what they could conceal after saying what they did.

The meetings were sometimes periodical. At some, there were never more than eight or ten, and always the same persons. In others, anybody who chose entered, and the room was so full that they were forced to stand. Some were there from enthusiasm and passion; others because *it was on their way to their work.* As in the time of the revolution, there were in these wine-shops some female patriots, who embraced the newcomers.

Other expressive facts came to light.

A man entered a shop, drank, and went out, saying: '*Wine-merchant, what is due, the revolution will pay.*'

At a wine-shop opposite the Rue de Charonne, revolutionary officers were elected. The ballots were gathered in caps.

Some working-men met at a fencing-master's, who gave lessons in the Rue de Cotte. There was a trophy of arms there, formed of wooden swords, canes, clubs, and foils. One day they took the buttons off the foils. A working-man said: '*We are twenty-five; but they don't count on me, because they look upon me as a machine.*' This machine was afterwards Quénisset.

All the little things which were premeditated, gradually acquired some strange notoriety. A woman sweeping her doorstep said to another woman: *For a long time they have been hard at work making cartridges.* Proclamations were read in the open street, addressed to the National Guards of the Departments. One of these proclamations was signed: *Burtot, wine-merchant.*

One day at a liquor-dealer's door in the Lenoir market, a man with a heavy beard and an Italian accent mounted on a block and read aloud a singular writing which seemed to emanate from a secret power. Groups formed about him and applauded. The passages which stirred the crowd most were caught and noted down. ' . . . Our doctrines are trammelled, our proclamations are torn down, our posters are watched and thrown into prison . . . ' ' . . . The recent fall in cottons has converted many moderates . . . ' ' . . . The future of the peoples is being worked out in our obscure ranks.' ' . . . Behold the statement of the matter: action or reaction, revolution or counter-revolution. For, in our times, there is no belief longer in inertia or in immobility. For the people or against the people, that is the question. There is no other.' ' . . . The day that we no longer suit you, crush us, but until then help us to go forward.' All this in broad day.

Other acts, bolder still, were suspected by the people on account of their very boldness. On the 4th of April 1832, a passer-by mounted the block at the corner of the Rue Sainte Marguerite, and cried: I am a *Babouvist!* But under Babeuf the people scented Gisquet.

Among other things, this man said:

'Down with property! The opposition of the left are cowards and traitors. When they want to be right, they preach revolution. They are democrats that they may not be beaten, and royalists that they may not fight. The republicans are feathered beasts. Distrust the republicans, citizen labourers.'

'Silence, citizen spy!' cried a working-man.

This put an end to the discourse.

Mysterious incidents occurred.

At nightfall, a working-man met 'a well-dressed man' near the canal, who said to him: 'Where are you going, citizen?' 'Monsieur,' said the working-man, 'I have not the honour of knowing you.' 'I know you very well.' And the man added: 'Don't be afraid. I am the officer of the Committee. They are suspicious that you are not very sure. You know that if you reveal anything, we have an eye upon you.' Then he gave the working-man a grip of the hand and went away, saying: 'We shall meet again soon.'

The police, on the scout, overheard, not merely in the wine-shops, but in the street, singular dialogues: 'Get yourself admitted very quick,' said a weaver to a cabinet-maker.

'Why?'

'There is going to be some shooting.'

Two passers in rags exchanged these remarkable phrases, big with apparent Jacquerie.

'Who governs us?'

'Monsieur Philippe.'

'No, it's the bourgeoisie.'

You would be mistaken if you supposed that we used the word Jacquerie in bad part. The Jacques were the poor.

Another time, two men were heard passing by, one of whom said to the other: 'We have a good plan of attack.'

Of a private conversation between four men crouching in a ditch at the fork of the road by the Barrière du Trône, there was caught only this:

'All that is possible will be done that he may promenade in Paris no more.'

Who was *he?* Threatening obscurity.

'The principal chiefs', as they said in the Faubourg, kept out of sight. They were believed to meet to concert together, in a wine-shop near Point Saint Eustache. One named Aug—, chief of the Tailors' Benevolent Society, Rue Mondétour, was thought to act as principal intermediary between the chiefs and the Faubourg Saint Antoine. Nevertheless, there was always much obscurity about these chiefs, and no actual fact could weaken the singular boldness of the response afterwards made by a prisoner before the Court of Peers.

'Who was your chief?'

'I knew none, and I recognised none.'

Still it was hardly more than words, transparent, but vague; sometimes rumours in the air, they-says, hearsay. Other indications were discovered.

A carpenter, engaged on the Rue de Reuilly in nailing the boards of a fence about a lot on which a house was building, found in the lot a fragment of a torn letter, on which the following lines were still legible.

'. . . The Committee must take measures to prevent recruiting in the sections for the different societies . . .'

And in a postscript:

'We have learned that there are muskets at No. 5 [*bis*] Rue du Faubourg Poissonière, to the number of five or six thousand, at an armourer's in that court. The section has no arms.'

What excited the carpenter and made him show the thing to his neighbours was that a few steps further on he picked up another paper also torn, but still more significant, the form of which we reproduce on account of the historic interest of these strange documents:

Q	C	D	S	*Learn this list by heart.* *Afterwards, tear it up. Men* *who are admitted will do the* *same when you have* *transmitted them their orders.* *Health and fraternity,* *u og a'fe L.*

Those who were at the time in the secret of this discovery, did not know till afterwards the meaning of these four capitals; *quinturions*, *centurions*, *decurions*, *scouts*, and the sense of those letters: *u og a'fe* which was a date, and which meant *this 15th April 1832*. Under each capital were inscribed names followed by very characteristic indications. Thus: Q. *Baunerel.* 8 muskets. 83 cartridges. Sure man. C. *Boubière.* 1 pistol. 40 cartridges. D. *Rollet.* 1 foil. 1 pistol. 1 pound of powder. S. *Teissier.* 1 sabre. 1 cartridge-box. Exact. *Terreur.* 8 muskets. Brave, etc.

Finally this carpenter found, in the same enclosure also, a third paper on which was written in pencil, but very legibly, this enigmatic list:

Unity. Blanchard: dry-tree. 6.
Barra. Soize. Salle au Comte.
Kosciusko. Aubry the butcher?
J. J. R.
Caius Gracchus.
Right of revision. Dufond. Four.
Fall of the Girondins. Derbac. Maubuée.
Washington. Pinson. 1 pist. 86 cart.
Marseillaise.
Sover. of the people. Michel. Quincampoix. Sabre.
Hoche.
Marceau. Plato. Dry-tree.
Warsaw. Tilly, crier of *Le Populaire*.

The honest bourgeois who finally came into possession of this list knew its signification. It appeared that this list gave the complete nomenclature of the sections of the Fourth Arrondissement of the Society of the Rights of Man, with the names and residences of the chiefs of sections. At this day, when all these facts then unknown are matter of history only, they can be published. It should be added that the foundation of the society of the Rights of Man seems to have been posterior to the time when this paper was found. Perhaps it was merely a draft.

Meanwhile, after rumours and speeches, after written indications, material facts began to leak out.

In the Rue Popincourt, at an old curiosity shop, there were seized in a bureau drawer seven sheets of grey paper all evenly folded in quarto; these sheets enclosed twenty-six squares of the same grey paper folded in the form of cartridges, and a card upon which was written:

Saltpetre	12 ounces
Sulphur	2 ounces
Charcoal	2 ounces and a half
Water	2 ounces

The official report of the seizure stated that the drawer exhaled a strong odour of powder.

A mason going home, after his day's work, forgot a little package on a bench near the Bridge of Austerlitz. This package was carried to the guardhouse. It was opened and disclosed two printed dialogues, signed *Lahautière*, a song entitled: *Working-men, associate*, and a tin box full of cartridges.

A working-man, drinking with a comrade, made him put his hand on him to see how warm he was; the other felt a pistol under his vest.

In a ditch on the boulevard, between Père Lachaise and the Barrière du Trône, at the most solitary spot, some children, playing, discovered under a heap of chips and rubbish a bag which contained a bullet-mould, a wooden mandrel for making cartridges, a wooden mortar in which there were some grains of hunting powder, and a little melting pot the interior of which showed unmistakable traces of melted lead.

Some policemen, penetrating suddenly at five o'clock in the morning into the house of a man, named Pardon, who was afterwards sectionary of the section of the Barricade Merry, and was killed in the insurrection of April, 1834, found him standing not far from his bed, with cartridges in his hands, which he was in the act of making.

About the hour when working-men rest, two men were seen to meet between the Barrière Picpus and the Barrière Charenton in a little cross alley between two walls near a wine-dealer's who had a card-table before his door. One took a pistol from under his blouse and handed it to the other. At the moment of handing it to him he perceived that the perspiration from his breast had communicated some moisture to the powder. He primed the pistol, and added some powder to that which was already in the pan. Then the two men went away.

A man named Gallais, afterwards killed in the Rue Beaubourg in the affair of April, boasted that he had seven hundred cartridges and twenty-four gun-flints at home.

The government received word one day that arms had just been distributed in the Faubourg and two hundred thousand cartridges. The week afterwards thirty thousand cartridges were distributed. A remarkable thing, the police could not seize one. An intercepted letter contained: 'The day is not distant when in four hours by the clock, eighty thousand patriots will be under arms.'

All this fermentation was public, we might almost say tranquil. The imminent insurrection gathered its storm calmly in the face of the government. No singularity was wanting in this crisis, still subterranean, but already perceptible. Bourgeois talked quietly with working-men about the preparations. They would say: 'How is the *émeute* coming on?' in the same tone in which they would have said: 'How is your wife?'

A furniture dealer, Rue Moreau, asked: 'Well, when do you attack?'

Another shopkeeper said:

'You will attack very soon, I know. A month ago there were fifteen thousand of you, now there are twenty-five thousand of you.' He offered his gun, and a neighbour offered a little pistol which he wanted to sell for seven francs.

The revolutionary fever, however, was increasing. No point of Paris or of France was exempt from it. The artery pulsated everywhere. Like those membranes which are born of certain inflammations and formed in the human body, the network of the secret societies began to spread over the country. From the association of the Friends of the People, public and secret at the same time, sprang the Society of the Rights of Man, which dated one of its orders of the day thus: *Pluviôse, year 40 of the Republican Era*, which was to survive even the decrees of the Court of Assizes pronouncing its dissolution, and which had no hesitation in giving its sections such significant names as these:

The Pikes
Tocsin
Alarm Gun
The Vagrant
Forward March
Robespierre
Phrygian Cap
21st January
The Beggars
Level
Ça ira

The Society of the Rights of Man produced the Society of Action. These were the more impatient who left it and ran forward. Other associations sought to recruit from the large mother societies. The sectionaries complained of being pestered by this. Thus arose The *Gallic Society* and *the Organising Committee of the Municipalities.* Thus the associations for *the Freedom of the Press*, for *Individual Freedom*, for *the Instruction of the People*, *against Direct Taxes.* Then the society of the Equalitist Working-men which divided into three fractions, the Equalitists, the Communists and the Reformers. Then the Army of the Bastilles, a sort of cohort with a military organisation, four men commanded by a corporal, ten by a sergeant, twenty by a second lieutenant, forty by a lieutenant; there were never more than five hundred men who knew each other. A creation in which precaution was combined with boldness, and which seems marked with the genius of Venice. The central committee, which was the head, had two arms, the Society of Action and the Army of the Bastilles. A legitimist association, the Chevaliers of Fidelity, moved among these republican affiliations. But it was denounced and repudiated.

The Parisian societies ramified into the principal cities. Lyons, Nantes, Lisle, and Marseilles had their Society of the Rights of Man, the Carbonari, the Free Men. Aix had a revolutionary society which was called the Cougourde. We have already pronounced this word.

At Paris the Faubourg Saint Marceau was hardly less noisy than the Faubourg Saint Antoine, and the schools not less excited than the Faubourgs. A café in the Rue St Hyacinthe, and the drinking and smoking-room of the Seven Billiards, Rue des Mathurin St Jacques, served as rallying places for the students. The Society of the Friends of the ABC, affiliated with the Mutualists of Angers and with the Cougourde of Aix, met, as he have seen, at the Café Musain. These same young people also gathered, as we have said, in a restaurant wine-shop near the Rue Mondétour which was called Corinthe. These meetings were secret, others were as public as possible, and we may judge of their boldness by this fragment of an interrogatory during one of the subsequent trials: 'Where was this meeting held?' 'Rue de la Paix.' 'In whose house?' 'In the street.' 'What sections were there?' 'But one.' 'Which one?' 'The Manuel section.' 'Who was the chief?' 'I.' 'You are too young to have formed alone the grave resolution of attacking the government. Whence came your instructions?' 'From the central committee.'

The army was mined at the same time as the population, as was proved afterwards by the movements of Béford, Lunéville, and Epinal. They counted on the fifty-second regiment, the fifth, the eighth, the thirty-seventh, and the twentieth light. In Burgundy and in the cities of the South the tree of Liberty was planted. That is to say, a pole surmounted by a red cap.

Such was the situation.

This situation was, as we said in the beginning, rendered tangible and emphatic by the Faubourg Saint Antoine more than by any other portion of the population. There was the stitch in the side.

This old Faubourg, populous as an ant-hill, industrious, courageous, and choleric as a hive, was thrilling with the expectation and the desire for a commotion. Everything was in agitation, and yet labour was not interrupted on that account. Nothing can give an idea of that vivid yet dark phase of affairs. There are in that Faubourg bitter distresses hidden under garret roofs; there are there also ardent and rare intelligencies. And it is especially in reference to distress and intelligence that it is dangerous for extremes to meet.

The Faubourg Saint Antoine had still other causes of excitement, for it felt the rebound of the commercial crises, of the failures, the strikes, and stoppages, inherent in great political disturbances. In time of revolution misery is at once cause and effect. The blow which it strikes returns upon itself. This population, full of proud virtue, filled with latent caloric to the highest point, always ready for an armed contest, prompt to explode, irritated, deep, mined, seemed only waiting for the fall of a spark. Whenever certain sparks are floating over the horizon, driven by the wind of events, we cannot but think of the Faubourg Saint Antoine and the terrible chance which has placed that powder-mill of sufferings and ideas at the gates of Paris.

The wine-shops of the Faubourg Antoine, more than once referred to in the preceding sketch, have a notoriety which is historic. In times of trouble their words are more intoxicating than their wine. A sort of prophetic spirit and an odour of the future circulates in them, swelling hearts and enlarging souls. The wine-shops of the Faubourg Antoine resemble those taverns of Mount Aventine, over the Sybil's cave, and communicating with the deep and sacred afflatus; taverns whose tables were almost tripods, and where men drank what Ennius calls *the sibylline wine*.

The Faubourg Saint Antoine is a reservoir of people. Revolutionary agitation makes fissures in it through which flows popular sovereignty. This sovereignty may do harm; it makes mistakes like everything else; but, even when led astray, it is still grand. We may say of it as of the blind Cyclops, *Ingens.*

In '93, according as the idea which was afloat was good or bad, according as it was the day of fanaticism or of enthusiasm, there came from the Faubourg Saint Antoine sometimes savage legions, sometimes heroic bands.

Savage. We must explain this word. What was the aim of those bristling men who in the demiurgic days of revolutionary chaos, ragged, howling, wild, with tomahawk raised, and pike aloft, rushed over old overturned Paris? They desired the end of oppressions, the end of tyrannies, the end of the sword, labour for man, instruction for children, social gentleness for woman, liberty, equality, fraternity, bread for all, ideas for all, the Edenisation of the world, Progress; and this holy, good, and gentle thing, progress, pushed to the wall and beside themselves, they demanded, terrible, half naked, a club in their grasp, and a roar in their mouth. They were savages, yes; but the savages of civilisation.

They proclaimed the right furiously; they desired, were it through fear and trembling, to force the human race into paradise. They seemed barbarians, and they were saviours. With the mask of night they demanded the light.

In contrast with these men, wild, we admit, and terrible, but wild and terrible for the good, there are other men, smiling, embroidered, gilded, beribboned, bestarred, in silk stockings, in white feathers, in yellow gloves, in varnished shoes, who, leaning upon a velvet table by the corner of a marble mantel, softly insist upon the maintenance and the preservation of the past, the middle ages, divine right, fanaticism, ignorance, slavery, the death penalty, and war, glorifying politely and in mild tones the sabre, the stake, and the scaffold. As for us, if we were compelled to choose between the barbarians of civilisation, and the civilisees of barbarism, we would choose the barbarians.

But, thanks to heaven, other choice is possible. No abrupt fall is necessary, forward more than backward. Neither despotism, nor terrorism. We desire progress with gentle slope.

God provides for this. The smoothing of acclivities is the whole policy of God.

6. Enjolras and his lieutenants

Not far from this period, Enjolras, in view of possible events, took a sort of mysterious account of stock.

All were in conventicle at the Café Musain.

Enjolras said, mingling with his words a few semi-enigmatic but significant metaphors:

'It is well to know where we are and on whom we can rely. If we desire fighting men, we must make them. Have the wherewith to strike. That can do no harm. Travellers have a better chance of catching a thrust of a horn when there are bulls in the road than when there are none. Let us then take a little account of the herd. How many are there of us? We cannot put this work off till tomorrow. Revolutionists ought always to be ready; progress has no time to lose. Let us not trust to the moment. Let us not be taken unprepared. We must go over all the seams which we have made, and see if they hold. This business should be probed to the bottom today. Courfeyrac, you will see the Polytechnicians. It is their day out. Today, Wednesday. Feuilly, will you not see the men of the Glacière? Combeferre has promised me to go to Picpus. There is really an excellent swarm there. Bahorel will visit the Estrapade. Prouvaire, the masons are growing lukewarm; you will bring us news from the lodge in the Rue de Grenelle Saint Honoré. Joly will go to Dupuytren's clinique, and feel the pulse of the Medical School. Bossuet will make a little tour in the Palace of Justice and chat with the young lawyers. I will take charge of the Cougourde.'

'Then it is all arranged,' said Courfeyrac.

'No.'

'What more is there then?'

'A very important thing.'

'What is it?' inquired Combeferre.

'The Barrière du Maine,' answered Enjolras.

Enjolras remained a moment, as it were, absorbed in his reflections, then resumed:

'At the Barrière du Maine there are marble cutters, painters, assistants in sculptors' studios. It is an enthusiastic family, but subject to chills. I do not know what has ailed them for some time. They are thinking of other things. They are fading out. They spend their time in playing dominoes. Somebody must go and talk to them a little, and firmly too. They meet at Richefeu's. They can be found there between noon and one o'clock. We must blow upon these embers. I had counted on that absent-minded Marius for this, for on the whole he is good, but he does not come any more. I must have somebody for the Barrière du Maine. I have nobody left.'

'I,' said Grantaire, 'I am here.'

'You?'

'I.'

'You to indoctrinate republicans! you, to warm up, in the name of principles, hearts that have grown cold!'

'Why not?'

'Is it possible that you can be good for anything?'

'Yes, I have a vague ambition for it,' said Grantaire.

'You don't believe in anything.'

'I believe in you.'

'Grantaire, do you want to do me a service?'

'Anything. Polish your boots.'

'Well, don't meddle with our affairs. Sleep off your bitters.'

'You are an ingrate, Enjolras.'

'You would be a fine man to go to the Barrière du Maine! you would be capable of it!'

'I am capable of going down the Rue des Grès, of crossing the Place Saint Michel, of striking off through the Rue Monsieur le Prince, of taking the Rue de Vaugirard, of passing the Carmes, of turning into the Rue d'Assas, of reaching the Rue du Cherche Midi, of leaving behind me the Conseil de Guerre, of hurrying through the Rue des Vieilles Tuileries, of striding through the Boulevard, of following the Chaussée du Maine, of crossing over the Barrière, and of entering Richefeu's. I am capable of that. My shoes are capable of it.'

'Do you know anything about these comrades at Richefeu's?'

'Not much. We are on good terms, though.'

'What will you say to them?'

'I will talk to them about Robespierre, faith. About Danton, about principles.'

'You!'

'I. But you don't do me justice. When I am about it, I am terrible. I have read Prudhomme, I know the Contrat Social, I know my Constitution of the year Two by heart. "The Liberty of the citizen ends where the Liberty of another citizen begins." Do you take me for a brute? I have an old assignat in my drawer. The Rights of Man, the sovereignty of the people, zounds! I am even a little of a Hébertist. I can repeat, for six hours at a time, watch in hand, superb things.'

'Be serious,' said Enjolras.

'I am savage,' answered Grantaire.

Enjolras thought for a few seconds, and made the gesture of a man who forms his resolution.

'Grantaire,' said he gravely, 'I consent to try you. You shall go to the Barrière du Maine.'

Grantaire lived in a furnished room quite near the Café Musain. He went out, and came back in five minutes. He had been home to put on a Robespierre waistcoat.

'Red,' said he as he came in, looking straight at Enjolras.

Then, with the flat of his huge hand, he smoothed the two scarlet points of his waistcoat over his breast.

And, approaching Enjolras, he whispered in his ear:

'Set your mind at ease.'

He jammed down his hat, resolutely, and went out.

A quarter of an hour later, the back room of the Café Musain was deserted. All the Friends of the ABC had gone, each his own way, to their business. Enjolras, who had reserved the Cougourde for himself, went out last.

Those of the Cougourde of Aix who were at Paris met at that time on the Plain of Issy, in one of the abandoned quarries so numerous on that side of Paris.

Enjolras, on his way towards this place of rendezvous, passed the situation in review. The gravity of events was plainly visible. When events, premonitory of some latent social malady, are moving heavily along, the least complication stops them and shackles them. A phenomenon whence come overthrows and new births. Enjolras caught glimpses of a luminous uprising under the dark skirts of the future. Who knows? the moment was perhaps approaching. The people seizing their rights again, what a beautiful spectacle! the Revolution majestically resuming possession of France, and saying to the world: to be continued tomorrow! Enjolras was content. The furnace was heating. He had, at that very instant, a powder-train of friends extended over Paris. He was composing in his thought, with the philosophic and penetrating eloquence of Combeferre, the cosmopolitan enthusiasm of Feuilly, Courfeyrac's animation, Bahorel's laughter, Jean Prouvaire's melancholy, Joly's science, and Bossuet's sarcasms, a sort of electric spark taking fire in all directions at once. All in the work. Surely, the result would answer to the effort. This was well. This led him to think of Grantaire. 'Stop,' said he to himself, 'the Barrière du Maine hardly takes me out of my way. Suppose I go as far as Richefeu's? Let us get a glimpse of what Grantaire is doing, and how he is getting along.' One o'clock sounded from the belfry of Vaugirard when Enjolras reached the Richefeu smoking-room. He pushed open the door, went in, folded his arms, letting the door swing to so that it hit his shoulders, and looked into the room full of tables, men, and smoke.

A voice was ringing out in the mist, sharply answered by another voice. It was Grantaire talking with an adversary, whom he had found.

Grantaire was seated, opposite another figure, at a table of Saint Anne marble strewed with bran, and dotted with dominoes: he was striking the marble with his fist, and what Enjolras heard was this:

'Double six.'

'Four.'

'The beast! I can't play.'

'You are done for. Two.'

'Six.'

'Three.'

'Ace.'

'It is my lay.'

'Four points.'

'Hardly.'

'Yours.'

'I made an awful blunder.'

'You are doing well.'

'Fifteen.'

'Seven more.'

'That makes me twenty-two. [Musing.] Twenty-two!'

'You didn't expect the double six. If I had laid it in the beginning, it would have changed the whole game.'

'Two again.'

'Ace.'

'Ace! Well, five.'

'I haven't any.'

'You laid, I believe?'

'Yes.'

'Blank.'

'Has he any chance! Ah! you have one chance! [Long reverie.] Two.'

'Ace.'

'Neither a five, no; an ace. That is bothering for you.'

'Domino.'

'Dogs on it!'

BOOK 2: ÉPONINE

1. *The Field of the Lark*

Marius had seen the unexpected denouement of the ambuscade upon the track of which he had put Javert; but hardly had Javert left the old ruin, carrying away his prisoners in three coaches, when Marius also slipped out of the house. It was only nine o'clock in the evening. Marius went to Courfeyrac's. Courfeyrac was no longer the imperturbable inhabitant of the Latin Quarter; he had gone to live in the Rue de la Verrerie 'for political reasons'; this quarter was one of those in which the insurrection was fond of installing itself in those days. Marius said to Courfeyrac: 'I have come to sleep with you.' Courfeyrac drew a mattress from his bed, where there were two, laid it on the floor, and said: 'There you are.'

The next day, by seven o'clock in the morning, Marius went back to the tenement, paid his rent, and what was due to Ma'am Bougon, had his books, bed, table, bureau, and his two chairs loaded upon a hand-cart, and went off without leaving his address, so that when Javert came back in the forenoon to question Marius about the events of the evening, he found only Ma'am Bougon, who answered him, 'moved!'

Ma'am Bougon was convinced that Marius was somehow an accomplice of the robbers seized the night before. 'Who would have thought so?' she exclaimed among the portresses of the quarter, 'a young man who had so much the appearance of a girl!'

Marius had two reasons for this prompt removal. The first was, that he now had a horror of that house, where he had seen, so near at hand, and in all its most repulsive and most ferocious development, a social deformity perhaps still more hideous than the evil rich man: the evil poor. The second was, that he did not wish to figure in the trial which would probably follow, and be brought forward to testify against Thénardier.

Javert thought that the young man, whose name he had not retained, had been frightened and had escaped, or, perhaps, had not even returned home at the time of the ambuscade; still he made some effort to find him, but he did not succeed.

A month rolled away, then another. Marius was still with Courfeyrac. He knew from a young attorney, an habitual attendant in the ante-rooms of the court, that Thénardier was in solitary confinement. Every Monday Marius sent to the clerk of La Force five francs for Thénardier.

Marius, having now no money, borrowed the five francs of Courfeyrac. It was the first time in his life that he had borrowed money. This periodical five francs was a double enigma, to Courfeyrac who furnished them, and to Thénardier who received them. 'To whom can it go?' thought Courfeyrac. 'Where can it come from?' Thénardier asked himself.

Marius, moreover, was in sore affliction. Everything had relapsed into darkness. He no longer saw anything before him; his life was again plunged into that mystery in which he had been blindly groping. He had for a moment seen close at hand in that obscurity, the young girl whom he loved, the old man who seemed her father, these unknown beings who were his only interest and his only hope in this world; and at the moment he had thought to hold them fast, a breath had swept all those shadows away. Not a spark of certainty or truth had escaped even from that most fearful shock. No conjecture was possible. He knew not even the name which he had thought he knew. Certainly it was no longer Ursula. And the Lark was a nickname. And what should he think of the old man? Was he really hiding from the police? The white-haired working-man whom Marius had met in the neighbourhood of the Invalides recurred to his mind. It now became probable that that working-man and M. Leblanc were the same man. He disguised himself then? This man had heroic sides and equivocal sides. Why had he not called for help? why had he escaped? was he, yes or no, the father of the young girl? Finally, was he really the man whom Thénardier thought he recognised? Could Thénardier have been mistaken? So many problems without issue. All this, it is true, detracted nothing from the angelic charms of the young girl of the Luxembourg. Bitter wretchedness; Marius had a passion in his heart, and night over his eyes. He was pushed, he was drawn, and he could not stir. All had vanished, except love. Even of love, he had lost the instincts and the sudden illuminations. Ordinarily, this flame which consumes us, illumines us also a little, and sheds some useful light without. Those vague promptings of passion, Marius no longer even heard. Never did he say to himself: Suppose I go there? suppose I try this? She whom he could no longer call Ursula was evidently somewhere; nothing indicated to Marius the direction in which he must seek for her. His whole life was now resumed in two words: an absolute uncertainty in an impenetrable mist. To see her again, Her; he aspired to this continually; he hoped for it no longer.

To crown all, want returned. He felt close upon him, behind him, that icy breath. During all these torments, and now for a long time, he had discontinued his work, and nothing is more dangerous than discontinued labour; it is habit lost. A habit easy to abandon, difficult to resume.

A certain amount of reverie is good, like a narcotic in discreet doses. It soothes the fever, sometimes high, of the brain at work, and produces in the mind a soft and fresh vapour which corrects the too angular contours of pure thought, fills up the gaps and intervals here and there, binds them together, and blunts the sharp corners of ideas. But too much reverie submerges and drowns. Woe to the brain-worker who allows himself to fall entirely from thought into reverie! He thinks that he shall rise again easily, and he says that, after all, it is the same thing. An error!

Thought is the labour of the intellect, reverie is its pleasure. To replace thought by reverie is to confound poison with nourishment.

Marius, we remember, had begun in this way. Passion supervened, and had at last precipitated him into bottomless and aimless chimæras. One no longer goes out of the house except to walk and dream. Sluggish birth. A tumultuous and stagnant gulf. And, as work diminishes, necessities increase. This is a law. Man, in the dreamy state, is naturally prodigal and luxurious; the relaxed mind cannot lead a severe life. There is, in this way of living, some good mingled with the evil, for if the softening be fatal, the generosity is wholesome and good. But the poor man who is generous and noble, and who does not work, is lost. His resources dry up, his necessities mount up.

Fatal slope, down which the firmest and the noblest are drawn, as well as the weakest and the most vicious, and which leads to one of these two pits, suicide or crime.

By continually going out for reverie, there comes a day when you go out to throw yourself into the water.

The excess of reverie produces men like Escousse and Lebras.

Marius was descending this slope with slow steps, his eyes fixed upon her whom he saw no more. What we have here written seems strange, and still it is true. The memory of an absent being grows bright in the darkness of the heart; the more it has disappeared the more radiant it is; the despairing and gloomy soul sees that light in its horizon; star of the interior night. She, this was all the thought of Marius. He dreamed of nothing else; he felt confusedly that his old coat was becoming an impossible coat and that his new coat was becoming an old coat, that his shirts were wearing out, that his hat was wearing out, that his boots were wearing out, that is to say, that his life was wearing out, and he said to himself, 'If I could only see her again before I die.'

A single sweet idea remained to him, that she had loved him, that her eyes had told him so, that she did not know his name but that she knew his soul, and that, perhaps, where she was, whatever that mysterious place might be, she loved him still. Who knows but she was dreaming of him as he was dreaming of her? Sometimes in the inexplicable hours, such as every heart has which loves, having reasons for sorrow only, yet feeling nevertheless a vague thrill of joy, he said to himself: It is her thoughts which come to me! Then he added, my thoughts reach her also, perhaps!

This illusion, at which he shook his head the moment afterwards, succeeded notwithstanding in casting some ray into his soul, which occasionally resembled hope. From time to time, especially at that evening hour which saddens dreamers most of all, he dropped upon a quire of paper, which he devoted to that purpose, the purest, the most impersonal, the most ideal of the reveries with which love filled his brain. He called that 'writing to her',

We must not suppose that his reason was disordered. Quite the contrary. He had lost the capability of work, and of moving firmly towards a definite end, but he was more clear-sighted and correct than ever. Marius saw, in a calm and real light, although a singular one, what was going on under his eyes, even the most indifferent facts or men; he said the right word about everything with a sort of honest languor and candid disinterestedness. His judgement, almost detached from hope, soared and floated aloft.

In this situation of mind nothing escaped him, nothing deceived him, and he saw at every moment the bottom of life, humanity, and destiny. Happy, even in anguish, is he to whom God has given a soul worthy of love and of grief! He who has not seen the things of this world, and the hearts of men by this double light, has seen nothing, and knows nothing of the truth.

The soul which loves and which suffers is in the sublime state.

The days passed, however, one after another, and there was nothing new. It seemed to him, merely, that the dreary space which remained for him to run through was contracting with every instant. He thought that he already saw distinctly the brink of the bottomless precipice.

'What!' he repeated to himself, 'shall I never see her again before!'

If you go up the Rue Saint Jacques, leave the barrière at your side, and follow the old interior boulevard to the left for some distance, you come to the

Rue de la Santé, then La Glacière, and, a little before reaching the small stream of the Gobelins, you find a sort of field, which is, in the long and monotonous circuit of the boulevards of Paris, the only spot where Ruysdael would be tempted to sit down.

That indescribable something from which grace springs is there, a green meadow crossed by tight drawn ropes, on which rags are drying in the wind, an old market-garden farmhouse built in the time of Louis XIII, with its large roof grotesquely pierced with dormer windows, broken palisade fences, a small pond between the poplars, women, laughter, voices; in the horizon the Pantheon, the tree of the Deaf-mutes, the Val de Grâce, black, squat, fantastic, amusing, magnificent, and in the background the severe square summits of the towers of Notre Dame.

As the place is worth seeing, nobody goes there. Hardly a cart or a wagon once in a quarter of an hour.

It happened one day that Marius' solitary walks conducted him to this spot near this pond. That day there was a rarity on the boulevard, a passer. Marius, vaguely struck with the almost sylvan charm of the spot, asked this traveller: 'What is the name of this place?'

The traveller answered: 'It is the Field of the Lark.'

And he added: 'It was here that Ulbach killed the shepherdess of Ivry.'

But after that word, the 'Lark', Marius had heard nothing more. There are such sudden congelations in the dreamy state, which a word is sufficient to produce. The whole mind condenses abruptly about one idea, and ceases to be capable of any other perception.

The Lark was the appellation which, in the depths of Marius' melancholy, had replaced Ursula. 'Yes,' said he in the kind of unreasoning stupor peculiar to these mysterious asides, 'this is her field. I shall learn here where she lives.'

This was absurd, but irresistible.

And he came every day to this Field of the Lark.

2. *Embryonic formation of crimes in the incubation of prisons*

Javert's triumph in the Gorbeau tenement had seemed complete, but it was not so.

In the first place, and this was his principal regret, Javert had not made the prisoner prisoner. The victim who slips away is more suspicious than the assassin; and it was probable that this personage, so precious a capture to the bandits, would be a not less valuable prize to the authorities.

And then, Montparnasse had escaped Javert.

He must await another occasion to lay his hand upon 'that devilish dandy'. Montparnasse, in fact, having met Eponine, who was standing sentry under the trees of the boulevard, had led her away, liking rather to be Némorin with the daughter than to be Schinderhannes with the father. Well for him that he did so. He was free. As to Eponine, Javert 'nabbed' her; trifling consolation. Eponine had rejoined Azelma at Les Madelonnettes.

Finally, on the trip from the Gorbeau tenement to La Force, one of the principal prisoners, Claquesous, had been lost. Nobody knew how it was done, the officers and sergeants 'didn't understand it', he had changed into vapour, he had glided out of the handcuffs, he had slipped through the cracks of the carriage, the fiacre was leaky, and had fled; nothing could be said, save that on reaching the prison there was no Claquesous. There were either fairies or police in the matter. Had Claquesous melted away into the darkness like a snowflake in the water? Was there some secret connivance of the officers? Did this man belong to the double enigma of disorder and of order? Was he concentric with infraction and with repression? Had this sphinx forepaws in crime and hind-paws in authority? Javert in no wise accepted these combinations, and his hair rose on end in view of such an exposure; but his squad contained other inspectors besides himself, more deeply initiated, perhaps, than himself, although his subordinates, in the secrets of the prefecture, and Claquesous was so great a scoundrel that he might be a very good officer. To be on such intimate juggling relations with darkness is excellent for brigandage and admirable for the police. There are such two-edged rascals. However it might be, Claquesous was lost, and was not found again. Javert appeared more irritated than astonished at it.

As to Marius, 'that dolt of a lawyer'. who was 'probably frightened', and whose name Javert had forgotten, Javert cared little for him. Besides he was a lawyer, they are always found again. But was he a lawyer merely?

The trial commenced.

The police judge thought it desirable not to put one of the men of the Patron-Minette band into solitary confinement, hoping for some blabbing. This was Brujon, the long-haired man of the Rue du Petit Banquier. He was left in the Charlemagne court, and the watchmen kept their eyes upon him.

This name, Brujon, is one of the traditions of La Force. In the hideous court called the Bâtiment Neuf, which the administration named Court Saint Bernard, and which the robbers named La Fosse aux Lions, upon that wall covered with filth and with mould, which rises on the left to the height of the roofs, near an old rusty iron door which leads into the former chapel of the ducal hôtel of La Force, now become a dormitory for brigands, a dozen years ago there could still be seen a sort of bastille coarsely cut in the stone with a nail, and below it this signature:

BRUJON, 1811

The Brujon of 1811 was the father of the Brujon of 1832.

This last, of whom only a glimpse was caught in the Gorbeau ambuscade, was a sprightly young fellow, very cunning and very adroit, with a flurried and plaintive appearance. It was on account of this flurried air that the judge had selected him, thinking that he would be of more use in the Charlemagne court than in a solitary cell.

Robbers do not cease operations because they are in the hands of justice. They are not disconcerted so easily. Being in prison for one crime does not prevent the commencement of another crime. They are artists who have a picture in the parlour, and who labour none the less for that on a new work in their studio.

Brujon seemed stupefied by the prison. He was sometimes seen whole hours in the Charlemagne court, standing near the sutler's window, and staring like an idiot at that dirty list of prices of supplies which began with: *garlic, 62 centimes,* and ended with: *cigars, cinq centimes.* Or instead, he would pass his time in trembling and making his teeth chatter, saying that he had a fever, and inquiring if one of the twenty-eight beds in the fever ward was not vacant.

Suddenly, about the second fortnight in February, 1832, it was discovered that Brujon, that sleepy fellow, had sent out, through the agents of the house, not in his own name, but in the name of three of his comrades, three different commissions, which had cost him in all fifty sous, a tremendous expense which attracted the attention of the prison brigadier.

He inquired into it, and by consulting the price list of commissions hung up in the convicts' waiting-room, he found that the fifty sous were made up thus: three commissions; one to the Pantheon, ten sous; one to the Val de Grâce, fifteen sous; and one to the Barrière de Grenelle, twenty-five sous. This was the dearest of the whole list. Now the Pantheon, the Val de Grâce, and the Barrière de Grenelle happened to be the residences of three of the most dreaded prowlers of the barriers, Kruideniers alias Bizarro, Glorieux, a liberated convict, and Barre Carosse, upon whom this incident fixed the eyes of the police. They thought they divined that these men were affiliated with Patron Minette, two of whose chiefs, Babet and Gueulemer, were secured. It was supposed that Brujon's messages sent, not addressed to any houses, but to persons who were waiting for them in the street, must have been notices of some projected crime. There were still other indications; they arrested the three prowlers, and thought they had foiled Brujon's machination, whatever it was.

About a week after these measures were taken, one night, a watchman, who was watching the dormitory in the lower part of the New Building, at the instant of putting his chestnut into the chestnut-box – this is the means employed to make sure that the watchmen do their duty with exactness; every hour a chestnut must fall into every box nailed on the doors of the dormitories – a watchman then saw through the peep-hole of the dormitory, Brujon sitting up in his bed and writing something by the light of the reflector. The warden entered, Brujon was put into the dungeon for a month, but they could not find what he had written. The police knew nothing more.

It is certain, however, that the next day 'a postilion' was thrown from the Charlemagne court into the Fosse aux Lions, over the five-storey building which separates the two courts.

Prisoners call a ball of bread artistically kneaded, which is sent *into Ireland,* that is to say, over the roof of a prison, from one court to the other, a postilion. Etymology: over England; from one country to the other; *into Ireland.* This ball falls in the court. He who picks it up opens it, and finds a letter in it addressed to some prisoner in the court. If it be a convict who finds it, he hands the letter to its destination; if it be a warden, or one of those secretly bribed prisoners who are called sheep in the prisons and foxes in the galleys, the letter is carried to the office and delivered to the police.

This time the postilion reached its address, although he for whom the message was destined was then *in solitary.* Its recipient was none other than Babet, one of the four heads of Patron Minette.

The postilion contained a paper rolled up, on which there were only these two lines:

'Babet, there is an affair on hand in the Rue Plumet. A grating in a garden.'

This was the thing that Brujon had written in the night.

In spite of spies, both male and female, Babet found means to send the letter from La Force to La Salpêtrière to 'a friend' of his who was shut up there. This girl in her turn transmitted the letter to another whom she knew, named Magnon, who was closely watched by the police, but not yet arrested. This Magnon, whose name the reader has already seen, had some relations with the Thénardiers which will be related hereafter, and could, by going to see Eponine, serve as a bridge between La Salpêtrière and Les Madelonnettes.

It happened just at that very moment, the proofs in the prosecution of Thénardier failing in regard to his daughters, that Eponine and Azelma were released.

When Eponine came out, Magnon, who was watching for her at the door of Les Madelonnettes, handed her Brujon's note to Babet, charging her to find out about the affair.

Eponine went to the Rue Plumet, reconnoitred the grating and the garden, looked at the house, spied, watched, and, a few days after, carried to Magnon, who lived in the Rue Clocheperce, a biscuit, which Magnon transmitted to Babet's mistress at La Salpêtrière. A biscuit, in the dark symbolism of the prisons, signifies: *nothing to do.*

So that in less than a week after that, Babet and Brujon meeting on the way from La Force, as one was going 'to examination', and the other was returning from it: 'Well,' asked Brujon, 'the Rue P?' 'Biscuit,' answered Babet.

This was the end of that fœtus of crime, engendered by Brujon in La Force.

This abortion, however, led to results entirely foreign to Brujon's programme. We shall see them.

Often, when thinking to knot one thread, we tie another.

3. *An apparition to Father Mabeuf*

Marius now visited nobody, but he sometimes happened to meet Father Mabeuf.

While Marius was slowly descending those dismal steps, which one might call cellar stairs, and which lead into places without light where we hear the happy walking above us, M. Mabeuf also was descending.

The *Flora of Cauteretz* had absolutely no sale more. The experiments upon indigo had not succeeded in the little garden of Austerlitz, which was very much exposed. M. Mabeuf could only cultivate a few rare plants which like moisture and shade. He was not discouraged, however. He had obtained a bit of ground in the Jardin des Plantes, with a good exposure, to carry on, 'at his own cost', his experiments upon indigo. For this he had put the plates of his *Flora* into pawn. He had reduced his breakfast to two eggs, and he left one of them for his old servant, whose wages he had not paid for fifteen months. And often his breakfast was his only meal. He laughed no more with his childlike laugh, he had become morose, and he now received no visits. Marius was right in not thinking to come. Sometimes, at the hour when M. Mabeuf went to the Jardin des Plantes, the old man and the young man met on the Boulevard de l'Hôpital. They did not speak, but sadly nodded their heads. It is a bitter thing that there should be a moment when misery unbinds. They had been two friends, they were two passers.

The bookseller, Royol, was dead. M. Mabeuf now knew only his books, his garden, and his indigo; those were to him the three forms which happiness, pleasure, and hope had taken. This fed his life. He said to himself: 'When I have made my blue balls, I shall be rich, I will take my plates out of pawn, I will bring my *Flora* into vogue through charlatanism, by big payments and by announcements in the journals, and I will buy, I well know where, a copy of Pierre de Médine's *Art de Naviguer*, with woodcuts, edition of 1559.' In the meantime he worked all day on his indigo bed, and at night returned home to water his garden, and read his books. M. Mabeuf was at this time very nearly eighty years old.

One night he saw a singular apparition.

He had come home while it was still broad day. Mother Plutarch, whose health was poor, was sick and gone to bed. He had dined on a bone on which a little meat was left, and a bit of bread which he had found on the kitchen table, and had sat down on a block of stone, which took the place of a seat in his garden.

Near this seat there rose, in the fashion of the old orchard-gardens, a sort of hut, in a ruinous condition, of joists and boards, a warren on the ground floor, a fruit-house above. There were no rabbits in the warren, but there were a few apples in the fruit-house. A remnant of the winter's store.

M. Mabeuf had begun to look through, reading by the way, with the help of his spectacles, two books which enchanted him, and in which he was even absorbed, a more serious thing at his age. His natural timidity fitted him, to a certain extent, to accept superstitions. The first of these books was the famous treatise of President Delancre, *On the inconstancy of Demons*, the other was the quarto of Mutor de la Rubaudière, *On the devils of Vauvert and the goblins of La Bièvé.* This last book interested him the more, since his garden was one of the spots formerly haunted by goblins. Twilight was beginning to whiten all above and to blacken all below. As he read, Father Mabeuf was looking over the book which he held in his hand, at his plants, and among others at a magnificent rhododendron which was one of his consolations; there had been four days of drought, wind, and sun, without a drop of rain; the stalks bent over, the buds hung down, the leaves were falling, they all needed to be watered; the rhododendron especially was a sad sight. Father Mabeuf was one of those to whom plants have souls. The old man had worked all day on his indigo bed, he was exhausted with fatigue, he got up nevertheless, put his books upon the bench, and walked, bent over and with tottering steps, to the well, but when he had grasped the chain, he could not even draw it far enough to unhook it. Then he turned and looked with a look of anguish towards the sky which was filling with stars.

The evening had that serenity which buries the sorrows of man under a strangely dreary yet eternal joy. The night promised to be as dry as the day had been.

'Stars everywhere!' thought the old man; 'not the smallest cloud! not a drop of water.'

And his head, which had been raised for a moment, fell back upon his breast.

He raised it again and looked at the sky, murmuring:

'A drop of dew! a little pity!'

He endeavoured once more to unhook the well-chain, but he could not.

At this moment he heard a voice which said:

'Father Mabeuf, would you like to have me water your garden?'

At the same time he heard a sound like that of a passing deer in the hedge, and he saw springing out of the shrubbery a sort of tall, slender girl, who came and stood before him, looking boldly at him. She had less the appearance of a human being than of a form which had just been born of the twilight.

Before Father Mabeuf, who was easily startled, and who was, as we have said, subject to fear, could answer a word, this being, whose motions seemed grotesquely abrupt in the obscurity, had unhooked the chain, plunged in and drawn out the bucket, and filled the watering-pot, and the goodman saw this apparition with bare feet and a ragged skirt running along the beds, distributing life about her. The sound of the water upon the leaves filled Father Mabeuf's soul with transport. It seemed to him that now the rhododendron was happy.

When the first bucket was emptied, the girl drew a second, then a third. She watered the whole garden.

Moving thus along the walks, her outline appearing entirely black, shaking her torn shawl over her long angular arms, she seemed something like a bat.

When she had ended, Father Mabeuf approached her with tears in his eyes, and laid his hand upon her forehead.

'God will bless you,' said he, 'you are an angel, since you care for flowers.'

'No,' she answered, 'I am the devil, but that is all the same to me.'

The old man exclaimed, without waiting for and without hearing her answer:

'What a pity that I am so unfortunate and so poor, and that I cannot do anything for you!'

'You can do something,' said she.

'What?'

'Tell me where M. Marius lives.'

The old man did not understand.

'What Monsieur Marius?'

He raised his glassy eye and appeared to be looking far something that had vanished.

'A young man who used to come here.'

Meanwhile M. Mabeuf had fumbled in his memory.

'Ah! yes,' he exclaimed, 'I know what you mean. Listen, now! Monsieur Marius – the Baron Marius Pontmercy, yes! he lives – or rather he does not live there now – ah! well, I don't know.'

While he spoke, he had bent over to tie up a branch of the rhododendron, and he continued:

'Ah! I remember now. He passes up the boulevard very often, and goes toward La Glacière, Rue Croulebarbe. The Field of the Lark. Go that way. He isn't hard to find.'

When M. Mabeuf rose up, there was nobody there; the girl had disappeared.

He was decidedly a little frightened.

'Really,' thought he, 'if my garden was not watered, I should think it was a spirit.'

An hour later when he had gone to bed, this returned to him, and, as he was falling asleep, at that troubled moment when thought, like that fabulous bird which changes itself into fish to pass through the sea, gradually takes the form of dream to pass through sleep, he said to himself confusedly:

'Indeed, this much resembles what Rubaudière relates of the goblins. Could it be a goblin?'

4. An apparition to Marius

A FEW DAYS after this visit of a 'spirit' to Father Mabeuf, one morning – it was Monday, the day on which Marius borrowed the hundred-sous piece of Courfeyrac for Thénardier – Marius had put this hundred-sous piece into his pocket, and before carrying it to the prison office, he had gone 'to take a little walk,' hoping that it would enable him to work on his return. It was eternally so. As soon as he rose in the morning, he sat down before a book and a sheet of paper to work upon some translation; the work he had on hand at that time was the translation into French of a celebrated quarrel between two Germans, the controversy between Gans and Savigny; he took Savigny, he took Gans, read four lines, tried to write one of them, could not, saw a star between his paper and his eyes, and rose from his chair, saying: 'I will go out. That will put me in trim.'

And he would go to the Field of the Lark.

There he saw the star more than ever, and Savigny and Gans less than ever.

He returned, tried to resume his work, and did not succeed, he found no means of tying a single one of the broken threads in his brain; then he would say: 'I will not go out tomorrow. It prevents my working.' Yet he went out every day.

He lived in the Field of the Lark rather than in Courfeyrac's room. This was his real address: Boulevard de la Santé, seventh tree from the Rue Croulebarbe.

That morning, he had left this seventh tree, and sat down on the bank of the brook of the Gobelins. The bright sun was gleaming through the new and glossy leaves.

He was thinking of 'Her!' And his dreaminess, becoming reproachful, fell back upon himself; he thought sorrowfully of the idleness, the paralysis of the soul, which was growing up within him, and of that night which was thickening before him hour by hour so rapidly that he had already ceased to see the sun.

Meanwhile, through this painful evolution of indistinct ideas which were not even a soliloquy, so much had action become enfeebled within him, and he no longer had even the strength to develop his grief – through this melancholy distraction, the sensations of the world without reached him. He heard behind and below him, on both banks of the stream, the washerwomen of the Gobelins beating their linen; and over his head, the birds chattering and singing in the elms. On the one hand the sound of liberty, of happy unconcern, of winged leisure; on the other, the sound of labour. A thing which made him muse profoundly, and almost reflect, these two joyous sounds.

All at once, in the midst of his ecstasy of exhaustion, he heard a voice which was known to him, say:

'Ah! there he is!'

He raised his eyes and recognised the unfortunate child who had come to his room one morning, the elder of the Thénardier girls, Eponine; he now knew her name. Singular fact, she had become more wretched and more beautiful, two steps which seemed impossible She had accomplished a double progress towards the light, and towards distress. She was barefooted and in rags, as on the day when she had so resolutely entered his room, only her rags were two months older; the holes were larger, the tatters dirtier. It was the same rough voice, the same forehead tanned and wrinkled by exposure; the same free, wild, and wandering gaze. She had, in addition to her former expression, that mixture of fear and sorrow which the experience of a prison adds to misery.

She had spears of straw and grass in her hair, not like Ophelia from having gone mad through the contagion of Hamlet's madness, but because she had slept in some stable loft.

And with all this, she was beautiful. What a star thou art, O youth!

Meantime, she had stopped before Marius, with an expression of pleasure upon her livid face, and something which resembled a smile.

She stood for a few seconds, as if she could not speak.

'I have found you, then?' said she at last. 'Father Mabeuf was right; it was on this boulevard. How I have looked for you? if you only knew? Do you know? I have been in the jug. A fortnight! They have let me out! seeing that there was nothing against me, and then I was not of the age of discernment. It lacked two months. Oh! how I have looked for you! it is six weeks now. You don't live down there any longer?'

'No,' said Marius.

'Oh! I understand. On account of the affair. Such scares are disagreeable. You have moved. What! why do you wear such an old hat as that? a young man like you ought to have fine clothes. Do you know, Monsieur Marius? Father Mabeuf calls you Baron Marius, I forget what more. It's not true that you are a baron? barons are old fellows, they go to the Luxembourg in front of the chateau where there is the most sun, they read the *Quotidienne* for a sou. I went once for a letter to a baron's like that. He was more than a hundred years old. But tell me, where do you live now?'

Marius did not answer.

'Ah!' she continued, 'you have a hole in your shirt. I must mend it for you.'

She resumed with an expression which gradually grew darker:

'You don't seem to be glad to see me?'

Marius said nothing; she herself was silent for a moment, then exclaimed:

'But if I would, I could easily make you glad!'

'How?' inquired Marius. 'What does that mean?'

'Ah! you used to speak more kindly to me!' replied she.

'Well, what is it that you mean?'

She bit her lip; she seemed to hesitate, as if passing through a kind of interior struggle. At last, she appeared to decide upon her course.

'So much the worse, it makes no difference. You look sad, I want you to be glad. But promise me that you will laugh, I want to see you laugh and hear you say: Ah, well! that is good. Poor Monsieur Marius! you know, you promised me that you would give me whatever I should ask – '

'Yes! but tell me!'

She looked into Marius' eyes and said:

'I have the address.'

Marius turned pale. All his blood flowed back to his heart.

'What address?'

'The address you asked me for!'

She added as if she were making an effort:

'The address – you know well enough!'

'Yes!' stammered Marius.

'Of the young lady!'

Having pronounced this word, she sighed deeply.

Marius sprang up from the bank on which he was sitting, and took her wildly by the hand.

'Oh! come! show me the way, tell me! ask me for whatever you will! Where is it?'

'Come with me,' she answered. 'I am not sure of the street and the number; it is away on the other side from here, but I know the house very well. I will show you.'

She withdrew her hand and added in a tone which would have pierced the heart of an observer, but which did not even touch the intoxicated and transported Marius:

'Oh! how glad you are!'

A cloud passed over Marius' brow. He seized Eponine by the arm:

'Swear to me one thing!'

'Swear?' said she, 'what does that mean? Ah! you want me to swear?'

And she laughed.

'Your father! promise me, Eponine! swear to me that you will not give this address to your father!'

She turned towards him with an astounded appearance.

'Eponine! How do you know that my name is Eponine?'

'Promise what I ask you!'

But she did not seem to understand.

'That is nice! you called me Eponine!'

Marius caught her by both arms at once.

'But answer me now, in heaven's name! pay attention to what I am saying, swear to me that you will not give the address you know to your father!'

'My father?' said she. 'Oh! yes, my father! do not be concerned on his account. He is in solitary. Besides, do I busy myself about my father!'

'But you don't promise me!' exclaimed Marius.

'Let me go then!' said she, bursting into a laugh, 'how you shake me! Yes! yes! I promise you that! I swear to you that! What is it to me? I won't give the address to my father. There! will that do? is that it?'

'Nor to anybody?' said Marius.

'Nor to anybody.'

'Now,' added Marius, 'show me the way.'

'Right away?'

'Right away.'

'Come. Oh! how glad he is!' said she.

After a few steps, she stopped.

'You follow too near me, Monsieur Marius. Let me go forward, and follow me like that, without seeming to. It won't do for a fine young man, like you, to be seen with a woman like me.'

No tongue could tell all that there was in that word, woman, thus uttered by this child.

She went on a few steps, and stopped again; Marius rejoined her. She spoke to him aside and without turning:

'By the way, you know you have promised me something?'

Marius fumbled in his pocket. He had nothing in the world but the five francs intended for Thénardier. He took it, and put it into Eponine's hand.

She opened her fingers and let the piece fall on the ground, and, looking at him with a gloomy look:

'I don't want your money,' said she.

BOOK 3: THE HOUSE IN THE RUE PLUMET

1. *The secret house*

TOWARDS THE MIDDLE of the last century, a velvet-capped president of the Parliament of Paris having a mistress and concealing it, for in those days the great lords exhibited their mistresses and the bourgeois concealed theirs, had '*une petite maison*' built in the Faubourg Saint Germain, in the deserted Rue de Blomet, now called the Rue Plumet, not far from the spot which then went by the name of the *Combat des Animaux*.

This was a summerhouse of but two storeys; two rooms on the ground floor, two chambers in the second storey, a kitchen below, a boudoir above, a garret next the roof, the whole fronted by a garden with a large iron grated gate opening on the street. This garden contained about an acre. This was all that the passers-by could see; but in the rear of the house there was a small yard, at the further end of which there was a low building, two rooms only and a cellar, a convenience intended to conceal a child and nurse in case of need. This building communicated, from the rear, by a masked door opening secretly, with a long narrow passage, paved, winding, open to the sky, bordered by two high walls, and which, concealed with wonderful art, and as it were lost between the enclosures of the gardens and fields, all the corners and turnings of which it followed, came to an end at another door, also concealed, which opened a third of a mile away, almost in another quarter, upon the unbuilt end of the Rue de Babylone.

The president came in this way, so that those even who might have watched and followed him, and those who might have observed that the president went somewhere mysteriously every day, could not have suspected that going to the Rue de Babylone was going to the Rue Blomet. By skilful purchases of land, the ingenious magistrate was enabled to have this secret route to his house made upon his own ground, and consequently without supervision. He had afterwards sold off the lots of ground bordering on the passage in little parcels for flower and vegetable gardens, and the proprietors of these lots of ground supposed on both sides that what they saw was a partition wall, and did not even suspect the existence of that long ribbon of pavement winding between two walls among their beds and fruit trees. The birds alone saw this curiosity. It is probable that the larks and the sparrows of the last century had a good deal of chattering about the president.

The house, built of stone in the Mansard style, wainscoted, and furnished in the Watteau style, rock-work within, peruke without, walled about with a triple hedge of flowers, had a discreet, coquettish, and solemn appearance about it, suitable to a caprice of love and of magistracy.

This house and this passage, which have since disappeared, were still in existence fifteen years ago. In '93, a coppersmith bought the house to pull it down, but not being able to pay the price for it, the nation sent him into bankruptcy. So that it was the house that pulled down the coppersmith. Thereafter the house remained empty, and fell slowly into ruin, like all dwellings to which the presence of man no longer communicates life. It remained, furnished with its old furniture, and always for sale or to let, and the ten or twelve persons who passed through the Rue Plumet in the course of a year were notified of this by a yellow and illegible piece of paper which had hung upon the railing of the garden since 1810.

Towards the end of the Restoration, these same passers might have noticed that the paper had disappeared, and that, also, the shutters of the upper storey were open. The house was indeed occupied. The windows had 'little curtains', a sign that there was a woman there.

In the month of October 1829, a man of a certain age had appeared and hired the house as it stood, including, of course, the building in the rear, and the passage which ran out to the Rue de Babylone. He had the secret openings of the two doors of this passage repaired. The house, as we have just said, was still nearly furnished with the president's old furniture. The new tenant had ordered a few repairs, added here and there what was lacking, put in a few flags in the yard, a few bricks in the basement, a few steps in the staircase, a few tiles in the floors, a few panes in the windows, and finally came and installed himself with a young girl and an aged servant, without any noise, rather like somebody stealing in than like a man who enters his own house. The neighbours did not gossip about it, for the reason that there were no neighbours.

This tenant, to partial extent, was Jean Valjean; the young girl was Cosette. The servant was a spinster named Toussaint whom Jean Valjean had saved from the hospital and misery, and who was old, stuttering, and a native of a province, three qualities which had determined Jean Valjean to take her with him. He hired the house under the name of Monsieur Fauchelevent, gentleman. In what has been related hitherto, the reader doubtless recognised Jean Valjean even before Thénardier did.

Why had Jean Valjean left the convent of the Petit Picpus? What had happened?

Nothing had happened.

As we remember, Jean Valjean was happy in the convent, so happy that his conscience at last began to be troubled. He saw Cosette every day, he felt paternity springing up and developing within him more and more, he brooded this child with his soul, he said to himself that she was his, that nothing could take her from him, that this would be so indefinitely, that certainly she would become a nun, being every day gently led on towards it, that thus the convent was henceforth the universe to her as well as to him, that he would grow old there and she would grow up there, that she would grow old there and he would die there; that finally, ravishing hope, no separation was possible. In reflecting upon this, he at last began to find difficulties. He questioned himself. He asked himself if all this happiness were really his own, if it were not made up of the happiness of another, of the happiness of this child whom he was appropriating and plundering, he, an old man; if this was not a robbery? He said to himself that this child had a right to know what life was before renouncing it; that to cut her off, in advance, and, in some sort, without consulting her, from all pleasure, under pretence of saving her from all trial, to take advantage of her ignorance and isolation to give her an artificial vocation, was to outrage a human creature and to lie to God. And who knows but, thinking over all this someday, and being a nun with regret, Cosette might come to hate him? a final thought, which was almost selfish and less heroic than the others, but which was insupportable to him. He resolved to leave the convent.

He resolved it, he recognised with despair that it must be done. As to objections, there were none. Five years of sojourn between those four walls, and of absence from among men, had necessarily destroyed or dispersed the elements of alarm. He might return tranquilly among men. He had grown old, and all had changed. Who would recognise him now? And then, to look at the worst, there was no danger save for himself, and he had no right to condemn Cosette to the cloister for the reason that he had been condemned to the galleys. What, moreover, is danger in presence of duty? Finally, nothing prevented him from being prudent, and taking proper precautions.

As to Cosette's education, it was almost finished and complete.

His determination once formed, he awaited an opportunity. It was not slow to present itself. Old Fauchelevent died.

Jean Valjean asked an audience of the reverend prioress, and told her that having received a small inheritance on the death of his brother, which enabled him to live henceforth without labour, he would leave the service of the convent, and take away his daughter; but that, as it was not just that Cosette, not taking her vows, should have been educated gratuitously, he humbly begged the reverend prioress to allow him to offer the community, as indemnity for the five years which Cosette had passed there, the sum of five thousand francs.

Thus Jean Valjean left the convent of the Perpetual Adoration.

On leaving the convent, he took in his own hands, and would not entrust to any assistant, the little box, the key of which he always had about him. This box puzzled Cosette, on account of the odour of embalming which came from it.

Let us say at once, that henceforth this box never left him more. He always had it in his room. It was the first, and sometimes the only thing that he carried away in his changes of abode. Cosette laughed about it, and called this box *the inseparable*, saying: 'I am jealous of it.'

Jean Valjean nevertheless did not appear again in the open city without deep anxiety.

He discovered the house in the Rue Plumet, and buried himself in it. He was henceforth in possession of the name of Ultimus Fauchelevent.

At the same time he hired two other lodgings in Paris, in order to attract less attention than if he always remained in the same quarter, to be able to change his abode on occasion, at the slightest anxiety which he might feel, and finally, that he might not again find himself in such a strait as on the night when he had so miraculously escaped from Javert. These two lodgings were two very humble dwellings, and of a poor appearance, in two quarters widely distant from each other, one in the Rue de l'Ouest, the other in the Rue de l'Homme Armé.

He went from time to time, now to the Rue de l'Homme Armé, and now to the Rue de l'Ouest, to spend a month or six weeks, with Cosette, without taking Toussaint. He was waited upon by the porters, and gave himself out for a man of some means of the suburbs, having a foothold in the city. This lofty virtue had three domiciles in Paris in order to escape from the police.

2. *Jean Valjean a National Guard*

STILL, properly speaking, he lived in the Rue Plumet, and he had ordered his life there in the following manner:

Cosette with the servant occupied the house; she had the large bedroom with painted piers, the boudoir with gilded mouldings, the president's parlour furnished with tapestry and huge armchairs; she had the garden. Jean Valjean had a bed put into Cosette's chamber with a canopy of antique damask in three colours, and an old and beautiful Persian carpet, bought at Mother Gaucher's in the Rue du Figuier Saint Paul, and, to soften the severity of these magnificent relics, he had added to this curiosity shop all the little lively and graceful pieces of furniture used by young girls, an *étagère*, a bookcase and gilt books, a writing-case, a blotting-case, a work-table inlaid with pearl, a silver-gilt dressing-case, a dressing table in Japan porcelain. Long damask curtains of three colours, on a red ground, matching those of the bed, hung at the second storey windows. On the first floor, tapestry curtains. All winter Cosette's Petite Maison was warmed from top to bottom. For his part, he lived in the sort of porter's lodge in the back-yard, with a mattress on a cot bedstead, a white wood table, two straw chairs, an earthen water-pitcher, a few books upon a board, his dear box in a corner, never any fire. He dined with Cosette, and there was a black loaf on the table for him. He said to Toussaint, when she entered their service: 'Mademoiselle is the mistress of the house.' 'And you, m–monsieur?' replied Toussaint, astounded. 'Me, I am much better than the master, I am the father.'

Cosette had been trained to housekeeping in the convent, and she regulated the expenses, which were very moderate, Every day Jean Valjean took Cosette's arm, and went to walk with her. They went to the least frequented walk of the Luxembourg, and every Sunday to mass, always at Saint Jacques du Haut Pas, because it was quite distant. As that is a very poor quarter, he gave much alms there, and the unfortunate surrounded him in the church, which had given him the title of the superscription of the epistle of the Thénardiers: *To the benevolent gentleman of the church of Saint Jacques du Haut Pas.* He was fond of taking Cosette to visit the needy and the sick. No stranger came into the house in the Rue Plumet. Toussaint brought the provisions, and Jean Valjean himself went after the water to a watering trough which was near by on the boulevard. They kept the wood and the wine in a kind of semi-subterranean vault covered with rock-work, which was near the door on the Rue de Babylone, and which had formerly served the president as a grotto; for, in the time of the Folies and the Petites Maisons, there was no love without a grotto.

There was on the Rue de Babylone door a box for letters and papers; but the three occupants of the summerhouse on the Rue Plumet receiving neither papers nor letters, the entire use of the box, formerly the agent of amours and the confidant of a legal spark, was now limited to the notices of the receiver of taxes and the Guard warnings. For M. Fauchelevent belonged to the National Guard: he had not been able to escape the close meshes of the enrolment of 1831. The municipal investigation made at that time had extended even to the convent of the Petit Picpus, a sort of impenetrable and holy cloud from which

Jean Valjean had come forth venerable in the eyes of his magistracy, and, in consequence, worthy of mounting guard.

Three or four times a year, Jean Valjean donned his uniform, and performed his duties; very willingly moreover; it was a good disguise for him, which associated him with everybody else while leaving him solitary. Jean Valjean had completed his sixtieth year, the age of legal exemption; but he did not appear more than fifty; moreover, he had no desire to escape from his sergeant-major and to cavil with the Count de Lobau; he had no civil standing; he was concealing his name, he was concealing his identity, he was concealing his age, he was concealing everything; and, we have just said, he was very willingly a National Guard. To resemble the crowd who pay their taxes, this was his whole ambition. This man had for his ideal within, the angel – without, the bourgeois.

We must note one incident, however. When Jean Valjean went out with Cosette, he dressed as we have seen, and had much the air of an old officer. When he went out alone, and this was most usually in the evening, he was always clad in the waistcoat and trousers of a working-man, and wore a cap which hid his face. Was this precaution, or humility? Both at once. Cosette was accustomed to the enigmatic aspect of her destiny, and hardly noticed her father's singularities. As for Toussaint, she venerated Jean Valjean, and thought everything good that he did. One day, her butcher, who had caught sight of Jean Valjean, said to her: 'That is a funny body.' She answered: 'He is a s–saint!'

Neither Jean Valjean, nor Cosette, nor Toussaint, ever came in or went out except by the gate on the Rue de Babylone. Unless one had seen them through the grated gate of the garden, it would have been difficult to guess that they lived in the Rue Plumet. This gate always remained closed. Jean Valjean had left the garden uncultivated, that it might not attract attention.

In this, he deceived himself, perhaps.

3. *Foliis ac frondibus*

THIS GARDEN, thus abandoned to itself for more than half a century, had become very strange and very pleasant. The passers-by of forty years ago stopped in the street to look at it, without suspecting the secrets which it concealed behind its fresh green thickets. More than one dreamer of that day has many a time allowed his eyes and his thoughts indiscreetly to penetrate through the bars of the ancient gate which was padlocked, twisted, tottering; secured by two green and mossy pillars, and grotesquely crowned with a pediment of indecipherable arabesque.

There was a stone seat in a corner, one or two mouldy statues, some trellises loosened by time and rotting upon the wall; no walks, moreover, nor turf; dog-grass everywhere. Horticulture had departed, and nature had returned. Weeds were abundant, a wonderful hap for a poor bit of earth. The heyday of the gilliflowers was splendid. Nothing in this garden opposed the sacred effort of things towards life; venerable growth was at home there. The trees bent over towards the briers, the briers mounted towards the trees, the shrub had climbed, the branch had bowed, that which runs upon the ground had attempted to find that which blooms in the air, that which floats in the wind had stooped towards that which trails in the moss; trunks, branches, leaves, twigs, tufts, tendrils, shoots, thorns, were mingled, crossed, married, confounded; vegetation, in a close and strong embrace, had celebrated and accomplished there under the satisfied eye of the Creator, in this enclosure of three hundred feet square, the sacred mystery of its fraternity, symbol of human fraternity. This garden was no longer a garden; it was a colossal bush, that is to say, something which is as impenetrable as a forest, populous as a city, tremulous as a nest, dark as a cathedral, odorous as a bouquet, solitary as a tomb, full of life as a multitude.

In Floréal, this enormous shrub, free behind its grating and within its four walls, warmed into the deep labour of universal germination, thrilled at the rising sun almost like a stag which inhales the air of universal love and feels the April sap mounting and boiling in his veins, and shaking its immense green antlers in the wind, scattered over the moist ground, over the broken statues, over the sinking staircase of the summerhouse, and even over the pavement of the deserted street, flowers in stars, dew in pearls, fecundity, beauty, life, joy, perfume. At noon, a thousand white butterflies took refuge in it, and it was a heavenly sight to see this living snow of summer whirling about in flakes in the shade. There, in this gay darkness of verdure, a multitude of innocent voices spoke softly to the soul, and what the warbling had forgotten to say, the humming completed. At night, a dreamy vapour arose from the garden and wrapped it around; a shroud of mist, a calm and celestial sadness, covered it; the intoxicating odour of honeysuckles and bindweed rose on all sides like an exquisite and subtle poison; you heard the last appeals of the woodpecker, and the wagtails drowsing under the branches; you felt the sacred intimacy of bird and tree; by day the wings rejoiced the leaves; by night the leaves protected the wings.

In winter, the bush was black, wet, bristling, shivering, and let the house be seen in part. You perceived, instead of the flowers in the branches and the dew in the flowers, the long silver ribbons of the snails upon the thick and cold carpet of yellow leaves; but in every way, under every aspect, in every season, spring, winter, summer, autumn, this little enclosure exhaled melancholy, contemplation, solitude, liberty, the absence of man, the presence of God, and the old rusty grating appeared to say: 'This garden is mine!'

In vain was the pavement of Paris all about it, the classic and splendid residences of the Rue de Varennes within a few steps, the dome of the Invalides quite near, the Chamber of Deputies not far off; in vain did the carriages of the Rue de Bourgogne and the Rue Saint Dominique roll pompously in its neighbourhood, in vain did the yellow, brown, white, and red omnibuses pass each other in the adjoining square, the Rue Plumet was a solitude; and the death of the old proprietors, the passage of a revolution, the downfall of ancient fortunes, absence, oblivion, forty years of abandonment and of widowhood, had sufficed to call back into this privileged place the ferns, the mulleins, the hemlocks, the milfoils, the tall weeds, the great flaunting plants with large leaves of a pale greenish drab, the lizards, the beetles, the restless and rapid insects; to bring out of the depths of the earth, and display within these four walls, an indescribably wild and savage grandeur; and that nature, who disavows the mean arrangements of man, and who always gives her whole self where she gives herself at all, as well in the ant as in the eagle, should come to display herself in a poor little Parisian garden with as much severity and majesty as in a virgin forest of the New World.

Nothing is really small; whoever is open to the deep penetration of nature knows this. Although indeed no absolute satisfaction may be vouchsafed to philosophy, no more in circumscribing the cause than in limiting the effect, the contemplator falls into unfathomable ecstasies in view of all these decompositions of forces resulting in unity. All works for all.

Algebra applies to the clouds; the radiance of the star benefits the rose; no thinker would dare to say that the perfume of the hawthorn is useless to the constellations. Who then can calculate the path of the molecule? how do we know that the creations of worlds are not determined by the fall of grains of sand? Who then understands the reciprocal flux and reflux of the infinitely great and the infinitely small, the echoing of causes in the abysses of being, and the avalanches of creation? A flesh-worm is of account; the small is great, the great is small; all is in equilibrium in necessity; fearful vision for the mind. There are marvellous relations between beings and things; in this inexhaustible whole, from sun to grub, there is no scorn; all need each other. Light does not carry terrestrial perfumes into the azure depths without knowing what it does with them; night distributes the stellar essence to the sleeping plants. Every bird which flies has the thread of the infinite in its claw. Germination includes the hatching of a meteor and the tap of a swallow's bill breaking the egg, and it leads forward the birth of an earthworm and the advent of Socrates. Where the telescope ends, the microscope begins. Which of the two has the grander view? Choose. A bit of mould is a pleiad of flowers; a nebula is an anthill of stars. The same promiscuity, and still more wonderful, between the things of the intellect and the things of matter. Elements and principles are mingled, combined, espoused, multiplied one by another, to such a degree as to bring the material world and the moral world into the same light. Phenomena are perpetually folded back upon themselves. In the vast cosmical changes, the universal life comes and goes in unknown quantities, rolling all in the invisible mystery of the emanations, losing no dream from no single sleep, sowing an animalcule here, crumbling a star there, oscillating and winding, making a force of light and an element of thought, disseminated and indivisible, dissolving all, save that geometrical point, the me; reducing everything to the soul-atom; making everything blossom into God; entangling, from the highest to the lowest, all activities in the obscurity of a dizzying mechanism, hanging the flight of an insect upon the movement of the earth, subordinating, who knows? were it only by the identity of the law, the evolutions of the comet in the firmament to the circling of the infusoria in the drop of water. A machine made of mind. Enormous gearing, whose first motor is the gnat, and whose last wheel is the zodiac.

4. Change of grating

It seemed as if this garden, first made to conceal licentious mysteries, had been transformed and rendered fit for the shelter of chaste mysteries. There were no longer in it either bowers, or lawns, or arbours, or grottoes; there was a magnificent dishevelled obscurity falling like a veil upon all sides; Paphos had become Eden again. Some secret repentance had purified this retreat. This flower-girl now offered its flowers to the soul. This coquettish garden, once so very free, had returned to virginity and modesty. A president assisted by a gardener, a goodman who thought he was a second Lamoignon, and another goodman who thought he was a second Lenôtre, had distorted it, pruned it, crumpled it, bedizened it, fashioned it for gallantry; nature had taken it again, had filled it with shade, and had arranged it for love.

There was also in this solitude a heart which was all ready. Love had only to show himself; there was a temple there composed of verdure, of grass, of moss, of the sighs of birds, of soft shade, of agitated branches, and a soul made up of gentleness, of faith, of candour, of hope, of aspiration, and of illusion.

Cosette had left the convent, still almost a child; she was a little more than fourteen years old, and she was 'at the ungrateful age'; as we have said, apart from her eyes, she seemed rather homely than pretty; she had, however, no ungraceful features, but she was awkward, thin, timid, and bold at the same time, a big child in short.

Her education was finished; that is to say, she had been taught religion, and also, and above all, devotion; then 'history', that is, the thing which they call thus in the convent, geography, grammar, the participles, the kings of France, a little music, to draw profiles, etc., but further than this she was ignorant of everything, which is a charm and a peril. The soul of a young girl ought not to be left in obscurity; in after life there spring up too sudden and too vivid mirages, as in a camera obscura. She should be gently and discreetly enlightened, rather by the reflection of realities than by their direct and stern light. A useful and graciously severe half-light which dissipates puerile fear and prevents a fall. Nothing but the maternal instinct, a wonderful intuition into which enter the memories of the maiden and the experience of the woman, knows how this half-light should be applied, and of what it should be formed. Nothing supplies this instinct. To form the mind of a young girl, all the nuns in the world are not equal to one mother.

Cosette had had no mother. She had only had many mothers, in the plural.

As to Jean Valjean, there was indeed within him all manner of tenderness and all manner of solicitude; but he was only an old man who knew nothing at all.

Now, in this work of education, in this serious matter of the preparation of a woman for life, how much knowledge is needed to struggle against that great ignorance which we call innocence.

Nothing prepares a young girl for passions like the convent. The convent turns the thoughts in the direction of the unknown. The heart, thrown back upon itself, makes for itself a channel, being unable to overflow, and deepens, being unable to expand. From thence visions, suppositions, conjectures, romances sketched out, longings for adventures, fantastic constructions, whole castles built in the interior obscurity of the mind, dark and secret dwellings where the passions find an immediate lodging as soon as the grating is crossed and they are permitted to enter. The convent is a compression which, in order to triumph over the human heart, must continue through the whole life.

On leaving the convent, Cosette could have found nothing more grateful and more dangerous than the house on the Rue Plumet. It was the continuation of solitude with the beginning of liberty; an enclosed garden, but a sharp, rich, voluptuous, and odorous nature; the same dreams as in the convent, but with glimpses of young men; a grating, but upon the street.

Still, we repeat, when she came there she was but a child. Jean Valjean gave her this uncultivated garden. 'Do whatever you like with it,' said he to her. It delighted Cosette; she ransacked every thicket and turned over every stone, she sought for 'animals'; she played while she dreamed; she loved this garden for the insects which she found in the grass under her feet, while she loved it for the stars which she saw in the branches over her head.

And then she loved her father, that is to say, Jean Valjean, with all her heart, with a frank filial passion which made the good man a welcome and very pleasant companion for her. We remember that M. Madeleine was a great reader; Jean Valjean had continued it; through this he had come to talk very well; he had the secret wealth and the eloquence of a humble and earnest intellect which has secured its own culture. He retained just enough harshness to flavour his goodness; he had a rough mind and a gentle heart. At the Luxembourg in their conversations, he gave long explanations of everything, drawing from what he had read, drawing also from what he had suffered. As she listened, Cosette's eyes wandered dreamily.

This simple man was sufficient for Cosette's thought, even as this wild garden was to her eyes. When she had had a good chase after the butterflies, she would come up to him breathless and say, 'Oh! how I have run!' He would kiss her forehead.

Cosette adored the good man. She was always running after him. Where Jean Valjean was, was happiness. As Jean Valjean did not live in the summerhouse or the garden, she found more pleasure in the paved back-yard than in the enclosure full of flowers, and in the little bedroom furnished with straw chairs than in the great parlour hung with tapestry, where she could recline on silken armchairs. Jean Valjean sometimes said to her, smiling with the happiness of being teased: 'Why don't you go home? why don't you leave me alone?'

She would give him those charming little scoldings which are so full of grace coming from the daughter to the father.

'Father, I am very cold in your house; why don't you put in a carpet and a stove here?'

'Dear child, there are many people who are better than I, who have not even a roof over their heads.'

'Then why do I have a fire and all things comfortable?'

'Because you are a woman and a child.'

'Pshaw! men then ought to be cold and uncomfortable?'

'Some men.'

'Well, I will come here so often that you will be obliged to have a fire.'

Again she said to him:

'Father, why do you eat miserable bread like that?'

'Because, my daughter.'

'Well, if you eat it, I shall eat it.'

Then, so that Cosette should not eat black bread, Jean Valjean ate white bread.

Cosette had but vague remembrance of her childhood. She prayed morning and evening for her mother, whom she had never known. The Thénardiers had remained to her like two hideous faces of some dream. She remembered that she had been 'one day, at night', into a wood after water. She thought that that was very far from Paris. It seemed to her that she had commenced life in an abyss, and that Jean Valjean had drawn her out of it. Her childhood impressed her as a time when there were only centipedes, spiders, and snakes about her. When she was dozing at night, before going to sleep, as she had no very clear idea of being Jean Valjean's daughter, and that he was her father, she imagined that her mother's soul had passed into this goodman and come to live with her.

When he sat down, she would rest her cheek on his white hair and silently drop a tear, saying to herself: 'This is perhaps my mother, this man!'

Cosette, although this may be a strange statement, in her profound ignorance as a girl brought up in a convent, maternity moreover being absolutely unintelligible to virginity, had come to imagine that she had had as little of a mother as possible. She did not even know her name. Whenever she happened to ask Jean Valjean what it was, Jean Valjean was silent. If she repeated her question, he answered by a smile. Once she insisted; the smile ended with a tear.

This silence of Jean Valjean's covered Fantine with night.

Was this prudence? was it respect? was it a fear to give up that name to the chances of another memory than his own?

While Cosette was a little girl, Jean Valjean had been fond of talking with her about her mother; when she was a young maiden, this was impossible for him. It seemed to him that he no longer dared. Was this on account of Cosette? was it on account of Fantine? He felt a sort of religious horror at introducing that shade into Cosette's thoughts, and at bringing in the dead as a third sharer of their destiny. The more sacred that shade was to him, the more formidable it seemed to him. He thought of Fantine and felt overwhelmed with silence. He saw dimly in the darkness something which resembled a finger on a mouth. Had all that modesty which had once been Fantine's and which, during her life, had been forced out of her by violence, returned after her death to take its place over her, to watch, indignant, over the peace of the dead woman, and to guard her fiercely in her tomb? Did Jean Valjean, without knowing it, feel its influence? We who believe in death are not of those who would reject this mysterious explanation. Hence the impossibility of pronouncing, even at Cosette's desire, this name: Fantine.

One day Cosette said to him:

'Father, I saw my mother in a dream last night. She had two great wings. My mother must have attained to sanctity in her life.'

'Through martyrdom,' answered Jean Valjean.

Still, Jean Valjean was happy.

When Cosette went out with him, she leaned upon his arm, proud, happy, in the fulness of her heart. Jean Valjean, at all these marks of a tenderness so exclusive and so fully satisfied with him alone, felt his thought melt into delight. The poor man shuddered, overflowed with an angelic joy; he declared in his transport that this would last through life; he said to himself that he really had not suffered enough to deserve such radiant happiness, and he thanked God, in the depths of his soul, for having permitted that he, a miserable man, should be so loved by this innocent being.

5. The rose discovers that she is an engine of war

ONE DAY Cosette happened to look in her mirror, and she said to herself: 'What!' It seemed to her almost that she was pretty. This threw her into strange anxiety. Up to this moment she had never thought of her face. She had seen herself in her glass, but she had not looked at herself. And then, she had often been told that she was homely; Jean Valjean alone would quietly say: 'Why no!

why! no!' However that might be, Cosette had always thought herself homely, and had grown up in that idea with the pliant resignation of childhood. And now suddenly her mirror said like Jean Valjean: 'Why no!' She had no sleep that night. 'If I were pretty!' thought she, 'how funny it would be if I should be pretty!' And she called to mind those of her companions whose beauty had made an impression in the convent, and said: 'What! I should be like Mademoiselle Such-a-one!'

The next day she looked at herself, but not by chance, and she doubted. 'Where were my wits gone ?' said she, 'no, I am homely.' She had merely slept badly, her eyes were dark and she was pale. She had not felt very happy the evening before, in the thought that she was beautiful, but she was sad at thinking so no longer. She did not look at herself again, and for more than a fortnight she tried to dress her hair with her back to the mirror.

In the evening after dinner, she regularly made tapestry or did some convent work in the parlour, while Jean Valjean read by her side. Once, on raising her eyes from her work, she was very much surprised at the anxious way in which her father was looking at her.

At another time, she was passing along the street, and it seemed to her that somebody behind her, whom she did not see, said: 'Pretty woman! but badly dressed.' 'Pshaw!' thought she, 'that is not me. I am well dressed and homely.' She had on at the time her plush hat and merino dress.

At last, she was in the garden one day, and heard poor old Toussaint saying: 'Monsieur, do you notice how pretty mademoiselle is growing? 'Cosette did not hear what her father answered. Toussaint's words threw her into a sort of commotion. She ran out of the garden, went up to her room, hurried to the glass, it was three months since she had looked at herself, and uttered a cry. She was dazzled by herself.

She was beautiful and handsome; she could not help being of Toussaint's and her mirror's opinion. Her form was complete, her skin had become white, her hair had grown lustrous, an unknown splendour was lighted up in her blue eyes. The consciousness of her beauty came to her entire, in a moment, like broad daylight when it bursts upon us; others noticed it moreover, Toussaint said so, it was of her evidently that the passer had spoken, there was no more doubt; she went down into the garden again, thinking herself a queen, hearing the birds sing, it was in winter, seeing the sky golden, the sunshine in the trees, flowers among the shrubbery, wild, mad, in an inexpressible rapture.

For his part, Jean Valjean felt a deep and undefinable anguish in his heart.

He had in fact, for sometime past, been contemplating with terror that beauty which appeared every day more radiant upon Cosette's sweet face. A dawn, charming to all others, dreary to him.

Cosette had been beautiful for some time before she perceived it. But, from the first day, this unexpected light which slowly rose and by degrees enveloped the young girl's whole person, wounded Jean Valjean's gloomy eyes. He felt that it was a change in a happy life, so happy that he dared not stir for fear of disturbing something. This man who had passed through every distress, who was still all bleeding from the lacerations of his destiny, who had been almost evil, and who had become almost holy, who, after having dragged the chain of the galleys, now dragged the invisible but heavy chain of indefinite infamy, this man whom the law had not released, and who might be at any instant retaken, and led back from the obscurity of his virtue to the broad light of public shame, this man accepted all, excused all, pardoned all, blessed all, wished well to all, and only asked of Providence, of men, of the laws, of society, of nature, of the world, this one thing, that Cosette should love him!

That Cosette should continue to love him! That God would not prevent the heart of this child from coming to him, and remaining his! Loved by Cosette, he felt himself healed, refreshed, soothed, satisfied, rewarded, crowned. Loved by Cosette, he was content! he asked nothing more. Had anybody said to him: 'Do you desire anything better?' he would have answered: 'No.' Had God said to him: 'Do you desire heaven?' he would have answered: 'I should be the loser.'

Whatever might affect this condition, were it only on the surface, made him shudder as if it were the commencement of another. He had never known very clearly what the beauty of a woman was; but, by instinct, he understood, that it was terrible.

This beauty which was blooming out more and more triumphant and superb beside him, under his eyes, upon the ingenuous and fearful brow of this child – he looked upon it, from the depths of his ugliness, his old age, his misery, his reprobation, and his dejection, with dismay.

He said to himself: 'How beautiful she is! What will become of me?'

Here in fact was the difference between his tenderness and the tenderness of a mother. What he saw with anguish, a mother would have seen with delight.

The first symptoms were not slow to manifest themselves.

From the morrow of the day on which she had said: 'Really, I am handsome!' Cosette gave attention to her dress. She recalled the words of the passer: 'Pretty, but badly dressed,' breath of an oracle which had passed by her and vanished after depositing in her heart one of the two germs which must afterwards fill the whole life of the woman, coquetry. Love is the other.

With faith in her beauty, the entire feminine soul blossomed within her. She was horrified at the merino and ashamed of the plush. Her father had never refused her anything She knew at once the whole science of the hat, the dress, the cloak, the boot, the cuff, the stuff which sits well, the colour which is becoming, that science which makes the Parisian woman something so charming, so deep, and so dangerous. The phrase *heady woman* was invented for her.

In less than a month little Cosette was, in that Thebaid of the Rue de Babylone, not only one of the prettiest women, which is something, but one of 'the best dressed' in Paris, which is much more. She would have liked to meet 'her passer' to hear what he would say, and 'to show him!' The truth is that she was ravishing in every point, and that she distinguished marvellously well between a Gerard hat and an Herbaut hat.

Jean Valjean beheld these ravages with anxiety. He, who felt that he could never more than creep, or walk at the most, saw wings growing on Cosette.

Still, merely by simple inspection of Cosette's toilette, a woman would have recognised that she had no mother. Certain little proprieties, certain special conventionalities, were not observed by Cosette. A mother, for instance, would have told her that a young girl does not wear damask.

The first day that Cosette went out with her dress and mantle of black damask and her white crape hat she came to take Jean Valjean's arm, gay, radiant, rosy, proud, and brilliant. 'Father,' said she, 'how do you like this?' Jean Valjean answered in a voice which resembled the bitter voice of envy: 'Charming!' He seemed as usual during the walk. When they came back he asked Cosette:

'Are you not going to wear your dress and hat any more?'

This occurred in Cosette's room. Cosette turned towards the wardrobe where her boarding-school dress was hanging.

'That disguise!' said she. 'Father, what would you have me do with it? Oh! to be sure, no, I shall never wear those horrid things again. With that machine on my head, I look like Madame Mad-dog.'

Jean Valjean sighed deeply.

From that day, he noticed that Cosette, who previously was always asking to stay in, saying: 'Father, I enjoy myself better here with you,' was now always asking to go out. Indeed, what is the use of having a pretty face and a delightful dress, if you do not show them?

He also noticed that Cosette no longer had the same taste for the back-yard. She now preferred to stay in the garden, walking even without displeasure before the grating. Jean Valjean, ferocious, did not set his foot in the garden. He stayed in his back-yard, like a dog.

Cosette, by learning that she was beautiful, lost the grace of not knowing it; an exquisite grace, for beauty heightened by artlessness is ineffable, and nothing is so adorable as dazzling, innocence, going on her way, and holding in her hand, all unconscious, the key of a paradise. But what she lost in ingenuous grace, she gained in pensive and serious charm. Her whole person, pervaded by the joys of youth, innocence, and beauty, breathed a splendid melancholy.

It was at this period that Marius, after the lapse of six months, saw her again at the Luxembourg.

6. The battle commences

Cosette, in her seclusion, like Marius in his, was all ready to take fire. Destiny, with its mysterious and fatal patience, was slowly bringing these two beings near each other, fully charged and all languishing with the stormy electricities of passion – these two souls which held love as two clouds hold lightning, and which were to meet and mingle in a glance like clouds in a flash.

The power of a glance has been so much abused in love stories, that it has come to be disbelieved in. Few people dare now to say that two beings have fallen in love because they have looked at each other. Yet it is in this way that love begins, and in this way only. The rest is only the rest, and comes afterwards. Nothing is more real than these great shocks which two souls give each other in exchanging this spark.

At that particular moment when Cosette unconsciously looked with this glance which so affected Marius, Marius had no suspicion that he also had a glance which affected Cosette.

She received from him the same harm and the same blessing.

For a long time now she had seen and scrutinised him as young girls scrutinise and see, while looking another way. Marius still thought Cosette ugly, while Cosette already began to think Marius beautiful. But as he paid no attention to her, this young man was quite indifferent to her.

Still she could not help saying to herself that he had beautiful hair, beautiful eyes, beautiful teeth, a charming voice, when she heard him talking with his comrades; that he walked with an awkward gait, if you will, but with a grace of his own; that he did not appear altogether stupid; that his whole person was noble, gentle, natural, and proud, and finally that he had a poor appearance, but that he had a good appearance.

On the day their eyes met and at last said abruptly to both those first obscure and ineffable things which the glance stammers out, Cosette at first did not comprehend. She went back pensively to the house in the Rue de l'Ouest, to which Jean Valjean, according to his custom, had gone to spend six weeks. The next day, on waking, she thought of this unknown young man, so long indifferent and icy, who now seemed to give some attention to her, and it did not seem to her that this attention was in the least degree pleasant. She was rather a little angry at this disdainful beau. An undercurrent of war was excited in her. It seemed to her, and she felt a pleasure in it still altogether childish, that at last she should be avenged.

Knowing that she was beautiful, she felt thoroughly, although in an indistinct way, that she had a weapon. Women play with their beauty as children do with their knives. They wound themselves with it.

We remember Marius' hesitations, his palpitations, his terrors. He remained at his seat and did not approach, which vexed Cosette. One day she said to Jean Valjean: 'Father, let us walk a little this way.' Seeing that Marius was not coming to her, she went to him. In such a case, every woman resembles Mahomet. And then, oddly enough, the first symptom of true love in a young man is timidity, in a young woman, boldness. This is surprising, and yet nothing is more natural. It is the two sexes tending to unite, and each acquiring the qualities of the other.

That day Cosette's glance made Marius mad, Marius' glance made Cosette tremble. Marius went away confident, and Cosette anxious. From that day onward, they adored each other.

The first thing that Cosette felt was a vague yet deep sadness. It seemed to her that since yesterday her soul had become black. She no longer recognised herself. The whiteness of soul of young girls, which is composed of coldness and gaiety, is like snow. It melts before love, which is its sun.

Cosette did not know what love was. She had never heard the word uttered in its earthly sense. In the books of profane music which came into the convent, *amour* was replaced by *tambour*, or *Pandour*. This made puzzles which exercised the imagination of the great girls, such as: *Oh! how delightful is the tambour!* or: *Pity is not a Pandour!* But Cosette had left while yet too young to be much concerned about the 'tambour'. She did not know, therefore, what name to give to what she now experienced. Is one less sick for not knowing the name of the disease?

She loved with so much the more passion as she loved with ignorance. She did not know whether it were good or evil, beneficient or dangerous, necessary or accidental, eternal or transitory, permitted or prohibited: she loved. She would have been very much astonished if anybody had said to her: 'You are sleepless; that is forbidden! You do not eat! that is very wrong! You have sinkings and palpitations of the heart! that is not right. You blush and you turn pale when a certain being dressed in black appears at the end of a certain green walk! that is abominable!' She would not have understood it, and she would have answered: 'How can I be to blame in a thing in which I can do nothing, and of which I know nothing?'

It proved that the love which presented itself was precisely that which best suited the condition of her soul. It was a sort of far-off worship, a mute contemplation, a deification by an unknown votary. It was the apprehension of adolescence by adolescence, the dream of her nights become a romance and remaining a dream, the wished-for phantom realised at last, and made flesh, but still having neither name, nor wrong, nor stain, nor need, nor defect; in a word, a lover distant and dwelling in the ideal, a chimæra having a form. Any closer and more palpable encounter would at this first period have terrified Cosette, still half buried in the magnifying mirage of the cloister. She had all the terrors of children and all the terrors of nuns commingled. The spirit of the convent, with which she had been imbued for five years, was still slowly evaporating from her whole person, and made everything tremulous about her. In this condition, it was not a lover that she needed, it was not even an admirer, it was a vision. She began to adore Marius as something charming, luminous, and impossible.

As extreme artlessness meets extreme coquetry, she smiled upon him, very frankly.

She waited impatiently every day the hour for her walk, she found Marius there, she felt herself inexpressibly happy, and sincerely believed that she uttered her whole thought when she said to Jean Valjean: 'What a delightful garden the Luxembourg is!'

Marius and Cosette were in the dark in regard to each other. They did not speak, they did not bow, they were not acquainted; they saw each other; and, like the stars in the sky separated by millions of leagues, they lived by gazing upon each other.

Thus it was that Cosette gradually became a woman, and beautiful and loving, grew with the consciousness of her beauty, and in ignorance of her love. Coquettish withal, through innocence.

7. *To sadness, sadness and a half*

EVERY CONDITION has its instinct. The old and eternal mother, Nature, silently warned Jean Valjean of the presence of Marius. Jean Valjean shuddered in the darkest of his mind. Jean Valjean saw nothing, knew nothing, but still gazed with persistent fixedness at the darkness which surrounded him, as if he perceived on one side something which was building, and on the other something which was falling down. Marius, also warned, and, according to the deep law of God, by this same mother, Nature, did all that he could to hide himself from the 'father'. It happened, however, that Jean Valjean sometimes perceived him. Marius' ways were no longer at all natural. He had an equivocal prudence and an awkward boldness. He ceased to come near them as formerly; he sat down at a distance, and remained there in an ecstasy; he had a book and pretended to be reading; why did he pretend? Formerly he came with his old coat, now he had his new coat on every day; it was not very certain that he did not curl his hair, he had strange eyes, he wore gloves; in short, Jean Valjean cordially detested this young man.

Cosette gave no ground for suspicion. Without knowing exactly what affected her, she had a very definite feeling that it was something, and that it must be concealed.

There was between the taste for dress which had arisen in Cosette and the habit of wearing new coats which had grown upon this unknown man, a parallelism which made Jean Valjean anxious. It was an accident perhaps, doubtless, certainly, but a threatening accident.

He had never opened his mouth to Cosette about the unknown man. One day, however, he could not contain himself, and with that uncertain despair which hastily drops the plummet into its unhappiness, he said to her: 'What a pedantic air that young man has!'

Cosette, a year before, an unconcerned little girl, would have answered: 'Why no, he is charming.' Ten years later, with the love of Marius in her heart, she would have answered: 'Pedantic and insupportable to the sight! you are quite right!' At the period of life and of heart in which she then was, she merely answered with supreme calmness: 'That young man!'

As if she saw him for the first time in her life.

'How stupid I am!' thought Jean Valjean. 'She had not even noticed him. I have shown him to her myself.'

O simplicity of the old! depth of the young!

There is another law of these young years of suffering and care, of these sharp struggles of the first love against the first obstacles, the young girl does not allow herself to be caught in any toil, the young man falls into all. Jean Valjean had commenced a sullen war against Marius, which Marius, with the sublime folly of his passion and his age, did not guess. Jean Valjean spread around him a multitude of snares; he changed his hours, he changed his seat, he forgot his handkerchief, he went to the Luxembourg alone; Marius fell headlong into every trap; and to all these interrogation points planted upon his path by Jean Valjean he answered ingenuously, yes. Meanwhile Cosette was still walled in in her apparent unconcern and her imperturbable tranquillity, so that Jean Valjean came to this conclusion: 'This booby is madly in love with Cosette, but Cosette does not even know of his existence!'

There was nevertheless a painful tremor in the heart. The moment when Cosette would fall in love might come at any instant. Does not everything begin by indifference?

Once only Cosette made a mistake, and startled him. He rose from the seat to go, after sitting there three hours, and she said: 'So soon!'

Jean Valjean had not discontinued the promenades in the Luxembourg, not wishing to do anything singular, and above all dreading to excite any suspicion in Cosette; but during those hours so sweet to the two lovers, while Cosette was sending her smile to the intoxicated Marius, who perceived nothing but that, and now saw nothing in the world save one radiant, adored face, Jean Valjean fixed upon Marius glaring and terrible eyes. He who had come to believe that he was no longer capable of a malevolent feeling, had moments in which, when Marius was there, he thought that he was again becoming savage and ferocious, and felt opening and upheaving against this young man those old depths of his soul where there had once been so much wrath. It seemed to him almost as if the unknown craters were forming within him again.

What? he was there, that creature. What did he come for? He came to pry, to scent, to examine, to attempt: he came to say, 'Eh, why not?' he came to prowl about his, Jean Valjean's life! – to prowl about his happiness, to clutch it and carry it away!

Jean Valjean added: 'Yes, that is it! what is he looking for? an adventure? What does he want? an amour! An amour! – and as for me! What! I, after having been the most miserable of men, shall be the most unfortunate; I shall have spent sixty years of life upon my knees; I shall have suffered all that a man can suffer; I shall have grown old without having been young; I shall have lived with no family, no relatives, no friends, no wife, no children! I shall have left my blood on every stone, on every thorn, on every post, along every wall; I shall have been mild, although the world was harsh to me, and good, although it was evil; I shall have become an honest man in spite of all; I shall have repented of the wrong which I have done, and pardoned the wrongs which have been done to me, and the moment that I am rewarded, the moment that it is over, the moment that I reach the end, the moment that I have what I desire, rightfully and justly; I have paid for it, I have earned it; it will all disappear, it will all vanish, and I shall lose Cosette, and I shall lose my life, my joy, my soul, because a great booby has been pleased to come and lounge about the Luxembourg.'

Then his eyes filled with a strange and dismal light. It was no longer a man looking upon a man; it was not an enemy looking upon an enemy. It was a dog looking upon a robber.

We know the rest. The insanity of Marius continued. One day he followed Cosette to the Rue de l'Ouest. Another day he spoke to the porter: the porter in his turn spoke, and said to Jean Valjean: 'Monsieur, who is that curious young man who has been asking for you?' The next day, Jean Valjean cast that glance at Marius which Marius finally perceived. A week after, Jean Valjean had moved. He resolved that he would never set his foot again either in the Luxembourg or in the Rue de l'Ouest. He returned to the Rue Plumet.

Cosette did not complain, she said nothing, she asked no questions, she did not seek to know any reason; she was already at that point at which one fears discovery and self-betrayal. Jean Valjean had no experience of this misery, the only misery which is charming, and the only misery which he did not know; for this reason, he did not understand the deep significance of Cosette's silence. He noticed only that she had become sad, and he became gloomy. There was on either side an armed inexperience.

Once he made a trial. He asked Cosette:

'Would you like to go to the Luxembourg?'

A light illumined Cosette's pale face.

'Yes,' said she.

They went. Three months had passed. Marius went there no longer. Marius was not there.

The next day, Jean Valjean asked Cosette again:

'Would you like to go to the Luxembourg?'

She answered sadly and quietly:

'No!'

Jean Valjean was hurt by this sadness, and harrowed by this gentleness.

What was taking place in this spirit so young, and already so impenetrable? What was in course of accomplishment in it? what was happening to Cosette's soul? Sometimes, instead of going to bed, Jean Valjean sat by his bedside with his head in his hands, and he spent whole nights asking himself: 'What is there in Cosette's mind?' and thinking what things she could be thinking about.

Oh! in those hours, what mournful looks he turned towards the cloister, that chaste summit, that abode of angels, that inaccessible glacier of virtue! With what despairing rapture he contemplated that convent garden, full of unknown flowers and secluded maidens, where all perfumes and all souls rose straight towards Heaven! How he worshipped that Eden, now closed for ever, from which he had voluntarily departed, and from which he had foolishly descended! How he regretted his self-denial, his madness in having brought Cosette back to the world, poor hero of sacrifice, caught and thrown to the ground by his very devotedness! How he said to himself: 'What have I done?'

Still nothing of this was exhibited towards Cosette: neither capriciousness nor severity. Always the same serene and kind face. Jean Valjean's manner was more tender and more paternal than ever. If anything could have raised a suspicion that there was less happiness, it was the greater gentleness.

For her part, Cosette was languishing. She suffered from the absence of Marius, as she had rejoiced in his presence, in a peculiar way, without really knowing it. When Jean Valjean ceased to take her on their usual walk, her woman's instinct murmured confusedly in the depths of her heart, that she must not appear to cling to the Luxembourg; and that if it were indifferent to her, her father would take her back there. But days, weeks, and months passed away. Jean Valjean had tacitly accepted Cosette's tacit consent. She regretted it. It was too late. The day she returned to the Luxembourg, Marius was no longer there. Marius then had disappeared; it was all over; what could she do? Would she ever find him again? She felt a constriction of her heart, which nothing relaxed, and which was increasing every day; she no longer knew whether it was winter or summer, sunshine or rain, whether the birds sang, whether it was the season for dahlias or daisies, whether the Luxembourg was more charming than the Tuileries, whether the linen which the washerwoman brought home was starched too much, or not enough, whether Toussaint did 'her marketing' well or ill; and she became dejected, absorbed, intent upon a single thought, her eye wild and fixed, as when one looks into the night at the deep black place where an apparition has vanished.

Still she did not let Jean Valjean see anything, except her paleness. She kept her face sweet for him.

This paleness was more than sufficient to make Jean Valjean anxious. Sometimes he asked her:

'What is the matter with you?'

She answered:

'Nothing.'

And after a silence, as she felt that he was sad also, she continued:

'And you, father, is not something the matter with you?'

'Me? nothing,' said he.

These two beings, who had loved each other so exclusively, and with so touching a love, and who had lived so long for each other, were now suffering by each other, and through each other; without speaking of it, without harsh feeling, and smiling the while.

8. The chain

THE MORE UNHAPPY of the two was Jean Valjean. Youth, even in its sorrows, always has a brilliancy of its own.

At certain moments, Jean Valjean suffered so much that he became puerile. It is the peculiarity of grief to bring out the childish side of man. He felt irresistibly that Cosette was escaping him. He would have been glad to put forth an effort, to hold her fast, to rouse her enthusiasm by something external and striking. These ideas, puerile, as we have just said, and at the same time senile, gave him by their very childishness a just idea of the influence of gewgaws over the imagination of young girls. He chanced once to see a general pass in the street on horseback in full uniform, Count Coutard, Commandant of Paris. He envied this gilded man; he thought what happiness it would be to be able to put on that coat which was an incontestable thing, that if Cosette saw him thus it would dazzle her, that when he should give his arm to Cosette and pass before the gate of the Tuileries they would present arms to him, and that that would so satisfy Cosette that it would destroy her inclination to look at the young men.

An unexpected shock came to him in the midst of these sad thoughts.

In the isolated life which they were leading, and since they had come to live in the Rue Plumet, they had formed a habit. They sometimes made a pleasure excursion to go and see the sun rise, a gentle joy suited to those who are entering upon life and those who are leaving it.

A walk at early dawn, to him who loves solitude, is equivalent to a walk at night, with the gaiety of nature added. The streets are empty and the birds are singing. Cosette, herself a bird, usually awoke early. These morning excursions were arranged the evening before. He proposed, she accepted. They were planned as a conspiracy, they went out before day, and these were so many pleasant hours for Cosette. Such innocent eccentricities have a charm for the young.

Jean Valjean's inclination was, we know, to go to unfrequented spots, to solitary nooks, to neglected places. There were at that time in the neighbourhood of the barrières of Paris some poor fields, almost in the city, where there grew in summer a scanty crop of wheat, and which in autumn, after this was gathered, appeared not to have been harvested, but stripped. Jean Valjean had a predilection for these fields. Cosette did not dislike them. To him it was solitude, to her it was liberty. There she became a little girl again, she could run and almost play, she took off her hat, laid it on Jean Valjean's knees, and gathered flowers. She looked at the butterflies upon the blossoms, but did not catch them; gentleness and tenderness are born with love, and the young girl who has in her heart a trembling and fragile ideal, feels pity for a butterfly's wing. She wove garlands of wild poppies which she put upon her head, and which, lit up and illuminated in the sunshine, and blazing like a flame, made a crown of fire for her fresh and rosy face.

Even after their life had been saddened, they continued their habit of morning walks.

So one October morning, tempted by the deep serenity of the autumn of 1831, they had gone out, and found themselves at daybreak near the Barrière du

Maine. It was not day, it was dawn; a wild and ravishing moment. A few constellations here and there in the deep pale heavens, the earth all black, the sky all white, a shivering in the spears of grass, everywhere the mysterious thrill of the twilight. A lark, which seemed among the stars, was singing at this enormous height, and one would have said that this hymn from littleness to the infinite was calming the immensity. In the east the Val de Grâce carved out upon the clear horizon, with the sharpness of steel, its obscure mass; Venus was rising in splendour behind that dome like a soul escaping from a dark edifice.

All was peace and silence; nobody upon the highway; on the footpaths a few scattered working-men, hardly visible, going to their work.

Jean Valjean was seated in the sidewalk, upon some timbers lying by the gate of a lumber-yard. He had his face turned towards the road, and his back towards the light; he had forgotten the sun which was just rising; he had fallen into one of those deep meditations in which the whole mind is absorbed, which even imprison the senses, and which are equivalent to four walls. There are some meditations which may be called vertical; when one is at the bottom it takes time to return to the surface of the earth. Jean Valjean had descended into one of these reveries. He was thinking of Cosette, of the happiness possible if nothing came between her and him, of that light with which she filled his life, a light which was the atmosphere of his soul. He was almost happy in this reverie. Cosette, standing near him, was watching the clouds as they became ruddy.

Suddenly, Cosette exclaimed: 'Father, I should think somebody was coming down there.' Jean Valjean looked up.

Cosette was right.

The highway which leads to the ancient Barrière du Maine is a prolongation, as everybody knows, of the Rue de Sèvres, and is intersected at a right angle by the interior boulevard. At the corner of the highway and the boulevard, at the point where they diverge, a sound was heard, difficult of explanation at such an hour, and a kind of moving confusion appeared. Some shapeless thing which came from the boulevard was entering upon the highway.

It grew larger, it seemed to move in order, still it was bristling and quivering; it looked like a wagon, but they could not make out the load. There were horses, wheels, cries; whips were cracking. By degrees the features became definite, although enveloped in darkness. It was in fact a wagon which had just turned out of the boulevard into the road, and which was making its way towards the barrière, near which Jean Valjean was; a second, of the same appearance, followed it, then a third, then a fourth; seven vehicles turned in in succession, the horses' heads touching the rear of the wagons. Dark forms were moving upon these wagons, flashes were seen in the twilight as if of drawn swords, a clanking was heard which resembled the rattling of chains; it advanced, the voices grew louder, and it was as terrible a thing as comes forth from the cavern of dreams.

As it approached it took form, and outlined itself behind the trees with the pallor of an apparition; the mass whitened; daylight, which was rising little by little, spread a pallid gleam over this crawling thing, which was at once sepulchral and alive, the heads of the shadows became the faces of corpses, and it was this:

Seven wagons were moving in file upon the road. Six of them were of a peculiar structure. They resembled coopers' drays; they were a sort of long ladder placed upon two wheels, forming thills at the forward end. Each dray, or better, each ladder, was drawn by four horses tandem. Upon these ladders strange clusters of men were carried. In the little light that there was, these men were not seen, they were only guessed. Twenty-four on each wagon, twelve on each sides back to back, their faces towards the passers-by, their legs hanging down, these men were travelling thus; and they had behind them something which clanked and which was a chain, and at their necks something which shone and which was an iron collar. Each had his collar, but the chain was for all; so that these twenty-four men, if they should chance to get down from the dray and walk, would be made subject to a sort of inexorable unity, and have to wriggle over the ground with the chain for a backbone, very much like centipedes. In front and rear of each wagon, two men, armed with muskets, stood, each having an end of the chain under his foot. The collars were square. The seventh wagon, a huge cart with racks, but without a cover, had four wheels and six horses, and carried a resounding pile of iron kettles, melting pots, furnaces, and chains, over which were scattered a number of men, who were bound and lying at full length, and who appeared to be sick. This cart, entirely exposed to view, was furnished with broken hurdles which seemed to have served in the ancient punishments.

These wagons kept the middle of the street. At either side marched a row of guards of infamous appearance, wearing three-pronged hats like the soldiers of the Directory, stained, torn, filthy, muffled up in Invalides' uniforms and hearse-boys' trousers, half grey and half blue, almost in tatters, with red epaulets, yellow cross-belts, sheath-knives, muskets, and clubs: a species of servant-soldiers. These *sbirri* seemed a compound of the abjectness of the beggar and the authority of the executioner. The one who appeared to be their chief had a horsewhip in his hand. All these details, blurred by the twilight, were becoming clearer and clearer in the growing light. At the head and the rear of the convoy, gendarmes marched on horseback, solemn, and with drawn swords.

This cortège was so long that when the first wagon reached the barrière, the last had hardly turned out of the boulevard.

A crowd, come from nobody knows where, and gathered in a twinkling, as is frequently the case in Paris, were pushing along the two sides of the highway and looking on. In the neighbouring lanes there were heard people shouting and calling each other, and the wooden shoes of the market gardeners who were running to see.

The men heaped upon the drays were silent as they were jolted along. They were livid with the chill of the morning. They all had tow trousers, and their bare feet were in wooden shoes. The rest of their costume was according to the fancy of misery. Their dress was hideously variegated: nothing is more dismal than the harlequin of rags. Felt hats jammed out of shape, glazed caps, horrible cloth caps, and beside the linen monkey-jacket, the black coat out at the elbows; several had women's hats; others had baskets on their heads; hairy breasts could be seen, and through the holes in their clothing tattooings could be discerned; temples of love, burning hearts, cupids, eruptions, and red sores could also be seen. Two or three had a rope of straw fixed to the bars of the dray, and hung beneath them like a stirrup, which sustained their feet. One of them held in his hand and carried to his mouth something which looked like a black stone, which he seemed to be gnawing; it was bread which he was eating. There were none but dry eyes among them; they were rayless, or lighted with an evil light. The troop of escort was cursing, the chained did not whisper; from time to time there was heard the sound of the blow of a club upon their shoulders or their heads; some of these men were yawning; their rags were terrible; their feet hung down, their shoulders swung, their heads struck together, their irons rattled, their eyes glared fiercely, their fists were clenched or opened inertly like the hands of the dead; behind the convoy a troop of children were bursting with laughter.

This file of wagons, whatever it was, was dismal. It was evident that tomorrow, that in an hour, a shower might spring up, that it would be followed by another, and another, and that the worn-out clothing would be soaked through, that once wet, these men would never get dry, that once chilled, they would never get warm again, that their tow trousers would be fastened to their skin by the rain, that water would fill their wooden shoes, that blows of the whip could not prevent the chattering of their jaws, that the chain would continue to hold them by the neck, that their feet would continue to swing; and it was impossible not to shudder at seeing these human creatures thus bound and passive under the chilling clouds of autumn, and given up to the rain, to the wind, to all the fury of the elements, like trees and stones.

The clubs did not spare even the sick, who lay tied with ropes and motionless in the seventh wagon, and who seemed to have been thrown there like sacks filled with misery.

Suddenly, the sun appeared; the immense radiance of the Orient burst forth, and one would have said that it set all these savage heads on fire. Their tongues were loosed, a conflagration of sneers, of oaths, and songs burst forth. The broad horizontal light cut the whole file in two, illuminating their heads and their bodies, leaving their feet and the wheels in the dark. Their thoughts appeared upon their faces; the moment was appalling; demons visible with their masks fallen off, ferocious souls laid bare. Lighted up, this group was still dark. Some, who were gay, had quills in their mouths from which they blew vermin among the crowd, selecting the women; the dawn intensified these mournful profiles by the blackness of the shade; not one of these beings who was not deformed by misery; and it was so monstrous that one would have said that it changed the sunbeams into the gleam of the lightning's flash. The wagon load which led the cortège had struck up and were singing at the top of their voices with a ghastly joviality a medley of Desaugiers, then famous, *la Vestale;* the trees shivered drearily on the sidewalks, the bourgeois listened with faces of idiotic bliss to these obscenities chanted by spectres.

Every form of distress was present in this chaos of a cortège; there was the facial angle of every beast, old men, youths, bald heads, grey beards, cynical monstrosities, dogged resignation, savage grimaces, insane attitudes, snouts set-off with caps, heads like those of young girls with corkscrews over their temples, child faces horrifying on that account, thin skeleton faces which lacked nothing but death. On the first wagon was a negro, who, perhaps, had been a slave and could compare chains. The fearful leveller, disgrace, had passed over these brows; at this degree of abasement the last transformation had taken place in all to its utmost degree; and ignorance, changed into stupidity, was the equal of intelligence changed into despair. No possible choice among these men who seemed by their appearance the élite of the mire. It was clear that the marshal, whoever he was, of this foul procession had not classified them. These beings had been bound and coupled pell-mell, probably in alphabetic disorder, and loaded haphazard upon these wagons. The aggregation of horrors, however, always ends by evolving a resultant; every addition of misfortune gives a total; there came from each chain a common soul, and each cartload had its own physiognomy. Beside the one which was singing, there was one which was howling; a third was begging; one was seen gnashing its teeth; another was threatening the bystanders, another blaspheming God; the last was silent as the tomb. Dante would have thought he saw the seven circles of Hell on their passage.

A passage from condemnation towards punishment, made drearily, not upon the formidable flashing car of the Apocalypse, but more dismal still, upon a hangman's cart.

One of the guard, who had a hook on the end of his club, from time to time made a semblance of stirring up this heap of human ordure. An old woman in the crowd pointed them out with her finger to a little boy five years old, and said: '*Whelp, that will teach you!*'

As the songs and the blasphemy increased, he who seemed the captain of the escort cracked his whip, and upon that signal, a fearful, sullen, and promiscuous cudgelling, which sounded like hail, fell upon the seven wagons; many roared and foamed; which redoubled the joy of the *gamins* who had collected, a swarm of flies upon these wounds.

Jean Valjean's eye had become frightful. It was no longer an eye; it was that deep window, which takes the place of the look in certain unfortunate beings, who seem unconscious of reality, and from which flashes out the reflection of horrors and catastrophes. He was not looking upon a sight; a vision was appearing to him. He endeavoured to rise, to flee, to escape; he could not move a limb. Sometimes things which you see, clutch you and hold you. He was spell-bound, stupefied, petrified, asking himself, through a vague unutterable anguish, what was the meaning of this sepulchral persecution, and whence came this pandemonium which was pursuing him. All at once he raised his hand to his forehead, a common gesture with those to whom memory suddenly returns; he remembered that this was really the route, that this detour was usual to avoid meeting the king, which was always possible on the Fontainebleau road, and that, thirty-five years before, he had passed through this barrière.

Cosette, though from another cause, was equally terrified. She did not comprehend; her breath failed her; what she saw did not seem possible to her; at last she exclaimed:

'Father! what can there be in those wagons?'

Jean Valjean answered:

'Convicts.'

'And where are they going?'

'To the galleys.'

At this moment the cudgelling, multiplied by a hundred hands, reached its climax; blows with the flat of the sword joined in; it was a fury of whips and clubs; the galley slaves crouched down, a hideous obedience was produced by the punishment, and all were silent with the look of chained wolves. Cosette trembled in every limb; she continued:

'Father, are they still men?'

'Sometimes,' said the wretched man.

It was in fact the chain which, setting out before day from Bicêtre, took the Mans road to avoid Fontainebleau, where the king then was. This detour made the terrible journey last three or four days longer; but to spare the royal person the sight of the punishment, it may well be prolonged.

Jean Valjean returned home overwhelmed. Such encounters are shocks, and the memory which they leave resembles a convulsion.

Jean Valjean, however, on the way back to the Rue de Babylone with Cosette, did not notice that she asked him other questions regarding what they had just seen; perhaps he was himself too much absorbed in his own dejection to heed her words or to answer them. But at night, as Cosette was leaving him to go to bed, he heard her say in an undertone, and as if talking to herself: 'It seems to me that if I should meet one of those men in my path, O my God, I should die just from seeing him near me!'

Fortunately it happened that on the morrow of this tragic day there were, in consequence of some official celebration, fêtes in Paris, a review in the Champ de Mars, rowing matches upon the Seine, theatricals in the Champs Elysées, fireworks at l'Etoile, illuminations everywhere. Jean Valjean, doing violence to his habits, took Cosette to these festivities, for the purpose of diverting her mind from the memories of the day before, and of effacing under the laughing tumult of all Paris, the abominable thing which had passed before her. The review, which enlivened the fête, made the display of uniforms quite natural; Jean Valjean put on his National Guard uniform with the vague interior feeling of a man who is taking refuge. Yet the object of this walk seemed attained. Cosette, whose law it was to please her father, and for whom, moreover, every sight was new, accepted the diversion with the easy and blithe grace of youth, and did not look too disdainfully upon that promiscuous bowl of joy which is called a public fête; so that Jean Valjean could believe that he had succeeded, and that no trace remained of the hideous vision.

Some days later, one morning, when the sun was bright, and they were both upon the garden steps, another infraction of the rules which Jean Valjean seemed to have imposed upon himself, and of the habit of staying in her room which sadness had imposed upon Cosette, Cosette, in her dressing-gown, was standing in that undress of the morning hour which is charmingly becoming to young girls, and which has the appearance of a cloud upon a star; and, with her head in the light, rosy from having slept well, under the tender gaze of the gentle goodman, she was picking a daisy in pieces. Cosette was ignorant of the transporting legend, *I love thee a little, passionately*, etc.; who should have taught it to her? She was fingering this flower, by instinct, innocently, without suspecting that to pick a daisy in pieces is to pluck a heart. Were there a fourth Grace named Melancholy, and were it smiling, she would have seemed that Grace.

Jean Valjean was fascinated by the contemplation of her slender fingers upon that flower, forgetting everything in the radiance of this child. A redbreast was twittering in the shrubbery beside them. White clouds were crossing the sky so gaily that one would have said they had just been set at liberty.

Cosette continued picking her flower attentively; she seemed to be thinking of something; but that must have been pleasant. Suddenly she turned her head over her shoulder with the delicate motion of the swan, and said to Jean Valjean: 'Father, what are they then, the galley slaves? '

BOOK 4: AID FROM BELOW MAY BE AID FROM ABOVE

1. Wound without, cure within

Thus their life gradually darkened.

There was left to them but one distraction, and this had formerly been a pleasure: that was to carry bread to those who were hungry, and clothing to those who were cold. In these visits to the poor, in which Cosette often accompanied Jean Valjean, they found some remnant of their former light-heartedness; and, sometimes, when they had had a good day, when many sorrows had been relieved and many little children revived and made warm, Cosette, in the evening, was a little gay. It was at this period that they visited the Jondrette den.

The day after that visit, Jean Valjean appeared in the cottage in the morning, with his ordinary calmness, but with a large wound on his left arm, very much inflamed and very venomous, which resembled a burn, and which he explained in some fashion. This wound confined him within doors more than a month with fever. He would see no physician. When Cosette urged it: 'Call the dog-doctor,' said he.

Cosette dressed it night and morning with so divine a grace and so angelic a pleasure in being useful to him, that Jean Valjean felt all his old happiness return, his fears and his anxieties dissipate, and he looked upon Cosette, saying: 'Oh! the good wound! Oh! the kind hurt!'

Cosette, as her father was sick, had deserted the summerhouse, and regained her taste for the little lodge and the backyard. She spent almost all her time with Jean Valjean, and read to him the books which he liked. In general, books of travels. Jean Valjean was born anew; his happiness revived with inexpressible radiance; the Luxembourg, the unknown young prowler, Cosette's coldness, all these clouds of his soul faded away. He now said to himself: 'I imagined all that. I am an old fool.'

His happiness was so great, that the frightful discovery of the Thénardiers, made in the Jondrette den, and so unexpectedly, had in some sort glided over him. He had succeeded in escaping; his trace was lost, what mattered the rest! he thought of it only to grieve over those wretches. 'They are now in prison, and can do no harm in future,' thought he, 'but what a pitiful family in distress!'

As to the hideous vision of the Barrière du Maine, Cosette had never mentioned it again.

At the convent, Sister Sainte Mechthilde had taught Cosette music. Cosette had the voice of a warbler with a soul, and sometimes in the evening, in the humble lodging of the wounded man, she sang plaintive songs which rejoiced Jean Valjean.

Spring came. The garden was so wonderful at that season of the year, that Jean Valjean said to Cosette: 'You never go there, I wish you would walk in it.'

'As you will, father,' said Cosette.

And, out of obedience to her father, she resumed her walks in the garden, oftenest alone, for, as we have remarked, Jean Valjean, who probably dreaded being seen through the gate, hardly ever went there.

Jean Valjean's wound had been a diversion.

When Cosette saw that her father was suffering less, and that he was getting well, and that he seemed happy, she felt a contentment that she did not even notice, so gently and naturally did it come upon her. It was then the month of March, the days were growing longer, winter was departing, winter always carries with it something of our sadness; then April came, that daybreak of summer, fresh like every dawn, gay like every childhood; weeping a little sometimes like the infant that it is. Nature in this month has charming gleams which pass from the sky, the clouds, the trees, the fields, and the flowers, into the heart of man.

Cosette was still too young for this April joy, which resembled her, not to find its way to her heart. Insensibly, and without a suspicion on her part, the darkness passed away from her mind. In the spring it becomes light in sad souls, as at noon it becomes light in cellars. And Cosette was not now very sad. So it was, however, but she did not notice it. In the morning, about ten o'clock, after breakfast, when she had succeeded in enticing her father into the garden for a quarter of an hour, and while she was walking in the sun in front of the steps, supporting his wounded arm, she did not perceive that she was laughing every moment, and that she was happy.

Jean Valjean saw her, with intoxication, again become fresh and rosy.

'Oh! the blessed wound!' repeated he in a whisper.

And he was grateful to the Thénardiers.

As soon as his wound was cured, he resumed his solitary and twilight walks.

It would be a mistake to believe that one can walk in this way alone in the uninhabited regions of Paris, and not meet with some adventure.

2. *Mother Plutarch is not embarrassed on the explanation of a phenomenon*

One evening little Gavroche had had no dinner; he remembered that he had had no dinner also the day before; this was becoming tiresome. He resolved that he would try for some supper. He went wandering about beyond La Salpêtrière, in the deserted spots; those are the places for good luck; where there is nobody, can be found something. He came to a settlement which appeared to him to be the village of Austerlitz.

In one of his preceding strolls, he had noticed an old garden there haunted by an old man and an old woman, and in this garden a passable apple tree. Beside this apple tree, there was a sort of fruit-loft poorly enclosed where the conquest of an apple might be made. An apple is a supper; an apple is life. What ruined Adam might save Gavroche. The garden was upon a solitary lane unpaved and bordered with bushes for lack of houses; a hedge separated it from the lane.

Gavroche directed his steps towards the garden; he found the lane, he recognised the apple tree, he verified the fruit-loft, he examined the hedge; a hedge is a stride. Day was declining, not a cat in the lane, the time was good. Gavroche sketched out the escalade, then suddenly stopped. Somebody was talking in the garden. Gavroche looked through one of the openings of the hedge.

Within two steps of him, at the foot of the hedge on the other side, precisely at the point where the hole he was meditating would have taken him, lay a stone which made a kind of seat, and on this seat the old man of the garden was sitting with the old woman standing before him. The old woman was muttering. Gavroche, who was anything but discreet, listened.

'Monsieur Mabeuf!' said the old woman.

'Mabeuf!' thought Gavroche, 'that is a funny name.'

The old man who was addressed made no motion. The old woman repeated:

'Monsieur Mabeuf.'

The old man, without raising his eyes from the ground, determined to answer:

'What, Mother Plutarch?'

'Mother Plutarch!' thought Gavroche, 'another funny name.'

Mother Plutarch resumed, and the old man was forced to enter into the conversation:

'The landlord is dissatisfied.'

'Why so?'

'There are three quarters due.'

'In three months there will be four.'

'He says that he will turn you out of doors to sleep.'

'I shall go.'

'The grocery woman wants to be paid. She holds on to her wood. What will you keep warm with this winter? We shall have no wood.'

'There is the sun.'

'The butcher refuses credit, he will not give us any more meat.'

'That is all right. I do not digest meat well. It is too heavy.'

'What shall we have for dinner?'

'Bread.'

'The baker demands something on account, and says no money, no bread.'

'Very well.'

'What will you eat?'

'We have the apples from the apple tree.'

'But, monsieur, we can't live like that without money.'

'I have not any.'

The old woman went away, the old man remained alone. He began to reflect. Gavroche was reflecting on his side. It was almost night.

The first result of Gavroche's reflection was that instead of climbing over the hedge he crept under. The branches separated a little at the bottom of the bushes.

'Heigho,' exclaimed Gavroche internally, 'an alcove!' and he hid in it. He almost touched Father Mabeuf's seat. He heard the octogenarian breathe.

Then, for dinner, he tried to sleep.

Sleep of a cat, sleep with one eye. Even while crouching there Gavroche kept watch.

The whiteness of the twilight sky blanched the earth, and the lane made a livid line between two rows of dusky bushes.

Suddenly, upon that whitened band two dim forms appeared. One came before – the other, at some distance, behind.

'There are two fellows,' growled Gavroche.

The first form seemed some old bourgeois bent and thoughtful, dressed more than simply, walking with the slow pace of an aged man, and taking his ease in the starry evening.

The second was straight, firm, and slight. It regulated its step by the step of the first; but in the unwonted slowness of the gait, dexterity and agility were manifest. This form had, in addition to something wild and startling, the whole appearance of what was then called a dandy; the hat was of the latest style, the coat was black, well cut, probably of fine cloth, and closely fitted to the form. The head was held up with a robust grace, and, under the hat, could be seen in the twilight the pale profile of a young man. This profile had a rose in its mouth. The second form was well known to Gavroche: it was Montparnasse.

As to the other, he could have said nothing about it, except that it was an old goodman.

Gavroche immediately applied himself to observation.

One of these two passers evidently had designs upon the other. Gavroche was well situated to see the issue. The alcove had very conveniently become a hiding-place.

Montparnasse hiding, at such an hour, in such a place – it was threatening. Gavroche felt his *gamin*'s heart moved with pity for the old man.

What could he do? intervene? one weakness in aid of another? That would be ludicrous to Montparnasse. Gavroche could not conceal it from himself that, to this formidable bandit of eighteen, the old man first, the child afterwards, would be but two mouthfuls.

While Gavroche was deliberating, the attack was made, sharp and hideous. The attack of a tiger on a wild ass, a spider on a fly. Montparnasse, on a sudden, threw away the rose, sprang upon the old man, collared him, grasped him and fastened to him, and Gavroche could hardly restrain a cry. A moment afterwards, one of these men was under the other, exhausted, panting, struggling, with a knee of marble upon his breast. Only it was not altogether as Gavroche had expected. The one on the ground was Montparnasse; the one above was the goodman. All this happened a few steps from Gavroche.

The old man had received the shock, and had returned it, and returned it so terribly that in the twinkling of an eye the assailant and assailed had changed parts.

'There is a brave Invalide!' thought Gavroche.

And he could not help clapping his hands. But it was a clapping of hands thrown away. It did not reach the two combatants, absorbed and deafened by each other, and mingling their breath in the contest.

There was silence. Montparnasse ceased to struggle. Gavroche said this aside: 'Can he be dead?'

The goodman had not spoken a word, nor uttered a cry. He arose, and Gavroche heard him say to Montparnasse:

'Get up.'

Montparnasse got up, but the goodman held him. Montparnasse had the humiliated and furious attitude of a wolf caught by a sheep.

Gavroche looked and listened, endeavouring to double his eyes by his ears. He was enormously amused.

He was rewarded for his conscientious anxiety as a spectator. He was able to seize upon the wing the following dialogue, which borrowed a strangely tragic tone from the darkness. The goodman questioned. Montparnasse responded.

'How old are you?'

'Nineteen.'

'You are strong and well. Why don't you work?'

'It is fatiguing.'

'What is your business?'

'Loafer.'

'Speak seriously. Can I do anything for you? What would you like to be?'

'A robber.'

There was a silence. The old man seemed to be thinking deeply. He was motionless, yet did not release Montparnasse.

From time to time the young bandit, vigorous and nimble, made the efforts of a beast caught in a snare. He gave a spring, attempted a trip, twisted his limbs desperately, endeavoured to escape. The old man did not appear to perceive it, and with a single hand held his two arms with the sovereign indifference of absolute strength.

The old man's reverie continued for some time, then, looking steadily upon Montparnasse, he gently raised his voice and addressed to him, in that obscurity in which they were, a sort of solemn allocution of which Gavroche did not lose a syllable:

'My child, you are entering by laziness into the most laborious of existences. Ah! you declare yourself a loafer! prepare to labour. Have you seen a terrible machine called the rolling-mill? Beware of it, it is a cunning and ferocious thing; if it but catch the skirt of your coat, you are drawn in entirely. This machine is idleness. Stop, while there is yet time, and save yourself! otherwise, it is all over; you will soon be between the wheels. Once caught hope for nothing more. To fatigue, idler! no more rest. The implacable iron hand of labour has seized you. Earn a living, have a task, accomplish a duty, you do not wish it! To be like others is tiresome! Well! you will be different. Labour is the law; he who spurns it as tiresome will have it as a punishment. You are unwilling to be a working-man, you will be a slave. Labour releases you on the one hand only to retake you on the other; you are unwilling to be her friend, you will be her negro. Ah! you have refused the honest weariness of men, you shall have the sweat of the damned. While others sing, you will rave. You will see from afar, from below, other men at work; it will seem to you that they are at rest. The labourer, the reaper, the sailor, the blacksmith, will appear to you in the light like the blessed in a paradise. What a radiance in the anvil! To drive the plough, to bind the sheaf, is happiness. The bark free before the wind, what a festival! You, idler, dig, draw, roll, march! Drag your halter, you are a beast of burden in the train of hell! Ah! to do nothing, that is your aim. Well! not a week, not a day, not an hour, without crushing exhaustion. You can lift nothing but with anguish. Every minute which elapses will make your muscles crack. What will be a feather for others will be a rock for you. The simplest things will become steep. Life will make itself a monster about you. To go, to come, to breathe, so many terrible labours. Your lungs will feel like a hundred-pound weight. To go here rather than there will be a problem to solve. Any other man who wishes to go out, opens his door, it is done, he is out of doors. You, if you wish to go out, must pierce your wall. To go into the street, what does everybody do? Everybody goes down the staircase! but you, you will tear up your bed clothes, you will make a rope of them strip by strip, then you will pass through your window and you will hang on that thread over an abyss, and it will be at night, in the storm, in the rain, in the tempest, and, if the rope is too short, you will have but one way to descend, to fall. To fall at a venture, into the abyss, from whatever height, upon what? Upon whatever is below, upon the unknown. Or you will climb through the flue of a chimney, at the risk of burning yourself; or you will crawl through a sewer, at the risk of being drowned. I do not speak of the holes which you must conceal, of the stones which you must take out and put back twenty times a day, of the mortar which you must hide in your mattress. A lock presents itself; the bourgeois has in his pocket his key, made by a locksmith. You, if you want to pass out, are condemned to make a frightful masterpiece; you will take a big sou, you will cut it into two slices; with what tools? You will invent them. That is your business. Then you will hollow out the interior of these two slices, preserving the outside carefully, and you will cut all around the edge a screw-thread, so that they will fit closely one upon the other, like a bottom and a cover. The bottom and the top thus screwed together, nobody will suspect anything. To the watchmen, for you will be watched, it will be a big sou; to you, it will be a box. What will you put in this box? A little bit of steel. A watch-spring in which you will cut teeth, and which will be a saw. With this saw, as long as a pin, and hidden in this sou, you will have to cut the bolt of the lock, the slide of the bolt, the clasp of the padlock, and the bar which you will have at your window, and the iron ring which you will have on your leg. This masterpiece finished, this prodigy accomplished, all those miracles of art, of address, of skill, of patience, executed, if it comes to be known that you are the author, what will be your reward? the dungeon. Behold your future. Idleness, pleasure, what abysses! To do nothing is a dreary course to take, be sure of it. To live idle upon the substance of society! To be useless, that is to say, noxious! This leads straight to the lowest depth of misery.

'Woe to him who would be a parasite! he will be vermin. Ah! it is not pleasant to you to work? Ah! you have but one thought: to eat, and drink, and sleep in luxury. You will drink water, you will eat black bread, you will sleep upon a board, with irons riveted to your limbs, the chill of which you will feel at night upon your flesh! You will break those irons, you will flee. Very well. You will drag yourself on your belly in the bushes, and eat grass like the beasts of the forest. And you will be retaken. And then you will spend years in a dungeon, fastened to a wall, groping for a drink from your pitcher, gnawing a frightful loaf of darkness which the dogs would not touch, eating beans which the worms have eaten before you. You will be a woodlouse in a cellar. Oh! take pity on yourself, miserable child, young thing, a suckling not twenty years ago, who doubtless have a mother still alive! I conjure you, listen to me. You desire fine black clothes, shining pumps, to curl your hair, to put sweet-scented oil upon your locks, to please your women, to be handsome. You will be close shorn, with a red coat and wooden shoes. You wish a ring on your finger, you will have an iron collar on your neck. And if you look at a woman, a blow of the club. And you will go in there at twenty, and you will come out at fifty! You will enter young, rosy, fresh, with your eyes bright and all your teeth white, and your beautiful youthful hair; you will come out broken, bent, wrinkled, toothless, horrible, with white hair! Oh! my child, you are taking a mistaken road, laziness is giving you bad advice; the hardest of all labour is robbery. Trust me, do not undertake this dreadful drudgery of being an idler. To become a rascal is not comfortable. It is not so hard to be an honest man. Go, now, and think of what I have said to you. And now, what did you want of me? my purse? here it is.'

And the old man, releasing Montparnasse, put his purse in his hand, which Montparnasse weighed for a moment; after which, with the same mechanical precaution as if he had stolen it, Montparnasse let it glide gently into the back pocket of his coat.

All this said and done, the goodman turned his back and quietly resumed his walk.

'Blockhead!' murmured Montparnasse.

Who was this goodman? the reader has doubtless guessed.

Montparnasse, in stupefaction, watched him till he disappeared in the twilight. This contemplation was fatal to him.

While the old man was moving away, Gavroche was approaching.

Gavroche, with a side glance, made sure that Father Mabeuf, perhaps asleep, was still sitting on the seat. Then the urchin came out of his bushes, and began to creep along in the shade, behind the motionless Montparnasse. He reached Montparnasse thus without being seen or heard, gently insinuated his hand into the back pocket of the fine black cloth coat, took the purse, withdrew his hand, and, creeping off again, glided away like an adder into the darkness. Montparnasse, who had no reason to be upon his guard, and who was reflecting for the first time in his life, perceived nothing of it. Gavroche, when he had reached the point where Father Mabeuf was, threw the purse over the hedge, and fled at full speed.

The purse fell on the foot of Father Mabeuf. This shock awoke him. He stooped down, and picked up the purse. He did not understand it at all, and he opened it. It was a purse with two compartments; in one there were some small coins; in the other, there were six napoleons.

M. Mabeuf, very much startled, carried the thing to his governess.

'This falls from the sky,' said Mother Plutarch.

BOOK 5: THE END OF WHICH IS UNLIKE THE BEGINNING

1. Solitude and the barracks

Cosette's grief, so poignant still, and so acute four or five months before, had, without her knowledge even, entered upon convalescence. Nature, spring, her youth, her love for her father, the gaiety of the birds and the flowers, were filtering little by little, day by day, drop by drop, into this soul so pure and so young, something which almost resembled oblivion. Was the fire dying out entirely? or was it merely becoming a bed of embers? The truth is, that she had scarcely anything left of that sorrowful and consuming feeling.

One day she suddenly thought of Marius: 'What!' said she, 'I do not think of him now.'

In the course of that very week she noticed, passing before the grated gate of the garden, a very handsome officer of lancers, waist like a wasp, ravishing uniform, cheeks like a young girl's, sabre under his arm, waxed moustaches, polished schapska. Moreover, fair hair, full blue eyes, plump, vain, insolent and pretty face; the very opposite of Marius. A cigar in his mouth. Cosette thought that this officer doubtless belonged to the regiment in barracks on the Rue de Babylone.

The next day, she saw him pass again. She noticed the hour.

Dating from this time, was it chance? she saw him pass almost every day.

The officer's comrades perceived that there was, in this garden so 'badly kept', behind that wretched old-fashioned grating, a pretty creature that always happened to be visible on the passage of the handsome lieutenant, who is not unknown to the reader, and whose name was Théodule Gillenormand.

'Stop!' said they to him. 'Here is a little girl who has her eye upon you; why don't you look at her?'

'Do you suppose I have the time,' answered the lancer, 'to look at all the girls who look at me?'

This was the very time when Marius was descending gloomily towards agony, and saying: 'If I could only see her again before I die!' Had his wish been realised, had he seen Cosette at that moment looking at a lancer, he would not have been able to utter a word, and would have expired of grief.

Whose fault was it? Nobody's.

Marius was of that temperament which sinks into grief, and remains there; Cosette was of that which plunges in, and comes out again.

Cosette indeed was passing that dangerous moment, the fatal phase of feminine reverie abandoned to itself, when the heart of an isolated young girl resembles the tendrils of a vine which seize hold, as chance determines, of the capital of a column or the signpost of a tavern. A hurried and decisive moment, critical for every orphan, whether she be poor or whether she be rich, for riches do not defend against a bad choice; misalliances are formed very high; the real misalliance is that of souls; and, even as more than one unknown young man, without name, or birth, or fortune, is a marble column which sustains a temple of grand sentiments and grand ideas, so you may find a satisfied and opulent man of the world, with polished boots and varnished speech, who, if you look, not at the exterior but the interior, that is to say, at what is reserved for the wife, is nothing but a stupid joist, darkly haunted by violent, impure, and debauched passions; the signpost of a tavern.

What was there in Cosette's soul? A soothed or sleeping passion; love in a wavering state; something which was limpid, shining, disturbed to a certain depth, gloomy below. The image of the handsome officer was reflected from the surface. Was there a memory at the bottom? deep at the bottom? Perhaps. Cosette did not know.

A singular incident followed.

2. *Fears of Cosette*

In the first fortnight in April, Jean Valjean went on a journey. This, we know, happened with him from time to time, at very long intervals. He remained absent one or two days at the most. Where did he go? nobody knew, not even Cosette. Once only, on one of these trips, she had accompanied him in a fiacre as far as the corner of a little cul-de-sac, on which she read: *Impasse de la Planchette*. There he got out, and the fiacre took Cosette back to the Rue de Babylone. It was generally when money was needed for the household expenses that Jean Valjean made these little journeys.

Jean Valjean then was absent. He had said: 'I shall be back in three days.'

In the evening, Cosette was alone in the parlour. To amuse herself, she had opened her piano and began to sing, playing an accompaniment, the chorus from *Euryanthe*: *Hunters wandering in the woods!* which is perhaps the finest piece in all music.

All at once it seemed to her that she heard a step in the garden.

It could not be her father, he was absent; it could not be Toussaint, she was in bed. It was ten o'clock at night.

She went to the window shutter which was closed and put her ear to it.

It appeared to her that it was a man's step, and that he was treading very softly.

She ran immediately up to the first storey, into her room, opened a slide in her blind, and looked into the garden. The moon was full. She could see as plainly as in broad day.

There was nobody there.

She opened the window. The garden was absolutely silent, and all that she could see of the street was as deserted as it always was.

Cosette thought she had been mistaken. She had imagined she heard this noise. It was a hallucination produced by Weber's sombre and majestic chorus, which opens before the mind startling depths, which trembles before the eye like a bewildering forest, and in which we hear the crackling of the dead branches beneath the anxious step of the hunters dimly seen in the twilight.

She thought no more about it.

Moreover, Cosette by nature was not easily startled. There was in her veins the blood of the gypsy and of the adventuress who goes barefoot. It must be remembered she was rather a lark than a dove. She was wild and brave at heart.

The next day, not so late, at nightfall, she was walking in the garden. In the midst of the confused thoughts which filled her mind, she thought she heard for a moment a sound like the sound of the evening before, as if somebody were walking in the darkness under the trees, not very far from her, but she said to herself that nothing is more like a step in the grass than the rustling of two limbs against each other, and she paid no attention to it. Moreover, she saw nothing.

She left 'the bush'; she had to cross a little green grass-plot to reach the steps. The moon, which had just risen behind her, projected, as Cosette came out from the shrubbery, her shadow before her upon this grass-plot.

Cosette stood still, terrified.

By the side of her shadow, the moon marked out distinctly upon the sward another shadow singularly frightful and terrible, a shadow with a round hat.

It was like the shadow of a man who might have been standing in the edge of the shrubbery, a few steps behind Cosette.

For a moment she was unable to speak, or cry, or call, or stir, or turn her head.

At last she summoned up all her courage and resolutely turned round.

There was nobody there.

She looked upon the ground. The shadow had disappeared.

She returned into the shrubbery, boldly hunted through the corners, went as far as the gate, and found nothing.

She felt her blood run cold. Was this also a hallucination? What! two days in succession? One hallucination may pass, but two hallucinations? What made her most anxious was that the shadow was certainly not a phantom. Phantoms never wear round hats.

The next day Jean Valjean returned. Cosette narrated to him what she thought she had heard and seen. She expected to be reassured, and that her father would shrug his shoulders and say: 'You are a foolish little girl.'

Jean Valjean became anxious.

'It may be nothing,' said he to her.

He left her under some pretext and went into the garden, and she saw him examining the gate very closely.

In the night she awoke; now she was certain, and she distinctly heard somebody walking very near the steps under her window. She ran to her slide and opened it. There was in fact a man in the garden with a big club in his hand. Just as she was about to cry out, the moon lighted up the man's face. It was her father.

She went back to bed, saying: 'So he is really anxious!'

Jean Valjean passed that night in the garden and the two nights following. Cosette saw him through the hole in her shutter.

The third night the moon was smaller and rose later, it might have been one o'clock in the morning, she heard a loud burst of laughter and her father's voice calling her:

'Cosette!'

She sprang out of bed, threw on her dressing-gown, and opened her window.

Her father was below on the grass-plot.

'I woke you up to show you,' said he. 'Look, here is your shadow in a round hat.'

And he pointed to a shadow on the sward made by the moon, and which really bore a close resemblance to the appearance of a man in a round hat. It was a figure produced by a sheet-iron stove-pipe with a cap, which rose above a neighbouring roof.

Cosette also began to laugh, all her gloomy suppositions fell to the ground, and the next day, while breakfasting with her father, she made merry over the mysterious garden haunted by shadows of stove-pipes.

Jean Valjean became entirely calm again; as to Cosette, she did not notice very carefully whether the stove-pipe was really in the direction of the shadow which she had seen, or thought she saw, and whether the moon was in the same part of the sky. She made no question about the oddity of a stove-pipe which is afraid of being caught in the act, and which retires when you look at its shadow, for the shadow had disappeared when Cosette turned round, and Cosette had really believed that she was certain of that. Cosette was fully reassured. The demonstration appeared to her complete, and the idea that there could have been anybody walking in the garden that evening, or that night, no longer entered her head.

A few days afterwards, however, a new incident occurred.

3. Enriched by the commentaries of Toussaint

In the garden, near the grated gate, on the street, there was a stone seat protected from the gaze of the curious by a hedge, but which, nevertheless, by an effort, the arm of a passer could reach through the grating and the hedge.

One evening in this same month of April, Jean Valjean had gone out; Cosette, after sunset, had sat down on this seat. The wind was freshening in the trees, Cosette was musing; a vague sadness was coming over her little by little, that invincible sadness which evening gives and which comes perhaps, who knows? from the mystery of the tomb half-opened at that hour.

Fantine was perhaps in that shadow.

Cosette rose, slowly made the round of the garden, walking in the grass which was wet with dew, and saying to herself through the kind of melancholy somnambulism in which she was enveloped: 'One really needs wooden shoes for the garden at this hour. I shall catch cold.'

She returned to the seat.

Just as she was sitting down, she noticed in the place she had left a stone of considerable size which evidently was not there the moment before.

Cosette reflected upon this stone, asking herself what it meant. Suddenly, the idea that this stone did not come upon the seat of itself, that somebody had put it there, that an arm had passed through that grating, this idea came to her and made her afraid. It was a genuine fear this time; there was the stone. No doubt was possible, she did not touch it, fled without daring to look behind her, took refuge in the house, and immediately shut the glass-door of the stairs with shutter, bar, and bolt. She asked Toussaint:

'Has my father come in?'

'Not yet, mademoiselle.'

(We have noticed once for all Toussaint's stammering. Let us be permitted to indicate it no longer. We dislike the musical notation of an infirmity.)

Jean Valjean, a man given to thought and a night-walker, frequently did not return till quite late.

'Toussaint,' resumed Cosette, 'you are careful in the evening to bar the shutters well, upon the garden at least, and to really put the little iron things into the little rings which fasten?'

'Oh! never fear, mademoiselle.'

Toussaint did not fail, and Cosette well knew it, but she could not help adding:

'Because it is so solitary about here!'

'For that matter,' said Toussaint, 'that is true. We would be assassinated before we would have time to say Boo! And then, monsieur doesn't sleep in the house. But don't be afraid, mademoiselle, I fasten the windows like Bastilles. Lone women! I am sure it is enough to make us shudder! Just imagine it! to see men come into the room at night and say to you: Hush! and set themselves to cutting your throat. It isn't so much the dying, people die, that is all right, we know very well that we must die, but it is the horror of having such people touch you. And then their knives, they must cut badly! O God!'

'Be still,' said Cosette. 'Fasten everything well.'

Cosette, dismayed by the melodrama improvised by Toussaint, and perhaps also by the memory of the apparitions of the previous week which came back to her, did not even dare to say to her: 'Go and look at the stone which somebody has laid on the seat!' for fear of opening the garden door again, and lest 'the men' would come in. She had all the doors and windows carefully closed, made Toussaint go over the whole house from cellar to garret, shut herself up in her room, drew her bolts, looked under her bed, lay down, and slept badly. All night she saw the stone big as a mountain and full of caves.

At sunrise – the peculiarity of sunrise is to make us laugh at all our terrors of the night, and our laugh is always proportioned to the fear we have had – at sunrise Cosette, on waking, looked upon her fright as upon a nightmare, and said to herself. 'What have I been dreaming about? This is like those steps which I thought I heard at night last week in the garden! it is like the shadow of the stove-pipe! And am I going to be a coward now!'

The sun, which shone through the cracks of her shutters, and made the damask curtains purple, reassured her to such an extent that it all vanished from her thoughts, even the stone.

'There was no stone on the bench, any more than there was a man with a round hat in the garden; I dreamed the stone as I did the rest.'

She dressed herself, went down to the garden, ran to the bench and felt a cold sweat. The stone was there.

But this was only for a moment. What is fright by night is curiosity by day.

'Pshaw!' said she, 'now let us see.'

She raised the stone, which was pretty large. There was something underneath which resembled a letter.

It was a white paper envelope. Cosette seized it; there was no address on the one side, no wafer on the other. Still the envelope, although open, was not empty. Papers could be seen in it.

Cosette examined it. There was no more fright, there was curiosity no more; there was a beginning of anxious interest.

Cosette took out of the envelope what it contained, a quire of paper, each page of which was numbered and contained a few lines written in a rather pretty handwriting, thought Cosette, and very fine.

Cosette looked for a name, there was none; a signature, there was none. To whom was it addressed? to her probably, since a hand had placed the packet upon her seat. From whom did it come? An irresistible fascination took possession of her, she endeavoured to turn her eyes away from these leaves which trembled in her hand, she looked at the sky, the street, the acacias all steeped in light, some pigeons which were flying about a neighbouring roof, then all at once her eye eagerly sought the manuscript, and she said to herself that she must know what there was in it.

This is what she read:

4. A heart under a stone

THE REDUCTION of the universe to a single being, the expansion of a single being even to God, this is love.

*

Love is the salutation of the angel to the stars.

*

How sad is the soul when it is sad from love!

*

What a void is the absence of the being who alone fills the world! Oh! how true it is that the beloved being becomes God! One would conceive that God would be jealous if the Father of all had not evidently made creation for the soul, and the soul for love!

*

A glimpse of a smile under a white crape hat with a lilac coronet is enough, for the soul to enter into the palace of dreams.

*

God is behind all things, but all things hide God. Things are black, creatures are opaque. To love a being, is to render her transparent.

*

Certain thoughts are prayers. There are moments when, whatever be the attitude of the body, the soul is on its knees.

*

Separated lovers deceive absence by a thousand chimerical things which still have their reality. They are prevented from seeing each other, they cannot write to each other; they find a multitude of mysterious means of correspondence. They commission the song of the birds, the perfume of flowers, the laughter of children, the light of the sun, the sighs of the wind, the beams of the stars, the whole creation. And why not? All the works of God were made to serve love. Love is powerful enough to charge all nature with its messages.

O spring! thou art a letter which I write to her.

*

The future belongs still more to the heart than to the mind. To love is the only thing which can occupy and fill up eternity. The infinite requires the inexhaustible.

*

Love partakes of the soul itself. It is of the same nature. Like it, it is a divine spark; like it, it is incorruptible, indivisible, imperishable. It is a point of fire which is within us, which is immortal and infinite, which nothing can limit and which nothing can extinguish. We feel it burn even in the marrow of our bones, and we see it radiate even to the depths of the sky.

*

O love! adorations! light of two minds which comprehend each other, of two hearts which are interchanged, of two glances which interpenetrate! You will come to me, will you not, happiness? Walks together in the solitudes! days blessed and radiant! I have sometimes dreamed that from time to time hours detached themselves from the life of the angels and came here below to pass through the destiny of men.

*

God can add nothing to the happiness of those who love one another, but to give them unending duration. After a life of love, an eternity of love is an augmentation indeed; but to increase in its intensity the ineffable felicity which love gives to the soul in this world, is impossible, even with God. God is the plenitude of heaven; love is the plenitude of man.

*

You look at a star from two motives, because it is luminous and because it is impenetrable. You have at your side a softer radiance and a greater mystery, woman.

*

We all, whoever we may be, have our respirable beings. If they fail us, the air fails us, we stifle, then we die. To die for lack of love is horrible. The asphyxia of the soul.

*

When love has melted and mingled two beings into an angelic and sacred unity, the secret of life is found for them; they are then but the two terms of a single destiny; they are then but the two wings of a single spirit. Love, soar!

*

The day that a woman who is passing before you sheds a light upon you as she goes, you are lost, you love. You have then but one thing to do: to think of her so earnestly that she will be compelled to think of you.

*

What love begins can be finished only by God.

*

True love is in despair and in raptures over a glove lost or a handkerchief found, and it requires eternity for its devotion and its hopes. It is composed at the same time of the infinitely great and the infinitely small.

*

If you are stone, be loadstone, if you are plant, be sensitive, if you are man, be love.

*

Nothing suffices love. We have happiness, we wish for paradise; we have paradise, we wish for Heaven.

O ye who love each other, all this is in love. Be wise enough to find it. Love has, as much as Heaven, contemplation, and more than Heaven, passionate delight.

*

'Does she still come to the Luxembourg?' 'No, monsieur.' 'She hears mass in this church, does she not?' 'She comes here no more.' 'Does she still live in this house?' 'She has moved away!' 'Whither has she gone to live?' 'She did not say.'

What a gloomy thing, not to know the address of one's soul?

*

Love has its childlikenesses, the other passions have their littlenesses. Shame on the passions which render man little! Honour to that which makes him a child!

*

There is a strange thing, do you know it? I am in the night. There is a being who has gone away and carried the heavens with her.

Oh! to be laid side by side in the same tomb, hand clasped in hand, and from time to time, in the darkness, to caress a finger gently, that would suffice for my eternity.

*

You who suffer because you love, love still more. To die of love, is to live by it.

*

Love. A sombre starry transfiguration is mingled with this crucifixion. There is ecstasy in the agony.

*

O joy of the birds! it is because they have their nest that they have their song.

*

Love is a celestial respiration of the air of paradise.

*

Deep hearts, wise minds take life as God has made it; it is a long trial, an unintelligible preparation for the unknown destiny. This destiny, the true one, begins for man at the first step in the interior of the tomb. Then something appears to him, and he begins to discern the definite. The definite, think of this word. The living see the infinite; the definite reveals itself only to the dead. Meantime, love and suffer, hope and contemplate. Woe, alas! to him who shall have loved bodies, forms, appearances only. Death will take all from him. Try to love souls, you shall find them again.

*

I met in the street a very poor young man who was in love. His hat was old, his coat was threadbare – there were holes at his elbows; the water passed through his shoes and the stars through his soul.

*

What a grand thing, to be loved? What a grander thing still, to love? The heart becomes heroic through passion. It is no longer composed of anything but what is pure; it no longer rests upon anything but what is elevated and great. An unworthy thought can no more spring up in it than a nettle upon a glacier. The soul lofty and serene, inaccessible to common passions and common emotions, rising above the clouds and the shadows of this world, its follies, its falsehoods, its hates, its vanities, its miseries, inhabits the blue of the skies, and only feels more the deep and subterranean commotions of destiny, as the summit of the mountains feels the quaking of the earth.

Were there not someone who loved, the sun would be extinguished.

5. *Cosette after the letter*

During the reading, Cosette entered gradually into reverie. At the moment she raised her eyes from the last line of the last page, the handsome officer, it was his hour, passed triumphant before the grating. Cosette thought him hideous.

She began again to contemplate the letter. It was written in a ravishing handwriting, thought Cosette; in the same hand, but with different inks, sometimes very black, sometimes pale, as ink is put into the ink-stand, and consequently on different days. It was then a thought which had poured itself out there, sigh by sigh, irregularly, without order, without choice, without aim, at hazard. Cosette had never read anything like it. This manuscript, in which she found still more clearness than obscurity, had the effect upon her of a half-opened sanctuary. Each of these mysterious lines was resplendent to her eyes, and flooded her heart with a strange light. The education which she had received had always spoken to her of the soul and never of love, almost like one who should speak of the brand and not of the flame. This manuscript of fifteen pages revealed to her suddenly and sweetly the whole of love, the sorrow, the destiny, the life, the eternity, the beginning, the end. It was like a hand which had opened and thrown suddenly upon her a handful of sunbeams. She felt in these few lines a passionate, ardent, generous, honest nature, a consecrated will, an immense sorrow and a boundless hope, an oppressed heart, a glad ecstasy. What was this manuscript? a letter. A letter with no address, no name, no date, no signature, intense and disinterested, an enigma composed of truths, a message of love made to be brought by an angel and read by a virgin, a rendezvous given beyond the earth, a love-letter from a phantom to a shade. He was a calm yet exhausted absent one, who seemed ready to take refuge in death, and who sent to the absent Her the secret of destiny, the key of life, love. It had been written with the foot in the grave and the finger in Heaven. These lines, fallen one by one upon the paper, were what might be called drops of soul.

Now these pages, from whom could they come? Who could have written them?

Cosette did not hesitate for a moment. One single man.

He!

Day had revived in her mind; all had appeared again. She felt a wonderful joy and deep anguish. It was he! he who wrote to her! he who was there! he whose arm had passed through that grating! While she was forgetting him, he had found her again! But had she forgotten him? No, never! She was mad to have thought so for a moment. She had always loved him, always adored him. The fire had been covered and had smouldered for a time, but she clearly saw it had only sunk in the deeper, and now it burst out anew and fired her whole being. This letter was like a spark dropped from that other soul into hers. She felt the conflagration rekindling. She was penetrated by every word of the manuscript: 'Oh yes!' said she, 'how I recognise all this! This is what I had already read in his eyes.'

As she finished it for the third time, Lieutenant Théodule returned before the grating, and rattled his spurs on the pavement. Cosette mechanically raised her eyes. She thought him flat, stupid, silly, useless, conceited, odious, impertinent, and very ugly. The officer thought it his duty to smile. She turned away insulted and indignant. She would have been glad to have thrown something at his head.

She fled, went back to the house and shut herself up in her room to read over the manuscript again, to learn it by heart, and to muse. When she had read it well, she kissed it, and put it in her bosom.

It was done. Cosette had fallen back into the profound seraphic love. The abyss of Eden had reopened.

All that day Cosette was in a sort of stupefaction. She could hardly think, her ideas were like a tangled skein in her brain. She could really conjecture nothing, she hoped while yet trembling, what? vague things. She dared to promise herself nothing, and she would refuse herself nothing. Pallors passed over her face and chills over her body. It seemed to her at moments that she was entering the chimerical; she said to herself, 'is it real?' then she felt of the beloved paper under her dress, she pressed it against her heart, she felt its corners upon her flesh, and if Jean Valjean had seen her at that moment, he would have shuddered before that luminous and unknown joy which flashed from her eyes. 'Oh yes!' thought she, 'it is indeed he! this comes from him for me!'

And she said to herself, that an intervention of angels, that a celestial chance had restored him to her.

O transfigurations of love! O dreams! this celestial chance, this intervention of angels, was that bullet of bread thrown by one robber to another robber, from the Charlemagne court to La Fosse aux Lions, over the roofs of La Force.

6. The old are made to go out when convenient

WHEN EVENING CAME, Jean Valjean went out; Cosette dressed herself. She arranged her hair in the manner which best became her, and she put on a dress the neck of which, as it had received one cut of the scissors too much, and as, by this slope, it allowed the turn of the neck to be seen, was, as young girls say, 'a little immodest'. It was not the least in the world immodest, but it was prettier than otherwise. She did all this without knowing why.

Did she intend to go out? no.

Did she expect a visit? no.

At dusk, she went down to the garden. Toussaint was busy in her kitchen, which looked out upon the back-yard.

She began to walk under the branches, putting them aside with her hand from time to time, because there were some that were very low.

She thus reached the seat.

The stone was still there.

She sat down, and laid her soft white hand upon that stone as if she would caress it and thank it.

All at once, she had that indefinable impression which we feel, though we see nothing, when there is somebody standing behind us.

She turned her head and arose.

It was he.

He was bareheaded. He appeared pale and thin. She hardly discerned his black dress. The twilight dimmed his fine forehead, and covered his eyes with darkness. He had, under a veil of incomparable sweetness, something of death and of night. His face was lighted by the light of a dying day, and by the thought of a departing soul.

It seemed as if he was not yet a phantom, and was now no longer a man.

His hat was lying a few steps distant in the shrubbery.

Cosette, ready to faint, did not utter a cry. She drew back slowly, for she felt herself attracted forward. He did not stir. Through the sad and ineffable something which enwrapped him, she felt the look of his eyes, which she did not see.

Cosette, in retreating, encountered a tree, and leaned against it. But for this tree, she would have fallen.

Then she heard his voice, that voice which she had never really heard, hardly rising above the rustling of the leaves, and murmuring:

'Pardon me, I am here. My heart is bursting, I could not live as I was, I have come. Have you read what I placed there, on this seat? do you recognise me at all? do not be afraid of me. It is a long time now, do you remember the day when you looked upon me? it was at the Luxembourg, near the Gladiator. And the day when you passed before me? it was the 16th of June and the 2nd of July. It will soon be a year. For a very long time now, I have not seen you at all. I asked the chairkeeper, she told me that she saw you no more. You lived in the Rue de l'Ouest, on the third floor front, in a new house, you see that I know! I followed you. What was I to do? And then you disappeared. I thought I saw you pass once when I was reading the papers under the arches of the Odéon. I ran. But no. It was a person who had a hat like yours. At night, I come here. Do not be afraid, nobody sees me. I come for a near look at your windows. I walk very softly that you may not hear, for perhaps you would be afraid. The other evening I was behind you, you turned round, I fled. Once I heard you sing. I was happy. Does it disturb you that I should hear you sing through the shutters? it can do you no harm. It cannot, can it? See, you are my angel, let me come sometimes; I believe I am going to die. If you but knew! I adore you! Pardon me, I am talking to you, I do not know what I am saying to you, perhaps I annoy you, do I annoy you?'

'O mother!' said she.

And she sank down upon herself as if she were dying.

He caught her, she fell, he caught her in his arms, he grasped her tightly, unconscious of what he was doing. He supported her even while tottering himself. He felt as if his head were enveloped in smoke; flashes of light passed through his eyelids; his ideas vanished; it seemed to him that he was performing a religious act, and that he was committing a profanation. Moreover, he did not feel one passionate emotion for this ravishing woman, whose form he felt against his heart. He was lost in love.

She took his hand and laid it on her heart. He felt the paper there, and stammered:

'You love me, then?'

She answered in a voice so low that it was no more than a breath which could scarcely be heard:

'Hush! you know it!'

And she hid her blushing head in the bosom of the proud and intoxicated young man.

He fell upon the seat, she by his side. There were no more words. The stars were beginning to shine. How was it that their lips met? How is it that the bird sings, that the snow melts, that the rose opens, that May blooms, that the dawn whitens behind the black trees on the shivering summit of the hills?

One kiss, and that was all.

Both trembled, and they looked at each other in the darkness with brilliant eyes.

They felt neither the fresh night, nor the cold stone, nor the damp ground, nor the wet grass, they looked at each other, and their hearts were full of thought. They had clasped hands, without knowing it.

She did not ask him, she did not even think of it, in what way and by what means he had succeeded in penetrating into the garden. It seemed so natural to her that he should be there!

From time to time Marius' knee touched Cosette's knee, which gave them both a thrill.

At intervals, Cosette faltered out a word. Her soul trembled upon her lips like a drop of dew upon a flower.

Gradually they began to talk. Overflow succeeded to silence, which is fullness. The night was serene and splendid above their heads. These two beings, pure as spirits, told each other all their dreams, their frenzies, their ecstasies, their chimeras, their despondencies, how they had adored each other from afar, how they had longed for each other, their despair when they had ceased to see each other. They confided to each other in an intimacy of the ideal, which even now nothing could have increased, all that was most hidden and most mysterious of themselves. They related to each other, with a candid faith in their illusions, all that love, youth, and that remnant of childhood was theirs, suggested to their thought. These two hearts poured themselves out into each other, so that at the end of an hour, it was the young man who had the young girl's soul and the young girl who had the soul of the young man. They interpenetrated, they enchanted, they dazzled each other.

When they had finished, when they had told each other everything, she laid her head upon his shoulder, and asked him:

'What is your name?'

'My name is Marius,' said he. 'And yours?'

'My name is Cosette.'

BOOK 6: LITTLE GAVROCHE

1. A malevolent trick of the wind

SINCE 1823, and while the Montfermeil chop-house was gradually foundering and being swallowed up, not in the abyss of a bankruptcy, but in the sink of petty debts, the Thénardier couple had had two more children; both male. This made five; two girls and three boys. It was a good many.

The Thénardiess had disembarrassed herself of the two last, while yet at an early age and quite small, with singular good fortune.

Disembarrassed is the word. There was in this woman but a fragment of nature. A phenomenon, moreover, of which there is more than one example. Like Madame la Maréchale de La Mothe Houdancourt, the Thénardiess was a mother only to her daughters. Her maternity ended there. Her hatred of the human race began with her boys. On the side towards her sons, her malignity was precipitous, and her heart had at that spot a fearful escarpment. As we have seen, she detested the eldest; she execrated the two others. Why? Because. The most terrible of motives and the most unanswerable of responses: Because. 'I have no use for a squalling pack of children,' said this mother.

We must explain how the Thénardiers had succeeded in disencumbering themselves of their two youngest children, and even in deriving a profit from them.

This Magnon girl, spoken of some pages back, was the same who had succeeded in getting her two children endowed by goodman Gillenormand. She lived on the Quai des Célestins, at the corner of that ancient Rue du Petit Musc which has done what it could to change its evil renown into good odour. Many will remember that great epidemic of croup which desolated, thirty-five years ago, the quarters bordering on the Seine at Paris, and of which science took advantage to experiment on a large scale as to the efficacy of insufflations of alum, now so happily replaced by the tincture of iodine externally applied. In that epidemic, Magnon lost her two boys, still very young, on the same day, one in the morning, the other at night. This was a blow. These children were precious to their mother; they represented eighty francs a month. These eighty francs were paid with great exactness, in the name of M. Gillenormand, by his rent-agent, M. Barge, retired constable, Rue du Roi de Sicile. The children dead, the income was buried. Magnon sought for an expedient. In that dark masonry of evil of which she was a part, everything is known, secrets are kept, and each aids the other. Magnon needed two children! the Thénardiess had two. Same sex, same age. Good arrangement for one, good investment for the other. The little Thénardiers became the little Magnons. Magnon left the Quai des Célestins and went to live in the Rue Clocheperce. In Paris, the identity which binds an individual to himself is broken from one street to another.

The government, not being notified, did not object, and the substitution took place in the most natural way in the world. Only Thénardier demanded, for this loan of children, ten francs a month, which Magnon promised, and even paid. It need not be said that Monsieur Gillenormand continued to pay. He came twice a year, to see the little ones. He did not perceive the change. 'Monsieur,' said Magnon to him, 'how much they look like you.'

Thénardier, to whom avatars were easy, seized this opportunity to become Jondrette. His two girls and Gavroche had hardly had time to perceive that they had two little brothers. At a certain depth of misery, men are possessed by a sort of spectral indifference, and look upon their fellow beings as upon goblins. Your nearest relatives are often but vague forms of shadow for you, hardly distinct from the nebulous background of life, and easily reblended with the invisible.

On the evening of the day she had delivered her two little ones to Magnon, expressing her willingness freely to renounce them for ever, the Thénardiess had, or feigned to have, a scruple. She said to her husband: 'But this is abandoning one's children!' Thénardier, magisterial and phlegmatic, cauterised the scruple with this phrase: 'Jean Jacques Rousseau did better!' From scruple the mother passed to anxiety: 'But suppose the police come to torment us? What we have done here, Monsieur Thénardier, say now, is it lawful?' Thénardier answered: 'Everything is lawful. Nobody will see it but the sky. Moreover, with children who have not a sou, nobody has any interest to look closely into it.'

Magnon had a kind of elegance in crime. She made a toilette. She shared her rooms, furnished in a gaudy yet wretched style, with a shrewd Frenchified English thief. This naturalised Parisian English woman, recommendable by very rich connections, intimately acquainted with the medals of the Bibliothèque and the diamonds of Mademoiselle Mars, afterwards became famous in the judicial records. She was called *Mamselle Miss.*

The two little ones who had fallen to Magnon had nothing to complain of. Recommended by the eighty francs, they were taken care of, as everything is which is a matter of business; not badly clothed, not badly fed, treated almost like 'little gentlemen', better with the false mother than with the true. Magnon acted the lady and did not talk argot before them.

They passed some years thus: Thénardier augured well of it. It occurred to him one day to say to Magnon who brought him his monthly ten francs, '*The father* must give them an education.'

Suddenly, these two poor children, till then well cared for, even by their ill fortune, were abruptly thrown out into life, and compelled to begin it.

A numerous arrest of malefactors like that of the Jondrette garret, necessarily complicated with ulterior searches and seizures, is really a disaster for this hideous occult counter-society which lives beneath public society; an event like this involves every description of misfortune in that gloomy world. The catastrophe of the Thénardiers produced the catastrophe of Magnon.

One day, a short time after Magnon handed Eponine the note relative to the Rue Plumet, there was a sudden descent of the police in the Rue Clocheperce. Magnon was arrested as well as Mamselle Miss, and the whole household, which was suspicious, was included in the haul. The two little boys were playing at the time in a back-yard, and saw nothing of the raid. When they wanted to go in, they found the door closed and the house empty. A cobbler, whose shop was opposite, called them and handed them a paper which 'their mother' had left for them. On the paper there was an address: M. Barge, rent-agent, Rue du Roi de Sicile, No. 8. The man of the shop said to them: 'You don't live here any more. Go there – it is near by – the first street to the left. Ask your way with this paper.'

The children started, the elder leading the younger, and holding in his hand the paper which was to be their guide. He was cold, and his benumbed little fingers had but an awkward grasp, and held the paper loosely. As they were turning out of the Rue Clocheperce, a gust of wind snatched it from him, and, as night was coming on, the child could not find it again.

They began to wander, as chance led them, in the streets.

2. *In which Little Gavroche takes advantage of Napoleon the Great*

Spring in Paris is often accompanied with keen and sharp north winds, by which one is not exactly frozen, but frost-bitten; these winds, which mar the most beautiful days, have precisely the effect of those currents of cold air which enter a warm room through the cracks of an ill-closed window or door. It seems as if the dreary door of winter were partly open and the wind were coming in at it. In the spring of 1832, the time when the first great epidemic of this century broke out in Europe, these winds were sharper and more piercing than ever. A door still more icy than that of winter was ajar. The door of the sepulchre. The breath of the cholera was felt in those winds.

In the meteorological point of view, these cold winds had this peculiarity, that they did not exclude a strong electric tension. Storms accompanied by thunder and lightning were frequent during this time.

One evening when these winds were blowing harshly, to that degree that January seemed returned, and the bourgeois had resumed their cloaks, little Gavroche, always shivering cheerfully under his rags, was standing, as if in ecstasy, before a wig-maker's shop in the neighbourhood of the Orme Saint Gervais. He was adorned with a woman's woollen shawl, picked up nobody knows where, of which he had made a muffler. Little Gavroche appeared to be intensely admiring a wax bride, with bare neck and a head-dress of orange flowers, which was revolving behind the sash, exhibiting, between two lamps, its smile to the passers; but in reality he was watching the shop to see if he could not 'chiper' a cake of soap from the front, which he would afterwards sell for a sou to a hairdresser in the banlieue. It often happened that he breakfasted upon one of these cakes. He called this kind of work, for which he had some talent, 'shaving the barbers'.

As he was contemplating the bride and squinting at the cake of soap, he muttered between his teeth: 'Tuesday. It isn't Tuesday. Is it Tuesday? Perhaps it is Tuesday. Yes, it is Tuesday.'

Nobody ever discovered to what this monologue related.

If, perchance, this soliloquy referred to the last time he had dined, it was three days before, for it was then Friday.

The barber in his shop, warmed by a good stove, was shaving a customer and casting from time to time a look towards this enemy, this frozen and brazen *gamin*, who had both hands in his pockets, but his wits evidently out of their sheath.

While Gavroche was examining the bride, the windows, and the Windsor soap, two children of unequal height, rather neatly dressed, and still smaller than he, one appearing to be seven years old, the other five, timidly turned the knob of the door and entered the shop, asking for something, charity, perhaps, in a plaintive manner which rather resembled a groan than a prayer. They both spoke at once, and their words were unintelligible because sobs choked the voice of the younger, and the cold made the elder's teeth chatter. The barber turned with a furious face, and without leaving his razor, crowding back the elder with his left hand and the little one with his knee, pushed them into the street and shut the door, saying:

'Coming and freezing people for nothing!'

The two children went on, crying. Meanwhile a cloud had come up; it began to rain.

Little Gavroche ran after them and accosted them:

'What is the matter with you, little brats?'

'We don't know where to sleep,' answered the elder.

'Is that all?' said Gavroche. 'That is nothing. Does anybody cry for that? Are they canaries then?'

And assuming, through his slightly bantering superiority, a tone of softened authority and gentle protection:

'*Momacques*, come with me.'

'Yes, monsieur,' said the elder.

And the two children followed him as they would have followed an archbishop. They had stopped crying.

Gavroche led them up the Rue Saint Antoine in the direction of the Bastille.

Gavroche, as he travelled on, cast an indignant and retrospective glance at the barber's shop.

'He has no heart, that *merlan*,' he muttered. 'He is an *Angliche*.'

A girl, seeing them all three marching in a row, Gavroche at the head, broke into a loud laugh. This laugh was lacking in respect for the group.

'Good-day, Mamselle Omnibus,' said Gavroche to her.

A moment afterwards, the barber recurring to him, he added:

'I am mistaken in the animal; he isn't a *merlan*, he is a snake. Wig-maker, I am going after a locksmith, and I will have a rattle made for your tail.'

This barber had made him aggressive. He apostrophised, as he leaped across a brook, a portress with a beard fit to meet Faust upon the Brocken, who had her broom in her hand.

'Madame,' said he to her, 'you have come out with your horse, have you?'

And upon this, he splashed the polished boots of a passer with mud.

'Whelp!' cried the man, furious.

Gavroche lifted his nose above his shawl.

'Monsieur complains?'

'Of you!' said the passer.

'The bureau is closed,' said Gavroche. 'I receive no more complaints.'

Meanwhile, continuing up the street, he saw, quite frozen under a *porte-cochère*, a beggar girl of thirteen or fourteen, whose clothes were so short that her knees could be seen. The little girl was beginning to be too big a girl for that. Growth plays you such tricks. The skirt becomes short at the moment that nudity becomes indecent.

'Poor girl!' said Gavroche. 'She hasn't even any breeches. But here, take this.'

And, taking off all that good woollen which he had about his neck, he threw it upon the bony and purple shoulders of the beggar girl, where the muffler again became a shawl.

The little girl looked at him with an astonished appearance, and received the shawl in silence. At a certain depth of distress, the poor, in their stupor, groan no longer over evil, and are no longer thankful for good.

This done:

'Brrr!' said Gavroche, shivering worse than St Martin, who, at least, kept half his cloak.

At this brrr! the storm, redoubling its fury, became violent. These malignant skies punish good actions.

'Ah,' exclaimed Gavroche, 'what does this mean? It rains again! Good God, if this continues, I withdraw my subscription.'

And he continued his walk.

'It's all the same,' added he, casting a glance at the beggar girl who was cuddling herself under the shawl, 'there is somebody who has a famous peel.'

And, looking at the cloud, he cried:

'Caught!'

The two children limped along behind him.

As they were passing, by one of those thick grated lattices which indicate a baker's shop, for bread like gold is kept behind iron gratings, Gavroche turned:

'Ah, ha, *mômes*, have we dined?'

'Monsieur,' answered the elder, 'we have not eaten since early this morning.'

'You are then without father or mother?' resumed Gavroche, majestically.

'Excuse us, monsieur, we have a papa and mamma, but we don't know where they are.'

'Sometimes that's better than knowing,' said Gavroche, who was a thinker.

'It is two hours now,' continued the elder, 'that we have been walking; we have been looking for things in every corner, but we can find nothing.'

'I know,' said Gavroche. 'The dogs eat up everything.'

He resumed, after a moment's silence:

'Ah! we have lost our authors. We don't know now what we have done with them. That won't do, *gamins*. It is stupid to get lost like that for people of any age. Ah, yes, we must *licher* for all that.'

Still he asked them no questions. To be without a home, what could be more natural?

The elder of the two *mômes*, almost entirely restored to the quick unconcern of childhood, made this exclamation:

'It is very queer for all that. Mamma, who promised to take us to look for some blessed box, on Palm Sunday.'

'Neurs,' answered Gavroche.

'Mamma,' added the elder, 'is a lady who lives with Mamselle Miss.'

'Tanflûte,' replied Gavroche.

Meanwhile he had stopped, and for a few minutes he had been groping and fumbling in all sorts of recesses which he had in his rags.

Finally he raised his head with an air which was only intended for one of satisfaction, but which was in reality triumphant.

'Let us compose ourselves, *momignards*. Here is enough for supper for three.'

And he took a sou from one of his pockets.

Without giving the two little boys time for amazement, he pushed them both before him into the baker's shop, and laid his sou on the counter, crying:

'Boy! five centimes' worth of bread.'

The man, who was the master baker himself, took a loaf and a knife.

'In three pieces, boy!' resumed Gavroche, and he added with dignity: 'There are three of us.'

And seeing that the baker, after having examined the three costumes, had taken a black loaf, he thrust his finger deep into his nose with a respiration as imperious as if he had had the great Frederick's pinch of snuff at the end of his thumb, and threw full in the baker's face this indignant apostrophe:

'Whossachuav?'

Those of our readers who may be tempted to see in this summons of Gavroche to the baker a Russian or Polish word, or one of those savage cries which the Iowas and the Botocudos hurl at each other from one bank of a stream to the other in their solitudes, are informed that it is a phrase which they use every day (they, our readers), and which takes the place of this phrase: what is that you have? The baker understood perfectly well, and answered:

'Why! it is bread, very good bread of the second quality.'

'You mean *larton brutal*,'* replied Gavroche, with a calm cold disdain. 'White bread, boy! *larton savonne!* I am treating.'

The baker could not help smiling, and while he was cutting the white bread, he looked at them in a compassionate manner which offended Gavroche.

'Come, paper cap!' said he, 'what are you fathoming us like that for?'

All three placed end to end would hardly have made a fathom.

When the bread was cut, the baker put the sou in his drawer and Gavroche said to the two children:

'*Morfilez.*'

The little boys looked at him confounded.

Gavroche began to laugh:

'Ah! stop, that is true, they don't know yet, they are so small.'

And he added:

'Eat.'

* Black bread

At the same time he handed each of them a piece of bread.

And, thinking that the elder, who appeared to him more worthy of his conversation, deserved some special encouragement and ought to be relieved of all hesitation in regard to satisfying his appetite, he added, giving him the largest piece:

'Stick that in your gun.'

There was one piece smaller than the other two; he took it for himself.

The poor children were starving, Gavroche included. While they were tearing the bread with their fine teeth, they encumbered the shop of the baker who, now that he had received his pay, was regarding them ill-humouredly.

'Come into the street,' said Gavroche.

They went on in the direction of the Bastille.

From time to time when they were passing before a lighted shop, the smaller one stopped to look at the time by a leaden watch suspended from his neck by a string.

'Here is decidedly a real canary,' said Gavroche.

Then he thoughtfully muttered between his teeth:

'It's all the same, if I had any *mômes*, I would hug them tighter than this.'

As they finished their pieces of bread and reached the corner of that gloomy Rue des Ballets, at the end of which the low and forbidding wicket of La Force is seen:

'Hullo, is that you, Gavroche?' said somebody.

'Hullo, is that you, Montparnasse?' said Gavroche.

A man had just accosted the *gamin*, and this man was none other than Montparnasse, disguised with blue eye-glasses, but recognisable by Gavroche.

'Mastiff!' continued Gavroche, 'you have a peel the colour of a flaxseed poultice and blue spectacles like a doctor. You are in style, 'pon the word of an old man.'

'Hush!' said Montparnasse, 'not so loud.'

And he hastily drew Gavroche out of the light of the shops.

The two little boys followed mechanically, holding each other by the hand.

When they were under the black arch of a *porte-cochère*, sheltered from sight and from the rain:

'Do you know where I am going?' inquired Montparnasse.

'To the Abbey of Monte à Regret,' * said Gavroche.

'Joker!'

And Montparnasse continued:

'I am going to find Babet.'

'Ah!' said Gavroche, 'her name is Babet.' Montparnasse lowered his voice.

'Not her, his.'

'Ah Babet! '

'Yes, Babet.'

'I thought he was buckled.'

'He has slipped the buckle,' answered Montparnasse.

And he rapidly related to the *gamin* that, on the morning of that very day, Babet, having been transferred to the Conciergerie, had escaped by turning to the left instead of turning to the right in 'the vestibule of the Examination hall'.

* To the scaffold

Gavroche admired the skill.

'What a dentist!' said he.

Montparnasse added a few particulars in regard to Babet's escape and finished with:

'Oh! that is not all.'

Gavroche, while listening, had caught hold of a cane which Montparnasse had in his hand, he had pulled mechanically on the upper part, and the blade of a dagger appeared.

'Ah!' said he, pushing the dagger back hastily, 'you have brought your gendarme disguised as a bourgeois.'

Montparnasse gave him a wink.

'The deuce!' resumed Gavroche, 'then you are going to have a tussle with the *cognes*?'

'We don't know,' answered Montparnasse with an indifferent air. 'It is always well to have a pin about you.'

Gavroche insisted:

'What is it you are going to do tonight?'

Montparnasse took up the serious line anew and said, biting his syllables:

'Several things.'

And abruptly changing the conversation:

'By the way!'

'What?'

'A story of the other day. Just think of it. I meet a bourgeois. He makes me a present of a sermon and his purse. I put that in my pocket. A minute afterwards I feel in my pocket. There is nothing there.'

'Except the sermon,' said Gavroche.

'But you,' resumed Montparnasse, 'where are you going now?'

Gavroche showed his two protégés and said:

'I am going to put these children to bed.'

'Where do they sleep?'

'At my house.'

'Your house. Where is that?'

'At my house.'

'You have a room then?'

'Yes, I have a room.'

'And where is your room?'

'In the elephant,' said Gavroche.

Montparnasse, although by nature not easily astonished, could not restrain an exclamation:

'In the elephant?'

'Well, yes, in the elephant?' replied Gavroche, 'whossematruthat?'

This is also a word in the language which nobody writes and which everybody uses. Whossematruthat, signifies what is the matter with that?

The profound observation of the *gamin* recalled Montparnasse to calmness and to good sense. He appeared to return to more respectful sentiments for Gavroche's lodging.

'Indeed!' said he, 'yes, the elephant. Are you well off there?'

'Very well,' said Gavroche. 'There, really *chenument*. There are no draughts of wind as there are under the bridges.'

'How do you get in?'

'I get in.'

'There is a hole then?' inquired Montparnasse.

'Zounds! But it mustn't be told. It is between the forelegs. The *coqueurs* * haven't seen it.'

'And you climb up? Yes, I understand.'

'In a twinkling, crick, crack, it is done, all alone.'

After a moment, Gavroche added:

'For these little boys I shall have a ladder.'

Montparnasse began to laugh:

'Where the devil did you get these brats?'

Gavroche simply answered:

'They are some *momichards* a wig-maker made me a present of.'

Meanwhile Montparnasse had become thoughtful.

'You recognised me very easily,' he murmured.

He took from his pocket two little objects which were nothing but two quills wrapped in cotton and introduced one into each nostril. This made him a new nose.

'That changes you,' said Gavroche, 'you are not so ugly, you ought to keep so all the time.'

Montparnasse was a handsome fellow, but Gavroche was a scoffer.

'Joking aside,' asked Montparnasse, 'how do you like that?'

It was also another sound of voice. In the twinkling of an eye, Montparnasse had become unrecognisable.

'Oh! play us Punchinello!' exclaimed Gavroche.

The two little ones, who had not been listening till now, they had themselves been so busy in stuffing their fingers into their noses, were attracted by this name and looked upon Montparnasse with dawning joy and admiration.

Unfortunately Montparnasse was anxious.

He laid his hand on Gavroche's shoulder and said to him, dwelling upon his words:

'Listen to a digression, boy, if I were on the Square, with my *dogue*, my *dague*, and my *digue*, and if you were so prodigal as to offer me twenty great sous, I shouldn't refuse to *goupiner* † for them, but we are not on Mardi Gras.'

This grotesque phrase produced a singular effect upon the *gamin*. He turned hastily, cast his small sparkling eyes about him with intense attention, and perceived, within a few steps, a *sergent de ville*, whose back was turned to them. Gavroche let an 'ah, yes!' escape him, which he suppressed upon the spot, and shaking Montparnasse's hand:

'Well, good night,' said he, 'I am going to my elephant with my *mômes*. On the supposition that you should need me some night, you will come and find me there. I live in the second storey. There is no porter. You would ask for Monsieur Gavroche.'

'All right,' said Montparnasse.

And they separated, Montparnasse making his way towards the Grève and Gavroche towards the Bastille. The little five-year-old drawn along by his brother, whom Gavroche was drawing along, turned his head back several

* Spies, policemen † To labour

times to see 'Punchinello' going away.

The unintelligent phrase by which Montparnasse had warned Gavroche of the presence of the *sergent de ville*, contained no other talisman than the syllable *dig* repeated five or six times under various forms. This syllable *dig*, not pronounced singly, but artistically mingled with the words of a phrase, means: *Take care, we cannot talk freely*. There was furthermore in Montparnasse's phrase a literary beauty which escaped Gavroche, that is *my dogue, my dague, and my digue*, an expression of the argot of the Temple, which signifies *my dog, my knife, and my wife*, very much used among the Pitres and the Queues Rouges of the age of Louis XIV, when Molière wrote and Callot drew.

Twenty years ago, there was still to be seen in the south-east corner of the Place de la Bastille, near the canal basin dug in the ancient ditch of the prison citadel, a grotesque monument which has now faded away from the memory of Parisians, and which is worthy to leave some trace, for it was an idea of the 'member of the Institute, General-in-Chief of the Army of Egypt'.

We say monument, although it was only a rough model. But this rough model itself, a huge plan, a vast carcass of an idea of Napoleon which two or three successive gusts of wind had carried away and thrown each time further from us, had become historical, and had acquired a definiteness which contrasted with its provisional aspect. It was an elephant, forty feet high, constructed of framework and masonry, bearing on its back its tower, which resembled a house, formerly painted green by some house-painter, now painted black by the sun, the rain, and the weather. In that open and deserted corner of the Square, the broad front of the colossus, his trunk, his tusks, his size, his enormous rump, his four feet like columns, produced at night, under the starry sky, a startling and terrible outline. One knew not what it meant. It was a sort of symbol of the force of the people. It was gloomy, enigmatic, and immense. It was a mysterious and mighty phantom, visibly standing by the side of the invisible spectre of the Bastille.

Few strangers visited this edifice, no passer-by looked at it. It was falling into ruin; every season, the mortar which was detached from its sides made hideous wounds upon it. 'The ædiles', as they say in fashionable dialect, had forgotten it since 1814. It was there in its corner, gloomy, diseased, crumbling, surrounded by a rotten railing, continually besmeared by drunken coachmen; crevices marked up the belly, a lath was sticking out from the tail, the tall grass came far up between its legs; and as the level of the square had been rising for thirty years all about it, by that slow and continuous movement which insensibly raises the soil of great cities, it was in a hollow, and it seemed as if the earth sank under it. It was huge, contemned, repulsive, and superb; ugly to the eye of the bourgeois; melancholy to the eye of the thinker. It partook, to some extent, of a filth soon to be swept away, and, to some extent, of a majesty soon to be decapitated.

As we have said, night changed its appearance. Night is the true medium for everything which is shadowy. As soon as twilight fell, the old elephant became transfigured; he assumed a tranquil and terrible form in the fearful serenity of the darkness. Being of the past, he was of the night; and this obscurity was fitting to his greatness.

This monument, rude, squat, clumsy, harsh, severe, almost deformed, but certainly majestic, and impressed with a sort of magnificent and savage seriousness, has disappeared, leaving a peaceable reign to the kind of gigantic stove, adorned with its stove-pipe, which has taken the place of the forbidding nine-towered fortress, almost as the bourgeoisie replaces feudality. It is very natural that a stove should be the symbol of an epoch of which a tea-kettle contains the power. This period will pass away, it is already passing away; we are beginning to understand that, if there may be force in a boiler, there can be power only in a brain; in other words, that what leads and controls the world, is not locomotives, but ideas. Harness the locomotives to the ideas, very well; but do not take the horse for the horseman.

However, this may be, to return to the Place de la Bastille, the architect of the elephant had succeeded in making something grand with plaster; the architect of the stove-pipe has succeeded in making something petty with bronze.

This stove-pipe, which was baptised with a sonorous name and called the Column of July, this would-be monument of an abortive revolution, was still, in 1832, enveloped in an immense frame-work covering, which we for our part still regret, and by a large board enclosure, which completed the isolation of the elephant.

It was towards this corner of the square, dimly lighted by the reflection of a distant lamp, that the *gamin* directed the two '*mômes*.'

We must be permitted to stop here long enough to declare that we are within the simple reality, and that twenty years ago the police tribunals would have had to condemn upon a complaint for vagrancy and breach of a public monument, a child who should have been caught sleeping in the interior even of the elephant of the Bastille. This fact stated, we continue.

As they came near the colossus, Gavroche comprehended the effect which the infinitely great may produce upon the infinitely small, and said:

'Brats! don't be frightened.'

Then he entered through a gap in the fence into the enclosure of the elephant, and helped the *mômes* to crawl through the breach. The two children, a little frightened, followed Gavroche without saying a word, and trusted themselves to that little Providence in rags who had given them bread and promised them a lodging.

Lying by the side of the fence was a ladder, which, by day, was used by the working-men of the neighbouring wood-yard. Gavroche lifted it with singular vigour, and set it up against one of the elephant's fore legs. About the point where the ladder ended, a sort of black hole could be distinguished in the belly of the colossus.

Gavroche showed the ladder and the hole to his guests, and said to them:

'Mount and enter.'

The two little fellows looked at each other in terror.

'You are afraid, *mômes!*' exclaimed Gavroche.

And he added:

'You shall see.'

He clasped the elephant's wrinkled foot, and in a twinkling, without deigning to make use of the ladder, he reached the crevice. He entered it as an adder glides into a hole, and disappeared, and a moment afterwards the two children saw his pallid face dimly appearing like a faded and wan form, at the edge of the hole full of darkness.

'Well,' cried he,' why don't you come up, *momignards*? you'll see how nice it is! Come up,' said he, to the elder, 'I will give you a hand.'

The little ones urged each other forward. The *gamin* made them afraid and reassured them at the same time, and then it rained very hard. The elder ventured. The younger, seeing his brother go up, and himself left all alone between the paws of this huge beast, had a great desire to cry, but he did not dare.

The elder clambered up the rounds of the ladder. He tottered badly. Gavroche, while he was on his way, encouraged him with the exclamations of a fencing master to his scholars, or of a muleteer to his mules:

'Don't be afraid!'

'That's it!'

'Come on!'

'Put your foot there!'

'Your hand here!'

'Be brave!'

And when he came within his reach he caught him quickly and vigorously by the arm and drew him up.

'Gulped!' said he.

The *môme* had passed through the crevice.

'Now,' said Gavroche, 'wait for me. Monsieur, have the kindness to sit down.'

And, going out by the crevice as he had entered, he let himself glide with the agility of a monkey along the elephant's leg, he dropped upon his feet in the grass, caught the little five-year-old by the waist and set him half way up the ladder, then he began to mount up behind him, crying to the elder:

'I will push him; you pull him.'

In an instant the little fellow was lifted, pushed, dragged, pulled, stuffed, crammed into the hole without having had time to know what was going on. And Gavroche, entering after him, pushing back the ladder with a kick so that it fell upon the grass, began to clap his hands, and cried:

'Here we are! Hurrah for General Lafayette!'

This explosion over, he added:

'Brats, you are in my house.'

Gavroche was in fact at home.

O unexpected utility of the useless! charity of great things! goodness of giants! This monstrous monument which had contained a thought of the emperor, had become the box of a *gamin*. The *môme* had been accepted and sheltered by the colossus. The bourgeois in their Sunday clothes, who passed by the elephant of the Bastille, frequently said, eyeing it scornfully with their goggle eyes: 'What's the use of that?' The use of it was to save from the cold, the frost, the hail, the rain, to protect from the wintry wind, to preserve from sleeping in the mud, which breeds fever, and from sleeping in the snow, which breeds death, a little being with no father or mother, with no bread, no clothing, no asylum. The use of it was to receive the innocent whom society repelled. The use of it was to diminish the public crime. It was a den open for him to whom all doors were closed. It seemed as if the miserable old mastodon, invaded by vermin and oblivion, covered with warts, mould, and ulcers, tottering, worm-eaten, abandoned, condemned, a sort of colossal beggar asking in vain the alms of a benevolent look in the middle of the Square, had taken pity itself on this other beggar, the poor pigmy who went with no shoes to his feet, no roof over his head, blowing his fingers, clothed in rags, fed upon what is thrown away. This was the use of the elephant of the Bastille. This idea of

Napoleon, disdained by men, had been taken up by God. That which had been illustrious only, had become august. The emperor must have had, to realise what he meditated, porphyry, brass, iron, gold, marble; for God the old assemblage of boards, joists, and plaster was enough. The emperor had had a dream of genius; in this titanic elephant, armed, prodigious, brandishing his trunk, bearing his tower, and making the joyous and vivifying waters gush out on all sides about him, he desired to incarnate the people. God had done a grander thing with it, he lodged a child.

The hole by which Gavroche had entered was a break hardly visible from the outside, concealed as it was, and as we have said, under the belly of the elephant, and so narrow that hardly anything but cats and *mômes* could have passed through.

'Let us begin,' said Gavroche, 'by telling the porter that we are not in.'

And plunging into the obscurity with certainty, like one who is familiar with his room, he took a board and stopped the hole.

Gavroche plunged again into the obscurity. The children heard the sputtering of the taper plunged into the phosphoric bottle. The chemical taper was not yet in existence; the Fumade tinder-box represented progress at that period.

A sudden light made them wink; Gavroche had just lighted one of those bits of string soaked in resin which are called cellar-rats. The cellar-rats, which made more smoke than flame, rendered the inside of the elephant dimly visible.

Gavroche's two guests looked about them, and felt something like what one would feel who should be shut up in the great tun of Heidelberg, or better still, what Jonah must have felt in the Biblical belly of the whale. An entire and gigantic skeleton appeared to them, and enveloped them. Above, a long dusky beam, from which projected at regular distances massive encircling timbers, represented the vertebral column with its ribs, stalactites of plaster hung down like the viscera, and from one side to the other huge spider-webs made dusty diaphragms. Here and there in the corners great blackish spots were seen, which had the appearance of being alive, and which changed their places rapidly with a wild and startled motion.

The debris fallen from the elephant's back upon his belly had filled up the concavity, so that they could walk upon it as upon a floor.

The smaller one hugged close to his brother and said in a low tone:

'It is dark.'

This word made Gavroche cry out. The petrified air of the two *mômes* rendered a shock necessary.

'What is that you are driving at?' he exclaimed 'Are we humbugging? are we coming the disgusted? Must you have the Tuileries? would you be fools? Say, I inform you that I do not belong to the regiment of ninnies. Are you the brats of the pope's head-waiter?'

A little roughness is good for alarm. It is reassuring. The two children came close to Gavroche.

Gavroche, paternally softened by this confidence, passed 'from the grave to the gentle', and addressing himself to the smaller:

'Goosy,' said he to him, accenting the insult with a caressing tone, 'it is outside that it is dark. Outside it rains, here it doesn't rain; outside it is cold, here there isn't a speck of wind; outside there are heaps of folks, here there isn't anybody; outside there isn't even a moon, here there is my candle, by jinks!'

The two children began to regard the apartment with less fear; but Gavroche did not allow them much longer leisure for contemplation.

'Quick,' said he.

And he pushed them towards what we are very happy to be able to call the bottom of the chamber.

His bed was there.

Gavroche's bed was complete. That is to say, there was a mattress, a covering, and an alcove with curtains.

The mattress was a straw mat, the covering a large blanket of coarse grey wool, very warm and almost new. The alcove was like this:

Three rather long laths, sunk and firmly settled into the rubbish of the floor, that is to say of the belly of the elephant, two in front and one behind, and tied together by a string at the top, so as to form a pyramidal frame. This frame supported a fine trellis of brass wire which was simply hung over it, but artistically applied and kept in place by fastenings of iron wire, in such a way that it entirely enveloped the three laths. A row of large stones fixed upon the ground all about this trellis so as to let nothing pass. This trellis was nothing more nor less than a fragment of those copper nettings which are used to cover the bird-houses in menageries. Gavroche's bed under this netting was as if in a cage. Altogether it was like an Eskimo tent.

It was this netting which took the place of curtains.

Gavroche removed the stones a little which kept down the netting in front, and the two folds of the trellis which lay one over the other opened.

'*Mômes*, on your hands and knees!' said Gavroche.

He made his guests enter into the cage carefully, then he went in after them, creeping, pulled back the stones, and hermetically closed the opening.

They were all three stretched upon the straw.

Small as they were, none of them could have stood up in the alcove. Gavroche still held the cellar rat in his hand.

'Now,' said he, '*pioncez!* I am going to suppress the candelabra.'

'Monsieur,' inquired the elder of the two brothers, of Gavroche, pointing to the netting, 'what is that?'

'That,' said Gavroche gravely, 'is for the rats, *pioncez!*'

However, he felt it incumbent upon him to add a few words for the instruction of these beings of a tender age, and he continued:

'They are things from the Jardin des Plantes. They are used for ferocious animals. Tsaol [it is a whole] magazine full of them. Tsony [it is only] to mount over a wall, climb by a window and pass under a door. You get as much as you want.'

While he was talking, he wrapped a fold of the coverlet about the smaller one, who murmured:

'Oh! that is good! it is warm!'

Gavroche looked with satisfaction upon the coverlet.

'That is also from the Jardin des Plantes,' said he. 'I took that from the monkeys.'

And, showing the elder the mat upon which he was lying, a very thick mat and admirably made, he added:

'That was the giraffe's.'

After a pause, he continued:

'The beasts had all this. I took it from them. They didn't care. I told them: It is for the elephant.'

He was silent again and resumed:

'We get over the walls and we make fun of the government. That's all.'

The two children looked with a timid and stupefied respect upon this intrepid and inventive being, a vagabond like them, isolated like them, wretched like them, who was something wonderful and all-powerful, who seemed to them supernatural, and whose countenance was made up of all the grimaces of an old mountebank mingled with the most natural and most pleasant smile.

'Monsieur,' said the elder timidly, 'you are not afraid then of the *sergents de ville*?'

Gavroche merely answered:

'*Môme!* we don't say *sergents de ville*, we say *cognes*.'

The smaller boy had his eyes open, but he said nothing. As he was on the edge of the mat, the elder being in the middle, Gavroche tucked the coverlet under him as a mother would have done, and raised the mat under his head with some old rags in such a way as to make a pillow for the *môme*. Then he turned towards the elder:

'Eh! we are pretty well off, here!'

'Oh yes,' answered the elder, looking at Gavroche with the expression of a rescued angel.

The two poor little soaked children were beginning to get warm.

'Ah now,' continued Gavroche, 'what in the world were you crying for?'

And pointing out the little one to his brother:

'A youngster like that, I don't say, but a big boy like you, to cry is silly; it makes you look like a calf.'

'Well,' said the child, 'we had no room, no place to go.'

'Brat!' replied Gavroche, 'we don't say a room, we say a *piolle*.'

'And then we were afraid to be all alone like that in the night.'

'We don't say night, we say *sorgue*.'

'Thank you, monsieur,' said the child.

'Listen to me,' continued Gavroche, 'you must never whine any more for anything. I will take care of you. You will see what fun we have. In summer we will go to the Glacière with Navet, a comrade of mine, we will go in swimming in the Basin, we will run on the track before the Bridge of Austerlitz all naked, that makes the washerwomen mad. They scream, they scold, if you only knew how funny they are! We will go to see the skeleton man. He is alive. At the Champs Elysées. That parishioner is as thin as anything. And then I will take you to the theatre. I will take you to Frederick Lemaitre's. I have tickets, I know the actors, I even played once in a piece. We were *mômes* so high, we ran about under a cloth, that made the sea. I will have you engaged at my theatre. We will go and see the savages. They're not real, those savages. They have red tights which wrinkle, and you can see their elbows darned with white thread. After that, we will go to the Opera. We will go in with the claqueurs. The claque at the Opera is very select. I wouldn't go with the claque on the boulevards. At the Opera, just think, there are some who pay twenty sous, but they are fools. They call them dish-clouts. And then we will go to see the guillotining. I will show you the executioner. He lives in the Rue des Marais. Monsieur Sanson. There is a letter-box on his door. Oh! we have famous fun!'

At this moment, a drop of wax fell upon Gavroche's finger, and recalled him to the realities of life.

'The deuce!' said he, 'there's the match used up. Attention! I can't spend more than a sou a month for my illumination. When we go to bed, we must go to sleep. We haven't time to read the romances of Monsieur Paul de Kock. Besides the light might show through the cracks of the *porte-cochère*, and the *cognes* couldn't help seeing.'

'And then,' timidly observed the elder who alone dared to talk with Gavroche and reply to him, 'a spark might fall into the straw, we must take care not to burn the house up.'

'We don't say burn the house,' said Gavroche, 'we say *riffauder* the *bocard*.'

The storm redoubled. They heard, in the intervals of the thunder, the tempest beating against the back of the colossus.

'Pour away, old rain!' said Gavroche. 'It does amuse me to hear the decanter emptying along the house's legs. Winter is a fool; he throws away his goods, he loses his trouble, he can't wet us, and it makes him grumble, the old water-porter!'

This allusion to thunder, all the consequences of which Gavroche accepted as a philosopher of the nineteenth century, was followed by a very vivid flash, so blinding that something of it entered by the crevice into the belly of the elephant. Almost at the same instant the thunder burst forth very furiously. The two little boys uttered a cry, and rose so quickly that the trellis was almost thrown out of place; but Gavroche turned his bold face towards them, and took advantage of the clap of thunder to burst into a laugh.

'Be calm, children. Don't upset the edifice. That was fine thunder; give us some more. That wasn't any fool of a flash. Bravo God! by jinks! that is most as good as it is at the theatre.'

This said, he restored order in the trellis, gently pushed the two children to the head of the bed, pressed their knees to stretch them out at full length, and exclaimed:

'As God is lighting his candle, I can blow out mine. Children, we must sleep, my young humans. It is very bad not to sleep. It would make you *schlinguer* in your strainer, or, as the big bugs say, stink in your jaws. Wind yourselves up well in the peel! I'm going to extinguish. Are you all right?'

'Yes,' murmured the elder, 'I am right. I feel as if I had feathers under my head.'

'We don't say head,' cried Gavroche, 'we say *tronche*.'

The two children hugged close to each other. Gavroche finished arranging them upon the mat, and pulled the coverlet up to their ears, then repeated for the third time the injunction in hieratic language:

'*Pioncez!*'

And he blew out the taper.

Hardly was the light extinguished when a singular tremor began to agitate the trellis under which the three children were lying. It was a multitude of dull rubbings, which gave a metallic sound, as if claws and teeth were grinding the copper wire. This was accompanied by all sorts of little sharp cries.

The little boy of five, hearing this tumult over his head, and shivering with fear, pushed the elder brother with his elbow, but the elder brother had already '*pioncé*', according to Gavroche's order. Then the little boy, no longer capable of fearing him, ventured to accost Gavroche, but very low, and holding his breath:

'Monsieur?'

'Hey?' said Gavroche, who had just closed his eyes.

'What is that?'

'It is the rats,' answered Gavroche.

And he laid his head again upon the mat.

The rats, in fact, which swarmed by thousands in the carcase of the elephant, and which were those living black spots of which we have spoken, had been held in awe by the flame of the candle so long as it burned, but as soon as this cavern, which was, as it were, their city, had been restored to night, smelling there what the good story-teller Perrault calls 'some fresh meat', they had rushed in en masse upon Gavroche's tent, climbed to the top, and were biting its meshes as if they were seeking to get through this new-fashioned mosquito bar.

Still the little boy did not go to sleep.

'Monsieur!' he said again.

'Hey?' said Gavroche.

'What are the rats?'

'They are mice.'

This explanation reassured the child a little. He had seen some white mice in the course of his life, and he was not afraid of them. However, he raised his voice again:

'Monsieur?'

'Hey?' replied Gavroche.

'Why don't you have a cat?'

'I had one,' answered Gavroche, 'I brought one here, but they ate her up for me.'

This second explanation undid the work of the first, and the little fellow again began to tremble. The dialogue between him and Gavroche was resumed for the fourth time:

'Monsieur!'

'Hey?'

'Who was it that was eaten up?'.

'The cat.'

'Who was it that ate the cat?'

'The rats.'

'The mice?'

'Yes, the rats.'

The child, dismayed by these mice who ate cats, continued: 'Monsieur, would those mice eat us?'

'Golly!' said Gavroche.

The child's terror was complete. But Gavroche added:

'Don't be afraid! they can't get in. And then I am here. Here, take hold of my hand. Be still, and *pioncez!*'

Gavroche at the same time took the little fellow's hand across his brother. The child clasped this hand against his body, and felt safe. Courage and strength have such mysterious communications. It was once more silent about them, the sound of voices had startled and driven away the rats; in a few minutes they might have returned and done their worst in vain, the three *mômes*, plunged in slumber, heard nothing more.

The hours of the night passed away. Darkness covered the immense Place de la Bastille; a wintry wind, which mingled with the rain, blew in gusts, the patrolmen ransacked the doors, alleys, yards, and dark corners, and, looking for nocturnal vagabonds, passed silently by the elephant; the monster, standing, motionless, with open eyes in the darkness, appeared to be in reverie and well satisfied with his good deeds, and he sheltered from the heavens and from men the three poor sleeping children.

To understand what follows, we must remember that at that period the guardhouse of the Bastille was situated at the other extremity of the Square, and that what occurred near the elephant could neither be seen nor heard by the sentinel.

Towards the end of the hour which immediately precedes daybreak, a man turned out of the Rue Saint Antoine, running, crossed the Square, turned the great enclosure of the Column of July, and glided between the palisades under the belly of the elephant. Had any light whatever shone upon this man, from his thoroughly wet clothing, one would have guessed that he had passed the night in the rain. When under the elephant he raised a grotesque call, which belongs to no human language and which a parrot alone could reproduce. He twice repeated this call, of which the following orthography gives but a very imperfect idea:

'Kirikikiou!'

At the second call, a clear, cheerful young voice answered from the belly of the elephant:

'Yes!'

Almost immediately the board which closed the hole moved away, and gave passage to a child, who descended along the elephant's leg and dropped lightly near the man. It was Gavroche. The man was Montparnasse.

As to this call, *kirikikiou*, it was undoubtedly what the child meant by, *You will ask for Monsieur Gavroche*.

On hearing it he had waked with a spring, crawled out of his 'alcove', separating the netting a little, which he afterwards carefully closed again, then he had opened the trap and descended.

The man and the child recognised each other silently in the dark; Montparnasse merely said:

'We need you. Come and give us a lift.'

The *gamin* did not ask any other explanation.

'I'm on hand,' said he.

And they both took the direction of the Rue Saint Antoine, whence Montparnasse came, winding their way rapidly through the long file of market wagons which go down at that hour towards the market.

The market gardeners, crouching among the salads and vegetables, half asleep, buried up to the eyes in the boots of their wagons on account of the driving rain, did not even notice these strange passengers.

3. *The fortunes and misfortunes of escape*

WHAT HAD TAKEN PLACE that same night at La Force was this:

An escape had been concerted between Babet, Brujon, Gueulemer, and Thénardier, although Thénardier was in solitary. Babet had done the business for himself during the day, as we have seen from the account of Montparnasse to Gavroche. Montparnasse was to help them from without.

Brujon, having spent a month in a chamber of punishment, had had time, first, to twist a rope, secondly, to perfect a plan. Formerly these stern cells in which the discipline of the prison delivers the condemned to himself, were composed of four stone walls, a ceiling of stone, a pavement of tiles, a camp bed, a grated air-hole, a double iron door, and were called *dungeons;* but the dungeon has been thought too horrible; now it is composed of an iron door, a grated air-hole, a camp bed, a pavement of tiles, a ceiling of stone, four stone walls, and it is called *chamber of punishment.* There is a little light in them about noon. The inconvenience of these chambers, which, as we see, are not dungeons, is that they allow beings to reflect who should be made to work.

Brujon then had reflected, and he had gone out of the chamber of punishment with a rope. As he was reputed very dangerous in the Charlemagne Court, he was put into the Bâtiment Neuf. The first thing which he found in the Bâtiment Neuf was Gueulemer, the second was a nail; Gueulemer, that is to say crime, a nail, that is to say liberty.

Brujon, of whom it is time to give a complete idea, was, with an appearance of a delicate complexion and a profoundly premeditated languor, a polished, gallant, intelligent robber, with an enticing look and an atrocious smile. His look was a result of his will, and his smile of his nature. His first studies in his art were directed towards roofs; he had made a great improvement in the business of the lead strippers who despoil roofings and distrain eaves by the process called: *the double fat.*

What rendered the moment peculiarly favourable for an attempt at escape, was that some workmen were taking off and relaying, at that very time, a part of the slating of the prison. The Cour Saint Bernard was not entirely isolated from the Charlemagne Court and the Cour Saint Louis. There were scaffoldings and ladders up aloft; in other words, bridges and stairways leading towards deliverance.

Bâtiment Neuf, the most cracked and decrepit affair in the world, was the weak point of the prison. The walls were so much corroded by saltpetre that they had been obliged to put a facing of wood over the arches of the dormitories, because the stones detached themselves and fell upon the beds of the prisoners. Notwithstanding this decay, the blunder was committed of shutting up in the Bâtiment Neuf the most dangerous of the accused, of putting 'the hard cases' in there, as they say in prison language.

The Bâtiment Neuf contained four dormitories one above the other and an attic which was called the Bel Air. A large chimney, probably of some ancient kitchen of the Dukes de La Force, started from the ground floor, passed through the four storeys, cutting in two all the dormitories in which it appeared to be a kind of flattened pillar, and went out through the roof.

Gueulemer and Brujon were in the same dormitory. They had been put into the lower storey by precaution. It happened that the heads of their beds rested against the flue of the chimney.

Thénardier was exactly above them in the attic known as the Bel Air.

The passer who stops in the Rue Culture Sainte Catherine, beyond the barracks of the firemen, in front of the *porte-cochère* of the bath-house, sees a yard full of flowers and shrubs in boxes, at the further end of which is a little white rotunda with two wings enlivened by green blinds, the bucolic dream of Jean Jacques. Not more than ten years ago, above this rotunda there arose a black wall, enormous, hideous, and bare, against which it was built. This was the encircling wall of La Force.

This wall, behind this rotunda, was Milton seen behind Berquin.

High as it was, this wall was over-topped by a still blacker roof which could be seen behind. This was the roof of the Bâtiment Neuf. You noticed in it four dormer windows with gratings; these were the windows of the Bel Air. A chimney pierced the roof, the chimney which passed through the dormitories.

The Bel Air, this attic of the Bâtiment Neuf, was a kind of large garret hall, closed with triple gratings and double sheet iron doors studded with monstrous nails. Entering at the north end, you had on your left the four windows, and on your right, opposite the windows, four large square cages, with spaces between, separated by narrow passages, built breast-high of masonry with bars of iron to the roof.

Thénardier had been in solitary in one of these cages since the night of the 3rd of February. Nobody has ever discovered how, or by what contrivance, he had succeeded in procuring and hiding a bottle of that wine invented, it is said, by Desrues, with which a narcotic is mixed, and which the band of the *Endormeurs* has rendered celebrated.

There are in many prisons treacherous employees, half jailers and half thieves, who aid in escapes, who sell a faithless service to the police, and who make much more than their salary.

On this same night, then, on which little Gavroche had picked up the two wandering children, Brujon and Gueulemer, knowing that Babet, who had escaped that very morning, was waiting for them in the street as well as Montparnasse, got up softly and began to pierce the flue of the chimney which touched their beds, with the nail which Brujon had found. The fragments fell upon Brujon's bed, so that nobody heard them. The hail storm and the thunder shook the doors upon their hinges, and made a frightful and convenient uproar in the prison. Those of the prisoners who awoke made a feint of going to sleep again, and let Gueulemer and Brujon alone. Brujon was adroit; Gueulemer was vigorous. Before any sound had reached the watchman who was lying in the grated cell with a window opening into the sleeping-room, the wall was pierced, the chimney scaled, the iron trellis which closed the upper orifice of the flue forced, and the two formidable bandits were upon the roof. The rain and the wind redoubled, the roof was slippery.

'What a good *sorgue* for a *crampe*,' * said Brujon.

A gulf of six feet wide and eighty feet deep separated them from the encircling wall. At the bottom of this gulf they saw a sentinel's musket gleaming in the

* What a good night for an escape.

obscurity. They fastened one end of the rope which Brujon had woven in his cell, to the stumps of the bars of the chimney which they had just twisted off, threw the other end over the encircling wall, cleared the gulf at a bound, clung to the coping of the wall, bestrode it, let themselves glide one after the other down along the rope upon a little roof which adjoined the bath-house, pulled down their rope, leaped into the bath-house yard, crossed it, pushed open the porter's slide, near which hung the cord, pulled the cord, opened the *porte-cochère*, and were in the street.

It was not three-quarters of an hour since they had risen to their feet on their beds in the darkness, their nail in hand, their project in their heads.

A few moments afterwards they had rejoined Babet and Montparnasse, who were prowling about the neighbourhood.

In drawing down their rope, they had broken it, and there was a piece remaining fastened to the chimney on the roof. They had received no other damage than having pretty thoroughly skinned their hands.

That night Thénardier had received a warning, it never could be ascertained in what manner, and did not go to sleep.

About one o'clock in the morning, the night being very dark, he saw two shadows passing on the roof, in the rain and in the raging wind, before the window opposite his cage. One stopped at the window long enough for a look. It was Brujon. Thénardier recognised him, and understood. That was enough for him. Thénardier, described as an assassin, and detained under the charge of lying in wait by night with force and arms, was kept constantly in sight. A sentinel, who was relieved every two hours, marched with loaded gun before his cage. The Bel Air was lighted by a reflector. The prisoner had irons on his feet weighing fifty pounds. Every day, at four o'clock in the afternoon, a warden, escorted by two dogs – this was customary at that period – entered his cage, laid down near his bed a two pound loaf of black bread, a jug of water, and a dish full of very thin soup in which a few beans were swimming, examined his irons, and struck upon the bars. This man, with his dogs, returned twice in the night.

Thénardier had obtained permission to keep a kind of an iron spike which he used to nail his bread into a crack in the wall, 'in order', said he, 'to preserve it from the rats'. As Thénardier was constantly in sight, they imagined no danger from this spike. However, it was remembered afterwards that a warden had said: 'It would be better to let him have nothing but a wooden pike.'

At two o'clock in the morning, the sentinel, who was an old soldier, was relieved, and his place was taken by a conscript. A few moments afterwards, the man with the dogs made his visit, and went away without noticing anything, except the extreme youth and the 'peasant air' of the 'greenhorn.' Two hours afterwards, at four o'clock, when they came to relieve the conscript, they found him asleep, and lying on the ground like a log near Thénardier's cage. As to Thénardier, he was not there. His broken irons were on the floor. There was a hole in the ceiling of his cage, and above, another hole in the roof. A board had been torn from his bed, and doubtless carried away, for it was not found again. There was also seized in the cell a half empty bottle, containing the rest of the drugged wine with which the soldier had been put to sleep. The soldier's bayonet had disappeared.

At the moment of this discovery, it was supposed that Thénardier was out of all reach. The reality is, that he was no longer in the Bâtiment Neuf, but that he was still in great danger.

Thénardier on reaching the roof of the Bâtiment Neuf, found the remnant of Brujon's cord hanging to the bars of the upper trap of the chimney, but this broken end being much too short, he was unable to escape over the sentry's path as Brujon and Gueulemer had done.

On turning from the Rue des Ballets into the Rue du Roi de Sicile, on the right you meet almost immediately with a dirty recess. There was a house there in the last century, of which only the rear wall remains, a genuine ruin wall which rises to the height of the third storey among the neighbouring buildings. This ruin can be recognised by two large square windows which may still be seen; the one in the middle, nearer the right gable, is crossed by a worm-eaten joist fitted like a cap-piece for a shore. Through these windows could formerly be discerned a high and dismal wall, which was a part of the encircling wall of La Force.

The void which the demolished house has left upon the street is half filled by a palisade fence of rotten boards, supported by five stone posts. Hidden in this enclosure is a little shanty built against that part of the ruin which remains standing. The fence has a gate which a few years ago was fastened only by a latch.

Thénardier was upon the crest of this ruin a little after three o'clock in the morning.

How had he got there? That is what nobody has ever been able to explain or understand. The lightning must have both confused and helped him. Did he use the ladders and the scaffoldings of the slaters to get from roof to roof, from enclosure to enclosure, from compartment to compartment, to the buildings of the Charlemagne court, then the buildings of the Cour Saint Louis, the encircling wall, and from thence to the ruin on the Rue du Roi de Sicile? But there were gaps in this route which seemed to render it impossible. Did he lay down the plank from his bed as a bridge from the roof of the Bel Air to the encircling wall, and did he crawl on his belly along the coping of the wall, all round the prison as far as the ruin? But the encircling wall of La Force followed an indented and uneven line, it rose and fell, it sank down to the barracks of the firemen, it rose up to the bathing-house, it was cut by buildings, it was not of the same height on the Hôtel Lamoignon as on the Rue Pavée, it had slopes and right angles everywhere; and then the sentinels would have seen the dark outline of the fugitive; on this supposition again, the route taken by Thénardier is still almost inexplicable. By either way, an impossible flight. Had Thénardier, illuminated by that fearful thirst for liberty which changes precipices into ditches, iron gratings into osier screens, a cripple into an athlete, an old gouty into a bird, stupidity into instinct, instinct into intelligence, and intelligence into genius, had Thénardier invented and extemporised a third method? It has never been known.

One cannot always comprehend the marvels of escape. The man who escapes, let us repeat, is inspired; there is something of the star and the lightning in the mysterious gleam of flight; the effort towards deliverance is not less surprising than the flight towards the sublime; and we say of an escaped robber: How did he manage to scale that roof? just as it is said of Corneille: Where did he learn *that he would die?*

However this may be, dripping with sweat, soaked through by the rain, his clothes in strips, his hands skinned, his elbows bleeding, his knees torn, Thénardier had reached what children, in their figurative language, call the edge of the wall of the ruin, he had stretched himself on it at full length, and there his strength failed him. A steep escarpment, three storeys high, separated him from the pavement of the street.

The rope which he had was too short.

He was waiting there, pale, exhausted, having lost all the hope which he had had, still covered by night, but saying to himself that day was just about to dawn, dismayed at the idea of hearing in a few moments the neighbouring clock of Saint Paul's strike four, the hour when they would come to relieve the sentinel and would find him asleep under the broken roof, gazing with a kind of stupor through the fearful depth, by the glimmer of the lamps, upon the wet and black pavement, that longed for yet terrible pavement which was death yet which was liberty.

He asked himself if his three accomplices in escape had succeeded, if they had heard him, and if they would come to his aid. He listened. Except a patrolman, nobody had passed through the street since he had been there. Nearly all the travel of the gardeners of Montreuil, Charonne, Vincennes, and Bercy to the Market, is through the Rue Saint Antoine.

The clock struck four. Thénardier shuddered. A few moments afterwards, that wild and confused noise which follows upon the discovery of an escape, broke out in the prison. The sound of doors opening and shutting, the grinding of gratings upon their hinges, the tumult in the guardhouse, the harsh calls of the gate-keepers, the sound of the butts of muskets upon the pavement of the yards reached him. Lights moved up and down in the grated windows of the dormitories, a torch ran along the attic of the Bâtiment Neuf, the firemen of the barracks alongside had been called. Their caps, which the torches lighted up in the rain, were going to and fro along the roofs. At the same time Thénardier saw in the direction of the Bastille a whitish cloud throwing a dismal pallor over the lower part of the sky.

He was on the top of a wall ten inches wide, stretched out beneath the storm, with two precipices, at the right and at the left, unable to stir, giddy at the prospect of falling, and horror-stricken at the certainty of arrest, and his thoughts, like the pendulum of a clock, went from one of these ideas to the other: 'Dead if I fall, taken if I stay.'

In this anguish, he suddenly saw, the street being still wrapped in obscurity, a man who was gliding along the walls, and who came from the direction of the Rue Pavée, stop in the recess above which Thénardier was as it were suspended. This man was joined by a second, who was walking with the same precaution, then by a third, then by a fourth. When these men were together, one of them lifted the latch of the gate in the fence, and they all four entered the enclosure of the shanty. They were exactly under Thénardier. These men had evidently selected this recess so as to be able to talk without being seen by the passers or by the sentinel who guards the gate of La Force a few steps off. It must also be stated that the rain kept this sentinel blockaded in his sentry-box. Thénardier, not being able to distinguish their faces, listened to their words with the desperate attention of a wretch who feels that he is lost.

Something which resembled hope passed before Thénardier's eyes; these men spoke argot.

The first said, in a low voice, but distinctly:

'*Decarrons.* What is it we *maquillons icigo*?'*

The second answered:

* Let us go, what are we doing here?

'*Il lansquine* enough to put out the *riffe* of the *rabouin*. And then the *coqueurs* are going by, there is a *grivier* there who carries a *gaffe*, shall we let them *emballer* us *icicaille*?'*

These two words, *icigo* and *icicaille*, which both mean *ici* [here], and which belong, the first to the argot of the Barrières, the second to the argot of the Temple, were revelations to Thénardier. By *icigo* he recognised Brujon, who was a prowler of the Barrières, and by *icicaille* Babet, who, among all his other trades, had been a second-hand dealer at the Temple.

The ancient argot of the age of Louis XIV, is now spoken only at the Temple, and Babet was the only one who spoke it quite purely. Without *icicaille*, Thénardier would not have recognised him, for he had entirely disguised his voice.

Meanwhile the third had put in a word:

'Nothing is urgent yet, let us wait a little. How do we know that he doesn't need our help?'

By this, which was only French, Thénardier recognised Montparnasse, whose elegance consisted in understanding all argots and speaking none.

As to the fourth, he was silent, but his huge shoulders betrayed him. Thénardier had no hesitation. It was Gueulemer.

Brujon replied almost impetuously, but still in a low voice:

'What is it you *bonnez* us there? The *tapissier* couldn't draw his *crampe*. He don't know the *truc*, indeed! *Bouliner* his *limace* and *faucher* his *empaffes*, *maquiller* a *tortouse*, *caler boulins* in the *lourdes*, *braser* the *faffes*, *maquiller caroubles*, *faucher* the Bards, balance his *tortouse* outside, *planquer* himself, *camoufler* himself, one must be a *mariol*? The old man couldn't do it, he don't know how to *goupiner*!' †

Babet added, still in that prudent, classic argot which was spoken by Poulailler and Cartouche, and which is to the bold, new, strongly-coloured, and hazardous argot which Brujon used, what the language of Racine is to the language of André Chénier:

'Your *orgue tapissier* must have been made *marron* on the stairs. One must be *arcasien*. He is a *galifard*. He has been played the *harnache* by a *roussin*, perhaps even by a *roussi*, who has beaten him *comtois*. Lend your *oche*, Montparnasse, do you hear those *criblements* in the *college*? You have seen all those *camoufles*. He has *tombé*, come! He must be left to draw his twenty *longes*. I have no *taf*, I am no *taffeur*, that is *colombé*, but there is nothing more but to make the *lezards*, or otherwise they will make us *gambiller* for it. Don't *renauder*, come with *nousiergue*. Let us go and *picter* a *rouillarde encible*.' ‡

* It rains enough to put out the devil's fire. And then the police are going by. There is a soldier there who is standing sentinel. Shall we let them arrest us here?

† What is it you tell us there? The innkeeper couldn't escape. He don't know the trade, indeed! To tear up his shirt and cut up his bedclothes to make a rope, to make holes in the doors, to forge false papers, to make false keys, to cut his irons, to hang his rope outside, to hide himself, to disguise himself, one must be a devil! The old man couldn't do it, he don't know how to work.

‡ Your innkeeper must have been caught in the act. One must be a devil. He is an apprentice. He has been duped by a spy, perhaps even by a sheep, who made him his gossip. Listen, Montparnasse, do you hear those cries in the prison? You have seen all those lights. He is retaken, come! He must be left to get his twenty years. I have no fear, I am no coward, that is known, but there is nothing more to be done, or otherwise they will make us dance. Don't be angry, come with us. Let us go and drink a bottle of old wine together.

'Friends are not left in difficulty,' muttered Montparnasse.

'I *bonnis* you that he is *malade*,' replied Brujon. 'At the hour which *toque*, the *tapissier* isn't worth a *broque!* We can do nothing here. *Décarrons*. I expect every moment that a *cogne* will *cintrer* me in *pogne!*' *

Montparnasse resisted now but feebly; the truth is, that these four men, with that faithfulness which bandits exhibit in never abandoning each other, had been prowling all night about La Force at whatever risk, in hope of seeing Thénardier rise above some wall. But the night which was becoming really too fine, it was storming enough to keep all the streets empty, the cold which was growing upon them, their soaked clothing, their wet shoes, the alarming uproar which had just broken out in the prison, the passing hours, the patrolmen they had met, hope departing, fear returning, all this impelled them to retreat. Montparnasse himself, who was, perhaps, to some slight extent a son-in-law of Thénardier, yielded. A moment more, they were gone. Thénardier gasped upon his wall like the shipwrecked sailors of the *Méduse* on their raft when they saw the ship which had appeared, vanish in the horizon.

He dared not call them, a cry overheard might destroy all; he had an idea, a final one, a flash of light; he took from his pocket the end of Brujon's rope, which he had detached from the chimney of the Bâtiment Neuf, and threw it into the enclosure.

This rope fell at their feet.

'A widow!' † said Babet.

'My *tortouse*!' ‡ said Brujon.

'There is the innkeeper,' said Montparnasse.

They raised their eyes. Thénardier advanced his head a little.

'Quick!' said Montparnasse, 'have you the other end of the rope, Brujon?'

'Yes.'

'Tie the two ends together. We will throw him the rope, he will fasten it to the wall, he will have enough to get down.'

Thénardier ventured to speak:

'I am benumbed.'

'We will warm you.'

'I can't stir.'

'Let yourself slip down, we will catch you.'

'My hands are stiff.'

'Only tie the rope to the wall.'

'I can't.'

'One of us must get up,' said Montparnasse.

'Three storeys!' said Brujon.

An old plaster flue, which had served for a stove which had formerly been in use in the shanty, crept along the wall, rising almost to the spot at which they saw Thénardier. This flue, then very much cracked and full of seams, has since fallen, but its traces can still be seen. It was very small.

'We could get up by that,' said Montparnasse.

* I tell you that he is retaken. At the present time, the innkeeper isn't worth a penny. We can do nothing here. Let us go. I expect every moment that a *sergent de ville* will have me in his hand.

† A rope (argot of the Temple) ‡ My rope (argot of the Barrières)

'By that flue!' exclaimed Babet, 'an *orgue*,[1] never! it would take a *mion*.' [2]

'It would take a *môme*,'[3] added Brujon.

'Where can we find a brat?' said Gueulemer.

'Wait,' said Montparnasse. 'I have the thing.'

He opened the gate of the fence softly, made sure that nobody was passing in the street, went out carefully, shut the door after him, and started on a run in the direction of the Bastille.

Seven or eight minutes elapsed, eight thousand centuries to Thénardier; Babet, Brujon, and Gueulemer kept their teeth clenched; the door at last opened again, and Montparnasse appeared, out of breath, with Gavroche. The rain still kept the street entirely empty.

Little Gavroche entered the enclosure and looked upon these bandit forms with a quiet air. The water was dripping from his hair. Gueulemer addressed him:

'Brat, are you a man?'

Gavroche shrugged his shoulders and answered:

'*A môme* like *mézig* is an *orgue*, and *orgues* like *vousailles* are *mômes*' [4]

'How the *mion* plays with the spittoon!'[5] exclaimed Babet.

'The *môme pantinois* isn't *maquillé* of *ferlille lansquinée*,'[6] added Brujon.

'What is it you want?' said Gavroche.

Montparnasse answered:

'To climb up by this flue.'

'With this widow,'[7] said Babet.

'And *ligoter* the *tortouse*,'[8] continued Brujon.

'To the *monté* of the *montant*,'[9] resumed Babet.

'To the *pieu* of the *vanterne*,'[10] added Brujon.

'And then?' said Gavroche.

'That's all!' said Gueulemer.

The *gamin* examined the rope, the flue, the wall, the windows, and made that inexpressible and disdainful sound with the lips which signifies:

'What's that?'

'There is a man up there whom you will save,' replied Montparnasse.

'Will you?' added Brujon.

'Goosy!' answered the child, as if the question appeared to him absurd; and he took off his shoes.

Gueulemer caught up Gavroche with one hand, put him on the roof of the shanty, the worm-eaten boards of which bent beneath the child's weight, and handed him the rope which Brujon had tied together during the absence of Montparnasse. The *gamin* went towards the flue, which it was easy to enter, thanks to a large hole at the roof. Just as he was about to start, Thénardier, who saw safety and life approaching, bent over the edge of the wall; the first gleam of day lighted up his forehead reeking with sweat, his livid cheeks, his thin and savage nose, his grey bristly beard, and Gavroche recognised him:

1 A man 2 A child (argot of the Temple) 3 A child (argot of the Barrières)
4 A child like me is a man, and men like you are children. 5 How well the child's tongue is hung! 6 The Parisian child isn't made of wet straw. 7 This rope. 8 Fasten the rope 9 To the top of the wall 10 To the cross-bar of the window

'Hold on!' said he, 'it is my father! – Well, that don't hinder!'

And taking the rope in his teeth, he resolutely commenced the ascent.

He reached the top of the ruin, bestrode the old wall like a horse, and tied the rope firmly to the upper cross-bar of the window.

A moment afterwards Thénardier was in the street.

As soon as he had touched the pavement, as soon as he felt himself out of danger, he was no longer either fatigued, benumbed, or trembling; the terrible things through which he had passed vanished like a whiff of smoke, all that strange and ferocious intellect awoke, and found itself erect and free, ready to march forward. The man's first words were these:

'Now, who are we going to eat?'

It is needless to explain the meaning of this frightfully transparent word, which signifies all at once to kill, to assassinate, and to plunder. *Eat*, real meaning: *devour*.

'Let us hide first,' said Brujon, 'Finish in three words, and we will separate immediately. There was an affair which had a good look in the Rue Plumet, a deserted street, an isolated house, an old rusty grating upon a garden, some lone women.'

'Well, why not?' inquired Thénardier.

'Your *fée** Eponine, has been to see the thing,' answered Babet.

'And she brought a biscuit to Magnon,' added Gueulemer, 'nothing to *maquiller* there.' †

'The *fée* isn't *loffe*,'‡ said Thénardier. 'Still we must see.'

'Yes, yes,' said Brujon, 'we must see.'

Meantime none of these men appeared longer to see Gavroche who, during this colloquy, had seated himself upon one of the stone supports of the fence; he waited a few minutes, perhaps for his father to turn towards him, then he put on his shoes, and said:

'It is over? you have no more use for me? men! you are out of your trouble. I am going. I must go and get my *mômes* up.'

And he went away.

The five men went out of the enclosure one after another.

When Gavroche had disappeared at the turn of the Rue des Ballets, Babet took Thénardier aside.

'Did you notice that *mion*?' he asked him.

'What *mion*?'

'The *mion* who climbed up the wall and brought you the rope.'

'Not much.'

'Well, I don't know, but it seems to me that it was your son.'

'Pshaw!' said Thénardier, 'do you think so?'

* Your daughter † Nothing, to do there ‡ Stupid

BOOK 7: ARGOT

1. Origin

Pigritia IS A TERRIBLE word.

It engenders a world, *la pègre*, read robbery, and a hell, *la pegrenne*, read *hunger*.

So idleness is a mother.

She has a son, robbery, and a daughter, hunger.

Where are we now? In argot.

What is argot? It is at the same time the nation and the idiom, it is robbery under its two aspects; people and language.

When thirty-four years ago the narrator of this grave and gloomy story introduced into a work written with the same aim as the present,* a robber talking argot, there was amazement and clamour. 'What! how! argot! But argot is hideous! why, it is the language of convicts, of the galleys, of the prisons, of all that is most abominable in society!' etc., etc., etc.

We have never comprehended this sort of objection.

Since then two powerful romancers, one of whom is a profound observer of the human heart, the other an intrepid friend of the people, Balzac and Eugène Süe, having made bandits talk in their natural tongue as the author of *Le Dernier Jour d'un Condamné* had done in 1828, the same outcry was made. It was repeated: 'What do these writers mean by this revolting patois? Argot is horrid! argot makes us shudder!'

Who denies it? Undoubtedly.

Where the purpose is to probe a wound, an abyss, or a society, since when has it been a crime to descend too far, to go to the bottom? We had always thought that it was sometimes an act of courage, and at the very least a simple and useful act, worthy of the sympathetic attention which is merited by a duty accomplished and accepted. Not explore the whole, not study the whole, stop by the way, why? To stop is the part of the lead and not of the leadsman.

Certainly, to go into the lowest depths of the social order, where the earth ends and the mire begins, to search in those thick waters, to pursue, to seize and to throw out still throbbing upon the pavement this abject idiom which streams with filth as it is thus drawn to the light, this pustulous vocabulary in which each word seems a huge ring from some monster of the slime and the darkness, is neither an attractive task nor an easy task. Nothing is more mournful than to contemplate thus bare, by the light of thought, the fearful crawl of argot. It seems indeed as if it were a species of horrible beast made for the night, which has just been dragged from its cesspool. We seem to see a frightful living and bristling bush which trembles, moves, quivers, demands its darkness again, menaces, and stares. This word resembles a fang, that a quenched and bleeding eye; this phrase seems to move like the claw of a crab. All this is alive with the hideous vitality of things which are organised in disorganisation.

* *Le Dernier Jour d'un Condamné.*

Now, since when has horror excluded study? Since when has the sickness driven away the physician? Imagine a naturalist who should refuse to study the viper, the bat, the scorpion, the scolopendra, the tarantula, and who should cast them back into their darkness, saying: Oh! how ugly they are! The thinker who should turn away from argot would be like a surgeon who should turn away from an ulcer or a wart. He would be a philologist hesitating to examine a fact of language, a philosopher hesitating to scrutinise a fact of humanity. For, it must indeed be said to those who know it not, argot is both a literary phenomenon and a social result. What is argot properly speaking? Argot is the language of misery.

Here we may be stopped; facts may be generalised, which is sometimes a method of extenuating them; it may be said that all trades, all professions, one might almost add all the accidents of the social hierarchy and all the forms of the intellect, have their argot. The merchant who says: *merchantable London stout, fine quality Marseilles*, the stockbroker who says: *seller sixty, dividend off*, the gambler who says: *I'll see you ten better, will you fight the tiger?* the huissier of the Norman Isles who says: *the enfeoffor restricted to his lands cannot claim the fruits of these grounds during the heritable seisin of the renouncer's fixtures*, the philosopher who says: *phenomenal triplicity*, the whale hunter who says: *there she blows, there she breaches*, the phrenologist who says: *amativeness, combativeness, secretiveness*, the fencing master who says: *tierce, quarte, retreat*, the compositor who says: *a piece of pie*, all, compositor, fencing-master, phrenologist, whale-hunter, philosopher, huissier, gambler, stockbroker, merchant, speak argot. The cobbler who says: *my kid*, the shopkeeper who says: *my counter-jumper*, the barber who says: *my clerk*, the printer who says: *my devil*, speak argot. In strictness, and if we will be absolute, all the various methods of saying right and left, the sailor's *larboard* and *starboard*, the machinist's *court side* and *garden side*, the beadle's *Epistle side* and *Gospel side*, are argot. There is an argot of the affected as there was the argot of the *Précieuses*. The Hôtel de Rambouillet bordered to some extent upon the Cour des Miracles. There is an argot of duchesses, witness this phrase written in a love-letter by a very great lady and a very pretty woman of the Restoration: 'You will find in these postings a fultitude of reasons why I should libertise.' * Diplomatic ciphers are argot; the Pontifical Chancellory, in saying 26 for *Rome*, *grkztntgzyal* for *packet*, and *abfxustgrnogrkzu tu* XI for *Duke of Modena*, speaks argot. The physicians of the Middle Ages who, to say carrot, radish, and turnip, said: *opoponach, perfroschinum, reptitalmus, dracatholicum angelorum, postmegorum*, spoke argot. The sugar manufacturer who says: '*Rectified, loaf, clarified, crushed, lump, molasses, mixed, common, burned, caked*,' this honest manufacturer talks argot. A certain critical school of twenty years ago which said: '*The half of Shakespeare is plays upon words and puns*' – spoke argot. The poet and the artist who, with deep significance, will describe M. de Montmorency as 'bourgeois', if he is not familiar with poetry and statues, speak argot. The classic Academician who calls flowers *Flora*, fruits *Pomona*, the sea *Neptune*, love *the fires*, beauty *the attractions*, a horse a *courser*, the white or the tricoloured cockade *the rose of Bellona*, the three-cornered hat *the triangle of Mars*, the classic Academician speaks argot. Algebra, medicine, botany, have their argot. The language which is employed afloat, that wonderful language of the sea, so complete and so picturesque, which was spoken by Jean Bart, Duquesne, Suffren, and Duperré,

* You will find in this gossip a multitude of reasons why I should take my liberty.

which mingles with the whistling of the rigging, with the sound of the speaking trumpet, with the clash of the boarding-axe, with the rolling, with the wind, with the squall, with the cannon, is all a heroic and splendid argot which is to the savage argot of crime what the lion is to the jackal.

Undoubtedly. But, whatever can be said about it, this method of understanding the word argot is an extension, which even people in general will not admit. As for us, we continue to this word its old acceptation, precise, circumscribed, and definite, and we limit argot to argot. The real argot, the argot *par excellence*, if these words can be joined, the immemorial argot which was a realm, is nothing more nor less, we repeat, than the ugly, restless, sly, treacherous, venomous, cruel, crooked, vile, deep, deadly language of misery. There is, at the extremity of all debasements and all misfortunes, a last wretchedness which revolts and determines to enter into a struggle against the whole mass of fortunate things and reigning rights; a hideous struggle in which, sometimes by fraud, sometimes by force, at the same time sickly and fierce, it attacks social order with pin-thrusts through vice and with club strokes through crime. For the necessities of this struggle, misery has invented a language of battle which is argot.

To buoy up and to sustain above oblivion, above the abyss, were it only a fragment of any language whatever which man has spoken and which would otherwise be lost, that is to say one of the elements, good or evil, of which civilisation is composed or with which it is complicated, is to extend the data of social observation; it is to serve civilisation itself. This service, Plautus rendered, intentionally or unintentionally, by making two Carthaginian soldiers speak Phœnician; this service Molière rendered, by making so many of his personages speak Levantine and all manner of patois. Here objections are revived: the Phœnician, perfectly right! the Levantine, well and good! even patois, so be it! these are languages which have belonged to nations or provinces; but argot? what is the use of preserving argot? what is the use of 'buoying up' argot?

To this we shall answer but a word. Certainly, if the language which a nation or a province has spoken is worthy of interest, there is something still more worthy of attention and study in the language which a misery has spoken.

It is the language which has been spoken in France, for example, for more than four centuries, not merely by a particular form of misery, but by misery, every possible human misery.

And then, we insist, the study of social deformities and infirmities and their indication in order to cure them, is not a work in which choice is permissible. The historian of morals and ideas has a mission no less austere than that of the historian of events. The latter has the surface of civilisation, the struggles of the crowns, the births of princes, the marriages of kings, the battles, the assemblies, the great public men, the revolutions in the sunlight, all the exterior; the other historian has the interior, the foundation, the people who work, who suffer, and who wait, overburdened woman, agonising childhood, the dumb wars of man with man, the obscure ferocities, the prejudices, the established iniquities, the subterranean reactions of the law, the secret evolutions of souls, the vague shudderings of the multitudes, the starving, the barefooted, the bare-armed, the disinherited, the orphans, the unfortunate and the infamous, all the goblins that wander in darkness. He must descend with a heart at the same time full of charity and of severity, as a brother and as a judge, to those impenetrable casemates where crawl in confusion those who bleed and those who strike, those who weep and those who curse, those who fast and those who devour, those who suffer wrong, and those who commit it. Have these historians of hearts and souls lesser duties than the historians of exterior facts? Do you think that Dante has fewer things to say than Machiavelli? Is the under-world of civilisation, because it is deeper and more gloomy, less important than the upper? Do we really know the mountain when we do not know the cavern?

We must say, however, by the way, from some words of what precedes, a decided separation between the two classes of historians might be inferred, which does not exist in our mind. No man is a good historian of the open, visible, signal, and public life of the nations, if he is not, at the same time, to a certain extent, the historian of their deeper and hidden life; and no man is a good historian of the interior, if he know not to be, whenever there is need, the historian of the exterior. The history of morals and ideas interpenetrate the history of events, and vice versa. They are two orders of different facts which answer to each other, which are always linked with and often produce each other. All the lineaments which Providence traces upon the surface of a nation have their dark but distinct parallels, in the bottom, and all the convulsions of the bottom produce upheavals at the surface. True history dealing with all, the true historian deals with all.

Man is not a circle with a single centre; he is an ellipse with two foci. Facts are one, ideas are the other.

Argot is nothing more nor less than a wardrobe in which language, having some bad deed to do, disguises itself. It puts on word-masks and metaphoric rags.

In which way it becomes horrible.

We can hardly recognise it. Is it really the French tongue, the great human tongue? There it is ready to enter upon the scene and give the cue to crime, and fitted for all the employments of the repertory of evil. It walks no more, it hobbles; it limps upon the crutch of the Cour des Miracles, a crutch which can be metamorphosed into a club; it gives itself the name of vagrancy; all the spectres, its dressing-maids, have begrimed it; it drags itself along and rears its head, the two characteristics of the reptile. It is apt for all parts henceforth, made squint-eyed by the forger, verdigrised by the poisoner, charcoaled by the incendiary's soot; and the murderer puts on his red.

When we listen, on the side of honest people, at the door of society, we overhear the dialogue of those who are without. We distinguish questions and answers. We perceive, without understanding, a hideous murmur, sounding almost like human tones, but nearer a howling than speech. This is argot. The words are uncouth, and marked by an indescribably fantastic beastliness. We think we hear hydras talking.

It is the unintelligible in the dark. It gnashes and it whispers, completing twilight by enigma. It grows black in misfortune, it grows blacker still in crime; these two blacknesses amalgamated make Argot. Darkness in the atmosphere, darkness in the deeds, darkness in the voices. Appalling toad language, which comes and goes, hops, crawls, drivels, and moves monstrously in that boundless grey mist made up of rain, night, hunger, vice, lying, injustice, nakedness, asphyxia, and winter, the broad noonday of the miserable.

Let us have compassion on the chastened. Who, alas! are we ourselves? who am I who speak to you? who are you who listen to me? whence do we come? and is it quite certain that we did nothing before we were born? The earth is not without resemblance to a jail. Who knows that man is not a prisoner of Divine Justice?

Look closely into life. It is so constituted that we feel punishment everywhere.

Are you what is called a fortunate man? Well, you are sad every day. Each day has its great grief or its little care. Yesterday you were trembling for the health of one who is dear to you, today you fear for your own; tomorrow it will be an anxiety about money, the next day the slanders of a calumniator, the day after the misfortune of a friend; then the weather, then something broken or lost, then a pleasure for which you are reproached by your conscience or your vertebral column reproaches you; another time, the course of public affairs. Without counting heart troubles. And so on. One cloud is dissipated, another gathers. Hardly one day in a hundred of unbroken joy and of unbroken sunshine. And you are of that small number who are fortunate! As to other men, stagnant night is upon them.

Reflecting minds make little use of this expression: the happy and the unhappy. In this world, the vestibule of another evidently, there is none happy.

The true division of humanity is this: the luminous and the dark.

To diminish the number of the dark, to increase the number of the luminous, behold the aim. This is why we cry: education, knowledge! to learn to read is to kindle a fire; every syllable spelled sparkles.

But he who says light does not necessarily say joy. There is suffering in the light; in excess it burns. Flame is hostile to the wing. To burn and yet to fly, this is the miracle of genius.

When you know and when you love you shall suffer still. The day dawns in tears. The luminous weep, were it only over the dark.

2. *Roots*

Argot is the language of the dark.

Thought is aroused in its gloomiest depths, social philosophy is excited to its most poignant meditations, before this enigmatic dialect which is at once withered and rebellious. Here is chastisement visible. Each syllable has a branded look. The words of the common language here appear as if wrinkled and shrivelled under the red-hot iron of the executioner. Some seem still smoking. A phrase affects you like the branded shoulder of a robber suddenly laid bare. Ideas almost refuse to be expressed by these substantives condemned of justice. Its metaphor is sometimes so shameless that we feel it has worn the iron collar.

Still, in spite of all that and because of all that, this strange dialect has of right its compartment in that great impartial collection in which there is place for the rusty farthing as well as for the gold medal, and which is called literature. Argot, whether we consent to it or not, has its syntax and its poesy. It is a language. If, by the deformity of certain terms, we recognise that it was mumbled by Mandrin, by the splendour of certain metonomies, we feel that it was spoken by Villon.

This verse so exquisite and so famous:

Mais où sont les neiges d'antan? *

is a verse of argot. *Antan – ante annum* – is a word of the argot of Thunes which signifies *the past year*, and by extension *formerly*. There might still be read thirty-five years ago, at the time of the departure of the great chain in 1827, in one of the dungeons of Bicêtre, this maxim engraved on the wall with a nail by a king of Thunes condemned to the galleys: *Les dabs d'antan trimaient siempre pour la pierre du Cöesre*. Which means: *the kings of old time always went to be consecrated*. In the mind of that king, consecration was the galleys.

The word *decarade*, which expresses the departure of a heavy wagon at a gallop, is attributed to Villon, and it is worthy of him. This word, which strikes fire with four feet, resumes in a masterly onomatopœia the whole of La Fontaine's admirable verse:

Six forts chevaux tiraient un coche. †

In a purely literary point of view, few studies would be more curious and more prolific than that of argot. It is a complete language within a language, a sort of diseased excrescence, a sickly graft which has produced a vegetation, a parasite which has its roots in the old Gallic trunk, the sinister foliage of which creeps over an entire side of the language. This is what may be called the primary aspect, the general aspect of argot. But to those who study language as it should be studied, that is to say as geologists study the earth, argot appears, as it were, a true alluvium. According as we dig more or less deep, we find in argot, beneath the old popular French, Provençal, Spanish, Italian, Levantine, this language of the Mediterranean ports, English and German, Romance in its three varieties, French Romance, Italian Romance, Romance Romance, Latin, and finally Basque and Celtic. A deep and grotesque formation. A subterranean edifice built in common by all the miserable. Each accursed race has deposited its stratum, each suffering has dropped its stone, each heart has given its pebble. A multitude of evil, low, or embittered souls, who have passed through life and vanished in eternity, are preserved here almost entire and in some sort still visible under the form of a monstrous word.

Will you have Spanish? the old Gothic argot swarms with it. Here is *boffette*, blow, which comes from *bofeton; vantane*, window (afterwards *vanterne)*, which comes from *vantana; gat*, cat, which comes from *gato; acite*, oil, which comes from *aceyte*. Will you have Italian? Here is *spade*, sword, which comes from *spada; carvel*, boat, which comes from *caravella*. Will you have English? Here is *bichot*, bishop; *raille*, spy, which comes from *rascal, rascallion; pilche*, box, which comes from *pilcher*. Will you have German? Here is *caleur*, waiter, *kellner; hers*, master, *herzog* (duke). Will you have Latin? Here is *frangir*, to break, *frangere; affurer*, to rob, *fur; cadène*, chain, *catena;* there is a word which appears in all the languages of the continent with a sort of mysterious power and authority, the word *magnus;* the Scotchman makes of it his *mac*, which designates the chief of the clan, Mac Farlane, Mac Callummore, the great Farlane, the great Callummore; ‡ argot

* But where are the snows of *antan*? † Six sturdy horses drew a coach.

‡ It should, however, be observed that *mac* in Celtic means son.

makes of it the *meck*, and afterwards, the *meg*, that is to say God. Will you have Basque? Here is *gahisto*, the devil, which comes from *gaïztoa*, evil; *sorgabon*, a good night, which comes from *gabon*, good evening. Will you have Celtic? Here is *blavin*, handkerchief, which comes from *blavet*, gushing water; *mènesse*, woman (in a bad sense), which comes from *meinec*, full of stones; *barant*, brook, from *baranton*, fountain; *goffeur*, locksmith, from *goff*, blacksmith; *guedouze*, death, which comes from *guenn-du*, white-black. Finally, will you have history? argot calls crowns *maltesès*, a reminiscence of the coins which circulated on the galleys of Malta.

Besides the philological origins which we have just pointed out, argot has other still more natural roots, which spring, so to speak, from the mind of man itself.

First, the direct creation of words. In this is the mystery of languages. To paint by words which have forms, we know not how nor why. This is the primitive foundation of all human language – what might be called the granite. Argot swarms with words of this kind, root-words, made out of whole cloth, we know not where nor by whom, without etymology, without analogy, without derivation, solitary, barbarous, sometimes hideous words, which have a singular power of expression, and which are all alive. The executioner, *the taule;* the forest, *the sabri;* fear, flight, *taf;* the lackey, *the larbin;* the general, the préfet, the minister, *pharos;* the devil, *the rabouin.* There is nothing stranger than these words, which mask and yet reveal. Some of them, *the rabouin*, for example, are at the same time grotesque and terrible, and produce the effect of a cyclopian grimace.

Secondly, metaphor. It is the peculiarity of a language, the object of which is to tell everything and conceal everything, to abound in figures. Metaphor is an enigma which offers itself as a refuge to the robber who plots a blow, to the prisoner who plans an escape. No idiom is more metaphorical than argot, *to unscrew the coco* * to wring the neck; *to wind up*,† to eat; *to be sheaved*,‡ to be judged; *a rat*, a bread thief; *il lansquine*, it rains, an old and striking figure, which in some sort carries its date with it, which assimilates the long slanting lines of the rain with the thick and driving pikes of the lansquenets, and which includes in a single word the popular metonomy, *it rains pitchforks.* Sometimes, in proportion as argot passes from the first period to the second, words pass from the savage and primitive state to the metaphorical sense. The devil ceases to be *the rabouin* and becomes *the baker*, he who puts into the oven. This is more witty, but not so grand, something like Racine after Corneille, like Euripedes after Æschylus. Certain phrases of argot, which partake of both periods, and have at the same time the barbaric and the metaphorical character, resemble phantasmagorias. *Les sorgueurs vont sollicer des gails à la lune* (the prowlers are going to steal some horses by night). This passes before the mind like a group of spectres. We know not what we see.

Thirdly, expedient. Argot lives upon the language. It uses it at its caprice, it takes from it by chance, and contents itself often, when the necessity arises, with summarily and grossly distorting it. Sometimes with common words thus deformed, and mystified with words of pure argot, it forms picturesque expressions, in which we feel the mixture of the two preceding elements, direct creation and metaphor: *Le cab jaspine, je marronne que la roulotte de Pantin trime dans la sabri*, the dog barks, I suspect that the Paris diligence is passing in the

* *Dévisser le coco* † *Tortiller* ‡ *Etre gerbé*

woods. *Le dab est sinve, la dabuge est merlouis sière, la fée est bative*, the bourgeois is stupid, the bourgeoise is cunning, the daughter is pretty. Most commonly, in order to mislead listeners, argot contents itself with adding promiscuously to all the words of the language a sort of ignoble tail, a termination in *aille*, in *orgue*, in *iergue*, or in *uche*. Thus: *vouzierque trouvaille bonorgue ce gigotmuche?* [1] Do you like this leg of mutton? A phrase addressed by Cartouche to a turnkey, to know whether the amount offered for an escape satisfied him. The termination in *mar* is of modern date.

Argot, being the idiom of corruption, is easily corrupted. Moreover, as it always seeks disguise so soon as it perceives it is understood, it transforms itself. Unlike all other vegetation, every ray of light upon it kills what it touches. Thus argot goes on decomposed and recomposed incessantly; an obscure and rapid process which never ceases. It changes more in ten years than the language in ten centuries. Thus the *larton* [2] becomes the *lartif*; the *gail* [3] becomes the *gaye;* the *fertauche*,[4] the *fertille;* the *momignard*, the *momacque;* the *Figues*,[5] the *trusques;* the *chique*,[6] the *égrugeoir;* the *colabre*,[7] the *colas*. The devil is first *gahisto*, then the *rabouin*, then the baker; the priest is the *ratichon*, then the boar; the dagger is the twenty-two, then the *surin*, then the *lingre;* police officers are *railles*, then *roussins*, then *rousses*, then lacing merchants, then *couqueurs*, then *cognes;* the executioner is the *Taule*, then *Charlot*, then the *atigeur*, then the *becquilard*. In the seventeenth century, to fight was *to take some tobacco;* in the nineteenth it is to *chew the jaws*. Twenty different expressions have passed between these two extremes. Cartouche would speak Hebrew to Lacenaire. All the words of this language are perpetually in flight like the men who use them.

From time to time, however, and because of this very change, the ancient argot reappears and again becomes new. It has its centres in which it is continuous. The temple preserves the argot of the seventeenth century; Bicêtre, when it was a prison, preserved the argot of Thunes. There was heard the termination in *anche* of the old Thuners. *Boyanches tu?* [8] (do you drink?) *il croyanche* [9] (he believes). But perpetual movement, nevertheless, is the law.

If the philosopher succeeds in fixing for a moment for the observer this language, which is incessantly evaporating, he falls into painful yet useful meditations. No study is more efficacious and more prolific in instruction. Not a metaphor, not an etymology of argot which does not contain its lesson.

Among these men, *to beat* means *to feign;* they beat a sickness; craft is their strength.

To them the idea of man is inseparable from the idea of shade. The night is called *sorgue;* man, *orgue*. Man is a derivative of night.

They have acquired the habit of considering society as an atmosphere which kills them, as a fatal force, and they speak of their liberty as one would of his health. A man arrested is *sick;* a man condemned is *dead*.

What is most terrible to the prisoner in the four stone walls which enshroud him is a sort of icy chastity; he calls the dungeon the *castus*. In this funereal place, life without is always under its most cheerful aspect. The prisoner has irons on his feet; you might suppose that he would be thinking that people walk with their

1 *Trouvez-vous ce gigot bon?* 2 Bread 3 Horse 4 Straw 5 Clothes
6 The church 7 The neck 8 *Bois-tu* 9 *Il croit*

feet? no, he is thinking that people dance with their feet; so, let him succeed in sawing through his irons, his first idea is that now he can dance, and he calls the saw a *fandango*. A *name* is a *centre*; a deep assimilation. The bandit has two heads, one which regulates his actions and controls him during his whole life, another which he has on his shoulders on the day of his death; he calls the head which counsels him to crime the *sorbonne*, and the head which expiates it the *tronche*. When a man has nothing but rags on his body and vices in his heart, when he has reached that double degradation, material as well as moral, which characterises, in its two acceptations, the word beggarly, he is at an edge for crime; he is like a well-whetted knife; he has two edges, his distress and his wickedness; so argot does not say 'a vagabond'; it says a *réguisé*. What are the galleys? a brazier of damnation, a Hell. The convict calls himself a *fagot*. Finally, what name do the malefactors give to the prison? *the college*. A whole penitentiary system might spring from this word.

Would you know where most of the songs of the galleys have originated, those refrains called in special phrase the *lirlonfa*? Listen to this.

There was at the Châtelet de Paris a broad long cellar. This cellar was eight feet deep below the level of the Seine. It had neither windows nor ventilators, the only opening was the door; men could enter, but not air. This cellar had for a ceiling a stone arch, and for a floor, ten inches of mud. It had been paved with tiles; but, under the oozing of the waters, the pavement had rotted and broken up. Eight feet above the floor, a long massive beam crossed this vault from side to side; from this beam there hung, at intervals, chains three feet in length, and at the end of these chains there were iron collars. Men condemned to the galleys were put into this cellar until the day of their departure for Toulon. They were pushed under this timber, where each had his iron swinging in the darkness, waiting for him. The chains, those pendent arms, and the collars, those open hands, seized these wretches by the neck. They were riveted, and they were left there. The chain being too short, they could not lie down. They remained motionless in this cave, in this blackness, under this timber, almost hung, forced to monstrous exertions to reach their bread or their pitcher, the arch above their heads, the mud up to their knees, their ordure running down their legs, collapsing with fatigue, their hips and knees giving way, hanging by their hands to the chain to rest themselves, unable to sleep except standing, and awakened every moment by the strangling of the collar: some did not awake. In order to eat, they had to draw their bread, which was thrown into the mire, up the leg with the heel, within reach of the hand. How long did they continue thus? A month, two months, six months sometimes; one remained a year. It was the antechamber of the galleys. Men were put there for stealing a hare from the king. In this hell-sepulchre what did they do? What can be done in a sepulchre, they agonised, and what can be done in a hell, they sang. For where there is no more hope, song remains. In the waters of Malta, when a galley was approaching, they heard the song before they heard the oars. The poor poacher, Survincent, who had passed through the cellar-prison of the Châtelet said: *it was the rhymes which sustained me*. Uselessness of poetry. Of what use is rhyme? In this cellar almost all the argot songs took birth. It is from the dungeon of the Grand Châtelet de Paris that the melancholy galley refrain of Montgomery comes: *Timaloumisaine, timoulamaison*. Most of these songs are dreary; some are cheerful; one is tender:

Icicaille est le théâtre
Du petit dardant.*

The endeavour is vain, you cannot annihilate that eternal relic of the human heart, love.

In this world of dark deeds secrecy is preserved. Secrecy is the interest of all. Secresy to these wretches is the unity which serves as a basis of union. To violate secresy is to tear from each member of this savage community something of himself. To inform against, in the energetic language of argot, is called: *Manger le morceau.*† As if the informer seized a bit of the substance of all, and fed upon a morsel of the flesh of each.

What is to receive a blow? The hackneyed metaphor responds: *C'est voir trente-six chandelles.*‡ Here argot intervenes and says: *chandelle, camoufle.* Upon this, the common language gives as a synonym for blow, *camouflet.* Thus, by a sort of upward penetration, through the aid of metaphor, that incalculable trajectory, argot rises from the cavern to the Academy; and Poulailler saying: 'I light my *camoufle*,' makes Voltaire write: 'Langleviel La Beaumelle deserves a hundred *camouflets*!'

A search into argot is a discovery at every step. Study and research into this strange idiom lead to the mysterious point of intersection between popular society and outcast society.

The robber also has his food for powder, his matter for plunder, you, me, the world in general; the *pantre. (Pan,* everybody.)

Argot is speech become a convict.

That the thinking principle of man can be trampled down so low, that it can be bound and dragged there by the obscure tyrannies of fatality, that it can be tied with unknown fastenings in that gulf, this is appalling.

Oh, pitiful thought of the miserable!

Alas! will none come to the help of the human soul in this gloom? Is it its destiny for ever to await the mind, the liberator, the huge rider of Pegasus and the hippogriffs, the aurora-hued combatant who descends from the skies with wings, the radiant Knight of the future? Shall it always call to its aid the gleaming lance of the ideal in vain? is it condemned to hear the Evil coming terribly through the depths of the abyss, and to see nearer and nearer at hand, under the hideous water, that dragon-head, those jaws reeking with foam, that serpentine waving of claws, distensions, and rings? Must it remain there, with no ray, no hope, abandoned to that horrible approach, vaguely scented by the monster, shuddering, dishevelled, wringing its hands, forever chained to the rock of night, hopeless Andromeda, white and naked in the darkness?

* Here we have the theatre
Of the little archer (Cupid)

† To eat the morsel

‡ It is to see thirty-six candles; English, to see stars

3. Argot which weeps and argot which laughs

As we see, all argot, the argot of four hundred years ago as well as the argot of the present, is pervaded with that sombre spirit of symbolism which gives to its every word, sometimes an appearance of grief, sometimes an air of menace. We feel in it the old, savage gloom of those vagabonds of the Cour des Miracles who played cards with packs peculiar to themselves, some of which have been preserved. The eight of clubs, for instance, represented a large tree bearing eight enormous clover leaves, a sort of fantastic personification of the forest. At the foot of this tree a fire was seen at which three hares were roasting a hunter on a spit, and in the background, over another fire, was a smoking pot from which the head of a dog projected. Nothing can be more mournful than these pictured reprisals, upon a pack of cards, in the days of the stake for roasting contrabandists, and the cauldron for boiling counterfeiters. The various forms which thought assumed in the realm of argot, even song, even raillery, even menace, all had this impotent and exhausted character. All the songs, some melodies of which have been preserved, were humble and lamentable unto weeping. The *pègre* calls itself *the poor pègre*, and it is always the hare hiding, the mouse escaping, the bird flying. Scarcely does it complain, it contents itself with a sigh; one of its groans has come down to us: '*Je n'entrave que le dail comment meck, le daron des orgues, peut atiger ses mômes et ses momignards et les locher criblant sans être agité lui-même.*' * The miserable being, whenever he has time to reflect, imagines himself mean before the law and wretched before society; he prostrates himself, he begs, he turns towards pity; we feel that he recognises that he is wrong.

Towards the middle of the last century, there was a change. The prison songs, the robbers' ritornels acquired, so to speak, an insolent and jovial expression. The plaintive *maluré* was supplanted by the *larifla*. We find in the eighteenth century, in almost all the songs of the galleys, the chain-gangs, and the prisons, a diabolical and enigmatic gaiety. We hear this boisterous and ringing refrain, which one would say was lighted with a phosphorescent gleam, and which seems as if it were thrown forth upon the forest by a will-o'-the-wisp playing the fife:

Mirlababi surlababo
Mirliton ribonribette
Surlababi mirlababo
Mirliton ribonribo.

This was sung while cutting a man's throat in a cave or in the edge of a forest.

A serious symptom. In the eighteenth century the old melancholy of these gloomy classes is dissipated. They began to laugh. They ridicule the great *meg* and the great *dab*, Speaking of Louis XV they call the King of France 'the Marquis of Pantin.' They are almost cheerful. A sort of flickering light comes from these wretches, as if conscience ceased to weigh upon them. These pitiful tribes of the darkness have no longer the desperate audacity of deeds merely, they have the

* I do not understand how God, the father of men, can torture his children and his grandchildren, and hear them cry without being tortured himself.

reckless audacity of mind. A sign that they are losing the perception of their criminality, and that they feel even among thinkers and dreamers some mysterious support which is unconsciously given. A sign that pillage and robbery are beginning to infiltrate even into doctrines and sophisms, in such a way as to lose something of their ugliness by giving much of it to the sophisms and the doctrines. A sign in short, if no diversion arises, of some prodigious and speedy outburst.

Let us pause for a moment. Whom are we accusing here? is it the eighteenth century? is it its philosophy? Certainly not. The work of the eighteenth century is sound and good. The Encyclopædists, Diderot at their head, the physiocratists, Turgot at their head, the philosophers, Voltaire at their head, the utopists, Rousseau at their head: these are four sacred legions. To them the immense advance of humanity towards the light is due. They are the four vanguards of the human race going to the four cardinal points of progress, Diderot towards the beautiful, Turgot towards the useful, Voltaire towards the true, Rousseau towards the just. But beside and beneath the philosophers, there were the sophists, a poisonous vegetation mingled with the healthy growth, hemlock in the virgin forest. While the executioner was burning upon the chief staircase of the Palais de Justice the grand liberating books of the century, writers now forgotten were publishing, with the privilege of the king, many strangely disorganising writings greedily read by the outcast. Some of these publications, strange to say, patronised by a prince, are still in the *Bibliothèque Secrète.* These facts, deep rooted, but ignored, were unperceived on the surface. Sometimes the very obscurity of a fact is its danger. It is obscure because it is subterranean. Of all the writers, he perhaps who dug the most unwholesome gallery through the masses was Restif de La Bretonne.

This work, adapted to all Europe, committed greater ravages in Germany than anywhere else. In Germany, during a certain period, summed up by Schiller in his famous drama *The Robbers*, robbery and plunder, elevated into a protest against property and labour, appropriated certain elementary, specious and false ideas, just in appearance, absurd in reality, enwrapped themselves in these ideas, disappeared in them in some sort, took an abstract name, and passed into the state of theory, and in this wise circulated among the labouring, suffering, and honest multitudes, unknown even to the imprudent chemists who had prepared the mixture, unknown even to the masses who accepted it. Whenever a thing of this kind occurs, it is serious. Suffering engenders wrath; and while the prosperous classes blind themselves, or fall asleep, which also is to close the eyes, the hatred of the unfortunate classes lights its torch at some fretful or ill-formed mind which is dreaming in a corner, and begins to examine society. Examination by hatred, a terrible thing.

Hence, if the misfortune of the time so wills, those frightful commotions which were formerly called *Jacqueries*, in comparison with which purely political agitations are child's play, and which are not merely the struggle of the oppressed against the oppressor, but the revolt of discomfort against well-being. All falls then.

Jacqueries are people-quakes.

This danger, imminent perhaps in Europe towards the end of the eighteenth century, was cut short by the French Revolution, that immense act of probity.

The French Revolution, which is nothing more nor less than the ideal armed with the sword, started to its feet, and by the very movement, closed the door of evil and opened the door of good.

It cleared up the question, promulgated truth, drove away miasma, purified the century, crowned the people.

We may say of it that it created man a second time, in giving him a second soul, his rights.

The nineteenth century inherits and profits by its work, and today the social catastrophe which we just now indicated is simply impossible. Blind is he who prophesies it! Silly is he who dreads it! Revolution is vaccination for Jacquerie.

Thanks to the Revolution, social conditions are changed. The feudal and monarchical diseases are no longer in our blood. There is nothing more of the Middle Ages in our constitution. We live no longer in the times when frightful interior swarms made eruption, when men heard beneath their feet the obscure course of a sullen sound, when there appeared on the surface of civilisation some mysterious uprising of molehills, when the soil cracked, when the mouths of caverns opened, and when men saw monstrous heads spring suddenly from the earth.

The revolutionary sense is a moral sense. The sentiment of rights, developed, develops the sentiment of duty. The law of all is liberty, which ends where the liberty of others begins, according to Robespierre's admirable definition. Since '89, the entire people has been expanding in the sublimated individual; there is no poor man, who, having his rights, has not his ray; the starving man feels within himself the honour of France; the dignity of the citizen is an interior armour; he who is free is scrupulous; he who votes reigns. Hence incorruptibility; hence the abortion of unnoxious lusts; hence the eyes heroically cast down before temptations. The revolutionary purification is such that on a day of deliverance, a 14th of July, or a 10th of August, there is no longer a mob. The first cry of the enlightened and enlarging multitudes is: death to robbers! Progress is an honest man; the ideal and the absolute pick no pockets. By whom in 1848 were the chests escorted which contained the riches of the Tuileries? by the rag-pickers of the Faubourg Saint Antoine. The rag mounted guard over the treasure. Virtue made these tatters resplendent. There was there, in those chests, in boxes hardly closed, some even half open, amid a hundred dazzling caskets, that old crown of France all in diamonds, surmounted by the regent's carbuncle of royalty, which was worth thirty millions. Barefooted they guarded that crown.

No more Jacquerie then. I regret it on account of the able. That is the old terror which has had its last effect, and which can never henceforth be employed in politics. The great spring of the red spectre is broken. Everybody knows it now. The scarecrow no longer scares. The birds take liberties with the puppet, the beetles make free with it, the bourgeois laugh at it.

4. The two duties: to watch and to hope

THIS BEING SO, is all social danger dissipated? Certainly not. No Jacquerie. Society may be reassured on that account; the blood will rush to its head no more, but let it take thought as to the manner of its breathing. Apoplexy is no longer to be feared, but consumption is there. The consumption of society is called misery.

We die undermined as well as stricken down.

Let us not weary of repeating it, to think first of all of the outcast and sorrowful multitudes, to solace them, to give them air, to enlighten them, to love them, to enlarge their horizon magnificently, to lavish upon them education in all its forms, to offer them the example of labour, never the example of idleness, to diminish the weight of the individual burden by intensifying the idea of the universal object, to limit poverty without limiting wealth, to create vast fields of public and popular activity, to have, like Briareus, a hundred hands to stretch out on all sides to the exhausted and the feeble, to employ the collective power in the great duty of opening workshops for all arms, schools for all aptitudes and laboratories for all intelligences, to increase wages, to diminish suffering, to balance the ought and the have, that is to say, to proportion enjoyment to effort and gratification to need, in one word, to evolve from the social structure, for the benefit of those who suffer and those who are ignorant, more light and more comfort; this is, let sympathetic souls forget it not, the first of fraternal obligations, this is, let selfish hearts know it, the first of political necessities.

And, we must say, all that is only a beginning. The true statement is this: labour cannot be a law without being a right.

We do not dwell upon it; this is not the place.

If nature is called providence, society should be called foresight.

Intellectual and moral growth is not less indispensable than material amelioration. Knowledge is a viaticum, thought is of primary necessity, truth is nourishment as well as wheat. A reason, by fasting from knowledge and wisdom, becomes puny. Let us lament as over stomachs, over minds which do not eat. If there is anything more poignant than a body agonising for want of bread, it is a soul which is dying of hunger for light.

All progress is tending towards the solution. Someday we shall be astounded. The human race rising, the lower strata will quite naturally come out from the zone of distress. The abolition of misery will be brought about by a simple elevation of level.

This blessed solution, we should do wrong to distrust.

The past, it is true, is very strong at the present hour. It is reviving. This revivification of a corpse is surprising. Here it is walking and advancing. It seems victorious; this dead man is a conqueror. He comes with his legion, the superstitions, with his sword, despotism, with his banner, ignorance; within a little time he has won ten battles. He advances, he threatens, he laughs, he is at our doors. As for ourselves, we shall not despair. Let us sell the field whereon Hannibal is camped.

We who believe, what can we fear?

There is no backward flow of ideas more than of rivers.

But let those who desire not the future, think of it. In saying no to progress, it is not the future which they condemn, but themselves. They give themselves a melancholy disease; they inoculate themselves with the past. There is but one way of refusing Tomorrow, that is to die.

Now, no death, that of the body as late as possible, that of the soul never, is what we desire.

Yes, the enigma shall say its word, the sphinx shall speak, the problem shall be resolved. Yes, the people, rough-hewn by the eighteenth century, shall be completed by the nineteenth. An idiot is he who doubts it! The future birth, the speedy birth of universal well-being, is a divinely fatal phenomenon.

Immense pushings together rule human affairs and lead them all in a given time to the logical condition, that is to say, to equilibrium; that is to say to equity. A force composite of earth and of Heaven results from humanity and governs it; this force is a worker of miracles; miraculous issues are no more difficult to it than extraordinary changes. Aided by science which comes from man, and by the event which comes from Another, it is little dismayed by those contradictions in the posture of problems, which seem impossibilities to the vulgar. It is no less capable of making a solution leap forth from the comparison of ideas than a teaching from the comparison of facts, and we may expect everything from this mysterious power of progress, which some fine day confronts the Orient with the Occident in the depths of a sepulchre, and makes the Imaums talk with Bonaparte in the interior of the great pyramid.

In the meantime, no halt, no hesitation, no interruption in the grand march of minds. Social philosophy is essentially science and peace. Its aim is, and its result must be, to dissolve angers by the study of antagonisms. It examines, it scrutinises, it analyses; then it recomposes. It proceeds by way of reduction, eliminating hatred from all.

That a society may be swamped in a gale which breaks loose over men has been seen more than once; history is full of shipwrecks of peoples and of empires; customs, laws, religions, some fine day, the mysterious hurricane passes by and sweeps them all away. The civilisations of India, Chaldea, Persia, Assyria, Egypt, have disappeared, one after the other. Why? we know not. What are the causes of these disasters? we do not know. Could these societies have been saved? was it their own fault? did they persist in some fatal vice which destroyed them? how much of suicide is there in these terrible deaths of a nation and of a race? Questions without answer. Darkness covers the condemned civilisations. They were not seaworthy, for they were swallowed up; we have nothing more to say; and it is with a sort of bewilderment that we behold, far back in that ocean which is called the past, behind those colossal billows, the centuries, the foundering of those huge ships, Babylon, Nineveh, Tarsus, Thebes, Rome, under the terrible blast which comes from all the mouths of darkness. But darkness there, light here. We are ignorant of the diseases of the ancient civilisations, we know the infirmities of our own. We have everywhere upon it the rights of light; we contemplate its beauties and we lay bare its deformities. Where it is unsound we probe; and, once the disease is determined, the study of the cause leads to the discovery of the remedy. Our civilisation, the work of twenty centuries, is at once their monster and their prodigy; it is worth saving. It will be saved. To relieve it, is much already; to enlighten it, is something more. All the labours of modern social philosophy ought to converge towards this end. The thinker of today has a great duty, to auscultate civilisation.

We repeat it, this auscultation is encouraging; and it is by this persistence in encouragement that we would finish these few pages, austere interlude of a sorrowful drama. Beneath the mortality of society we feel the imperishability of humanity. Because it has here and there those wounds, craters, and those ringworms, solfataras, because of a volcano which breaks, and which throws out its pus, the globe does not die. The diseases of a people do not kill man.

And nevertheless, he who follows the social clinic shakes his head at times. The strongest, the tenderest, the most logical have their moments of fainting.

Will the future come? It seems that we may almost ask this question when we see such terrible shadow. Sullen face-to-face of the selfish and the miserable. On the part of the selfish, prejudices, the darkness of the education of wealth, appetite increasing through intoxication, a stupefaction of prosperity which deafens, a dread of suffering which, with some, is carried even to aversion for sufferers, an implacable satisfaction, the me so puffed up that it closes the soul; on the part of the miserable, covetousness, envy, hatred of seeing others enjoy, the deep yearnings of the human animal towards the gratifications, hearts full of gloom, sadness, want, fatality, ignorance impure and simple.

Must we continue to lift our eyes towards heaven? is the luminous point which we there discern of those which are quenched? The ideal is terrible to see, thus lost in the depths, minute, isolated, imperceptible, shining, but surrounded by all those great black menaces monstrously massed about it; yet in no more danger than a star in the jaws of the clouds.

BOOK 8: ENCHANTMENTS AND DESOLATIONS

1. *Sunshine*

The reader has understood that Eponine, having recognised through the grating the inhabitant of that Rue Plumet, to which Magnon had sent her, had begun by diverting the bandits from the Rue Plumet, had then conducted Marius thither, and that after several days of ecstasy before that grating, Marius, drawn by that force which pushes the iron towards the magnet and the lover towards the stones of which the house of her whom he loves is built, had finally entered Cosette's garden as Romeo did the garden of Juliet. It had even been easier for him than for Romeo; Romeo was obliged to scale a wall, Marius had only to push aside a little one of the bars of the decrepit grating, which was loosened in its rusty socket, like the teeth of old people. Marius was slender, and easily passed through.

As there was never anybody in the street, and as, moreover, Marius entered the garden only at night, he ran no risk of being seen.

From that blessed and holy hour when a kiss affianced these two souls, Marius came every evening. If, at this period of her life, Cosette had fallen into the love of a man who was unscrupulous and a libertine, she would have been ruined; for there are generous natures which give themselves, and Cosette was one. One of the magnanimities of woman is to yield. Love, at that height at which it is absolute, is associated with an inexpressibly celestial blindness of modesty. But what risks do you run, O noble souls! Often, you give the heart, we take the body. Your heart remains to you, and you look upon it in the darkness, and shudder. Love has no middle term; either it destroys, or it saves. All human destiny is this dilemma. This dilemma, destruction or salvation, no fatality proposes more inexorably than love. Love is life, if it be not death. Cradle; coffin also. The same sentiment says yes and no in the human heart. Of all the things which God has made, the human heart is that which sheds most light, and, alas! most night.

God willed that the love which Cosette met, should be one of those loves which save.

Through all the month of May of that year 1832, there were there, every night, in that poor, wild garden, under that shrubbery each day more odorous and more dense, two beings composed of every chastity and every innocence, overflowing with all the felicities of Heaven, more nearly archangels than men, pure, noble, intoxicated, radiant, who were resplendent to each other in the darkness. It seemed to Cosette that Marius had a crown, and to Marius that Cosette had a halo. They touched each other, they beheld each other, they clasped each other's hands, they pressed closely to each other; but there was a distance which they did not pass. Not that they respected it; they were ignorant of it. Marius felt a barrier, the purity of Cosette, and Cosette felt a support, the loyalty of Marius. The first kiss was the last also. Marius, since, had not gone beyond touching Cosette's hand, or her neckerchief, or her ringlets, with his lips. Cosette was to him a perfume, and not a woman. He breathed her. She refused nothing and he asked nothing. Cosette was happy, and Marius was satisfied. They lived in that ravishing condition which might be called the dazzling of a soul by a soul. It was that ineffable first embrace of two virginities in the ideal. Two swans meeting upon the Jungfrau.

At that hour of love, an hour when passion is absolutely silent under the omnipotence of ecstasy, Marius, the pure and seraphic Marius, would have been capable rather of visiting a public woman than of lifting Cosette's dress to the height of her ankle. Once, on a moonlight night, Cosette stooped to pick up something from the ground, her dress loosened and displayed the rounding of her bosom. Marius turned away his eyes.

What passed between these two beings? Nothing. They were adoring each other.

At night, when they were there, this garden seemed a living and sacred place. All the flowers opened about them, and proffered them their incense; they too opened their souls and poured them forth to the flowers: the lusty and vigorous vegetation trembled full of sap and intoxication about these two innocent creatures, and they spoke words of love at which the trees thrilled.

What were these words? Whispers, nothing more. These whispers were enough to arouse and excite all this nature. A magic power, which one can hardly understand by this prattle, which is made to be borne away and dissipated like whiffs of smoke by the wind under the leaves. Take from these murmurs of two lovers that melody which springs from the soul, and which accompanies them like a lyre, what remains is only a shade. You say: What! is that all? Yes, childish things, repetitions, laughs about nothing, inutilities, absurdities, all that is deepest and most sublime in the world! the only things which are worth being said and listened to.

These absurdities, these poverties, the man who has never heard them, the man who has never uttered them, is an imbecile and a wicked man.

Cosette said to Marius:

'Do you know my name is Euphrasie?'

'Euphrasie? Why no, your name is Cosette.'

'Oh! Cosette is such an ugly name that they gave me somehow when I was little. But my real name is Euphrasie. Don't you like that name, Euphrasie?'

'Yes – but Cosette is not ugly.'

'Do you like it better than Euphrasie?'

'Why – yes.'

'Then I like it better, too. It is true it is pretty, Cosette. Call me Cosette.'

And the smile which she added made of this dialogue an idyl worthy of a celestial grove.

At another time she looked at him steadily and exclaimed:

'Monsieur, you are handsome, you are beautiful, you are witty, you are not stupid in the least, you are much wiser than I, but I defy you with this word: I love you!'

And Marius, in a cloudless sky, thought he heard a strophe sung by a star.

Or again, she gave him a little tap because he coughed, and said to him:

'Do not cough, monsieur. I do not allow coughing here without permission. It is very naughty to cough and disturb me. I want you to be well, because, in the first place, if you were not well, I should be very unhappy. What will you have me do for you!'

And that was all purely divine.

Once Marius said to Cosette:

'Just think, I thought at one time that your name was Ursula.'

This made them laugh the whole evening.

In the midst of another conversation, he happened to exclaim:

'Oh! one day at the Luxembourg I would have been glad to break the rest of the bones of an Invalide!'

But he stopped short and went no further. He would have been obliged to speak to Cosette of her garter, and that was impossible for him. There was an unknown coast there, the flesh, before which this immense innocent love recoiled with a kind of sacred awe.

Marius imagined life with Cosette like this, without anything else: to come every evening to the Rue Plumet, to put aside the complaisant old bar of the president's grating, to sit side by side upon this seat, to behold through the trees the scintillation of the commencing night, to make the fold of the knee of his pantaloons intimate with the fullness of Cosette's dress, to caress her thumbnail, to say dearest to her, to inhale one after the other the odour of the same flower, for ever, indefinitely. During this time the clouds were passing above their heads. Every breath of wind bears away more dreams from man than clouds from the sky.

That this chaste, almost severe, love was absolutely without gallantry we will not say. 'To pay compliments' to her whom we love is the first method of caressing, a demi-audacity venturing. A compliment is something like a kiss through a veil. Pleasure sets her soft seal there, even while hiding herself. Before pleasure the heart recoils, to love better. Marius' soft words, all saturated as they were with chimæra, were, so to speak, sky-blue. The birds, when they are flying on high beside the angels, must hear such words. There was mingled with them, however, life, humanity, all the positiveness of which Marius was capable. It was what is said in the grotto, a prelude to what will be said in the alcove: a lyrical effusion, the strophe and the sonnet mingled, the gentle hyperboles of cooing, all the refinements of adoration arranged in a bouquet and exhaling a subtle celestial perfume, an ineffable warbling of heart to heart.

'Oh!' murmured Marius, 'how beautiful you are! I dare not look at you. That is why I stare at you. You are a grace. I do not know what is the matter with me. The hem of your dress, when the tip of your shoe appears, completely overwhelms me. And then what enchanting glow when I see a glimpse of your thought. You reason astonishingly. It seems to me at times that you are a dream. Speak, I am listening to you, I am wondering at you. O Cosette! how strange and charming it is! I am really mad. You are adorable, mademoiselle. I study your feet with the microscope and your soul with the telescope.'

And Cosette answered:

'I have been loving you a little more every minute since this morning.'

Questions and answers fared as they might in this dialogue, always falling naturally at last upon love, like those loaded toys which always fall upon their base.

Cosette's whole person was artlessness, ingenuousness, transparency, whiteness, candour, radiance. We might say of Cosette that she was pellucid. She gave to him who saw her a sensation of April and of dawn. There was dew in her eyes. Cosette was a condensation of auroral light in womanly form.

It was quite natural that Marius, adoring her, should admire her. But the truth is that this little schoolgirl, fresh from the convent mill, talked with an exquisite penetration and said at times all manner of true and delicate words. Her prattle was conversation. She made no mistakes, and saw clearly. Woman feels and speaks with the tender instinct of the heart, that infallibility. Nobody knows like a woman how to say things at the same time sweet and profound. Sweetness and death, this is all of woman; this is all of Heaven.

In this fullness of felicity, at every instant tears came to their eyes. An insect trodden upon, a feather falling from a nest, a twig of hawthorn broken, moved their pity, and their ecstasy, sweetly drowned in melancholy, seemed to ask nothing better than to weep. The most sovereign symptom of love, is a tenderness sometimes almost insupportable.

And, by the side of this – all these contradictions are the lightning play of love – they were fond of laughing, and laughed with a charming freedom, and so familiarly that they sometimes seemed almost like two boys. Nevertheless, though hearts intoxicated with chastity may be all unconscious, nature, who can never be forgotten, is always present. There she is, with her aim, animal yet sublime; and whatever may be the innocence of souls, we feel, in the most modest intercourse, the adorable and mysterious shade which separates a couple of lovers from a pair of friends.

They worshipped each other.

The permanent and the immutable continue. There is loving, there is smiling and laughing, and little pouts with the lips, and interlacing of the fingers, and fondling speech, yet that does not hinder eternity. Two lovers hide in the evening, in the twilight, in the invisible with the birds, with the roses, they fascinate each other in the shadow with their hearts which they throw into their eyes, they murmur, they whisper, and during all this time immense librations of stars fill infinity.

2. *The stupefaction of complete happiness*

Their existence was vague, bewildered with happiness. They did not perceive the cholera which decimated Paris that very month. They had been as confidential with each other as they could be, but this had not gone very far beyond their names. Marius had told Cosette that he was an orphan, that his name was Marius Pontmercy, that he was a lawyer, that he lived by writing things for publishers, that his father was a colonel, that he was a hero, and that he, Marius, had quarrelled with his grandfather who was rich. He had also said something about being a baron; but that had produced no effect upon Cosette. Marius baron! She did not comprehend. She did not know what that word meant. Marius was Marius. On her part she had confided to him that she had been brought up at the Convent of the Petit Picpus, that her mother was dead as well as his, that her father's name was M. Fauchelevent, that he was very kind, that he gave much to the poor, but that he was poor himself, and that he deprived himself of everything while he deprived her of nothing.

Strange to say, in the kind of symphony in which Marius had been living since he had seen Cosette, the past, even the most recent, had become so confused and distant to him that what Cosette told him satisfied him fully. He did not even think to speak to her of the night adventure at the Gorbeau tenement, the Thénardiers, the burning, and the strange attitude and the singular flight of her father. Marius had temporarily forgotten all that; he did not even know at night what he had done in the morning, nor where he had breakfasted, nor who had spoken to him; he had songs in his ear which rendered him deaf to every other thought; he existed only during the hours in which he saw Cosette. Then, as he was in Heaven, it was quite natural that he should forget the earth. They were both supporting with languor the undefinable burden of the immaterial pleasures. Thus live these somnambulists called lovers.

Alas! who has not experienced all these things? why comes there an hour when we leave this azure, and why does life continue afterwards?

Love almost replaces thought. Love is a burning forgetfulness of all else. Ask logic then of passion. There is no more an absolute logical chain in the human heart than there is a perfect geometrical figure in the celestial mechanics. To Cosette and Marius there was nothing in being beyond Marius and Cosette. The universe about them had fallen out of sight. They lived in a golden moment. There was nothing before, nothing after. It is doubtful if Marius thought whether Cosette had a father. He was so dazzled that all was effaced from his brain. Of what then did they talk, these lovers? We have seen, of the flowers, the swallows, the setting sun, the rising of the moon, of all important things. They had told all, except everything. The all of lovers is nothing. But the father, the realities, that garret, those bandits, that adventure, what was the use? and was he quite certain that that nightmare was real? They were two, they adored each other, there was nothing but that. Everything else was not. It is probable that this oblivion of the hell behind us is a part of arrival at paradise. Have we seen demons? are there any? have we trembled? have we suffered? We know nothing now about that. A rosy cloud rests upon it all.

These two beings, then, were living thus, very high, with all the improbability of nature; neither at the nadir nor at the zenith, between man and the seraph, above earth, below the ether, in the cloud; scarcely flesh and bone, soul and ecstasy from head to foot; too sublimated already to walk upon the earth, and yet too much weighed down with humanity to disappear in the sky, in suspension like atoms which are awaiting precipitation; apparently outside of destiny; ignoring that beaten track yesterday, today, tomorrow; astounded, swooping, floating; at times, light enough to soar into the infinity; almost ready for the eternal flight.

They were sleeping awake in this rocking cradle. O splendid lethargy of the real overwhelmed by the ideal!

Sometimes, beautiful as was Cosette, Marius closed his eyes before her. With closed eyes is the best way of looking at the soul.

Marius and Cosette did not ask where this would lead them. They looked upon themselves as arrived. It is a strange demand for men to ask that love should anywhither.

3. Shadow commences

JEAN VALJEAN suspected nothing.

Cosette, a little less dreamy than Marius, was cheerful, and that was enough to make Jean Valjean happy. The thoughts of Cosette, her tender preoccupations, the image of Marius which filled her soul, detracted nothing from the incomparable purity of her beautiful, chaste, and smiling forehead. She was at the age when the maiden bears her love as the angel bears her lily. And then when two lovers have an understanding they always get along well; any third person who might disturb their love, is kept in perfect blindness by a very few precautions, always the same for all lovers. Thus never any objections from Cosette to Jean Valjean. Did he wish to take a walk? yes, my dear father. Did he wish to remain at home? very well. Would he spend the evening with Cosette? she was in raptures. As he always retired at ten o'clock, at such times Marius would not come to the garden till after that hour, when from the street he would hear Cosette open the glass-door leading out on the steps. We need not say that Marius was never met by day. Jean Valjean no longer even thought that Marius was in existence. Once, only, one morning, he happened to say to Cosette: 'Why, you have something white on your back!' The evening before, Marius, in a transport, had pressed Cosette against the wall.

Old Toussaint, who went to bed early, thought of nothing but going to sleep, once her work was done, and was ignorant of all, like Jean Valjean.

Never did Marius set foot into the house. When he was with Cosette they hid themselves in a recess near the steps, so that they could neither be seen nor heard from the street, and they sat there, contenting themselves often, by way of conversation, with pressing each other's hands twenty times a minute while looking into the branches of the trees. At such moments, a thunderbolt might have fallen within thirty paces of them, and they would not have suspected it, so deeply was the reverie of the one absorbed and buried in the reverie of the other.

Limpid purities. Hours all white, almost all alike. Such loves as these are a collection of lily leaves and dove-down.

The whole garden was between them and the street. Whenever Marius came in and went out, he carefully replaced the bar of the grating in such a way that no derangement was visible.

He went away commonly about midnight, returning to Courfeyrac's. Courfeyrac said to Bahorel:

'Would you believe it? Marius comes home nowadays at one o'clock in the morning.'

Bahorel answered:

'What would you expect? every young person has his wild oats.'

At times Courfeyrac folded his arms, assumed a serious air, and said to Marius:

'You are getting dissipated, young man!'

Courfeyrac, a practical man, was not pleased at this reflection of an invisible paradise upon Marius; he had little taste for unpublished passions, he was impatient at them, and he occasionally would serve Marius with a summons to return to the real.

One morning, he threw out this admonition:

'My dear fellow, you strike me at present as being situated in the moon, kingdom of dream, province of illusion, capital Soap-Bubble. Come, be a good boy, what is her name?'

But nothing could make Marius 'confess'. You might have torn his nails out sooner than one of the two sacred syllables which composed that ineffable name, *Cosette.* True love is luminous as the dawn, and silent as the grave. Only there was, to Courfeyrac, this change in Marius, that he had a radiant taciturnity.

During this sweet month of May, Marius and Cosette knew these transcendent joys:

To quarrel and to say monsieur and mademoiselle, merely to say Marius and Cosette better afterwards;

To talk at length, and with most minute detail, of people who did not interest them in the least; a further proof that, in this ravishing opera which is called love, the libretto is almost nothing;

For Marius, to listen to Cosette talking dress;

For Cosette, to listen to Marius talking politics;

To hear, knee touching knee, the wagons roll along the Rue de Babylone;

To gaze upon the same planet in space, or the same worm glow in the grass;

To keep silence together; a pleasure still greater than to talk;

Etc., etc.

Meanwhile various complications were approaching.

One evening Marius was making his way to the rendezvous by the Boulevard des Invalides; he usually walked with his head bent down; as he was just turning the corner of the Rue Plumet, he heard someone saying very near him:

'Good evening, Monsieur Marius.'

He looked up, and recognised Eponine.

This produced a singular effect upon him. He had not thought even once of this girl since the day she brought him to the Rue Plumet, he had not seen her again, and she had completely gone out of his mind. He had motives of gratitude only towards her; he owed his present happiness to her, and still it was annoying to him to meet her.

It is a mistake to suppose that passion, when it is fortunate and pure, leads man to a state of perfection; it leads him simply, as we have said, to a state of forgetfulness. In this situation man forgets to be bad, but he also forgets to be good. Gratitude, duty, necessary and troublesome memories, vanish. At any other time Marius would have felt very differently towards Eponine. Absorbed in Cosette, he had not even clearly in his mind that this Eponine's name was Eponine Thénardier, and that she bore a name written in his father's will, that name to which he would have been, a few months before, so ardently devoted. We show Marius just as he was. His father himself, disappeared somewhat from his soul beneath the splendour of his love.

He answered with some embarrassment:

'What! is it you, Eponine?'

'Why do you speak to me so sternly? Have I done anything to you?'

'No,' answered he.

Certainly, he had nothing against her. Far from it. Only, he felt that he could not do otherwise, now that he had whispered to Cosette, than speak coldly to Eponine.

As he was silent, she exclaimed:

'Tell me now – '

Then she stopped. It seemed as if words failed this creature, once so reckless and so bold. She attempted to smile and could not. She resumed:

'Well? – '

Then she was silent again, and stood with her eyes cast down.

'Good evening, Monsieur Marius,' said she all at once abruptly, and she went away.

4. Cab rolls in English and yelps in argot

THE NEXT DAY, it was the 3rd of June, the 3rd of June 1832, a date which must be noted on account of the grave events which were at that time suspended over the horizon of Paris like thunderclouds. Marius, at nightfall, was following the same path as the evening before, with the same rapturous thoughts in his heart, when he perceived, under the trees of the boulevard, Eponine approaching him. Two days in succession, this was too much. He turned hastily, left the boulevard, changed his route, and went to the Rue Plumet through the Rue Monsieur.

This caused Eponine to follow him to the Rue Plumet, a thing which she had not done before. She had been content until then to see him on his way through the boulevard without even seeking to meet him. The evening previous, only, had she tried to speak to him.

Eponine followed him then, without a suspicion on his part. She saw him push aside the bar of the grating, and glide into the garden.

'Why!' said she, 'he is going into the house.'

She approached the grating, felt of the bars one after another, and easily recognised the one which Marius had displaced.

She murmured in an undertone, with a mournful accent:

'None of that, Lisette!'

She sat down upon the surbase of the grating, close beside the bar, as if she were guarding it. It was just at the point at which the grating joined the neighbouring wall. There was an obscure corner there, in which Eponine was entirely hidden.

She remained thus for more than an hour, without stirring and without breathing, a prey to her own thoughts.

About ten o'clock in the evening, one of the two or three passers in the Rue Plumet, a belated old bourgeois who was hurrying through this deserted and ill-famed place, keeping along by the garden grating, on reaching the angle which the grating made with the wall, heard a sullen and threatening voice which said:

'I wouldn't be surprised if he came every evening!'

He cast his eyes about him, saw nobody, dared not look into that dark corner, and was very much frightened. He doubled his pace.

This person had reason to hasten, for a very few moments afterwards six men, who were walking separately and at some distance from each other along the wall, and who might have been taken for a tipsy patrol, entered the Rue Plumet.

The first to arrive at the grating of the garden stopped and waited for the others; in a second they were all six together.

These men began to talk in a low voice.

'It is *icicaille*,' said one of them.

'Is there a *cab* [1] in the garden?' asked another.

'I don't know. At all events I have *levé* [2] a bullet which we will make him *morfiler*.' [3]

'Have you some mastic to *frangir* the *vanterne*? [4]

'Yes.'

'The grating is old,' added a fifth, who had a voice like a ventriloquist.

'So much the better,' said the second who had spoken. 'It will not *criblera* [5] under the *bastringue*,[6] and will not be so hard to *faucher*. [7]

The sixth, who had not yet opened his mouth, began to examine the grating as Eponine had done an hour before, grasping each bar successively and shaking it carefully. In this way he came to the bar which Marius had loosened. Just as he was about to lay hold of this bar, a hand, starting abruptly from the shadow, fell upon his arm, he felt himself pushed sharply back by the middle of his breast, and a roughened voice said to him without crying out:

'There is a *cab*.'

At the same time he saw a pale girl standing before him.

The man felt that commotion which is always given by the unexpected. He bristled up hideously; nothing is so frightful to see as ferocious beasts which are startled, their appearance when terrified is terrifying. He recoiled, and stammered:

'What is this creature?'

'Your daughter.'

It was indeed Eponine who was speaking to Thénardier.

On the appearance of Eponine the five others, that is to say, Claquesous, Gueulemer, Babet, Montparnasse and Brujon, approached without a sound, without haste, without saying a word, with the ominous slowness peculiar to these men of the night.

In their hands might be distinguished some strangely hideous tools. Gueulemer had one of those crooked crowbars which the prowlers call *fanchons*.

'Ah there, what are you doing here? what do you want of us? are you crazy?' exclaimed Thénardier, as much as one can exclaim in a whisper. 'What do you come and hinder us in our work for?'

Eponine began to laugh and sprang to his neck.

'I am here, my darling father, because I am here. Is there any law against sitting upon the stones in these days? It is you who shouldn't be here. What are you coming here for, since it is a biscuit? I told Magnon so. There is nothing to do here. But embrace me now, my dear good father! What a long time since I have seen you! You are out then?'

Thénardier tried to free himself from Eponine's arms, and muttered:

1 Dog 2 Brought. From the Spanish *llevar*. 3 Eat 4 *To break a pane* by means of a plaster of mastic, which, sticking to the window, holds the pieces of glass and prevents noise. 5 Cry 6 Saw 7 Cut

'Very well. You have embraced me. Yes, I am out. I am not in. Now, be off.'

But Eponine did not loose her hold and redoubled her caresses.

'My darling father, how did you do it? You must have a good deal of wit to get out of that! Tell me about it! And my mother? where is my mother? Give me some news of mamma.'

Thénardier answered:

'She is well, I don't know, let me alone, I tell you to be off.'

'I don't want to go away just now,' said Eponine, with the pettishness of a spoiled child, 'you send me away when here it is four months that I haven't seen you, and when I have hardly had time to embrace you.'

And she caught her father again by the neck.

'Ah! come now, this is foolish,' said Babet.

'Let us hurry!' said Gueulemer, 'the *coqueurs* may come along.'

The ventriloquist sang this distich:

> Nous n'sommes pas le jour de l'an,
> A bécoter papa, maman.*

Eponine turned towards the five bandits.

'Why, this is Monsieur Brujon. Good day, Monsieur Babet. Good day, Monsieur Claquesous. Don't you remember me, Monsieur Gueulemer? How goes it, Montparnasse?'

'Yes, they recognise you,' said Thénardier. 'But good-day, good-night, keep off! don't disturb us!'

'It is the hour for foxes, and not for pullets,' said Montparnasse.

'You see well enough that we are going to *goupiner icigo*,' † added Babet.

Eponine took Montparnasse's hand.

'Take care,' said he, 'you will cut yourself, I have a *lingre* ‡ open.'

'My darling Montparnasse,' answered Eponine very gently, 'we must have confidence in people. I am my father's daughter, perhaps. Monsieur Babet, Monsieur Gueulemer, it is I who was charged with finding out about this affair.'

It is remarkable that Eponine did not speak argot. Since she had known Marius, that horrid language had become impossible to her.

She pressed in her little hand, as bony and weak as the hand of a corpse, the great rough fingers of Gueulemer, and continued:

'You know very well that I am not a fool. Ordinarily you believe me. I have done you service on occasion. Well, I have learned all about this, you would expose yourself uselessly, do you see. I swear to you that there is nothing to be done in that house.'

'There are lone women,' said Gueulemer.

'No. The people have moved away.'

'The candles have not, anyhow!' said Babet.

And he showed Eponine, through the top of the trees, a light which was moving about in the garret of the cottage. It was Toussaint, who had sat up to hang out her clothes to dry.

Eponine made a final effort.

* 'Tis not the first of the new year
To hug papa and mamma dear.

† To work here ‡ Knife

'Well,' said she, 'they are very poor people, and it is a shanty where there isn't a sou.'

'Go to the devil!' cried Thénardier. 'When we have turned the house over, and when we have put the cellar at the top and the garret at the bottom, we will tell you what there is inside, and whether it is *balles*, *ronds*, or *broques*.' *

And he pushed her to pass by.

'My good friend Monsieur Montparnasse,' said Eponine, 'I beg you, you who are a good boy, don't go in!'

'Take care, you will cut yourself,' replied Montparnasse.

Thénardier added, with his decisive tone:

'Clear out, *fée*, and let men do their work!'

Eponine let go of Montparnasse's hand, which she had taken again, and said:

'You will go into that house then?'

'Just a little!' said the ventriloquist, with a sneer.

Then she placed her back against the grating, faced the six bandits who were armed to the teeth, and to whom the night gave faces of demons, and said in a low and firm voice:

'Well! I won't have it.'

They stopped astounded. The ventriloquist, however, finished his sneer. She resumed.

'Friends! listen to me. That isn't the thing. Now speak. In the first place, if you go into the garden, if you touch this grating, I shall cry out, I shall rap on doors, I shall wake everybody up, I shall have all six of you arrested, I shall call the *sergents de ville*.'

'She would do it,' said Thénardier in a low tone to Brujon and the ventriloquist.

She shook her head, and added:

'Beginning with my father!'

Thénardier approached.

'Not so near, goodman!' said she.

He drew back, muttering between his teeth: 'Why, what is the matter with her?' and he added:

'Slut!'

She began to laugh in a terrible way:

'As you will, you shall not go in. I am not the daughter of a dog, for I am the daughter of a wolf. There are six of you, what is that to me? You are men. Now, I am a woman. I am not afraid of you, not a bit. I tell you that you shall not go into this house, because it does not please me. If you approach, I shall bark. I told you so, I am the *cab*, I don't care for you. Go your ways, you annoy me. Go where you like, but don't come here, I forbid it! You have knives, I have feet and hands. That makes no difference, come on now!'

She took a step towards the bandits, she was terrible, she began to laugh.

'The devil! I am not afraid. This summer, I shall be hungry; this winter, I shall be cold. Are they fools, these geese of men, to think that they can make a girl afraid! Of what! afraid? Ah, pshaw, indeed! Because you have hussies of mistresses who hide under the bed when you raise your voice, it won't do here! I, I am not afraid of anything!'

* Francs, sous, or farthings

She kept her eye fixed upon Thénardier, and said:

'Not even of you, father!'

Then she went on, casting her ghastly bloodshot eyes over the bandits:

'What is it to me whether somebody picks me up tomorrow on the pavement of the Rue Plumet, beaten to death with a club by my father, or whether they find me in a year in the ditches of Saint Cloud, or at the Ile de Cygnes, among the old rotten rubbish and the dead dogs?'

She was obliged to stop; a dry cough seized her, her breath came like a rattle from her narrow and feeble chest.

She resumed:

'I have but to cry out, they come, bang! You are six; but I am everybody.'

Thénardier made a movement towards her.

' 'Proach not!' cried she.

He stopped, and said to her mildly:

'Well, no; I will not approach, but don't speak so loud. Daughter, you want then to hinder us in our work? Still we must earn our living. Have you no love for your father now?'

'You bother me,' said Eponine.

'Still we must live, we must eat – '

'Die.'

Saying which, she sat down on the surbase of the grating, humming:

Mon bras si dodu,
Ma jambe bien faite
Et le temps perdu.*

She had her elbow on her knee and her chin in her hand, and she was swinging her foot with an air of indifference. Her dress was full of holes, and showed her sharp shoulder-blades. The neighbouring lamp lit up her profile and her attitude. Nothing could be more resolute or more surprising.

The six assassins, sullen and abashed at being held in check by a girl, went under the protecting shade of the lantern and held counsel, with humiliated and furious shrugs of their shoulders.

She watched them the while with a quiet yet indomitable air.

'Something is the matter with her,' said Babet. 'Some reason. Is she in love with the *cab*? But it is a pity to lose it. Two women, an old fellow who lodges in a back-yard, there are pretty good curtains at the windows. The old fellow must be a *guinal*.† I think it is a good thing.'

'Well, go in the rest of you,' exclaimed Montparnasse. 'Do the thing. I will stay here with the girl, and if she trips – '

He made the open knife which he had in his hand gleam in the light of the lantern.

Thénardier said not a word and seemed ready for anything.

Brujon, who was something of an oracle, and who had, as we know, 'got up the thing', had not yet spoken. He appeared thoughtful. He had a reputation for recoiling from nothing, and they knew that he had plundered, from sheer

* So plump is my arm, / My leg so well formed, / Yet my time has no charm. † A Jew

bravado, a police station. Moreover he made verses and songs, which gave him a great authority.

Babet questioned him.

'You don't say anything, Brujon?'

Brujon remained silent a minute longer, then he shook his head in several different ways, and at last decided to speak.

'Here: I met two sparrows fighting this morning; tonight, I run against a woman quarrelling. All this is bad. Let us go away.'

They went away.

As they went, Montparnasse murmured:

'No matter, if they had said so, I would have made her feel the weight of my hand.'

Babet answered:

'Not I. I don't strike a lady.'

At the corner of the street, they stopped and exchanged this enigmatic dialogue in a smothered voice:

'Where are we going to sleep tonight?'

'Under *Pantin.*' *

'Have you the key of the grating with you, Thénardier?'

'Humph.'

Eponine, who had not taken her eyes off from them, saw them turn back the way they had come. She rose and began to creep along the walls and houses behind them. She followed them as far as the boulevard. There, they separated, and she saw these men sink away in the obscurity into which they seemed to melt.

5. Things of the night

AFTER THE DEPARTURE of the bandits, the Rue Plumet resumed its quiet night appearance.

What had just taken place in this street would not have astonished a forest. The trees, the copse, the heath, the branches roughly intertangled, the tall grass, have a darkly mysterious existence; this wild multitude sees there sudden apparitions of the invisible; there what is below man distinguishes through the dark what is above man; and there in the night meet things unknown by us living men. Nature, bristling and tawny, is startled at certain approaches in which she seems to feel the supernatural. The forces of the shadow know each other, and have mysterious balancings among themselves. Teeth and claws dread the intangible. Bloodthirsty brutality, voracious and starving appetites in quest of prey, instincts armed with nails and jaws which find in the belly their origin and their object, behold and snuff with anxiety the impassive spectral figure prowling beneath a shroud, standing in its dim shivering robe, and seeming to them to live with a dead and terrible life. These brutalities, which are matter only, confusedly dread having to do with the infinite dark condensed into an unknown being. A black figure barring the passage stops the wild beast short. That which comes from the graveyard intimidates and disconcerts that which comes from the den; the ferocious is afraid of the sinister: wolves recoil before a ghoul.

* *Pantin*, Paris.

6. Marius becomes so real as to give Cosette his address

WHILE THIS SPECIES of dog in human form was mounting guard over the grating, and the six bandits were slinking away before a girl, Marius was with Cosette.

Never had the sky been more studded with stars, or more charming, the trees more tremulous, the odour of the shrubs more penetrating; never had the birds gone to sleep in the leaves with a softer sound; never had all the harmonies of the universal serenity better responded to the interior music of love; never had Marius been more enamoured, more happy, more in ecstasy. But he had found Cosette sad. Cosette had been weeping. Her eyes were red.

It was the first cloud in this wonderful dream,

Marius' first word was:

'What is the matter?'

And she answered:

'See.'

Then she sat down on the seat near the stairs, and as he took his place all trembling beside her, she continued:

'My father told me this morning to hold myself in readiness, that he had business, and that perhaps we should go away.'

Marius shuddered from head to foot.

When we are at the end of life, to die means to go away; when we are at the beginning, to go away means to die.

For six weeks Marius, gradually, slowly, by degrees, had been each day taking possession of Cosette. A possession entirely ideal, but thorough. As we have entirely explained, in the first love, the soul is taken far before the body; afterwards the body is taken far before the soul; sometimes the soul is not taken at all; the Faublas and the Prudhommes add: because there is none; but the sarcasm is fortunately a blasphemy. Marius then possessed Cosette, as minds possess; but he wrapped her in his whole soul, and clasped her jealously with an incredible conviction. He possessed her smile, her breath, her perfume, the deep radiance of her blue eyes, the softness of her skin when he touched her hand, the charming mark that she had on her neck, all her thoughts. They had agreed never to go to sleep without dreaming of each other, and they had kept their word. He possessed all Cosette's dreams. He beheld untiringly, and he sometimes touched with his breath, the short hairs at the back of her neck, and he declared to himself that there was not one of those little hairs which did not belong to him, Marius. He gazed upon and adored the things which she wore, her knot of ribbon, her gloves, her cuffs, her slippers, as sacred objects of which he was master. He thought that he was lord of those pretty shell-combs which she had in her hair, and he said to himself even, dim and confused stammerings of dawning desire, that there was not a thread of her dress, not a mesh in her stockings, not a fold of her corset, which was not his. At Cosette's side, he felt near his wealth, near his property, near his despot, and near his slave. It seemed as if they so mingled their souls, that if they had desired to take them back again, it would have been impossible to identify them. 'This one is mine.' 'No, it is mine.' 'I assure you that you are mistaken. This is really I.' 'What you take for you, is I.' Marius was something which was a part of Cosette, and Cosette was something which was a part of Marius. Marius felt Cosette living within him. To have Cosette, to possess Cosette, this to him was not separable from breathing. Into the midst of this faith, of this intoxication, of this virginal possession, marvellous and absolute, of this sovereignty, these words: 'We are going away,' fell all at once, and the sharp voice of reality cried to him: 'Cosette is not yours!'

Marius awoke. For six weeks Marius had lived, as we have said, outside of life; this word, going away, brought him roughly back to it.

He could not find a word. She said to him in her turn.

'What is the matter?'

He answered so low that Cosette hardly heard him:

'I don't understand what you have said.'

She resumed:

'This morning my father told me to arrange all my little affairs and to be ready, that he would give me his clothes to pack, that he was obliged to take a journey, that we were going away, that we must have a large trunk for me and a small one for him, to get all that ready within a week from now, and that we should go perhaps to England.'

'But it is monstrous!' exclaimed Marius.

It is certain that at that moment, in Marius' mind, no abuse of power, no violence, no abomination of the most cruel tyrants, no action of Busiris, Tiberius, or Henry VIII, was equal in ferocity to this: M. Fauchelevent taking his daughter to England because he has business.

He asked in a feeble voice:

'And when should you start?'

'He didn't say when.'

'And when should you return?'

'He didn't say when.'

Marius arose, and said coldly:

'Cosette, shall you go?'

Cosette turned upon him her beautiful eyes full of anguish and answered with a sort of bewilderment:

'Where?'

'To England? shall you go?'

'Why do you speak so to me?'

'I ask you if you shall go?'

'What would you have me do?' said she, clasping her hands.

'So, you will go?'

'If my father goes?'

'So, you will go?'

Cosette took Marius' hand and pressed it without answering.

'Very well,' said Marius. 'Then I shall go elsewhere.'

Cosette felt the meaning of this word still more than she understood it. She turned so pale that her face became white in the darkness. She stammered:

'What do you mean?'

Marius looked at her, then slowly raised his eyes towards heaven and answered:

'Nothing.'

When his eyes were lowered, he saw Cosette smiling upon him. The smile of the woman whom we love has a brilliancy which we can see by night.

'How stupid we are! Marius, I have an idea.'

'What?'

'Go if we go! I will tell you where! Come and join me where I am!'

Marius was now a man entirely awakened. He had fallen back into reality. He cried to Cosette:

'Go with you? are you mad? But it takes money, and I have none! Go to England? Why I owe now, I don't know, more than ten louis to Courfeyrac, one of my friends whom you do not know! Why I have an old hat which is not worth three francs, I have a coat from which some of the buttons are gone in front, my shirt is all torn, my elbows are out, my boots let in the water; for six weeks I have not thought of it, and I have not told you about it. Cosette! I am a miserable wretch. You only see me at night, and you give me your love; if you should see me by day, you would give me a sou! Go to England? Ah! I have not the means to pay for a passport!'

He threw himself against a tree which was near by, standing with his arms above his head, his forehead against the bark, feeling neither the tree which was chafing his skin, nor the fever which was hammering his temples, motionless, and ready to fall, like a statue of Despair.

He was a long time thus. One might remain through eternity in such abysses. At last he turned. He heard behind him a little stifled sound, soft and sad.

It was Cosette sobbing.

She had been weeping more than two hours while Marius had been thinking.

He came to her, fell on his knees, and, prostrating himself slowly, he took the tip of her foot which peeped from under her dress and kissed it.

She allowed it in silence. There are moments when woman accepts, like a goddess sombre and resigned, the religion of love.

'Do not weep,' said he.

She murmured:

'Because I am perhaps going away, and you cannot come!'

He continued:

'Do you love me?'

She answered him by sobbing out that word of Paradise which is never more enrapturing than when it comes through tears:

'I adore you!'

He continued with a tone of voice which was an inexpressible caress:

'Do not weep. Tell me, will you do this for me, not to weep?'

'Do you love me too?' said she.

He caught her hand.

'Cosette, I have never given my word of honour to anybody, because I stand in awe of my word of honour. I feel that my father is at my side. Now, I give you my most sacred word of honour that, if you go away, I shall die.'

There was in the tone with which he pronounced these words a melancholy so solemn and so quiet, that Cosette trembled. She felt that chill which is given by a stern and true fact passing over us. From the shock she ceased weeping.

'Now listen,' said he, 'do not expect me tomorrow.'

'Why not?'

'Do not expect me till the day after tomorrow!'

'Oh! why not?'

'You will see.'

'A day without seeing you! Why, that is impossible.'

'Let us sacrifice one day to gain perhaps a whole life.'

And Marius added in an undertone, and aside:

'He is a man who changes none of his habits, and he has never received anybody till evening.'

'What man are you speaking of?' inquired Cosette.

'Me? I said nothing.'

'What is it you hope for, then?'

'Wait till day after tomorrow.'

'You wish it?'

'Yes, Cosette.'

She took his head in both her hands, rising on tiptoe to reach his height, and striving to see his hope in his eyes.

Marius continued:

'It occurs to me, you must know my address, something may happen, we don't know; I live with that friend named Courfeyrac, Rue de la Verrerie, number 16.'

He put his hand in his pocket, took out a penknife, and wrote with the blade upon the plastering of the wall:

16, Rue de la Verrerie.

Cosette, meanwhile, began to look into his eyes again.

'Tell me your idea. Marius, you have an idea. Tell me. Oh! tell me, so that I may pass a good night!'

'My idea is this: that it is impossible that God should wish to separate us. Expect me day after tomorrow.'

'What shall I do till then?' said Cosette. 'You, you are out doors, you go, you come! How happy men are. I have to stay alone. Oh! how sad I shall be! What is it you are going to do tomorrow evening, tell me?'

'I shall try a plan.'

'Then I will pray God, and I will think of you from now till then, that you may succeed. I will not ask any more questions, since you wish me not to. You are my master. I shall spend my evening tomorrow singing that music of Euryanthe which you love, and which you came to hear one evening behind my shutter. But day after tomorrow you will come early; I shall expect you at night, at nine o'clock precisely. I forewarn you. Oh dear! how sad it is that the days are long! You understand; – when the clock strikes nine, I shall be in the garden.'

'And I too.'

And without saying it, moved by the same thought, drawn on by those electric currents which put two lovers in continual communication, both intoxicated with pleasure even in their grief, they fell into each other's arms, without perceiving that their lips were joined, while their uplifted eyes, overflowing with ecstasy and full of tears, were fixed upon the stars.

When Marius went out, the street was empty. It was the moment when Eponine was following the bandits to the boulevard.

While Marius was thinking with his head against the tree, an idea had passed through his mind; an idea, alas! which he himself deemed senseless and impossible. He had formed a desperate resolution.

7. *The old heart and young heart in presence*

GRANDFATHER GILLENORMAND had, at this period, fully completed his ninety-first year. He still lived with Mademoiselle Gillenormand, Rue des Filles du Calvaire, No. 6, in that old house which belonged to him. He was, as we remember, one of those antique old men who await death still erect, whom age loads without making them stoop, and whom grief itself does not bend.

Still, for some time, his daughter had said: 'My father is failing.' He no longer beat the servants; he struck his cane with less animation on the landing of the stairs, when Basque was slow in opening the door. The revolution of July had hardly exasperated him for six months. He had seen almost tranquilly in the *Moniteur* this coupling of words: M. Humblot Conté, peer of France. The fact is, that the old man was filled with dejection. He did not bend, he did not yield; that was no more a part of his physical than of his moral nature; but he felt himself interiorly failing. Four years he had been waiting for Marius, with his foot down, that is just the word, in the conviction that that naughty little scapegrace would ring at his door someday or other: now he had come, in certain gloomy hours, to say to himself that even if Marius should delay, but little longer – It was not death that was insupportable to him; it was the idea that perhaps he should never see Marius again. Never see Marius again – that had not, even for an instant, entered into his thought until this day; now this idea began to appear to him, and it chilled him. Absence, as always happens when feelings are natural and true, had only increased his grandfather's love for the ungrateful child who had gone away like that. It is on December nights, with the thermometer at zero, that we think most of the sun. M. Gillenormand was, or thought himself, in any event, incapable of taking a step, he the grandfather, towards his grandson; 'I would die first,' said he. He acknowledged no fault on his part; but he thought of Marius only with a deep tenderness and the mute despair of an old goodman who is going away into the darkness.

He was beginning to lose his teeth, which added to his sadness.

M. Gillenormand, without however acknowledging it to himself, for he would have been furious and ashamed at it, had never loved a mistress as he loved Marius.

He had had hung in his room, at the foot of his bed, as the first thing which he wished to see on awaking, an old portrait of his other daughter, she who was dead, Madame Pontmercy, a portrait taken when she was eighteen years old. He looked at this portrait incessantly. He happened one day to say, while looking at it:

'I think it looks like the child.'

'Like my sister?' replied Mademoiselle Gillenormand. 'Why yes.'

The old man added:

'And like him also.'

Once, as he was sitting, his knees pressed together, and his eyes almost closed, in a posture of dejection, his daughter ventured to say to him:

'Father, are you still so angry with him?'

She stopped, not daring to go further.

'With whom?' asked he.

'With that poor Marius?'

He raised his old head, laid his thin and wrinkled fist upon the table, and cried in his most irritated and quivering tone:

'Poor Marius, you say? That gentleman is a rascal, a worthless knave, a little ungrateful vanity, with no heart, no soul, a proud, a wicked man!'

And he turned away that his daughter might not see the tear he had in his eyes.

Three days later, after a silence which had lasted for four hours, he said to his daughter snappishly:

'I have had the honour to beg Mademoiselle Gillenormand never to speak to me of him.'

Aunt Gillenormand gave up all attempts and came to this profound diagnosis: 'My father never loved my sister very much after her folly. It is clear that he detests Marius.'

'After her folly' meant: after she married the colonel.

Still, as may have been conjectured, Mademoiselle Gillenormand had failed in her attempt to substitute her favourite, the officer of lancers, for Marius. The supplanter Théodule had not succeeded. Monsieur Gillenormand had not accepted the *quid pro quo*. The void in the heart does not accommodate itself to a proxy. Théodule, for his part, even while snuffing the inheritance, revolted at the drudgery of pleasing. The goodman wearied the lancer, and the lancer shocked the goodman. Lieutenant Théodule was lively doubtless, but a babbler; frivolous, but vulgar; a good liver, but of bad company; he had mistresses, it is true, and he talked about them a good deal, that is also true; but he talked about them badly. All his qualities had a defect. Monsieur Gillenormand was wearied out with hearing him tell of all the favours that he had won in the neighbourhood of his barracks, Rue de Babylone. And then Lieutenant Théodule sometimes came in his uniform with the tricolour cockade. This rendered him altogether insupportable. Grandfather Gillenormand, at last, said to his daughter: 'I have had enough of him, your Théodule. I have little taste for warriors in time of peace. Entertain him yourself, if you like. I am not sure, but I like the sabrers even better than the trailers of the sabre. The clashing of blades in battle is not so wretched, after all, as the rattling of the sheaths on the pavement. And then, to harness himself like a bully, and to strap himself up like a flirt, to wear a corset under a cuirass, is to be ridiculous twice over. A genuine man keeps himself at an equal distance from swagger and roguery. Neither hector, nor heartless. Keep your Théodule for yourself.'

It was of no use for his daughter to say: 'Still he is your grand-nephew,' it turned out that Monsieur Gillenormand, who was grandfather to the ends of his nails, was not grand-uncle at all.

In reality, as he had good judgement and made the comparison, Théodule only served to increase his regret for Marius.

One evening, it was the 4th of June, which did not prevent Monsieur Gillenormand from having a blazing fire in his fireplace, he had said goodnight to his daughter who was sewing in the adjoining room. He was alone in his room with the rural scenery, his feet upon the andirons, half enveloped in his vast coromandel screen with nine folds, leaning upon his table on which two candles were burning under a green shade, buried in his tapestried armchair, a book in his hand, but not reading. He was dressed, according to his custom, *en incroyable*, and resembled an antique portrait of Garat. This would have caused him to be followed in the streets, but his daughter always covered him when he went out, with a huge bishop's doublet, which hid his dress. At home, except in getting up and going to bed, he never wore a dressing-gown. '*It gives an old look*,' said he.

Monsieur Gillenormand thought of Marius lovingly and bitterly; and, as usual, the bitterness predominated. An increase of tenderness always ended by boiling over and turning into indignation. He was at that point where we seek to adopt a course, and to accept what rends us. He was just explaining to himself that there was now no longer any reason for Marius to return, that if he had been going to return, he would have done so already, that he must give him up. He endeavoured to bring himself to the idea that it was over with, and that he would die without seeing 'that gentleman' again. But his whole nature revolted; his old paternity could not consent to it. 'What?' said he, this was his sorrowful refrain, 'he will not come back!' His bald head had fallen upon his breast, and he was vaguely fixing a lamentable and irritated look upon the embers on his hearth.

In the deepest of this reverie, his old domestic, Basque, came in and asked:

'Can monsieur receive Monsieur Marius?'

The old man straightened up, pallid and like a corpse which rises under a galvanic shock. All his blood had flown back to his heart. He faltered:

'Monsieur Marius what?'

'I don't know,' answered Basque, intimidated and thrown out of countenance by his master's appearance, 'I have not seen him. Nicolette just told me: There is a young man here, say that it is Monsieur Marius.'

M. Gillenormand stammered out in a whisper:

'Show him in.'

And he remained in the same attitude, his head shaking, his eyes fixed on the door. It opened. A young man entered. It was Marius.

Marius stopped at the door, as if waiting to be asked to come in.

His almost wretched dress was not perceived in the obscurity produced by the green shade. Only his face, calm and grave, but strangely sad, could be distinguished.

M. Gillenormand, as if congested with astonishment and joy, sat for some moments without seeing anything but a light, as when one is in presence of an apparition. He was almost fainting; he perceived Marius through a blinding haze. It was indeed he, it was indeed Marius!

At last! after four years! He seized him, so to speak, all over at a glance. He thought him beautiful, noble, striking, adult, a complete man, with graceful attitude and pleasing air. He would gladly have opened his arms, called him, rushed upon him, his heart melted in rapture, affectionate words welled and overflowed in his breast; indeed, all this tenderness started up and came to his lips, and, through the contrast which was the groundwork of his nature, there came forth a harsh word. He said abruptly:

'What is it you come here for?'

Marius answered with embarrassment:

'Monsieur – '

M. Gillenormand would have had Marius throw himself into his arms. He was displeased with Marius and with himself. He felt that he was rough, and that Marius was cold. It was to the goodman an insupportable and irritating anguish, to feel himself so tender and so much in tears within, while he could only be harsh without. The bitterness returned. He interrupted Marius with a sharp tone:

'Then what do you come for?'

This then signified: *If you don't come to embrace me.* Marius looked at his grandfather, whose pallor had changed to marble.

'Monsieur' –

The old man continued, in a stern voice:

'Do you come to ask my pardon? have you seen your fault?'

He thought to put Marius on the track, and that 'the child' was going to bend. Marius shuddered; it was the disavowal of his father which was asked of him; he cast down his eyes and answered:

'No, monsieur.'

'And then,' exclaimed the old man impetuously, with a grief which was bitter and full of anger, 'what do you want with me?'

Marius clasped his hands, took a step, and said in a feeble and trembling voice:

'Monsieur, have pity on me.'

This word moved M. Gillenormand; spoken sooner, it would have softened him, but it came too late. The grandfather arose; he supported himself upon his cane with both hands, his lips were white, his forehead quivered, but his tall stature commanded the stooping Marius.

'Pity on you, monsieur! The youth asks pity from the old man of ninety-one! You are entering life, I am leaving it; you go to the theatre, the ball, the café, the billiard-room; you have wit, you please the women, you are a handsome fellow, while I cannot leave my chimney corner in midsummer; you are rich, with the only riches there are, while I have all the poverties of old age; infirmity, isolation! You have your thirty-two teeth, a good stomach, a keen eye, strength, appetite, health, cheerfulness, a forest of black hair, while I have not even white hair left; I have lost my teeth, I am losing my legs, I am losing my memory, there are three names of streets which I am always confounding, the Rue Charlot, the Rue du Chaume, and the Rue Saint Claude, there is where I am; you have the whole future before you full of sunshine, while I am beginning not to see another drop of it, so deep am I getting into the night; you are in love, of course, I am not loved by anybody in the world; and you ask pity of me. Zounds, Molière forgot this. If that is the way you jest at the Palais, Messieurs Lawyers, I offer you my sincere compliments. You are funny fellows.'

And the nonagenarian resumed in an angry and stern voice:

'Come now, what do you want of me?'

'Monsieur,' said Marius, 'I know that my presence is displeasing to you, but I come only to ask one thing of you, and then I will go away immediately.'

'You are a fool!' said the old man. 'Who tells you to go away?'

This was the translation of those loving words which he had deep in his heart: *Come, ask my pardon now! Throw yourself on my neck!* M. Gillenormand felt that Marius was going to leave him in a few moments, that his unkind reception repelled him, that his harshness was driving him away; he said all this to himself, and his anguish increased; and as his anguish immediately turned into anger, his harshness augmented. He would have had Marius comprehend, and Marius did not comprehend; which rendered the goodman furious. He continued:

'What! you have left me! me, your grandfather, you have left my house to go nobody knows where; you have afflicted your aunt, you have been, that is clear, it is more pleasant, leading the life of a bachelor, playing the elegant, going home at all hours, amusing yourself; you have not given me a sign of life; you have contracted debts without even telling me to pay them; you have made yourself a breaker of windows and a rioter, and, at the end of four years, you come to my house, and have nothing to say but that!'

This violent method of pushing the grandson to tenderness produced only silence on the part of Marius. M. Gillenormand folded his arms, a posture which with him was particularly imperious, and apostrophised Marius bitterly.

'Let us make an end of it. You have come to ask something of me, say you? Well what? what is it? speak!'

'Monsieur,' said Marius, with the look of a man who feels that he is about to fall into an abyss, 'I come to ask your permission to marry.'

M. Gillenormand rang. Basque half opened the door.

'Send my daughter in.'

A second later – the door opened again. Mademoiselle Gillenormand did not come in, but showed herself. Marius was standing, mute, his arms hanging down, with the look of a criminal. M. Gillenormand was coming and going up and down the room. He turned towards his daughter and said to her:

'Nothing. It is Monsieur Marius. Bid him good evening. Monsieur wishes to marry. That is all. Go.'

The crisp, harsh tones of the old man's voice announced a strange fullness of feeling. The aunt looked at Marius with a bewildered air, appeared hardly to recognise him, allowed neither a motion nor a syllable to escape her, and disappeared at a breath from her father, quicker than a dry leaf before a hurricane.

Meanwhile Grandfather Gillenormand had returned and stood with his back to the fireplace.

'You marry! at twenty-one! You have arranged that! You have nothing but a permission to ask! a formality. Sit down, monsieur. Well, you have had a revolution since I had the honour to see you. The Jacobins have had the upper hand. You ought to be satisfied. You are a republican, are you not, since you are a baron? You arrange that. The republic is sauce to the barony. Are you decorated by July? – did you take a bit of the Louvre, monsieur? There is close by here, in the Rue Saint Antoine, opposite the Rue des Nonaindières, a ball encrusted in the wall of the third storey of a house with this inscription: July 28th, 1830. Go and see that. That produces a good effect. Ah! Pretty things those friends of yours do. By the way, are they not making a fountain in the square of the monument of M. the Duke de Berry? So you want to marry? Whom? can the question be asked without indiscretion?'

He stopped, and, before Marius had had time to answer, he added violently:

'Come now, you have a business? your fortune made? how much do you earn at your lawyer's trade?'

'Nothing,' said Marius, with a firmness and resolution which were almost savage.

'Nothing? you have nothing to live on but the twelve hundred livres which I send you?'

Marius made no answer. M. Gillenormand continued:

'Then I understand the girl is rich?'

'As I am.'

'What! no dowry?'

'No.'

'Some expectations?'

'I believe not.'

'With nothing to her back! and what is the father?'

'I do not know.'

'What is her name?'

'Mademoiselle Fauchelevent.'

'Fauchewhat?'

'Fauchelevent.'

'Pttt!' said the old man.

'Monsieur!' exclaimed Marius.

M. Gillenormand interrupted him with the tone of a man who is talking to himself.

'That is it, twenty-one, no business, twelve hundred livres a year, Madame the Baroness Pontmercy will go to market to buy two sous' worth of parsley.'

'Monsieur,' said Marius, in the desperation of the last vanishing hope, 'I supplicate you! I conjure you, in the name of heaven, with clasped hands, monsieur, I throw myself at your feet, allow me to marry her!'

The old man burst into a shrill, dreary laugh, through which he coughed and spoke.

'Ha, ha, ha! you said to yourself, "The devil! I will go and find that old wig, that silly dolt! What a pity that I am not twenty-five! how I would toss him a good respectful notice! how I would give him the go-by. Never mind, I will say to him: Old idiot, you are too happy to see me, I desire to marry, I desire to espouse mamselle no matter whom, daughter of monsieur no matter what, I have no shoes, she has no chemise, all right; I desire to throw to the dogs my career, my future, my youth, my life; I desire to make a plunge into misery with a wife at my neck, that is my idea, you must consent to it! and the old fossil will consent." Go, my boy, as you like, tie your stone to yourself, espouse your Pousselevent, your Couplevent – Never, monsieur! never!'

'Father!'

'Never!'

At the tone in which this 'never' was pronounced Marius lost all hope. He walked the room with slow steps, his head bowed down, tottering, more like a man who is dying than like one who is going away. M. Gillenormand followed him with his eyes, and, at the moment the door opened and Marius was going out, he took four steps with the senile vivacity of impetuous and self-willed old men, seized Marius by the collar, drew him back forcibly into the room, threw him into an armchair, and said to him:

'Tell me about it!'

It was that single word, *father*, dropped by Marius, which had caused this revolution.

Marius looked at him in bewilderment. The changing countenance of M. Gillenormand expressed nothing now but a rough and ineffable good-nature. The guardian had given place to the grandfather.

'Come, let us see, speak, tell me about your love scrapes, jabber, tell me all! Lord! how foolish these young folks are!'

'Father,' resumed Marius –

The old man's whole face shone with an unspeakable radiance.

'Yes! that is it! call me father, and you shall see!'

There was now something so kind, so sweet, so open, so paternal, in this abruptness, that Marius, in this sudden passage from discouragement to hope, was, as it were, intoxicated, stupefied. He was sitting near the tables, the light of the candle made the wretchedness of his dress apparent, and the grandfather gazed at it in astonishment.

'Well, father,' said Marius –

'Come now,' interrupted M. Gillenormand, 'then you really haven't a sou? you are dressed like a robber.'

He fumbled in a drawer and took out a purse, which he laid upon the table:

'Here, there is a hundred louis, buy yourself a hat.'

'Father,' pursued Marius, 'my good father, if you knew. I love her. You don't realise it; the first time that I saw her was at the Luxembourg, she came there; in the beginning I did not pay much attention to her, and then I do not know how it came about, I fell in love with her. Oh I how wretched it has made me! Now at last I see her every day, at her own house, her father does not know it, only think that they are going away, we see each other in the garden in the evening, her father wants to take her to England, then I said to myself: I will go and see my grandfather and tell him about it. I should go crazy in the first place, I should die, I should make myself sick, I should throw myself into the river. I must marry her because I should go crazy. Now, that is the whole truth, I do not believe that I have forgotten anything. She lives in a garden where there is a railing, in the Rue Plumet. It is near the Invalides.'

Grandfather Gillenormand, radiant with joy, had sat down by Marius' side. While listening to him and enjoying the sound of his voice, he enjoyed at the same time a long pinch of snuff. At that word, Rue Plumet, he checked his inspiration and let the rest of his snuff fall on his knees.

'Rue Plumet! – you say Rue Plumet? – Let us see now! – Are there not some barracks down there? Why yes, that is it. Your cousin Théodule has told me about her. The lancer, the officer. A lassie, my good friend, a lassie! – Lord yes, Rue Plumet. That is what used to be called Rue Blomet. It comes back to me now. I have heard tell about this little girl of the grating in the Rue Plumet. In a garden, a Pamela. Your taste is not bad. They say she is nice. Between ourselves, I believe that ninny of a lancer has paid his court to her a little. I do not know how far it went. After all that does not amount to anything. And then, we must not believe him. He is a boaster. Marius! I think it is very well for a young man like you to be in love. It belongs to your age. I like you better in love than as a Jacobin. I like you better taken by a petticoat, Lord! by twenty petticoats, than by Monsieur de Robespierre. For my part, I do myself this justice that in the matter of *sans culottes*, I have never liked anything but women. Pretty women are pretty women, the devil! there is no objection to that. As to the little girl, she receives you unknown to papa. That is all right. I have had adventures like that myself. More than one. Do you know how we do? we don't take the thing ferociously; we don't rush into the tragic; we don't conclude with marriage and with Monsieur the Mayor and his scarf. We are altogether a shrewd fellow. We have good sense. Slip over it, mortals, don't marry. We come and find grandfather who is a good man at heart, and who almost always has a few rolls of louis in an old drawer; we say to him: "Grandfather, that's how it is." And grandfather says: "That is all natural. Youth must fare and old age must wear. I have been young, you will be old. Go on, my boy, you will repay this to your grandson. There are two hundred pistoles. Amuse yourself, roundly! Nothing better! that is the way the thing should be done. We don't marry, but that doesn't hinder." You understand me?'

Marius, petrified and unable to articulate a word, shook his head.

The goodman burst into a laugh, winked his old eye, gave him a tap on the knee, looked straight into his eyes with a significant and sparkling expression, and said to him with the most amorous shrug of the shoulders:

'Stupid! make her your mistress.'

Marius turned pale. He had understood nothing of all that his grandfather had been saying. This rigmarole of Rue Blomet, of Pamela, of barracks, of a lancer, had passed before Marius like a phantasmagoria. Nothing of all could relate to Cosette, who was a lily. The goodman was wandering. But this wandering had terminated in a word which Marius did understand, and which was a deadly insult to Cosette. That phrase, *make her your mistress*, entered the heart of the chaste young man like a sword.

He rose, picked up his hat which was on the floor, and walked towards the door with a firm and assured step. There he turned, bowed profoundly before his grandfather, raised his head again, and said:

'Five years ago you outraged my father; today you have outraged my wife. I ask nothing more of you, monsieur. Adieu.'

Grandfather Gillenormand, astounded, opened his mouth, stretched out his arms, attempted to rise, but before he could utter a word, the door closed and Marius had disappeared.

The old man was for a few moments motionless, and as it were thunder-stricken, unable to speak or breathe, as if a hand were clutching his throat. At last he tore himself from his chair, ran to the door as fast as a man who is ninety-one can run, opened it and cried:

'Help! help!'

His daughter appeared, then the servants. He continued with a pitiful rattle in his voice:

'Run after him! catch him! what have I done to him! he is mad! he is going away! Oh! my God! oh! my God! – this time he will not come back!'

He went to the window which looked upon the street, opened it with his tremulous old hands, hung more than half his body outside, while Basque and Nicolette held him from behind, and cried:

'Marius! Marius! Marius! Marius!'

But Marius was already out of hearing, and was at that very moment turning the corner of the Rue Saint Louis.

The nonagenarian carried his hands to his temples two or three times, with an expression of anguish, drew back tottering, and sank into an armchair, pulseless, voiceless, tearless, shaking his head, and moving his lips with a stupid air, having now nothing in his eyes or in his heart but something deep and mournful, which resembled night.

BOOK 9: WHERE ARE THEY GOING?

1. *Jean Valjean*

THAT VERY DAY, towards four o'clock in the afternoon, Jean Valjean was sitting alone upon the reverse of one of the most solitary embankments of the Champ de Mars. Whether from prudence, or from a desire for meditation, or simply as a result of one of those insensible changes of habits which creep little by little into all lives, he now rarely went out with Cosette. He wore his working-man's waistcoat, brown linen trousers, and his cap with the long visor hid his face. He was now calm and happy in regard to Cosette; what had for some time alarmed and disturbed him was dissipated; but within a week or two anxieties of a different nature had come upon him. One day, when walking on the boulevard, he had seen Thénardier; thanks to his disguise, Thénardier had not recognised him; but since then Jean Valjean had seen him again several times, and he was now certain that Thénardier was prowling about the quarter. This was sufficient to make him take a serious step. Thénardier there! this was all dangers at once. Moreover, Paris was not quiet: the political troubles had this inconvenience for him who had anything in his life to conceal, that the police had become very active, and very secret, and that in seeking to track out a man like Pépin or Morey, they would be very likely to discover a man like Jean Valjean. Jean Valjean had decided to leave Paris, and even France, and to pass over to England. He had told Cosette. In less than a week he wished to be gone. He was sitting on the embankment in the Champ de Mars, revolving all manner of thoughts in his mind, Thénardier, the police, the journey, and the difficulty of procuring a passport.

On all these points he was anxious.

Finally, an inexplicable circumstance which had just burst upon him, and with which he was still warm, had added to his alarm. On the morning of that very day, being the only one up in the house, and walking in the garden before Cosette's shutters were open, he had suddenly come upon this line scratched upon the wall, probably with a nail.

16, Rue de la Verrerie.

It was quite recent, the lines were white in the old black mortar, a tuft of nettles at the foot of the wall was powdered with fresh fine plaster. It had probably been written during the night. What was it? an address? a signal for others? a warning for him? At all events, it was evident that the garden had been violated, and that some persons unknown had penetrated into it. He recalled the strange incidents which had already alarmed the house. His mind worked upon this canvas. He took good care not to speak to Cosette of the line written on the wall, for fear of frightening her.

In the midst of these meditations, he perceived, by a shadow which the sun projected, that somebody had just stopped upon the crest of the embankment immediately behind him. He was about to turn round, when a folded paper fell upon his knees, as if a hand had dropped it from above his head. He took the paper, unfolded it, and read on it this word, written in large letters with a pencil:

REMOVE.

Jean Valjean rose hastily, there was no longer anybody on the embankment; he looked about him, and perceived a species of being larger than a child, smaller than a man, dressed in a grey blouse, and trousers of dirt-coloured cotton velvet, which jumped over the parapet and let itself slide into the ditch of the Champ de Mars.

Jean Valjean returned home immediately, full of thought.

2. *Marius*

MARIUS HAD LEFT M. Gillenormand's desolate. He had entered with a very small hope; he came out with an immense despair.

Still, and those who have observed the beginnings of the human heart will understand it, the lancer, the officer, the ninny, the cousin Théodule, had left no shadow in his mind. Not the slightest. The dramatic poet might apparently hope for some complications from this revelation, made in the very teeth of the grandson by the grandfather. But what the drama would gain, the truth would lose. Marius was at that age when we believe no ill; later comes the age when we believe all. Suspicions are nothing more nor less than wrinkles. Early youth has none. What overwhelms Othello glides over Candide. Suspect Cosette! There are a multitude of crimes which Marius could have more easily committed.

He began to walk the streets, the resource of those who suffer He thought of nothing which he could ever remember. At two o'clock in the morning he returned to Courfeyrac's, and threw himself, dressed as he was, upon his mattress. It was broad sunlight when he fell asleep, with that frightful, heavy slumber in which the ideas come and go in the brain. When he awoke, he saw standing in the room, their hats upon their heads, all ready to go out, and very busy, Courfeyrac, Enjolras, Feuilly, and Combeferre.

Courfeyrac said to him:

'Are you going to the funeral of General Lamarque?'

It seemed to him that Courfeyrac was speaking Chinese.

He went out sometime after them. He put into his pocket the pistols which Javert had confided to him at the time of the adventure of the 3rd of February, and which had remained in his hands. These pistols were still loaded. It would be difficult to say what obscure thought he had in his mind in taking them with him.

He rambled about all day without knowing where; it rained at intervals, he did not perceive it; for his dinner he bought a penny roll at a baker's, put it in his pocket, and forgot it. It would appear that he took a bath in the Seine without being conscious of it. There are moments when a man has a furnace in his brain. Marius was in one of those moments. He hoped nothing more, he feared nothing more; he had reached this condition since the evening before. He waited for night with feverish impatience, he had but one clear idea; that was, that at nine o'clock he should see Cosette. This last happiness was now his whole future; afterwards, darkness. At intervals, while walking along the most deserted boulevards, he seemed to hear strange sounds in Paris. He roused himself from his reverie, and said: 'Are they fighting?'

At nightfall, at precisely nine o'clock, as he had promised Cosette, he was in the Rue Plumet. When he approached the grating he forgot everything else. It was forty-eight hours since he had seen Cosette, he was going to see her again, every other thought faded away, and he felt now only a deep and wonderful joy. Those minutes in which we live centuries always have this sovereign and wonderful peculiarity, that for the moment while they are passing, they entirely fill the heart.

Marius displaced the grating, and sprang into the garden. Cosette was not at the place where she usually waited for him. He crossed the thicket and went to the recess near the steps. 'She is waiting for me there,' said he. Cosette was not there. He raised his eyes, and saw that the shutters of the house were closed. He took a turn around the garden, the garden was deserted. Then he returned to the house, and, mad with love, intoxicated, dismayed, exasperated with grief and anxiety, like a master who returns home in an untoward hour, he rapped on the shutters. He rapped, he rapped again, at the risk of seeing the window open and the forbidding face of the father appear and ask him: 'What do you want?' This was nothing compared with what he now began to see. When he had rapped, he raised his voice and called Cosette. 'Cosette!' cried he. 'Cosette!' repeated he imperiously. There was no answer. It was settled. Nobody in the garden; nobody in the house.

Marius fixed his despairing eyes upon that dismal house, as black, as silent, and more empty than a tomb. He looked at the stone seat where he had passed so many adorable hours with Cosette. Then he sat down upon the steps, his heart full of tenderness and resolution, he blessed his love in the depths of his thought, and he said to himself that since Cosette was gone, there was nothing more for him but to die.

Suddenly he heard a voice which appeared to come from the street, and which cried through the trees:

'Monsieur Marius!'

He arose.

'Hey?' said he.

'Monsieur Marius, is it you?'

'Yes.'

'Monsieur Marius,' added the voice, 'your friends are expecting you at the barricade, in the Rue de la Chanvrerie.'

This voice was not entirely unknown to him. It resembled the harsh and roughened voice of Eponine. Marius ran to the grating, pushed aside the movable bar, passed his head through, and saw somebody who appeared to him to be a young man rapidly disappearing in the twilight.

3. M. Mabeuf

Jean Valjean's purse was useless to M. Mabeuf. M. Mabeuf, in his venerable childlike austerity, had not accepted the gift of the stars; he did not admit that a star could coin itself into gold louis. He did not guess that what fell from the sky came from Gavroche. He carried the purse to the Commissary of Police of the quarter, as a lost article, placed by the finder at the disposition of claimants. The purse was lost, in fact. We need not say that nobody reclaimed it, and it did not help M. Mabeuf.

For the rest, M. Mabeuf had continued to descend.

The experiments upon indigo had succeeded no better at the Jardin des

Plantes than in his garden at Austerlitz. The year before, he owed his housekeeper her wages; now, we have seen, he owed three quarters of his rent. The pawnbroker, at the expiration of thirteen months, had sold the plates of his *Flora*. Some coppersmith had made saucepans of them. His plates gone, being no longer able even to complete the broken sets of his *Flora* which he still possessed, he had given up engravings and text at a wretched price to a second-hand bookseller, as *odd copies*. He had now nothing left of the work of his whole life. He began to eat up the money from these copies. When he saw that this slender resource was failing him, he renounced his garden and left it uncultivated. Before this, and for a long time before, he had given up the two eggs and the bit of beef which he used to eat from time to time. He dined on bread and potatoes. He had sold his last furniture, then all his spare bedding and clothing, then his collections of plants and his pictures; but he still had his most precious books, several of which were of great rarity, among other *Les Quadrins Historiques de la Bible*, edition of 1560, *La Concordance des Bibles* of Pierre de Besse, *Les Marguerites de la Marguerite* of Jean de la Haye with a dedication to the Queen of Navarre, the book *On the charge and dignity of the Ambassador* by the Sieur de Villiers Hotman, a *Florilegium Rabbinicum* of 1644, a Tibullus of 1567 with this splendid inscription: *Venetiis, in ædibus Manutianis*; finally a Diogenes Laertius, printed at Lyons in 1644, containing the famous variations of the manuscript 411, of the thirteenth century, in the Vatican, and those of the two manuscripts of Venice, 393 and 394, so fruitfully consulted by Henry Estienne, and all the passages in the Doric dialect which are found only in the celebrated manuscript of the twelfth century of the library of Naples. M. Mabeuf never made a fire in his room, and went to bed by daylight so as not to burn a candle. It seemed that he had now no neighbours, he was shunned when he went out; he was aware of it. The misery of a child is interesting to a mother, the misery of a young man is interesting to a young woman, the misery of an old man is interesting to nobody. This is of all miseries the coldest. Still Father Mabeuf had not entirely lost his childlike serenity. His eye regained some vivacity when it was fixed upon his books, and he smiled when he thought of the Diogenes Laertius, which was a unique copy. His glass bookcase was the only pïece of furniture which he had preserved beyond what was indispensable.

One day Mother Plutarch said to him:

'I have nothing to buy the dinner with.'

What she called the dinner was a loaf of bread and four or five potatoes.

'On credit?' said M. Mabeuf.

'You know well enough that they refuse me.'

M. Mabeuf opened his library, looked long at all his books one after another, as a father, compelled to decimate his children, would look at them before choosing, then took one of them hastily, put it under his arm, and went out. He returned two hours afterwards with nothing under his arm, laid thirty sous on the table, and said:

'You will get some dinner.'

From that moment, Mother Plutarch saw settling over the old man's white face a dark veil which was never lifted again.

The next day, the day after, every day, he had to begin again. M. Mabeuf went out with a book and came back with a piece of money. As the bookstall keepers saw that he was forced to sell, they bought from him for twenty sous what he had paid twenty francs for, sometimes to the same booksellers. Volume by volume, the whole library passed away. He said at times: 'I am eighty years old however,' as if he had some lingering hope of reaching the end of his days before reaching the end of his books. His sadness increased. Once, however, he had a pleasure. He went out with a Robert Estienne which he sold for thirty-five sous on the Quai Malaquais and returned with an Aldine which he had bought for forty sous in the Rue des Grès. 'I owe five sous,' said he to Mother Plutarch, glowing with joy.

That day he did not dine.

He belonged to the Society of Horticulture. His poverty was known there. The president of this society came to see him, promised to speak to the Minister of Agriculture and Commerce about him, and did so. 'Why, how now!' exclaimed the minister. 'I do believe! An old philosopher! a botanist! an inoffensive man! We must do something for him!' The next day M. Mabeuf received an invitation to dine at the minister's. Trembling with joy, he showed the letter to Mother Plutarch. 'We are saved!' said he. On the appointed day, he went to the minister's. He perceived that his ragged cravat, his large, old, square coat, and his shoes polished with egg, astonished the ushers. Nobody spoke to him, not even the minister. About ten o'clock in the evening, as he was still expecting a word, he heard the minister's wife, a beautiful lady in a low-necked dress, whom he had not dared to approach, asking: 'What can that old gentleman be?' He returned home on foot, at midnight, in a driving rain. He had sold an Elzevir to pay for a fiacre to go with.

He had acquired the habit, every evening before going to bed, of reading a few pages in his Diogenes Laertius. He knew Greek well enough to enjoy the peculiarities of the text which he possessed. He had now no other joy. Some weeks rolled by. Suddenly Mother Plutarch fell sick. There is one thing sadder than having nothing with which to buy bread from the baker; that is, having nothing with which to buy drugs from the apothecary. One night, the doctor had ordered a very dear potion. And then, the sickness was growing worse, a nurse was needed. M. Mabeuf opened his bookcase; there was nothing more there. The last volume had gone. The Diogenes Laertius alone remained.

He put the unique copy under his arm and went out, it was the 4th of June 1832, he went to the Porte Saint Jacques, to Royol's Successor's, and returned with a hundred francs. He laid the pile of five-franc pieces on the old servant's bedroom table, and went back to his room without saying a word.

The next day, by dawn, he was seated on the stone post in the garden, and he might have been seen from over the hedge all the morning motionless, his head bowed down, his eye vaguely fixed upon the withered beds. At intervals he wept; the old man did not seem to perceive it. In the afternoon, extraordinary sounds broke out in Paris. They resembled musket shots, and the clamour of a multitude.

Father Mabeuf raised his head. He saw a gardener going by, and asked:

'What is that?'

The gardener answered, his spade upon his shoulder, and in the most quiet tone:

'It's the *émeutes.*'

'What *émeutes*?'

'Yes. They are fighting.'

'What are they fighting for?'

'Oh! Lordy!' said the gardener.

'Whereabouts?' continued M. Mabeuf.

'Near the Arsenal.'

Father Mabeuf went into the house, took his hat, looked mechanically for a book to put under his arm, did not find any, said: 'Ah! it is true!' and went away with a bewildered air.

BOOK 10: JUNE 5TH, 1832

1. *The surface of the question*

Of what is the *émeute* composed? Of nothing and of everything. Of an electricity gradually evolved, of a flame suddenly leaping forth, of a wandering force, of a passing wind. This wind meets talking tongues, dreaming brains, suffering souls, burning passions, howling miseries, and sweeps them away.

Whither?

At hazard. Across the state, across the laws, across the prosperity and the insolence of others.

Irritated convictions, eager enthusiasms, excited indignations, the repressed instincts of war, exalted young courage, noble impulses; curiosity, the taste for change, the thirst for the unexpected, that sentiment which gives us pleasure in reading the bill of a new play, and which makes the ringing of the prompter's bell at the theatre a welcome sound; vague hatreds, spites, disappointments, every vanity which believes that destiny has caused it to fail; discomforts, empty dreams, ambitions shut in by high walls, whoever hopes for an issue from a downfall; finally, at the very bottom, the mob, that mud which takes fire, such are the elements of the *émeute*.

Whatever is greatest and whatever is most infamous; the beings who prowl about outside of everything, awaiting an opportunity, bohemians, people without occupation, loafers about the street-corners, those who sleep at night in a desert of houses, with no other roof than the cold clouds of the sky, those who ask their bread each day from chance and not from labour, the unknown ones of misery and nothingness, the bare arms, the bare feet, belong to the *émeute*.

Whoever feels in his soul a secret revolt against any act whatever of the state, of life or of fate, borders on the *émeute*, and, so soon as it appears, begins to shiver, and to feel himself uplifted by the whirlwind.

The *émeute* is a sort of waterspout in the social atmosphere which suddenly takes form in certain conditions of temperature, and which, in its whirling, mounts, runs, thunders, tears up, razes, crushes, demolishes, uproots, dragging with it the grand natures and the paltry, the strong man and the feeble mind, the trunk of the tree and the blade of straw.

Woe to him whom it sweeps away, as well as to him whom it comes to smite! It breaks them one against the other.

It communicates to those whom it seizes a mysterious and extraordinary power. It fills the first comer with the force of events; it makes projectiles of everything. It makes a bullet of a pebble, and a general of a street porter.

If we may believe certain oracles of crafty politics, from the governmental point of view, something of the *émeute* is desirable. System: the *émeute* strengthens those governments which it does not overthrow. It tests the army, it concentrates the bourgeoisie; it calls out the muscles of the police; it determines the strength of the social frame. It is a gymnastic training; it is almost hygienic. Power is healthier after an *émeute*, as a man is after a rubbing.

The *émeute*, thirty years ago, was looked upon from still other points of view.

There is a theory for everything which proclaims itself 'common sense;' Philinte against Alceste; mediation offered between the true and the false; explanation, admonition, a somewhat haughty extenuation which, because it is a mixture of blame and excuse, thinks itself wisdom, and is often only pedantry. An entire political school, called the compromise school, has sprung from this. Between cold water and warm water, this is the party of tepid water. This school, with its pretended depth, wholly superficial, which dissects effect without going back to the causes, from the height of a half-science, chides the agitations of the public square.

To hear this school: 'The *émeutes* with which the achievement of 1830 was complicated, robbed that great event of a portion of its purity. The revolution of July had been a fine breeze of the popular wind, quickly followed by blue sky. They brought back the cloudy sky. They degraded that revolution, at first so remarkable for unanimity, into a quarrel. In the revolution of July, as in all sudden progress, there were some secret fractures; the *émeute* rendered them sensible. We might say: 'Ah! this is broken.' After the revolution of July, the deliverance only was felt; after the *émeutes*, the catastrophe was felt.

'Every *émeute* closes the shops, depresses the funds, terrifies the stockboard, suspends commerce, shackles business, precipitates failures; no more money, private fortunes shaken, the public credit disturbed, manufactures disconcerted, capital hoarded, labour depreciated, fear everywhere; reactions in all the cities. Hence yawning gulfs. It has been calculated that the first day of an *émeute* costs France twenty millions, the second forty, the third sixty. An *émeute* of three days costs a hundred and twenty millions, that is to say, looking only at the financial result, is equivalent to a disaster, a shipwreck, or the loss of a battle, which should annihilate a fleet of sixty vessels of the line.

'Beyond a doubt, historically, *émeutes* had their beauty; the war of the pavements is no less grand and no less pathetic than the war of the thickets; in the one there is the soul of forests; in the other the heart of cities; one has Jean Chouan, the other has Jeanne. The *émeutes* illuminated, with red light, but splendidly, all the most original outgrowths of the Parisian character, generosity, devotion, stormy gaiety, students proving that bravery is part of intelligence, the National Guard unwavering, bivouacs of shopkeepers, fortresses of *gamins*, scorn of death among the people on the street. Schools and legions came in conflict. After all, between the combatants, there was only a difference of age; they were the same race; they are the same stoical men who die at twenty for their ideas, at forty for their families. The army, always sad in civil wars, opposed prudence to audacity. The *émeutes*, at the same time that they manifested the intrepidity of the people, effected the education of the courage of the bourgeois.

'Very well. But is it all worth the bloodshed? And to the bloodshed add the future darkened, progress incriminated, anxiety among the best men, noble liberals despairing, foreign absolutism delighted with these wounds inflicted on the revolution by itself, the vanquished of 1830 triumphing and saying: "We told you so!" Add Paris enlarged perhaps, but France surely diminished. Add, for we must tell all, the massacres which too often dishonoured the victory of order grown ferocious over liberty grown mad. Taken altogether, *émeutes* have been disastrous.'

Thus speaks this almost wisdom with which the bourgeoisie, that almost people, so gladly contents itself.

As for us, we reject this too broad and consequently too convenient word, *émeute*. Between a popular movement and a popular movement, we make a distinction. We do not ask whether an *émeute* cost as much as a battle. In the first place wherefore a battle? Here arises the question of war. Is war less a scourge than the *émeute* a calamity? And then, are all *émeutes* calamities? And what if the 14th of July did cost a hundred and twenty millions? The establishment of Philip V in Spain cost France two thousand millions. Even at the same price, we should prefer the 14th of July. Moreover, we put aside these figures, which seem to be reasons, and which are only words. An *émeute* given, we examine it in itself. In all that is said by the theoretic objection above set forth, only the effect is in question, we seek for the cause.

We specify.

2. *The bottom of the question*

THERE IS THE *émeute*, there is the insurrection; they are two angers; one is wrong, the other is right. In democratic states, the only governments founded in justice, it sometimes happens that a fraction usurps; then the whole rises up, and the necessary vindication of its right may go so far as to take up arms. In all questions which spring from the collective sovereignty, the war of the whole against the fraction is insurrection; the attack of the fraction against the whole is an *émeute*; according as the Tuileries contain the King or contain the Convention, they are justly or unjustly attacked. The same cannon pointed against the multitude is wrong the 10th of August, and right the 14th of Vendémiaire. Similar in appearance, different at bottom; the Swiss defend the false. Bonaparte defends the true. What universal suffrage has done in its freedom and its sovereignty cannot be undone by the street. So, in the affairs of pure civilisation; the instinct of the masses, yesterday clear-sighted, may tomorrow be clouded. The same fury is lawful against Terray, and absurd against Turgot. The breaking of machines, the pillaging of storehouses, the tearing up of rails, the demolition of docks, the false means of the multitudes, the denials of justice by the people to progress, Ramus assassinated by the students, Rousseau driven out of Switzerland with stones, is the *émeute*. Israel against Moses, Athens against Phocion, Rome against Scipio, is the *émeute*; Paris against the Bastille is insurrection. The soldiers against Alexander, the sailors against Christopher Columbus, this is the same revolt; an impious revolt; why? Because Alexander does for Asia with the sword what Christopher Columbus does for America with the compass; Alexander, like Columbus, finds a world. These gifts of a world to civilisation are such extensions of light that all resistance to them is criminal. Sometimes the people counterfeits fidelity to itself. The mob is traitor to the people. Is there, for instance, anything more strange than that long and bloody protest of the contraband saltmakers, a legitimate chronic revolt, which, at the decisive moment, on the day of safety, at the hour of the people's victory, espouses the throne, turns Chouan, and from insurrection against makes itself an *émeute* for! Dreary masterpieces of ignorance! The contraband saltmaker escapes the royal gallows, and, with a bit of rope at his neck, mounts the white cockade. Death to the excise gives birth to Vive le Roi. Saint Bartholomew assassins, September murderers, Avignon massacrers, assassins of Coligny, assassins of Madame de Lamballe, assassins of Brune, Miquelets, Verdets, Cadenettes, companions of Jéhu, Chevaliers du Brassard, such is *émeute*. La Vendée is a great catholic *émeute*. The sound of the advancing right knows itself, it does not always get clear of the quaking of the overthrown masses; there are foolish rages, there are cracked bells; every tocsin does not ring with the ring of bronze. The clash of passions and of ignorances is different from the shock of progress. Rise, if you will, but to grow. Show me to which side you are going. There is no insurrection but forward. Every other rising is evil; every violent step backwards is an *émeute*; to retreat is an act of violence against the human race. Insurrection is the Truth's access of fury; the paving-stones which insurrection tears up, throw off the spark of right. These stones leave to the *émeute* only their mud. Danton against Louis XVI is insurrection, Hébert against Danton is *émeute*.

Hence it is that, if insurrection, in given cases, may be, as Lafayette said, the most sacred of duties, an *émeute* may be the most deadly of crimes.

There is also some difference in the intensity of caloric; the insurrection is often a volcano, the *émeute* is often a fire of straw.

The revolt, as we have said, is sometimes on the part of power. Polignac is an *émeuter*; Camille Desmoulins is a governor.

Sometimes, insurrection is resurrection.

The solution of everything by universal suffrage being a fact entirely modern, and all history anterior to that fact being, for four thousand years, filled with violated right and the suffering of the people, each period of history brings with it such protest as is possible to it. Under the Cæsars there was no insurrection, but there was Juvenal.

The *facit indignatio* replaces the Gracchi.

Under the Cæsars there is the exile of Syene; there is also the man of the *Annales*.

We do not speak of the sublime exile of Patmos, who also overwhelms the real world with a protest in the name of the ideal, makes of vision a tremendous satire, and throws upon Nineveh-Rome, upon Babylon-Rome, upon Sodom-Rome, the flaming reverberation of the Apocalypse.

John upon his rock is the Sphinx upon her pedestal; we cannot comprehend him; he is a Jew, and it is Hebrew; but the man who wrote the *Annales* is a Latin; let us rather say he is a Roman.

As the Neros reign darkly, they should be pictured so. Work with the graver only would be pale; into the grooves should be poured a concentrated prose which bites.

Despots are an aid to thinkers. Speech enchained is speech terrible. The writer doubles and triples his style when silence is imposed by a master upon the people. There springs from this silence a certain mysterious fullness which filters and freezes into brass in the thoughts. Compression in the history produces conciseness in the historian. The granitic solidity of some celebrated prose is only a condensation produced by the tyrant. Tyranny constrains the writer to shortenings of diameter which are increases of strength. The Ciceronian period, hardly sufficient upon Verres, would lose its edge upon Caligula. Less roundness in the phrase, more intensity in the blow. Tacitus thinks with his arm drawn back.

The nobility of a great heart, condensed into justice and truth, strikes like a thunderbolt.

Be it said in passing, it is noteworthy that Tacitus was not historically superimposed upon Cæsar. The Tiberii were reserved for him. Cæsar and Tacitus are two successive phenomena whose meeting seems mysteriously avoided by Him who, in putting the centuries on the stage, rules the entrances and the exits. Cæsar is grand, Tacitus is grand; God spares these two grandeurs by not dashing them against each other. The judge, striking Cæsar, might strike too hard, and be unjust. God did not will it. The great wars of Africa and Spain, the destruction of the Cilician pirates, civilisation introduced into Gaul, into Britain, into Germany, all this glory covers the Rubicon. There is a delicacy of divine justice here, hesitating to let loose the terrible historian upon the illustrious usurper, saving Cæsar from Tacitus, and according to the genius the extenuating circumstances.

Certainly, despotism is always despotism, even under the despot of genius. There is corruption under illustrious tyrants, but the moral pestilence is more hideous still under infamous tyrants. In these reigns nothing veils the shame; and makers of examples, Tacitus as well as Juvenal, belabour to best purpose in presence of the human race, this ignominy without excuse.

Rome smells worse under Vitellius than under Sylla. Under Claudius and under Domitian, there is a deformity of baseness corresponding to the ugliness of the tyrant. The foulness of the slaves is a direct result of the despot; a miasma exhales from these crouching consciences which reflect the master; the public powers are unclean; hearts are small, consciences are sunken, souls are puny; this is so under Caracalla, this is so under Commodus, this is so under Heliogabalus, while there comes from the Roman Senate under Cæsar only the rank odour peculiar to the eagle's eyrie.

Hence the coming, apparently late, of the Tacituses and of the Juvenals; it is at the hour of evidence that the demonstrator appears.

But Juvenal and Tacitus, even like Isaiah in the biblical times, even like Dante in the Middle Ages, are men; the *émeute* and the insurrection are the multitude, which sometimes is wrong, sometimes is right.

In the most usual cases *émeute* springs from a material fact; insurrection is always a moral phenomenon. The *émeute* is Masaniello; the insurrection is Spartacus. Insurrection borders on the mind, *émeute* on the stomach; Gaster is irritated; but Gaster, certainly, is not always wrong. In cases of famine, *émeute*, Buzançais, for instance, has a true, pathetic, and just point of departure. Still it remains *émeute*. Why? because having reason at bottom, it was wrong in form. Savage, although right, violent, although strong, it struck at hazard; it marched like the blind elephant, crushing; it left behind it the corpses of old men, women, and children; it poured out, without knowing why, the blood of the inoffensive and the innocent. To nurture the people is a good end; to massacre it is an evil means.

Every armed protest, even the most legitimate, even the 10th of August, even the 14th of July, ends with the same trouble. Before the right is evolved, there is tumult and foam. In the beginning insurrection is an *émeute*, even as the river is a torrent. Ordinarily it ends in this ocean, revolution. Sometimes, however, coming from those high mountains which rule the moral horizon, justice, wisdom, reason, right, made of the purest snow of the ideal, after a long fall from rock to rock, after having reflected the sky in its transparency and been swollen by a hundred affluents in the majestic path of triumph, insurrection suddenly loses itself in some bourgeois quagmire, like the Rhine in a marsh.

All this is of the past, the future is different. Universal suffrage is so far admirable that it dissolves the *émeute* in its principle, and by giving a vote to insurrection, it takes away its arms. The vanishing of war, of the war of the streets as well as the war of the frontiers, such is inevitable progress. Whatever may be Today, peace is Tomorrow.

However, insurrection, *émeute*, in what the first differs from the second, the bourgeois, properly speaking, knows little of these shades. To him, all is sedition, rebellion pure and simple, revolt of the dog against the master, attempt to bite which must be punished by chain and kennel, barking, yelping, till the day when the dog's head, suddenly enlarged, stands out dimly in the darkness with a lion's face.

Then the bourgeois cries; *Vive le peuple!*

This explanation given, what, for history, is the movement of June, 1832? is it an *émeute*? is it an insurrection?

It is an insurrection.

We may happen, in this presentation of a fearful event, sometimes to say the *émeute*, but only to denote the surface facts, and always maintaining the distinction between the form *émeute* and the substance insurrection.

This movement of 1832 had, in its rapid explosion and in its dismal extinction, so much grandeur that those even who see in it only an *émeute* do not speak of it without respect. To them it is like a remnant of 1830. 'Excited imaginations,' say they, 'do not calm down in a day. A revolution is not cut off square. It has always some necessary undulations before returning to the condition of peace like a mountain on descending towards the plain. There are no Alps without their Jura, nor Pyrenees without Asturias.'

This pathetic crisis of contemporary history, which the memory of Parisians calls the '*epoch of émeutes*,' is surely a characteristic period amid the stormy periods of this century. A last word before resuming the narrative.

The events which we are about to relate belong to that dramatic and living reality which the historian sometimes neglects, for lack of time and space. In them, however, we insist, in them is the life, the palpitation, the quivering of humanity. Little incidents, we believe we have said, are, so to speak, the foliage of great events and are lost in the distance of history. The epoch known as that 'of *émeutes*' abounds in details of this kind. The judicial investigations, for other reasons than history, did not reveal everything, nor perhaps get to the bottom of everything. We shall therefore bring to light, among the known and public circumstances, some things which have never been known, deeds, over some of which oblivion has passed; over others, death. Most of the actors in those gigantic scenes have disappeared; from the morrow they were silent; but what we shall relate, we can say that we saw. We shall change some names, for history relates and does not inform against, but we shall paint reality. From the nature of the book which we are writing, we only show one side and an episode, and that certainly the least known, of the days of the 5th and 6th of June 1832; but we shall do it in such a way that the reader may catch a glimpse, under the gloomy veil which we are about to lift, of the real countenance of that fearful public tragedy.

3. A burial: opportunity for rebirth

In the spring of 1832, although for three months the cholera had chilled all hearts and thrown over their agitation an inexpressibly mournful calm, Paris had for a long time been ready for a commotion. As we have said, the great city resembles a piece of artillery; when it is loaded the falling of a spark is enough, the shot goes off. In June 1832, the spark was the death of General Lamarque.

Lamarque was a man of renown and of action. He had had successively, under the Empire and under the Restoration, the two braveries necessary to the two epochs, the bravery of the battlefield and the bravery of the rostrum. He was eloquent as he had been valiant; men felt a sword in his speech. Like Foy, his predecessor, after having upheld command, he upheld liberty. He sat between the left and the extreme left, loved by the people because he accepted the chances of the future, loved by the masses because he had served the emperor well. He was, with Counts Gérard and Drouet, one of Napoleon's marshals *in petto*. The treaties of 1815 regarded him as a personal offence. He hated Wellington with a direct hatred which pleased the multitude; and for seventeen years, hardly noticing intermediate events, he had majestically preserved the sadness of Waterloo. In his death-agony, at his latest hour, he had pressed against his breast a sword which was presented to him by the officers of the Hundred Days. Napoleon died pronouncing the word *armée*, Lamarque pronouncing the word *patrie*.

His death, which had been looked for, was dreaded by the people as a loss, and by the government as an opportunity. This death was a mourning. Like everything which is bitter, mourning may turn into revolt. This is what happened.

The eve and the morning of the 5th of June, the day fixed for the funeral of Lamarque, the Faubourg Saint Antoine, through the edge of which the procession was to pass, assumed a formidable aspect. That tumultuous network of streets was full of rumour. Men armed themselves as they could. Some joiners carried their bench-claw 'to stave in the doors'. One of them had made a dagger of a shoe-hook by breaking off the hook and sharpening the stump. Another, in the fever 'to attack', had slept for three nights without undressing. A carpenter named Lombier met a comrade, who asked him: 'Where are you going?' 'Well! I have no arms.' 'What then?' 'I am going to my yard to look for my compasses.' 'What for?' 'I don't know,' said Lombier. A certain Jacqueline, a man of business, hailed every working-man who passed by with: 'Come, you!' He bought ten sous' worth of wine, and said: 'Have you any work? ' 'No.' 'Go to Filspierre's, between the Barrière Montreuil and the Barrière Charonne, you will find work.' They found at Filspierre's cartridges and arms. Certain known chiefs *did the post*, that is to say, ran from one house to another to assemble their people. At Barthélemy's, near the Barrière du Trone, and at Capet's, at the Petit

Chapeau, the drinkers accosted each other seriously. They were heard to say: '*Where is your pistol?*' '*Under my blouse.*' '*And yours?*' '*Under my shirt.*' On the Rue Traversière, in front of the Roland workshop, and in the Cour de la Maison Brûlée, in front of Bernier's machine-shop, groups were whispering. Among the most ardent, a certain Mavot was noticed, who never worked more than a week in one shop, the masters sending him away, 'because they had to dispute with him every day'. Mavot was killed the next day in the barricade, in the Rue Ménilmontant. Pretot, who was also to die in the conflict, seconded Mavot, and to this question: 'What is your object?' answered: '*Insurrection.*' Some working-men, gathered at the corner of the Rue de Bercy, were waiting for a man named Lemarin, revolutionary officer for the Faubourg Saint Marceau. Orders were passed about almost publicly.

On the 5th of June, then, a day of mingled rain and sunshine, the procession of General Lamarque passed through Paris with the official military pomp, somewhat increased by way of precaution. Two battalions, drums muffled, muskets reversed, ten thousand National Guards, their sabres at their sides, the batteries of artillery of the National Guard, escorted the coffin. The hearse was drawn by young men. The officers of the Invalides followed immediately bearing branches of laurel. Then came a countless multitude, strange and agitated, the sectionaries of the Friends of the People, the Law School, the Medical School, refugees from all nations, Spanish, Italian, German, Polish flags, horizontal tricoloured flags, every possible banner, children waving green branches, stone-cutters and carpenters, who were on a strike at that very moment, printers recognisable by their paper caps, walking two by two, three by three, uttering cries, almost all brandishing clubs, a few swords, without order, and yet with a single soul, now a rout, now a column. Some platoons chose chiefs; a man, armed with a pair of pistols openly worn, seemed to be passing others in review as they filed off before him. On the cross alleys of the boulevards, in the branches of the trees, on the balconies, at the windows, on the roofs, were swarms of heads, men, women, children; their eyes were full of anxiety. An armed multitude was passing by, a terrified multitude was looking on.

The government also was observing. It was observing, with its hand upon the hilt of the sword. One might have seen, all ready to march, with full cartridge-boxes, guns and musquetoons loaded, in the Place Louis XV, four squadrons of carbineers, in the saddle, trumpets at their heads, in the Latin Quarter and at the Jardin des Plantes, the Municipal Guard, *en échelon* from street to street, at the Halle aux Vins a squadron of dragoons, at La Grève one half of the 12th Light, the other half at the Bastille, the 6th dragoons at the Célestins, the Court of the Louvre full of artillery. The rest of the troops were stationed in the barracks, without counting the regiments in the environs of Paris. Anxious authority held suspended over the threatening multitude twenty-four thousand soldiers in the city, and thirty thousand in the banlieue.

Divers rumours circulated in the cortège. They talked of legitimist intrigues; they talked of the Duke of Reichstadt, whom God was marking for death at that very moment when the populace was designating him for empire. A personage still unknown announced that at the appointed hour two foremen, who had been won over, would open to the people the doors of a manufactory of arms. The dominant expression on the uncovered foreheads of most of those present, was one of subdued enthusiasm. Here and there in this multitude, a prey to so many violent, but noble, emotions, could also be seen some genuine faces of malefactors and ignoble mouths, which said 'pillage!' There are certain agitations which stir up the bottom of the marsh, and which make clouds of mud rise in the water. A phenomenon to which 'well-regulated' police are not strangers.

The cortège made its way, with a feverish slowness, from the house of death, along the boulevards as far as the Bastille. It rained from time to time; the rain had no effect upon that throng. Several incidents, the coffin drawn around the Vêndome column, the stones thrown at the Duke de Fitz-James who was seen on a balcony with his hat on, the Gallic cock torn from a popular flag and dragged in the mud, a *sergent de ville* wounded by a sword thrust at the Porte Saint Martin, an officer of the 12th Light saying aloud: 'I am a republican,' the Polytechnic School unlooked for after its forced countersign, the cries: *Vive l'ecole polytechnique! Vive la république!* marked the progress of the procession. At the Bastille, long and formidable files of the curious from the Faubourg Saint Antoine made their junction with the cortège, and a certain terrible ebullition began to upheave the multitude.

One man was heard saying to another: 'Do you see that man with the red beard? it is he who will say when we must draw.' It would appear that that same red beard was found afterwards with the same office in another *émeute*; the Quénisset affair.

The hearse passed the Bastille, followed the canal, crossed the little bridge, and reached the esplanade of the Bridge of Austerlitz. There it stopped. At this moment a bird's-eye view of this multitude would have presented the appearance of a comet, the head of which was at the esplanade, while the tail, spreading over the Quai Bourdon, covered the Bastille, and stretched along the boulevard as far as the Porte Saint Martin. A circle was formed about the hearse. The vast assemblage became silent. Lafayette spoke and bade farewell to Lamarque. It was a touching and august moment, all heads were uncovered, all hearts throbbed. Suddenly a man on horseback, dressed in black, appeared in the midst of the throng with a red flag, others say with a pike surmounted by a red cap. Lafayette turned away his head. Exelmans left the cortège.

This red flag raised a storm and disappeared in it. From the Boulevard Bourdon to the Bridge of Austerlitz one of those shouts which resemble billows moved the multitude. Two prodigious shouts arose: *Lamarque to the Pantheon! Lafayette to the Hôtel de Ville!* Some young men, amid the cheers of the throng, harnessed themselves, and began to draw Lamarque in the hearse over the bridge of Austerlitz, and Lafayette in a fiacre along the Quai Morland.

In the crowd which surrounded and cheered Lafayette, was noticed and pointed out a German, named Ludwig Snyder, who afterwards died a centenarian, who had also been in the war of 1776, and who had fought at Trenton under Washington, and under Lafayette at Brandywine.

Meanwhile, on the left bank, the municipal cavalry was in motion, and had just barred the bridge, on the right bank the dragoons left the Célestins and deployed along the Quai Morland. The men who were drawing Lafayette suddenly perceived them at the corner of the Quai, and cried: 'the dragoons!' The dragoons were advancing at a walk, in silence, their pistols in their holsters, their sabres in their sheaths, their musketoons in their rests, with an air of gloomy expectation.

At two hundred paces from the little bridge, they halted. The fiacre in which

Lafayette was, made its way up to them, they opened their ranks, let it pass, and closed again behind it. At that moment the dragoons and the multitude came together. The women fled in terror.

What took place in that fatal moment? nobody could tell. It was the dark moment when two clouds mingle. Some say that a trumpet-flourish sounding the charge was heard from the direction of the Arsenal, others that a dagger-thrust was given by a child to a dragoon. The fact is that three shots were suddenly fired, the first killed the chief of the squadron, Cholet, the second killed an old deaf woman who was closing her window in the Rue Contrescarpe, the third singed the epaulet of an officer; a woman cried: 'They are beginning too soon!' and all at once there was seen, from the side opposite the Quai Morland, a squadron of dragoons which had remained in barracks turning out on the gallop, with swords drawn, from the Rue Bassompierre and the Boulevard Bourdon, and sweeping all before them.

There are no more words, the tempest breaks loose, stones fall like hail, musketry bursts forth, many rush headlong down the bank and cross the little arm of the Seine now filled up, the yards of the Ile Louviers, that vast ready-made citadel, bristle with combatants, they tear up stakes, they fire pistol-shots, a barricade is planned out, the young men crowded back, pass the Bridge of Austerlitz with the hearse at a run, and charge on the Municipal Guard, the carbineers rush up, the dragoons ply the sabre, the mass scatters in every direction, a rumour of war flies to the four corners of Paris, men cry: 'To arms!' they run, they tumble, they fly, they resist. Wrath sweeps along the *émeute* as the wind sweeps along a fire.

4. The ebullitions of former times

Nothing is more extraordinary than the first swarming of an *émeute*. Everything bursts out everywhere at once. Was it foreseen? yes. Was it prepared? no. Whence does it spring? from the pavements. Whence does it fall? from the clouds. Here the insurrection has the character of a plot; there of an improvisation. The first comer takes possession of a current of the multitude and leads it whither he will. A beginning full of terror with which is mingled a sort of frightful gaiety. At first there are clamours, the shops close, the displays of the merchants disappear; then some isolated shots; people flee; butts of guns strike against *porte-cochères*; you hear the servant girls laughing in the yards of the houses and saying: *There is going to be a row!*

A quarter of an hour had not elapsed and here is what had taken place nearly at the same time at twenty different points in Paris.

In the Rue Sainte Croix de la Bretonnerie, some twenty young men, with beards and long hair, entered a smoking-room and came out again a moment afterwards, bearing a horizontal tricolour flag covered with crape, and having at their head three men armed, one with a sword, another with a gun, the third with a pike.

In the Rue des Nonaindières, a well-dressed bourgeois, who was pursy, had a sonorous voice, a bald head, a high forehead, a black beard, and one of those rough moustaches which cannot be smoothed down, offered cartridges publicly to the passers-by.

In the Rue Sainte Pierre Montmartre, some men with bare arms paraded a black flag on which these words could be read in white letters: *Republic or death*. In the Rue des Jeûneurs, the Rue du Cadran, the Rue Montorgueil, and the Rue Mandar, appeared groups waving flags on which were visible in letters of gold, the word *section* with a number. One of these flags was red and blue with an imperceptible white stripe between.

A manufactory of arms was rifled, on the Boulevard Saint Martin, and three armourer's shops, the first in the Rue Beaubourg, the second in the Rue Michel le Comte, the third in the Rue du Temple. In a few minutes the thousand hands of the multitude seized and carried off two hundred and thirty muskets nearly all double-barrelled, sixty-four swords, eighty-three pistols. To arm more people, one took the gun, another the bayonet.

Opposite the Quai de la Grève, young men armed with muskets installed themselves with the women to shoot. One of them had a musket with a match-lock. They rang, entered, and set to making cartridges. One of these women said: '*I did not know what cartridges were, my husband told me to.*'

A throng broke into a curiosity shop in the Rue des Vieilles Haudriettes and took some yataghans and Turkish arms.

The corpse of a mason killed by a musket shot was lying in the Rue de la Perle.

And then, right bank, left bank, on the quais, on the boulevards, in the Latin quarter, in the region of the markets, breathless men, working-men, students, sectionaries, read proclamations, cried: 'To arms!' broke the street lamps, unharnessed wagons, tore up the pavements, broke in the doors of the houses, uprooted the trees, ransacked the cellars, rolled hogsheads, heaped up paving stones, pebbles, pieces of furniture, boards, made barricades.

They forced the bourgeois to help them. They went into the women's houses, they made them give up the sword and the gun of their absent husbands, and wrote over the door with Spanish white: '*The arms are delivered.*' Some signed 'with their names' receipts for the gun and sword, and said: '*Send for them tomorrow to the mairie.*' They disarmed the solitary sentinels in the streets and the National Guards going to their municipality. They tore off the officers' epaulets. In the Rue du Cimetière Saint Nicolas, an officer of the National Guard, pursued by a troop armed with clubs and foils, took refuge with great difficulty in a house which he was able to leave only at night, and in disguise.

In the Quartier St Jacques, the students came out of their hôtels in swarms, and went up the Rue Saint Hyacinthe to the Café du Progrès or down to the Café des Sept Billards, on the Rue des Mathurins. There, before the doors, some young men standing upon the posts distributed arms. They pillaged the lumberyard on the Rue Transnonain to make barricades. At a single point, the inhabitants resisted, at the corner of the Rues Sainte Avoye and Simon le Franc where they destroyed the barricade themselves. At a single point, the insurgents gave way; they abandoned a barricade commenced in the Rue du Temple after having fired upon a detachment of the National Guard, and fled through the Rue de la Corderie. The detachment picked up in the barricade a red flag, a package of cartridges, and three hundred pistol balls. The National Guards tore up the flag and carried the shreds at the point of their bayonets.

All that we are here relating slowly and successively took place at once in all points of the city in the midst of a vast tumult, like a multitude of flashes in a single peal of thunder.

In less than an hour twenty-seven barricades rose from the ground in the single quarter of the markets. At the centre was that famous house, No. 50, which was the fortress of Jeanne and her hundred and six companions, and which, flanked on one side by a barricade at Saint Merry, and on the other by a barricade on the Rue Maubuée, commanded three streets, the Rue des Arcis, the Rue Saint Martin, and the Rue Aubry le Boucher on which it fronted. Two barricades at right angles ran back, one from the Rue Montorgueil to the Grande Truanderie, the other from the Rue Geoffroy Langevin to the Rue Sainte Avoye. Without counting innumerable barricades in twenty other quarters of Paris, in the Marais, at Mount Sainte Geneviève; one, on the Rue Ménilmontant, where could be seen a *porte-cochère* torn from its hinges; another near the little bridge of the Hôtel Dieu made with an *écossaise* unhitched and overturned, within three hundred yards of the prefecture of police.

At the barricade on the Rue des Ménétriers, a well-dressed man distributed money to the labourers. At the barricade on the Rue Grenetat a horseman appeared and handed to him who appeared to be the chief of the barricade a roll which looked like a roll of money. '*This*,' said he, '*is to pay the expenses, wine, et cœtera*.' A young man of a light complexion, without a cravat, went from one barricade to another carrying orders. Another, with drawn sword and a blue police cap on his head, was stationing sentinels. In the interior, within the barricades, wine-shops and porters' lodges were converted into guardhouses. Moreover, the *émeute* was conducted according to the soundest military tactics. The narrow, uneven, sinuous streets, full of turns and corners, were admirably chosen; the environs of the markets in particular, a network of streets more intricate than a forest. The Society of the Friends of the People, it was said, had assumed the direction of the insurrection in the Quartier Sainte Avoye. A man, killed in Rue du Ponceau who was searched, had a plan of Paris upon him.

What had really assumed the direction of the *émeute* was a sort of unknown impetuosity which was in the atmosphere. The insurrection, abruptly, had built the barricades with one hand, and with the other seized nearly all the posts of the garrison. In less than three hours, like a train of powder which takes fire, the insurgents had invaded and occupied, on the right bank, the Arsenal, the Mayor's office of the Place Royale, all the Marais, the Popincourt manufactory of arms, the Galiote, the Château d'Eau, all the streets near the markets; on the left bank, the barracks of the Véterans, Sainte Pélagie, the Place Maubert, the powder-mill of the Deux Moulins, all the Barrières. At five o'clock in the afternoon they were masters of the Bastille, the Lingerie, the Blancs Manteaux; their scouts touched the Place des Victoires, and threatened the Bank, the barracks of the Petits Pères, and the Hôtel des Postes. The third of Paris was in the *émeute*.

At all points the struggle had commenced on a gigantic scale; and from the disarmings, from the domiciliary visits, from the armourers' shops hastily invaded, there was this result, that the combat which was commenced by throwing stones, was continued by throwing balls.

About six o'clock in the afternoon, the Arcade du Saumon became a field of battle. The *émeute* was at one end, the troops at the end opposite. They fired from one grating to the other. An observer, a dreamer, the author of this book, who had gone to get a near view of the volcano, found himself caught in the arcade between the two fires. He had nothing but the projection of the pilasters which separate the shops to protect him from the balls; he was nearly half an hour in this delicate situation.

Meanwhile the drums beat the long roll, the National Guards dressed and armed themselves in haste, the legions left the mairies, the regiments left their barracks. Opposite the Arcade de l'Ancre, a drummer received a thrust from a dagger. Another, on the Rue du Cygne, was assailed by some thirty young men, who destroyed his drum and took away his sword. Another was killed in the Rue Grenier Saint Lazare. In the Rue Michel le Comte three officers fell dead one after another. Several Municipal Guards, wounded in the Rue des Lombards, turned back.

In front of the Cour Batave, a detachment of National Guards found a red flag bearing this inscription: *Republican revolution, No. 127*. Was it a revolution, in fact?

The insurrection had made the centre of Paris a sort of inextricable, tortuous, colossal citadel.

There was the focus, there was evidently the question. All the rest were only skirmishes. What proved that there all would be decided, was that they were not yet fighting there.

In some regiments, the soldiers were doubtful, which added to the frightful obscurity of the crisis. They remembered the popular ovation which in July, 1830, had greeted the neutrality of the 53rd of the line. Two intrepid men, who had been proved by the great wars, Marshal de Lobau and General Bugeaud, commanded, Bugeaud under Lobau. Enormous patrols, composed of battalions of the line surrounded by entire companies of the National Guard, and preceded by a commissary of police with his badge, went out reconnoitring the insurgent streets. On their side, the insurgents placed pickets at the corners of the streets and boldly sent patrols outside of the barricades. They kept watch on both sides. The government, with an army in its hand, hesitated; night was coming on, and the tocsin of Saint Merry began to be heard. The Minister of War of the time, Marshal Soult, who had seen Austerlitz, beheld this with gloomy countenance.

These old sailors, accustomed to correct manœuvring, and having no resource or guide, save tactics, that compass of battles, are completely lost in presence of that immense foam which is called the wrath of the people. The wind of revolutions is not tractable.

The National Guard of the banlieue hurried together in disorder. A battalion of the 12th Light ran down from Saint Denis, the 14th of the Line arrived from Courbevoie, the batteries of the Military School had taken position at the Carrousel; artillery came from Vincennes.

Solitude reigned at the Tuileries. Louis Philippe was full of serenity.

5. *Originality of Paris*

WITHIN TWO YEARS, as we have said, Paris had seen more than one insurrection. Outside of the insurgent quarters, nothing is usually more strangely calm than the physiognomy of Paris during an *émeute*. Paris accustoms itself very quickly to everything – it is only an *émeute* – and Paris is so busy that it does not trouble itself for so slight a thing. These colossal cities alone can contain at the same time a civil war, and an indescribably strange tranquillity. Usually, when the insurrection begins, when the drum, the long-roll, the genérale, are heard, the shopkeeper merely says:

'It seems there is some squabble in the Rue Saint Martin.'

Or:

'Faubourg Saint Antoine.'

Often he adds with unconcern:

'Somewhere down that way.'

Afterwards, when he distinguishes the dismal and thrilling uproar of musketry and the firing of platoons, the shopkeeper says:

'It is getting warm, then! Hullo, it is getting warm!'

A moment afterwards, if the *émeute* approaches and increases, he precipitately shuts his shop, and hastily puts on his uniform; that is to say, places his goods in safety and risks his person.

There is firing at the street corners, in an arcade, in a cul-de-sac; barricades are taken, lost, and retaken; blood flows, the fronts of the houses are riddled with grape, balls kill people in their beds, corpses encumber the pavement. A few streets off, you hear the clicking of billiard balls in the cafés.

The theatres open their doors and play comedies; the curious chat and laugh two steps from these streets full of war. The fiacres jog along; passers are going to dine in the city. Sometimes in the very quarter where there is fighting. In 1831 a fusilade was suspended to let a wedding party pass by.

At the time of the insurrection of the 12th of May 1839, in the Rue Saint Martin, a little infirm old man, drawing a handcart surmounted by a tricoloured rag, in which there were decanters filled with some liquid, went back and forth from the barricade to the troops and from the troops to the barricade, impartially offering glasses of cocoa – now to the government, now to anarchy.

Nothing is more strange; and this is the peculiar characteristic of the *émeutes* of Paris, which is not found in any other capital. Two things are requisite for it, the greatness of Paris and its gaiety. It requires the city of Voltaire and of Napoleon.

This time, however, in the armed contest of the 5th of June 1832, the great city felt something which was, perhaps, stronger than herself. She was afraid. You saw everywhere, in the most distant and the most 'disinterested' quarters, doors, windows, and shutters closed in broad day. The courageous armed, the poltroons hid. The careless and busy wayfarer disappeared. Many streets were as empty as at four o'clock in the morning. Alarming stories were circulated, ominous rumours were spread. 'That *they* were masters of the Bank'; 'that, merely at the cloisters of Saint Merry, there were six hundred, entrenched and fortified in the church'; 'that the Line was doubtful'; 'that Armand Carrel had been to see Marshal Clausel, and that the marshal had said: *Have one regiment in the place first*'; 'that Lafayette was sick, but that he had said to them notwithstanding: *I am with you. I will follow you anywhere where there is room for a chair*'; 'that it was necessary to keep on their guard; that in the night there would be people who would pillage the isolated houses in the deserted quarters of Paris (in this the imagination of the police was recognised, that Anne Radcliffe mixed with government)'; 'that a battery had been planted in the Rue Aubry le Boucher'; 'that Lobau and Bugeaud were consulting and that at midnight, or at daybreak at the latest, four columns would march at once upon the centre of the *émeute*, the first coming from the Bastille, the second from the Porte Saint Martin, the third from La Grève, the fourth from the markets'; 'that perhaps also the troops would evacuate Paris and retire to the Champ de Mars'; 'that nobody knew what might happen, but that certainly, this time, it was serious.' They were concerned about Marshal Soult's hesitation. 'Why doesn't he attack right away?' It is certain that he was deeply absorbed. The old lion seemed to scent in that darkness some unknown monster.

Evening came, the theatres did not open; the patrols made their round spitefully; passers were searched; the suspicious were arrested. At nine o'clock there were more than eight hundred persons under arrest; the prefecture of police was crowded, the Conciergerie was crowded, La Force was crowded. At the Conciergerie, in particular, the long vault which is called the Rue de Paris was strewn with bundles of straw, on which lay a throng of prisoners, whom the man of Lyons, Lagrange, harangued valiantly. The rustling of all this straw, stirred by all these men, was like the sound of a shower. Elsewhere the prisoners lay in the open air in the prison yards, piled one upon another. Anxiety was everywhere, and a certain tremor, little known to Paris.

People barricaded themselves in their houses; wives and mothers were terrified; you heard only this: *Oh ! my God! he has not come back!* In the distance there was heard very rarely the rumbling of a wagon. People listened, on their door-sills, to the rumours, the cries, the tumults, the dull and indistinct sounds, things of which they said: *That is the cavalry*, or: *Those are the ammunition wagons galloping down*, the trumpets, the drums, the musketry, and above all, that mournful tocsin of Saint Merry. They expected the first cannon-shot. Men rose up at the corners of the streets and disappeared, crying: 'Go home!' And they hastened to bolt their doors. They said: 'How will it end?' From moment to moment, as night fell, Paris seemed coloured more dismally with the fearful flame of the *émeute*.

BOOK II: THE ATOM FRATERNISES WITH THE HURRICANE

1. Some insight into the origin of Gavroche's poetry – influence of an Academician upon that poetry

AT THE MOMENT the insurrection, springing up at the shock of the people with the troops in front of the Arsenal, determined a backward movement in the multitude which was following the hearse and which, for the whole length of the boulevards, weighed, so to say, upon the head of the procession, there was a frightful reflux. The mass wavered, the ranks broke, all ran, darted, slipped away, some with cries of attack, others with the pallor of flight. The great river which covered the boulevards divided in a twinkling, overflowed on the right and on the left, and poured in torrents into two hundred streets at once with the rushing of an opened mill-sluice. At this moment a ragged child who was coming down the Rue Ménilmontant, holding in his hand a branch of laburnum in bloom, which he had just gathered on the heights of Belleville, caught sight, before a second-hand dealer's shop, of an old horse pistol. He threw his flowering branch upon the pavement, and cried:

'Mother What's-your-name, I'll borrow your machine.'

And he ran off with the pistol.

Two minutes later, a flood of terrified bourgeois who were fleeing through the Rue Amelot and the Rue Basse, met the child who was brandishing his pistol and singing:

La nuit on ne voit rien,
Le jour on voit très bien,
D'un écrit apocryphe
Le bourgeois s'ébouriffe,
Pratiquez la vertu,
Tutu chapeau pointu!

It was little Gavroche going to war.

On the boulevard he perceived that the pistol had no hammer.

Whose was this refrain which served him to time his march, and all the other songs which, on occasion, he was fond of singing? we do not know. Who knows? his own perhaps. Gavroche besides kept up with all the popular airs in circulation, and mingled with them his own warbling. A sprite and a devil, he made a medley of the voices of nature and the voices of Paris. He combined the repertory of the birds with the repertory of the workshops. He knew some painter's boys, a tribe contiguous to his own. He had been, as it appears, three months a printer's apprentice. He had done an errand one day for Monsieur Baour-Lormian, one of the Forty. Gavroche was a *gamin* of letters.

Gavroche moreover had no suspicion that on that wretched rainy night when he had offered the hospitality of his elephant to two brats, it was for his own brothers that he had acted the part of Providence. His brothers in the evening, his father in the morning; such had been his night. On leaving the Rue des Ballets at early dawn, he had returned in haste to the elephant, artistically extracted the two *mômes*, shared with them such breakfast as he could invent, then went away, confiding them to that good mother, the street, who had almost brought him up himself. On leaving them, he had given them rendezvous for the evening at the same place, and left them this discourse as a farewell: '*I cut stick, otherwise spoken, I esbigne, or, as they say at the court, I haul off. Brats, if you don't find papa and mamma, come back here tonight. I will strike you up some supper and put you to bed.*' The two children, picked up by some *sergent de ville* and put in the retreat, or stolen by some mountebank, or simply lost in the immense Chinese Parisian turmoil, had not returned. The lower strata of the existing social world are full of these lost traces. Gavroche had not seen them since. Ten or twelve weeks had elapsed since that night. More than once he had scratched the top of his head and said: 'Where the devil are my two children?'

Meanwhile he had reached, pistol in hand, the Rue du Pont aux Choux. He noticed that there was now, in that street, but one shop open, and, a matter worthy of reflection, a pastrycook's shop. This was a providential opportunity to eat one more apple-puff before entering the unknown. Gavroche stopped, fumbled in his trousers, felt in his fob, turned out his pockets, found nothing in them, not a sou, and began to cry: 'Help!'

It is hard to lack the final cake.

Gavroche none the less continued on his way.

Two minutes later, he was in the Rue Saint Louis. While passing through the Rue du Parc Royal he felt the need of some compensation for the impossible apple-puff, and he gave himself the immense pleasure of tearing down the theatre posters in broad day.

A little further along, seeing a group of well-to-do persons pass by, who appeared to him to be men of property, he shrugged his shoulders, and spat out at random this mouthful of philosophic bile:

'These rich men, how fat they are! they stuff themselves. They wallow in good dinners. Ask them what they do with their money. They don't know anything about it. They eat it, they do! How much of it the belly carries away.'

2. *Gavroche on the march*

THE BRANDISHING of a pistol without a hammer, holding it in one's hand in the open street, is such a public function that Gavroche felt his spirits rise higher with every step. He cried, between the snatches of the Marseillaise which he was singing:

'It's all going well. I suffer a good deal in my left paw, I am broken with my rheumatism, but I am content, citizens. The bourgeois have nothing to do but to behave themselves, I am going to sneeze subversive couplets at them. What are the detectives? they are dogs. By jinks! don't let us fail in respect for dogs. Now I wish I had one to my pistol.* I come from the boulevard, my friends, it is getting hot, it is boiling over a little, it is simmering. It is time to skim the pot. Forward, men! let their impure blood water the furrows! I give my days for my country. I shall never see my concubine again, n–e–ver, over, yes. Never! but it's all the same, let us be joyful! let us fight, egad! I have had enough of despotism.'

At that moment, the horse of a lancer of the National Guard, who was passing, having fallen down, Gavroche laid his pistol on the pavement, and raised up the man, then he helped to raise the horse. After which he picked up his pistol, and resumed his way.

In the Rue de Thorigny, all was peace and silence. This apathy, suited to the Marais, contrasted with the vast surrounding uproar. Four gossips were chatting upon a doorstep.

Scotland has her trios of witches, but Paris has her quartettes of gossips; and the 'thou shalt be king', would be quite as ominously cast at Bonaparte in the Baudoyer Square as at Macbeth in the heath of Armuyr. It would be almost the same croaking.

The gossips of the Rue de Thorigny were busy only with their own affairs. They were three portresses and a rag-picker with her basket and hook.

The four seemed standing at the four corners of old age, which are decay, decrepitude, ruin, and sorrow.

The rag-picker was humble. In this outdoor society, the rag-picker bows, the portress patronises. That is a result of the sweepings which are, as the portresses will, fat or lean, according to the fancy of her who makes the head. There may be kindness in the broom.

This rag-picker was a grateful basket, and she smiled, what a smile! to the

* The French call the hammer of a pistol, the *dog* of it.

three portresses. Such things as this were said:

'Ah, now, your cat is always spiteful, is she?'

'Luddy! cats, you know, are naturally the enemies of dogs. It is the dogs that complain.'

'And folks, too.'

'Still, cats' fleas don't get on folks.'

'That's not the trouble, dogs are dangerous. I remember one year there was so many dogs they had to put it in the papers. It was the time they had the big sheep at the Tuileries to draw the King of Rome's little wagon. Do you remember the King of Rome?'

'Me, I liked the Duke of Bourdeaux better.'

'For my part, I knew Louis XVII. I like Louis XVII better.'

'How dear meat is, Ma'am Patagon!'

'Oh! don't speak of it, the butchering is horrid. Horridly horrid. They have nothing but tough meat nowadays.'

Here the rag-picker intervened!

'Ladies, business is very dull. The garbage heaps are shabby. Folks don't throw anything away in these days. They eat everything.'

'There are poorer people than you, Vargoulême.'

'Oh, that is true!' replied the rag-picker, with deference, 'for my part I have an occupation.'

There was a pause, and the rag-picker, yielding to that necessity for display which lies deepest in the human heart, added:

'In the morning when I get home, I pick over the basketful, I make my sorties (probably sortings). That makes heaps in my room. I put the rags in a basket, the cores in a tub, the linens in my closet, the woollens in my bureau, the old papers in the corner of the window, the things good to eat into my plate, the bits of glass in the fireplace, the old shoes behind the door, and the bones under my bed.'

Gavroche, who had stopped behind, was listening.

'Old women,' said he, 'what business have you now talking politics?'

A volley assailed him, composed of a quadruple hoot.

'There is another scoundrel!'

'What has he got in his stump? A pistol.'

'I want to know, that beggar of a *môme*!'

'They are never quiet if they are not upsetting the government.'

Gavroche, in disdain, made no other reply than merely to lift the end of his nose with his thumb while he opened his hand to its full extent.

The rag-picker cried:

'Spiteful go-bare-paws!'

She who answered to the name of Ma'am Patagon clapped her hands in horror.

'There is going to be troubles, that's sure. That rascal over there with a beard, I used to see him go by every morning with a young thing in a pink cap under his arm; today I see him go by, he was giving his arm to a musket. Ma'am Bacheux says that there was a revolution last week at – at – at – where is the place? – at Pontoise. And then see him there with his pistol, that horrid blackguard? It seems the Célestins are all full of cannon. What would you have the government do with the scapegraces who do nothing but invent ways to disturb people, when we are beginning to be a little quiet, after all the troubles we have had, good

Lord God, that poor queen that I see go by in the cart! And all this is going to make snuff dearer still. It is infamous! and surely I will go to see you guillotined, you scoundrel.'

'You sniffle, my ancient,' said Gavroche. 'Blow your promontory.'

And he passed on.

When he reached the Rue Pavée, the rag-picker recurred to his mind, and he soliloquised thus:

'You do wrong to insult the Revolutionists, Mother Heap-in-the-corner. This pistol is in your interest. It is so that you may have more things good to eat in your basket.'

Suddenly he heard a noise behind him: it was the portress Patagon who had followed him, and who, from a distance, was shaking her fist at him, crying:

'You are nothing but a bastard!'

'Yes,' said Gavroche, 'I amuse myself at that in a profound manner.'

Soon after, he passed the Hôtel Lamoignon. There he shouted out this appeal:

'*En route* for battle!'

And he was seized with a fit of melancholy. He looked at his pistol with a reproachful air, which seemed an endeavour to soften it:

'I go off,' said he to it, 'but you do not go off.'

One dog may distract attention from another. A very lean cur was passing. Gavroche was moved to pity.

'My poor bow-wow,' said he, 'have you swallowed a barrel, then, that all the hoops show?'

Then he bent his steps towards the Orme Saint Gervais.

3. Just indignation of a barber

THE WORTHY BARBER, who drove away the two little boys to whom Gavroche opened the paternal intestines of the elephant, was at this moment in his shop, busy shaving an old legionary soldier who had served under the empire. They were chatting. The barber had naturally spoken to the veteran of the *émeute*, then of General Lamarque, and from Lamarque they had come to the emperor. Hence a conversation between a barber and a soldier which Prudhomme, if he had been present, would have enriched with arabesques, and which he would have entitled: *Dialogue of the razor and the sabre.*

'Monsieur,' said the wig-maker, 'how did the emperor mount on horseback?'

'Badly. He didn't know how to fall. So he never fell.'

'Did he have fine horses? he must have had fine horses!'

'The day he gave me the cross, I noticed his animal. She was a running mare, perfectly white. Her ears were very wide apart, saddle deep, head fine, marked with a black star, neck very long, knees strongly jointed, ribs protruding, shoulders sloping, hind quarters powerful. A little more than fifteen hands high.'

'A pretty horse,' said the barber.

'It was the animal of his majesty.'

The barber felt that after this word a little silence was proper, he conformed to it, then resumed:

'The emperor was never wounded but once, was he, monsieur?'

The old soldier answered with the calm and sovereign tone of a man who was there:

'In the heel. At Ratisbon. I never saw him so well dressed as he was that day. He was as neat as a penny.'

'And you, Monsieur Veteran, you must have been wounded often?'

'I?' said the soldier, 'ah! no great thing, I got two sabre slashes in my neck at Marengo, a ball in my right arm at Austerlitz, another in my left hip at Jena, at Friedland a bayonet thrust – there, – at Moscow seven or eight lance thrusts, no matter where, at Lutzen a shell burst which crushed my finger – Ah! and then at Waterloo a bullet in my leg. That is all.'

'How beautiful it is,' exclaimed the barber with a pindaric accent, 'to die on the field of battle! Upon my word, rather than die in my bed, of sickness, slowly, a little every day, with drugs, plasters, syringes, and medicine, I would prefer a cannon ball in my belly.'

'You are not fastidious,' said the soldier.

He had hardly finished when a frightful crash shook the shop. A pane of the window had been suddenly shattered,

The barber became pallid.

'O God!' cried he, 'there is one!'

'What?'

'A cannon ball.'

'Here it is,' said the soldier.

And he picked up something which was rolling on the floor, It was a stone.

The barber ran to the broken window and saw Gavroche, who was running with all his might towards the Saint Jean market. On passing the barber's shop, Gavroche, who had the two *mômes* on his mind, could not resist the desire to bid him good day, and had sent a stone through his sash.

'See!' screamed the barber, who from white had become blue, 'he makes mischief for the sake of mischief. What has anybody done to that *gamin?*'

4. The child wonders at the old man

MEANWHILE GAVROCHE at the Saint Jean market, where the guard was already disarmed, had just – effected his junction – with a band led by Enjolras, Courfeyrac, Combeferre, and Feuilly. They were almost armed. Bahorel and Jean Prouvaire had joined them and enlarged the group. Enjolras had a double-barrelled fowling piece. Combeferre a National Guard's musket bearing the number of the legion, and at his waist two pistols which could be seen, his coat being unbuttoned Jean Prouvaire an old cavalry musketoon, Bahorel a carbine Courfeyrac was brandishing an unsheathed sword-cane. Feuilly, a drawn sabre in his hand, marched in the van, crying: 'Poland for ever!'

They came from the Quai Morland cravatless, hatless, breathless, soaked by the rain, lightning in their eyes. Gavroche approached them calmly:

'Where are we going?'

'Come on,' said Courfeyrac.

Behind Feuilly marched, or rather bounded, Bahorel, a fish in the water of the *émeute*. He had a crimson waistcoat, and those words which crush everything. His waistcoat overcame a passer, who cried out in desperation:

'There are the reds!'

'The red, the reds!' replied Bahorel. 'A comical fear, bourgeois. As for me, I don't tremble before a red poppy, the little red hood inspires me with no dismay. Bourgeois, believe me, leave the fear of red to horned cattle.'

He caught sight of a piece of wall on which was placarded the most peaceful sheet of paper in the world, a permission to eat eggs, a charge for Lent, addressed by the Archbishop of Paris to his *ouailles* [flock].

Bahorel exclaimed:

'*Ouailles;* polite way of saying *oies*' [geese].

And he tore the charge from the wall. This conquered Gavroche. From that moment, Gavroche began to study Bahorel.

'Bahorel,' observed Enjolras, 'you are wrong. You should have let that charge alone, it is not with it that we have to do. You are expending your wrath uselessly. Economise your ammunition. We don't fire out of rank, – no more with the soul than with the gun.'

'Each in his own way, Enjolras,' retorted Bahorel. 'This bishop's prosing annoys me, I want to eat eggs without anybody's permission. You have the cold burning style; I amuse myself. Besides, I am not exhausting myself, I am gaining new energy; and if I tore down that charge, by Hercules! it was to give me an appetite.'

This word, *Hercules*, struck Gavroche. He sought every opportunity to instruct himself, and this tearer-down of posters had his esteem. He asked him:

'What does that mean, *Hercules?*'

Bahorel answered:

'It means holy name of a dog in Latin.'

Here Bahorel recognised at a window a pale young man with a black beard, who was looking at them as they were passing, probably a Friend of the ABC. He cried to him:

'Quick, cartridges! *para bellum.*'

'*Bel homme!* [Handsome man!] that is true,' said Gavroche, who now understood Latin.

A tumultuous cortège accompanied them, students, artists, young men affiliated to the Cougourde d'Aix, workingmen, rivermen, armed with clubs and bayonets; a few, like Combeferre, with pistols thrust into their waistbands. An old man, who appeared very old, was marching with this band. He was not armed, and he was hurrying, that he should not be left behind, although he had a thoughtful expression. Gavroche perceived him:

'Whossat?' said he to Courfeyrac.

'That is an old man.'

It was M. Mabeuf.

5. The old man

We must tell what had happened.

Enjolras and his friends were on the Boulevard Bourdon, near the warehouses, at the moment the dragoons charged. Enjolras, Courfeyrac, and Combeferre were among those who took to the Rue Bassomipierre, crying: 'To the barricades!' In the Rue Lesdiguières they met an old man trudging along. What attracted their attention was, that this goodman was walking zigzag, as if he were drunk. Moreover, he had his hat in his hand, although it had been raining all the morning, and was raining hard at that very moment. Courfeyrac recognised Father Mabeuf. He knew him from having seen him many times accompanying Marius to his door. Knowing the peaceful and more than timid habits of the old church-warden-bookworm, and astounded at seeing him in the midst of this tumult, within two steps of the cavalry charges, almost in the midst of a fusilade, bareheaded in the rain, and walking among the bullets, he went up to him, and the *émeuter* of five-and-twenty and the octogenarian exchanged this dialogue:

'Monsieur Mabeuf, go home.'

'What for?'

'There is going to be a row.'

'Very well.'

'Sabre strokes, musket shots, Monsieur Mabeuf.'

'Very well.'

'Cannon shots.'

'Very well. Where are you going, you boys?'

'We are going to pitch the government over.'

'Very well.'

And he followed them. From that moment he had not uttered a word. His step had suddenly become firm; some workingmen had offered him an arm, he refused with a shake of the head. He advanced almost to the front rank of the column, having at once the motion of a man who is walking, and the countenance of a man who is asleep.

'What a desperate goodman!' murmured the students. The rumour ran through the assemblage that he was – an ancient Conventionist – an old regicide. The company had turned into the Rue de la Verrerie.

Little Gavroche marched on with all his might with this song, which made him a sort of clarion. He sang:

Voici la lune qui paraît,
Quand irons-nous dans la forêt?
Demandait Charlot à Charlotte.

Tou tou tou
Pour Chatou.
Je n'ai qu'un Dieu, qu'un roi, qu'un liard et qu'une botte.

Pour avour bu de grand matin
La rosée à même le thym,
Deux moineaux étaient en ribote.

Zi zi zi
Pour Passy.
Je n'ai qu'un Dieu, qu'un roi, qu'un liard et qu'une botte.

Et ces deux pauvres petits loups
Comme deux grives étaient soûls;
Un tigre en riait dans sa grotte.

Don don don
Pour Meudon.
Je n'ai qu'un Dieu, qu'un roi, qu'un liard et qu'une botte.

L'un jurait et l'autre sacrait.
Quand irons-nous dans la forêt?
Demandait Charlot à Charlotte.

Tin tin tin
Pour Pantin.
Je n'ai qu'un Dieu, qu'un roi, qu'un liard et qu'une botte.*

They made their way towards Saint Merry.

6. *Recruits*

THE BAND INCREASED at every moment. Towards the Rue des Billettes a man of tall stature, who was turning grey, whose rough and bold mien Courfeyrac, Enjolras, and Combeferre noticed, but whom none of them knew, joined them. Gavroche, busy singing, whistling, humming, going forward and rapping on the shutters of the shops with the butt of his hammerless pistol, paid no attention to this man.

It happened that, in the Rue de la Verrerie, they passed by Courfeyrac's door.

'That is lucky,' said Courfeyrac, 'I have forgotten my purse, and I have lost my hat.' He left the company and went up to his room, four stairs at a time. He took an old hat and his purse. He took also a large square box, of the size of a big valise, which was hidden among his dirty clothes. As he was running down again, the portress hailed him:

'Monsieur de Courfeyrac?'

'Portress, what is your name?' responded Courfeyrac.

The portress stood aghast.

'Why, you know it very well; I am the portress, my name is Mother Veuvain.'

'Well, if you call me Monsieur de Courfeyrac again, I shall call you Mother de Veuvain. Now, speak, what is it? What do you want?'

'There is somebody who wishes to speak to you.'

'Who is it?'

* See the moon is shining, when shall we go into the woods? asked Charley of Charlotte.
Too, too, too, for Chatou. I have but one God, one king, one farthing, and one boot.
For having drunk in early morn, dew and thyme, two sparrows were in a fuddle.
Zi, zi, zi, for Passy. I have but one God, one king, one farthing and one boot.
And these two poor little wolves were as drunk as two thrushes;
a tiger laughed at it in his cave.
Don, don, don, for Meudon. I have but one God, one king, one farthing and one boot.
One swore and the other cursed. When shall we go into the woods,
asked Charley of Charlotte.
Tin, tin, tin, for Pantin. I have but one God, one king, one farthing and one boot.

'I don't know.'

'Where is he?'

'In my lodge.'

'The devil!' said Courfeyrac.

'But he has been waiting more than an hour for you to come home!' replied the portress.

At the same time, a sort of young working-man, thin, pale, small, freckled, dressed in a torn blouse and patched pantaloons of ribbed velvet, and who had rather the appearance of a girl in boy's clothes than of a man, came out of the lodge and said to Courfeyrac in a voice which, to be sure, was not the least in the world a woman's voice.

'Monsieur Marius, if you please?'

'He is not in.'

'Will he be in this evening?'

'I don't know anything about it.'

And Courfeyrac added: 'As for myself, I shall not be in.'

The young man looked fixedly at him, and asked him:

'Why so?'

'Because.'

'Where are you going then?'

'What is that to you?'

'Do you want me to carry your box?'

'I am going to the barricades.'

'Do you want me to go with you?'

'If you like,' answered Courfeyrac. 'The road is free; the streets belong to everybody.'

And he ran off to rejoin his friends. When he had rejoined them, he gave the box to one of them to carry. It was not until a quarter of an hour afterwards that he perceived that the young man had in fact followed them.

A mob does not go precisely where it wishes. We have explained that a gust of wind carries it along. They went beyond Saint Merry and found themselves, without really knowing how, in the Rue Saint Denis.

BOOK 12: CORINTH

1. *History of Corinth from its foundation*

THE PARISIANS who, today, upon entering the Rue Rambuteau from the side of the markets, notice on their right, opposite the Rue Mondétour, a basket-maker's shop, with a basket for a sign, in the shape of the Emperor Napoleon the Great, with this inscription:

NAPOLÉON EST FAIT,
TOUT EN OSIER, *

do not suspect the terrible scenes which this very place saw thirty years ago.

Here were the Rue de la Chanvrerie, which the old signs spelled Chanverrerie, and the celebrated wine-shop called Corinth.

The reader will remember all that has been said about the barricade erected on this spot and eclipsed elsewhere by the barricade of Saint Merry. Upon this famous barricade of the Rue de la Chanvrerie, now fallen into deep obscurity, we are about to throw some little light.

Permit us to recur, for the sake of clearness, to the simple means already employed by us for Waterloo. Those who would picture to themselves with sufficient exactness the confused blocks of houses which stood at that period near the Pointe Saint Eustache, at the northeast corner of the markets of Paris, where is now the mouth of the Rue Rambuteau, have only to figure to themselves, touching the Rue Saint Denis at its summit, and the markets at its base, an N, of which the two vertical strokes would be the Rue de la Grande Truanderie and the Rue de la Chanvrerie, and the Rue de la Petite Truanderie would make the transverse stroke. The old Rue Mondétour cut the three strokes at the most awkward angles. So that the labyrinthine entanglement of these four streets sufficed to make, in a space of four hundred square yards, between the markets and the Rue Saint Denis, in one direction, and between the Rue du Cygne and the Rue des Prêcheurs in the other direction, seven islets of houses, oddly intersecting, of various sizes, placed crosswise and as if by chance, and separated but slightly, like blocks of stone in a stone yard, by narrow crevices.

We say narrow crevices, and we cannot give a more just idea of those obscure, contracted, angular lanes, bordered by ruins eight storeys high. These houses were so dilapidated, that in the Rues de la Chanvrerie and de la Petite Truanderie, the fronts were shored up with beams, reaching from one house to another. The street was narrow and the gutter wide, the passer walked along a pavement which was always wet, beside shops that were like cellars, great stone blocks encircled with iron, immense garbage heaps, and alley gates armed with enormous and venerable gratings. The Rue Rambuteau has devastated all this.

The name Mondétour pictures marvellously well the windings of all this

* Napoleon is made, all of willow braid.

route. A little further along you found them still better expressed by the *Rue Pirouette*, which ran into the Rue Mondétour.

The passer-by who came from the Rue Saint Denis into the Rue de la Chanvrerie saw it gradually narrow away before him as if he had entered an elongated funnel. At the end of the street, which was very short, he found the passage barred on the market side, and he would have thought himself in a cul-de-sac, if he had not perceived on the right and on the left two black openings by which he could escape. These were the Rue Mondétour, which communicated on the one side with the Rue des Prêcheurs, on the other with the Rues du Cygne and Petite Truanderie. At the end of this sort of cul-de-sac, at the corner of the opening on the right, might be seen a house lower than the rest, and forming a kind of cape on the street.

In this house, only two storeys high, had been festively installed for three hundred years an illustrious wine-shop. This wine-shop raised a joyful sound in the very place which old Théophile has rendered famous in these two lines:

Là branle le squelette horrible
D'un pauvre amant qui se pendit. *

The location was good. The proprietorship descended from father to son.

In the times of Mathurin Régnier, this wine-shop was called the *Pot aux Roses* (the Pot of Roses), and as rebuses were in fashion, it had for a sign a post *(poteau)* painted rose colour. In the last century, the worthy Natoire, one of the fantastic masters now held in disdain by the rigid school, having got tipsy several times in this wine-shop at the same table where Régnier had got drunk, out of gratitude painted a bunch of Corinth grapes upon the rose-coloured post. The landlord, from joy, changed his sign and had gilded below the bunch these words: *The Grape of Corinth.* Hence the name Corinth. Nothing is more natural to drinkers than an ellipsis. The ellipsis is the zigzag of phrase. Corinth gradually dethroned the *Pot aux Roses.* The last landlord of the dynasty, Father Hucheloup, not even knowing the tradition, had the post painted blue.

A basement room in which was the counter, a room on the first floor in which was the billiard table, a spiral wooden staircase piercing the ceiling, wine on the tables, smoke on the walls, candles in broad day, such was the wine-shop. A stairway with a trap-door in the basement-room led to the cellar. On the second floor were the rooms of the Hucheloups. You ascended by a stairway, which was rather a ladder than a stairway, the only entrance to which was by a back door in the large room on the first floor. In the attic, two garret rooms, with dormer windows, nests for servants. The kitchen divided the ground-floor with the counting-room.

Father Hucheloup was perhaps a born chemist, he was certainly a cook; people not only drank in his wine-shop, they ate there. Hucheloup had invented an excellent dish which was found only at his house; it was stuffed carps which he called *carpes au gras*. This was eaten by the light of a tallow candle, or a lamp of the time of Louis XVI, upon tables on which an oil-cloth was nailed for a tablecloth. Men came there from a distance. Hucheloup, one fine morning, thought proper to advertise by-passers of his 'speciality'; he dipped a brush in a

* There rattles the horrible skeleton of a poor lover who hung himself.

pot of blacking, and as he had an orthography of his own, even as he had a cuisine of his own, he improvised upon his wall this remarkable inscription:

CARPES HO GRAS.

One winter, the showers and the storms took a fancy to efface the S which terminated the first word and the G which commenced the third; it was left like this:

CARPE HO RAS.

Time and the rain aiding, a humble gastronomic advertisement had become a profound piece of advice.

So that it happened that, not knowing French, Father Hucheloup had known Latin, that he had brought philosophy out of his kitchen, and that, desiring simply to eclipse Carême, he had equalled Horace. And what was striking was that this also meant: Enter my wine-shop.

Nothing of all this is at present in existence. The Mondétour labyrinth was ripped up and opened wide in 1847, and probably is now no more. The Rue de la Chanvrerie and Corinth have disappeared under the pavements of the Rue Rambuteau.

As we have said, Corinth was one of the meeting, if not rallying places, of Courfeyrac and his friends. It was Grantaire who had discovered Corinth. He had entered on account of *Carpe Horas*, and he returned on account of *Carpes au Gras.* They drank there, they ate there, they shouted there; they paid little, they paid poorly, they did not pay at all, they were always welcome. Father Hucheloup was a goodman.

Hucheloup, a goodman, we have just said, was a cook with moustaches: an amusing variety. He had always an ill-humoured face, seemed to wish to intimidate his customers, grumbled at people who came to his house, and appeared more disposed to pick a quarrel with them than to serve them their soup. And still, we maintain, they were always welcome. This oddity had brought custom to his shop, and led young men to him, saying to each other: 'Come and hear Father Hucheloup grumble.' He had been a fencing-master. He would suddenly burst out laughing. Coarse voice, good devil. His was a comic heart, with a tragic face; he asked nothing better than to frighten you, much like those snuff-boxes which have the shape of a pistol. The discharge is a sneeze.

His wife was Mother Hucheloup, a bearded creature, and very ugly.

Towards 1830, Father Hucheloup died. With him the secret of the *carpes au gras* was lost. His widow, scarcely consolable, continued the wine-shop. But the cuisine degenerated and became execrable, the wine, which had always been bad became frightful. Courfeyrac and his friends continued to go to Corinth, however – 'from pity,' said Bossuet.

Widow Hucheloup was short-winded and deformed, with memories of the country. She relieved their tiresomeness by her pronunciation. She had a way of her own of saying things which spiced her village and springtime reminiscences. It had once been her fortune, she affirmed, to hear 'the lead-breasts sing in the hawkthorns.'

The room on the first floor, in which was 'the restaurant', was a long and wide room, encumbered with stools, crickets, chairs, benches, and tables, and a rickety old billiard-table. It was reached by the spiral staircase which terminated at the corner of the room in a square hole like the hatchway of a ship.

This room, lighted by a single narrow window and by a lamp which was always burning, had the appearance of a garret. All the pieces of furniture on four legs behaved as if they had but three. The whitewashed walls had no ornament except this quatrain in honour of Ma'am Hucheloup:

> Elle etonne à dix pas, elle épouvante à deux,
> Une verrue habite en son nez hasardeux;
> On tremble à chaque instant qu'elle ne vous la mouche
> Et qu'un beau jour son nez ne tombe dans sa bouche. *

This was written in charcoal upon the wall.

Ma'am Hucheloup, the original, went back and forth from morning till night before this quatrain in perfect tranquillity. Two servants, called Chowder and Fricassee, and for whom nobody had ever known any other names, helped Ma'am Hucheloup to put upon the tables the pitchers of blue wine and the various broths which were served to the hungry in earthen dishes. Chowder, fat, round, red, and boisterous, former favourite sultana of the defunct Hucheloup, was uglier than any mythological monster; still, as it is fitting that the servant should always keep behind the mistress, she was less ugly than Ma'am Hucheloup. Fricassee, long, delicate, white with a lymphatic whiteness, rings around her eyes, eyelids drooping, always exhausted and dejected, subject to what might be called chronic weariness, up first, in bed last, served everybody, even the other servant, mildly and in silence, smiling through fatigue with a sort of vague sleepy smile.

Before entering the restaurant room, you might read upon the door this line written in chalk by Courfeyrac:

> Régale si tu peux et mange si tu l'oses.†

2. *Preliminary gaiety*

LAIGLE DE MEAUX, we know, lived more with Joly than elsewhere. He had a lodging as the bird has a branch. The two friends lived together, ate together, slept together. Everything was in common with them, even Musichetta a little. They were what, among the Chapeau Brothers, are called *bini*. On the morning of the 5th of June, they went to breakfast at Corinth. Joly, whose head was stopped up, had a bad cold, which Laigle was beginning to share. Laigle's coat was threadbare, but Joly was well dressed.

It was about nine o'clock in the morning when they opened the door of Corinth.

They went up to the first floor.

* She astounds at ten paces, she terrifies at two, a wart inhabits her dangerous nose; you tremble every moment lest she blow it at you, and lest some fine day her nose may fall into her mouth. † Feast if you can and eat if you dare.

Chowder and Fricassee received them: 'Oysters, cheese, and ham,' said Laigle.

And they sat down at a table.

The wine-shop was empty; they two only were there.

Fricassee, recognising Joly and Laigle, put a bottle of wine on the table.

As they were at their first oysters, a head appeared at the hatchway of the stairs, and a voice said:

'I was passing. I smelt in the street a delicious odour of Brie cheese. I have come in.'

It was Grantaire.

Grantaire took a stool and sat down at the table.

Fricassee, seeing Grantaire, put two bottles of wine on the table.

That made three.

'Are you going to drink those two bottles?' inquired Laigle of Grantaire.

Grantaire answered:

'All are ingenious, you alone are ingenuous. Two bottles never astonished a man.'

The others had begun by eating. Grantaire began by drinking. A half bottle was quickly swallowed.

'Have you a hole in your stomach?' resumed Laigle.

'You surely have one in your elbow,' said Grantaire.

And, after emptying his glass, he added:

'Ah now, Laigle of the funeral orations, your coat is old.'

'I hope so,' replied Laigle. 'That makes us agree so well, my coat and I. It has got all my wrinkles, it doesn't bind me anywhere, it has fitted itself to all my deformities, it is complaisant to all my motions; I feel it only because it keeps me warm. Old coats are the same thing as old friends.'

'That's true,' exclaimed Joly, joining in the dialogue, 'an old *habit* [coat] is an old *abi* [friend].'

'Especially,' said Grantaire, 'in the mouth of a man whose head is stopped up.'

'Grantaire,' asked Laigle, 'do you come from the boulevard?'

'No.'

'We just saw the head of the procession pass, Joly and I.'

'It is a barvellous spectacle,' said Joly.

'How quiet this street is!' exclaimed Laigle. 'Who would suspect that Paris is all topsy-turvy? You see this was formerly all monasteries about here! Du Breul and Sauval give the list of them, and the Abbé Lebeuf. They were all around here, they swarmed, the shod, the unshod, the shaven, the bearded, the greys, the blacks, the whites, the Franciscans, the Minimi, the Capuchins, the Carmelites, the Lesser Augustines, the Greater Augustines, the Old Augustines. They littered.'

'Don't talk about monks,' interrupted Grantaire, 'it makes me want to scratch.'

Then he exclaimed:

'Peugh! I have just swallowed a bad oyster. Here's the hypochondria upon me again. The oysters are spoiled, the servants are ugly. I hate human kind. I passed just now in the Rue Richelieu before the great public library. This heap of oyster shells, which they call a library, disgusts me to think of. How much paper! how much ink! how much scribbling! Somebody has written all that! What booby was it who said that man is a biped without feathers? And then, I met a pretty girl whom I know, beautiful as spring, worthy to be called Floréal, and delighted, transported, happy, with the angels, the poor creature, because yesterday a horrid banker, pitted with smallpox, deigned to fancy her. Alas! woman watches the publican no less than the fop; cats chase mice as well as birds. This damsel, less than two months ago, was a good girl in a garret, she fixed the little rings of copper in the eyelets of corsets, how do you call it? She sewed, she had a bed, she lived with a flower-pot, she was contented. Now she is a bankeress. This transformation was wrought last night. I met the victim this morning, full of joy. The hideous part of it is, that the wench was quite as pretty today as yesterday. Her financier didn't appear on her face. Roses have this much more or less than women, that the traces which worms leave on them are visible. Ah! there is no morality upon the earth; I call to witness the myrtle, the symbol of love, the laurel, the symbol of war, the olive, that goose, the symbol of peace, the apple, which almost strangled Adam with its seed, and the fig, the grandfather of petticoats. As to rights, do you want to know what rights are? The Gauls covet Clusium, Rome protects Clusium, and asks them what Clusium has done to them. Brennus answers: 'What Alba did to you, what Fidenæ did to you, what the Æqui, the Volsci, and the Sabines did to you. They were your neighbours. The Clusians are ours. We understand neighbourhood as you do. You stole Alba, we take Clusium.' Rome says: 'You will not take Clusium.' Brennus took Rome. Then he cried: '*Væ victis!*' That is what rights are. Ah! in this world, what beasts of prey! what eagles! it makes me crawl all over.'

He reached his glass to Joly, who filled it again, then he drank, and proceeded, almost without having been interrupted by this glass of wine, which nobody perceived, not even himself.

'Brennus, who takes Rome, is an eagle; the banker, who takes the grisette, is an eagle. No more shame here than there. Then let us believe in nothing. There is but one reality: to drink. Whatever may be your opinion whether you are for the lean cock, like the Canton of Uri, or for the fat cock, like the Canton of Glaris, matters little, drink. You talk to me of the boulevard, of the procession, et cætera. Ah now, there is going to be a revolution again, is there? This poverty of means on the part of God astonishes me. He has to keep greasing the grooves of events continually. It hitches, it does not go. Quick, a revolution. God has his hands black with this villanous cart-grease all the time. In his place, I would work more simply, I wouldn't be winding up my machine every minute, I would lead the human race smoothly, I would knit the facts stitch to stitch, without breaking the thread, I would have no emergency, I would have no extraordinary repertory. What you fellows call progress moves by two springs, men and events. But sad to say, from time to time the exceptional is necessary. For events as well as for men, the stock company is not enough; geniuses are needed among men, and revolutions among events. Great accidents are the law; the order of things cannot get along without them; and, to see the apparitions of comets, one would be tempted to believe that Heaven itself is in need of star actors. At the moment you least expect it, God placards a meteor on the wall of the firmament. Some strange star comes along, underlined by an enormous tail. And that makes Cæsar die. Brutus strikes him with a knife, and God with a comet. Crack, there is an aurora borealis, there is a revolution, there is a great man; '93 in big letters. Napoleon with a line to himself, the comet of 1811 at the top of the poster. Ah! the beautiful blue poster, all studded with unexpected flourishes! Boom! boom! extraordinary spectacle. Look up, loungers. All is dishevelled, the star as well as the drama. Good God, it is too much, and it is not enough. These resources, used in emergency, seem magnificence, and are poverty. My friends, Providence is put to his trumps. A revolution, what does that prove? That God is hard up. He makes a *coup d'état*, because there is a solution of continuity between the present and the future, and because he, God, is unable to join the two ends. In fact, that confirms me in my conjectures about the condition of Jehovah's fortune; and to see so much discomfort above and below, so much rascality and odiousness and stinginess and distress in the heavens and on the earth, from the bird which has not a grain of millet to me who have not a hundred thousand livres of income, to see human destiny, which is very much worn out, and even royal destiny, which shows the warp, witness the Prince of Condé hung, to see winter, which is nothing but a rent in the zenith through which the wind blows, to see so many tatters even in the brand new purple of the morning on the tops of the hills, to see the dew drops, those false pearls, to see the frost, that paste, to see humanity ripped, and events patched, and so many spots on the sun, and so many holes in the moon, to see so much misery everywhere, I suspect that God is not rich. He keeps up appearances, it is true, but I feel the pinch. He gives a revolution as a merchant, whose credit is low, gives a ball. We must not judge the gods from appearances. Beneath the gilding of the sky I catch a glimpse of a poor universe. Creation is bankrupt. That is why I am a malcontent. See, it is the fifth of June, it is very dark; since morning I have been waiting for the daybreak, it has not come, and I will bet that it won't come all day. It is a negligence of a badly paid clerk. Yes, everything is badly arranged, nothing fits anything, this old world is all rickety, I range myself with the opposition. Everything goes cross-grained; the universe is a tease. It is like children, those who want it haven't it, those who don't want it have it. Total: I scoff. Besides, Laigle de Meaux, that bald-head, afflicts my sight. It humiliates me to think that I am the same age as that knee. Still, I criticise, but I don't insult. The universe is what it is. I speak here without malice, and to ease my conscience. Receive, Father Eternal, the assurance of my distinguished consideration. Oh! by all the saints of Olympus and by all the gods of Paradise, I was not made to be a Parisian, that is to say, to ricochet for ever, like a shuttlecock between two battledores, from the company of loafers to the company of rioters! I was made to be a Turk, looking all day long at Oriental jades executing those exquisite dances of Egypt, as lascivious as the dreams of a chaste man, or a Beauce peasant, or a Venetian gentleman surrounded by gentledames, or a little German prince, furnishing the half of a foot soldier to the Germanic Confederation, and occupying his leisure in drying his socks upon his hedge, that is to say, upon his frontier! Such is the destiny for which I was born! Yes, I said Turk, and I don't unsay it. I don't understand why the Turks are commonly held in bad repute; there is some good in Mahomet; respect for the inventor of seraglios with houris, and paradises with odalisques! Let us not insult Mahometanism, the only religion that is adorned with a hen-roost! On that, I insist upon drinking. The earth is a great folly. And it appears that they are going to fight, all these idiots, to get their heads broken, to massacre one another, in midsummer, in the month of June, when they might go off with some creature under their arm, to scent in the fields the huge cup of tea of the new mown hay! Really, they are too silly. An old broken lamp which I saw just now at a second-hand shop suggests me a reflection. It is time to enlighten the human race. Yes, here I am again sad. What a thing it is to swallow an oyster or a revolution the wrong way! I am getting dismal. Oh! the frightful old world! They strive with one another, they plunder one another, they prostitute one another, they kill one another, they get used to one another!'

And Grantaire, after this fit of eloquence, had a fit of coughing, which he deserved.

'Speakig of revolutiod,' said Joly, 'it appears that Barius is decidedly abourous.'

'Does anybody know of whom?' inquired Laigle.

'Do.'

'No?'

'Do! I tell you.'

'Marius's amours!' exclaimed Grantaire, 'I see them now. Marius is a fog, and he must have found a vapour. Marius is of the race of poets. He who says poet, says fool. *Tymbrœus Apollo.* Marius and his Mary, or his Maria; or his Marietta, or his Marion, they must make droll lovers. I imagine how it is. Ecstasies where they forget to kiss. Chaste upon the earth, but coupling in the infinite. They are souls which have senses. They sleep together in the stars.'

Grantaire was entering on his second bottle, and perhaps his second harangue, when a new actor emerged from the square hole of the stairway. It was a boy of less than ten years, ragged, very small, yellow, a mug of a face, a keen eye, monstrous long hair, wet to the skin, a complacent look.

The child, choosing without hesitation among the three, although he evidently knew none of them, addressed himself to Laigle de Meaux.

'Are you Monsieur Bossuet?' asked he.

'That is my nickname,' answered Laigle. 'What do you want of me?'

'This is it. A big light-complexioned fellow on the boulevard said to me: Do you know Mother Hucheloup? I said: Yes, Rue Chanvrerie, the widow of the old man. He said to me. Go there. You will find Monsieur Bossuet there, and you will tell him from me: A – B – C. It is a joke that somebody is playing on you, isn't it? He gave me ten sous.'

'Joly, lend me ten sous,' said Laigle, and turning towards Grantaire: 'Grantaire, lend me ten sous.'

This made twenty sous which Laigle gave the child.

'Thank you, monsieur,' said the little fellow.

'What is your name?' asked Laigle.

'Navet, Gavroche's friend.'

'Stop with us,' said Laigle.

'Breakfast with us,' said Grantaire.

The child answered:

'I can't, I am with the procession, I am the one to cry, Down with Polignac.'

And giving his foot a long scrape behind him, which is the most respectful of all possible bows, he went away.

The child gone, Grantaire resumed:

'This is the pure *gamin.* There are many varieties in the *gamin* genus. The notary *gamin* is called *saute-ruisseau*, the cook *gamin is* called *marmiton*, the baker *gamin is* called *mitron*, the lackey *gamin* is called *groom*, the sailor *gamin* is called *mousse*, the soldier *gamin* is called *tapin*, the painter *gamin is* called *rapin*, the trader *gamin* is called *trottin*, the courtier *gamin is* called *menin*, the king *gamin* is called *dauphin*, the god *gamin* is called *bambino*.'

Meanwhile Laigle was meditating; he said in an undertone:

'A – B – C, that is to say: Lamarque's funeral.'

'The big light-complexioned man,' observed Grantaire, 'is Enjolras, who sent to notify you.'

'Shall we go?' said Bossuet.

'It raids,' said Joly. 'I have sword to go through fire, dot water. I dod't wadt to catch cold.'

'I stay here,' said Grantaire. 'I prefer a breakfast to a hearse.'

'Conclusion: we stay,' resumed Laigle. 'Well, let us drink then. Besides we can miss the funeral, without missing the *émeute*.'

'Ah! the ébeute, I am id for that,' exclaimed Joly.

Laigle rubbed his hands:

'Now they are going to retouch the Revolution of 1830. In fact, it binds the people in the armholes.'

'It don't make much difference with me, your revolution,' said Grantaire. 'I don't execrate this government. It is the crown tempered with the night-cap. It is a sceptre terminating in an umbrella. In fact, today, I should think, in this weather Louis Philippe could make good use of his royalty at both ends, extend the sceptre end against the people, and open the umbrella end against the sky.'

The room was dark, great clouds were completing the suppression of the daylight. There was nobody in the wine-shop, nor in the street, everybody having gone 'to see the events.'

'Is it noon or midnight?' cried Bossuet. 'We can't see a speck. Fricassee, a light.'

Grantaire, melancholy, was drinking.

'Enjolras despises me,' murmured he. 'Enjolras said: Joly is sick. Grantaire is drunk. It was to Bossuet that he sent Navet. If he had come for me I would have followed him. So much the worse for Enjolras! I won't go to his funeral.'

This resolution taken, Bossuet, Joly, and Grantaire did not stir from the wine-shop. About two o'clock in the afternoon, the table on which they were leaning was covered with empty bottles. Two candles were burning, one in a perfectly green copper candlestick, the other in the neck of a cracked decanter. Grantaire had drawn Joly and Bossuet towards wine; Bossuet and Joly had led Grantaire towards joy.

As for Grantaire, since noon, he had got beyond wine, an indifferent source of dreams. Wine, with serious drunkards, has only a quiet success. There is, in point of inebriety, black magic and white magic; wine is only white magic. Grantaire was a daring drinker of dreams. The blackness of a fearful drunkenness yawning before him, far from checking him, drew him on. He had left the bottle behind and taken to the jug. The jug is the abyss. Having at his hand neither opium nor hashish, and wishing to fill his brain with mist, he had had recourse to that frightful mixture of brandy, stout, and absinth, which produces such terrible lethargy. It is from these three vapours, beer, brandy, and absinth, that the lead of the soul is formed. They are three darknesses; the celestial butterfly is drowned in them; and there arise, in a membranous smoke vaguely condensed into bat wings, three dumb furies, nightmare, night, death, flitting above the sleeping Psyche.

Grantaire was not yet at this dreary phase; far from it. He was extravagantly gay, and Bossuet and Joly kept pace with him. They touched glasses. Grantaire added to the eccentric accentuation of his words and ideas incoherency of gesture; he rested his left wrist upon his knee with dignity, his arms a-kimbo, and his cravat untied, bestriding a stool, his full glass in his right hand, he threw out to the fat servant Chowder these solemn words:

'Let the palace doors be opened! Let everybody belong to the Académie Française, and have the right of embracing Madame Hucheloup! let us drink.'

And turning towards Ma'am Hucheloup he added:

'Antique woman consecrated by use, approach that I may gaze upon thee!'

And Joly exclaimed:

'Chowder add Fricassee, dod't give Gradtaire ady bore to drigk. He spedds his bodey foolishly. He has already devoured sidce this bordigg in desperate prodigality two fragcs didety-five cedtibes.'

And Grantaire replied:

'Who has been unhooking the stars without my permission to put them on the table in the shape of candles?'

Bossuet, very drunk, had preserved his calmness.

He sat in the open window, wetting his back with the falling rain, and gazed at his two friends.

Suddenly he heard a tumult behind him, hurried steps, cries *to arms!* He turned, and saw in the Rue Saint Denis, at the end of the Rue de la Chanvrerie, Enjolras passing, carbine in hand, and Gavroche with his pistol, Feuilly with his sabre, Courfeyrac with his sword, Jean Prouvaire with his musketoon, Combeferre with his musket, Bahorel with his musket, and all the armed and stormy gathering which followed them.

The Rue de la Chanvrerie was hardly as long as the range of a carbine. Bossuet improvised a speaking trumpet with his two hands, and shouted:

'Courfeyrac! Courfeyrac! ahoy!'

Courfeyrac heard the call, perceived Bossuet, and came a few steps into the Rue de la Chanvrerie, crying a 'what do you want?' which was met on the way by a 'where are you going?'

'To make a barricade,' answered Courfeyrac.

'Well, here! this is a good place! make it here!'

'That is true, Eagle,' said Courfeyrac.

And at a sign from Courfeyrac, the band rushed into the Rue de la Chanvrerie.

3. Night begins to gather over Grantaire

THE PLACE was indeed admirably chosen, the entrance of the street wide, the further end contracted and like a cul-de-sac, Corinth throttling it, Rue Mondétour easy to bar at the right and left, no attack possible except from the Rue Saint Denis, that is from the front, and without cover. Bossuet tipsy had the *coup d'œil* of Hannibal fasting.

At the irruption of the mob, dismay seized the whole street, not a passer but had gone into eclipse. In a flash, at the end, on the right, on the left, shops, stalls, alley gates, windows, blinds, dormer-windows, shutters of every size, were closed from the ground to the roofs. One frightened old woman had fixed a mattress before her window on two clothes poles, as a shield against the musketry. The wine-shop was the only house which remained open; and that for a good reason, because the band had rushed into it. 'Oh my God! Oh my God!' sighed Ma'am Hucheloup.

Bossuet had gone down to meet Courfeyrac.

Joly, who had come to the window, cried:

'Courfeyrac, you bust take ad ubbrella. You will catch cold.'

Meanwhile, in a few minutes, twenty iron bars had been wrested from the grated front of the wine-shop, twenty yards of pavement had been torn up; Gavroche and Bahorel had seized on its passage and tipped over the dray of a lime merchant named Anceau, this dray contained three barrels full of lime, which they had placed under the piles of paving stones; Enjolras had opened the trap-door of the cellar and all the widow Hucheloup's empty casks had gone to flank the lime barrels; Feuilly, with his fingers accustomed to colour the delicate folds of fans, had buttressed the barrels and the dray with two massive heaps of stones. Stones improvised like the rest, and obtained nobody knows where. Some shoring-timbers had been pulled down from the front of a neighbouring house and laid upon the casks. When Bossuet and Courfeyrac turned round, half the street was already barred by a rampart higher than a man. There is nothing like the popular hand to build whatever can be built by demolishing.

Chowder and Fricassee had joined the labourers. Fricassee went back and forth loaded with rubbish. Her weariness contributed to the barricade. She served paving stones, as she would have served wine, with a sleepy air.

An omnibus with two white horses passed at the end of the street.

Bossuet sprang over the pavement, ran, stopped the driver, made the passengers get down, gave his hand 'to the ladies,' dismissed the conductor, and came back with the vehicle, leading the horses by the bridle.

'An omnibus,' said he, 'doesn't pass by Corinth. *Non licet omnibus adire Corinthum.*'

A moment later the horses were unhitched and going off at will through the Rue Mondetour, and the omnibus, lying on its side, completed the barring of the street.

Ma'am Hucheloup, completely upset, had taken refuge in the first storey.

Her eyes were wandering, and she looked without seeing, crying in a whisper. Her cries were dismayed and dared not come out of her throat.

'It is the end of the world,' she murmured.

Joly deposited a kiss upon Ma'am Hucheloup's coarse, red, and wrinkled neck, and said to Grantaire: 'My dear fellow, I have always considered a woman's neck an infinitely delicate thing.'

But Grantaire was attaining the highest regions of dithyramb. Chowder having come up to the first floor, Grantaire seized her by the waist and pulled her towards the window with long bursts of laughter.

'Chowder is ugly!' cried he; 'Chowder is the dream of ugliness! Chowder is a chimera. Listen to the secret of her birth: a Gothic Pygmalion who was making cathedral waterspouts, fell in love with one of them one fine morning, the most horrible of all. He implored Love to animate her, and that made Chowder. Behold her, citizens! her hair is the colour of chromate of lead, like that of Titian's mistress, and she is a good girl. I warrant you that she will fight well. Every good girl contains a hero. As for Mother Hucheloup, she is an old brave. Look at her moustaches! she inherited them from her husband. A hussaress, indeed, she will fight too. They two by themselves will frighten the banlieue. Comrades, we will overturn the government, as true as there are fifteen acids intermediate between margaric acid and formic acid, which I don't care a fig about. Messieurs, my father always detested me, because I could not understand mathematics. I only understand love and liberty. I am Grantaire, a good boy. Never having had any money, I have never got used to it, and by that means I have never felt the need of it; but if I had been rich, there would have been no more poor! you should have seen. Oh! if the good hearts had the fat purses, how much better everything would go! I imagine Jesus Christ with Rothschild's fortune! How much good he would have done! Chowder, embrace me! you are voluptuous and timid! you have cheeks which call for the kiss of a sister, and lips which demand the kiss of a lover.'

'Be still, wine-cask!' said Courfeyrac.

Grantaire answered:

'I am Capitoul and Master of Floral Games!'

Enjolras, who was standing on the crest of the barricade, musket in hand, raised his fine austere face. Enjolras, we know, had something of the Spartan and of the Puritan. He would have died at Thermopylæ with Leonidas, and would have burned Drogheda with Cromwell.

'Grantaire,' cried he, 'go sleep yourself sober away from here. This is the place for intoxication and not for drunkenness. Do not dishonour the barricade!'

This angry speech produced upon Grantaire a singular effect. One would have said that he had received a glass of cold water in his face. He appeared suddenly sobered. He sat down, leaned upon a table near the window, looked at Enjolras with an inexpressible gentleness, and said to him:

'Let me sleep here.'

'Go sleep elsewhere,' cried Enjolras.

But Grantaire, keeping his tender and troubled eyes fixed upon him, answered:

'Let me sleep here – until I die here.'

Enjolras regarded him with a disdainful eye:

'Grantaire, you are incapable of belief, of thought, of will, of life, and of death.'

Grantaire replied with a grave voice:

'You will see.'

He stammered out a few more unintelligible words, then his head fell heavily upon the table, and, a common effect of the second stage of inebriety into which Enjolras had rudely and suddenly pushed him, a moment later he was asleep.

4. Attempt at consolation upon the Widow Hucheloup

Bahorel, in ecstasies with the barricade, cried:

'There is the street in a low neck, how well it looks!'

Courfeyrac, even while helping to demolish the wine-shop, sought to console the widowed landlady.

'Mother Hucheloup, were you not complaining the other day that you had been summoned and fined because Fricassee had shaken a rug out of your window?'

'Yes, my good Monsieur Courfeyrac. Oh! my God! are you going to put that table also into your horror? And besides that, for the rug, and also for a flower-pot which fell from the attic into the street, the government fined me a hundred francs. If that isn't an abomination!'

'Well, Mother Hucheloup, we are avenging you.'

Mother Hucheloup, in this reparation which they were making her, did not seem to very well understand her advantage. She was satisfied after the manner of that Arab woman who, having received a blow from her husband, went to complain to her father, crying for vengeance and saying: 'Father, you owe my husband affront for affront.' The father asked: 'Upon which cheek did you receive the blow?' 'Upon the left cheek.' The father struck the right cheek, and said: 'Now you are satisfied. Go and tell your husband that he has struck my daughter, but that I have struck his wife.'

The rain had ceased. Recruits had arrived. Some working-men had brought under their blouses a keg of powder, a hamper containing bottles of vitriol, two or three carnival torches, and a basket full of lamps, 'relics of the king's fête', which fête was quite recent, having taken place the 1st of May. It was said that these supplies came from a grocer of the Faubourg Saint Antoine, named Pépin. They broke the only lamp in the Rue de la Chanvrerie, the lamp opposite the Rue Saint Denis, and all the lamps in the surrounding streets, Mondétour, du Cygne, des Prêcheurs, and de la Grande and de la Petite Truanderie.

Enjolras, Combeferre, and Courfeyrac, directed everything. Two barricades were now building at the same time, both resting on the house of Corinth and making a right angle; the larger one closed the Rue de la Chanvrerie, the other closed the Rue Mondétour in the direction of the Rue du Cygne. This last barricade, very narrow, was constructed only of casks and paving stones. There were about fifty labourers there, some thirty armed with muskets, for, on their way, they had effected a wholesale loan from an armourer's shop.

Nothing could be more fantastic and more motley than this band. One had a short-jacket, a cavalry sabre, and two horse-pistols; another was in shirt sleeves, with a round hat, and a powder-horn hung at his side; a third had a breast-plate of nine sheets of brown paper, and was armed with a saddler's awl. There was one of them who cried: '*Let us exterminate to the last man, and die on the point of our bayonets!*' This man had no bayonet. Another displayed over his coat a cross-belt and cartridge-box of the National Guard, with the box cover adorned with this inscription in red cloth: *Public Order.* Many muskets bearing the numbers of their legions, few hats, no cravats, many bare arms, some pikes. Add to this all ages, all faces, small pale young men, bronzed wharfmen. All were hurrying and, while helping each other, they talked about the possible chances – that they would have help by three o'clock in the morning – that they were sure of one regiment – that Paris would rise. Terrible subjects, with which were mingled a sort of cordial joviality. One would have said they were brothers, they did not know each other's names. Great perils have this beauty, that they bring to light the fraternity of strangers.

A fire had been kindled in the kitchen, and they were melting pitchers, dishes, forks, all the pewter ware of the wine-shop into bullets. They drank through it all. Percussion-caps and buckshot rolled pell-mell upon the tables with glasses of wine. In the billiard-room, Ma'am Hucheloup, Chowder, and Fricassée, variously modified by terror, one being stupefied, another breathless, the third alert, were tearing up old linen and making lint; three insurgents assisted them, three long-haired, bearded, and moustached wags who tore up the cloth with the fingers of a linen-draper, and who made them tremble.

The man of tall stature whom Courfeyrac, Combeferre, and Enjolras had noticed, at the moment he joined the company at the corner of the Rue des Eillettes, was working on the little barricade, and making himself useful there. Gavroche worked on the large one. As for the young man who had waited for Courfeyrac at his house, and had asked him for Monsieur Marius, he had disappeared very nearly at the moment the omnibus was overturned.

Gavroche, completely carried away and radiant, had charged himself with making all ready. He went, came, mounted, descended, remounted, bustled, sparkled. He seemed to be there for the encouragement of all. Had he a spur? yes, certainly, his misery; had he wings? yes, certainly, his joy. Gavroche was a whirlwind. They saw him incessantly, they heard him constantly. He filled the air, being everywhere at once. He was a kind of stimulating ubiquity; no stop possible with him. The enormous barricade felt him on its back. He vexed the loungers, he excited the idle, he reanimated the weary, he provoked the thoughtful, kept some in cheerfulness, others in breath, others in anger, all in motion, piqued a student, was biting to a working-man; took position, stopped, started on, flitted above the tumult and the effort, leaped from these to those, murmured, hummed, and stirred up the whole train; the fly on the revolutionary coach.

Perpetual motion was in his little arms, and perpetual clamour in his little lungs.

'Cheerly? more paving stones? more barrels? more machines? where are there any? A basket of plaster, to stop that hole. It is too small, your barricade. It must go higher. Pile on everything, brace it with everything. Break up the house. A barricade is Mother Gibou's tea-party. Hold on, there is a glass-door.'

This made the labourers exclaim:

'A glass-door? what do you want us to do with a glass-door, tubercle?'

'Hercules yourselves?' retorted Gavroche. 'A glass-door in a barricade is excellent. It doesn't prevent attacking it, but it bothers them in taking it. Then you have never hooked apples over a wall with broken bottles on it? A glass-door, it will cut the corns of the National Guards, when they try to climb over the barricade. Golly! glass is the devil. Ah, now you haven't an unbridled imagination, my comrades.'

Still, he was furious at his pistol without a hammer. He went from one to another, demanding: 'A musket? I want a musket? Why don't you give me a musket?'

'A musket for you?' said Combeferre.

'Well?' replied Gavroche, 'why not? I had one in 1830, in the dispute with Charles X.'

Enjolras shrugged his shoulders.

'When there are enough for the men, we will give them to the children.'

Gavroche turned fiercely, and answered him:

'If you are killed before me, I will take yours.'

'*Gamin!*' said Enjolras.

'Smooth-face?' said Gavroche.

A stray dandy who was lounging at the end of the street made a diversion.

Gavroche cried to him:

'Come with us, young man? Well, this poor old country you won't do anything for her then?'

The dandy fled.

5. *Preparations*

THE JOURNALS of the time which said that the barricade of the Rue de la Chanvrerie, that *almost inexpugnable construction* as they call it, attained the level of a second storey, were mistaken. The fact is, that it did not exceed an average height of six or seven feet. It was built in such a manner that the combatants could, at will, either disappear behind the wall, or look over it, and even scale the crest of it by means of a quadruple range of paving-stones superposed and arranged like steps on the inner side. The front of the barricade on the outside, composed of piles of paving-stones and of barrels bound together by timbers and boards which were interlocked in the wheels of the Anceau cart and the overturned omnibus, had a bristling and inextricable aspect.

An opening sufficient for a man to pass through had been left between the wall of the houses and the extremity of the barricade furthest from the wine-shop, so that a sortie was possible. The pole of the omnibus was turned directly up and held with ropes, and a red flag, fixed to this pole, floated over the barricade.

The little Mondétour barricade, hidden behind the wine-shop, was not visible. The two barricades united formed a staunch redoubt. Enjolras and Courfeyrac had not thought proper to barricade the other end of the Rue Mondétour which opens a passage to the markets through the Rue des Prêcheurs, wishing doubtless to preserve a possible communication with the outside, and having little dread of being attacked from the dangerous and difficult alley des Prêcheurs.

Except this passage remaining free, which constituted what Folard, in his strategic style, would have called a branch-trench, and bearing in mind also the narrow opening arranged on the Rue de la Chanvrerie, the interior of the barricade, where the wine-shop made a salient angle, presented an irregular quadrilateral closed on all sides. There was an interval of about twenty yards between the great barricade and the tall houses which formed the end of the street, so that we might say that the barricade leaned against these houses all inhabited, but closed from top to bottom.

All this labour was accomplished without hindrance in less than an hour, and without this handful of bold men seeing a bearskin-cap or a bayonet arise. The few bourgeois who still ventured at that period of the *émeute* into the Rue Saint Denis cast a glance down the Rue de la Chanvrerie, perceived the barricade, and redoubled their pace.

The two barricades finished, the flag run up, a table was dragged out of the wine-shop; and Courfeyrac mounted upon the table. Enjolras brought the square box and Courfeyrac opened it. This box was filled with cartridges. When they saw the cartridges, there was a shudder among the bravest, and a moment of silence.

Courfeyrac distributed them with a smile.

Each one received thirty cartridges. Many had powder and set about making others with the balls which they were moulding. As for the keg of powder, it was on a table by itself near the door, and it was reserved.

The long-roll which was running through all Paris was not discontinued, but it had got to be only a monotonous sound to which they paid no more attention. This sound sometimes receded, sometimes approached, with melancholy undulations.

They loaded their muskets and their carbines all together, without precipitation, with a solemn gravity. Enjolras placed three sentinels outside the barricades, one in the Rue de la Chanvrerie, the second in the Rue des Prêcheurs, the third at the corner of la Petite Truanderie.

Then, the barricades built, the posts assigned, the muskets loaded, the videttes placed, alone in these fearful streets in which there were now no passers, surrounded by these dumb, and as it were dead houses, which throbbed with no human motion, enwrapped by the deepening shadows of the twilight, which was beginning to fall, in the midst of this obscurity and this silence, through which they felt the advance of something inexpressibly tragical and terrifying, isolated, armed, determined, tranquil, they waited.

6. *While waiting*

In these hours of waiting what did they do? This we must tell – for this is history.

While the men were making cartridges and the women lint, while a large frying-pan, full of melted pewter and lead, destined for the bullet-mould, was smoking over a burning furnace, while the videttes were watching the barricades with arms in their hands, while Enjolras, whom nothing could distract, was watching the videttes, Combeferre, Courfeyrac, Jean Prouvaire, Feuilly, Bossuet, Joly, Bahorel, a few others besides, sought each other and got together, as in the most peaceful days of their student-chats, and in a corner of this wine-shop changed into a casemate, within two steps of the redoubt which they had thrown up, their carbines primed and loaded resting on the backs of their chairs, these gallant young men, so near their last hour, began to sing love-rhymes.

What rhymes? Here they are:

Vous rappelez-vous notre douce vie,
Lorsque nous étions si jeunes tous deux,
Et que nous n'avions au cœur d'autre envie
Que d'être bien mis et d'être amoureux.

Lorsqu'en ajoutant votre âge à mon âge,
Nous ne comptions pas à deux quarante ans,
Et que, dans notre humble et petit ménage,
Tout, même l'hiver, nous était printemps?

Beaux jours! Manuel était fier et sa
Paris s'asseyait à de saints banquets,
Foy lançait la foudre, et votre corsage
Avait une épingle où je me piquais.

Tout vous contemplait. Avocat sans causes,
Quand je vous menais au Prado dîner,
Vous étiez jolie au point que les roses
Me faisaient l'effet de se retourner.

Je les entendais dire: Est-elle belle!
Comme elle sent bon! quels cheveux à flots!
Sous son mantelet elle cache une aile,
Son bonnet charmant est à peine éclos.

J'errais avec toi, pressant ton bras souple.
Les passants croyaient que l'amour charmé
Avait marié, dans notre heureux couple,
Le doux mois d'avril au beau mois de mai.

Nous vivions cachés, contents, porte close,
Dévorant l'amour, bon fruit défendu;
Ma bouche n'avait pas dit une chose
Que déjà ton cœur avait répondu.

La Sorbonne était l'endroit bucolique
Où je t'adorais du soir au matin,
C'est ainsi qu'une âme amoureuse applique
La carte du Tendre au pays Latin.

O place Maubert! O place Dauphine!
Quand, dans le taudis frais et printanier,
Tu tirais ton bas sur ta jambe fine,
Je voyais un astre au fond du grenier.

J'ai fort lu Platon, mais rien ne m'en reste;
Mieux que Malebranche et que Lamennais
Tu me démontrais la bonté céleste
Avec une fleur que tu me donnais.

Je t'obéissais, tu m'étais soumise.
O grenier doré! te lacer! te voir!
Aller et venir dès l'aube en chemise,
Mirant ton front jeune à ton vieux miroir!

Et qui donc pourrait perdre la mémoire
De ces temps d'aurore et de firmament,
De rubans, de fleurs, de gaze et de moire,
Où l'amour bégaye un argot charmant?

Nos jardins étaient un pot de tulipe;
Tu masquais la vitre avec un jupon;
Je prenais le bol de terre de pipe,
Et je te donnais la tasse en japon.

Et ces grands malheurs qui nous faisaient rire!
Ton manchon brûlé, ton boa perdu!
Et ce cher portrait du divin Shakespeare
Qu'un soir pour souper nous avons vendu!

J'étais mendiant, et toi charitable;
Je baisais au vol tes bras frais et ronds.
Dante in folio nous servait de table
Pour manger gaîment un cent de marrons.

La première fois qu'en mon joyeux bouge
Je pris un baiser à ta lèvre en feu,
Quand tu t'en allas décoiffée et rouge,
Je restai tout pâle et je crus en Dieu!

Te rappeles-tu nos bonheurs sans nombre
Et tous ces fichus changés en chiffons?
Oh! que de soupirs, de nos cœurs pleins d'ombre,
Se sont envolés dans les cieux profonds!

The hour, the place, these memories of youth recalled, the few stars which began to shine in the sky, the funereal repose of these deserted streets, the imminence of the inexorable event, gave a pathetic charm to these rhymes, murmured in a low tone in the twilight by Jean Prouvaire, who, as we have said, was a sweet poet.

Meanwhile they had lighted a lamp at the little barricade, and at the large one, of those wax torches which are seen on Mardi Gras in front of the wagons loaded with masks, which are going to the Comtille. These torches, we have seen, came from the Faubourg Saint Antoine.

The torch had been placed in a kind of cage, closed in with paving-stones on three sides, to shelter it from the wind, and disposed in such a manner that all the light fell upon the flag. The street and the barricade remained plunged in obscurity and nothing could be seen but the red flag, fearfully lighted up, as if by an enormous dark lantern.

This light gave to the scarlet of the flag an indescribably terrible purple.

7. *The man recruited in the Rue des Billettes*

It was now quite night, nothing came. There were only confused sounds, and at intervals volleys of musketry; but rare, ill-sustained, and distant. This respite, which was thus prolonged, was a sign that the government was taking its time, and massing its forces. These fifty men were awaiting sixty thousand.

Enjolras felt himself possessed by that impatience which seizes strong souls on the threshold of formidable events. He went to find Gavroche who had set himself to making cartridges in the basement room by the doubtful light of two candles placed upon the counter through precaution on account of the powder scattered over the tables. These two candles threw no rays outside. The insurgents moreover had taken care not to have any lights in the upper storeys.

Gavroche at this moment was very much engaged, not exactly with his cartridges.

The man from the Rue les Billettes had just entered the basement room and had taken a seat at the table which was least lighted. An infantry musket of large model had fallen to his lot, and he held it between his knees. Gavroche hitherto, distracted by a hundred 'amusing' things, had not even seen this man.

When he came in, Gavroche mechanically followed him with his eyes, admiring his musket, then, suddenly, when the man had sat down, the *gamin* arose. Had anyone watched this man up to this time, he would have seen him observe everything in the barricade and in the band of insurgents with a singular attention; but since he had come into the room, he had fallen into a kind of meditation and appeared to see nothing more of what was going on. The *gamin* approached this thoughtful personage, and began to turn about him on the points of his toes as one walks when near somebody whom he fears to awake. At the same time, over his childish face, at once so saucy and so serious, so flighty and so profound, so cheerful and so touching, there passed all those grimaces of the old which signify: 'Oh bah! impossible! I am befogged! I am dreaming! can it be? no, it isn't! why yes! why no!' etc. Gavroche balanced himself upon his heels, clenched both fists in his pockets, twisted his neck like a bird, expended in one measureless pout all the sagacity of his lower lip. He was stupefied, uncertain, credulous, convinced, bewildered. He had the appearance of the chief of the eunuchs in the slave market discovering a Venus among dumpies, and the air of an amateur recognising a Raphael in a heap of daubs. Everything in him was at work, the instinct which scents and the intellect which combines. It was evident that an event had occurred with Gavroche.

It was in the deepest of this meditation that Enjolras accosted him.

'You are small,' said Enjolras, 'nobody will see you. Go out of the barricades, glide along by the houses, look about the streets a little, and come and tell me what is going on.'

Gavroche straightened himself up.

'Little folks are good for something then! that is very lucky! will go! meantime, trust the little folks, distrust the big – ' And Gavroche, raising his head and lowering his voice, added, pointing to the man of the Rue des Billettes:

'You see that big fellow there?'

'Well?'

'He is a spy.'

'You are sure?'

'It isn't a fortnight since he pulled me by the ear off the cornice of the Pont Royal where I was taking the air.'

Enjolras hastily left the *gamin*, and murmured a few words very low to a working-man from the wine docks who was there. The working-man went out of the room and returned almost immediately, accompanied by three others. The four men, four broad-shouldered porters, placed themselves, without doing anything which could attract his attention, behind the table on which the man of the Rue des Billettes was leaning. They were evidently ready to throw themselves upon him.

Then Enjolras approached the man and asked him:

'Who are you?'

At this abrupt question, the man gave a start. He looked straight to the bottom of Enjolras' frank eye and appeared to catch his thought. He smiled with a smile which, of all things in the world, was the most disdainful, the most energetic, and the most resolute, and answered with a haughty gravity:

'I see how it is – Well, yes!'

'You are a spy?'

'I am an officer of the government.'

'Your name is?'

'Javert.'

Enjolras made a sign to the four men. In a twinkling, before Javert had had time to turn around, he was collared, thrown down, bound, searched.

They found upon him a little round card framed between two glasses, and bearing on one side the arms of France, engraved with this legend: *Surveillance et vigilance*, and on the other side this endorsement: Javert, inspector of police, aged fifty-two, and the signature of the prefect of police of the time, M. Gisquet.

He had besides his watch and his purse, which contained a few gold pieces. They left him his purse and his watch. Under the watch, at the bottom of his fob, they felt and seized a paper in an envelope, which Enjolras opened, and on which he read these six lines, written by the prefect's own hand.

'As soon as his political mission is fulfilled, Inspector Javert will ascertain, by a special examination, whether it be true that malefactors have resorts on the slope of the right bank of the Seine, near the bridge of Jena.'

The search finished, they raised Javert, tied his arms behind his back, and fastened him in the middle of the basement-room to that celebrated post which had formerly given its name to the wine-shop.

Gavroche, who had witnessed the whole scene and approved the whole by silent nods of his head, approached Javert and said to him:

'The mouse has caught the cat.'

All this was executed so rapidly that it was finished as soon as it was perceived about the wine-shop. Javert had not uttered a cry. Seeing Javert tied to the post, Courfeyrac, Bossuet, Joly, Combeferre, and the men scattered about the two barricades, ran in.

Javert, backed up against the post, and so surrounded with ropes that he could make no movement, held up his head with the intrepid serenity of the man who has never lied.

'It is a spy,' said Enjolras.

And turning towards Javert:

'You will be shot ten minutes before the barricade is taken.'

Javert replied in his most imperious tone:

'Why not immediately?'

'We are economising powder.'

'Then do it with a knife.'

'Spy,' said the handsome Enjolras, 'we are judges, not assassins.'

Then he called Gavroche.

'You! go about your business! Do what I told you.'

'I am going,' cried Gavroche.

And stopping just as he was starting:

'By the way, you will give me his musket!' And he added: 'I leave you the musician, but I want the clarionet.'

The *gamin* made a military salute, and sprang gaily through the opening in the large barricade.

8. Several interrogation points concerning one Le Cabuc, who perhaps was not Le Cabuc

THE TRAGIC PICTURE which we have commenced would not be complete, the reader would not see in their exact and real relief these grand moments of social parturition and of revolutionary birth in which there is convulsion mingled with effort, were we to omit, in the outline here sketched, an incident full of epic and savage horror which occurred almost immediately after Gavroche's departure.

Mobs, as we know, are like snowballs, and gather a heap of tumultuous men as they roll. These men do not ask one another whence they come. Among the passers who had joined themselves to the company led by Enjolras, Combeferre, and Courfeyrac, there was a person wearing a porter's waistcoat worn out at the shoulders, who gesticulated and vociferated and had the appearance of a sort of savage drunkard. This man, who was named or nicknamed Le Cabuc, and who was moreover entirely unknown to those who attempted to recognise him, very drunk, or feigning to be, was seated with a few others at a table which they had brought outside of the wine-shop. This Cabuc, while inciting those to drink who were with him, seemed to gaze with an air of reflection upon the large house at the back of the barricade, the five storeys of which overlooked the whole street and faced towards the Rue Saint Denis. Suddenly he exclaimed:

'Comrades, do you know? it is from that house that we must fire. If we are at the windows, devil a one can come into the street.'

'Yes, but the house is shut up,' said one of the drinkers.

'Knock!'

'They won't open.'

'Stave the door in!'

Le Cabuc runs to the door, which had a very massive knocker, and raps. The door does not open. He raps a second time. Nobody answers. A third rap. The same silence.

'Is there anybody here?' cries Le Cabuc.

Nothing stirs.

Then he seizes a musket and begins to beat the door with the butt. It was an old alley door, arched, low, narrow, solid, entirely of oak, lined on the inside with sheet-iron and with iron braces, a genuine postern of a bastille. The blows made the house tremble, but did not shake the door.

Nevertheless it is probable that the inhabitants were alarmed, for they finally saw a little square window on the third storey light up and open, and there appeared at this window a candle, and the pious and frightened face of a grey-haired goodman who was the porter.

The man who was knocking, stopped.

'Messieurs,' asked the porter, 'what do you wish?'

'Open!' said Le Cabuc.

'Messieurs, that cannot be.'

'Open, I tell you!'

'Impossible, messieurs!'

Le Cabuc took his musket and aimed at the porter's head; but as he was below, and it was very dark, the porter did not see him.

'Yes, or no, will you open?'

'No, messieurs!'

'You say no?'

'I say no, my good – '

The porter did not finish. The musket went off; the ball entered under his chin and passed out at the back of the neck, passing through the jugular. The old man sank down without a sigh. The candle fell and was extinguished, and nothing could now be seen but an immovable head lying on the edge of the window, and a little whitish smoke floating towards the roof.

'That's it!' said Le Cabuc, letting the butt of his musket drop on the pavement.

Hardly had he uttered these words when he felt a hand pounce upon his shoulder with the weight of an eagle's talons, and heard a voice which said to him:

'On your knees.'

The murderer turned and saw before him the white cold face of Enjolras. Enjolras had a pistol in his hand.

At the explosion, he had come up.

He had grasped with his left hand Le Cabuc's collar, blouse, shirt, and suspenders.

'On your knees,' repeated he.

And with a majestic movement the slender young man of twenty bent the broad-shouldered and robust porter like a reed and made him kneel in the mud. Le Cabuc tried to resist, but he seemed to have been seized by a superhuman grasp.

Pale, his neck bare, his hair flying, Enjolras, with his woman's face, had at that moment an inexpressible something of the ancient Themis. His distended nostrils, his downcast eyes, gave to his implacable Greek profile that expression of wrath and that expression of chastity which from the point of view of the ancient world belonged to justice.

The whole barricade ran up, then all ranged in a circle at a distance, feeling that it was impossible to utter a word in presence of the act which they were about to witness.

Le Cabuc, vanquished, no longer attempted to defend himself, but trembled in every limb. Enjolras let go of him and took out his watch.

'Collect your thoughts,' said he. 'Pray or think. You have one minute.'

'Pardon!' murmured the murderer, then he bowed his head and mumbled some inarticulate oaths.

Enjolras did not take his eyes off his watch; he let the minute pass, then he put his watch back into his fob. This done, he took Le Cabuc, who was writhing against his knees and howling, by the hair, and placed the muzzle of his pistol at his ear. Many of those intrepid men, who had so tranquilly entered upon the most terrible of enterprises, turned away their heads.

They heard the explosion, the assassin fell face forward on the pavement, and Enjolras straightened up and cast about him his look determined and severe.

Then he pushed the body away with his foot, and said:

'Throw that outside.'

Three men lifted the body of the wretch, which was quivering with the last mechanical convulsions of the life that had flown, and threw it over the small barricade into the little Rue Mondétour.

Enjolras had remained thoughtful. Shadow, mysterious and grand, was slowly spreading over his fearful serenity. He suddenly raised his voice. There was a silence.

'Citizens,' said Enjolras, 'what that man did is horrible, and what I have done is terrible. He killed, that is why I killed him. I was forced to do it, for the insurrection must have its discipline. Assassination is a still greater crime here than elsewhere; we are under the eye of the revolution, we are the priests of the republic, we are the sacramental host of duty, and none must be able to calumniate our combat. I therefore judged and condemned that man to death. As for myself, compelled to do what I have done, but abhorring it, I have judged myself also, and you shall soon see to what I have sentenced myself.'

Those who heard shuddered.

'We will share your fate,' cried Combeferre.

'So be it,' added Enjolras. 'A word more. In executing that man, I obeyed necessity; but necessity is a monster of the old world, the name of necessity is Fatality. Now the law of progress is, that monsters disappear before angels, and that Fatality vanish before Fraternity. This is not a moment to pronounce the word love. No matter, I pronounce it, and I glorify it. Love, thine is the future. Death, I use thee, but I hate thee. Citizens, there shall be in the future neither darkness nor thunderbolts; neither ferocious ignorance nor blood for blood. As Satan shall be no more, so Michael shall be no more. In the future no man shall slay his fellow, the earth shall be radiant, the human race shall love. It will come, citizens, that day when all shall be concord, harmony, light, joy, and life; it will come, and it is that it may come that we are going to die.'

Enjolras was silent. His virgin lips closed; and he remained some time standing on the spot where he had spilled blood, in marble immobility. His fixed eye made all about him speak low.

Jean Prouvaire and Combeferre silently grasped hands, and, leaning upon one another in the corner of the barricade, considered, with an admiration not unmingled with compassion, this severe young man, executioner and priest, luminous like the crystal, and rock also.

Let us say right here that later, after the action, when the corpses were carried to the Morgue and searched, there was a police officer's card found on Le Cabuc. The author of this book had in his own hands, in 1848, the special report made on that subject to the prefect of police in 1832.

Let us add that, if we are to believe a police tradition, strange, but probably well founded, Le Cabuc was Claquesous. The fact is, that after the death of Le Cabuc, nothing more was heard of Claquesous. Claquesous left no trace on his disappearance, he would seem to have been amalgamated with the invisible. His life had been darkness, his end was night.

The whole insurgent group were still under the emotion of this tragic trial, so quickly instituted and so quickly terminated, when Courfeyrac again saw in the barricade the small young man who in the morning had called at his house for Marius.

This boy, who had a bold and reckless air, had come at night to rejoin the insurgents.

BOOK 13: MARIUS ENTERS THE SHADOW

1. From the Rue Plumet to the Quartier Saint Denis

THAT VOICE which through the twilight had called Marius to the barricade of the Rue de la Chanvrerie, sounded to him like the voice of destiny. He wished to die, the opportunity presented itself; he was knocking at the door of the tomb, a hand in the shadow held out the key. These dreary clefts in the darkness before despair are tempting. Marius pushed aside the bar which had let him pass so many times, came out of the garden, and said: 'Let us go!'

Mad with grief, feeling no longer anything fixed or solid in his brain, incapable of accepting anything henceforth from fate, after these two months passed in the intoxications of youth and of love, whelmed at once beneath all the reveries of despair, he had now but one desire: to make an end of it very quick.

He began to walk rapidly. It happened that he was armed, having Javert's pistols with him.

The young man whom he thought he had seen was lost from his eyes in the streets.

Marius, who had left the Rue Plumet by the boulevard, crossed the Esplanade and the Bridge of the Invalides, the Champs Elysées, the Place Louis XV, and entered the Rue de Rivoli. The stores were open, the gas was burning under the arches, women were buying in the shops, people were taking ices at the Café Laiter, they were eating little cakes at the Pâtisserie Anglaise. However, a few post chaises were setting off at a gallop from the Hôtel des Princes and the Hôtel Meurice.

Marius entered through the Delorme Arcade into the Rue Saint Honoré. The shops here were closed, the merchants were chatting before their half-open doors, people were moving about, the lamps were burning, above the first storeys all the windows were lighted as usual. There was cavalry in the square of the Palais Royal.

Marius followed the Rue St Honoré. As he receded from the Palais Royal, there were fewer lighted windows; the shops were entirely closed, nobody was chatting in the doors, the street grew gloomy, and at the same time the throng grew dense. For the passers now were a throng. Nobody was seen to speak in this throng, and still there came from it a deep and dull hum.

Towards the Fontaine de l'Arbre Sec, there were 'gatherings', immovable and sombre groups, which, among the comers and goers, were like stones in the middle of a running stream.

At the entrance of the Rue des Prouvaires, the throng no longer moved. It was a resisting, massive, solid, compact, almost impenetrable block of people, heaped together and talking in whispers. Black coats and round hats had almost disappeared. Frocks, blouses, caps, bristly and dirty faces. This multitude undulated confusedly in the misty night. Its whispering had the harsh sound of a roar. Although nobody was walking, a trampling was heard in the mud. Beyond this dense mass, in the Rue du Roule, in the Rue des Prouvaires, and in the prolongation of the Rue Saint Honoré, there was not a single window in which a candle was burning. In those streets the files of the lamps were seen stretching away solitary and decreasing. The lamps of that day resembled great red stars hanging from ropes, and threw a shadow on the pavement which had the form of a large spider. These streets were not empty. Muskets could be distinguished in stacks, bayonets moving and troops bivouacking. The curious did not pass this bound. There circulation ceased. There the multitude ended and the army began.

Marius willed with the will of a man who no longer hopes. He had been called, he must go. He found means to pass through the multitude, and to pass through the bivouac of the troops, he avoided the patrols, evaded the sentinels. He made a detour, reached the Rue de Béthisy, and made his way towards the markets. At the corner of the Rue des Bourdonnais the lamps ended.

After having crossed the belt of the multitude and passed the fringe of troops, he found himself in the midst of something terrible. Not a passer more, not a soldier, not a light; nobody. Solitude, silence, night; a mysterious chill which seized upon him. To enter a street was to enter a cellar.

He continued to advance.

He took a few steps. Somebody passed near him running. Was it a man? a woman? were there several? He could not have told. It had passed and had vanished.

By a circuitous route, he came to a little street which he judged to be the Rue de la Poterie; about the middle of this alley he ran against some obstacle. He put out his hands. It was an overturned cart; his foot recognised puddles of water, mud-holes, paving-stones, scattered and heaped up. A barricade had been planned there and abandoned. He climbed over the stones and found himself on the other side of the obstruction. He walked very near the posts and guided himself by the walls of the houses. A little beyond the barricade, he seemed to catch a glimpse of something white in front of him. He approached, it took form. It was two white horses; the omnibus horses unharnessed by Bossuet in the morning, which had wandered at chance from street to street all day long, and had finally stopped there, with the exhausted patience of brutes, who no more comprehend the ways of man than man comprehends the ways of Providence.

Marius left the horses behind him. As he came to a street which struck him as being the Rue du Contrat Social, a shot from a musket coming nobody knows whence, passing at random through the obscurity, whistled close by him, and the ball pierced a copper shaving-dish suspended before a barber's shop. This shaving-dish with the bullet-hole could still be seen, in 1846, in the Rue du Contrat Social, at the corner of the pillars of the markets.

This musket-shot was life still. From that moment he met nothing more.

This whole route resembled a descent down dark stairs.

Marius none the less went forward.

2. *Paris – an owl's eye view*

A BEING who could have soared above Paris at that moment with the wing of the bat or the owl would have had a gloomy spectacle beneath his eyes.

All that old quarter of the markets, which is like a city within the city, which is traversed by the Rues Saint Denis and Saint Martin, where a thousand little streets cross each other, and of which the insurgents had made their stronghold and their field of arms, would have appeared to him like an enormous black hole dug out in the centre of Paris. There the eye fell into an abyss. Thanks to the broken lamps, thanks to the closed windows, there ceased all radiance, all life, all sound, all motion. The invisible police of the *émeute* watched everywhere, and maintained order, that is night. To drown the smallness of their number in a vast obscurity and to multiply each combatant by the possibilities which that obscurity contains, are the necessary tactics of insurrection. At nightfall, every window in which a candle was lighted had received a ball. The light was extinguished, sometimes the inhabitant killed. Thus nothing stirred. There was nothing there but fright, mourning, stupor in the houses; in the streets a sort of sacred horror. Even the long ranges of windows and of storeys were not perceptible, the notching of the chimneys and the roofs, the dim reflections which gleam on the wet and muddy pavement. The eye which might have looked from above into that mass of shade would have caught a glimpse here and there perhaps, from point to point, of indistinct lights, bringing out broken and fantastic lines, outlines of singular constructions, something like ghostly gleams, coming and going among ruins; these were the barricades. The rest was a lake of obscurity, misty, heavy, funereal, above which rose, motionless and dismal silhouettes, the tower Saint Jacques, the church Saint Merry, and two or three others of those great buildings of which man makes giants and of which night makes phantoms.

All about this deserted and disquieted labyrinth, in the quarters where the circulation of Paris was not stopped, and where a few rare lamps shone out, the aerial observer might have distinguished the metallic scintillation of sabres and bayonets, the sullen rumbling of artillery, and the swarming of silent battalions augmenting from moment to moment; a formidable girdle which was tightening and slowly closing about the *émeute*.

The invested quarter was now only a sort of monstrous cavern; everything in it appeared to be sleeping or motionless, and, as we have just seen, none of the streets on which you might have entered, offered anything but darkness.

A savage darkness, full of snares, full of unknown and formidable encounters, where it was fearful to penetrate and appalling to stay, where those who entered shuddered before those who were awaiting them, where those who waited trembled before those who were to come. Invisible combatants entrenched at every street-corner; the grave hidden in ambush in the thickness of the night. It was finished. No other light to be hoped for there henceforth save the flash of musketry, no other meeting save the sudden and rapid apparition of death. Where? how? when? nobody knew; but it was certain and inevitable. There, in that place marked out for the contest, the government and the insurrection, the National Guard and the popular societies, the bourgeoisie and the *émeute* were to grope their way. For those as for these, the necessity was the same. To leave that place slain or victors, the only possible issue henceforth. A situation so extreme, an obscurity so overpowering, that the most timid felt themselves filled with resolution and the boldest with terror.

Moreover, on both sides, fury, rancour, equal determination. For those to advance was to die, and nobody thought of retreat; for these to stay was to die, and nobody thought of flight.

All must be decided on the morrow, the triumph must be on this side or on that, the insurrection must be a revolution or a blunder. The government understood it as well as the factions; the least bourgeois felt it. Hence a feeling of anguish which mingled with the impenetrable darkness of this quarter where all was to be decided; hence a redoubling of anxiety about this silence whence a catastrophe was to issue But one sound could be heard, a sound heart-rending as a death rattle, menacing as a malediction, the tocsin of Saint Merry. Nothing was so blood-chilling as the clamour of this wild and desperate bell wailing in the darkness.

As often happens, nature seemed to have put herself in accord with what men were about to do. Nothing disturbed the funereal harmonies of that whole. The stars had disappeared, heavy clouds filled the whole horizon with their melancholy folds. There was a black sky over those dead streets, as if an immense pall had unfolded itself over that immense tomb.

While a battle as yet entirely political was preparing in this same locality, which had already seen so many revolutionary events, while the youth, the secret associations, the schools, in the name of principles, and the middle class, in the name of interests, were approaching to dash against each other, to close with and to overthrow each other, while each was hurrying and calling the final and decisive hour of the crisis, afar off and outside of that fatal quarter, in the deepest of the unfathomable caverns of that old, miserable Paris, which is disappearing under the splendour of the happy and opulent Paris, the gloomy voice of the people was heard sullenly growling.

A fearful and sacred voice, which is composed of the roar of the brute and the speech of God, which terrifies the feeble and which warns the wise, which comes at the same time from below like the voice of the lion and from above like the voice of the thunder.

3. The extreme limit

MARIUS HAD ARRIVED at the markets.

There all was more calm, more obscure, and more motionless still than in the neighbouring streets. One would have said that the icy peace of the grave had come forth from the earth and spread over the sky.

A red glare, however, cut out upon this dark background the high roofs of the houses which barred the Rue de la Chanvrerie on the side towards Saint Eustache. It was the reflection of the torch which was blazing in the barricade of Corinth. Marius directed his steps towards this glare. It led him to the Beet Market, and he dimly saw the dark mouth of the Rue des Prêcheurs. He entered it. The vidette of the insurgents who was on guard at the other end did not perceive him. He felt that he was very near what he had come to seek, and he walked upon tiptoe. He reached in this way the elbow of that short end of the Rue Mondétour, which was, as we remember, the only communication preserved by Enjolras with the outside. Round the corner of the last house on his left, cautiously advancing his head, he looked into this end of the Rue Mondétour.

A little beyond the black corner of the alley and the Rue de la Chanvrerie, which threw a broad shadow, in which he was himself buried, he perceived a light upon the pavement, a portion of the wine-shop, and behind, a lamp twinkling in a kind of shapeless wall, and men crouching down with muskets on their knees. All this was within twenty yards of him. It was the interior of the barricade.

The houses on the right of the alley hid from him the rest of the wine-shop, the great barricade, and the flag.

Marius had but one step more to take.

Then the unhappy young man sat down upon a stone, folded his arms, and thought of his father.

He thought of that heroic Colonel Pontmercy who had been so brave a soldier, who had defended the frontier of France under the republic, and reached the frontier of Asia under the emperor, who had seen Genoa, Alessandria, Milan, Turin, Madrid, Vienna, Dresden, Berlin, Moscow, who had left upon every field of victory in Europe drops of that same blood which he, Marius, had in his veins, who had grown grey before his time in discipline and in command, who had lived with his sword-belt buckled, his epaulets falling on his breast, his cockade blackened by powder, his forehead wrinkled by the cap, in the barracks, in the camp, in the bivouac, in the ambulance, and who after twenty years had returned from the great wars with his cheek scarred, his face smiling, simple, tranquil, admirable, pure as a child, having done everything for France and nothing against her.

He said to himself that his day had come to him also, that his hour had at last struck, that after his father, he also was to be brave, intrepid, bold, to run amidst bullets, to bare his breast to the bayonets, to pour out his blood, to seek the enemy, to seek death, that he was to wage war in his turn and to enter upon the field of battle, and that that field of battle upon which he was about to enter, was the street, and that war which he was about to wage, was civil war!

He saw civil war yawning like an abyss before him, and that in it he was to fall.

Then he shuddered.

He thought of that sword of his father which his grandfather had sold to a junk-shop, and which he himself had so painfully regretted. He said to himself that it was well that that chaste and valiant sword had escaped from him, and gone off in anger into the darkness; that if it had fled thus, it was because it was intelligent and because it foresaw the future; because it foreboded the *émeute*, the war of the gutters, the war of the pavements, the firing from cellar windows, blows given and received from behind; because, coming from Marengo and Friedland, it would not go to the Rue de la Chanvrerie, because after what it had done with the father, it would not do this with the son! He said to himself that if that sword were there, if, having received it from the bedside of his dead father, he had dared to take it and bring it away for this night combat between Frenchmen at the street corners, most surely it would have burned his hands, and flamed before him like the sword of the angel! He said to himself that it was fortunate that it was not there and that it had disappeared, that it was well, that it was just, that his grandfather had been the true guardian of his father's glory, and that it was better that the colonel's sword had been cried at auction, sold to a dealer, thrown among old iron, than that it should be used today to pierce the side of the country.

And then he began to weep bitterly.

It was horrible. But what could he do? Live without Cosette, he could not. Since she had gone away, he must surely die. Had he not given her his word of honour that he should die? She had gone away knowing that; therefore it pleased her that Marius should die. And then it was clear that she no longer loved him, since she had gone away thus, without notifying him, without a word, without a letter, and she knew his address! What use in life and why live longer? And then, indeed! to have come so far, and to recoil! to have approached the danger, and to flee! to have come and looked into the barricade and to slink away! to slink away all trembling, saying: 'in fact, I have had enough of this, I have seen, that is sufficient, it is civil war, I am going away!' To abandon his friends who were expecting him! who perhaps had need of him! who were a handful against an army! To fail in all things at the same time, in his love, his friendship, his word! To give his poltroonery the pretext of patriotism! But this was impossible, and if his father's ghost were there in the shadow and saw him recoil, he would strike him with the flat of his sword and cry to him: 'Advance, coward!'

A prey to the swaying of his thoughts, he bowed his head.

Suddenly he straightened up. A sort of splendid rectification was wrought in his spirit. There was an expansion of thought fitted to the confinity of the tomb; to be near death makes us see the truth. The vision of the act upon which he felt himself, perhaps on the point of entering, appeared to him no longer lamentable, but superb. The war of the street was suddenly transfigured by some indescribable interior throe of the soul, before the eye of his mind. All the tumultuous interrogation points of his reverie thronged upon him, but without troubling him. He left none without an answer.

Let us see, why should his father be indignant? are there not cases when insurrection rises to the dignity of duty? what would there be then belittling to the son of Colonel Pontmercy in the impending combat? It is no longer Montmirail or Champaubert; it is something else. It is no longer a question of a sacred territory, but of a holy idea. The country laments, so be it; but humanity applauds. Besides is it true that the country mourns? France bleeds, but liberty smiles; and before the smile of liberty, France forgets her wound. And then, looking at the matter from a still higher stand, why do men talk of civil war?

Civil war? What does this mean? Is there any foreign war? Is not every war between men, war between brothers? War is modified only by its aim. There is neither foreign war, nor civil war; there is only unjust war and just war. Until the day when the great human concordat shall be concluded, war, that at least which is the struggle of the hurrying future against the lingering past, may be necessary. What reproach can be brought against such war! War becomes shame, the sword becomes a dagger, only when it assassinates right, progress, reason, civilisation, truth. Then, civil war or foreign war, it is iniquitous; its name is crime. Outside of that holy thing, justice, by what right does one form of war despise another? by what right does the sword of Washington disown the pike of Camille Desmoulins? Leonidas against the foreigner, Timoleon against the tyrant, which is the greater? one is the defender, the other is the liberator. Shall we brand, without troubling ourselves with the object, every resort to arms in the interior of a city? then mark with infamy Brutus, Marcel, Arnold of Blankenheim, Coligny. War of the thickets? war of the streets? Why not? it was the war of Ambiorix, of Artaveld, of Marnix, of Pelagius. But Ambiorix fought against Rome, Artaveld against France, Marnix against Spain, Pelagius against the Moors; all against the foreigner. Well, monarchy is the foreigner; oppression is the foreigner; divine right is the foreigner. Despotism violates the moral frontier, as invasion violates the geographical frontier. To drive out the tyrant or to drive out the English is, in either case, to retake your territory. There comes an hour when protest no longer suffices; after philosophy there must be action; the strong hand finishes what the idea has planned; *Prometheus Bound* begins, Aristogeiton completes; the *Encyclopédie* enlightens souls, the 10th of August electrifies them. After Æschylus, Thrasybulus; after Diderot, Danton. The multitudes have a tendency to accept a master. Their mass deposits apathy. A mob easily totalises itself into obedience. Men must be aroused, pushed, shocked by the very benefits of their deliverance, their eyes wounded with the truth, light thrown them in terrible handfuls. They should be blinded a little for their own safety; this dazzling wakens them. Hence the necessity for tocsins and for wars. Great warriors must arise, illuminate the nations by boldness, and shake free this sad humanity which is covered with shadow by divine right. Cæsarean glory, force, fanaticism, irresponsible power, and absolute dominion, a mob stupidly occupied with gazing, in their twilight splendour, at these gloomy triumphs of the night. Down with the tyrant! But what? of whom do you speak? do you call Louis Philippe the tyrant? no; no more than Louis XVI. They are both what history is accustomed to call good kings; but principles cannot be parcelled out, the logic of the true is rectilinear, the peculiarity of truth is to be without complaisance; no compromise, then; all encroachment upon man must be repressed; there is divine right in Louis XVI, there is *parce que Bourbon* in Louis Philippe; both represent in a certain degree the confiscation of the right; and to wipe out the universal usurpation, it is necessary to fight them; it is necessary, France always taking the initiative. When the master falls in France, he falls everywhere. In short, to re-establish social truth, to give back to liberty her throne, to give back the people to the people, to give back sovereignty to man, to replace the purple upon the head of France, to restore in their fullness reason and equity, to suppress every germ of antagonism by restoring every man to himself, to abolish the obstacle which royalty opposes to the immense universal concord, to replace the human race on a level with right, what cause more just, and, consequently, what war more grand? These wars construct peace. An enormous fortress of prejudices, of privileges, of superstitions, of lies, of exactions, of abuses, of violence, of iniquity, of darkness, is still standing upon the world with its towers of hatred. It must be thrown down. This monstrous pile must be made to fall. To conquer at Austerlitz is grand; to take the Bastille is immense.

There is nobody who has not remarked it in himself, the soul, and this is the marvel of its complicate unity and ubiquity, has the wonderful faculty of reasoning almost coolly in the most desperate extremities; and it often happens that disconsolate passion and deep despair, in the very agony of their darkest soliloquies, weigh subjects and discuss theses. Logic is mingled with convulsion, and the thread of a syllogism floats unbroken in the dreary storm of thought. This was Marius' state of mind.

Even while thinking thus, overwhelmed but resolute, hesitating, however, and, indeed, shuddering in view of what he was about to do, his gaze wandered into the interior of the barricade. The insurgents were chatting in undertone, without moving about; and that quasi-silence was felt which marks the last phase of delay. Above them, at a third storey window, Marius distinguished a sort of spectator or witness who seemed to him singularly attentive. It was the porter killed by Le Cabuc. From below, by the reflection of the torch hidden among the paving-stones, this head was dimly perceptible. Nothing was more strange in that gloomy and uncertain light, than that livid, motionless, astonished face with its bristling hair, its staring eyes, and its gaping mouth, leaning over the street in an attitude of curiosity. One would have said that he who was dead was gazing at those who were about to die. A long trail of blood which had flowed from this head, descended in ruddy streaks from the window to the height of the first storey, where it stopped.

BOOK 14: THE GRANDEURS OF DESPAIR

1. The flag: first act

NOTHING CAME YET. The clock of Saint Merry had struck ten. Enjolras and Combeferre had sat down, carbine in hand, near the opening of the great barricade. They were not talking, they were listening; seeking to catch even the faintest and most distant sound of a march.

Suddenly, in the midst of this dismal calm, a clear, young, cheerful voice, which seemed to come from the Rue Saint Denis, arose and began to sing distinctly to the old popular air, *Au clair de la lune*, these lines which ended in a sort of cry similar to the crow of a cock:

Mon nez est en larmes,
Mon ami Bugeaud,
Prêt-moi tes gendarmes
Pour leur dire un mot.
En capote bleue,
La poule au shako,
Voici la banlieue!
Co-cocorico! *

They grasped each other by the hand:

'It is Gavroche,' said Enjolras.

'He is warning us,' said Combeferre.

A headlong run startled the empty street; they saw a creature nimbler than a clown climb over the omnibus, and Gavroche bounded into the barricade all breathless, saying:

'My musket! Here they are.'

An electric thrill ran through the whole barricade, and a moving of hands was heard, feeling for their muskets.

* My nose is in tears,
My good friend Bugeaud,
Just lend me your spears
To tell them my woe.
In blue cassimere
And feathered shako,
The banlieue is here!
Co-cocorico!

'Do you want my carbine?' said Enjolras to the *gamin*.

'I want the big musket,' answered Gavroche.

And he took Javert's musket.

Two sentinels had been driven back, and had come in almost at the same time as Gavroche. They were the sentinel from the end of the street, and the vidette from la Petite Truanderie. The vidette in the little Rue des Prêcheurs remained at his post, which indicated that nothing was coming from the direction of the bridges and the markets.

The Rue de la Chanvrerie, in which a few paving-stones were dimly visible by the reflection of the light which was thrown upon the flag, offered to the insurgents the appearance of a great black porch opening into a cloud of smoke.

Every man had taken his post for the combat.

Forty-three insurgents, among them Enjolras, Combeferre, Courfeyrac, Bossuet, Joly, Bahorel, and Gavroche, were on their knees in the great barricade, their heads even with the crest of the wall, the barrels of their muskets and their carbines pointed over the paving-stones as through loopholes, watchful, silent, ready to fire. Six, commanded by Feuilly, were stationed with their muskets at their shoulders, in the windows of the two upper storeys of Corinth.

A few moments more elapsed, then a sound of steps, measured, heavy, numerous, was distinctly heard from the direction of Saint Leu. This sound, at first faint, then distinct, then heavy and sonorous, approached slowly, without halt, without interruption, with a tranquil and terrible continuity. Nothing but this could be heard. It was at once the silence and the sound of the statue of the Commander, but this stony tread was so indescribably enormous and so multiplex, that it called up at the same time the idea of a throng and of a spectre. You would have thought you heard the stride of the fearful statue Legion. This tread approached; it approached still nearer, and stopped. They seemed to hear at the end of the street the breathing of many men. They saw nothing, however, only they discovered at the very end, in that dense obscurity, a multitude of metallic threads, as fine as needles and almost imperceptible, which moved about like those indescribable phosphoric networks which we perceive under our closed eyelids at the moment of going to sleep, in the first mists of slumber. They were bayonets and musket barrels dimly lighted up by the distant reflection of the torch.

There was still a pause, as if on both sides they were awaiting. Suddenly, from the depth of that shadow, a voice, so much the more ominous, because nobody could be seen, and because it seemed as if it were the obscurity itself which was speaking, cried:

'Who is there?'

At the same time they heard the click of the levelled muskets. Enjolras answered in a lofty and ringing tone:

'French Revolution!'

'Fire!' said the voice.

A flash empurpled all the façades on the street, as if the door of a furnace were opened and suddenly closed.

A fearful explosion burst over the barricade. The red flag fell. The volley had been so heavy and so dense that it had cut the staff, that is to say, the very point of the pole of the omnibus. Some balls, which ricocheted from the cornices of the houses, entered the barricade and wounded several men.

The impression produced by this first charge was freezing. The attack was impetuous, and such as to make the boldest ponder. It was evident that they had to do with a whole regiment at least.

'Comrades,' cried Courfeyrac, 'don't waste the powder. Let us wait to reply till they come into the street.'

'And, first of all,' said Enjolras, 'let us hoist the flag again!'

He picked up the flag which had fallen just at his feet.

They heard from without the rattling of the ramrods in the muskets: the troops were reloading.

Enjolras continued:

'Who is there here who has courage? who replants the flag on the barricade?'

Nobody answered. To mount the barricade at the moment when without doubt it was aimed at anew, was simply death. The bravest hesitates to sentence himself, Enjolras himself felt a shudder. He repeated:

'Nobody volunteers!'

2. *The flag: second act*

Since they had arrived at Corinth and had commenced building the barricade, hardly any attention had been paid to Father Mabeuf. M. Mabeuf, however, had not left the company. He had entered the ground floor of the wine-shop and sat down behind the counter. There he had been, so to speak, annihilated in himself. He no longer seemed to look or to think. Courfeyrac and others had accosted him two or three times, warning him of the danger, entreating him to withdraw, but he had not appeared to hear them. When nobody was speaking to him, his lips moved as if he were answering somebody, and as soon as anybody addressed a word to him, his lips became still and his eyes lost all appearance of life. Some hours before the barricade was attacked, he had taken a position which he had not left since, his hands upon his knees and his head bent forward as if he were looking into an abyss. Nothing had been able to draw him out of this attitude; it appeared as if his mind were not in the barricade. When everybody had gone to take his place for the combat, there remained in the basement room only Javert tied to the post, an insurgent with drawn sabre watching Javert, and he, Mabeuf. At the moment of the attack, at the discharge, the physical shock reached him, and, as it were, awakened him; he rose suddenly, crossed the room, and at the instant when Enjolras repeated his appeal: 'Nobody volunteers?' they saw the old man appear in the doorway of the wine-shop.

His presence produced some commotion in the group. A cry arose:

'It is the Voter! it is the Conventionist! it is the Representative of the people!'

It is probable that he did not hear.

He walked straight to Enjolras, the insurgents fell back before him with a religious awe, he snatched the flag from Enjolras, who drew back petrified, and then, nobody daring to stop him, or to aid him, this old man of eighty, with shaking head but firm foot, began to climb slowly up the stairway of paving-stones built into the barricade. It was so gloomy and so grand that all about him cried: 'Hats off!' At each step it was frightful; his white hair, his decrepit face, his large forehead bald and wrinkled, his hollow eyes, his quivering and open mouth, his old arm raising the red banner, surged up out of the shadow and grew grand in the bloody light of the torch, and they seemed to see the ghost of '93 rising out of the earth, the flag of terror in its hand.

When he was on the top of the last step, when this trembling and terrible phantom, standing upon that mound of rubbish before twelve hundred invisible muskets, rose up, in the face of death and as if he were stronger than it, the whole barricade had in the darkness a supernatural and colossal appearance.

There was one of those silences which occur only in presence of prodigies.

In the midst of this silence the old man waved the red flag and cried:

'*Vive la révolution! Vive la république!* fraternity! equality! and death!'

They heard from the barricade a low and rapid muttering like the murmur of a hurried priest dispatching a prayer. It was probably the commissary of police who was making the legal summons at the other end of the street.

Then the same ringing voice which had cried: 'Who is there?' cried:

'Disperse!'

M. Mabeuf, pallid, haggard, his eyes illumined by the mournful fires of insanity, raised the flag above his head and repeated:

'*Vive la république!*'

'Fire!' said the voice.

A second discharge, like a shower of grape, beat against the barricade.

The old man fell upon his knees, then rose up, let the flag drop, and fell backwards upon the pavement within, like a log, at full length with his arms crossed.

Streams of blood ran from beneath him. His old face, pale and sad, seemed to behold the sky.

One of those emotions superior to man, which make us forget even to defend ourselves, seized the insurgents, and they approached the corpse with a respectful dismay.

'What men these regicides are!' said Enjolras.

Courfeyrac bent over to Enjolras' ear.

'This is only for you, and I don't wish to diminish the enthusiasm. But he was anything but a regicide. I knew him. His name was Father Mabeuf. I don't know what ailed him today. But he was a brave blockhead. Just look at his head.'

'Blockhead and Brutus heart,' answered Enjolras.

Then he raised his voice:

'Citizens! This is the example which the old give to the young. We hesitated, he came! we fell back, he advanced! Behold what those who tremble with old age teach those who tremble with fear! This patriarch is august in the sight of the country. He has had a long life and a magnificent death! Now let us protect his corpse, let everyone defend this old man dead as he would defend his father living, and let his presence among us make the barricade impregnable!'

A murmur of gloomy and determined adhesion followed these words.

Enjolras stooped down, raised the old man's head, and timidly kissed him on the forehead, then separating his arms, and handling the dead with a tender care, as if he feared to hurt him, he took off his coat, showed the bleeding holes to all, and said:

'There now is our flag.'

3. *Gavroche would have done better to accept Enjolras' carbine*

THEY THREW A LONG BLACK SHAWL belonging to the widow Hucheloup over Father Mabeuf. Six men made a barrow of their muskets, they laid the corpse upon it, and they bore it, bareheaded, with a solemn slowness, to the large table in the basement room.

These men, completely absorbed in the grave and sacred thing which they were doing, no longer thought of the perilous situation in which they were.

When the corpse passed near Javert, who was still impassible, Enjolras said to the spy:

'You! directly.'

During this time little Gavroche, who alone had not left his post and had remained on the watch, thought he saw some men approaching the barricade with a stealthy step. Suddenly he cried:

'Take care!'

Courfeyrac, Enjolras, Jean Prouvaire, Combeferre, Joly, Bahorel, Bossuet, all sprang tumultuously from the wine-shop. There was hardly a moment to spare. They perceived a sparkling breadth of bayonets undulating above the barricade. Municipal Guards of tall stature were penetrating, some by climbing over the omnibus, others by the opening, pushing before them the *gamin*, who fell back, but did not fly.

The moment was critical. It was that first fearful instant of the inundation, when the stream rises to the level of the bank and when the water begins to infiltrate through the fissures in the dyke. A second more, and the barricade had been taken.

Bahorel sprang upon the first Municipal Guard who entered, and killed him at the very muzzle of his carbine; the second killed Bahorel with his bayonet. Another had already prostrated Courfeyrac, who was crying 'Help!' The largest of all, a kind of colossus, marched upon Gavroche with fixed bayonet. The *gamin* took Javert's enormous musket in his little arms, aimed it resolutely at the giant, and pulled the trigger. Nothing went off. Javert had not loaded his musket. The Municipal Guard burst into a laugh and raised his bayonet over the child.

Before the bayonet touched Gavroche the musket dropped from the soldier's hands, a ball had struck the Municipal Guard in the middle of the forehead, and he fell on his back. A second ball struck the other Guard, who had assailed Courfeyrac, full in the breast, and threw him upon the pavement.

It was Marius who had just entered the barricade.

4. *The keg of powder*

MARIUS, STILL HIDDEN in the corner of the Rue Mondétour, had watched the first phase of the combat, irresolute and shuddering. However, he was not able long to resist that mysterious and sovereign infatuation which we may call the appeal of the abyss. Before the imminence of the danger, before the death of M. Mabeuf, that fatal enigma, before Bahorel slain, Courfeyrac crying 'Help!' that child threatened, his friends to succour or to avenge, all hesitation had vanished, and he had rushed into the conflict, his two pistols in his hands. By the first shot he had saved Gavroche, and by the second delivered Courfeyrac.

At the shots, at the cries of the wounded Guards, the assailants had scaled the entrenchment, upon the summit of which could now be seen thronging Municipal Guards, soldiers of the Line, National Guards of the banlieue, musket in hand. They already covered more than two-thirds of the wall, but they did not leap into the enclosure; they seemed to hesitate, fearing some snare. They looked into the obscure barricade as one would look into a den of lions. The light of the torch only lighted up their bayonets, their bearskin caps, and the upper part of their anxious and angry faces.

Marius had now no arms, he had thrown away his discharged pistols, but he had noticed the keg of powder in the basement room near the door.

As he turned half round, looking in that direction, a soldier aimed at him. At the moment the soldier aimed at Marius, a hand was laid upon the muzzle of the musket, and stopped it. It was somebody who had sprung forward, the young working-man with velvet pantaloons. The shot went off, passed through the hand, and perhaps also through the working-man, for he fell, but the ball did not reach Marius. All this in the smoke, rather guessed than seen. Marius, who was entering the basement room, hardly noticed it. Still he had caught a dim glimpse of that musket directed at him, and that hand which had stopped it, and he had heard the shot. But in moments like that the things which we see, waver and rush headlong, and we stop for nothing. We feel ourselves vaguely pushed towards still deeper shadow, and all is cloud.

The insurgents, surprised, but not dismayed, had rallied. Enjolras had cried: 'Wait! don't fire at random!' In the first confusion, in fact, they might hit one another. Most of them had gone up to the window of the second storey and to the dormer windows, whence they commanded the assailants. The most determined, with Enjolras, Courfeyrac, Jean Prouvaire, and Combeferre, had haughtily placed their backs to the houses in the rear, openly facing the ranks of soldiers and guards which crowded the barricade.

All this was accomplished without precipitation, with that strange and threatening gravity which precedes mêlées. On both sides they were taking aim, the muzzles of the guns almost touching; they were so near that they could talk with each other in an ordinary tone. Just as the spark was about to fly, an officer in a gorget and with huge epaulets, extended his sword and said:

'Take aim!'

'Fire!' said Enjolras.

The two explosions were simultaneous, and everything disappeared in the smoke.

A stinging and stifling smoke amid which writhed, with dull and feeble groans, the wounded and the dying.

When the smoke cleared away, on both sides the combatants were seen, thinned out, but still in the same places, and reloading their pieces in silence.

Suddenly, a thundering voice was heard, crying:

'Begone, or I'll blow up the barricade!'

All turned in the direction whence the voice came.

Marius had entered the basement room, and had taken the keg of powder, then he had profited by the smoke and the kind of obscure fog which filled the entrenched enclosure, to glide along the barricade as far as that cage of paving-stones in which the torch was fixed. To pull out the torch, to put the keg of powder in its place, to push the pile of paving-stones upon the keg, which stove it in, with a sort of terrible self-control – all this had been for Marius the work of stooping down and rising up; and now all, National Guards, Municipal Guards, officers, soldiers, grouped at the other extremity of the barricade, beheld him with horror, his foot upon the stones, the torch in his hand, his stern face lighted by a deadly resolution, bending the flame of the torch towards that formidable pile in which they discerned the broken barrel of powder, and uttering that terrific cry:

'Begone, or I'll blow up the barricade!'

Marius upon this barricade, after the octogenarian, was the vision of the young revolution after the apparition of the old.

'Blow up the barricade!' said a sergeant, 'and yourself also!'

Marius answered:

'And myself also.'

And he approached the torch to the keg of powder.

But there was no longer anybody on the wall. The assailants, leaving their dead and wounded, fled pell-mell and in disorder towards the extremity of the street, and were again lost in the night. It was a rout.

The barricade was redeemed.

5. *End of Jean Prouvaire's rhyme*

ALL FLOCKED ROUND Marius. Courfeyrac sprang to his neck.

'You here!'

'How fortunate!' said Combeferre.

'You came in good time!' said Bossuet.

'Without you I should have been dead!' continued Courfeyrac.

'Without you I'd been gobbled!' added Gavroche.

Marius inquired:

'Where is the chief?'

'You are the chief,' said Enjolras.

Marius had all day had a furnace in his brain, now it was a whirlwind. This whirlwind which was within him, affected him as if it was without, and were sweeping him along. It. seemed to him that he was already at an immense distance from life. His two luminous months of joy and of love, terminating abruptly upon this frightful precipice, Cosette lost to him, this barricade, M. Mabeuf dying for the republic, himself a chief of insurgents, all these things appeared a monstrous nightmare. He was obliged to make a mental effort to assure himself that all this which surrounded him was real. Marius had lived too little as yet to know that nothing is more imminent than the impossible, and that what we must always foresee is the unforeseen. He was a spectator of his own drama, as of a play which one does not comprehend.

In this mist in which his mind was struggling, he did not recognise Javert, who, bound to his post, had not moved his head during the attack upon the barricade, and who beheld the revolt going on about him with the resignation of a martyr and the majesty of a judge. Marius did not even perceive him.

Meanwhile the assailants made no movement, they were heard marching and swarming at the end of the street, but they did not venture forward, either that they were awaiting orders, or that before rushing anew upon that impregnable redoubt, they were awaiting reinforcements. The insurgents had posted sentinels, and some who were students in medicine had set about dressing the wounded.

They had thrown the tables out of the wine-shop, with the exception of two reserved for lint and cartridges, and that on which lay Father Mabeuf; they added them to the barricade, and had replaced them in the basement room by the mattresses from the beds of the widow Hucheloup, and the servants. Upon these mattresses they had laid the wounded; as for the three poor creatures who lived in Corinth, nobody knew what had become of them. They found them at last, however, hidden in the cellar.

A bitter emotion came to darken their joy over the redeemed barricade.

They called the roll. One of the insurgents was missing and who? One of the dearest. One of the most valiant, Jean Prouvaire. They sought him among the wounded, he was not there. They sought him among the dead, he was not there. He was evidently a prisoner.

Combeferre said to Enjolras:

'They have our friend; we have their officer. Have you set your heart on the death of this spy?'

'Yes,' said Enjolras; 'but less than on the life of Jean Prouvaire.'

This passed in the basement room near Javert's post.

'Well,' replied Combeferre, 'I am going to tie my handkerchief to my cane, and go with a flag of truce to offer to give them their man for ours.'

'Listen,' said Enjolras, laying his hand on Combeferre's arm.

There was a significant clicking of arms at the end of the street.

They heard a manly voice cry:

'*Vive la France! Vive l'avenir!*'

They recognised Prouvaire's voice.

There was a flash and an explosion.

Silence reigned again.

'They have killed him,' exclaimed Combeferre.

Enjolras looked at Javert and said to him:

'Your friends have just shot you.'

6. The agony of death after the agony of life

A PECULIARITY of this kind of war is that the attack on the barricades is almost always made in front, and that in general the assailants abstain from turning the positions, whether it be that they dread ambuscades, or that they fear to become entangled in the crooked streets. The whole attention of the insurgents therefore was directed to the great barricade, which was evidently the point still threatened, and where the struggle must infallibly recommence. Marius, however, thought of the little barricade and went to it. It was deserted, and was guarded only by the lamp which flickered between the stones. The little Rue Mondétour, moreover, and the branch streets de la Petite Truanderie and du Cygne, were perfectly quiet.

As Marius, the inspection made, was retiring, he heard his name faintly pronounced in the obscurity:

'Monsieur Marius!'

He shuddered, for he recognised the voice which had called him two hours before, through the grating in the Rue Plumet.

Only this voice now seemed to be but a breath.

He looked about him and saw nobody.

Marius thought he was deceived, and that it was an illusion added by his mind to the extraordinary realities which were thronging about him. He started to leave the retired recess in which the barricade was situated.

'Monsieur Marius!' repeated the voice.

This time he could not doubt, he had heard distinctly; he looked, and saw nothing.

'At your feet,' said the voice.

He stooped and saw a form in the shadow, which was dragging itself towards him. It was crawling along the pavement. It was this that had spoken to him.

The lamp enabled him to distinguish a blouse, a pair of torn pantaloons of coarse velvet, bare feet, and something which resembled a pool of blood. Marius caught a glimpse of a pale face which rose towards him and said to him:

'You do not know me?'

'No.'

'Eponine.'

Marius bent down quickly. It was indeed that unhappy child. She was dressed as a man.

'How came you here? what are you doing there?'

'I am dying,' said she.

There are words and incidents which rouse beings who are crushed. Marius exclaimed, with a start:

'You are wounded! Wait, I will carry you into the room! They will dress your wounds! Is it serious? how shall I take you up so as not to hurt you? Where are you hurt? Help! my God! But what did you come here for?'

And he tried to pass his arm under her to lift her.

In lifting her he touched her hand.

She uttered a feeble cry.

'Have I hurt you?' asked Marius.

'A little.'

'But I have only touched your hand.'

She raised her hand into Marius' sight, and Marius saw in the centre of that hand a black hole.

'What is the matter with your hand?' said he.

'It is pierced.'

'Pierced?'

'Yes.'

'By what?'

'By a ball.'

'How?'

'Did you see a musket aimed at you?'

'Yes, and a hand which stopped it.'

'That was mine.'

Marius shuddered.

'What madness! Poor child! But that is not so bad, if that is all, it is nothing, let me carry you to a bed. They will care for you, people don't die from a shot in the hand.'

She murmured:

'The ball passed through my hand, but it went out through my back. It is useless to take me from here. I will tell you how you can care for me, better than a surgeon. Sit down by me on that stone.'

He obeyed: she laid her head on Marius' knees, and without looking at him, she said:

'Oh! how good it is! How kind he is! That is it! I don't suffer any more!'

She remained a moment in silence, then she turned her head with effort and looked at Marius.

'Do you know, Monsieur Marius? It worried me that you should go into that garden, it was silly, since it was I who had shown you the house, and then indeed I ought surely to have known that a young man like you – '

She stopped, and, leaping over the gloomy transitions which were doubtless in her mind, she added with a heartrending smile:

'You thought me ugly, didn't you?'

She continued:

'See, you are lost! Nobody will get out of the barricade, now. It was I who led you into this, it was! You are going to die, I am sure. And still when I saw him aiming at you, I put up my hand upon the muzzle of the musket. How droll it is! But it was because I wanted to die before you. When I got this ball, I dragged myself here, nobody saw me, nobody picked me up. I waited for you, I said: He will not come then? Oh! if you knew, I bit my blouse, I suffered so much! Now I am well. Do you remember the day when I came into your room, and when I looked at myself in your mirror, and the day when I met you on the boulevard near some work-women? How the birds sang! It was not very long ago. You gave me a hundred sous, and I said to you: I don't want your money. Did you pick up your piece? You are not rich. I didn't think to tell you to pick it up. The sun shone bright, I was not cold. Do you remember, Monsieur Marius? Oh! I am happy! we are all going to die.'

She had a wandering, grave, and touching air. Her torn blouse showed her bare throat. While she was talking she rested her wounded hand upon her breast where there was another hole, from which there came with each pulsation a flow of blood like a jet of wine from an open bung.

Marius gazed upon this unfortunate creature with profound compassion.

'Oh!' she exclaimed suddenly, 'it is coming back. I am stifling!'

She seized her blouse and bit it, and her legs writhed upon the pavement.

At this moment the chicken voice of little Gavroche resounded through the barricade. The child had mounted upon a table to load his musket and was gaily singing the song then so popular:

En voyant Lafayette.
Le gendarme répète:
Sauvons-nous! sauvons-nous! sauvons-nous!

Eponine raised herself up, and listened, then she murmured:

'It is he.'

And turning towards Marius:

'My brother is here. He must not see me. He would scold me.'

'Your brother?' asked Marius, who thought in the bitterest and most sorrowful depths of his heart, of the duties which his father had bequeathed him towards the Thénardiers, 'who is your brother?'

'That little boy.'

'The one who is singing?'

'Yes.'

Marius started.

'Oh! don't go away!' said she, 'it will not be long now!'

She was sitting almost upright, but her voice was very low and broken by hiccoughs. At intervals the death-rattle interrupted her. She approached her face as near as she could to Marius' face. She added with a strange expression:

'Listen, I don't want to deceive you. I have a letter in my pocket for you. Since yesterday. I was told to put it in the post. I kept it. I didn't want it to reach you. But you would not like it of me perhaps when we meet again so soon. We do meet again, don't we? Take your letter.'

She grasped Marius' hand convulsively with her wounded hand, but she seemed no longer to feel the pain. She put Marius' hand into the pocket of her blouse. Marius really felt a paper there.

'Take it,' said she.

Marius took the letter.

She made a sign of satisfaction and of consent.

'Now for my pains, promise me – '

And she hesitated.

'What?' asked Marius.

'Promise me!'

'I promise you.'

'Promise to kiss me on the forehead when I am dead. I shall feel it.'

She let her head fall back upon Marius' knees and her eyelids closed. He thought that poor soul had gone. Eponine lay motionless; but just when Marius supposed her for ever asleep, she slowly opened her eyes in which the gloomy deepness of death appeared, and said to him with an accent the sweetness of which already seemed to come from another world:

'And then, do you know, Monsieur Marius, I believe I was a little in love with you.'

She essayed to smile again and expired.

7. *Gavroche a profound calculator of distances*

Marius kept his promise. He kissed that livid forehead from which oozed an icy sweat. This was not an infidelity to Cosette; it was a thoughtful and gentle farewell to an unhappy soul.

He had not taken the letter which Eponine had given him without a thrill. He had felt at once the presence of an event. He was impatient to read it. The heart of man is thus made; the unfortunate child had hardly closed her eyes when Marius thought to unfold this paper. He laid her gently upon the ground, and went away. Something told him that he could not read that letter in sight of this corpse.

He went to a candle in the basement-room. It was a little note, folded and sealed with the elegant care of woman. The address was in a woman's hand, and ran:

'To Monsieur, Monsieur Marius Pontmercy, at M. Courfeyrac's, Rue de la Verrerie, No. 16.'

He broke the seal and read:

'My beloved, alas! my father wishes to start immediately. We shall be tonight in the Rue de l'Homme Armé, No. 7. In a week we shall be in England. COSETTE. June 4th.'

Such was the innocence of this love that Marius did not even know Cosette's handwriting.

What happened may be told in a few words. Eponine had done it all. After the evening of the 3rd of June, she had had a double thought, to thwart the projects of her father and the bandits upon the house in the Rue Plumet, and to separate Marius from Cosette. She had changed rags with the first young rogue who thought it amusing to dress as a woman while Eponine disguised herself as a man. It was she who, in the Champ de Mars, had given Jean Valjean the expressive warning: *Remove.* Jean Valjean returned home, and said to Cosette: *We start tonight, and we are going to the Rue de l'Homme Armé with Toussaint. Next week we shall be in London.* Cosette, prostrated by this unexpected blow, had hastily written two lines to Marius. But how should she get the letter to the post? She did not go out alone, and Toussaint, surprised at such an errand, would surely show the letter to M. Fauchelevent. In this anxiety, Cosette saw, through the grating, Eponine in men's clothes, who was now prowling continually about the garden. Cosette called 'this young working-man' and handed him five francs and the letter, saying to him: 'carry this letter to its address right away.' Eponine put the letter in her pocket. The next day, June 5th, she went to Courfeyrac's to ask for Marius, not to give him the letter, but, a thing which every jealous and loving soul will understand, 'to see'. There she waited for Marius, or, at least, for Courfeyrac – still to see. When Courfeyrac said to her: we are going to the barricades, an idea flashed across her mind. To throw herself into that death as she would have thrown herself into any other, and to push Marius into it. She followed Courfeyrac, made sure of the post where they were building the barricade; and very sure, since Marius had received no notice and she had intercepted the letter, that he would at nightfall be at his usual evening rendezvous, she went to the Rue Plumet, waited there for Marius, and sent him, in the name of his friends, that appeal which must, she thought, lead him to the barricade. She counted upon Marius' despair when he should not find Cosette; she was not mistaken. She returned herself to the Rue de la Chanvrerie. We have seen what she did there. She died with that tragic joy of jealous hearts which drag the being they love into death with them, saying: nobody shall have him!

Marius covered Cosette's letter with kisses. She loved him then? He had for a moment the idea that now he need not die. Then he said to himself: 'She is going away. Her father takes her to England, and my grandfather refuses to consent to the marriage. Nothing is changed in the fatality.' Dreamers, like Marius, have these supreme depressions, and paths hence are chosen in despair. The fatigue of life is insupportable; death is sooner over. Then he thought that there were two duties remaining for him to fulfil: to inform Cosette of his death and to send her a last farewell, and to save from the imminent catastrophe which was approaching, this poor child, Eponine's brother and Thenardier's son.

He had a pocket-book with him; the same that had contained the pages upon which he had written so many thoughts of love for Cosette. He tore out a leaf and wrote with a pencil these few lines:

'Our marriage was impossible. I have asked my grandfather, he has refused; I am without fortune, and you also. I ran to your house, I did not find you, you know the promise that I gave you? I keep it, I die, I love you. When you read this, my soul will be near you, and will smile upon you.'

Having nothing to seal this letter with, he merely folded the paper, and wrote upon it this address:

'*To Mademoiselle Cosette Fauchelevent, at M. Faucheleveuf's, Rue de l'Homme Armé, No. 7.*'

The letter folded, he remained a moment in thought, took his pocket-book again, opened it, and wrote these four lines on the first page with the same pencil:

'My name is Marius Pontmercy. Carry my corpse to my grandfather's, M. Gillenormand, Rue des Filles du Calvaire, No. 6, in the Marais.'

He put the book into his coat-pocket, then he called Gavroche. The *gamin*, at the sound of Marius' voice, ran up with his joyous and devoted face:

'Will you do something for me?'

'Anything,' said Gavroche. 'God of the good God! without you, I should have been cooked, sure.'

'You see this letter?'

'Yes.'

'Take it. Go out of the barricade immediately (Gavroche, disturbed, began to scratch his ear), and tomorrow morning you will carry it to its address, to Mademoiselle Cosette, at M. Fauchelevent's, Rue de l'Homme Armé No. 7.'

The heroic boy answered:

'Ah, well, but in that time they'll take the barricade, and I shan't be here.'

'The barricade will not be attacked again before daybreak, according to all appearance, and will not be taken before tomorrow noon.'

The new respite which the assailants allowed the barricade was, in fact, prolonged. It was one of those intermissions frequent in night combats, which are always followed by a redoubled fury.

'Well,' said Gavroche, 'suppose I go and carry your letter in the morning?'

'It will be too late. The barricade will probably be blockaded; all the streets will be guarded, and you cannot get out. Go, right away!'

Gavroche had nothing more to say; he stood there, undecided, and sadly scratching his ear. Suddenly, with one of his birdlike motions, he took the letter:

'All right,' said he.

And he started off on a run by the little Rue Mondétour.

Gavroche had an idea which decided him, but which he did not tell, for fear Marius would make some objection to it.

That idea was this:

'It is hardly midnight, the Rue de l'Homme Armé is not far, I will carry the letter right away, and I shall get back in time.'

BOOK 15: THE RUE L'HOMME ARMÉ

1. *Blotter, Blabber*

WHAT ARE THE CONVULSIONS of a city compared with the *émeutes* of the soul? Man is a still deeper depth than the people. Jean Valjean, at that very moment, was a prey to a frightful uprising. All the gulfs were reopened within him. He also, like Paris, was shuddering on the threshold of a formidable and obscure revolution. A few hours had sufficed. His destiny and his conscience were suddenly covered with shadow. Of him also, as of Paris, we might say: the two principles are face to face. The angel of light and the angel of darkness are to wrestle on the bridge of the abyss. Which of the two shall hurl down the other? which shall sweep him away?

On the eve of that same day, June 5th, Jean Valjean, accompanied by Cosette and Toussaint, had installed himself in the Rue de l'Homme Armé. A sudden turn of fortune awaited him there.

Cosette had not left the Rue Plumet without an attempt at resistance. For the first time since they had lived together, Cosette's will and Jean Valjean's will had shown themselves distinct, and had been, if not conflicting, at least contradictory. There was objection on one side and inflexibility on the other. The abrupt advice: *remove*, thrown to Jean Valjean by an unknown hand, had so far alarmed him as to render him absolute. He believed himself tracked out and pursued. Cosette had to yield.

They both arrived in the Rue de l'Homme Armé without opening their mouths or saying a word, absorbed in their personal meditations; Jean Valjean so anxious that he did not perceive Cosette's sadness, Cosette so sad that she did not perceive Jean Valjean's anxiety.

Jean Valjean had brought Toussaint, which he had never done in his preceding absences. He saw that possibly he should not return to the Rue Plumet, and he could neither leave Toussaint behind, nor tell her his secret. Besides he felt that she was devoted and safe. Between domestic and master, treason begins with curiosity. But Toussaint, as if she had been predestined to be the servant of Jean Valjean, was not curious. She said through her stuttering, in her Barneville peasant's speech: 'I am from same to same; I think my act; the remainder is not my labour.' (I am so; I do my work; the rest is not my affair.)

In this departure from the Rue Plumet, which was almost a flight, Jean Valjean carried nothing but the little embalmed valise christened by Cosette the *inseparable*. Full trunks would have required porters, and porters are witnesses. They had a coach come to the door on the Rue Babylone, and they went away.

It was with great difficulty that Toussaint obtained permission to pack up a little linen and clothing and a few toilet articles. Cosette herself carried only her writing-desk and her blotter.

Jean Valjean, to increase the solitude and mystery of this disappearance, had arranged so as not to leave the cottage on the Rue Plumet till the close of the day, which left Cosette time to write her note to Marius. They arrived in the Rue de l'Homme Armé after nightfall.

They went silently to bed.

The lodging in the Rue de l'Homme Armé was situated in a rear court, on the second storey, and consisted of two bedrooms, a dining-room, and a kitchen adjoining the dining-room, with a loft where there was a cot-bed which fell to Toussaint. The dining-room was at the same time the ante-chamber, and separated the two bedrooms. The apartments contained all necessary furniture.

We are reassured almost as foolishly as we are alarmed; human nature is so constituted. Hardly was Jean Valjean in the Rue de l'Homme Armé, before his anxiety grew less, and by degrees was dissipated. There are quieting spots which act in some sort mechanically upon the mind. Obscure street, peaceful inhabitants. Jean Valjean felt some strange contagion of tranquillity in that lane of the ancient Paris, so narrow that it was barred to carriages by a tranverse joist laid upon two posts, dumb and deaf in the midst of the noisy city, twilight in broad day, and, so to speak, incapable of emotions between its two rows of lofty, century-old houses which are silent like the patriarchs that they are. There is stagnant oblivion in this street. Jean Valjean breathed there. By what means could anybody find him there?

His first care was to place the *inseparable* by his side.

He slept well. Night counsels; we may add: night calms. Next morning he awoke almost cheerful. He thought the dining-room charming, although it was hideous, furnished with an old round table, a low sideboard surmounted by a hanging mirror, a worm-eaten armchair, and a few other chairs loaded down with Toussaint's bundles. Through an opening in one of these bundles, Jean Valjean's National Guard uniform could be seen.

As for Cosette, she had Toussaint bring a bowl of soup to her room, and did not make her appearance till evening.

About five o'clock, Toussaint, who was coming and going, very busy with this little removal, set a cold fowl on the dining-room table, which Cosette, out of deference to her father, consented to look at.

This done, Cosette, upon pretext of a severe headache, said good night to Jean Valjean, and shut herself up in her bedroom. Jean Valjean ate a chicken's wing with a good appetite, and, leaning on the tables, clearing his brow little by little, was regaining his sense of security.

While he was making this frugal dinner, he became confusedly aware, on two or three occasions, of the stammering of Toussaint, who said to him: 'Monsieur, there is a row; they are fighting in Paris.' But, absorbed in a multitude of interior combinations, he paid no attention to it. To tell the truth, he had not heard.

He arose, and began to walk from the window to the door, and from the door to the window, growing calmer and calmer.

With calmness, Cosette, his single engrossing care, returned to his thoughts. Not that he was troubled about this headache, a petty derangement of the nerves, a young girl's pouting, the cloud of a moment, in a day or two it would be gone; but he thought of the future, and, as usual, he thought of it pleasantly. After all, he saw no obstacle to their happy life resuming its course. At certain hours, everything seems impossible; at other hours, everything appears easy; Jean Valjean was in one of those happy hours. They come ordinarily after the evil ones, like day after night, by that law of succession and contrast which lies at the very foundation of nature, and which superficial minds call antithesis. In this peaceful street, in which he had taken refuge, Jean Valjean was relieved from all that had troubled him for sometime past. From the very fact that he had seen a good deal of darkness, he began to perceive a little blue sky. To have left the Rue Plumet without complication and without accident, was already a piece of good fortune. Perhaps it would be prudent to leave the country, were it only for a few months, and go to London. Well, they would go. To be in France, to be in England, what did that matter, if he had Cosette with him? Cosette was his nation. Cosette sufficed for his happiness; the idea that perhaps he did not suffice for Cosette's happiness, this idea, once his fever and his bane, did not even present itself to his mind. All his past griefs had disappeared, and he was in the full tide of optimism. Cosette, being near him, seemed to belong to him; an optical effect which everybody has experienced. He arranged in his own mind, and with every possible facility, the departure for England with Cosette, and he saw his happiness reconstructed, no matter where, in the perspective of his reverie.

While yet walking up and down, with slow steps, his eye suddenly met something strange.

He perceived facing him, in the inclined mirror which hung above the sideboard, and he distinctly read the lines which follow:

'My beloved, alas! my father wishes to start immediately. We shall be tonight in the Rue de l'Homme Armé No. 7. In a week we shall be in London. COSETTE. June 4th.'

Jean Valjean stood aghast.

Cosette, on arriving, had laid her blotter on the sideboard before the mirror, and, wholly absorbed in her sorrowful anguish, had forgotten it there, without even noticing that she left it wide open, and open exactly at the page upon which she had dried the five lines written by her, and which she had given in charge to the young workman passing through the Rue Plumet. The writing was imprinted upon the blotter.

The mirror reflected the writing.

There resulted what is called in geometry the symmetrical image; so that the writing reversed on the blotter was corrected by the mirror, and presented its original form; and Jean Valjean had beneath his eyes the letter written in the evening by Cosette to Marius.

It was simple and withering.

Jean Valjean went to the mirror. He read the five lines again, but he did not believe it. They produced upon him the effect of an apparition in a flash of lightning. It was a hallucination. It was impossible. It was not.

Little by little his perception became more precise; he looked at Cosette's blotter, and the consciousness of the real fact returned to him. He took the blotter and said: 'It comes from that.' He feverishly examined the five lines imprinted on the blotter, the reversal of the letters made a fantastic scrawl of them, and he saw no sense in them. Then he said to himself: 'But that does not mean anything, there is nothing written there.' And he drew a long breath, with an inexpressible sense of relief. Who has not felt these silly joys in moments of horror? The soul does not give itself up to despair until it has exhausted all illusions.

He held the blotter in his hand and gazed at it, stupidly happy, almost laughing at the hallucination of which he had been the dupe. All at once his eyes fell upon the mirror, and he saw the vision again. This time it was not a mirage. The second sight of a vision is a reality, it was palpable, it was the writing restored by the mirror. He understood.

Jean Valjean tottered, let the blotter fall, and sank down into the old armchair by the sideboard, his head drooping, his eye glassy, bewildered. He said to himself that it was clear, and that the light of the world was for ever eclipsed, and that Cosette had written that to somebody. Then he heard his soul, again become terrible, give a sullen roar in the darkness. Go, then, and take from the lion the dog which he has in his cage.

A circumstance strange and sad, Marius at that moment had not yet Cosette's letter; chance had brought it, like a traitor, to Jean Valjean before delivering it to Marius.

Jean Valjean till this day had never been vanquished when put to the proof. He had been subjected to fearful trials; no violence of ill fortune had been spared him; the ferocity of fate, armed with every vengeance and with every scorn of society, had taken him for a subject and had greedily pursued him. He had neither recoiled nor flinched before anything. He had accepted, when he must, every extremity; he had sacrificed his reconquered inviolability of manhood, given up his liberty, risked his head, lost all, suffered all, and he had remained so disinterested and stoical that at times one might have believed him translated, like a martyr. His conscience, inured to all possible assaults of adversity, might seem for ever impregnable. Well, he who could have seen his inward monitor would have been compelled to admit that at this hour it was growing feeble.

For, of all the tortures which he had undergone in that inquisition of destiny, this was the most fearful. Never had such pincers seized him. He felt the mysterious quiver of every latent sensibility. He felt the laceration of the unknown fibre. Alas, the supreme ordeal, let us say rather, the only ordeal, is the loss of the beloved being.

Poor old Jean Valjean did not, certainly, love Cosette otherwise than as a father; but, as we have already mentioned, into this paternity the very bereavement of his life had introduced every love; he loved Cosette as his daughter, and he loved her as his mother, and he loved her as his sister; and, as he had never had either sweetheart or wife, as nature is a creditor who accepts no protest, that sentiment, also, the most indestructible of all, was mingled with the others, vague, ignorant, pure with the purity of blindness, unconscious, celestial, angelic, divine; less like a sentiment than like an instinct, less like an instinct than like an attraction, imperceptible and invisible, but real; and love, properly speaking, existed in his enormous tenderness for Cosette as does the vein of gold in the mountain, dark and virgin.

Remember that condition of heart which we have already pointed out. No marriage was possible between them, not even that of souls; and still it was certain that their destinies were espoused. Except Cosette, that is to say, except a childhood, Jean Valjean, in all his long life, had known nothing of those objects which man can love. The passions and the loves which succeed one another, had not left on him those successive greens, a light green over a dark green, which we notice upon leaves that pass the winter, and upon men who pass their fifty years. In short, and we have more than once insisted upon it, all that interior fusion, all that whole, the resultant of which was a lofty virtue, ended in making of Jean Valjean a father for Cosette. A strange father forged out of the grandfather, the son, the brother, and the husband, which there was in Jean Valjean; a father in whom there was even a mother; a father who loved Cosette, and who adored her, and to whom that child was light, was home, was family, was country, was paradise.

So, when he saw that it was positively ended, that she escaped him, that she glided from his hands, that she eluded him, that it was cloud, that it was water, when he had before his eyes this crushing evidence; another is the aim of her heart, another is the desire of her life, there is a beloved; I am only the father; I no longer exist; when he could no more doubt when he said to himself: 'She is going away out of me!' the grief which he felt surpassed the possible. To have done all that he had done to come to this! and, what! to be nothing! Then, as we have just said, he felt from head to foot a shudder of revolt. He felt even to the roots of his hair the immense awakening of selfishness, and the Me howled in the abyss of this soul.

There are interior subsoilings. The penetration of a torturing certainty into man does not occur without breaking up and pulverising certain deep elements which are sometimes the man himself. Grief, when it reaches this stage, is a panic of all the forces of the soul. These are fatal crises. Few among us come through them without change, and firm in duty. When the limit of suffering is overpassed, the most imperturbable virtue is disconcerted. Jean Valjean took up the blotter, and convinced himself anew; he bent as if petrified over the five undeniable lines, with eye fixed; and such a cloud formed within him that one might have believed the whole interior of that soul was crumbling.

He examined this revelation, through the magnifying powers of reverie, with an apparent and frightful calmness, for it is a terrible thing when the calmness of man reaches the rigidity of the statue.

He measured the appalling step which his destiny had taken without a suspicion on his part; he recalled his fears of the previous summer, so foolishly dissipated: he recognised the precipice; it was still the same; only Jean Valjean was no longer on the brink, he was at the bottom.

A bitter and monstrous thing, he had fallen without perceiving it. All the light of his life had gone out, he believing that he constantly saw the sun.

His instinct did not hesitate. He put together certain circumstances, certain dates, certain blushes, and certain pallors of Cosette, and he said to himself: 'It is he.' The divination of despair is a sort of mysterious bow which never misses its aim. With his first conjecture, he hit Marius. He did not know the name, but he found the man at once. He perceived distinctly, at the bottom of the implacable evocation of memory, the unknown prowler of the Luxembourg, that wretched seeker of amours, that romantic idler, that imbecile, that coward, for it is cowardice to come and make sweet eyes at girls who are beside their father who loves them.

After he had fully determined that that young man was at the bottom of this state of affairs, and that it all came from him, he, Jean Valjean, the regenerated man, the man who had laboured so much upon his soul, the man who had made so many efforts to resolve all life, all misery, and all misfortune into love; he looked within himself, and there he saw a spectre, Hatred.

Great griefs contain dejection. They discourage existence. The man into whom they enter feels something go out of him. In youth, their visit is dismal; in later years it is ominous. Alas! when the blood is hot, when the hair is black, when the head is erect upon the body like the flame upon the torch, when the sheaf of destiny is still full, when the heart, filled with a fortunate love, still has pulsations which can be responded to, when we have before us the time to retrieve, when all women are before us, and all smiles, and all the future, and all the horizon, when the strength of life is complete, if despair is a fearful thing, what is it then in old age, when the years rush along, growing bleaker and bleaker, at the twilight hour, when we begin to see the stars of the tomb!

While he was thinking, Toussaint entered. Jean Valjean arose, and asked her:

'In what direction is it? Do you know?'

Toussaint, astonished, could only answer:

'If you please?'

Jean Valjean resumed:

'Didn't you tell me just now that they were fighting?'

'Oh! yes, monsieur,' answered Toussaint. 'It is over by Saint Merry.'

There are some mechanical impulses which come to us, without our knowledge even, from our deepest thoughts. It was doubtless under the influence of an impulse of this kind, and of which he was hardly conscious, that Jean Valjean five minutes afterwards found himself in the street.

He was bare-headed, seated upon the stone block by the door of his house. He seemed to be listening.

The night had come.

2. *The gamin an enemy of light*

How much time did he pass thus? What were the ebbs and the flows of that tragic meditation? did he straighten up? did he remain bowed? had he been bent so far as to break? could he yet straighten himself, and regain a foothold in his conscience upon something solid? He himself probably could not have told.

The street was empty. A few anxious bourgeois, who were rapidly returning home, hardly perceived him. Every man for himself in times of peril. The lamplighter came as usual to light the lamp which hung exactly opposite the door of No. 7, and went away. Jean Valjean, to one who had examined him in that shadow, would not have seemed a living man. There he was, seated upon the block by his door, immovable as a goblin of ice. There is congelation in despair. The tocsin was heard, and vague stormy sounds were heard. In the midst of all this convulsive clamour of the bell mingled with the *émeute*, the clock of St Paul's struck eleven, gravely and without haste, for the tocsin is man; the hour is God. The passing of the hour had no effect upon Jean Valjean; Jean Valjean did not stir. However, almost at that very moment, there was a sharp explosion in the direction of the markets, a second followed, more violent still; it was probably that attack on the barricade of the Rue de la Chanvrerie which we have just seen repulsed by Marius. At this double discharge, the fury of which seemed increased by the stupor of the night, Jean Valjean was startled; he looked up in the direction whence the sound came; then he sank down upon the block, folded his arms, and his head dropped slowly upon his breast.

He resumed his dark dialogue with himself.

Suddenly he raised his eyes, somebody was walking in the street, he heard steps near him, he looked, and, by the light of the lamp, in the direction of the Archives, he perceived a livid face, young and radiant.

Gavroche had just arrived in the Rue de l'Homme Armé.

Gavroche was looking in the air, and appeared to be searching for something. He saw Jean Valjean perfectly, but he took no notice of him.

Gavroche, after looking into the air, looked on the ground; he raised himself on tiptoe and felt of the doors and windows of the ground floors; they were all closed, bolted, and chained. After having found five or six houses barricaded in this way, the *gamin* shrugged his shoulders, and took counsel with himself in these terms:

'Golly!'

Then he began to look into the air again.

Jean Valjean, who, the instant before, in the state of mind in which he was, would not have spoken nor even replied to anybody, felt irresistibly impelled to address a word to this child.

'Small boy,' said he, 'what is the matter with you?'

'The matter is that I am hungry,' answered Gavroche tartly. And he added: 'Small yourself.'

Jean Valjean felt in his pocket and took out a five-franc piece.

But Gavroche, who was of the wagtail species, and who passed quickly from one action to another, had picked up a stone. He had noticed a lamp.

'Hold on,' said he, 'you have your lamps here still. You are not regular, my friends. It is disorderly. Break me that.'

And he threw the stone into the lamp, the glass from which fell with such a clatter that some bourgeois, hid behind their curtains in the opposite house, cried: 'There is 'Ninety-three!'

The lamp swung violently and went out. The street became suddenly dark.

'That's it, old street,' said Gavroche, 'put on your nightcap.'

And turning towards Jean Valjean:

'What do you call that gigantic monument that you have got there at the end of the street? That's the Archives, isn't it? They ought to chip off these big fools of columns slightly, and make a genteel barricade of them.'

Jean Valjean approached Gavroche.

'Poor creature,' said he, in an undertone, and speaking to himself, 'he is hungry.'

And he put the hundred-sous piece into his hand.

Gavroche cocked up his nose, astonished at the size of this big sou; he looked at it in the dark, and the whiteness of the big sou dazzled him. He knew five-franc pieces by hearsay; their reputation was agreeable to him; he was delighted to see one so near. He said: 'Let us contemplate the tiger.'

He gazed at it for a few moments in ecstasy; then, turning towards Jean Valjean, he handed him the piece, and said majestically:

'Bourgeois, I prefer to break lamps. Take back your wild beast. You don't corrupt me. It has five claws; but it don't scratch me.'

'Have you a mother?' inquired Jean Valjean.

Gavroche answered:

'Perhaps more than you have.'

'Well,' replied Jean Valjean, 'keep this money for your mother.'

Gavroche felt softened. Besides he had just noticed that the man who was talking to him, had no hat, and that inspired him with confidence.

'Really,' said he, 'it isn't to prevent my breaking the lamps?'

'Break all you like.'

'You are a fine fellow,' said Gavroche.

And he put the five-franc piece into one of his pockets.

His confidence increasing, he added:

'Do you belong in the street?'

'Yes; why?'

'Could you show me number seven?'

'What do you want with number seven?'

Here the boy stopped; he feared that he had said too much; he plunged his nails vigorously into his hair, and merely answered:

'Ah! that's it.'

An idea flashed across Jean Valjean's mind. Anguish has such lucidities. He said to the child:

'Have you brought the letter I am waiting for?'

'You?' said Gavroche. 'You are not a woman.'

'The letter is for Mademoiselle Cosette; isn't it?'

'Cosette?' muttered Gavroche, 'Yes, I believe it is that funny name.'

'Well,' resumed Jean Valjean, 'I am to deliver the letter to her. Give it to me.'

'In that case you must know that I am sent from the barricade?'

'Of course,' said Jean Valjean.

Gavroche thrust his hand into another of his pockets, and drew out a folded paper.

Then he gave a military salute.

'Respect for the despatch,' said he. 'It comes from the provisional government.'

'Give it to me,' said Jean Valjean.

Gavroche held the paper raised above his head.

'Don't imagine that this is a love-letter. It is for a woman, but it is for the people. We men, we are fighting and we respect the sex. We don't do as they do in high life, where there are lions who send love-letters to camels.'

'Give it to me.'

'The fact is,' continued Gavroche, 'you look to me like a fine fellow.'

'Give it to me quick.'

'Take it.'

And he handed the paper to Jean Valjean.

'And hurry yourself, Monsieur What's-your-name, for Mamselle What's-her-namess is waiting.'

Gavroche was proud of having produced this word.

Jean Valjean asked:

'Is it to Saint Merry that the answer is to be sent?'

'In that case,' exclaimed Gavroche, 'you would make one of those cakes vulgarly called blunders. That letter comes from the barricade in the Rue de la Chanvrerie, and I am going back there. Good night, citizen.'

This said, Gavroche went away, or rather, resumed his flight like an escaped bird towards the spot whence he came. He replunged into the obscurity as if he made a hole in it, with the rapidity and precision of a projectile; the little Rue de l'Homme Armé again became silent and solitary; in a twinkling, this strange child, who had within him shadow and dream, was buried in the dusk of those rows of black houses, and was lost therein like smoke in the darkness; and one might have thought him dissipated and vanished, if, a few minutes after his disappearance, a loud crashing of glass and the splendid patatras of a lamp falling upon the pavement had not abruptly rewakened the indignant bourgeois. It was Gavroche passing along the Rue du Chaume.

3. *While Cosette and Toussaint sleep*

JEAN VALJEAN went in with Marius' letter.

He groped his way upstairs, pleased with the darkness like an owl which holds his prey, opened and softly closed the door, listened to see if he heard any sound, decided that, according to all appearances, Cosette and Toussaint were asleep, plunged three or four matches into the bottle of the Fumade tinder-box before he could raise a spark, his hand trembled so much; there was theft in what he was about to do. At last, his candle was lighted, he leaned his elbows on the table, unfolded the paper, and read.

In violent emotions, we do not read, we prostrate the paper which we hold, so to speak, we strangle it like a victim, we crush the paper, we bury the nails of our wrath or of our delight in it; we run to the end we leap to the beginning; the attention has a fever; it comprehends by wholesale, almost, the essential: it seizes a point, and all the rest disappears. In Marius' note to Cosette, Jean Valjean saw only these words.

'– I die. When you read this, my soul will be near you.' Before these two lines, he was horribly dazzled; he sat a moment as if crushed by the change of emotion which was wrought within him, he looked at Marius' note with a sort of drunken astonishment; he had before his eyes that splendour, the death of the hated being.

He uttered a hideous cry of inward joy. So, it was finished. The end came sooner than he had dared to hope. The being who encumbered his destiny was disappearing. He was going away of himself, freely, of his own accord. Without any intervention on his, Jean Valjean's part, without any fault of his, 'that man' was about to die. Perhaps even he was already dead. – Here his fever began to calculate. – No. He is not dead yet. The letter was evidently written to be read by Cosette in the morning; since those two discharges which were heard between eleven o'clock and midnight, there has been nothing; the barricade will not be seriously attacked till daybreak – but it is all the same, for the moment 'that man' meddled with this war, he was lost; he is caught in the net. Jean Valjean felt that he was delivered. He would then find himself once more alone with Cosette. Rivalry ceased; the future recommenced. He had only to keep the note in his pocket. Cosette would never know what had become of 'that man'.

'I have only to let things take their course. That man cannot escape. If he is not dead yet, it is certain that he will die. What happiness!'

All this said within himself, he became gloomy.

Then he went down and waked the porter.

About an hour afterwards, Jean Valjean went out in the full dress of a National Guard, and armed. The porter had easily found in the neighbourhood what was necessary to complete his equipment. He had a loaded musket and a cartridge-box full of cartridges. He went in the direction of the markets.

4. The excess of Gavroche's zeal

MEANWHILE AN ADVENTURE had just befallen Gavroche.

Gavroche, after having conscientiously stoned the lamp in the Rue du Chaume, came to the Rue des Vieilles Haudriettes, and not seeing 'a cat' there, thought it a good opportunity to strike up all the song of which he was capable. His march, far from being slackened by the singing, was accelerated. He began to scatter along the sleeping or terrified houses these incendiary couplets:

L'oiseau medit dans les charmilles,
Et pretend qu'hier Atala
Avec un russe s'en alla.
Où vont les belles filles,
Lon la.

Mon ami pierrot, tu babilles,
Parce que l'autre jour Mila
Cogna sa vitre, et m'appela.
Où vont, etc.

Les drôlesses sont fort gentilles,
Leur poison qu m'ensorcela
Griserait monsieur Orfila.
Où vont, etc.

J'aime l'amour et ses bisbilles,
J'aime Agnès, j'aime Paméla,
Lise en m'allumant se brûla.
Où vont, etc.

Jadis, quand je vis les mantilles
De Suzette et de Zéila,
Mon âme à leurs plis se mêla.
Où vont, etc.

Amour, quand, dans l'ombre où tu brilles,
Tu coiffes de roses Lola,
Je me damnerais pour cela.
Où vont, etc.

Jeanne, à ton miroir tu t'habilles!
Mon cœur un beau jour s'envola;
Je crois que c'est Jeanne qui l'a.
Où vont, etc.

Le soir, en sortant des quadrilles,
Je morte aux étoiles Stella
Et je leur dis; 'Regardez-la.'
Où vont, etc.

Gavroche, while yet singing, was lavish of pantomime. Action is the foundation of the refrain. His face, an inexhaustible repertory of masks, made more convulsive and more fantastic grimaces than the mouths of a torn cloth in a heavy wind. Unfortunately, as he was alone and in the night, it was neither seen nor visible. There are such lost riches.

Suddenly he stopped short. 'Let us interrupt the romance,' said he.

His cat-like eye had just distinguished in the recess of a *porte-cochère* what is called in painting a harmony: that is to say, a being and a thing; the thing was a hand-cart, the being was an Auvergnat who was sleeping in it.

The arms of the cart rested on the pavement and the Auvergnat's head rested on the tail-board of the cart. His body was curled up on the inclined plane and his feet touched the ground.

Gavroche, with his experience of the things of this world, recognised a drunken man. It was some corner-porter who had drunk too much and who was sleeping too much.

'This,' thought Gavroche, 'is what summer nights are good for. The Auvergnat is asleep in his cart. We take the cart for the republic and we leave the Auvergnat to the monarchy.'

His mind had just received this illumination:

'That cart would go jolly well on our barricade.'

The Auvergnat was snoring.

Gavroche drew the cart softly by the back end and the Auvergnat by the forward end, that is to say by the feet, and, in a minute, the Auvergnat, imperturbable, was lying flat on the pavement. The cart was delivered.

Gavroche, accustomed to face the unforeseen on all sides, always had everything about him. He felt in one of his pockets, and took out a scrap of paper and an end of a red pencil pilfered from some carpenter.

He wrote:

'*French Republic*

'Received your cart.'

And he signed, 'GAVROCHE.'

This done, he put the paper into the pocket of the still snoring Auvergnat's velvet waistcoat, seized the cross-piece with both hands, and started off in the direction of the markets, pushing the cart before him at a full gallop with a glorious triumphal uproar.

This was perilous. There was a post at the Imprimerie Royale. Gavroche did not think of it. This post was occupied by the National Guards of the banlieue. A certain watchfulness began to excite the squad, and their heads were lifted from their camp-beds. Two lamps broken one after another, that song sung at the top of the voice, it was a good deal for streets so cowardly, which long to go to sleep at sunset, and put their extinguisher upon their candle so early. For an hour the *gamin* had been making, in this peaceful district, the uproar of a fly in a bottle. The sergeant of the banlieue listened. He waited. He was a prudent man.

The furious rolling of the cart filled the measure of possible delay, and determined the sergeant to attempt a reconnaissance. 'There is a whole band here,' said he, 'we must go softly.'

It was clear that the hydra of anarchy had got out of its box, and was raging in the quarter.

And the sergeant ventured out of the post with stealthy tread.

All at once, Gavroche, pushing his cart, just as he was going to turn out of the Rue des Vieilles Haudriettes, found himself face to face with a uniform, a shako, a plume, and a musket.

For the second time, he stopped short.

'Hold on,' said he, 'that's him. Good morning, public order.'

Gavroche's astonishments were short and quickly thawed.

'Where are you going, vagabond?' cried the sergeant.

'Citizen,' said Gavroche, 'I haven't called you bourgeois yet. What do you insult me for?'

'Where are you going, rascal?'

'Monsieur,' resumed Gavroche, 'may have been a man of wit yesterday, but you were discharged this morning.'

'I want to know where you are going, scoundrel?'

Gavroche answered.

'You talk genteelly. Really, nobody would guess your age. You ought to sell all your hairs at a hundred francs apiece. That would make you five hundred francs.'

'Where are you going? where are you going? where are you going, bandit?

Gavroche replied:

'Those are naughty words. The first time anybody gives you a suck, they should wipe your mouth better.'

The sergeant crossed his bayonet.

'Will you tell me where you are going, at last, wretch?'

'My general,' said Gavroche, 'I am going after the doctor for my wife, who is put to bed.'

'To arms!' cried the sergeant.

To save yourself by means of that which has ruined you is the masterpiece of great men; Gavroche measured the entire situation at a glance. It was the cart which had compromised him, it was for the cart to protect him.

At the moment the sergeant was about to rush upon Gavroche the cart became a projectile, and, hurled with all the *gamin*'s might, ran against him furiously, and the sergeant, struck full in the stomach, fell backward into the gutter while his musket went off in the air. At the sergeant's cry, the men of the post had rushed out pell-mell; the sound of the musket produced a general discharge at random, after which they reloaded and began again.

This musketry at blindman's buff lasted a full quarter of an hour, and killed several squares of glass.

Meanwhile Gavroche, who had run back desperately, stopped five or six streets off, and sat down breathless upon the block at the corner of the Enfants Rouges.

He listened attentively.

After breathing a few moments, he turned in the direction in which the firing was raging, raised his left hand to the level of his nose, and threw it forward three times, striking the back of his head with his right hand at the same time: a sovereign gesture into which the Parisian *gamin* has condensed French irony, and which is evidently effective, since it has lasted already for a half century.

This cheerfulness was marred by a bitter reflection:

'Yes,' said he, 'I grin, I twist myself, I run over with joy; but I am losing my way, I shall have to make a detour. If I only get to the barricade in time.

Thereupon, he resumed his course.

And, while yet running:

'Ah yes, where was I?' said he.

He began again to sing his song, as he plunged rapidly through the streets, and this receded into the darkness:

Mais il reste encor des bastilles,
Et je vais mettre le holà
Dans l'ordre public que voilà.
    Où vont les belles filles,
        Lon la.

Quelqu'un vent-il jouer aux quilles?
Tout l'ancien monde s'écroula
Quand la grosse boule roula.
    Où vont, etc.

Vieux bon peuple, a coups de béquilles,
Cassons ce Louvre où s'étala
La monarchie en falbala.
    Où vont, etc.

Nous en avons forcé les grilles,
Le roi Charles-Dix ce jour-là
Tenait mal et se décolla.
    Où vont, etc.

The taking up of arms at the post was not without result. The cart was conquered, the drunkard was taken prisoner. One was put on the wood-pile; the other was afterwards tried before a court-martial, as an accomplice. The public ministry of the time availed itself of this circumstance to show its indefatigable zeal for the defence of society.

Gavroche's adventure, preserved among the traditions of the quarter of the Temple, is one of the most terrible reminiscences of the old bourgeois of the Marais, and is entitled in their memory: Nocturnal attack on the post of the Imprimerie Royale.

PART FIVE: JEAN VALJEAN

BOOK I: WAR BETWEEN FOUR WALLS

1. *The Charybdis of the Faubourg Saint Antoine and the Scylla of the Faubourg du Temple*

The two most memorable barricades which the observer of social diseases might mention do not belong to the period in which the action of this book is placed. These two barricades, symbols both, under two different aspects, of a terrible situation, rose from the earth at the time of the fatal insurrection of June, 1848, the grandest street war which history has seen.

It sometimes happens that, even against principles, even against liberty, equality, and fraternity, even against universal suffrage, even against the government of all by all, from the depths of its anguish, of its discouragements, of its privations, of its fevers, of its distresses, of its miasmas, of its ignorance, of its darkness, that great madman, the rabble, protests, and the populace gives battle to the people.

The vagabonds attack the common right; the ochlocracy rises against the demos.

Those are mournful days; for there is always a certain amount of right even in this madness, there is suicide in this duel, and these words, which are intended for insults, vagabonds, rabble, ochlocracy, populace, indicate, alas! rather the fault of those who reign than the fault of those who suffer; rather the fault of the privileged than the fault of the outcasts.

As for us, we never pronounce these words save with sorrow and with respect, for when philosophy fathoms the facts to which they correspond, it often finds in them many grandeurs among the miseries. Athens was an ochlocracy; the vagabonds made Holland; the populace more than once saved Rome; and the rabble followed Jesus Christ.

There is no thinker who has not sometimes contemplated the nether magnificences.

It was of this rabble, doubtless, that St Jerome thought, and of all those poor people, and of all those vagabonds, and of all those wretches, whence sprang the apostles and the martyrs, when he uttered those mysterious words: *Fex urbis, lex orbis.*

The exasperations of this multitude which suffers and which bleeds, its violences in misconstruction of the principles which are its life, its forcible resistance to the law, are popular *coups d'état,* and must be repressed. The honest man devotes himself to it, and, for very love for that multitude, he battles against it. But how excusable he feels it, even while opposing it; how he venerates it, even while resisting it! It is one of those rare moments when, in doing what we have to do, we feel something which disconcerts and which almost dissuades from going further; we persist, we are compelled to; but the conscience, though satisfied, is sad, and the performance of the duty is marred by an oppression of heart.

June, 1848, was, let us hasten to say, a thing apart, and almost impossible to class in the philosophy of history. All that we have just said must be set aside when we consider that extraordinary *émeute* in which was felt the sacred anxiety of labour demanding its rights. It must be put down, and that was duty, for it attacked the republic. But, at bottom, what was June 1848? A revolt of the people against itself.

When the subject is not lost sight of, there is no digression; let us then be permitted for a moment to arrest the reader's attention upon the two absolutely unique barricades of which we have just spoken, and which characterised that insurrection.

One obstructed the entrance to the Faubourg Saint Antoine; the other defended the approaches of the Faubourg du Temple; those before whom arose, under the bright blue sky of June, these two frightful masterpieces of civil war, will never forget them.

The barricade Saint Antoine was monstrous; it was three storeys high and seven hundred feet long. It barred from one corner to the other the vast mouth of the Faubourg, that is to say, three streets; ravined, jagged, notched, abrupt, indented with an immense rent, buttressed with mounds which were themselves bastions, pushing out capes here and there, strongly supported by the two great promontories of houses of the Faubourg, it rose like a cyclopean embankment at the foot of the terrible square which saw the 14th of July. Nineteen barricades stood at intervals along the streets in the rear of this mother barricade. Merely from seeing it, you felt in the Faubourg the immense agonising suffering which had reached that extreme moment when distress rushes into catastrophe. Of what was this barricade made? Of the ruins of three six-storey houses, torn down for the purpose, said some. Of the prodigy of all passions, said others. It had the woeful aspect of all the works of hatred: Ruin. You might say: who built that? You might also say; who destroyed that? It was the improvisation of ebullition. Here! that door! that grating! that shed! that casement! that broken furnace! that cracked pot! Bring all! throw on all! push, roll, dig, dismantle. overturn, tear down all! It was the collaboration of the pavement, the pebble, the timber, the iron bar, the chip, the broken square, the stripped chair, the cabbage stump, the scrap, the rag, and the malediction. It was great and it was little. It was the bottomless pit parodied upon the spot by chaos come again. The mass with the atom; the side wall thrown down and the broken dish; a menacing fraternisation of all rubbish. Sisyphus had cast in his rock and Job his potsherd. Upon the whole, terrible. It was the acropolis of the ragamuffins. Carts overturned roughened the slope; an immense dray was displayed there, crosswise, the axle pointing to the sky, and seemed a scar upon that tumultuous façade; an omnibus, cheerily hoisted by main strength to the very top of the pile, as if the architects of that savagery would add sauciness to terror, presented its unharnessed pole to unknown horses of the air. This gigantic mass, the alluvium of *émeute*, brought before the mind an Ossa upon Pelion of all the revolutions; '93 upon '89, the 9th Thermidor upon the 10th of August, the 18th Brumaire upon the 21st of January, Vendémiaire upon Prairial, 1848 upon 1830. The place deserved the pains, and that barricade was worthy to appear on the very spot where the Bastille had disappeared. Were the ocean to make dykes, it would build them thus. The fury of the flood was imprinted upon that misshapen obstruction. What flood? The multitude. You would have thought you saw uproar petrified. You would have thought you heard, upon that barricade, as if there they had been upon their hive, the humming of the enormous black bees of progress by force. Was it a thicket? was it a Bacchanal? was it a fortress? Dizziness seemed to have built it by flappings of its wing. There was something of the cloaca in this redoubt, and something of Olympus in this jumble. You saw there, in a chaos full of despair, rafters from roofs, patches from garrets with their wall paper, window sashes with all their glass planted in the rubbish, awaiting artillery, chimneys torn down, wardrobes, tables, benches, a howling topsy-turvy, and those thousand beggarly things, the refuse even of the mendicant, which contain at once fury and nothingness. One would have said that it was the tatters of a people, tatters of wood, of iron, of bronze, of stone, and that the Faubourg Saint Antoine had swept them there to its door by one colossal sweep of the broom, making of its misery its barricade. Logs shaped like chopping blocks, dislocated chains, wooden frames with brackets having the form of gibbets, wheels projecting horizontally from the rubbish, amalgamated with this edifice of anarchy the forbidding form of the old tortures suffered by the people. The barricade Saint Antoine made a weapon of everything; all that civil war can throw at the head of society came from it; it was not battle, it was paroxysm; the carbines which defended that stronghold, among which were some blunderbusses, scattered bits of delftware, knucklebones, coat buttons, even table castors, dangerous projectiles on account of the copper. This barricade was furious; it threw up to the clouds an inexpressible clamour; at certain moments, defying the army, it covered itself with multitude and with tempest; a mob of flaming heads crowned it; a swarming filled it; its crest was thorny with muskets, with swords, with clubs, with axes, with pikes, and with bayonets; a huge red flag fluttered in the wind; there were heard cries of command, songs of attack, the roll of the drum, the sobs of woman, and the dark wild laughter of the starving. It was huge and living; and, as from the back of an electric beast, there came from it a crackling of thunders. The spirit of revolution covered with its cloud that summit whereon growled this voice of the people which is like the voice of God; a strange majesty emanated from that titanic hodful of refuse. It was a garbage heap, and it was Sinaï.

As we have before said, it attacked in the name of the Revolution, what? the Revolution. This barricade, chance, disorder, bewilderment, misunderstanding, the unknown, had opposed to it the Constituent Assembly, the sovereignty of the people, universal suffrage, the nation, the republic; and it was the Carmagnole defying the Marseillaise.

An insane, but heroic defiance, for this old Faubourg is a hero.

The Faubourg and its redoubt lent each other aid. The Faubourg put its shoulder to the redoubt, the redoubt braced itself upon the Faubourg. The huge barricade extended like a cliff upon which broke the strategy of the generals of Africa. Its caverns, its excrescences, its warts, its humps, made grimaces, so to speak, and sneered beneath the smoke. Grape vanished there in the shapeless; shells sank in, were swallowed up, were engulfed; bullets succeeded only in boring holes; of what use to cannonade chaos? And regiments, accustomed to the most savage sights of war, looked with anxious eye upon this kind of wild beast redoubt, by its bristling, a wild boar, and by its enormity, a mountain.

A mile from there, at the corner of the Rue du Temple which runs into the boulevard near the Château d'Eau, if you advanced your head boldly beyond the point formed by the front of the Dallemagne warehouse, you perceived in the distance, beyond the canal, in the street which mounts the slopes of Belleville, at the culminating point of the hill, a strange wall reaching the second storey of the house fronts, a sort of hyphen between the houses on the right and the houses on the left, as if the street had folded back its highest wall, to shut itself abruptly in. This wall was built of paving-stones. It was straight, correct, cold, perpendicular, levelled with the square, built by the line, aligned by the plummet. Cement doubtless there was none, but as in certain Roman walls, that did not weaken its rigid architecture. From its height its depth could be guessed. The entablature was mathematically parallel to the base. Here and there could be distinguished, on the grey surface, loopholes almost invisible, which resembled black threads. These loopholes were separated from each other by equal intervals. The street was deserted as far as could be seen. Every window and every door closed. In the background rose this obstruction, which made of the street a cul-de-sac; an immovable and quiet wall; nobody could be seen, nothing could be heard; not a cry, not a sound, not a breath. A sepulchre.

The dazzling June sun flooded this terrible thing with light.

This was the barricade of the Faubourg du Temple.

As soon as the ground was reached and it was seen, it was impossible, even for the boldest, not to become thoughtful before this mysterious apparition. It was fitted, dovetailed, imbricated, rectilinear, symmetrical, and deathly. There was in it science and darkness. You felt that the chief of that barricade was a geometer or a spectre. You beheld it and you spoke low.

From time to time, if anybody, soldier, officer, or representative of the people, ventured to cross the solitary street, a sharp and low whistling was heard, and the passer fell wounded or dead, or, if he escaped, a ball was seen to bury itself in some closed shutter, in a space between the stores, in the plastering of a wall. Sometimes a large ball. For the men of the barricade had made of two pieces of cast-iron gas-pipe, stopped at one end with oakum and fire-clay, two small guns. No useless expenditure of powder. Almost every shot told. There were a few corpses here and there, and pools of blood upon the pavement. I recollect a white butterfly flying back and forth in the street. Summer does not abdicate.

In the vicinity, the pavements of the *porte-cochères* were covered with wounded.

You felt yourself beneath the eye of somebody whom you did not see, and that the whole length of the street was held under aim.

Massed behind the sort of saddleback which the narrow bridge over the canal makes at the entrance to the Faubourg du Temple, the soldiers of the attacking column, calm and collected, looked upon this dismal redoubt, this immobility, this impassability, whence death came forth. Some crept on the ground as far as the top of the curve of the bridge, taking care that their shakos did not show over it.

The valiant Colonel Monteynard admired this barricade with a shudder. '*How that is built!*' said he to a representative. '*Not one stone projects beyond another. It is porcelain.*' At that moment a ball broke the cross on his breast, and he fell.

'The cowards!' it was said. 'But let them show themselves! let us see them! they dare not? they hide? The barricade of the Faubourg du Temple, defended by eighty men, attacked by ten thousand, held out three days. On the fourth day, they did as at Zaatcha and at Constantine; they pierced through the houses, they went along the roofs, the barricade was taken. Not one of the eighty cowards thought of flight; all were killed, except the chief, Barthélemy, of whom we shall speak presently.

The barricade St Antoine was the tumult of thunders; the barricade du Temple was silence. There was between these two redoubts the difference between the terrible and the ominous. The one seemed a gaping mouth; the other a mask.

Admitting that the gloomy and gigantic insurrection of June was composed of an anger and an enigma; you felt in the first barricade the dragon, and behind the second the sphinx.

These two fortresses were built by two men, one named Cournet, the other Barthélemy. Cournet made the barricade Saint Antoine; Barthélemy the barricade du Temple. Each was the image of him who built it.

Cournet was a man of tall stature; he had broad shoulders, a red face, a muscular arm, a bold heart, a loyal soul, a sincere and terrible eye. Intrepid, energetic, irascible, stormy, the most cordial of men, the most formidable of warriors. War, conflict, the mêlée, were the air he breathed, and put him in good-humour. He had been a naval officer, and, from his carriage and his voice, you would have guessed that he sprang from the ocean, and that he came from the tempest; he continued the hurricane in battle. Save in genius, there was in Cournet something of Danton, as, save in divinity, there was in Danton something of Hercules.

Barthélemy, thin, puny, pale, taciturn, was a kind of tragic *gamin* who, struck by a *sergent de ville*, watched for him, waited for him, and killed him, and, at seventeen, was sent to the galleys. He came out, and built this barricade.

Later, a terrible thing, at London, both outlaws, Barthélemy killed Cournet. It was a mournful duel. Some time after, caught in the meshes of one of those mysterious fatalities in which passion is mingled, catastrophes in which French justice sees extenuating circumstances, and in which English justice sees only death, Barthélemy was hung. The gloomy social edifice is so constructed, that, thanks to material privation, thanks to moral darkness, this unfortunate being who contained an intelligence, firm certainly, great perhaps, began with the galleys in France, and ended with the gallows in England. Barthélemy, on all occasions, hoisted but one flag; the black flag.

2. *What can be done in the abyss but to talk*

SIXTEEN YEARS tell in the subterranean education of the *émeute*, and June 1848 understood it far better than June 1832. Thus the barricade of the Rue de la Chanvrerie was only a rough draught and an embryo compared with the two colossal barricades which we have just sketched; but, for the period, it was formidable.

The insurgents, under the eye of Enjolras, for Marius no longer looked to anything, turned the night to advantage. The barricade was not only repaired, but made larger. They raised it two feet. Iron bars planted in the paving stones resembled lances in rest. All sorts of rubbish added, and brought from all sides, increased the exterior intricacy. The redoubt was skilfully made over into a wall within and a thicket without.

They rebuilt the stairway of paving-stones, which permitted ascent, as upon a citadel wall,

They put the barricade in order, cleared up the basement room, took the kitchen for a hospital, completed the dressing of the wounds; gathered up the powder scattered over the floor and the tables, cast bullets, made cartridges, scraped lint, distributed the arms of the fallen, cleaned the interior of the redoubt, picked up the fragments, carried away the corpses.

They deposited the dead in a heap in the little Rue Mondétour, of which they were still masters. The pavement was red for a long time at that spot. Among the dead were four National Guards of the banlieue. Enjolras had their uniforms laid aside.

Enjolras advised two hours of sleep. Advice from Enjolras was an order. Still, three or four only profited by it. Feuilly employed these two hours in engraving this inscription on the wall which fronted the wine-shop:

VIVENT LES PEUPLES!

These three words, graven in the stone with a nail, were still legible on that wall in 1848.

The three women took advantage of the night's respite to disappear finally, which made the insurgents breathe more freely.

They found refuge in some neighbouring house.

Most of the wounded could and would still fight. There were, upon a straw mattress and some bunches of straw, in the kitchen now become a hospital, five men severely wounded, two of whom were Municipal Guards. The wounds of the Municipal Guards were dressed first.

Nothing now remained in the basement room but Mabeuf, under his black cloth, and Javert bound to the post.

'This is the dead-room,' said Enjolras.

In the interior of this room, feebly lighted by a candle, at the very end the funereal table being behind the post like a horizontal bar, a sort of large dim cross was produced by Javert standing, and Mabeuf lying.

The pole of the omnibus, although maimed by the musketry, was still high enough for them to hang a flag upon it.

Enjolras, who had this quality of a chief, always to do as he said, fastened the pierced and bloody coat of the slain old man to this pole.

No meals could now be had. There was neither bread nor meat. The fifty men of the barricade, in the sixteen hours that they had been there, had very soon exhausted the meagre provisions of the wine-shop. In a given time, every barricade which holds out, inevitably becomes the raft of le Méduse. They must resign themselves to famine. They were in the early hours of that Spartan day of the 6th of June, when, in the barricade Saint Merry, Jeanne, surrounded by insurgents who were asking for bread, to all those warriors, crying: 'Something to eat!' answered: 'What for? it is three o'clock. At four o'clock we shall be dead.'

As they could eat nothing, Enjolras forbade drinking. He prohibited wine, and put them on allowance of brandy.

They found in the cellar some fifteen bottles, full and hermetically sealed. Enjolras and Combeferre examined them. As they came up Combeferre said: 'It is some of the old stock of Father Hucheloup who began as a grocer.'

'It ought to be genuine wine,' observed Bossuet. 'It is lucky that Grantaire is asleep. If he were on his feet, we should have hard work to save those bottles.' Enjolras, in spite of the murmurs, put his veto upon the fifteen bottles, and in order that no one should touch them, and that they might be as it were consecrated, he had them placed under the table on which Father Mabeuf lay.

About two o'clock in the morning, they took a count. There were left thirty-seven of them.

Day was beginning to dawn. They had just extinguished the torch which had been replaced in its socket of paving-stones. The interior of the barricade, that little court taken in on the street, was drowned in darkness, and seemed, through the dim twilight horror, the deck of a disabled ship. The combatants going back and forth, moved about in it like black forms. Above this frightful nest of shadow, the storeys of the mute houses were lividly outlined; at the very top the wan chimneys appeared. The sky had that charming undecided hue, which is perhaps white, and perhaps blue. Some birds were flying with joyful notes. The tall house which formed the rear of the barricade, being towards the east, had a rosy reflection upon its roof. At the window on the third storey, the morning breeze played with the grey hairs on the dead man's head.

'I am delighted that the torch is extinguished,' said Courfeyrac to Feuilly. 'That torch, startled in the wind, annoyed me. It appeared to be afraid. The light of a torch resembles the wisdom of a coward; it is not clear, because it trembles.'

The dawn awakens minds as well as birds; all were chatting.

Joly, seeing a cat prowling about a water-spout, extracted philosophy therefrom.

'What is the cat?' he exclaimed. 'It is a correction. God, having made the mouse, said: "Hold here, I have made a blunder." And he made the cat. The cat is the erratum of the mouse. The mouse, plus the cat, is the revised and corrected proof of creation.'

Combeferre, surrounded by students and workmen, spoke of the dead, of Jean Prouvaire, of Bahorel, of Mabeuf, and even of Le Cabuc, and of the stern sadness of Enjolras. He said:

'Harmodius and Aristogeiton, Brutus, Chereas, Stephanus, Cromwell, Charlotte Corday, Sand – all, after the blow, had their moment of anguish. Our hearts are so fluctuating, and human life is such a mystery that, even in a civic murder, even in a liberating murder, if there be such, the remorse of having stricken a man surpasses the joy of having served the human race.'

And, such is the course of conversation, a moment afterwards, by a transition from Jean Prouvaire's rhymes, Combeferre was comparing the translators of the Georgics, Raux with Cournand, Cournand with Delille, pointing out the few passages translated by Malfilâtre, particularly the prodigies at the death of Cæsar; and from this word, Cæsar, they came to Brutus.

'Caesar,' said Combeferre, 'fell justly. Cicero was severe upon Caesar, and he was right. This severity is not diatribe. When Zoïlus insults Homer, when Mævius insults Virgil, when Visé insults Molière, when Pope insults Shakespeare, when Fréron insults Voltaire, it is an old law of envy and hatred which is at work; genius attracts insult, great men are always barked at more or less. But Zoïlus and Cicero are two. Cicero is a judge through the soul, even as Brutus is a judge through the sword. I condemn, for my own part, that final justice, the sword; but antiquity admitted it. Cæsar, the violator of the Rubicon, conferring, as coming from himself, the dignities which came from the people, not rising upon the entrance of the senate, acted, as Eutropius says, the part of a king and almost of a tyrant, *regia ac penè tyrannica.* He was a great man; so much the worse, or so much the better; the lesson is the greater. His twenty-three wounds touch me less than the spittle in the face of Jesus Christ. Cæsar was stabbed by senators; Christ was slapped by lackeys. In the greater outrage, we feel the God.'

Bossuet, overlooking the talkers from the top of a heap of paving-stones, exclaimed, carbine in hand:

'O Cydathenæum, O Myrrhinus, O Probalinthe, O graces of Æantides. Oh! who will give me to pronounce the verses of Homer like a Greek of Laurium or of Edapteon?'

3. Light and darkness

ENJOLRAS HAD GONE to make a reconnaissance. He went out by the little Rue Mondétour, creeping along by the houses.

The insurgents, we must say, were full of hope. The manner in which they had repelled the attack during the night, had led them almost to contempt in advance for the attack at daybreak. They awaited it, and smiled at it. They had no more doubt of their success than of their cause. Moreover, help was evidently about to come. They counted on it. With that facility for triumphant prophecy which is a part of the strength of the fighting Frenchman, they divided into three distinct phases the day which was opening: at six o'clock in the morning a regiment, 'which had been laboured with', would come over. At noon, insurrection of all Paris; at sundown, revolution.

They heard the tocsin of Saint Merry, which had not been silent a moment since the evening; a proof that the other barricade, the great one, that of Jeanne, still held out.

All these hopes were communicated from one to another in a sort of cheerful yet terrible whisper, which resembled the buzz of a hive of bees at war.

Enjolras reappeared. He returned from his gloomy eagle's walk in the obscurity without. He listened for a moment to all this joy with folded arms, one hand over his mouth. Then, fresh and rosy in the growing whiteness of the morning, he said:

'The whole army of Paris fights. A third of that army is pressing upon the barricade in which you are. Besides the National Guard, I distinguished the shakos of the Fifth of the line and the colours of the Sixth Legion. You will be attacked in an hour. As for the people, they were boiling yesterday, but this morning they do not stir. Nothing to expect, nothing to hope. No more from a Faubourg than from a regiment. You are abandoned.'

These words fell upon the buzzing of the groups, and wrought the effect which the first drops of the tempest produce upon the swarm. All were dumb. There was a moment of inexpressible silence, when you might have heard the flight of death.

This moment was short.

A voice, from the most obscure depths of the groups, cried to Enjolras:

'So be it. Let us make the barricade twenty feet high, and let us all stand by it. Citizens, let us offer the protest of corpses. Let us show that, if the people abandon the republicans, the republicans do not abandon the people.'

These words relieved the minds of all from the painful cloud of personal anxieties. They were greeted by an enthusiastic acclamation,

The name of the man who thus spoke was never known; it was some obscure blouse-wearer, an unknown, a forgotten man, a passing hero, that great anonymous always found in human crises and in social births, who, at the proper instant, speaks the decisive word supremely, and who vanishes into the darkness after having for a moment represented, in the light of a flash, the people and God.

This inexorable resolution so filled the air of June 6, 1832, that, almost at the same hour, in the barricade of Saint Merry, the insurgents raised this shout which was proved on the trial, and which has become historical: 'Let them come to our aid or let them not come, what matter? Let us die here to the last man.'

As we see, the two barricades, although essentially isolated, communicated.

4. Five less, one more

AFTER THE MAN of the people, who decreed 'the protest of corpses,' had spoken and given the formula of the common soul, from all lips arose a strangely satisfied and terrible cry, funereal in meaning and triumphant in tone: 'Long live death! Let us all stay!'

'Why all?' said Enjolras.

'All! all!'

Enjolras resumed:

'The position is good, the barricade is fine. Thirty men are enough. Why sacrifice forty?'

They replied:

'Because nobody wants to go away.'

'Citizens,' cried Enjolras, and there was in his voice almost an angry tremor, 'the republic is not rich enough in men to incur useless expenditures. Vainglory is a squandering. If it is the duty of some to go away, that duty should be performed as well as any other.'

Enjolras, the man of principle, had over his co-religionists that sort of omnipotence which emanates from the absolute. Still, notwithstanding this omnipotence, there was a murmur.

Chief to his finger-ends, Enjolras, seeing that they murmured, insisted. He resumed haughtily:

'Let those who fear to be one of but thirty, say so.'

The murmurs redoubled.

'Besides,' observed a voice from one of the groups, 'to go away is easily said. The barricade is hemmed in.'

'Not towards the markets,' said Enjolras. 'The Rue Mondétour is open, and by the Rue des Prêcheurs one can reach the Marché des Innocents.'

'And there,' put in another voice from the group, 'he will be taken. He will fall upon some grand guard of the line or the banlieue. They will see a man going by in a cap and blouse. "Where do you come from, fellow? you belong to the barricade, don't you?" And they look at your hands. You smell of powder. Shot.'

Enjolras, without answering, touched Combeferre's shoulder, and they both went into the basement room.

They came back a moment afterwards. Enjolras held out in his hands the four uniforms which he had reserved. Combeferre followed him, bringing the cross belts and shakos.

'With this uniform,' said Enjolras, 'you can mingle with the ranks and escape. Here are enough for four.'

And he threw the four uniforms upon the unpaved ground.

No wavering in the stoical auditory. Combeferre spoke:

'Come,' said he, 'we must have a little pity. Do you know what the question is now? It is a question of women. Let us see. Are there any wives, yes or no? are there any children, yes or no? Are there, yes or no, any mothers, who rock the cradle with their foot and who have heaps of little ones about them? Let him among you who has never seen the breast of a nursing-woman hold up his hand. Ah! you wish to die, I wish it also, I, who am speaking to you, but I do not wish to feel the ghosts of women wringing their hands about me. Die, so be it, but do not make others die. Suicides like those which will be accomplished here are sublime; but suicide is strict, and can have no extension; and as soon as it touches those next you, the name of suicide is murder. Think of the little flaxen heads, and think of the white hairs. Listen, but a moment ago, Enjolras, he just told me of it, saw at the corner of the Rue du Cygne a lighted casement, a candle in a poor window, in the fifth storey, and on the glass the quivering shadow of the head of an old woman who appeared to have passed the night in watching and to be still waiting. She is perhaps the mother of one of you. Well, let that man go away, and let him hasten to say to his mother: "Mother, here I am!" Let him feel at ease, the work here will be done just as well. When a man supports his relatives by his labour, he has no right to sacrifice himself. That is deserting his family. And those who have daughters, and those who have sisters! Do you think of it? You get killed, here you are dead, very well, and tomorrow? Young girls who have no bread, that is terrible. Man begs, woman sells. Ah! those charming beings, so graceful and so sweet, who have bonnets of flowers, who fill the house with chastity, who sing, who prattle, who are like a living perfume, who prove the existence of angels in heaven by the purity of maidens on the earth, that Jeanne, that Lise, that Mimi, those adorable and noble creatures who are your benediction and your pride, oh, God, they will be hungry! What would you have me say to you? There is a market for human flesh; and it is not with your shadowy hands, fluttering about them, that you can prevent them from entering it! Think of the street, think of the pavement covered with passers, think of the shops before which women walk to and fro with bare shoulders, through the mud. Those women also have been pure. Think of your sisters, those who have them. Misery, prostitution, the *sergents de ville*, Saint Lazare, such will be the fall of those delicate beautiful girls, those fragile wonders of modesty, grace, and beauty, fresher than the lilacs of the month of May. Ah! you are killed! ah! you are no longer with them! Very well; you desired to deliver the people from monarchy, you give your maidens to the police. Friends, beware, have compassion. Women, hapless women, are not in the habit of reflecting much. We boast that women have not received the education of men, we prevent them from reading, we prevent them from thinking, we prevent them from interesting themselves in politics; will you prevent them from going tonight to the Morgue and identifying your corpses? Come, those who have families must be good fellows and give us a grasp of the hand and go away, and leave us to the business here all alone. I know well that it requires courage to go, it is difficult; but the more difficult it is, the more praiseworthy. You say: I have a musket, I am at the barricade, come the worst, I stay. Come the worst, that is very soon said. My friends, there is a morrow; you will not be here on that morrow, but your families will. And what suffering! See, a pretty, healthy child that has cheeks like an apple, that babbles, that prattles, that jabbers, that laughs, that smells sweet under the kiss, do you know what becomes of him when he is abandoned? I saw one, very small, no taller than that. His father was dead. Some poor people had taken him in from charity, but they had no bread for themselves. The child was always hungry. It was winter. He did not cry. They saw him go up to the stove where there was never any fire, and the pipe of which, you know, was plastered with yellow clay. The child picked off some of that clay with his little fingers and ate it. His breathing was hard, his face livid, his legs soft, his belly big. He said nothing. They spoke to him, he did not answer. He died. He was brought to the Necker Hospital to die, where I saw him. I was surgeon at that hospital. Now, if there are any fathers among you, fathers whose delight it is to take a walk on Sunday holding in their great strong hand the little hand of their child, let each of those fathers imagine that that child is his own. That poor bird, I remember him well, it seems to me that I see him now, when he lay naked upon the dissecting table, his ribs projecting under his skin like graves under the grass of a churchyard. We found a kind of mud in his stomach. There were ashes in his teeth. Come, let us search with our conscience and take counsel with our hearts. Statistics show that the mortality of abandoned children is fifty-five per cent. I repeat it, it is a question of wives, it is a question of mothers, it is a question of young girls, it is a question of babes. Do I speak to you for yourselves? We know very well what you are; we know very well that you are all brave, good heavens! we know very well that your souls are filled with joy and glory at giving your life for the great cause; we know very well that you feel that you are elected to die usefully and magnificently, and that each of you clings to his share of the triumph. Well and good. But you are not alone in this world. There are other beings of whom we must think. We must not be selfish.'

All bowed their heads with a gloomy air.

Strange contradictions of the human heart in its most sublime moments! Combeferre, who spoke thus, was not an orphan. He remembered the mothers of others, and he forgot his own. He was going to be killed. He was 'selfish.'

Marius, fasting, feverish, successively driven from every hope, stranded upon grief, most dismal of shipwrecks, saturated with violent emotions and feeling the end approach, was sinking deeper and deeper into that visionary stupor which always precedes the fatal hour when voluntarily accepted.

A physiologist might have studied in him the growing symptoms of that febrile absorption known and classified by science, and which is to suffering what ecstasy is to pleasure. Despair also has its ecstasy. Marius had reached that point. He witnessed it all as from without; as we have said, the things which were occurring before him, seemed afar off; he perceived the whole, but did not distinguish the details. He saw the comers and goers through a bewildering glare. He heard the voices speak as from the depth of an abyss.

Still this moved him. There was one point in this scene which pierced through to him, and which woke him. He had now but one idea, to die, and he would not be diverted from it; but he thought, in his funereal somnambulism, that while destroying oneself it is not forbidden to save another.

He raised his voice:

'Enjolras and Combeferre are right,' said he; 'no useless sacrifice. I add my voice to theirs, and we must hasten. Combeferre has given the criteria. There are among you some who have families, mothers, sisters, wives, children. Let those leave the ranks.'

Nobody stirred.

'Married men and supports of families, out of the ranks!' repeated Marius.

His authority was great. Enjolras was indeed the chief of the barricade, but Marius was its saviour.

'I order it,' cried Enjolras.

'I beseech you,' said Marius.

Then, roused by the words of Combeferre, shaken by the order of Enjolras, moved by the prayer of Marius, those heroic men began to inform against each other. 'That is true,' said a young man to a middle-aged man. 'You are the father of a family. Go away.' 'It is you rather,' answered the man, 'you have two sisters whom you support.' And an unparalleled conflict broke out. It was as to which should not allow himself to be laid at the door of the tomb.

'Make haste,' said Courfeyrac, 'in a quarter of an hour it will be too late.'

'Citizens,' continued Enjolras, 'this is the republic, and universal suffrage reigns. Designate yourselves those who ought to go.'

They obeyed. In a few minutes five were unanimously designated and left the ranks.

'There are five!' exclaimed Marius.

There were only four uniforms.

'Well,' resumed the five, 'one must stay.'

And it was who should stay, and who should find reasons why the others should not stay. The generous quarrel recommenced.

'You, you have a wife who loves you.' 'As for you, you have your old mother.' 'You have neither father nor mother, what will become of your three little brothers?' 'You are the father of five children.' 'You have a right to live, you are seventeen, it is too soon.'

These grand revolutionary barricades were rendezvous of heroisms. The improbable there was natural. These men were not astonished at each other.

'Be quick,' repeated Courfeyrac.

Somebody cried out from the group, to Marius:

'Designate yourself, which must stay.'

'Yes,' said the five, 'choose. We will obey you.'

Marius now believed no emotion possible. Still at this idea: to select a man for death, all his blood flowed back towards his heart. He would have turned pale if he could have been paler.

He advanced towards the five, who smiled upon him, and each, his eye full of that grand flame which we see in the depth of history over the Thermopylæs, cried to him:

'Me! me! me!'

And Marius, in a stupor, counted them; there were still five! Then his eyes fell upon the four uniforms.

At this moment a fifth uniform dropped, as if from heaven, upon the four others.

The fifth man was saved.

Marius raised his eyes and saw M. Fauchelevent.

Jean Valjean had just entered the barricade.

Whether by information obtained, or by instinct, or by chance, he came by the little Rue Mondétour. Thanks to his National Guard dress, he had passed easily.

The sentry placed by the insurgents in the Rue Mondétour, had not given the signal of alarm for a single National Guard. He permitted him to get into the street, saying to himself: 'He is a reinforcement, probably, and at the very worst a prisoner.' The moment was too serious for the sentinel to be diverted from his duty and his post of observation.

At the moment Jean Valjean entered the redoubt, nobody had noticed him, all eyes being fixed upon the five chosen ones and upon the four uniforms. Jean Valjean, himself, saw and understood, and, silently, he stripped off his coat, and threw it upon the pile with the others.

The commotion was indescribable.

'Who is this man?' asked Bossuet.

'He is,' answered Combeferre, 'a man who saves others.'

Marius added in a grave voice:

'I know him.'

This assurance was enough for all.

Enjolras turned towards Jean Valjean:

'Citizen, you are welcome.'

And he added:

'You know that we are going to die.'

Jean Valjean, without answering, helped the insurgent whom he saved to put on his uniform.

5. What horizon is visible from the top of the barricade

THE SITUATION OF ALL, in this hour of death and in this inexorable place, found its resultant and summit in the supreme melancholy of Enjolras.

Enjolras had within himself the plenitude of revolution; he was incomplete notwithstanding, as much as the absolute can be; he clung too much to Saint Just, and not enough to Anacharsis Clootz; still his mind, in the society of the Friends of the ABC, had at last received a certain polarisation from the ideas of Combeferre; for some time, he had been leaving little by little the narrow form of dogma, and allowing himself to tread the broad paths of progress, and he had come to accept, as its definitive and magnificent evolution, the transformation of the great French Republic into the immense human republic. As to the immediate means, in a condition of violence, he wished them to be violent; in that he had not varied; and he was still of that epic and formidable school, which is summed up in this word: 'Ninety-three.

Enjolras was standing on the paving-stone steps, his elbow upon the muzzle of his carbine. He was thinking; he started, as at the passing of a gust; places where death is have such tripodal effects. There came from his eyes, full of the interior sight, a kind of stifled fire. Suddenly he raised his head, his fair hair waved backwards like that of the angel upon his sombre car of stars, it was the mane of a startled lion flaming with a halo, and Enjolras exclaimed:

'Citizens, do you picture to yourselves the future? The streets of the cities flooded with light, green branches upon the thresholds, the nations sisters, men just, the old men blessing the children, the past loving the present, thinkers in full liberty, believers in full equality, for religion the heavens, God priest direct, human conscience become the altar, no more hatred, the fraternity of the workshop and the school, for reward and for penalty notoriety, to all, labour, for all, law, over all, peace, no more bloodshed, no more war, mothers happy! To subdue matter is the first step; to realise the ideal is the second. Reflect upon what progress has already done. Once the early human races looked with terror upon the hydra which blew upon the waters, the dragon which vomited fire, the griffin, monster of the air, which flew with the wings of an eagle and the claws of a tiger; fearful animals which were above man. Man, however, has laid his snares, the sacred snares of intelligence, and has at last caught the monsters. We have tamed the hydra, and he is called the steamer; we have tamed the dragon, and he is called the locomotive; we are on the point of taming the griffin, we have him already, and he is called the balloon. The day when this promethean work shall be finished, and when man shall have definitively harnessed to his will the triple chimæra of the ancients, the hydra, the dragon, and the griffin, he will be master of the water, the fire, and the air, and he will be to the rest of the animated creation what the ancient gods were formerly to him. Courage, and forward! Citizens, whither are we tending? To science made government, to the force of things, recognised as the only public force, to the natural law having its sanction and its penalty in itself and promulgated by its self-evidence, to a dawn of truth, corresponding with the dawn of the day. We are tending towards the union of the peoples; we are tending towards the unity of man. No more fictions; no more parasites. The real governed by the true, such is the aim. Civilisation will hold its courts on the summit of Europe, and later at the centre of the continents, in a grand parliament of intelligence. Something like this has been seen already. The Amphictyons had two sessions a year, one at Delphi, place of the gods, the other at Thermopylæ, place of the heroes. Europe will have her Amphictyons; the globe will have its Amphictyons. France bears within her the sublime future. This is the gestation of the nineteenth century. That which was sketched by Greece is worth being finished by France. Listen to me, then, Feuilly, valiant working-man, man of the people, man of the peoples. I venerate thee. Yes, thou seest clearly future ages; yes, thou art right. Thou hadst neither father nor mother, Feuilly; thou hast adopted humanity for thy mother, and the right for thy father. Thou art going to die here; that is, to triumph. Citizens, whatever may happen today, through our defeat as well as through our victory, we are going to effect a revolution. Just as conflagrations light up the whole city, revolutions light up the whole human race. And what revolution shall we effect? I have just said, the revolution of the True. From the political point of view, there is but one single principle: the sovereignty of man over himself. This sovereignty of myself over myself is called Liberty. Where two or several of these sovereignties associate the state begins. But in this association there is no abdication. Each sovereignty gives up a certain portion of itself to form the common right. That portion is the same for all. This identity of concession which each makes to all, is Equality. The common right is nothing more nor less than the protection of all radiating upon the right of each. This protection of all over each is called Fraternity. The point of intersection of all these aggregated sovereignties is called Society. This intersection being a junction, this point is a knot. Hence what is called the social tie. Some say social contract; which is the same thing, the word contract being etymologically formed with the idea of tie.

Let us understand each other in regard to equality; for, if liberty is the summit, equality is the base. Equality, citizens, is not all vegetation on a level, a society of big spears of grass and little oaks; a neighbourhood of jealousies emasculating each other; it is, civilly, all aptitudes having equal opportunity; politically, all votes having equal weight; religiously, all consciences having equal rights. Equality has an organ: gratuitous and obligatory instruction. The right to the alphabet, we must begin by that. The primary school obligatory upon all, the higher school offered to all, such is the law. From the identical school springs equal society. Yes, instruction! Light! Light! all comes from light, and all returns to it. Citizens, the nineteenth century is grand, but the twentieth century will be happy. Then there will be nothing more like old history. Men will no longer have to fear, as now, a conquest, an invasion, a usurpation, a rivalry of nations with the armed hand, an interruption of civilisation depending on a marriage of kings, a birth in the hereditary tyrannies, a partition of the peoples by a Congress, a dismemberment by the downfall of a dynasty, a combat of two religions meeting head to head, like two goats of darkness, upon the bridge of the infinite; they will no longer have to fear famine, speculation, prostitution from distress, misery from lack of work, and the scaffold, and the sword, and the battle, and all the brigandages of chance in the forest of events. We might almost say: there will be no events more. Men will be happy. The human race will fulfil its law as the terrestrial globe fulfils its; harmony will be re-established between the soul and the star; the soul will gravitate about the truth like the star about the light. Friends, the hour in which we live, and in which I speak to you, is a gloomy hour, but of such is the terrible price of the future. Revolution is a toll-gate. Oh! the human race shall be delivered, uplifted, and consoled! We affirm it on this barricade. Whence shall arise the shout of love, if it be not from the summit of sacrifice? O my brothers, here is the place of junction between those who think and those who suffer; this barricade is made neither of paving-stones, nor of timbers, nor of iron; it is made of two mounds, a mound of ideas and a mound of sorrows. Misery here encounters the ideal. Here day embraces night, and says: I will die with thee and thou shalt be born again with me. From the pressure of all desolations faith gushes forth. Sufferings bring their agony here, and ideas their immortality. This agony and this immortality are to mingle and compose our death. Brothers, he who dies here dies in the radiance of the future, and we are entering a grave illuminated by the dawn.'

Enjolras broke off rather than ceased, his lips moved noiselessly, as if he were continuing to speak to himself, and they looked at him with attention, endeavouring still to hear. There was no applause; but they whispered for a long time. Speech being breath, the rustling of intellects resembles the rustling of leaves.

6. Marius haggard, Javert laconic

LET US TELL what was passing in Marius' thoughts.

Remember the condition of his mind. As we have just mentioned, all was now to him a dream. His understanding was troubled. Marius, we must insist, was under the shadow of the great black wings which open above the dying. He felt that he had entered the tomb, it seemed to him that he was already on the other side of the wall, and he no longer saw the faces of the living save with the eyes of one dead.

How came M. Fauchelevent there? Why was he there? What did he come to do? Marius put none of these questions. Besides, our despair having this peculiarity that it enwraps others as well as ourselves, it seemed logical to him that everybody should come to die.

Only he thought of Cosette with an oppression of the heart.

Moreover M. Fauchelevent did not speak to him, did not look at him, and had not even the appearance of hearing him when Marius said: I know him.

As for Marius, this attitude of M. Fauchelevent was a relief to him, and if we might employ such a word for such impressions, we should say, pleased him. He had always felt it absolutely impossible to address a word to that enigmatic man, who to him was at once equivocal and imposing. It was also a very long time since he had seen him; which, with Marius' timid and reserved nature, increased the impossibility still more.

The five men designated went out of the barricade by the little Rue Mondétour; they resembled National Guards perfectly; one of them went away weeping. Before starting, they embraced those who remained.

When the five men sent away into life had gone, Enjolras thought of the one condemned to death. He went into the basement room. Javert, tied to the pillar, was thinking.

'Do you need anything?' Enjolras asked him.

Javert answered:

'When shall you kill me?'

'Wait. We need all our cartridges at present.'

'Then, give me a drink,' said Javert.

Enjolras presented him with a glass of water himself, and, as Javert was bound, he helped him to drink.

'Is that all?' resumed Enjolras.

'I am uncomfortable at this post,' answered Javert. 'It was not affectionate to leave me to pass the night here. Tie me as you please, but you can surely lay me on a table. Like the other.'

And with a motion of his head he indicated M. Mabeuf's body.

There was, it will be remembered, at the back of the room, a long wide table, upon which they had cast balls and made cartridges. All the cartridges being made and all the powder used up, this table was free.

At Enjolras' order, four insurgents untied Javert from the post. While they were untying him, a fifth held a bayonet to his breast. They left his hands tied behind his back, they put a small yet strong whipcord about his feet, which permitted him to take fifteen-inch steps like those who are mounting the scaffold, and they made him walk to the table at the back of the room, on which they extended him, tightly bound by the middle of his body.

For greater security, by means of a rope fixed to his neck, they added to the system of bonds which rendered all escape impossible, that species of ligature, called in the prisons a martingale, which, starting from the back of the neck, divides over the stomach, and is fastened to the hands after passing between the legs.

While they were binding Javert, a man, on the threshold of the door, gazed at him with singular attention. The shade which this man produced made Javert turn his head. He raised his eyes and recognised Jean Valjean. He did not even start, he haughtily dropped his eyelids, and merely said: 'It is very natural.'

7. *The situation grows serious*

It was growing light rapidly. But not a window was opened, not a door stood ajar; it was the dawn, not the hour of awakening. The extremity of the Rue de la Chanvrerie opposite the barricade had been evacuated by the troops, as we have said; it seemed free, and lay open for wayfarers with an ominous tranquillity. The Rue Saint Denis was as silent as the avenue of the Sphinxes at Thebes. Not a living being at the corners, which were whitening in a reflection of the sun. Nothing is so dismal as this brightness of deserted streets.

They saw nothing, but they heard. A mysterious movement was taking place at some distance. It was evident that the critical moment was at hand. As in the evening the sentries were driven in; but this time all.

The barricade was stronger than at the time of the first attack. Since the departure of the five, it had been raised still higher.

On the report of the sentry who had been observing the region of the markets, Enjolras, for fear of a surprise from the rear, formed an important resolution. He had barricaded the little passage of the Rue Mondétour, which till then had been open. For this purpose they unpaved the length of a few more houses. In this way, the barricade, walled in upon three streets, in front upon the Rue de la Chanvrerie, at the left upon the Rue du Cygne and la Petite Truanderie, at the right upon the Rue Mondétour, was really almost impregnable; it is true that they were fatally shut in. It had three fronts, but no longer an outlet. 'A fortress, but mousetrap,' said Courfeyrac with a laugh.

Enjolras had piled up near the door of the wine-shop some thirty paving-stones, 'torn up uselessly', said Bossuet.

The silence was now so profound on the side from which the attack must come, that Enjolras made each man resume his post for combat.

A ration of brandy was distributed to all.

Nothing is more singular than a barricade which is preparing for an assault. Each man chooses his place, as at a play. They lean on their sides, their elbows, their shoulders. There are some who make themselves stalls with paving-stones. There is a corner of a wall which is annoying, they move away from it; here is a redan which may be a protection, they take shelter in it. The left-handed are precious; they take places which are inconvenient for the rest. Many make arrangements to fight sitting down. They wish to be at their ease in killing, and comfortable in dying. In the deadly war of June 1848, an insurgent, who had a terrible aim, and who fought from the top of a terrace, on a roof, had a Voltaire armchair carried up there; a charge of grape found him in it.

As soon as the chief has ordered the decks cleared for the fight, all disorderly movements cease; no more skirmishing with one another; no more coteries; no more asides; no more standing apart; that which is in all minds converges, and changes into expectation of the assailant. A barricade before danger, chaos; in danger, discipline. Peril produces order.

As soon as Enjolras had taken his double-barrelled carbine and placed himself on a kind of battlement which he had reserved, all were silent. A little dry snapping sound was heard confusedly along the wall of paving-stones. They were cocking their muskets.

Moreover, their bearing was firmer and more confident than ever; excess of sacrifice is a support; they had hope no longer, but they had despair. Despair, final arm, which sometimes gives victory; Virgil has said so. Supreme resources spring from extreme resolutions. To embark in death is sometimes the means of escaping a shipwreck; and the coffin-lid becomes a plank of safety.

As on the evening before, the attention of all was turned, and we might almost say threw its weight upon the end of the street, now lighted and visible.

They had not long to wait. Activity distinctly recommenced in the direction Saint Leu, but it did not resemble the movement of the first attack. A rattle of chains, the menacing jolt of a mass, a clicking of brass bounding over the pavement, a sort of solemn uproar, announced that an ominous body of iron was approaching. There was a shudder in the midst of those peaceful old streets, cut through and built up for the fruitful circulation of interests and ideas, and which were not made for the monstrous rumbling of the wheels of war.

The stare of all the combatants upon the extremity of the street became wild.

A piece of artillery appeared.

The gunners pushed forward the piece; it was all ready to be loaded; the fore wheels had been removed; two supported the carriage, four were at the wheels, others followed with the caisson. The smoke of the burning match was seen.

'Fire!' cried Enjolras.

The whole barricade flashed fire, the explosion was terrible; an avalanche of smoke covered and effaced the gun and the men; in a few seconds the cloud dissipated, and the cannon and the men reappeared; those in charge of the piece placed it in position in front of the barricade, slowly, correctly, and without haste. Not a man had been touched. Then the gunner, bearing his weight on the breech, to elevate the range, began to point the cannon with the gravity of an astronomer adjusting a telescope.

'Bravo for the gunners!' cried Bossuet.

And the whole barricade clapped hands.

A moment afterwards, placed squarely in the very middle of the street, astride of the gutter, the gun was in battery. A formidable mouth was opened upon the barricade.

'Come, be lively!' said Courfeyrac. 'There is the brute. After the fillip, the knock-down. The army stretches out its big paw to us. The barricade is going to be seriously shaken. The musketry feels, the artillery takes.'

'It is a bronze eight-pounder, new model,' added Combeferre. 'Those pieces, however little they exceed the proportion of ten parts of tin to a hundred of copper, are liable to burst. The excess of tin makes them too tender. In that case they have hollows and chambers in the vent. To obviate this danger, and to be able to force out the load, it would be necessary, perhaps, to return to the process of the fourteenth century, hooping, and to strengthen the piece exteriorly, by a succession of steel rings unsoldered, from the breech to the trunnion. In the meanwhile, they remedy the defect as they can; they find out where the holes and the hollows in the bore of a cannon are by means of a searcher. But there is a better way, that is the movable star of Gribeauval.'

'In the sixteenth century,' observed Bossuet, 'they rifled their cannon.'

'Yes,' answered Combeferre, 'that augments the ballistic power, but diminishes the accuracy of the aim. In a short range, the trajectory has not the stiffness desirable, the parabola is exaggerated, the path of the projectile is not rectilinear enough to permit it to hit the intermediate objects, a necessity of combat, however, the importance of which increases with the proximity of the enemy and the rapidity of the firing. This want of tension in the curve of the projectile, in the rifled cannon of the sixteenth century, is due to the feebleness of the charge; feeble charges, for this kind of arm, are required by the necessities of balistics, such, for instance, as the preservation of the carriages. Upon the whole, artillery, that despot, cannot do all it would; strength is a great weakness. A cannon ball makes only two thousand miles an hour; light makes two hundred thousand miles a second. Such is the superiority of Jesus Christ over Napoleon.'

'Reload arms,' said Enjolras.

How was the facing of the barricade going to behave under fire? would the shot make a breach? That was the question. While the insurgents were reloading their muskets, the gunners loaded the cannon.

There was intense anxiety in the redoubt.

The gun went off; the detonation burst upon them.

'Present!' cried a cheerful voice.

And at the same time with the ball, Gavroche tumbled into the barricade.

He came by way of the Rue du Cygne, and he had nimbly clambered over the minor barricade, which fronted upon the labyrinth of the Petite Truanderie.

Gavroche produced more effect in the barricade than the ball.

The ball lost itself in the jumble of the rubbish. At the very utmost it broke a wheel of the omnibus, and finished the old Anceau cart. Seeing which, the barricade began to laugh.

'Proceed,' cried Bossuet to the gunners.

8. The gunners produce a serious impression

THEY SURROUNDED Gavroche.

But he had no time to tell anything. Marius, shuddering, took him aside.

'What have you come here for?'

'Hold on!' said the boy. 'What have you come for?'

And he looked straight at Marius with his epic effrontery. His eyes grew large with the proud light which was in them.

Marius continued, in a stern tone:

'Who told you to come back? At least you carried my letter to its address?'

Gavroche had some little remorse in relation to that letter. In his haste to return to the barricade, he had got rid of it rather than delivered it. He was compelled to acknowledge to himself that he had entrusted it rather rashly to that stranger, whose face even he could not distinguish. True, this man was bareheaded, but that was not enough. On the whole, he had some little interior remonstrances on this subject, and he feared Marius' reproaches. He took, to get out of the trouble, the simplest course; he lied abominably.

'Citizen, I carried the letter to the porter. The lady was asleep. She will get the letter when she wakes up.'

Marius, in sending this letter, had two objects: to say farewell to Cosette, and to save Gavroche. He was obliged to be content with the half of what he intended.

The sending of his letter, and the presence of M. Fauchelevent in the barricade, this coincidence occurred to his mind. He pointed out M. Fauchelevent to Gavroche.

'Do you know that man?'

'No,' said Gavroche.

Gavroche, in fact, as we have just mentioned, had only seen Jean Valjean in the night.

The troubled and sickly conjectures which had arisen in Marius' mind were dissipated. Did he know M. Fauchelevent's opinions? M. Fauchelevent was a republican, perhaps. Hence his very natural presence in this conflict.

Meanwhile Gavroche was already at the other end of the barricade, crying 'My musket!'

Courfeyrac ordered it to be given him.

Gavroche warned his 'comrades', as he called them, that the barricade was surrounded. He had had great difficulty in getting through. A battalion of the line, whose muskets were stacked in la Petite Truanderie, were observing the side on the Rue du Cygne; on the opposite side the municipal guard occupied the Rue des Prêcheurs. In front, they had the bulk of the army.

This information given, Gavroche added:

'I authorise you to give them a dose of pills.'

Meanwhile Enjolras, on his battlement, was watching, listening with intense attention.

The assailants, dissatisfied doubtless with the effect of their fire, had not repeated it.

A company of infantry of the line had come in and occupied the extremity of the street, in the rear of the gun. The soldiers tore up the pavement, and with the stones constructed a little low wall, a sort of breastwork, which was hardly more than eighteen inches high, and which fronted the barricade. At the corner on the left of this breastwork, they saw the head of the column of a battalion of the banlieue massed in the Rue St Denis.

Enjolras, on the watch, thought he distinguished the peculiar sound which is made when canisters of grape are taken from the caisson, and he saw the gunner change the aim and incline the piece slightly to the left. Then the cannoneers began to load. The gunner seized the linstock himself and brought it near the touch-hole.

'Heads down, keep close to the wall!' cried Enjolras, 'and all on your knees along the barricade!'

The insurgents, who were scattered in front of the wine-shop, and who had left their posts of combat on Gavroche's arrival, rushed pell-mell towards the barricade; but before Enjolras' order was executed, the discharge took place with the fearful rattle of grapeshot. It was so in fact.

The charge was directed at the opening of the redoubt, it ricocheted upon the wall, and this terrible ricochet killed two men and wounded three.

If that continued, the barricade was no longer tenable. It was not proof against grape.

There was a sound of consternation.

'Let us prevent the second shot, at any rate,' said Enjolras.

And, lowering his carbine, he aimed at the gunner, who, at that moment, bending over the breech of the gun, was correcting and finally adjusting the aim.

This gunner was a fine-looking sergeant of artillery, quite young, of fair complexion, with a very mild face, and the intelligent air peculiar to that predestined and formidable arm which, by perfecting itself in horror, must end in killing war.

Combeferre, standing near Enjolras, looked at this young man.

'What a pity!' said Combeferre. 'What a hideous thing these butcheries are! Come, when there are no more kings, there will be no more war. Enjolras, you are aiming at that sergeant, you are not looking at him. Just think that he is a charming young man; he is intrepid; you see that he is a thinker; these young artillery-men are well educated; he has a father, a mother, a family; he is in love, probably; he is at most twenty-five years old; he might be your brother.'

'He is,' said Enjolras.

'Yes,' said Combeferre, 'and mine also. Well, don't let us kill him.'

'Let me alone. We must do what we must.'

And a tear rolled slowly down Enjolras' marble cheek.

At the same time he pressed the trigger of his carbine. The flash leaped forth. The artillery-man turned twice round, his arms stretched out before him, and his head raised as if to drink the air, then he fell over on his side upon the gun, and lay there motionless. His back could be seen, from the centre of which a stream of blood gushed upwards. The ball had entered his breast and passed through his body. He was dead.

It was necessary to carry him away and to replace him. It was indeed some minutes gained.

9. Use of that old poacher skill, and that infallible shot which influenced the conviction of 1796

THERE WAS CONFUSION in the counsel of the barricade. The gun was about to be fired again. They could not hold out a quarter of an hour in that storm of grape. It was absolutely necessary to deaden the blows.

Enjolras threw out his command:

'We must put a mattress there.'

'We have none,' said Combeferre, 'the wounded are on them.'

Jean Valjean, seated apart on a block, at the corner of the wine-shop, his musket between his knees, had, up to this moment, taken no part in what was going on. He seemed not to hear the combatants about him say: 'There is a musket which is doing nothing.'

At the order given by Enjolras, he got up.

It will be remembered that on the arrival of the company in the Rue de la Chanvrerie, an old woman, foreseeing bullets, had put her mattress before her window. This window, a garret window, was on the roof of a house of six storeys standing a little outside of the barricade. The mattress, placed crosswise, rested at the bottom upon two clothes-poles, and was sustained above by two ropes which, in the distance, seemed like threads, and which were fastened to nails driven into the window casing. These two ropes could be seen distinctly against the sky like hairs.

'Can somebody lend me a double-barrelled carbine?' said Jean Valjean.

Enjolras, who had just reloaded his, handed it to him.

Jean Valjean aimed at the window and fired.

One of the two ropes of the mattress was cut.

The mattress now hung only by one thread.

Jean Valjean fired the second barrel. The second rope struck the glass of the window. The mattress slid down between the two poles and fell into the street.

The barricade applauded.

All cried:

'There is a mattress.'

'Yes,' said Combeferre, 'but who will go after it?'

The mattress had, in fact, fallen outside of the barricade, between the besieged and the besiegers. Now, the death of the gunner having exasperated the troops, the soldiers, for some moments, had been lying on their faces behind the line of paving-stones which they had raised, and, to make up for the compulsory silence of the gun, which was quiet while its service was being reorganised, they had opened fire on the barricade. The insurgents made no response to this musketry, to spare their ammunition. The fusillade was broken against the barricade; but the street, which it filled with balls, was terrible.

Jean Valjean went out at the opening, entered the street, passed through the storm of balls, went to the mattress, picked it up, put it on his back, and returned to the barricade.

He put the mattress into the opening himself. He fixed it against the wall in such a way that the artillerymen did not see it.

This done, they awaited the charge of grape.

They had not long to wait.

The cannon vomited its package of shot with a roar. But there was no ricochet. The grape miscarried upon the mattress. The desired effect was obtained. The barricade was preserved.

'Citizen,' said Enjolras to Jean Valjean, 'the republic thanks you.'

Bossuet admired and laughed. He exclaimed:

'It is immoral that a mattress should have so much power. Triumph of that which yields over that which thunders. But it is all the same; glory to the mattress which nullifies a cannon.'

10. Dawn

AT THAT MOMENT Cosette awoke.

Her room was small, neat, retired, with a long window to the east, looking upon the back-yard of the house.

Cosette knew nothing of what was going on in Paris. She had not been out of her room in the evening, and she had already withdrawn to it when Toussaint said: 'It appears that there is a row.'

Cosette had slept few hours, but well. She had had sweet dreams which was partly owing perhaps to her little bed being very white. Somebody who was Marius had appeared to her surrounded by a halo. She awoke with the sun in her eyes, which at first produced the effect of a continuation of her dream.

Her first emotion, on coming out of this dream, was joyous. Cosette felt entirely reassured. She was passing through, as Jean Valjean had done a few hours before, that reaction of the soul which absolutely refuses woe. She began to hope with all her might without knowing why. Then came an oppression of the heart. 'Here were three days now that she had not seen Marius. But she said to herself that he must have received her letter, that he knew where she was, and that he had so much tact, that he would find means to reach her.' 'And that certainly today, and perhaps this very morning.' 'It was broad day, but the rays of light were very horizontal, she thought it was very early; that she must get up, however, to receive Marius.'

She felt that she could not live without Marius, and that, consequently, that was enough, and that Marius would come. No objection was admissible. All that was certain. It was monstrous enough already to have suffered three days. Marius absent three days, it was horrible in the good God. Now this cruel sport of Heaven was an ordeal that was over. Marius was coming, and would bring good news. Thus is youth constituted; it quickly wipes its eyes; it believes sorrow useless and does not accept it. Youth is the smile of the future before an unknown being which is itself. It is natural for it to be happy. It seems as though it breathed hope.

Besides, Cosette could not succeed in recalling what Marius had said to her on the subject of this absence which was to last but one day, or what explanation he had given her about it. Everybody has noticed with what address a piece of money which you drop on the floor, runs and hides, and what art it has in rendering itself undiscoverable. There are thoughts which play us the same trick; they hide in a corner of our brain; it is all over; they are lost; impossible to put the memory back upon them. Cosette was a little vexed at the useless petty efforts which her recollection made. She said to herself that it was very naughty of her and very wicked to have forgotten words uttered by Marius.

She got up and performed the two ablutions, of the soul and the body, her prayer and her toilette.

We may, in extreme cases, introduce the reader into a nuptial chamber, not into a maiden's chamber. Verse would hardly dare, prose ought not.

It is the interior of a flower yet unblown, it is a whiteness in the shade, it is the inmost cell of a closed lily which ought not to be looked upon by man, while yet it has not been looked upon by the sun. Woman in the bud is sacred. The innocent bed which is thrown open, the adorable semi-nudity which is afraid of itself, the white foot which takes refuge in a slipper, the bosom which veils itself before a mirror as if that mirror were an eye; the chemise which hastens up to hide the shoulder at the snapping of a piece of furniture, or at the passing of a wagon, the ribbons tied, the clasps hooked, the lacings drawn, the starts, the shivers of cold and of modesty, the exquisite shyness in every movement, the almost winged anxiety where there is no cause for fear; the successive phases of the dress as charming as the clouds of the dawn; it is not fitting that all this should be described, and it is too much, indeed, to refer to it.

The eye of man should be more religious still before the rising of a young maiden than before the rising of a star. The possibility of touch should increase respect. The down of peach, the dust of the plum, the radiated crystal of the snow, the butterfly's wing powdered with feathers, are gross things in presence of that chastity which does not even know that it is chaste. The young maiden is only the gleam of a dream, and is not yet statue. Her alcove is hidden in the shadows of the ideal. The indiscreet touch of the eye defaces this dim penumbra. Here, to gaze is to profane.

We will show nothing, then, of all that pleasant little confusion on Cosette's awakening.

An Eastern tale relates that the rose was made white by God, but that Adam having looked at it at the moment it was half opened, it was ashamed and blushed. We are of those who feel themselves speechless before young maidens and flowers, finding them venerable.

Cosette dressed herself very quickly, combed and arranged her hair, which was a very simple thing at that time, when women did not puff out their ringlets and plaits with cushions and rolls, and did not put crinoline in their hair. Then she opened the window and looked all about, hoping to discover something of the street, a corner of a house, a patch of pavement, and to be able to watch for Marius there. But she could see nothing of the street. The back-yard was surrounded with high walls, and a few gardens only were in view. Cosette pronounced these gardens hideous; for the first time in her life she found flowers ugly. The least bit of a street gutter would have been more to her mind. She finally began to look at the sky, as if she thought that Marius might come that way also.

Suddenly, she melted into tears. Not that it was fickleness of soul; but, hopes cut off by faintness of heart, such was her situation. She vaguely felt some indefinable horror. Things float in the air in fact. She said to herself that she was not sure of anything; that to lose from sight, was to lose; and the idea that Marius might indeed return to her from the sky, appeared no longer charming, but dismal.

Then, such are these clouds, calmness returned to her, and hope, and a sort of smile, unconscious, but trusting in God.

Everybody was still in bed in the house. A rural silence reigned. No shutter had been opened. The porter's box was closed. Toussaint was not up, and Cosette very naturally thought that her father was asleep. She must have suffered indeed, and she must have been still suffering, for she said to herself that her father had been unkind; but she counted on Marius. The eclipse of such a light was entirely impossible. At intervals she heard at some distance a kind of sullen jar, and she said: 'It is singular that people are opening and shutting *porte-cochères* so early.' It was the cannon battering the barricade.

There was, a few feet below Cosette's window, in the old black cornice of the wall, a nest of martins; the corbel of this nest made a little projection beyond the cornice, so that the inside of this little paradise could be seen from above. The mother was there, opening her wings like a fan over her brood; the father flew about, went away, then returned, bringing in his bill food and kisses. The rising day gilded this happy thing, the great law Multiply was there, smiling and august, and this sweet mystery was blossoming in the glory of the morning. Cosette, her hair in the sunshine, her soul in chimera, made luminous by love within, and the dawn without, bent over as if mechanically, and, almost without daring to acknowledge to herself that she was thinking of Marius at the same time, began to look at these birds, this family, this male and this female, this mother and these little ones, with the deep restlessness which a nest gives to a maiden.

11. *The shot that misses nothing and kills nobody*

The fire of the assailants continued. The musketry and the grape alternated, without much damage indeed. The top of the façade of Corinth alone suffered; the window of the first storey and the dormer windows on the roof, riddled with shot and ball, were slowly demolished. The combatants who were posted there, had to withdraw. Besides, this is the art of attacking barricades; to tease for a long time, in order to exhaust the ammunition of the insurgents, if they commit the blunder of replying. When it is perceived, from the slackening of their fire, that they have no longer either balls or powder, the assault is made. Enjolras did not fall into this snare; the barricade did not reply.

At each platoon fire, Gavroche thrust out his cheek with his tongue, a mark of lofty disdain:

'That's right,' said he, 'tear up the cloth. We want lint.'

Courfeyrac jested with the grape about its lack of effect, and said to the cannon:

'You are getting diffuse, my goodman.'

In a battle people force themselves upon acquaintance, as at a ball. It is probable that this silence of the redoubt began to perplex the besiegers, and make them fear some unlooked-for accident, and that they felt the need of seeing through that heap of paving-stones, and knowing what was going on behind that impassable wall, which was receiving their fire without answering it. The insurgents suddenly perceived a casque shining in the sun upon a neighbouring roof. A sapper was backed up against a tall chimney, and seemed to be there as a sentinel. He looked directly into the barricade.

'There is a troublesome overseer,' said Enjolras.

Jean Valjean had returned his carbine to Enjolras, but he had his musket.

Without saying a word, he aimed at the sapper, and, a second afterwards, the casque, struck by a ball, fell noisily into the street. The startled soldier hastened to disappear.

A second observer took his place. This was an officer. Jean Valjean, who had reloaded his musket, aimed at the new comer, and sent the officer's casque to keep company with the soldier's. The officer was not obstinate, and withdrew very quickly. This time the warning was understood. Nobody appeared upon the roof again, and they gave up watching the barricade.

'Why didn't you kill the man?' asked Bossuet of Jean Valjean.

Jean Valjean did not answer.

12. *Disorder a partisan of order*

Bossuet murmured in Combeferre's ear:

'He has not answered my question.'

'He is a man who does kindness by musket shots,' said Combeferre.

Those who retain some recollection of that now distant period, know that the National Guard of the banlieue was valiant against the insurrections. It was particularly eager and intrepid in the days of June, 1832. Many a good wineshopkeeper of Pantin, of the Vertus or of La Cunette, whose 'establishment' was without custom in consequence of the *émeute*, became leonine on seeing his dancing-hall deserted, and died to preserve order represented by the tavern. In those days, at once bourgeois and heroic, in presence of ideas which had their knights, interests had their paladins. The prosaic motive detracted nothing from the bravery of the action. The decrease of a pile of crowns made bankers sing the Marseillaise. They poured out their blood lyrically for the counter; and with a Lacedæmonian enthusiasm they defended the shop, that immense diminutive of one's native land.

In reality we must say, there was nothing in all this which was not very serious. It was the social elements entering into conflict, while awaiting the day when they shall enter into equilibrium.

Another sign of that time was anarchy mingled with governmentalism (barbarous name of the correct party). Men were for order without discipline. The drum beat unawares, at the command of some colonel of the National Guard, capricious rollcalls; many a captain went to the fire by inspiration; many a National Guard fought 'from fancy', and on his own account. In the critical moments, on the 'days', they took counsel less of their chiefs than of their instincts. There were in the army of order genuine guerrillas, some of the sword like Fannicot; others of the pen, like Henri Fonfrède.

Civilisation, unfortunately represented at that epoch rather by an aggregation of interests than by a group of principles, was, or thought itself in peril; it raised the cry of alarm; every man making himself a centre, defended it, aided it, and protected it, in his own way; and anybody and everybody took it upon himself to save society.

Zeal sometimes goes to the extent of extermination. Such a platoon of National Guards constituted themselves, of their own private authority, a court-martial, and condemned and executed an insurgent prisoner in five minutes. It was an improvisation of this kind which had killed Jean Prouvaire. Ferocious Lynch law, with which no party has the right to reproach others, for it is applied by the republic in America as well as by monarchy in Europe. This Lynch law is liable to mistakes. During an *émeute*, a young poet, named Paul Aimé Garnier, was pursued in the Place Royale at the point of the bayonet, and only escaped by taking refuge under the *porte-cochère* of Number 6. The cry was: *There is another of those Saint Simonians!* and there was an attempt to kill him. Now, he had under his arm a volume of the memoirs of the Duke de Saint Simon. A National Guard had read upon this book the name: *Saint Simon*, and cried: 'Kill him.'

On the 6th of June 1832, a company of National Guards of the banlieue, commanded by Captain Fannicot, before mentioned, got themselves, through whim and for sport's sake, decimated in the Rue de la Chanvrerie. The fact, singular as it may seem, was proven by the judicial investigation entered upon after the insurrection of 1832. Captain Fannicot, a bold and impatient bourgeois, a kind of condottiere of the order of those we have just characterised, a fanatical and insubordinate governmentalist, could not resist the impulse to open fire before the hour, and the ambition of taking the barricade by himself all alone, that is, with his company. Exasperated by the successive appearance of the red flag and the old coat which he took for the black flag, he loudly blamed the generals and chiefs of corps, who were holding counsel, and did not deem that the moment for the decisive assault had come, and were leaving, according to a celebrated expression of one of them, 'the insurrection to cook in its own juice'. As for him, he thought the barricade ripe, and, as what is ripe ought to fall, he made the attempt.

He commanded men as resolute as himself, 'madmen', said a witness. His company, the same which had shot the poet Jean Prouvaire, was the first of the battalion posted at the corner of the street. At the moment when it was least expected, the captain hurled his men against the barricade. This movement, executed with more zeal than strategy, cost the Fannicot company dear. Before it had passed over two-thirds of the street, it was greeted by a general discharge from the barricade. Four, the most daring, who were running in advance, were shot down at the muzzles of the muskets, at the very foot of the redoubt; and this courageous mob of National Guards, very brave men, but who had no military tenacity, had to fall back, after some hesitation, leaving fifteen dead upon the pavement. The moment of hesitation gave the insurgents time to reload, and a second discharge, very murderous, reached the company before it was able to regain the corner of the street, its shelter. At one moment it was taken between two storms of balls, and it received the volley of the piece in battery which, receiving no orders, had not discontinued its fire. The intrepid and imprudent Fannicot was one of the killed by this volley. He was slain by the cannon, that is to say, by order.

This attack, more furious than serious, irritated Enjolras. 'The fools!' said he. 'They are getting their men killed and using up our ammunition, for nothing.'

Enjolras spoke like the true general of *émeute* that he was. Insurrection and repression do not contend with equal arms. Insurrection, readily exhaustible, has but a certain number of shots to fire, and but a certain number of combatants to expend. A cartridge-box emptied, a man killed, are not replaced. Repression, having the army, does not count men, and, having Vincennes, does not count shots. Repression has as many regiments as the barricade has men, and as many arsenals as the barricade has cartridge-boxes. Thus they are struggles of one against a hundred, which always end in the destruction of the barricade; unless revolution, abruptly appearing, casts into the balance its flaming archangel's sword. That happens. Then everything rises, the pavements begin to ferment, the redoubts of the people swarm, Paris thrills sovereignly, the *quid divinum* is set free, a 10th of August is in the air, a 29th of July is in the air, a marvellous light appears, the yawning jaws of force recoil, and the army, that lion, sees before it, erect and tranquil, this prophet, France.

13. Gleams which pass

In the chaos of sentiments and passions which defend a barricade, there is something of everything; there is bravery, youth, honour, enthusiasm, the ideal, conviction, the eager fury of the gamester, and above all, intervals of hope.

One of those intervals, one of those vague thrills of hope, suddenly crossed, at the most unexpected moment, the barricade of the Rue de la Chanvrerie.

'Hark!' abruptly exclaimed Enjolras, who was constantly on the alert, 'it seems to me that Paris is waking.'

It is certain that on the morning of the 6th of June the insurrection had, for an hour or two, a certain recrudescence. The obstinacy of the tocsin of Saint Merry reanimated some dull hopes. In the Rue du Poirier, in the Rue des Gravilliers, barricades were planned out. In front of the Porte Saint Martin, a young man, armed with a carbine, attacked singly a squadron of cavalry. Without any shelter, in the open boulevard, he dropped on one knee, raised his weapon to his shoulder, fired, killed the chief of the squadron, and turned round saying: '*There is another who will do us no more harm.*' He was sabred. In the Rue Saint Denis, a woman fired upon the Municipal Guard from behind a Venetian blind. The slats of the blind were seen to tremble at each report. A boy of fourteen was arrested in the Rue de la Cossonerie with his pockets full of cartridges. Several posts were attacked. At the entrance of the Rue Bertin Poiree, a very sharp and entirely unexpected fusilade greeted a regiment of cuirassiers, at the head of which marched General Cavaignac de Baragne. In the Rue Planche Mibray they threw upon the troops, from the roofs, old fragments of household vessels and utensils; a bad sign; and when this fact was reported to Marshal Soult, the old lieutenant of Napoleon grew thoughtful, remembering the saying of Suchet at Saragossa: '*We are lost when the old women empty their pots upon our heads.*'

These general symptoms which were manifested just when it was supposed the *émeute* was localised, this fever of wrath which was regaining the upper hand, these sparks which flew here and there above those deep masses of combustible material which are called the Faubourgs of Paris, all taken together rendered the military chiefs anxious. They hastened to extinguish these beginnings of conflagration. They delayed, until these sparks should be quenched, the attack on the barricades Maubuée, de la Chanvrerie, and Saint Merry, that they might have them only to deal with, and might be able to finish all at one blow. Columns were thrown into the streets in fermentation, sweeping the large ones, probing the small, on the right, on the left, sometimes slowly and with precaution, sometimes at a double quick step. The troops beat in the doors of the houses from which there had been firing; at the same time manoeuvres of cavalry dispersed the groups on the boulevards. This repression was not accomplished without noise, nor without that tumultuous uproar peculiar to shocks between the army and the people. This was what Enjolras caught, in the intervals of the cannonade and the musketry. Besides, he had seen some wounded passing at the end of the street upon litters, and said to Courfeyrac: 'Those wounded do not come from our fire.'

The hope did not last long; the gleam was soon eclipsed. In less than half an hour that which was in the air vanished; it was like heat lightning, and the insurgents felt that kind of leaden pall fall upon them which the indifference of the people casts over the wilful when abandoned.

The general movement, which seemed to have been vaguely projected, had miscarried; and the attention of the Minister of War and the strategy of the generals could now be concentrated upon the three or four barricades remaining standing.

The sun rose above the horizon.

An insurgent called to Enjolras:

'We are hungry here. Are we really going to die like this without eating?'

Enjolras, still leaning upon his battlement, without taking his eyes off the extremity of the street, nodded his head.

14. In which will be found the name of Enjolras' mistress

Courfeyrac, seated on a paving-stone beside Enjolras, continued his insults to the cannon, and every time that that gloomy cloud of projectiles which is known by the name of grape passed by, with its monstrous sound, he received it with an outburst of irony.

'You are tiring your lungs, my poor old brute, you trouble me, you are wasting your racket. That is not thunder; no, it is a cough.'

And those about him laughed.

Courfeyrac and Bossuet, whose valiant good-humour increased with the danger, like Madame Scarron, replaced food by pleasantry, and, as they had no wine, poured out cheerfulness for all.

'I admire Enjolras,' said Bossuet. 'His impassive boldness astonishes me. He lives alone, which renders him perhaps a little sad. Enjolras suffers for his greatness, which binds him to widowhood. The rest of us have all, more or less, mistresses who make fools of us, that is to say braves. When we are as amorous as a tiger, the least we can do is to fight like a lion. It is a way of avenging ourselves for the tricks which Mesdames our grisettes play us. Roland gets himself killed to spite Angelica; all our heroisms come from our women. A man without a woman, is a pistol without a hammer; it is the woman who makes the man go off. Now, Enjolras has no woman. He is not in love, and he finds a way to be intrepid. It is a marvellous thing that a man can be as cold as ice and as bold as fire.'

Enjolras did not appear to listen, but had anybody been near him he would have heard him murmur in an undertone, '*Patria*.'

Bossuet was laughing still when Courfeyrac exclaimed:

'Something new!'

And, assuming the manner of an usher announcing an arrival, he added:

'My name is Eight-Pounder.'

In fact, a new personage had just entered upon the scene. It was a second piece of ordnance.

The artillerymen quickly executed the manœuvres, and placed this second piece in battery near the first.

This suggested the conclusion.

A few moments afterwards, the two pieces, rapidly served, opened directly upon the redoubt; the platoon firing of the line and the banlieue supported the artillery.

Another cannonade was heard at some distance. At the same time that two cannon were raging against the redoubt in the Rue de la Chanvrerie, two other pieces of ordnance, pointed, one on the Rue Saint Denis, the other on the Rue Aubry le Boucher, were riddling the barricade St Merry. The four cannon made dreary echo to one another.

The bayings of the dismal dogs of war answered each other.

Of the two pieces which were now battering the barricade in the Rue de la Chanvrerie, one fired grape, the other ball.

The gun which threw balls was elevated a little, and the range was calculated so that the ball struck the extreme edge of the upper ridge of the barricade, dismantled it, and crumbled the paving-stones over the insurgents in showers.

This peculiar aim was intended to drive the combatants from the summit of the redoubt, and to force them to crowd together in the interior, that is, it announced the assault.

The combatants once driven from the top of the barricade by the balls and from the windows of the wine-shop by the grape, the attacking columns could venture into the street without being watched, perhaps even without being under fire, suddenly scale the redoubt, as on the evening before, and, who knows? take it by surprise.

'We must at all events diminish the inconvenience of those pieces,' said Enjolras, and he cried: 'fire upon the cannoneers!'

All were ready. The barricade, which had been silent for a long time, opened fire desperately; seven or eight discharges succeeded each other with a sort of rage and joy; the street was filled with a blinding smoke, and after a few minutes, through this haze pierced by flame, they could confusedly make out two thirds of the cannoneers lying under the wheels of the guns. Those who remained standing continued to serve the pieces with rigid composure, but the fire was slackened.

'This goes well,' said Bossuet to Enjolras. 'Success.'

Enjolras shook his head and answered:

'A quarter of an hour more of this success, and there will not be ten cartridges in the barricade.'

It would seem that Gavroche heard this remark.

15. Gavroche outside

COURFEYRAC SUDDENLY PERCEIVED somebody at the foot of the barricade, outside in the street, under the balls.

Gavroche had taken a basket from the wine-shop, had gone out by the opening, and was quietly occupied in emptying into his basket the full cartridge-boxes of the National Guards who had been killed on the slope of the redoubt.

'What are you doing there?' said Courfeyrac.

Gavroche cocked up his nose.

'Citizen, I am filling my basket.'

'Why, don't you see the grape?'

Gavroche answered:

'Well, it rains. What then?'

Courfeyrac cried:

'Come back!'

'Directly,' said Gavroche.

And with a bound, he sprang into the street.

It will be remembered that the Fannicot company, on retiring, had left behind them a trail of corpses.

Some twenty dead lay scattered along the whole length of the street on the pavement. Twenty cartridge-boxes for Gavroche, a supply of cartridges for the barricade.

The smoke in the street was like a fog. Whoever has seen a cloud fall into a mountain gorge between two steep slopes can imagine this smoke crowded and as if thickened by two gloomy lines of tall houses. It rose slowly and was constantly renewed; hence a gradual darkening which even rendered broad day pallid. The combatants could hardly perceive each other from end to end of the street, although it was very short.

This obscurity, probably desired and calculated upon by the leaders who were to direct the assault upon the barricade, was of use to Gavroche.

Under the folds of this veil of smoke, and thanks to his small size, he could advance far into the street without being seen. He emptied the first seven or eight cartridge-boxes without much danger.

He crawled on his belly, ran on his hands and feet, took his basket in his teeth, twisted, glided, writhed, wormed his way from one body to another, and emptied a cartridge-box as a monkey opens a nut.

From the barricade, of which he was still within hearing, they dared not call to him to return, for fear of attracting attention to him.

On one corpse, that of a corporal, he found a powder-flask.

'In case of thirst,' said he as he put it into his pocket.

By successive advances, he reached a point where the fog from the firing became transparent.

So that the sharp-shooters of the line drawn up and on the alert behind their wall of paving-stones, and the sharp-shooters of the banlieue massed at the corner of the street, suddenly discovered something moving in the smoke.

Just as Gavroche was relieving a sergeant who lay near a stone-block of his cartridges, a ball struck the body.

'The deuce!' said Gavroche. 'So they are killing my dead for me.'

A second ball splintered the pavement beside him. A third upset his basket.

Gavroche looked and saw that it came from the banlieue.

He rose up straight, on his feet, his hair in the wind, his hands upon his hips, his eye fixed upon the National Guards who were firing, and he sang:

> On est laid à Nanterre,
> C'est la faute à Voltaire;
> Et bête à Palaiseau,
> C'est la faute à Rousseau.

Then he picked up his basket, put into it the cartridge which had fallen out, without losing a single one, and, advancing towards the fusilade, began to empty another cartridge-box. There a fourth ball just missed him again. Gavroche sang:

> Je ne suis pas notaire,
> C'est la faute à Voltaire;
> Je suis petit oiseau,
> C'est la faute à Rousseau.

A fifth ball succeeded only in drawing a third couplet from him:

> Joie est mon caractère,
> C'est fa faute à Voltaire;
> Misère est mon trousseau,
> C'est la faute à Rousseau.

This continued thus for some time.

The sight was appalling and fascinating. Gavroche, fired at, mocked the firing. He appeared to be very much amused. It was the sparrow pecking at the hunters. He replied to each discharge by a couplet. They aimed at him incessantly, they always missed him. The National Guards and the soldiers laughed as they aimed at him. He lay down, then rose up, hid himself in a doorway, then sprang out, disappeared, reappeared, escaped, returned, retorted upon the volleys by wry faces, and meanwhile pillaged cartridges, emptied cartridge-boxes, and filled his basket. The insurgents, breathless with anxiety, followed him with their eyes. The barricade was trembling; he was singing. It was not a child; it was not a man; it was a strange fairy *gamin*. One would have said the invulnerable dwarf of the mêlée. The bullets ran after him; he was more nimble than they. He was playing an indescribably terrible game of hide-and-seek with death; every time the flat-nosed face of the spectre approached, the *gamin* snapped his fingers.

One bullet, however, better aimed or more treacherous than the others, reached the Will-o'-the-wisp child. They saw Gavroche totter, then he fell. The whole barricade gave a cry; but there was an Antæus in this pigmy; for the *gamin* to touch the pavement is like the giant touching the earth; Gavroche had fallen only to rise again; he sat up, a long stream of blood rolled down his face, he raised both arms in air, looked in the direction whence the shot came, and began to sing:

> Je suis tombé par terre,
> C'est la faute à Voltaire,
> La nez daus le ruisseau,
> C'est la faute à –

He did not finish. A second ball from the same marksman cut him short. This time he fell with his face upon the pavement, and did not stir again. That little great soul had taken flight.

16. How brother becomes father

There were at that very moment in the garden of the Luxembourg – for the eye of the drama should be everywhere present – two children holding each other by the hand. One might have been seven years old, the other five. Having been soaked in the rain, they were walking in the paths on the sunny side; the elder was leading the little one; they were pale and in rags; they looked like wild birds. The smaller said: 'I want something to eat.'

The elder, already something of a protector, led his brother with his left hand and had a stick in his right hand.

They were alone in the garden. The garden was empty, the gates being closed by order of the police on account of the insurrection. The troops which had bivouacked there had been called away by the necessities of the combat.

How came these children there? Had they haply escaped from some half-open guardhouse; was there perchance in the neighbourhood, at the Barrière d'Enfer, or on the esplanade of the Observatoire, or in the neighbouring square overlooked by the pediment on which we read: *Invenerunt parvulum pannis involutum*, some mountebank's tent from which they had fled; had they perchance, the evening before, evaded the eye of the garden-keepers at the hour of closing, and had they passed the night in some one of those boxes in which people read the papers? The fact is, that they were wandering, and that they seemed free. To be wandering and to seem free is to be lost. These poor little ones were lost indeed.

These two children were the very same about whom Gavroche had been in trouble, and whom the reader remembers. Children of the Thénardiers, rented out to Magnon, attributed to M. Gillenormand, and now leaves fallen from all these rootless branches, and whirled over the ground by the wind.

Their clothing, neat in Magnon's time, and which served her as a prospectus in the sight of M. Gillenormand, had become tatters.

These creatures belonged henceforth to the statistics of 'abandoned children', whom the police report, collect, scatter, and find again on the streets of Paris.

It required the commotion of such a day for these little outcasts to be in this garden. If the officers had noticed them, they would have driven away these rags. Poor children cannot enter the public gardens; still one would think that, as children, they had a right in the flowers.

These were there, thanks to the closed gates. They were in violation of the rules. They had slipped into the garden, and they had stayed there. Closed gates do not dismiss the keepers, the oversight is supposed to continue, but it is relaxed and at its ease; and the keepers, also excited by the public anxiety and busier with matters without than within, no longer paid attention to the garden, and had not seen the two delinquents.

It had rained the night before, and even a little that morning. But in June showers are of no account. It is with difficulty that we can realise, an hour after a storm, that this fine fair day has been rainy. The ground in summer is as soon dry as the cheek of a child.

At this time of the solstice, the light of the full noon is, so to speak, piercing. It seizes upon everything. It applies itself and spreads itself over the earth with a sort of suction. One would say that the sun was thirsty. A shower is a glass of water; a rain is swallowed immediately. In the morning all is streaming, in the afternoon all is dusty.

Nothing is so admirable as a verdure washed by the rain and wiped by the sunbeam; it is warm freshness. The gardens and the meadows, having water at their roots and sunshine in their flowers, become vases of incense, and exhale all their perfumes at once. All these laugh, sing, and proffer themselves. We feel sweet intoxication. Spring is a provisional paradise; sunshine helps to make man patient.

There are people who ask nothing more; living beings who, having the blue sky, say: 'it is enough!' dreamers absorbed in marvel, drawing from idolatry of nature an indifference to good and evil, contemplators of the cosmos radiantly diverted from man, who do not understand how anybody can busy himself with the hunger of these, with the thirst of those, with the nakedness of the poor in winter, with the lymphatic curvature of a little backbone, with the pallet, with the garret, with the dungeon, and with the rags of shivering little girls, when he might dream under the trees; peaceful and terrible souls, pitilessly content. A strange thing, the infinite is enough for them. This great need of man, the finite, which admits of embrace, they ignore. The finite, which admits of progress, sublime toil, they do not think of. The indefinite, which is born of the combination human and divine, of the infinite and the finite, escapes them. Provided they are face to face with immensity, they smile. Never joy, always ecstasy. To lose themselves is their life. The history of humanity to them is only a fragmentary plan; All is not there, the true All is still beyond; what is the use of busying ourselves with this incident, man? Man suffers, it is possible; but look at Aldebaran rising yonder! The mother has no milk, the newborn dies, I know nothing about that, but look at this marvellous rosette formed by a transverse section of the sapwood of the firtree when examined by the microscope! compare me that with the most beautiful Mechlin lace! These thinkers forget to love. The zodiac has such success with them that it prevents them from seeing the weeping child. God eclipses the soul. There is a family of such minds, at once little and great. Horace belonged to it, Goethe belonged to it, La Fontaine perhaps; magnificent egotists of the infinite, tranquil spectators of grief, who do not see Nero if the weather is fine, from whom the sunshine hides the stake, who would behold the guillotine at work, watching for an effect of light, who hear neither the cry, nor the sob, nor the death-rattle, nor the tocsin, to whom all is well, since there is a month of May, who, so long as there are clouds of purple and gold above their heads, declare themselves content, and who are determined to be happy until the light of the stars and the song of the birds are exhausted.

They are of a dark radiance. They do not suspect that they are to be pitied. Certainly they are. He who does not weep does not see. We should admire and pity them, as we would pity and admire a being at once light and darkness, with no eyes under his brows and a star in the middle of his forehead.

In the indifference of these thinkers, according to some lies a superior philosophy. So be it; but in this superiority there is some infirmity. One may be immortal and a cripple; Vulcan for instance. One may be more than man and less than man. The immense incomplete exists in nature. Who knows that the sun is not blind?

But then, what! in whom trust? *Solem quis dicere falsum audeat?* Thus certain geniuses themselves, certain Most High mortals, star men, may have been deceived! That which is on high, at the top, at the summit, in the zenith, that which sends over the earth so much light, may see little, may see badly, may see nothing! Is not that disheartening? No. But what is there, then, above the sun? The God.

On the 6th June 1832, towards eleven o'clock in the morning, the Luxembourg, solitary and unpeopled, was delightful. The quincunxes and the parterres projected themselves into the light in balms and dazzlings. The branches, wild with the noonday brilliance, seemed seeking to embrace each other. There was in the sycamores a chattering of linnets, the sparrows were jubilant, the woodpeckers climbed up the horse-chestnuts, tapping with their beaks the wrinkles in the bark. The flower beds accepted the legitimate royalty of the lilies; the most august of perfumes is that which comes from whiteness. You inhaled the spicy odour of the pinks. The old rooks of Marie de' Medici were amorous in the great trees. The sun gilded, empurpled, and kindled the tulips, which are nothing more nor less than all varieties of flame made flowers. All about the tulip beds whirled the bees, sparks from these flame-flowers. All was grace and gaiety, even the coming rain; that old offender, by whom the honeysuckles and the lilies of the valley would profit, produced no disquiet; the swallows flew low, charming menace. He who was there breathed happiness; life was sweet; all this nature exhaled candour, help, assistance, paternity, caress, dawn. The thoughts which fell from the sky were as soft as the child's little hand which you kiss.

The statues under the trees, bare and white, had robes of shade torn by light; these goddesses were all tattered by the sunshine; it hung from them in shreds on all sides. Around the great basin, the earth was already so dry as to be almost baked. There was wind enough to raise here and there little *émeutes* of sand. A few yellow leaves, relics of the last autumn, chased one another joyously, and seemed to be playing the *gamin.*

The abundance of light was inexpressibly comforting. Life, sap, warmth, odour, overflowed; you felt beneath creation the enormity of its source; in all these breezes saturated with love, in this coming and going of reflections and reverberations, in this prodigious expenditure of rays, in this indefinite outlay of fluid gold, you felt the prodigality of the inexhaustible; and behind this splendour, as behind a curtain of flame, you caught a glimpse of God, the millionaire of stars.

Thanks to the sand, there was not a trace of mud; thanks to the rain, there was not a speck of dust. The bouquets had just been washed; all the velvets, all the satins, all the enamels, all the golds, which spring from the earth in the form of flowers, were irreproachable. This magnificence was tidy. The great silence of happy nature filled the garden. A celestial silence compatible with a thousand melodies, cooings of nests, hummings of swarms, palpitations of the wind. All the harmony of the season was accomplished in a graceful whole; the entrances and exits of spring took place in the desired order; the lilacs ended, the jessamines began; some flowers were belated, some insects in advance; the vanguard of the red butterflies of June fraternised with the rearguard of the white butterflies of May. The plane trees were getting a new skin. The breeze scooped out waves in the magnificent vastness of the horse-chestnuts. It was resplendent. A veteran of the adjoining barracks, looking through the grating, said: 'There is spring under arms, and in full dress.'

All nature was breakfasting; creation was at table; it was the hour; the great blue cloth was spread in the sky, and the great green cloth over the earth; the sun shone *à giorno.* God was serving up the universal repast. Every creature had its food or its fodder. The ringdove found hempseed, the chaffinch found millet, the goldfinch found chickweed, the redbreast found worms, the bee found flowers, the fly found infusoria, the grosbeak found flies. They ate one another a little, to be sure, which is the mystery of evil mingled with good; but not an animal had an empty stomach.

The two little abandoned creatures were near the great basin, and, slightly disturbed by all this light, they endeavoured to hide, an instinct of the poor and feeble before magnificence even impersonal, and they kept behind the shelter for the swans.

Here and there, at intervals, when the wind fell, they confusedly heard cries, a hum, a kind of tumultuous rattle, which was the musketry, and sullen jars, which were reports of cannon. There was smoke above the roofs in the direction of the markets. A bell, which appeared to be calling, sounded in the distance.

These children did not seem to notice these sounds. The smaller one repeated from time to time in an under tone: 'I want something to eat.'

Almost at the same moment with the two children, another couple approached the great basin. This was a goodman of fifty, who was leading by the hand a goodman of six. Doubtless a father with his son. The goodman of six had a big bun in his hand.

At that period, certain adjoining houses, in the Rue Madame and the Rue d'Enfer, had keys to the Luxembourg which the occupants used when the gates were closed, a favour since suppressed. This father and this son probably came from one of those houses.

The two poor little fellows saw 'this Monsieur' coming, and hid themselves a little more closely.

He was a bourgeois. The same, perhaps, whom one day Marius, in spite of his love fever, had heard, near this same great basin, counselling his son 'to beware of extremes'. He had an affable and lofty manner, and a mouth which, never closing, was always smiling. This mechanical smile, produced by too much jaw and too little skin, shows the teeth rather than the soul. The child, with his bitten bun, which he did not finish, seemed stuffed. The boy was dressed as a National Guard, on account of the *émeute*, and the father remained in citizen's clothes for the sake of prudence.

The father and son stopped near the basin in which the two swans were sporting. This bourgeois appeared to have a special admiration for the swans. He resembled them in this respect, that he walked like them.

For the moment, the swans were swimming, which is their principal talent, and they were superb.

If the two poor little fellows had listened, and had been of an age to understand, they might have gathered up the words of a grave man. The father said to the son:

'The sage lives content with little. Behold me, my son. I do not love pomp. Never am I seen with coats bedizened with gold and gems; I leave this false splendour to badly organised minds.'

Here the deep sounds, which came from the direction of the markets, broke out with a redoubling of bell and of uproar.

'What is that?' inquired the child.

The father answered:

'They are saturnalia.'

Just then he noticed the two little ragged fellows standing motionless behind the green cottage of the swans.

'There is the beginning,' said he.

And after a moment, he added:

'Anarchy is entering this garden.'

Meanwhile the son bit the bun, spat it out, and suddenly began to cry.

'What are you crying for?' asked the father.

'I am not hungry any more,' said the child.

The father's smile grew broad.

'You don't need to be hungry, to eat a cake.'

'I am sick of my cake. It is stale.'

'You don't want any more of it?'

'No.'

The father showed him the swans.

'Throw it to those palmipeds.'

The child hesitated. Not to want any more of one's cake, is no reason for giving it away.

The father continued:

'Be humane. We must take pity on the animals.'

And, taking the cake from his son, he threw it into the basin. The cake fell near the edge.

The swans were at a distance, in the centre of the basin, and busy with some prey. They saw neither the bourgeois nor the bun.

The bourgeois, feeling that the cake was in danger of being lost, and aroused by this useless shipwreck, devoted himself to a telegraphic agitation which finally attracted the attention of the swans.

They perceived something floating, veered about like the ships they are, and directed themselves slowly towards the bun with that serene majesty which is fitting to white animals.

'*Cygnes* [swans] understand *signes* [signs],' said the bourgeois, delighted at his wit.

Just then the distant tumult in the city suddenly increased again. This time it was ominous. There are some gusts of wind which speak more distinctly than others. That which blew at that moment brought clearly the rolls of drums, shouts, platoon firing, and the dismal replies of the tocsin and the cannon. This was coincident with a black cloud which abruptly shut out the sun.

The swans had not yet reached the bun.

'Come home,' said the father, 'they are attacking the Tuileries.'

He seized his son's hand again. Then he continued:

'From the Tuileries to the Luxembourg, there is only the distance which separates royalty from the peerage; it is not far. It is going to rain musket-balls.'

He looked at the cloud.

'And perhaps also the rain itself is going to rain; the heavens are joining in; the younger branch is condemned. Come home, quick.'

'I should like to see the swans eat the bun,' said the child.

The father answered:

'That would be an imprudence.'

And he led away his little bourgeois.

The son, regretting the swans, turned his head towards the basin, until a turn in the rows of trees hid it from him.

Meanwhile, at the same time with the swans, the two little wanderers had approached the bun. It was floating on the water. The smaller was looking at the cake, the larger was looking at the bourgeois who was going away.

The father and the son entered the labyrinth of walks which leads to the grand stairway of the cluster of trees on the side towards the Rue Madame.

As soon as they were out of sight, the elder quickly lay down with his face over the rounded edge of the basin, and, holding by it with his left hand, hanging over the water, almost falling in, with his right hand reached his stick towards the cake. The swans, seeing the enemy, made haste, and in making haste produced an effect with their breasts which was useful to the little fisher; the water flowed back before the swans, and one of those smooth concentric waves pushed the bun gently towards the child's stick. As the swans came up, the stick touched the cake. The child made a quick movement, drew in the bun, frightened the swans, seized the cake, and got up. The cake was soaked; but they were hungry and thirsty. The eldest broke the bun into two pieces, one large and one small, took the small one for himself, gave the large one to his little brother, and said to him:

'*Stick that in your gun.*'

17. *Mortuus pater filium moriturum expectat*

MARIUS HAD SPRUNG out of the barricade. Combeferre had followed him. But it was too late. Gavroche was dead. Combeferre brought back the basket of cartridges; Marius brought back the child.

'Alas!' thought he, 'what the father had done for his father he was returning to the son; only Thénardier had brought back his father living, while he brought back the child dead.'

When Marius re-entered the redoubt with Gavroche in his arms, his face, like the child's, was covered with blood.

Just as he had stooped down to pick up Gavroche, a ball grazed his skull; he did not perceive it.

Courfeyrac took off his cravat and bound up Marius' forehead.

They laid Gavroche on the same table with Mabeuf, and they stretched the black shawl over the two bodies. It was large enough for the old man and the child.

Combeferre distributed the cartridges from the basket which he had brought back.

This gave each man fifteen shots.

Jean Valjean was still at the same place, motionless upon his block. When Combeferre presented him his fifteen cartridges, he shook his head.

'There is a rare eccentric,' said Combeferre in a low tone to Enjolras. 'He finds means not to fight in this barricade.'

'Which does not prevent him from defending it,' answered Enjolras.

'Heroism has its originals,' replied Combeferre.

And Courfeyrac, who had overheard, added:

'He is a different kind from Father Mabeuf.'

A notable fact, the fire which was battering the barricade hardly disturbed the interior. Those who have never passed through the whirlwind of this kind of war can have no idea of the singular moments of tranquillity which are mingled with these convulsions. Men come and go, they chat, they joke, they lounge. An acquaintance of ours heard a combatant say to him in the midst of the grape: *This is like a bachelor's breakfast.* The redoubt in the Rue de la Chanvrerie, we repeat, seemed very calm within. Every turn and every phase of fortune had been or would soon be exhausted. The position, from critical had become threatening, and from threatening was probably becoming desperate. In proportion as the condition of affairs grew gloomy the heroic gleam empurpled the barricade more and more. Enjolras, grave, commanded it, in the attitude of a young Spartan devoting his drawn sword to the sombre genius Epidotas.

Combeferre, with apron at his waist, was dressing the wounded; Bossuet and Feuilly were making cartridges with the flask of powder taken by Gavroche from the dead corporal, and Bossuet said to Feuilly: *We shall soon take the diligence for another planet;* Courfeyrac, upon the few paving-stones which he had reserved for himself near Enjolras, was disposing and arranging a whole arsenal, his sword-cane, his musket, two horse-pistols, and a pocket pistol, with the care of a girl who is putting a little work-box in order. Jean Valjean was looking in silence at the opposite wall. A working-man was fastening on his head with a string a large straw hat belonging to Mother Hucheloup, *for fear of sun-stroke,* said he. The young men of the Cougourde d'Aix were chatting gaily with one another, as if they were in a hurry to talk patois for the last time. Joly, who had taken down the widow Hucheloup's mirror, was examining his tongue in it. A few combatants, having discovered some crusts of bread, almost mouldy, in a drawer, were eating them greedily. Marius was anxious about what his father would say to him.

18. The vulture becomes prey

We must dwell upon a psychological fact, peculiar to barricades. Nothing which characterises this surprising war of the streets should be omitted.

Whatever be that strange interior tranquillity of which we have just spoken, the barricade, for those who are within, is none the less a vision.

There is an apocalypse in civil war, all the mists of the unknown are mingled with these savage flames, revolutions are sphinxes, and he who has passed through a barricade, believes he has passed through a dream.

What is felt in those places, as we have indicated in reference to Marius, and as we shall see in what follows, is more and is less than life. Once out of the barricade, a man no longer knows what he has seen in it. He was terrible, he does not know it. He was surrounded by combating ideas which had human faces; he had his head in the light of the future. There were corpses lying and phantoms standing. The hours were colossal, and seemed hours of eternity. He lived in death. Shadows passed by. What were they? He saw hands on which there was blood; it was an appalling uproar, it was also a hideous silence; there were open mouths which shouted, and other open mouths which held their peace; he was in the smoke, in the night, perhaps. He thinks he has touched the ominous ooze of the unknown depths; he sees something red in his nails. He remembers nothing more.

Let us return to the Rue de la Chanvrerie.

Suddenly between two discharges they heard the distant sound of a clock striking.

'It is noon,' said Combeferre.

The twelve strokes had not sounded when Enjolras sprang to his feet, and flung down from the top of the barricade this thundering shout:

'Carry some paving-stones into the house. Fortify the windows with them. Half the men to the muskets, the other half to the stones. Not a minute to lose.'

A platoon of sappers, their axes on their shoulders, had just appeared in order of battle at the end of the street.

This could only be the head of a column; and of what column? The column of attack, evidently. The sappers, whose duty it is to demolish the barricade, must always precede the soldiers whose duty it is to scale it.

They were evidently close upon the moment which Monsieur de Clermont

Tonnerre, in 1822, called 'the twist of the necklace'.

Enjolras' order was executed with the correct haste peculiar to ships and barricades, the only places of combat whence escape is impossible. In less than a minute, two-thirds of the paving-stones which Enjolras had had piled up at the door of Corinth were carried up to the first storey and to the garret; and before a second minute had elapsed, these stones, artistically laid one upon another, walled up half the height of the window on the first storey and the dormer windows of the attic. A few openings carefully arranged by Feuilly, chief builder, allowed musket barrels to pass through. This armament of the windows could be performed the more easily since the grape had ceased. The two pieces were now firing balls upon the centre of the wall, in order to make a hole, and if it were possible, a breach for the assault.

When the paving-stones, destined for the last defence, were in position, Enjolras had them carry up to the first storey the bottles which he had placed under the table where Mabeuf was.

'Who will drink that?' Bossuet asked him.

'They,' answered Enjolras.

Then they barricaded the basement window, and they held in readiness the iron cross-pieces which served to bar the door of the wine-shop on the inside at night.

The fortress was complete. The barricade was the rampart, the wine-shop was the donjon.

With the paving-stones which remained, they closed up the opening beside the barricade.

As the defenders of a barricade are always obliged to husband their ammunition, and as the besiegers know it, the besiegers perfect their arrangements with a sort of provoking leisure, expose themselves to fire before the time, but in appearance more than in reality, and take their ease. The preparations for attack are always made with a certain methodical slowness, after which, the thunderbolt.

This slowness allowed Enjolras to look over the whole, and to perfect the whole. He felt that since such men were to die, their death should be a masterpiece.

He said to Marius: 'We are the two chiefs; I will give the last orders within. You stay outside and watch.'

Marius posted himself for observation upon the crest of the barricade.

Enjolras had the door of the kitchen, which, we remember, was the hospital, nailed up.

'No spattering on the wounded,' said he.

He gave his last instructions in the basement-room in a quick, but deep and calm voice; Feuilly listened, and answered in the name of all.

'First storey, hold your axes ready to cut the staircase. Have you them?'

'Yes,' said Feuilly.

'How many?'

'Two axes and a pole-axe.'

'Very well. There are twenty-six effective men left.'

'How many muskets are there?'

'Thirty-four.'

'Eight too many. Keep these eight muskets loaded like the rest, and at hand.

Swords and pistols in your belts. Twenty men to the barricade. Six in ambush at the dormer windows and at the window on the first storey to fire upon the assailants through the loopholes in the paving-stones. Let there be no useless labourer here. Immediately, when the drum beats the charge, let the twenty from below rush to the barricade. The first there will get the best places.'

These dispositions made, he turned towards Javert, and said to him:

'I won't forget you.'

And, laying a pistol on the table, he added:

'The last man to leave this room will blow out the spy's brains!'

'Here?' inquired a voice.

'No, do not leave this corpse with ours. You can climb over the little barricade on the Rue Mondétour. It is only four feet high. The man is well tied. You will take him there, and execute him there.'

There was one man, at that moment, who was more impassable than Enjolras; it was Javert.

Here Jean Valjean appeared.

He was in the throng of insurgents. He stepped forward, and said to Enjolras:

'You are the commander?'

'Yes.'

'You thanked me just now.'

'In the name of the republic. The barricade has two saviours, Marius Pontmercy and you.'

'Do you think that I deserve a reward?'

'Certainly.'

'Well, I ask one.'

'What?'

'To blow out that man's brains myself.'

Javert raised his head, saw Jean Valjean, made an imperceptible movement, and said:

'That is appropriate.'

As for Enjolras, he had begun to reload his carbine; he cast his eyes about him:

'No objection.'

And turning towards Jean Valjean: 'Take the spy.'

Jean Valjean, in fact, took possession of Javert by sitting down on the end of the table. He caught up the pistol, and a slight click announced that he had cocked it.

Almost at the same moment, they heard a flourish of trumpets.

'Come on!' cried Marius, from the top of the barricade.

Javert began to laugh with that noiseless laugh which was peculiar to him, and, looking fixedly upon the insurgents, said to them:

'Your health is hardly better than mine.'

'All outside?' cried Enjolras.

The insurgents sprang forward in a tumult, and, as they went out, they received in the back, allow us the expression, this speech from Javert:

'Farewell till immediately!'

19. Jean Valjean takes his revenge

WHEN JEAN VALJEAN was alone with Javert, he untied the rope that held the prisoner by the middle of the body, the knot of which was under the table. Then he motioned to him to get up.

Javert obeyed, with that undefinable smile into which the supremacy of enchained authority is condensed.

Jean Valjean took Javert by the martingale as you would take a beast of burden by a strap, and, drawing him after him, went out of the wine-shop slowly, for Javert, with his legs fettered, could take only very short steps.

Jean Valjean had the pistol in his hand.

They crossed thus the interior trapezium of the barricade. The insurgents, intent upon the imminent attack, were looking the other way.

Marius, alone, placed towards the left extremity of the wall, saw them pass. This group of the victim and the executioner borrowed a light from the sepulchral gleam which he had in his soul.

Jean Valjean, with some difficulty, bound as Javert was, but without letting go of him for a single instant, made him scale the little entrenchment on the Rue Mondétour.

When they had climbed over this wall, they found themselves alone in the little street. Nobody saw them now. The corner of the house hid them from the insurgents. The corpses carried out from the barricades made a terrible mound a few steps off.

They distinguished in a heap of dead, a livid face, a flowing head of hair, a wounded hand, and a woman's breast half naked. It was Eponine.

Javert looked aside at this dead body, and, perfectly calm, said in an undertone:

'It seems to me that I know that girl.'

Then he turned towards Jean Valjean.

Jean Valjean put the pistol under his arm, and fixed upon Javert a look which had no need of words to say: 'Javert, it is I.'

Javert answered:

'Take your revenge.'

Jean Valjean took a knife out of his pocket, and opened it.

'*A surin!*' exclaimed Javert. 'You are right. That suits you better.'

Jean Valjean cut the martingale which Javert had about his neck, then he cut the ropes which he had on his wrists, then, stooping down, he cut the cord which he had on his feet; and, rising, he said to him:

'You are free.'

Javert was not easily astonished. Still, complete master as he was of himself, he could not escape an emotion. He stood aghast and motionless.

Jean Valjean continued:

'I don't expect to leave this place. Still, if by chance I should, I live, under the name of Fauchelevent, in the Rue de l'Homme Armé, Number Seven.'

Javert had the scowl of a tiger half opening a corner of his mouth, and he muttered between his teeth:

'Take care.'

'Go,' said Jean Valjean.

Javert resumed:

'You said Fauchelevent, Rue de l'Homme Armé?'

'Number Seven.'

Javert repeated in an undertone: 'Number seven.' He buttoned his coat, restored the military stiffness between his shoulders, turned half round, folded his arms, supporting his chin with one hand, and walked off in the direction of the markets. Jean Valjean followed him with his eyes. After a few steps, Javert turned back, and cried to Jean Valjean:

'You annoy me. Kill me rather.'

Javert did not notice that his tone was more respectful towards Jean Valjean.

'Go away,' said Jean Valjean.

Javert receded with slow steps. A moment afterwards, he turned the corner of the Rue des Prêcheurs.

When Javert was gone, Jean Valjean fired the pistol in the air. Then he re-entered the barricade and said: 'It is done.'

Meanwhile what had taken place is this:

Marius, busy rather with the street than the wine-shop, had not until then looked attentively at the spy who was bound in the dusky rear of the basement-room.

When he saw him in broad day clambering over the barricade on his way to die, he recognised him. A sudden reminiscence came into his mind. He remembered the inspector of the Rue de Pontoise, and the two pistols which he had handed him and which he had used, he, Marius, in this very barricades and not only did he recollect the face, but he recalled the name.

This reminiscence, however, was misty and indistinct, like all his ideas. It was not an affirmation which he made to himself, it was a question which he put: 'Is not this that inspector of police who told me his name was Javert?'

Perhaps there was still time to interfere for this man? But he must first know if it were indeed that Javert.

Marius called to Enjolras, who had just taken his place at the other end of the barricade,

'Enjolras!'

'What?'

'What is that man's name?'

'Who?'

'The police officer. Do you know his name?'

'Of course. He told us.'

'What is his name?'

'Javert.'

Marius sprang up.

At that moment they heard the pistol-shot.

Jean Valjean reappeared and cried: 'It is done.'

A dreary chill passed through the heart of Marius.

20. *The dead are right and the living are not wrong*

THE DEATH-AGONY of the barricade was approaching.

All things concurred in the tragic majesty of this supreme moment; a thousand mysterious disturbances in the air, the breath of armed masses set in motion in streets which they could not see, the intermittent gallop of cavalry, the heavy concussion of artillery on the march, the platoon firing and the cannonades crossing each other in the labyrinth of Paris, the smoke of the battle rising all golden above the roofs, mysterious cries, distant, vaguely terrible flashes of menace everywhere, the tocsin of Saint Merry which now had the sound of a sob, the softness of the season, the splendour of the sky full of sunshine and of clouds, the beauty of the day, and the appalling silence of the houses.

For, since evening, the two rows of houses in the Rue de la Chanvrerie had become two walls; savage walls. Doors closed, windows closed, shutters closed.

In those days, so different from these in which we live, when the hour had come in which the people wished to make an end of a state of affairs which had lasted too long, of a granted charter or of a constitutional country, when the universal anger was diffused in the atmosphere, when the city consented to the upheaval of its pavements, when insurrection made the bourgeoisie smile by whispering its watchword in its ear, then the inhabitant filled with *émeute*, so to speak, was the auxiliary of the combatant, and the house fraternised with the impromptu fortress which leaned upon it. When the condition of affairs was not ripe, when the insurrection was not decidedly acceptable, when the mass disavowed the movement, it was all over with the combatants, the city changed into a desert about the revolt, souls were chilled, asylums were walled up, and the street became a defile to aid the army in taking the barricade.

A people cannot be surprised into a more rapid progress than it wills. Woe to him who attempts to force its hand! A people does not allow itself to be used. Then it abandons the insurrection to itself. The insurgents become pestiferous. A house is an escarpment, a door is a refusal, a façade is a wall. This wall sees, hears, and will not. It might open and save you. No. This wall is a judge. It looks upon you and condemns you. How gloomy are these closed houses! They seem dead, they are living. Life, which is as it were suspended in them, still exists. Nobody has come out of them for twenty-four hours, but nobody is missing. In the interior of this rock, people go and come, they lie down, they get up; they are at home there; they drink and they eat; they are afraid there, a fearful thing! Fear excuses this terrible inhospitality; it tempers it with timidity, a mitigating circumstance. Sometimes even, and this has been seen, fear becomes passion; fright may change into fury, as prudence into rage; hence this saying so profound: *The madmen of moderation*. There are flamings of supreme dismay from which rage springs like a dismal smoke. 'What do these people want? They are never contented. They compromise peaceable men. As if we had not had revolutions enough like this! What do they come here for? Let them get out of it themselves. So much the worse for them. It is their own fault. They have only got what they deserve. It doesn't concern us. Here is our poor street riddled with balls. They are a parcel of scamps. Above all, don't open the door.' And the house puts on the semblance of a tomb. The insurgent before that door is in his last agony; he sees the grape and the drawn sabres coming; if he calls, he knows that they hear him, but that they will not come; there are walls which might protect him, there are men who might save him; and those walls have ears of flesh, and those men have bowels of stone.

Whom shall he accuse?

Nobody, and everybody.

The imperfect age in which we live.

It is always at her own risk and peril that Utopia transforms herself into insurrection, and from a philosophic protest becomes an armed protest, from Minerva, Pallas. The Utopia which grows impatient and becomes *émeute* knows what awaits her; almost always she is too soon. Then she resigns herself, and stoically accepts, instead of triumph, catastrophe. She serves, without complaining, and exonerating them even, those who deny her, and it is her magnanimity to consent to abandonment. She is indomitable against hindrance, and gentle towards ingratitude.

But is it ingratitude?

Yes, from the point of view of the race.

No, from the point of view of the individual.

Progress is the mode of man. The general life of the human race is called Progress; the collective advance of the human race is called Progress. Progress marches; it makes the great human and terrestrial journey towards the celestial and the divine; it has its halts where it rallies the belated flock; it has its stations where it meditates, in sight of some splendid Canaan suddenly unveiling its horizon; it has its nights when it sleeps; and it is one of the bitter anxieties of the thinker to see the shadow upon the human soul, and to feel in the darkness progress asleep, without being able to waken it.

'*God is dead perhaps*,' said Gérard de Nerval one day, to him who writes these lines, confounding progress with God, and mistaking the interruption of the movement for the death of the Being.

He who despairs is wrong. Progress infallibly awakens, and, in short, we might say that it advances even in sleep, for it has grown. When we see it standing again, we find it taller. To be always peaceful belongs to progress no more than to the river; raise no obstruction, cast in no rock; the obstacle makes water foam and humanity seethe. Hence troubles; but after these troubles, we recognise that there has been some ground gained. Until order, which is nothing more nor less than universal peace, be established, until harmony and unity reign, progress will have revolutions for stations.

What then is progress? We have just said. The permanent life of the peoples.

Now, it sometimes happens that the momentary life of individuals offers resistance to the eternal life of the human race.

Let us acknowledge it without bitterness, the individual has his distinct interest, and may without offence set up that interest and defend it: the present has its excusable quantum of selfishness; the life of the moment has its rights, and is not bound to sacrifice itself continually to the future. The generation which has now its turn of passing over the earth is not compelled to abridge it for the generations, its equals after all, which are to have their turn afterwards. 'I exist,' murmurs that somebody whose name is All. 'I am young and I am in love, I am old and I want to rest, I am the father of a family, I am working, I am prospering, I am doing a good business, I have houses to rent, I have money in the government, I am happy. I have a wife and children, I love all this, I desire to live, let me alone.' Hence, at certain periods, a deep chill upon the magnanimous vanguard of the human race.

Utopia, moreover, we must admit, departs from its radiant sphere in making war. The truth of tomorrow, she borrows her process, battle, from the lie of yesterday. She, the future, acts like the past. She, the pure idea, becomes an act of force. She compromises her heroism by a violence for which it is just that she should answer; a violence of opportunity and of expediency, contrary to principles, and for which she is fatally punished. Utopia insurrection fights, the old military code in her hand; she shoots spies, she executes traitors, she suppresses living beings and casts them into the unknown dark. She uses death, a solemn thing. It seems as though Utopia had lost faith in the radiation of light, her irresistible and incorruptible strength. She strikes with the sword. Now, no sword is simple. Every blade has two edges; he who wounds with one wounds himself with the other.

This reservation made, and made in all severity, it is impossible for us not to admire, whether they succeed or not, the glorious combatants of the future, the professors of Utopia. Even when they fail, they are venerable, and it is perhaps in failure that they have the greater majesty. Victory, when it is according to progress, deserves the applause of the peoples; but a heroic defeat deserves their compassion. One is magnificent, the other is sublime. For ourselves, who prefer martyrdom to success, John Brown is greater than Washington, and Pisacane is greater than Garibaldi.

Surely some must be on the side of the vanquished.

Men are unjust towards these great essayists of the future when they fail.

The revolutionists are accused of striking terror. Every barricade seems an outrage. Their theories are incriminated, their aim is suspected, their afterthought is dreaded, their conscience is denounced. They are reproached with raising, building, and heaping up against the reigning social state a mound of miseries, of sorrows, of iniquities, of griefs, of despairs, and with tearing up blocks of darkness from the lower depths with which to entrench themselves and to fight. Men cry to them: 'You are unpaving hell!' They might answer: 'That is why our barricade is made of good intentions.'

The best, certainly, is the peaceable solution. On the whole, let us admit, when we see the pavement, we think of the bear, and his is a willingness about which society is not at ease. But the salvation of society depends upon itself; to its own willingness we appeal. No violent remedy is necessary. Study evil lovingly, determine it, then cure it. To that we urge.

However this may be, even when fallen, especially when fallen, august are they who, upon all points of the world, with eyes fixed on France, struggle for the great work with the inflexible logic of the ideal; they give their life a pure gift for progress; they accomplish the will of Providence; they perform a religious act. At the appointed hour, with as much disinterestedness as an actor who reaches his cue, obedient to the divine scenario, they enter into the tomb. And this hopeless combat, and this stoical disappearance, they accept to lead to its splendid and supreme universal consequences the magnificent movement of man, irresistibly commenced on the 14th of July 1789; these soldiers are priests. The French Revolution is an act of God.

Still, there are, and it is proper to add this distinction to the distinctions already indicated in another chapter, there are accepted insurrections which are called revolutions; there are rejected revolutions which are called *émeutes*. An insurrection breaking out is an idea passing its examination before the people. If the people drops its black ball, the idea is withered fruit; the insurrection is an affray.

To go to war upon every summons and whenever Utopia desires it, is not the part of the peoples. The nations have not always and at every hour the temperament of heroes and of martyrs.

They are positive. A priori, insurrection repels them; first, because it often results in disaster, secondly, because it always has an abstraction for its point of departure.

For, and this is beautiful, it is always for the ideal, and for the ideal alone, that those devote themselves who do devote themselves. An insurrection is an enthusiasm. Enthusiasm may work itself into anger; hence the resort to arms. But every insurrection which is directed against a government or a régime aims still higher. Thus, for instance, let us repeat what the chiefs of the insurrection of 1832, and in particular the young enthusiasts of the Rue de la Chanvrerie, fought against, was not exactly Louis Philippe. Most of them, speaking frankly, rendered justice to the qualities of this king, midway between the monarchy and the revolution; none hated him. But they attacked the younger branch of divine right in Louis Philippe as they had attacked the elder branch in Charles X; and what they desired to overthrow in overthrowing royalty in France, as we have explained, was the usurpation of man over man, and of privilege over right, in the whole world. Paris without a king has, as a consequence, the world without despots. They reasoned in this way. Their aim was distant doubtless, vague perhaps, and receding before effort, but great.

Thus it is. And men sacrifice themselves for these visions, which, to the sacrificed, are illusions almost always, but illusions with which, upon the whole, all human certainty is mingled. The insurgent poetises and gilds the insurrection. He throws himself into these tragic things, intoxicated with what he is going to do. Who knows? they will succeed perhaps. They are but few; they have against them a whole army; but they defend right, natural law, that sovereignty of each over himself, of which there is no abdication possible, justice, truth, and in case of need they die like the three hundred Spartans. They think not of Don Quixote, but of Leonidas. And they go forward, and, once engaged, they do not recoil, and they hurl themselves headlong, hoping for unparalleled victory, revolution completed, progress set at liberty, the aggrandisement of the human race, universal deliverance; and seeing at the worst a Thermopylæ.

These passages at arms for progress often fail; why, we have just told. The throng is restive under the sway of the paladins. The heavy masses, the multitudes, fragile on account of their very weight, dread uncertainties; and there is uncertainty in the ideal.

Moreover, let it not be forgotten, interests are there, little friendly to the ideal and the emotional. Sometimes the stomach paralyses the heart.

The grandeur and the beauty of France are that she cares less for the belly than other peoples; she knots the rope about her loins more easily. She is first awake, last asleep. She goes in advance. She is a pioneer.

That is because she is an artist.

The ideal is nothing more nor less than the culminating point of logic, even as the beautiful is nothing more nor less than the summit of the true. The artist people is thus the consistent people. To love beauty is to see light. This is why the torch of Europe, that is to say, civilisation, was first borne by Greece, who passed it to Italy, who passed it to France. Divine pioneer peoples! *Vitai lampada tradunt!*

An admirable thing, the poetry of a people is the element of its progress. The amount of civilisation is measured by the amount of imagination. Only a civilising people must remain a manly people. Corinth, yes; Sybaris, no. He who becomes effeminate becomes corrupt. We must be neither dilettanti nor virtuosi; but we must be artists. In the matter of civilisation, we must not refine, but we must sublime. On this condition, we give the human race the pattern of the ideal.

The modern ideal has its type in art, and its means in science. It is through science that we shall realise that august vision of the poets: social beauty. We shall reproduce Eden by A^+B. At the point which civilisation has reached, the exact is a necessary element of the splendid, and the artistic sentiment is not merely served, but completed by the scientific organ; dream must calculate. Art, which is the conqueror, must have its fulcrum in science, which is the mover. The solidity of the mounting is important. The modern spirit is the genius of Greece with the genius of India for its vehicle; Alexander upon the elephant.

Races petrified in dogma or demoralised by lucre are unfit to lead civilisation. Genuflexion before the idol or the dollar atrophies the muscle which walks and the will which goes. Hieratic or mercantile absorption diminishes the radiance of a people, lowers its horizon by lowering its level, and deprives it of that intelligence of the universal aim, at the same time human and divine, which makes the missionary nations. Babylon has no ideal. Carthage has no ideal. Athens and Rome have and preserve, even through all the thick night of centuries, haloes of civilisation.

France is of the same quality of people as Greece and Italy. She is Athenian by the beautiful, and Roman by the great. In addition she is good. She gives herself. She is oftener than other peoples in the spirit of devotion and sacrifice. Only this spirit takes her and leaves her. And here lies the great peril for those who run when she wishes to walk, or who walk when she wishes to stop. France has her relapses of materialism, and, at certain moments, the ideas which obstruct that sublime brain lose all that recalls French greatness, and are Of the dimensions of a Missouri or of a South Carolina. What is to be done? The giantess is playing the dwarf; immense France has her childish whims. That is all.

To this nothing can be said. A people, like a star, has the right of eclipse. And all is well, provided the light return and the eclipse do not degenerate into night. Dawn and resurrection are synonyms. The reappearance of the light is identical with the persistence of the Me.

Let us lay down these things with calmness. Death on the barricade, or a grave in exile, is an acceptable alternative for devotion. The true name of devotion is disinterestedness. Let the abandoned submit to abandonment, let the exile submit to exile, and let us content ourselves with imploring the great peoples not to recede too far, when they do recede. They must not, under pretext of a return to reason, go too far in the descent.

Matter is, the moment is, interest is, the belly is; but the belly must not be the only wisdom. The momentary life has its rights, we admit, but the permanent life has its also. Alas! to have risen does not prevent falling. We see this in history oftener than we would wish. A nation is illustrious; it tastes the ideal; then it bites the filth, and finds it good; and if we ask why it abandons Socrates for Falstaff, it answers: 'Because I love statesmen.'

A word more before returning to the conflict.

A battle like this which we are now describing is nothing but a convulsive movement towards the ideal. Enfettered progress is sickly, and it has these tragic epilepsies. This disease of progress, civil war, we have had to encounter upon our passage. It is one of the fatal phases, at once act and interlude, of this drama the pivot of which is a social outcast, and the true title of which is: *Progess.*

Progress!

This cry which we often raise, is our whole thought; and, at the present point of this drama, the idea that it contains having still more than one ordeal to undergo, it is permitted us perhaps, if not to lift the veil from it, at least to let the light shine clearly through.

The book which the reader has now before his eyes is, from one end to the other, in its whole and in its details, whatever may be the intermissions, the exceptions, or the defaults, the march from evil to good, from injustice to justice, from the false to the true, from night to day, from appetite to conscience, from rottenness to life, from brutality to duty, from Hell to Heaven, from nothingness to God. Starting point: matter; goal: the soul. Hydra at the beginning, angel at the end.

21. *The heroes*

SUDDENLY THE DRUM beat the charge.

The attack was a hurricane. In the evening, in the obscurity, the barricade had been approached silently as if by a boa. Now, in broad day, in this open street, surprise was entirely impossible; the strong hand, moreover, was unmasked, the cannon had commenced the roar, the army rushed upon the barricade. Fury was now skill. A powerful column of infantry of the line, intersected at equal intervals by National Guards and Municipal Guards on foot, and supported by deep masses heard but unseen, turned into the street at a quick step, drums beating, trumpets sounding, bayonets fixed, sappers at their head, and, unswerving under the projectiles, came straight upon the barricade with the weight of a bronze column upon a wall.

The wall held well.

The insurgents fired impetuously. The barricade scaled was like a mane of flashes. The assault was so sudden that for a moment it was overflowed by assailants; but it shook off the soldiers as the lion does the dogs, and it was covered with besiegers only as the cliff is with foam, to reappear, a moment afterwards, steep, black, and formidable.

The column, compelled to fall back, remained massed in the street, unsheltered, but terrible, and replied to the redoubt by a fearful fusilade. Whoever has seen fireworks remembers that sheaf made by a crossing of flashes which is called the bouquet. Imagine the bouquet, not now vertical, but horizontal, bearing a ball, a buckshot, or a bullet, at the point of each of its jets of fire, and scattering death in its clusters of thunder. The barricade was beneath it.

On both sides equal resolution. Bravery there was almost barbaric, and was mingled with a sort of heroic ferocity which began with the sacrifice of itself. Those were the days when a National Guard fought like a Zouave. The troops desired to make an end of it; the insurrection desired to struggle. The acceptance of death in full youth and in full health makes a frenzy of intrepidity. Every man in this mêlée felt the aggrandisement given by the supreme hour. The street was covered with dead.

Enjolras was at one end of the barricade, and Marius at the other. Enjolras, who carried the whole barricade in his head, reserved and sheltered himself; three soldiers fell one after the other under his battlement, without even having perceived him; Marius fought without shelter. He took no aim. He stood with more than half his body above the summit of the redoubt. There is no wilder prodigal than a miser who takes the bit in his teeth; there is no man more fearful in action than a dreamer. Marius was terrible and pensive. He was in the battle as in a dream. One would have said a phantom firing a musket.

The cartridges of the besieged were becoming exhausted; not so their sarcasms. In this whirlwind of the sepulchre in which they were, they laughed.

Courfeyrac was bareheaded.

'What have you done with your hat?' inquired Bossuet.

Courfeyrac answered:

'They have knocked it off at last by their cannonade.'

Or indeed they said haughty things.

'Does anybody understand these men,' exclaimed Feuilly bitterly (and he cited the names, well-known names, famous even, some of the old army), 'who promised to join us, and took an oath to help us, and who were bound to it in honour, and who are our generals, and who abandon us!'

And Combeferre simply answered with a grave smile:

'There are people who observe the rules of honour as we observe the stars, from afar off.'

The interior of the barricade was so strewn with torn cartridges that one would have said it had been snowing.

The assailants had the numbers; the insurgents the position. They were on the top of a wall, and they shot down the soldiers at the muzzles of their muskets, as they stumbled over the dead and wounded and became entangled in the escarpment. This barricade, built as it was, and admirably supported, was really one of those positions in which a handful of men hold a legion in check. Still, constantly reinforced and increasing under the shower of balls, the attacking column inexorably approached, and now, little by little, step by step, but with certainty, the army hugged the barricade as the screw hugs the winepress.

There was assault after assault. The horror continued to increase.

Then resounded over this pile of paving-stones, in this Rue de la Chanvrerie, a struggle worthy the walls of Troy. These men, wan, tattered, and exhausted, who had not eaten for twenty-four hours, who had not slept, who had but few more shots to fire, who felt their pockets empty of cartridges, nearly all wounded, their heads or arms bound with a smutty and blackened cloth, with holes in their coats whence the blood was flowing, scarcely armed with worthless muskets and with old hacked swords, became Titans. The barricade was ten times approached, assaulted, scaled, and never taken.

To form an idea of this struggle, imagine fire applied to a mass of terrible valour, and that you are witnessing the conflagration. It was not a combat, it was the interior of a furnace; there mouths breathed flame; there faces were wonderful. There the human form seemed impossible, the combatants flashed flames, and it was terrible to see going and coming in that lurid smoke these salamanders of the fray. The successive and simultaneous scenes of this grand slaughter, we decline to paint. The epic alone has a right to fill twelve thousand lines with one battle.

One would have said it was that hell of Brahminism, the most formidable of the seventeen abysses, which the Veda calls the Forest of Swords.

They fought breast to breast, foot to foot, with pistols, with sabres, with fists, at a distance, close at hand, from above, from below, from everywhere, from the roofs of the house, from the windows of the wine-shop, from the gratings of the cellars into which some had slipped. They were one against sixty. The facade of Corinth, half demolished, was hideous. The window, riddled with grape, had lost glass and sash, and was now nothing but a shapeless hole, confusedly blocked with paving-stones. Bossuet was killed; Feuilly was killed; Courfeyrac was killed; Joly was killed; Combeferre, pierced by three bayonet-thrusts in the breast, just as he was lifting a wounded soldier, had only time to look to heaven, and expired.

Marius, still fighting, was so hacked with wounds, particularly about his head, that the countenance was lost in blood, and you would have said that he had his face covered with a red handkerchief.

Enjolras alone was untouched. When his weapon failed, he reached his hand to right or left, and an insurgent put whatever weapon he could in his grasp. Of four swords, one more than Francis I. at Marignan, he now had but one stump remaining.

Homer says: 'Diomed slays Axylus, son of Teuthras, who dwelt in happy Arisbe; Euryalus, son of Mecisteus, exterminates Dresos and Opheltios, Aesepus, and that Pedasus whom the Naiad Abarbarea conceived by the irreproachable Bucolion; Ulysses overthrows Pidutes of Percote; Antilochus, Ablerus; Polypætes, Astyalus; Polydamas, Otus of Cyllene; and Teucer, Aretaon. Meganthius dies beneath the spear of Euripylus. Agamemnon, king of heroes, prostrates Elatus born in the lofty city which the sounding Satnio laves.' In our old poems of exploits, Esplandian attacks the giant Marquis Swantibore with a two-edged flame, while he defends himself by stoning the knight with the towers which he tears up. Our ancient mural frescoes show us the two dukes of Brittany and of Bourbon, armed, mailed, and crested for war, on horseback, and meeting each other, battle-axe in hand, masked with iron, booted with iron, gloved with iron, one caparisoned with ermine, the other draped with azure; Brittany with his lion between the two horns of his crown, Bourbon with a monstrous fleur-de-lis on the vizor of his casque. But to be superb, it is not necessary to bear like Yvon, the ducal morion, to handle, like Espiandian, a living flame, or like Phyles, father of Polydamas, to have brought from Ephyræ a fine armour, a present from the king of men Euphetes; it is enough to give life for a conviction or for a loyalty. That little artless soldier, yesterday a peasant of Beauce or Limousin, who prowls, cabbage-knife at his side, about the children's nurses in the Luxembourg, that pale young student bending over a piece of anatomy or a book, a fair-haired youth who trims his beard with scissors, take them both, breathe upon them a breath of duty, place them opposite each other in the Boucherat square or in the Cul-de-sac Blanche Mibray, and let the one fight for his flag, and the other for his ideal, and let them both imagine that they are fighting for the country; the strife will be colossal; and the shadow which will be thrown upon that great epic field where humanity is struggling, by this blue-coat and this saw-bones in quarrel, will equal the shadow which is cast by Megaryon, King of Lycia, full of tigers, wrestling body to body with the immense Ajax, equal of the gods.

22. *Foot to foot*

WHEN THERE WERE NONE of the chiefs alive save Enjolras and Marius, who were at the extremities of the barricade, the centre, which Courfeyrac, Joly, Bossuet, Feuilly, and Combeferre had so long sustained, gave way. The artillery, without making a practicable breach, had deeply indented the centre of the redoubt; there, the summit of the wall had disappeared under the balls, and had tumbled down; and the rubbish which had fallen, sometimes on the interior, sometimes on the exterior, had finally made, as it was heaped up, on either side of the wall, a kind of talus, both on the inside, and on the outside. The exterior talus offered an inclined plane for attack.

A final assault was now attempted, and this assault succeeded. The mass bristling with bayonets and hurled at a double-quick step, came on irresistible, and the dense battle-front of the attacking column appeared in the smoke at the top of the escarpment. This time, it was finished. The group of insurgents who defended the centre fell back pell-mell.

Then grim love of life was roused in some. Covered by the aim of that forest of muskets, several were now unwilling to die.

This is a moment when the instinct of self-preservation raises a howl, and the animal reappears in the man. They were pushed back to the high six-storey house which formed the rear of the redoubt. This house might be safety. This house was barricaded, and, as it were, walled in from top to bottom. Before the troops of the line would be in the interior of the redoubt, there was time for a door to open and shut, a flash was enough for that, and the door of this house, suddenly half opened and closed again immediately, to these despairing men was life. In the rear of this house, there were streets, possible flight, space. They began to strike this door with the butts of their muskets, and with kicks, calling, shouting, begging, wringing their hands. Nobody opened. From the window on the third storey, the death's head looked at them.

But Enjolras and Marius, with seven or eight who had been rallied about them, sprang forward and protected them. Enjolras cried to the soldiers: 'Keep back!' and an officer not obeying, Enjolras killed the officer. He was now in the little interior court of the redoubt, with his back to the house of Corinth, his sword in one hand, his carbine in the other, keeping the door of the wine-shop open while he barred it against the assailants. He cried to the despairing: 'There is but one door open. This one.' And, covering them with his body, alone facing a battalion, he made them pass in behind him. All rushed in. Enjolras executing with his carbine, which he now used as a cane, what cudgel-players call *la rose couverte*, beat down the bayonets about him and before him, and entered last of all; and for an instant it was horrible, the soldiers struggling to get in, the insurgents to close the door. The door was closed with such violence that, in shutting into its frame, it exposed, cut off, and adhering to the casement, the thumb and fingers of a soldier who had caught hold of it.

Marius remained without. A ball had broken his shoulder-blade; he felt that he was fainting, and that he was falling. At that moment, his eyes already closed, he experienced the shock of a vigorous hand seizing him, and his fainting fit, in which he lost consciousness, left him hardly time for this thought, mingled with the last memory of Cosette: 'I am taken prisoner. I shall be shot.'

Enjolras, not seeing Marius among those who had taken refuge in the wine-shop, had the same idea. But they had reached that moment when each has only time to think of his own death. Enjolras fixed the bar of the door and bolted it, and fastened it with a double turn of lock and padlock, while they were beating furiously on the outside, the soldiers with the butts of their muskets, the sappers with their axes. The assailants were massed upon this door. The siege of the wine-shop was now beginning.

The soldiers, we must say, were greatly irritated.

The death of the sergeant of artillery had angered them; and then, a more deadly thing, during the few hours which preceded the attack, it had been told among them that the insurgents mutilated prisoners, and that there was in the wine-shop the body of a soldier headless. This sort of unfortunate rumour is the ordinary accompaniment of civil wars, and it was a false report of this kind which, at a later day, caused the catastrophe of the Rue Transnonain.

When the door was barricaded, Enjolras said to the rest:

'Let us sell ourselves dearly.'

Then he approached the table upon which Mabeuf and Gavroche were extended. Two straight and rigid forms could be seen under the black cloth, one large, the other small, and the two faces were vaguely outlined beneath the stiff folds of the shroud. A hand projected from below the pall, and hung towards the floor. It was the old man's.

Enjolras bent down and kissed that venerable hand, as in the evening he had kissed the forehead.

They were the only kisses which he had given in his life.

We must be brief. The barricade had struggled like a gate of Thebes; the wine-shop struggled like a house of Saragossa. Such resistances are dogged. No quarter. No parley possible. They are willing to die provided they kill. When Suchet says: 'Capitulate,' Palafox answers: 'After the war with cannon, war with the knife.' Nothing was wanting to the storming of the Hucheloup wine-shop: neither the paving-stones raining from the window and the roof upon the besiegers, and exasperating the soldiers by their horrible mangling, nor the shots from the cellars and the garret windows, nor fury of attack, nor rage of defence; nor, finally, when the door yielded, the frenzied madness of the extermination. The assailants, on rushing into the wine-shop, their feet entangled in the panels of the door, which were beaten in and scattered over the floor, found no combatant there. The spiral stairway, which had been cut down with the axe, lay in the middle of the basement room, a few wounded had just expired, all who were not killed were in the first storey, and there, through the hole in the ceiling, which had been the entrance for the stairway, a terrific firing broke out. It was the last of the cartridges. When they were gone, when these terrible men in their death-agony had no longer either powder or ball, each took two of those bottles reserved by Enjolras, of which we have spoken, and they defended the ascent with these frightfully fragile clubs. They were bottles of aquafortis. We describe these gloomy facts of the carnage as they are. The besieged, alas, make a weapon of everything. Greek fire did not dishonour Archimedes, boiling pitch did not dishonour Bayard. All war is appalling, and there is nothing to choose in it. The fire of the besiegers, although difficult and from below upwards, was murderous. The edge of the hole in the ceiling was very soon surrounded with the heads of the dead, from which flowed long red and reeking lines. The uproar was inexpressible; a stifled and burning smoke made night almost over this combat. Words fail to express horror when it reaches this degree. There were men no longer in this now infernal conflict. They were no longer giants against colossi. It resembled Milton and Dante rather than Homer. Demons attacked, spectres resisted.

It was the heroism of monsters.

23. Orestes fasting and Pylades drunk

AT LAST, mounting on each other's shoulders, helping themselves by the skeleton of the staircase, climbing up the walls, hanging to the ceiling, cutting to pieces, at the very edge of the hatchway, the last to resist, some twenty of the besiegers, soldiers, National Guards, Municipal Guards, pell-mell, most disfigured by wounds in the face in this terrible ascent, blinded with blood, furious, become savages, made an irruption into the room of the first storey. There was now but a single man there on his feet, Enjolras. Without cartridges, without a sword, he had now in his hand only the barrel of his carbine, the stock of which he had broken over the heads of those who were entering. He had put the billiard table between the assailants and himself; he had retreated to the corner of the room, and there, with proud eye, haughty head, and that stump of a weapon in his grasp, he was still so formidable that a large space was left about him. A cry arose:

'This is the chief. It is he who killed the artilleryman. A he has put himself there, it is a good place. Let him stay. Let us shoot him on the spot.'

'Shoot me,' said Enjolras.

And, throwing away the stump of his carbine, and folding his arms, he presented his breast.

The boldness that dies well always moves men. As soon as Enjolras had folded his arms, accepting the end, the uproar of the conflict ceased in the room, and that chaos suddenly hushed into a sort of sepulchral solemnity. It seemed as if the menacing majesty of Enjolras, disarmed and motionless, weighed upon that tumult, and as if, merely by the authority of his tranquil eye, this young man, who alone had no wound, superb, bloody, fascinating, indifferent as if he were invulnerable, compelled that sinister mob to kill him respectfully. His beauty, at that moment, augmented by his dignity, was a resplendence, and, as if he could no more be fatigued than wounded, after the terrible twenty-four hours which had just elapsed, he was fresh and rosy. It was of him perhaps that the witness spoke who said afterwards before the court-martial: 'There was one insurgent whom I heard called Apollo.' A National Guard who was aiming at Enjolras, dropped his weapon, saying: 'It seems to me that I am shooting a flower.'

Twelve men formed in platoon in the corner opposite Enjolras and made their muskets ready in silence.

Then a sergeant cried: 'Take aim!'

An officer intervened.

'Wait.'

And addressing Enjolras:

'Do you wish your eyes bandaged?'

'No.'

'Was it really you who killed the sergeant of artillery?

'Yes.'

Within a few seconds Grantaire had awakened.

Grantaire, it will be remembered, had been asleep since the day previous in the upper room of the wine-shop, sitting in a chair, leaning heavily forward on a table.

He realised, in all its energy, strength, the old metaphor: dead drunk. The hideous potion, absinthe, stout and alcohol, had thrown him into a lethargy. His table being small, and of no use in the barricade, they had left it to him. He had continued in the same posture, his breast doubled over the table, his head lying flat upon his arms, surrounded by glasses, jugs, and bottles. He slept with that crushing sleep of the torpid bear and the overfed leech. Nothing had affected him, neither the musketry, nor the balls, nor the grape which penetrated through the casement into the room in which he was. Nor the prodigious uproar of the assault. Only, he responded sometimes to the cannon with a snore. He seemed waiting there for a ball to come and save him the trouble of awaking. Several corpses lay about him; and, at the first glance, nothing distinguished him from those deep sleepers of death.

Noise does not waken a drunkard; silence wakens him. This peculiarity has been observed more than once. The fall of everything about him augmented Grantaire's oblivion; destruction was a lullaby to him. The kind of halt in the tumult before Enjolras was a shock to this heavy sleep. It was the effect of a wagon at a gallop stopping short. The sleepers are roused by it. Grantaire rose up with a start, stretched his arms, rubbed his eyes, looked, gaped, and understood.

Drunkenness ending is like a curtain torn away. We see altogether, and at a single glance, all that is concealed. Everything is suddenly presented to the memory; and the drunkard who knows nothing of what has taken place for twenty-four hours, has no sooner opened his eyes than he is aware of all that has passed. His ideas come back to him with an abrupt lucidity, the effacement of drunkenness, a sort of lye-wash which blinds the brain, dissipates, and give place to clear and precise impressions of the reality.

Retired as he was in a corner and as it were sheltered behind the billiard-table, the soldiers, their eyes fixed upon Enjolras, had not even noticed Grantaire, and the sergeant was preparing to repeat the order: 'Take aim!' when suddenly they heard a powerful voice cry out beside them:

'*Vive la République!* I belong to it.'

Grantaire had arisen.

The immense glare of the whole combat which he had missed, and in which he had not been, appeared in the flashing eye of the transfigured drunkard.

He repeated: *'Vive la République!'* crossed the room with a firm step, and took his place before the muskets beside Enjolras.

'Two at one shot,' said he.

And, turning towards Enjolras gently, he said to him:

'Will you permit it?'

Enjolras grasped his hand with a smile.

This smile was not finished when the report was heard.

Enjolras, pierced by eight balls, remained backed against the wall as if the balls had nailed him there. Only he bowed his head.

Grantaire, stricken down, fell at his feet.

A few moments afterwards, the soldiers dislodged the last insurgents who had taken refuge in the top of the house. They fired through a wooden lattice into the garret. They fought in the attics. They threw the bodies out of the windows, some living. Two voltigeurs, who were trying to raise the shattered omnibus, were killed by two shots from a carbine fired from the dormer-windows. A man in a blouse was pitched out headlong, with a bayonet thrust in his belly, and his death-rattle was finished upon the ground. A soldier and an insurgent slipped together on the slope of the tiled roof, and would not let go of each other, and fell, clasped in a wild embrace. Similar struggle in the cellar. Cries, shots, savage stamping. Then silence. The barricade was taken.

The soldiers commenced the search of the houses round about and the pursuit of the fugitives.

24. *Prisoner*

MARIUS WAS in fact a prisoner. Prisoner of Jean Valjean.

The hand which had seized him from behind at the moment he was falling, and the grasp of which he had felt in losing consciousness, was the hand of Jean Valjean.

Jean Valjean had taken no other part in the combat than to expose himself. Save for him, in that supreme phase of the death-struggle, nobody would have thought of the wounded. Thanks to him, everywhere present in the carnage like a providence, those who fell were taken up, carried into the basement-room, and their wounds dressed. In the intervals, he repaired the barricade. But nothing which could resemble a blow, an attack, or even a personal defence, came from his hands. He was silent; and gave aid. Moreover, he had only a few scratches. The balls refused him. If suicide were a part of what had occurred to him in coming to this sepulchre, in that respect he had not succeeded. But we doubt whether he had thought of suicide, an irreligious act.

Jean Valjean, in the thick cloud of the combat, did not appear to see Marius; the fact is, that he did not take his eyes from him. When a shot struck down Marius, Jean Valjean bounded with the agility of a tiger, dropped upon him as upon a prey, and carried him away.

The whirlwind of the attack at that instant concentrated so fiercely upon Enjolras and the door of the wine-shop, that nobody saw Jean Valjean cross the unpaved field of the barricade, holding the senseless Marius in his arms, and disappear behind the corner of the house of Corinth.

It will be remembered that this corner was a sort of cape on the street; it sheltered from balls and grape, and from sight also, a few square feet of ground. Thus, there is sometimes in conflagrations a room which does not burn; and in the most furious seas, beyond a promontory or at the end of a cul-de-sac of shoals, a placid little haven. It was in this recess of the interior trapezium of the barricade that Eponine had died.

There Jean Valjean stopped: he let Marius slide to the ground, set his back to the wall, and cast his eyes about him.

The situation was appalling.

For the moment, for two or three minutes, perhaps, this skirt of wall was a shelter; but how escape from this massacre? He remembered the anguish in which he was in the Rue Polonceau, eight years before, and how he had succeeded in escaping; that was difficult then, today it was impossible. Before him he had that deaf and implacable house of six storeys, which seemed inhabited only by the dead man, leaning over his window; on his right he had the low barricade, which closed the Petite Truanderie; to clamber over this obstacle appeared easy, but above the crest of the wall a range of bayonet-points could be seen. A company of the line was posted beyond this barricade, on the watch. It was evident that to cross the barricade was to meet the fire of a platoon, and that every head which should venture to rise above the top of the wall of paving-stones would serve as a target for sixty muskets. At his left he had the field of the combat. Death was behind the corner of the wall.

What should he do?

A bird alone could have extricated himself from that place.

And he must decide upon the spot, find an expedient, adopt his course. They were fighting a few steps from him; by good luck all were fiercely intent upon a single point, the door of the wine-shop; but let one soldier, a single one, conceive the idea of turning the house, of attacking it in flank, and all was over.

Jean Valjean looked at the house in front of him, he looked at the barricade by the side of him, then he looked upon the ground, with the violence of the last extremity, in desperation, and as if he would have made a hole in it with his eyes.

Beneath his persistent look, something vaguely tangible in such an agony outlined itself and took form at his feet, as if there were a power in the eye to develop the thing desired. He perceived a few steps from him, at the foot of the little wall so pitilessly watched and guarded on the outside, under some fallen paving-stones which partly hid it, an iron grating laid flat and level with the ground. This grating, made of strong transverse bars, was about two feet square. The stone frame which held it had been torn up, and it was as it were unset. Through the bars a glimpse could be caught of an obscure opening, something like the flue of a chimney or the main of a cistern. Jean Valjean sprang forward. His old science of escape mounted to his brain like a flash. To remove the stones, to lift the grating, to load Marius, who was as inert as a dead body, upon his shoulders, to descend, with that burden upon his back, by the aid of his elbows and knees, into this kind of well, fortunately not very deep, to let fall over his head the heavy iron trapdoor upon which the stones were shaken back again, to find a foothold upon a flagged surface ten feet below the ground, this was executed like what is done in delirium, with the strength of a giant and the rapidity of an eagle; it required but very few moments.

Jean Valjean found himself, with Marius still senseless, in a sort of long underground passage.

There, deep peace, absolute silence, night.

The impression which he had formerly felt in falling from the street into the convent came back to him. Only, what he was now carrying away was not Cosette; it was Marius.

He could now hardly hear above him, like a vague murmur, the fearful tumult of the wine-shop taken by assault.

BOOK 2: THE INTESTINE OF LEVIATHAN

1. The earth impoverished by the sea

PARIS THROWS FIVE MILLIONS a year into the sea. And this without metaphor. How, and in what manner? day and night. With what object? without any object. With what thought? without thinking of it. For what return? for nothing. By means of what organ? by means of its intestine. What is its intestine? its sewer.

Five millions is the most moderate of the approximate figures which the estimates of special science give.

Science, after long experiment, now knows that the most fertilising and the most effective of manures is that of man. The Chinese, we must say to our shame, knew it before us. No Chinese peasant, Eckeberg tells us, goes to the city without carrying back, at the two ends of his bamboo, two buckets full of what we call filth. Thanks to human fertilisation, the earth in China is still as young as in the days of Abraham. Chinese wheat yields a hundred and twenty fold. There is no guano comparable in fertility to the detritus of a capital. A great city is the most powerful of stercoraries. To employ the city to enrich the plain would be a sure success. If our gold is filth, on the other hand, our filth is gold.

What is done with this filth, gold? It is swept into the abyss.

We fit out convoys of ships, at great expense, to gather up at the south pole the droppings of petrels and penguins, and the incalculable element of wealth which we have under our own hand, we send to the sea. All the human and animal manure which the world loses, restored to the land instead of being thrown into the water, would suffice to nourish the world.

These heaps of garbage at the corners of the stone blocks, these tumbrils of mire jolting through the streets at night, these horrid scavengers' carts, these fetid streams of subterranean slime which the pavement hides from you, do you know what all this is? It is the flowering meadow, it is the green grass, it is marjoram and thyme and sage, it is game, it is cattle, it is the satisfied low of huge oxen at evening, it is perfumed hay, it is golden corn, it is bread on your table, it is warm blood in your veins, it is health, it is joy, it is life. Thus wills that mysterious creation which is transformation upon earth and transfiguration in heaven.

Put that into the great crucible; your abundance shall spring from it. The nutrition of the plains makes the nourishment of men.

You have the power to throw away this wealth, and to think me ridiculous into the bargain. That will cap the climax of your ignorance.

Statistics show that France, alone, makes a liquidation of a hundred millions every year into the Atlantic from the mouths of her rivers. Mark this: with that hundred millions you might pay a quarter of the expenses of the government. The cleverness of man is such that he prefers to throw this hundred millions into the gutter. It is the very substance of the people which is carried away, here drop by drop, there in floods, by the wretched vomiting of our sewers into the rivers, and the gigantic collection of our rivers into the ocean. Each hiccough of our cloaca costs us a thousand francs. From this two results: the land impoverished and the water infected. Hunger rising from the furrow and disease rising from the river.

It is notorious, for instance, that at this hour the Thames is poisoning London.

As for Paris, it has been necessary within a few years past, to carry most of the mouths of the sewers down the stream below the last bridge.

A double tubular arrangement, provided with valves and sluiceways, sucking up and flowing back, a system of elementary drainage, as simple as the lungs of man, and which is already in full operation in several villages in England, would suffice to bring into our cities the pure water of the fields and send back into our fields the rich water of the cities; and this easy see-saw, the simplest in the world, would retain in our possession the hundred millions thrown away. We are thinking of something else.

The present system does harm in endeavouring to do good. The intention is good, the result is sad. Men think they are purging the city, they are emaciating the population. A sewer is a mistake. When drainage everywhere, with its double function, restoring what it takes away, shall have replaced the sewer, that simple impoverishing washing, then, this being combined with the data of a new social economy, the products of the earth will be increased tenfold, and the problem of misery will be wonderfully diminished. Add the suppression of parasitism, it will be solved.

In the meantime, the public wealth runs off into the river, and the leakage continues. Leakage is the word. Europe is ruining herself in this way by exhaustion.

As for France, we have just named her figure. Now, Paris containing a twenty-fifth of the total French population, and the Parisian guano being the richest of all, we are within the truth in estimating at five millions the portion of Paris in the loss of the hundred millions which France annually throws away. These five millions, employed in aid and in enjoyment, would double the splendour of Paris. The city expends them in cloacæ. So that we may say that the great prodigality of Paris, her marvellous fête, her Beaujon folly, her orgy, her full-handed outpouring of gold, her pageant, her luxury, her magnificence, is her sewer.

It is in this way that, in the blindness of a vicious political economy, we drown and let float downstream and be lost in the depths, the welfare of all. There should be Saint Cloud nettings for the public fortune.

Economically, the fact may be summed up thus: Paris a leaky basket.

Paris, that model city, that pattern of well-formed capitals of which every people endeavours to have a copy, that metropolis, of the ideal, that august country of the initiative, of impulse and enterprise, that centre and that abode of mind, that nation city, that hive of the future, that marvellous compound of Babylon and Corinth, from the point of view which we have just indicated, would make a peasant of Fo-Kian shrug his shoulders.

Imitate Paris, you will ruin yourself.

Moreover, particularly in this immemorial and senseless waste, Paris herself imitates.

These surprising absurdities are not new; there is no young folly in this. The ancients acted like the moderns. 'The cloacæ of Rome,' says Liebig, 'absorbed all the well-being of the Roman peasant. When the Campagna of Rome was ruined by the Roman sewer, Rome exhausted Italy, and when she had put Italy into her cloaca, she poured Sicily in, then Sardinia, then Africa. The sewer of Rome engulfed the world. This cloaca offered its maw to the city and to the globe. *Urbi et orbi.* Eternal city, unfathomable sewer.

In these things, as well as in others, Rome sets the example.

This example, Paris follows, with all the stupidity peculiar to cities of genius.

For the necessities of the operation which we have just explained, Paris has another Paris under herself; a Paris of sewers; which has its streets, its crossings, its squares, its blind alleys, its arteries, and its circulation, which is slime, minus the human form.

For we must flatter nothing, not even a great people; where there is everything, there is ignominy by the side of sublimity; and, if Paris contains Athens, the City of light, Tyre, the city of power, Sparta, the city of manhood, Nineveh, the city of prodigy, it contains also Lutetia, the city of mire.

Besides, the seal of her power is there also, and the titanic sink of Paris realises, among monuments, that strange ideal realised in humanity by some men, such as Machiavelli, Bacon, and Mirabeau: the sublimity of abjectness.

The subsoil of Paris, if the eye could penetrate the surface, would present the aspect of a colossal madrepore. A sponge has hardly more defiles and passages than the tuft of earth of fifteen miles' circuit upon which rests the ancient great city. Without speaking of the catacombs, which are a cave apart, without speaking of the inextricable trellis of the gas-pipes, without counting the vast tubular system for the distribution of living water which ends in the hydrants, the sewers of themselves alone form a prodigious dark network under both banks; a labyrinth the descent of which is its clue.

There is seen, in the humid haze, the rat, which seems the product of the accouchement of Paris.

2. *The ancient history of the sewer*

IMAGINE PARIS taken off like a cover, a bird's-eye view of the subterranean network of the sewers will represent upon either bank a sort of huge branch engrafted upon the river. Upon the right bank, the belt-sewer will be the trunk of this branch, the secondary conduits will be the limbs, and the primary drains will be the twigs.

This figure is only general and half exact, the right angle, which is the ordinary angle of this kind of underground ramification, being very rare in vegetation.

We shall form an image more closely resembling this strange geometric plan by supposing that we see spread out upon a background of darkness some grotesque alphabet of the East jumbled as in a medley, the shapeless letters of which are joined to each other, apparently pell-mell and as if by chance, sometimes by their corners, sometimes by their extremities.

The sinks and the sewers played an important part in the Middle Ages, in the Lower Empire, and in the ancient East. In them pestilence was born, in them despots died. The multitudes regarded almost with a religious awe these beds of corruption, monstrous cradles of death. The pit of vermin of Benares is not less bewildering than the Pit of Lions of Babylon. Tiglath Pilezer, according to the Rabbinical books, swore by the sink of Nineveh. It was from the sewer of Münster that John of Leyden made his false moon rise, and it was from the cloaca pit of Kekhschab that his eastern Menæchmus, Mokannah, the veiled prophet of Khorassan, made his false sunrise.

The history of men is reflected in the history of cloacæ. The Gemoniæ describe Rome. The sewer of Paris has been a terrible thing in time past. It has been a sepulchre, it has been an asylum. Crime, intelligence, social protest, liberty of conscience, thought, theft, all that human laws pursue or have pursued, have hidden in this hole; the Maillotins in the fourteenth century, the Tire-laines in the fifteenth, the Huguenots in the sixteenth, the Illuminati of Morin in the seventeenth, the Chauffeurs in the eighteenth. A hundred years ago, the blow of the dagger by night came thence, the pickpocket in danger glided thither; the forest had its cave; Paris had its sewer. Vagabondage, that Gallic *picareria*, accepted the sewer as an affiliation of the Cour des Miracles, and at night, crafty and ferocious, returned into the Maubué vomitoria as into an alcove.

It was quite natural that those whose field of daily labour was the Cul-de-sac Vide-Gousset, or the Rue Coupe-Gorge, should have for their nightly abode the culvert of the Chemin Vert or the Hurepoix kennel. Hence a swarm of traditions. All manner of phantoms haunt these long solitary corridors; putridity and miasma everywhere; here and there a breathing-hole through which Villon within chats with Rabelais without.

The sewer, in old Paris, is the rendezvous of all drainages and all assays. Political economy sees in it a detritus, social philosophy sees in it a residuum.

The sewer is the conscience of the city. All things converge into it and are confronted with one another. In this lurid place there is darkness, but there are no secrets. Everything has its real form, or at least its definitive form. This can be said for the garbage-heap, that it is no liar. Frankness has taken refuge in it. Basil's mask is found there, but we see the pasteboard, and the strings, and the inside as well as the outside, and it is emphasised with honest mud. Scapin's false nose is close by. All the uncleannesses of civilisation, when once out of service, fall into this pit of truth, where the immense social slipping is brought to an end. They are swallowed up, but they are displayed in it. This pell-mell is a confession. Here, no more false appearances, no possible plastering, the filth takes off its shirt, absolute nakedness, rout of illusions and of mirages, nothing more but what is, wearing the sinister face of what is ending. Reality and disappearance. Here, the stump of a bottle confesses drunkenness, the handle of a basket tells of domestic life; here, the apple core which has had literary opinions becomes again an apple core; the face on the big sou freely covers itself with verdigris, the spittle of Caïaphas encounters Falstaff's vomit, the louis d'or which comes from the gaming-house jostles the nail from which hangs the suicide's bit of rope, a livid fœtus rolls by wrapped in the spangles which danced at the opera last Mardi Gras, a cap which has judged men wallows near a rottenness which was one of Peggy's petticoats; it is more than brotherhood, it is the closest intimacy. All that paints besmears. The last veil is rent. A sewer is a cynic. It tells all.

This sincerity of uncleanness pleases us, and is a relief to the soul. When a man has passed his time on the earth in enduring the spectacle of the grand airs which are assumed by reasons of state, oaths, political wisdom, human justice, professional honesty, the necessities of position, incorruptible robes, it is a consolation to enter a sewer and see the slime which befits it.

It is a lesson at the same time. As we have just said, history passes through the sewer. The Saint Bartholomews filter drop by drop through the pavements. The great public assassinations, the political and religious butcheries, traverse this vault of civilisation, and push their dead into it. To the reflecting eye, all the historic murderers are there, in the hideous gloom, on their knees, with a little of their shroud for an apron, dolefully sponging their work. Louis XI is there with Tristan, Francis I is there with Duprat, Charles IX is there with his mother, Richelieu is there with Louis XIII, Louvois is there, Letellier is there, Hébert and Maillard are there, scraping the stones, and endeavouring to efface all trace of their deeds. Beneath these vaults we hear the broom of these spectres. We breathe the enormous fetidness of social catastrophes. We see reddish reflections in the corners. There flows a terrible water, in which bloody hands have been washed.

The social observer should enter these shades. They are part of his laboratory. Philosophy is the microscope of thought. Everything desires to flee from it, but nothing escapes it. Tergiversation is useless. What phase of your character do you show in tergiversation? the shameful phase. Philosophy pursues evil with its rigid search, and does not permit it to glide away into nothingness. In the effacement of things which disappear, in the lessening of those which vanish, it recognises everything. It reconstructs the purple from the rag and the woman from the tatter. With the cloaca it reproduces the city, with the mire it reproduces its customs. From a fragment it infers the amphora, or the pitcher. It recognises by the print of a finger nail upon a parchment the difference between the Jewry of the Judengasse and the Jewry of the Ghetto. It finds in what remains what has been, the good, the ill, the false, the true, the stain of blood in the palace, the blot of ink in the cavern, the drop of grease in the brothel, trials undergone, temptations welcomed, orgies spewed out, the wrinkles which characters have received in abasing themselves, the trace of prostitution in souls which their own grossness has made capable of it, and, on the vest of the porters of Rome, the mark of Messalina's elbow.

3. Bruneseau

THE SEWER OF PARIS, in the Middle Ages, was legendary. In the sixteenth century, Henry II attempted an examination, which failed. Less than a hundred years ago, the cloaca, Mercier bears witness, was abandoned to itself, and became what it might.

Such was that ancient Paris, given up to quarrels, to indecisions, and to gropings. It was for a long time stupid enough. Afterwards, '89 showed how cities come to their wits. But, in the good old times, the capital had little head; she could not manage her affairs either morally or materially, nor better sweep away her filth than her abuses. Everything was an obstacle, everything raised a question. The sewer, for instance, was refractory to all itineracy. Men could no more succeed in guiding themselves through its channels than in understanding themselves in the city; above, the unintelligible, below, the inextricable; beneath the confusion of tongues there was the confusion of caves; Labyrinth lined Babel.

Sometimes, the sewer of Paris took it into its head to overflow, as if that unappreciated Nile were suddenly seized with wrath. There were, infamous to relate, inundations from the sewer. At intervals, this stomach of civilisation digested badly, the cloaca flowed back into the city's throat, and Paris had the aftertaste of its slime. These resemblances of the sewer to remorse had some good in them; they were warnings; very badly received, however; the city was indignant that its mire should have so much audacity, and did not countenance the return of the ordure. Drive it away better.

The inundation of 1802 is a present reminiscence with Parisians of eighty. The mire spread out in a cross in the Place des Victoires, where the statue of Louis XIV is; it entered the Rue Saint Honoré by the two mouths of the sewer of the Champs Elysées, the Rue Saint Florentin by the Saint Florentin sewer, the Rue Pierre à Poisson by the sewer of the Sonnerie, the Rue Popincourt by the sewer of the Chemin Vert, the Rue de la Roquette by the sewer of the Rue de Sappe; it covered the curbstones of the Rue des Champs Elysées to the depth of some fourteen inches; and, on the south, by the vomitoria of the Seine performing its function in the inverse way, it penetrated the Rue Mazarine, the Rue de l'Echaudé, and the Rue des Marais, where it stopped, having reached the length of a hundred and twenty yards, just a few steps from the house which Racine had lived in, respecting, in the seventeenth century, the poet more than the king. It attained its maximum depth in the Rue Saint Pierre, where it rose three feet above the flagging of the water-spouts, and its maximum extent in the Rue Saint Sabin, where it spread out over a length of two hundred and sixty-one yards.

At the commencement of this century, the sewer of Paris was still a mysterious place. Mire can never be in good repute; but here ill-fame reached even fright. Paris dimly realised that she had a terrible cave beneath her. People talked of it as of that monstrous bog of Thebes which swarmed with scolopendras fifteen feet long, and which might have served as a bathing-tub for Behemoth. The big boots of the sewer-men never ventured beyond certain known points. They were still very near the time when the scavengers' tumbrils, from the top of which Sainte Foix fraternised with the Marquis of Créqui, were simply emptied into the sewer. As for cleansing, that operation was confided to the showers, which obstructed more than they swept out. Rome still left some poetry to her cloaca, and called it Gemoniæ; Paris insulted hers and called it the Stink-Hole. Science and superstition were at one in regard to the horror. The Stink-Hole was not less revolting to hygiene than to legend. The Goblin Monk had appeared under the fetid arch of the Mouffetard sewer; the corpses of the Marmousets had been thrown into the sewer of the Barillerie; Fagon had attributed the fearful malignant fever of 1685 to the great gap in the sewer of the Marais which remained yawning until 1833, in the Rue Saint Louis, almost in front of the sign of the Gallant Messenger. The mouth of the sewer of the Rue de la Mortellerie was famous for the pestilence which came from it; with its pointed iron grating which looked like a row of teeth, it lay in that fatal street like the jaws of a dragon blowing hell upon men. The popular imagination seasoned the gloomy Parisian sink with an indefinably hideous mixture of the infinite. The sewer was bottomless. The sewer was the barathrum. The idea of exploring these leprous regions did not occur even to the police. To tempt that unknown, to throw the lead into that darkness, to go on a voyage of discovery in that abyss, who would have dared? It was frightful. Somebody came forward, however. The cloaca had its Columbus.

One day in 1805, on one of those rare visits which the emperor made to Paris, the Minister of the Interior came to the master's private audience. In the carrousel was heard the clatter of the swords of all those marvellous soldiers of the Grand Republic and the Grand Empire; there was a multitude of heroes at the door of Napoleon; men of the Rhine, of the Scheldt, of the Adige, and of the Nile; companions of Joubert, of Desaix, of Marceau, of Hoche, of Kléber; balloonists of Fleurus; grenadiers of Mayence, pontooniers of Genoa, hussars whom the Pyramids had beheld, artillerymen whom Junot's ball had bespattered, cuirassiers who had taken by assault the fleet at anchor in the Zuyder Zee; these had followed Bonaparte over the bridge of Lodi, those had been with Murat in the trenches of Mantua, others had preceded Lannes in the sunken road of Montebello. The whole army of that time was there, in the Court of the Tuileries, represented by a squad or a platoon, guarding Napoleon in repose; and it was the splendid epoch when the grand army had behind it Marengo and before it Austerlitz. 'Sire,' said the Minister of the Interior to Napoleon, 'I saw yesterday the boldest man in your empire.' 'Who is the man,' said the emperor quickly, 'and what has he done?' 'He wishes to do something, sire.' 'What?' 'To visit the sewers of Paris.'

That man existed, and his name was Bruneseau.

4. Details ignored

THE VISIT WAS MADE. It was a formidable campaign; a night battle against pestilence and asphyxia. It was at the same time a voyage of discoveries. One of the survivors of this exploration, an intelligent working-man, then very young, still related a few years ago the curious details which Bruneseau thought it his duty to omit in his report to the prefect of police, as unworthy the administrative style. Disinfecting processes were very rudimentary at that period. Hardly had Bruneseau passed the first branchings of the subterranean network, when eight out of the twenty labourers refused to go further. The operation was complicated; the visit involved the cleaning; it was necessary therefore to clean, and at the same time to measure; to note the entrance of water, to count the gratings and the mouths, to detail the branchings, to indicate the currents at the points of separation, to examine the respective borders of the various basins, to fathom the little sewers engrafted upon the principal sewer, to measure the height of each passage under the keystone, and the width, as well at the spring of the arch as at the level of the floor, finally to determine the ordinates of the levellings at a right angle with each entrance of water, either from the floor of the sewer, or from the surface of the street. They advanced with difficulty. It was not uncommon for the step ladders to plunge into three feet of mire. The lanterns flickered in the miasms. From time to time, they brought out a sewerman who had fainted. At certain places, a precipice. The soil had sunken, the pavement had crumbled, the sewer had changed into a blind well; they found no solid ground; one man suddenly disappeared; they had great difficulty in recovering him. By the advice of Fourcroy, they lighted from point to point, in the places sufficiently purified, great cages full of oakum and saturated with resin. The wall, in places, was-covered with shapeless fungi, and one would have said with tumours; the stone itself seemed diseased in this irrespirable medium.

Bruneseau, in his exploration, proceeded from the head towards the mouth. At the point of separation of the two water pipes from the Grand Hurleur, he deciphered upon a projecting stone the date 1550; this stone indicated the limit reached by Philibert Delorme, who was charged by Henry II with visiting the subterranean canals of Paris. This stone was the mark of the sixteenth century upon the sewer; Bruneseau also found the handiwork of the seventeenth century, in the conduit of the Ponceau and the conduit of the Rue Vieille du Temple, built between 1600 and 1650, and the handiwork of the eighteenth century in the western section of the collecting canal, banked up and arched in 1740. These two arches, especially the later one, that of 1740, were more cracked and more dilapidated than the masonry of the belt sewer, which dated from 1412, the epoch when the fresh-water brook of Ménilmontant was raised to the dignity of Grand Sewer of Paris, an advancement analogous to that of a peasant who should become first valet de chambre to the king; something like Gros Jean transformed into Lebel.

They thought they recognised here and there, chiefly under the Palais de Justice, some cells of ancient dungeons built in the sewer itself. Hideous *in pace*. An iron collar hung in one of these cells. They walled them all up. Some odd things were found; among other things the skeleton of an ourang-outang which disappeared from the Jardin des Plantes in 1800, a disappearance probably connected with the famous and incontestable appearance of the devil in the Rue des Bernardins in the last year of the eighteenth century. The poor devil finally drowned himself in the sewer.

Under the long arched passage which terminates at the Arche Marion, a ragpicker's basket, in perfect preservation, was the admiration of connoisseurs. Everywhere, the mud, which the workmen had come to handle boldly, abounded in precious objects, gold and silver trinkets, precious stones, coins. A giant who should have filtered this cloaca would have had the riches of centuries in his sieve. At the point of separation of the two branches of the Rue du Temple and the Rue Sainte Avoye, they picked up a singular Huguenot medal in copper, bearing on one side a hog wearing a cardinal's hat, and on the other a wolf with the tiara on his head.

The most surprising discovery was at the entrance of the Grand Sewer. This entrance had been formerly closed by a grating, of which the hinges only remained. Hanging to one of these hinges was a sort of shapeless and filthy rag, which, doubtless, caught there on its passage, had fluttered in the darkness, and was finally worn to tatters. Bruneseau approached his lantern to this strip and examined it. It was of very fine cambric, and they made out at the least worn of the corners a heraldic crown embroidered above these seven letters: LAVBESP. The crown was a marquis's crown, and the seven letters signified *Laubespine*. They recognised that what they had before their eyes was a piece of Marat's winding-sheet. Marat, in his youth, had had his amours. It was when he made a portion of the household of the Count d'Artois in the capacity of physician of the stables. From these amours, a matter of history, with a great lady, there remained to him this sheet. Waif or souvenir. At his death, as it was the only fine linen he had in the house, he was shrouded in it. Old women dressed out for the tomb, in this cloth in which there had been pleasure, the tragic Friend of the People. Bruneseau passed on. They left this scrap where it was; they did not make an end of it. Was this contempt or respect? Marat deserved both. And then, destiny was so imprinted upon it that they might hesitate to touch it. Besides, we should leave the things of the grave in the place which they choose. In short, the relic was strange. A marchioness had slept upon it; Marat had rotted in it; it had passed through the Pantheon to come at last to the rats of the sewer. This rag of the alcove, every fold of which Watteau would once have gladly sketched, had at last become worthy of Dante's fixed regard.

The complete visitation of the subterranean sewer system of Paris occupied seven years, from 1805 to 1812. While yet he was performing it, Bruneseau laid out, directed, and brought to an end some considerable works; in 1808 he lowered the floor of the Ponceau, and, creating new lines everywhere, he extended the sewer, in 1809, under the Rue St Denis as far as the Fontaine des Innocents; in 1810, under the Rue Froidmanteau and under La Salpêtrière; in 1811, under the Rue Neuve des Petits Pères, the Rue du Mail, the Rue de l'Echarpe, and the Place Royale; in 1812, under the Rue de la Paix and the Chaussée d'Antin. At the same time, he disinfected and purified the whole network. After the second year, Bruneseau was assisted by his son-in-law Nargaud.

Thus, at the beginning of this century, the old society cleansed its double bottom and made the toilette of its sewer. It was always so much cleaned.

Tortuous, fissured, unpaved, crackling, interrupted by quagmires, broken by fantastic elbows, rising and falling out of all Tule, fetid, savage, wild, submerged, in obscurity, with scars on its pavements and gashes on its walls, appalling, such was, seen retrospectively, the ancient sewer of Paris. Ramifications in every direction, crossings of trenches, branchings, goose-tracks, stars as if in mines, cœcums, cul-de-sacs, arches covered with saltpetre, infectious cesspools, a herpetic ooze upon the walls, drops falling from the ceiling, darkness; nothing equalled the horror of this old voiding crypt, the digestive apparatus of Babylon, cavern, grave, gulf pierced with streets, titanic molehill, in which the mind seems to see prowling through the shadow, in the ordure which has been splendour, that enormous blind mole, the past.

This, we repeat, was the sewer of former times.

5. *Present progress*

At present the sewer is neat, cold, straight, correct. It almost realises the ideal of what is understood in England by the word 'respectable.' It is comely and sober; drawn by the line; we might almost say fresh from the band-box. It is like a contractor become a councillor of state. We almost see clearly in it. The filth comports itself decently. At the first glance, we should readily take it for one of those underground passages formerly so common and so useful for the flight of monarchs and princes, in that good old time 'when the people loved their kings.' The present sewer is a beautiful sewer; the pure style reigns in it; the classic rectilinear alexandrine which, driven from poetry, appears to have taken refuge in architecture, seems mingled with every stone of that long darkling and whitish arch; each discharging mouth is an arcade; the Rue de Rivoli rules the school even in the cloaca. However, if the geometric line is in place anywhere, it surely is in the stercorary trenches of a great city. There, all should be subordinated to the shortest road. The sewer has now assumed a certain official aspect. The very police reports of which it is sometimes the object are no longer wanting in respect for it. The words which characterise it in the administrative language are elevated and dignified. What was called a gut is called a gallery; what was called a hole is called a vista. Villon would no longer recognise his old dwelling in case of need. This network of caves has still indeed its immemorial population of rodents, swarming more than ever; from time to time, a rat, an old moustache, risks his head at the window of the sewer and examines the Parisians; but these vermin themselves have grown tame, content as they are with their subterranean palace. The cloaca has now nothing of its primitive ferocity. The rain, which befouled the sewer of former times, washes the sewer of the present day. Do not trust in it too much, however. Miasmas still inhabit it. It is rather hypocritical than irreproachable. The prefecture of police and the health commission have laboured in vain. In spite of all the processes of purification, it exhales a vague odour, suspicious as Tartuffe, after confession.

Let us admit, as, all things considered, street-cleaning is a homage which the sewer pays to civilisation, and as, from this point of view, Tartuffe's conscience is an advance upon Augeas' stable, it is certain that the sewer of Paris has been ameliorated.

It is more than an advance; it is a transmutation. Between the ancient sewer and the present sewer, there is a revolution. Who has wrought this revolution?

The man whom everybody forgets, and whom we have named. Bruneseau.

6. Future progress

THE EXCAVATION OF THE SEWER of Paris has been no small work. The last ten centuries have laboured upon it, without being able to complete it any more than to finish Paris. The sewer, indeed, receives all the impulsions of the growth of Paris. It is, in the earth, a species of dark polyp with a thousand antennæ which grows beneath at the same time that the city grows above. Whenever the city opens a street, the sewer puts out an arm. The old monarchy had constructed only twenty-five thousand four hundred and eighty yards of sewers; Paris was at that point on the 1st of January 1806. From that epoch, of which we shall speak again directly, the work was profitably and energetically resumed and continued; Napoleon built, the figures are interesting, five thousand two hundred and fifty-four yards; Louis XVIII, six thousand two hundred and forty-four; Charles X, eleven thousand eight hundred and fifty-one; Louis Philippe, ninety-seven thousand three hundred and fifty-five; the Republic of 1848, twenty-five thousand five hundred and seventy; the existing régime, seventy-seven thousand one hundred; in all, at the present hour, two hundred and forty-seven thousand eight hundred and twenty-eight yards; a hundred and forty miles of sewers; the enormous entrails of Paris. Obscure ramification always at work; unnoticed and immense construction.

As we see, the subterranean labyrinth of Paris is today more than tenfold what it was at the commencement of the century. It is hard to realise all the perseverance and effort which were necessary to bring this cloaca to the point of relative perfection where it now is. It was with great difficulty that the old monarchical provostship and, in the last ten years of the eighteenth century, the revolutionary mayoralty, had succeeded in piercing the thirteen miles of sewers which existed before 1806. All manner of obstacles hindered this operation, some peculiar to the nature of the soil, others inherent in the very prejudices of the labouring population of Paris. Paris is built upon a deposit singularly rebellious to the spade, the hoe, the drill, to human control. Nothing more difficult to pierce and to penetrate than that geological formation upon which is superposed the wonderful historical formation called Paris; as soon as, under whatever form, labour commences and ventures into that street of alluvium, subterraneous resistance abounds. There are liquid clays, living springs, hard rocks, those soft and deep mires which technical science calls Moutardes. The pick advances laboriously into these calcareous strata alternating with seams of very fine clay and laminar schistose beds, encrusted with oyster shells contemporary with the pre-adamite oceans. Sometimes a brook suddenly throws down an arch which has been commenced, and inundates the labourers; or a slide of marl loosens and rushes down with the fury of a cataract, crushing the largest of the sustaining timbers like glass. Quite recently at Villette, when it was necessary, without interrupting navigation and without emptying the canal, to lead the collecting sewer under the Saint Martin canal, a fissure opened in the head of the canal; the water suddenly rose in the works underground, beyond all the power of the pumps; they were obliged to seek the fissure, which was in the neck of the great basin, by means of a diver, and it was not without difficulty that it was stopped. Elsewhere, near the Seine, and even at some distance from the river, as, for instance, at Belleville, Grande Rue, and the Lunière arcade, we find quicksands in which we sink, and a man may be buried out of sight. Add asphyxia from the miasma, burial by the earth falling in, sudden settlings of the bottom. Add typhus, with which the labourers are slowly impregnated. In our day, after having excavated the gallery of Clichy, with a causeway to receive a principal water-pipe from the Ourcq, a work executed in a trench, over ten yards in depth; after having, in spite of slides, by means of excavations, often putrid, and by props, arched the Bièvre from the Boulevard de l'Hôpital to the Seine; after having, to deliver Paris from the swelling waters of Montmartre and to furnish an outlet for that fluvial sea of twenty-two acres which stagnated near the Barrière des Martyrs, after having, we say, constructed the line of sewers from the Barrière Blanche to the Aubervilliers road, in four months, working day and night, at a depth of twelve yards; after having, a thing which had not been seen before, executed entirely underground a sewer in the Rue Barre du Bec, without a trench, twenty feet below the surface, Superintendent Monnot died. After having arched three thousand yards of sewers in all parts of the city, from the Rue Traversière Saint Antoine to the Rue de l'Ourcine; after having, by the branching of the Arbalète, relieved the Censier Mouffetard Square from inundation by the rain; after having built the Saint Georges sewer upon stonework and concrete in the quicksand; after having directed the dangerous lowering of the floor of the Notre Dame de Nazareth branch, Engineer Duleau died. There are no bulletins for these acts of bravery, more profitable, however, than the stupid slaughter of the battlefield.

The sewers of Paris, in 1832, were far from being what they are today.

Bruneseau had made a beginning, but it required the cholera to determine the vast reconstruction which has since taken place. It is surprising to say, for instance, that, in 1821, a portion of the belt sewer, called the Grand Canal, as at Venice, was still stagnating in the open sky, in the Rue des Gourdes. It was only in 1823 that the city of Paris found in its pocket the forty-nine thousand eight hundred and ninety dollars and one cent necessary for the covering of this shame. The three absorbing wells of the Combat, the Cunette, and Saint Mandé, with their discharging mouths, their apparatus, their pits, and their depuratory branches, date only from 1836. The intestinal canal of Paris has been rebuilt anew, and, as we have said, increased more than tenfold within a quarter of a century.

Thirty years ago, at the period of the insurrection of the 5th and 6th of June, it was still, in many places, almost the ancient sewer. A very large number of streets, now vaulted, were then hollow causeways. You very often saw, at the low point in which the gutters of a street or a square terminated, large rectangular gratings with great bars, the iron of which shone, polished by the feet of the multitude, dangerous and slippery for wagons, and making the horses stumble. The official language of roads and bridges gave to these low points and gratings the expressive name of *Cassis*. In 1832, in many streets, the Rue de l'Etoile, the Rue Saint Louis, the Rue du Temple, the Rue Vieille du Temple, the Rue Notre Dame de Nazareth, the Rue Folie Méricourt, the Quai aux Fleurs, the Rue du Petit Musc, the Rue de Normandie, the Rue Pont aux Biches, the Rue des Marais, Faubourg Saint Martin, the Rue Notre Dame des Victoires, Faubourg Montmartre, the Rue Grange Batelière in the Champs Elysées, the Rue Jacob, the Rue de Tournon, the old Gothic cloaca still cynically showed its jaws. They were enormous, sluggish gaps of stone, sometimes surrounded by stone blocks, with monumental effrontery.

Paris, in 1806, was still almost at the figure of sewers established in May 1663: five thousand three hundred and twenty-eight fathoms. According to Bruneseau, on the 1st of January 1832, there were forty-four thousand and seventy-three yards. From 1806 to 1831, there were built annually, on an average, eight hundred and twenty yards; since then there have been constructed every year eight, and even ten thousand yards of galleries, in masonry of small materials laid in hydraulic cement on a foundation of concrete.

At thirty-five dollars a yard, the hundred and forty miles of sewers of the present Paris represent nine millions.

Besides the economical progress which we pointed out in commencing, grave problems of public hygiene are connected with this immense question: the sewer of Paris.

Paris is between two sheets, a sheet of water and a sheet of air. The sheet of water lying at a considerable depth under ground, but already reached by two borings, is furnished by the bed of green sand lying between the chalk and the jurassic limestone; this bed may be represented by a disk with a radius of seventy miles; a multitude of rivers and brooks filter into it; we drink the Seine, the Marne, the Yonne, the Oise, the Aisne, the Cher, the Vienne, and the Loire, in a glass of water from the well of Grenelle. The sheet of water is salubrious; it comes, first from heaven, then from the earth; the sheet of air is unwholesome, it comes from the sewer. All the miasmas of the cloaca are mingled with the respiration of the city; hence that foul breath. The air taken from above a dunghill, this has been scientifically determined, is purer than the air taken from above Paris. In a given time, progress aiding, mechanisms being perfected, and light increasing, the sheet of water will be employed to purify the sheet of air. That is to say, to wash the sewer. By washing the sewer, of course, we understand: restitution of the mire to the land; return of the muck to the soil, and the manure to the fields. There will result, from this simple act, to the whole social community, a diminution of misery and an augmentation of health. At the present hour, the radiation of the diseases of Paris extends a hundred and fifty miles about the Louvre, taken as the hub of this pestilential wheel.

We might say that, for ten centuries, the cloaca has been the disease of Paris. The sewer is the taint which the city has in her blood. The popular instinct is never mistaken. The trade of sewerman was formerly almost as perilous, and almost as repulsive to the people, as the trade of knacker so long stricken with horror, and abandoned to the executioner. It required high wages to persuade a mason to disappear in that fetid ooze; the well-digger's ladder hesitated to plunge into it; it was said proverbially: *to descend into the sewer is to enter the grave;* and all manner of hideous legends, as we have said, covered this colossal drain with dismay; awful sink, which bears the traces of the revolutions of the globe as well as of the revolutions of men, and in which we find vestiges of all the cataclysms from the shellfish of the deluge down to the rag of Marat.

BOOK 3: MIRE, BUT SOUL

1. The cloaca and its surprises

It was in the sewer of Paris that Jean Valjean found himself.

Further resemblance of Paris with the sea. As in the ocean, the diver can disappear.

The transition was marvellous. From the very centre of the city, Jean Valjean had gone out of the city, and, in the twinkling of an eye, the time of lifting a cover and closing it again, he had passed from broad day to complete obscurity, from noon to midnight, from uproar to silence, from the whirl of the thunder to the stagnation of the tomb, and, by a mutation much more prodigious still than that of the Rue Polonceau, from the most extreme peril to the most absolute security.

Sudden fall into a cave; disappearance in the dungeon of Paris; to leave that street in which death was everywhere for this kind of sepulchre in which there was life was an astounding crisis. He remained for some seconds as if stunned; listening, stupefied. The spring trap of safety had suddenly opened beneath him. Celestial goodness had in some sort taken him by treachery. Adorable ambuscades of Providence!

Only, the wounded man did not stir, and Jean Valjean did not know whether what he was carrying away in this grave were alive or dead.

His first sensation was blindness. Suddenly he saw nothing more. It seemed to him also that in one minute he had become deaf. He heard nothing more. The frenzied storm of murder which was raging a few feet above him only reached him, as we have said, thanks to the thickness of the earth which separated him from it, stifled and indistinct, and like a rumbling at a great depth. He felt that it was solid under his feet; that was all; but that was enough. He reached out one hand, then the other, and touched the wall on both sides, and realised that the passage was narrow; he slipped, and realised that the pavement was wet. He advanced one foot with precaution, fearing a hole, a pit, some gulf; he made sure that the flagging continued. A whiff of fetidness informed him where he was.

After a few moments, he ceased to be blind. A little light fell from the air-hole through which he had slipped in, and his eye became accustomed to this cave. He began to distinguish something. The passage in which he was earthed, no other word better expresses the condition, was walled up behind him. It was one of those cul-de-sacs technically called branchments. Before him, there was another wall, a wall of night. The light from the air-hole died out ten or twelve paces from the point at which Jean Valjean stood, and scarcely produced a pallid whiteness over a few yards of the damp wall of the sewer. Beyond, the opaqueness was massive; to penetrate it appeared horrible, and to enter it seemed like being engulfed. He could, however, force his way into that wall of mist, and he must do it. He must even hasten. Jean Valjean thought that that grating, noticed by him under the paving-stones, might also be noticed by the soldiers, and that all depended upon that chance. They also could descend into the well and explore it. There was not a minute to be lost. He had laid Marius upon the ground, he gathered him up, this is again the right word, replaced him upon his shoulders, and began his journey. He resolutely entered that obscurity.

The truth is, that they were not so safe as Jean Valjean supposed. Perils of another kind, and not less great, awaited them perhaps. After the flashing whirl of the combat, the cavern of miasmas and pitfalls; after chaos, the cloaca. Jean Valjean had fallen from one circle of Hell to another.

At the end of fifty paces he was obliged to stop. A question presented itself. The passage terminated in another which it met transversely. These two roads were offered. Which should be take? should he turn to the left or to the right? How guide himself in this black labyrinth. This labyrinth, as we have remarked, has a clue: its descent. To follow the descent is to go to the river.

Jean Valjean understood this at once.

He said to himself that he was probably in the sewer of the markets; that, if he should choose the left and follow the descent, he would come in less than a quarter of an hour to some mouth upon the Seine between the Pont au Change and the Pont Neuf, that is to say, he would reappear in broad day in the most populous portion of Paris. He might come out in some gathering of corner idlers. Amazement of the passers-by at seeing two bloody men come out of the ground under their feet. Arrival of *sergent de ville*, call to arms in the next guardhouse. He would be seized before getting out. It was better to plunge into the labyrinth, to trust to this darkness, and to rely on Providence for the issue.

He chose the right, and went up the ascent.

When he had turned the corner of the gallery, the distant gleam of the air-hole disappeared, the curtain of obscurity fell back over him, and he again became blind. He went forward none the less, and as rapidly as he could. Marius' arms were passed about his neck, and his feet hung behind him. He held both arms with one hand, and groped for the wall with the other. Marius' cheek touched his and stuck to it, being bloody. He felt a warm stream, which came from Marius, flow over him and penetrate his clothing. Still, a moist warmth at his ear, which touched the wounded man's mouth, indicated respiration, and consequently life. The passage through which Jean Valjean was now moving was not so small as the first. Jean Valjean walked in it with difficulty. The rains of the previous day had not yet run off, and made a little stream in the centre of the floor, and he was compelled to hug the wall, to keep his feet out of the water. Thus he went on in midnight. He resembled the creatures of night groping in the invisible, and lost underground in the veins of the darkness.

However, little by little, whether that some distant air-holes sent a little floating light into this opaque mist, or that his eyes became accustomed to the obscurity, some dim vision came back to him, and he again began to receive a confused perception, now of the wall which he was touching, and now of the arch under which he was passing. The pupil dilates in the night, and at last finds day in it, even as the soul dilates in misfortune, and at last finds God in it.

To find his way was difficult.

The track of the sewers echoes, so to speak, the track of the streets which overlie them. There were in the Paris of that day two thousand two hundred streets. Picture to yourselves below them that forest of dark branches which is called the sewer. The sewers existing at that epoch, placed end to end, would have given a length of thirty miles. We have already said that the present network, thanks to the extraordinary activity of the last thirty years, is not less than a hundred and forty miles.

Jean Valjean began with a mistake. He thought that he was under the Rue Saint Denis, and it was unfortunate that he was not there. There is beneath the Rue Saint Denis an old stone sewer, which dates from Louis XIII, and which goes straight to the collecting sewer, called the Grand Sewer, with a single elbow, on the right, at the height of the ancient Cour des Miracles, and a single branch, the Saint Martin sewer, the four arms of which cut each other in a cross. But the gallery of the Petite Truanderie, the entrance to which was near the wine-shop of Corinth, never communicated with the underground passage in the Rue Saint Denis; it runs into the Montmartre sewer, and it was in that that Jean Valjean was entangled. There, opportunities of losing oneself abound. The Montmartre sewer is one of the most labyrinthian of the ancient network. Luckily Jean Valjean had left behind him the sewer of the markets, the geometrical plan of which represents a multitude of interlocked top-gallant-masts; but he had before him more than one embarrassing encounter and more than one street corner – for these are streets – presenting itself in the obscurity like a point of interrogation; first, at his left, the vast Plâtrière sewer, a kind of Chinese puzzle, pushing and jumbling its chaos of T's and Z's beneath the Hôtel des Postes and the rotunda of the grain-market to the Seine, where it terminates in a Y; secondly, at his right, the crooked corridor of the Rue du Cadran, with its three teeth, which are so many blind ditches; thirdly, at his left, the branch of the Mail, complicated, almost at its entrance, by a kind of fork, and, after zigzag upon zigzag, terminating in the great voiding crypt of the Louvre, truncated and ramified in all directions; finally, at the right, the cul-de-sac passage of the Rue des Jeûneurs, with countless little reducts here and there, before arriving at the central sewer, which alone could lead him to some outlet distant enough to be secure.

If Jean Valjean had had any notion of what we have here pointed out, he would have quickly perceived, merely from feeling the wall, that he was not in the underground gallery of the Rue Saint Denis. Instead of the old hewn stone, instead of the ancient architecture, haughty and royal even in the sewer, with floor and running courses of granite, and mortar of thick lime, which cost seventy-five dollars a yard, he would have felt beneath his hand the contemporary cheapness, the economical expedient, the millstone grit laid in hydraulic cement upon a bed of concrete, which cost thirty-five dollars a yard, the bourgeois masonry known as *small materials;* but he knew nothing of all this.

He went forward, with anxiety, but with calmness, seeing nothing, knowing nothing, plunged into chance, that is to say, swallowed up in Providence.

By degrees, we must say, some horror penetrated him. The shadow which enveloped him entered his mind. He was walking in an enigma. This aqueduct of the cloaca is formidable; it is dizzily intertangled. It is a dreary thing to be caught in this Paris of darkness. Jean Valjean was obliged to find and almost to invent his route without seeing it. In that unknown region, each step which he ventured might be the last. How should he get out? Should he find an outlet? Should he find it in time? Would this colossal subterranean sponge with cells of stone admit of being penetrated and pierced? Would he meet with some unlooked-for knot of obscurity? Would he encounter the inextricable and the insurmountable? Would Marius die of hæmorrhage, and he of hunger? Would they both perish there at last, and make two skeletons in some niche of that night? He did not know. He asked himself all this, and he could not answer. The intestine of Paris is an abyss. Like the prophet, he was in the belly of the monster.

Suddenly he was surprised. At the most unexpected moment, and without having diverged from a straight line, he discovered that he was no longer rising; the water of the brook struck coming against his heels instead of upon the top of his feet. The sewer now descended. What? would he then soon reach the Seine? This danger was great, but the peril of retreat was still greater. He continued to advance.

It was not towards the Seine that he was going. The saddleback which the topography of Paris forms upon the right bank, empties one of its slopes into the Seine and the other into the Grand Sewer. The crest of this saddle-back which determines the division of the waters follows a very capricious line. The culminating point, which is the point of separation of the flow, is in the Saint Avoye sewer, beyond the Rue Michel de Comte, in the sewer of the Louvre, near the boulevards, and in the Montmartre sewer, near the markets. It was at this culminating point that Jean Valjean had arrived. He was making his way towards the belt sewer; he was on the right road. But he knew nothing of it.

Whenever he came to a branch, he felt its angles, and if he found the opening not as wide as the corridor in which he was, he did not enter, and continued his route, deeming rightly that every narrower way must terminate in a cul-de-sac, and could only lead him away from his object, the outlet. He thus evaded the quadruple snare which was spread for him in the obscurity, by the four labyrinths which we have just enumerated.

At a certain moment he felt that he was getting away from under the Paris which was petrified by the *émeute*, in which the barricades had suppressed the circulation, and that he was coming beneath the Paris which was alive and normal. He heard suddenly above his head a sound like thunder, distant, but continuous. It was the rumbling of the vehicles.

He had been walking for about half an hour, at least by his own calculation, and had not yet thought of resting; only he had changed the hand which supported Marius. The darkness was deeper than ever, but this depth reassured him.

All at once he saw his shadow before him. It was marked out on a feeble ruddiness almost indistinct, which vaguely empurpled the floor at his feet, and the arch over his head, and which glided along at his right and his left on the two slimy walls of the corridor. In amazement he turned round.

Behind him, in the portion of the passage through which he had passed, at a distance which appeared to him immense, flamed, throwing its rays into the dense obscurity, a sort of horrible star which appeared to be looking at him.

It was the gloomy star of the police which was rising in the sewer.

Behind this star were moving without order eight or ten black forms, straight, indistinct, terrible.

2. *Explanation*

DURING THE DAY of the 6th of June, a battle of the sewers had been ordered. It was feared that they would be taken as a refuge by the vanquished, and prefect Gisquet was to ransack the occult Paris, while General Bugeaud was sweeping the public Paris; a connected double operation which demanded a double strategy of the public power, represented above by the army and below by the police. Three platoons of officers and sewermen explored the subterranean streets of Paris, the first, the right bank, the second, the left bank, the third, in the City.

The officers were armed with carbines, clubs, swords, and daggers.

That which was at this moment directed upon Jean Valjean, was the lantern of the patrol of the right bank.

This patrol had just visited the crooked gallery and the three blind alleys which are beneath the Rue du Cadran. While they were taking their candle to the bottom of these blind alleys, Jean Valjean had come to the entrance of the gallery upon his way, had found it narrower than the principal passage, and had not entered it. He had passed beyond. The policemen, on coming out from the Cadran gallery, had thought they heard the sound of steps in the direction of the belt sewer. It was in fact Jean Valjean's steps. The sergeant in command of the patrol lifted his lantern, and the squad began to look into the mist in the direction whence the sound came.

This was to Jean Valjean an indescribable moment.

Luckily, if he saw the lantern well, the lantern saw him badly. It was light and he was shadow. He was far off, and merged in the blackness of the place. He drew close to the side of the wall, and stopped.

Still, he formed no idea of what was moving there behind him. Lack of sleep, want of food, emotions, had thrown him also into the visionary state. He saw a flaring flame, and about that flame, goblins. What was it? He did not understand.

Jean Valjean having stopped, the noise ceased.

The men of the patrol listened and heard nothing, they looked and saw nothing. They consulted.

There was at that period a sort of square at this point of the Montmartre sewer, called *de service*, which has since been suppressed on account of the little interior lake which formed in it, by the damming up in heavy storms of the torrents of rain water. The patrol could gather in a group in this square.

Jean Valjean saw these goblins form a kind of circle. These mastiffs' heads drew near each other and whispered.

The result of this council held by the watchdogs was that they had been mistaken, that there had been no noise, that there was nobody there, that it was needless to trouble themselves with the belt sewer, that that would be time lost, but that they must hasten towards Saint Merry, that if there were anything to do and any 'bousingot' to track out, it was in that quarter.

From time to time parties put new soles to their old terms of insult. In 1832, the word *bousingot* filled the interim between the word *jacobin*, which was worn out, and the word *demagogue*, then almost unused, but which has since done such excellent service.

The sergeant gave the order to file left towards the descent to the Seine. If they had conceived the idea of dividing into two squads and going in both directions, Jean Valjean would have been caught. That hung by this thread. It is probable that the instructions from the prefecture, foreseeing the possibility of a combat and that the insurgents might be numerous, forbade the patrol to separate. The patrol resumed its march, leaving Jean Valjean behind. Of all these movements, Jean Valjean perceived nothing except the eclipse of the lantern, which suddenly turned back.

Before going away, the sergeant, to ease the police conscience, discharged his carbine in the direction they were abandoning, towards Jean Valjean. The detonation rolled from echo to echo in the vault like the rumbling of this titanic bowel. Some plastering which fell into the stream and spattered the water a few steps from Jean Valjean made him aware that the ball had struck the arch above his head.

Slow and measured steps resounded upon the floor for some time, more and more deadened by the progressive increase of the distance, the group of black forms sank away, a glimmer oscillated and floated, making a ruddy circle in the vault, which decreased, then disappeared, the silence became deep again, the obscurity became again complete, blindness and deafness resumed possession of the darkness; and Jean Valjean, not yet daring to stir, stood for a long time with his back to the wall, his ear intent and eye dilated, watching the vanishing of that phantom patrol.

3. The man spun

WE MUST DO THE POLICE of that period this justice that, even in the gravest public conjunctures, it imperturbably performed its duties watchful and sanitary. An *émeute* was not in its eyes a pretext for giving malefactors a loose rein, and for neglecting society because the government was in peril. The ordinary duty was performed correctly in addition to the extraordinary duty, and was not disturbed by it. In the midst of the beginning of an incalculable political event, under the pressure of a possible revolution, without allowing himself to be diverted by the insurrection and the barricade, an officer would 'spin' a thief.

Something precisely like this occurred in the afternoon of the 6th of June at the brink of the Seine, on the beach of the right bank, a little beyond the Pont des Invalides.

There is no beach there now. The appearance of the place has changed. On this beach, two men some distance apart seemed to be observing each other, one avoiding the other. The one who was going before was endeavouring to increase the distance, the one who came behind to lessen it.

It was like a game of chess played from a distance and silently. Neither seemed to hurry, and both walked slowly, as if either feared that by too much haste he would double the pace of his partner.

One would have said it was an appetite following a prey, without appearing to do it on purpose. The prey was crafty, and kept on its guard.

The requisite proportions between the tracked marten and the tracking hound were observed. He who was trying to escape had a feeble frame and a sorry mien; he who was trying to seize, a fellow of tall stature, was rough in aspect, and promised to be rough in encounter.

The first, feeling himself the weaker, was avoiding the second; but he avoided him in a very furious way; he who could have observed him would have seen in his eyes the gloomy hostility of flight, and all the menace which there is in fear.

The beach was solitary; there were no passers; not even a boatman nor a lighterman on the barges moored here and there.

These two men could not have been easily seen, except from the quay in front, and to him who might have examined them from that distance, the man who was going forward would have appeared like a bristly creature, tattered and skulking, restless and shivering under a ragged blouse, and the other, like a classic and official person, wearing the overcoat of authority buttoned to the chin.

The reader would perhaps recognise these two men, if he saw them nearer.

What was the object of the last?

Probably to put the first in a warmer dress.

When a man clad by the state pursues a man in rags, it is in order to make of him also a man clad by the state. Only the colour is the whole question. To be clad in blue is glorious; to be clad in red is disagreeable.

There is a purple of the depths.

It was probably some inconvenience and some purple of this kind that the first desired to escape.

If the other was allowing him to go on and did not yet seize him, it was, according to all appearance, in the hope of seeing him bring up at some significant rendezvous, some group of good prizes. This delicate operation is called 'spinning'.

What renders this conjecture the more probable is, that the closely buttoned man, perceiving from the shore a fiacre which was passing on the quay empty, beckoned to the driver; the driver understood, evidently recognised with whom he had to do, turned his horse, and began to follow the two men on the upper part of the quay at a walk. This was not noticed by the equivocal and ragged personage who was in front.

The fiacre rolled along the trees of the Champs Elysées. There could be seen moving above the parapet, the bust of the driver, whip in hand.

One of the secret instructions of the police to officers contains this article: 'Always have a vehicle within call, in case of need.'

While manœuvring, each on his side, with an irreproachable strategy, these two men approached a slope of the quay descending to the beach, which, at that time, allowed the coach-drivers coming from Passy to go to the river to water their horses. This slope has since been removed, for the sake of symmetry; the horses perish with thirst, but the eye is satisfied.

It seemed probable that the man in the blouse would go up by this slope in order to attempt escape into the Champs Elysées, a place ornamented with trees, but on the other hand thickly dotted with officers, and where his pursuer would have easily seized him with a strong hand.

This point of the quay is very near the house brought from Moret to Paris in 1824, by Colonel Brack, and called the house of Francis I. A guardhouse is quite near by.

To the great surprise of his observer, the man pursued did not take the slope of the watering-place. He continued to advance on the beach along the quay.

His position was visibly becoming critical.

If not to throw himself into the Seine, what was he going to do?

No means henceforth of getting up to the quay; no other slope, and no staircase; and they were very near the spot, marked by the turn of the Seine towards the Pont d'Iéna, where the beach, narrowing more and more, terminates in a slender tongue, and is lost under the water. There he would inevitably find himself blockaded between the steep wall on his right, the river on the left and in front, and authority upon his heels.

It is true that this end of the beach was masked from sight by a mound of rubbish from six to seven feet high, the product of some demolition. But did this man hope to hide with any effect behind this heap of fragments, which the other had only to turn. The expedient would have been puerile. He certainly did not dream of it. The innocence of robbers does not reach this extent.

The heap of rubbish made a sort of eminence at the edge of the water, which was prolonged like a promontory, as far as the wall of the quay.

The man pursued reached this little hill and doubled it, so that he ceased to be seen by the other.

The latter, not seeing, was not seen; he took advantage of this to abandon all dissimulation, and to walk very rapidly. In a few seconds he came to the mound of rubbish, and turned it. There, he stopped in amazement. The man whom he was hunting was gone.

Total eclipse of the man in the blouse.

The beach beyond the mound of rubbish had scarcely a length of thirty yards, then it plunged beneath the water which beat against the wall of the quay.

The fugitive could not have thrown himself into the Seine nor scaled the quay without being seen by him who was following him. What had become of him?

The man in the closely buttoned coat walked to the end of the beach, and stopped there a moment thoughtful, his fists convulsive, his eyes ferreting. Suddenly he slapped his forehead. He had noticed, at the point where the land and the water began, an iron grating broad and low, arched, with a heavy lock and three massive hinges. This grating, a sort of door cut into the bottom of the quay, opened upon the river as much as upon the beach. A blackish stream flowed from beneath it. This stream emptied into the Seine.

Beyond its heavy rusty bars could be distinguished a sort of corridor arched and obscure.

The man folded his arms and looked at the grating reproachfully.

This look not sufficing, he tried to push it; he shook it, it resisted firmly. It was probable that it had just been opened, although no sound had been heard, a singular circumstance with a grating so rusty; but it was certain that it had been closed again. That indicated that he before whom this door had just turned, had not a hook but a key.

This evident fact burst immediately upon the mind of the man who was exerting himself to shake the grating, and forced from him this indignant epiphonema:

'This is fine! a government key!'

Then, calming himself immediately, he expressed a whole world of interior ideas by this whiff of monosyllables accented almost ironically:

'Well! well! well! well!'

This said, hoping nobody knows what, either to see the man come out, or to see others go in, he posted himself on the watch behind the heap of rubbish, with the patient rage of a pointer.

For its part, the fiacre, which followed all his movements, had halted above him near the parapet. The driver, foreseeing a long stay, fitted the muzzles of his horses into the bag of wet oats, so well known to Parisians, to whom the governments, be it said in parenthesis, sometimes apply it. The few passers over the Pont d'Iéna, before going away, turned their heads to look for a moment at these two motionless features of the landscape, the man on the beach, the fiacre on the quay.

4. He also bears his cross

Jean Valjean had resumed his advance, and had not stopped again.

This advance became more and more laborious. The level of these arches varies; the medium height is about five feet six inches, and was calculated for the stature of a man; Jean Valjean was compelled to bend so as not to hit Marius against the arch; he had to stoop every second, then rise up, to grope incessantly for the wall. The moisture of the stones and the sliminess of the floor made them bad points of support, whether for the hand or the foot. He was wading in the hideous muck of the city. The occasional gleams from the air-holes appeared only at long intervals, and so ghastly were they that the noonday seemed but moonlight; all the rest was mist, miasma, opacity, blackness. Jean Valjean was hungry and thirsty; thirsty especially; and this place, like the sea, is one full of water where you cannot drink. His strength, which was prodigious, and very little diminished by age, thanks to his chaste and sober life, began to give way notwithstanding. Fatigue grew upon him, and as his strength diminished the weight of his load increased. Marius, dead perhaps, weighed heavily upon him as inert bodies do. Jean Valjean supported him in such a way that his breast was not compressed and his breathing could always be as free as possible. He felt the rapid gliding of the rats between his legs. One of them was so frightened as to bite him. There came to him from time to time through the aprons of the mouths of the sewer a breath of fresh air which revived him.

It might have been three o'clock in the afternoon when he arrived at the belt sewer.

He was first astonished at this sudden enlargement. He abruptly found himself in the gallery where his outstretched hands did not reach the two walls, and under an arch which his head did not touch. The Grand Sewer indeed is eight feet wide and seven high.

At the point where the Montmartre sewer joins the Grand Sewer, two other subterranean galleries, that of the Rue de Provence and that of the Abattoir, coming in, make a square. Between these four ways, a less sagacious man would have been undecided. Jean Valjean took the widest, that is to say, the belt sewer. But there the question returned: to descend, or to ascend. He thought that the condition of affairs was urgent, and that he must, at whatever risk, now reach the Seine. In other words, descend. He turned to the left.

Well for him that he did so. For it would be an error to suppose that the belt sewer has two outlets, the one towards Bercy, the other towards Passy, and that it is, as its name indicates, the subterranean belt of the Paris of the right bank. The Grand Sewer, which is, it must be remembered, nothing more nor less than the ancient brook of Ménilmontant, terminates, if we ascend it, in a cul-de-sac, that is to say, its ancient starting point, which was its spring, at the foot of the hill of Ménilmontant. It has no direct communication with the branch which gathers up the waters of Paris below the Popincourt quarter, and which empties into the Seine by the Amelot sewer above the ancient Ile Louviers. This branch, which completes the collecting sewer, is separated from it, under the Rue Ménilmontant even, by a solid wall which marks the point of separation of the waters up and down. Had Jean Valjean gone up the gallery, he would have come, after manifold efforts, exhausted by fatigue, expiring, in the darkness, to a wall. He would have been lost.

Strictly speaking, by going back a little, entering the passage of the Filles du Calvaire, if he did not hesitate at the subterranean goose-track of the Boucherat crossing, by taking the Saint Louis corridor, then, on the left, the Saint Gilles passage, then by turning to the right and avoiding the Saint Sébastien gallery, he might have come to the Amelot sewer, and thence, provided he had not gone astray in the sort of F which is beneath the Bastille, reached the outlet on the Seine near the Arsenal. But, for that, he must have been perfectly familiar in all its ramifications and in all its tubes with the huge madrepore of the sewer. Now, we must repeat, he knew nothing of this frightful system of paths along which he was making his way; and, had anybody asked him where he was, he would have answered: In the night.

His instinct served him well. To descend was, in fact, possible safety.

He left on his right the two passages which ramify in the form of a claw under the Rue Lafitte and the Rue Saint Georges, and the long forked corridor of the Chaussée d'Antin.

A little beyond an affluent which was probably the branching of the Madeleine, he stopped. He was very tired. A large airhole, probably the vista on the Rue d'Anjou, produced an almost vivid light. Jean Valjean, with the gentleness of movement of a brother for his wounded brother, laid Marius upon the side bank of the sewer. Marius' bloody face appeared, under the white gleam from the air-hole, as if at the bottom of a tomb. His eyes were closed, his hair adhered to his temples like brushes dried in red paint, his hands dropped down lifeless, his limbs were cold, there was coagulated blood at the corners of his mouth. A clot of blood had gathered in the tie of his cravat; his shirt was bedded in the wounds, the cloth of his coat chafed the gaping gashes in the living flesh. Jean Valjean, removing the garments with the ends of his fingers, laid his hand upon his breast; the heart still beat. Jean Valjean tore up his shirt, bandaged the wounds as well as he could, and staunched the flowing blood; then, bending in the twilight over Marius, who was still unconscious and almost lifeless, he looked at him with an inexpressible hatred.

In opening Marius' clothes, he had found two things in his pockets, the bread which had been forgotten there since the day previous, and Marius' pocket-book. He ate the bread and opened the pocket-book. On the first page he found the four lines written by Marius. They will be remembered:

'My name is Marius Pontmercy. Carry my corpse to my grandfather's, M. Gillenormand, Rue des Filles du Calvaire, No. 6, in the Marais.'

By the light of the air-hole, Jean Valjean read these four lines, and stopped a moment as if absorbed in himself, repeating in an undertone: 'Rue des Filles du Calvaire, Number Six, Monsieur Gillenormand.' He replaced the pocket-book in Marius' pocket. He had eaten, strength had returned to him: he took Marius on his back again, laid his head carefully upon his right shoulder, and began to descend the sewer.

The Grand Sewer, following the course of the valley of Ménilmontant, is almost two leagues in length. It is paved for a considerable part of its course.

This torch of the name of the streets of Paris with which we are illuminating Jean Valjean's subterranean advance for the reader, Jean Valjean did not have. Nothing told him what zone of the city he was passing through, nor what route he had followed. Only the growing pallor of the gleams of light which he saw from time to time, indicated that the sun was withdrawing from the pavement, and that the day would soon be gone; and the rumbling of the wagons above his head, from continuous having become intermittent, then having almost ceased, he concluded that he was under central Paris no longer, and that he was approaching some solitary region, in the vicinity of the outer boulevards or the furthest quays. Where there are fewer houses and fewer streets, the sewer has fewer air-holes. The darkness thickened about Jean Valjean. He none the less continued to advance, groping in the obscurity.

This obscurity suddenly became terrible.

5. *For sand as well as women there is a finesse which is perfidy*

He felt that he was entering the water, and that he had under his feet, pavement no longer, but mud.

It sometimes happens, on certain coasts of Brittany or Scotland, that a man, traveller or fisherman, walking on the beach at low tide far from the bank, suddenly notices that for several minutes he has been walking with some difficulty. The strand beneath his feet is like pitch; his soles stick to it; it is sand no longer, it is glue. The beach is perfectly dry, but at every step he takes, as soon as he lifts his foot, the print which it leaves fills with water. The eye, however, has noticed no change; the immense strand is smooth and tranquil, all the sand has the same appearance, nothing distinguishes the surface which is solid from the surface which is no longer so; the joyous little cloud of sand-fleas continues to leap tumultuously over the wayfarer's feet. The man pursues his way, goes forward, inclines towards the land, endeavours to get nearer the upland. He is not anxious. Anxious about what? Only, he feels somehow as if the weight of his feet increased with every step which he takes. Suddenly he sinks in. He sinks in two or three inches. Decidedly he is not on the right road; he stops to take his bearings. All at once, he looks at his feet. His feet have disappeared. The sand covers them. He draws his feet out of the sand, he will retrace his steps, he turns back, he sinks in deeper. The sand comes up to his ankles, he pulls himself out and throws himself to the left, the sand is half leg deep, he throws himself to the right, the sand comes up to his shins. Then he recognises with unspeakable terror that he is caught in the quicksand, and that he has beneath him the fearful medium in which man can no more walk than the fish can swim. He throws off his load if he has one, he lightens himself like a ship in distress; it is already too late, the sand is above his knees.

He calls, he waves his hat or his handkerchief, the sand gains on him more and more; if the beach is deserted, if the land is too far off, if the sandbank is of too ill-repute, if there is no hero in sight, it is all over, he is condemned to enlizement. He is condemned to that appalling interment, long, infallible, implacable, impossible to slacken or to hasten, which endures for hours, which will not end, which seizes you erect, free and in full health, which draws you by the feet, which, at every effort that you attempt, at every shout that you utter, drags you a little deeper, which appears to punish you for your resistance by a redoubling of its grasp, which sinks the man slowly into the earth while it leaves him all the time to look at the horizon, the trees, the green fields, the smoke of the villages in the plain, the sails of the ships upon the sea, the birds flying and singing, the sunshine, the sky. *Enlizement* is the grave become a tide and rising from the depths of the earth towards a living man. Each minute is an inexorable enshroudress. The victim attempts to sit down, to lie down, to creep; every movement he makes, inters him; he straightens up, he sinks in; he feels that he is being swallowed up; he howls, implores, cries to the clouds, wrings his hands, despairs. Behold him waist deep in the sand; the sand reaches his breast, he is now only a bust. He raises his arms, utters furious groans, clutches the beach with his nails, would hold by that straw, leans upon his elbows to pull himself out of this soft sheath, sobs frenziedly; the sand rises. The sand reaches his shoulders, the sand reaches his neck; the face alone is visible now. The mouth cries, the sand fills it; silence. The eyes still gaze, the sand shuts them; night. Then the forehead decreases, a little hair flutters above the sand; a hand protrudes, comes through the surface of the beach, moves and shakes, and disappears. Sinister effacement of a man.

Sometimes the horseman is enlized with his horse; sometimes the cartman is enlized with his cart; all horrible beneath the beach. It is a shipwreck elsewhere than in the water. It is the earth drowning man. The earth, filled with the ocean, becomes a trap. It presents itself as a plain and opens like a wave. Such treacheries has the abyss.

This fatal mishap, always possible upon one or another coast of the sea, was also possible, thirty years ago, in the sewer of Paris.

Before the important works commenced in 1833, the subterranean system of Paris was subject to sudden sinkings of the bottom.

The water filtered into certain underlying, particularly friable soils; the floor, which was of paving-stones, as in the old sewers, or of hydraulic cement upon concrete, as in the new galleries, having lost its support, bent. A bend in a floor of that kind is a crack, is a crumbling. The floor gave way over a certain space. This crevasse, a hiatus in a gulf of mud, was called technically *fontis*. What is a fontis? It is the quicksand of the sea-shore suddenly encountered under ground; it is the beach of Mont Saint Michel in a sewer. The diluted soil is as it were in fusion; all its molecules are in suspension in a soft medium; it is not land, and it is not water. Depth sometimes very great. Nothing more fearful than such a mischance. If the water predominates, death is prompt, there is swallowing up; if the earth predominates, death is slow, there is enlizement.

Can you picture to yourself such a death? If *enlizement* is terrible on the shore of the sea, what is it in the cloaca? Instead of the open air, the full light, the broad day, that clear horizon, those vast sounds, those free clouds whence rains life, those barks seen in the distance, that hope under every form, probable passers, succour possible until the last moment; instead of all that, deafness, blindness, a black arch, an interior of a tomb already prepared, death in the mire under a cover! the slow stifling by the filth, a stone box in which asphyxia opens its claw in the slime and takes you by the throat; fetidness mingled with the death rattle; mire instead of sand, sulphuretted hydrogen instead of the hurricane, ordure instead of the ocean? and to call, and to gnash your teeth, and writhe, and struggle, and agonise, with that huge city above your head knowing nothing of it all!

Inexpressible horror of dying thus! Death sometimes redeems its atrocity by a certain terrible dignity. At the stake, in the shipwreck, man may be great; in the flame as in the foam, a superb attitude is possible; you are transfigured while falling into that abyss. But not here. Death is unclean. It is humiliating to expire. The last flitting visions are abject. Mire is synonymous with shame. It is mean, ugly, infamous. To die in a butt of Malmsey, like Clarence, so be it; in the scavenger's pit, like d'Escoubleau, that is horrible. To struggle within it is hideous; at the very time that you are agonising, you are splashing. There is darkness enough for it to be Hell, and slime enough for it to be only a slough, and the dying man knows not whether he will become a spectre or a toad.

Everywhere else the grave is gloomy; here it is misshapen.

The depth of the fontis varied, as well as its length, and its density by reason of the more or less yielding character of the subsoil. Sometimes a fontis was three or four feet deep, sometimes eight or ten; sometimes no bottom could be found. The mire was here almost solid, there almost liquid. In the Lunière fontis, it would have taken a man a day to disappear, while he would have been devoured in five minutes by the Phélippeaux slough. The mire bears more or less according to its greater or less density. A child escapes where a man is lost. The first law of safety is to divest yourself of every kind of burden. To throw away his bag of tools, or his basket, or his hod, is the first thing that every sewerman does when he feels the soil giving way beneath him.

The fontis had various causes: friability of the soil; some crevasse at a depth beyond the reach of man; the violent showers of summer; the incessant storms of winter; the long misty rains. Sometimes the weight of the neighbouring houses upon a marly or sandy soil pressed out the arches of the subterranean galleries and made them yield, or it would happen that the floor gave way and cracked under this crushing pressure. The settling of the Pantheon obliterated in this manner, a century ago, a part of the excavations on Mount Saint Geneviève. When a sewer sank beneath the pressure of the houses, the difficulty, on certain occasions, disclosed itself above in the street by a kind of saw-tooth separation in the pavement; this rent was developed in a serpentine line for the whole length of the cracked arch, and then, the evil being visible, the remedy could be prompt. It often happened also that the interior damage was not revealed by any exterior scar. And, in that case, woe to the sewermen. Entering without precaution into the sunken sewer, they might perish. The old registers make mention of some working-men who were buried in this way in the fontis. They give several names; among others that of the sewerman who was engulfed in a sunken slough under the kennel on the Rue Carême Prenant, whose name was Blaise Poutrain; this Blaise Poutrain was brother of Nicholas Poutrain, who was the last gravedigger of the cemetery called Charnier des Innocents in 1785; the date at which that cemetery died.

There was also that young and charming Vicomte d'Escoubleau, of whom we have spoken, one of the heroes of the siege of Lerida, where they gave the assault in silk stockings, headed by violins. d'Escoubleau, surprised one night with his cousin, the Duchess de Sourdis, was drowned in a quagmire of the Beautreillis sewer, in which he had taken refuge to escape from the duke. Madame de Sourdis, when this death was described to her, called for her smelling-bottle, and forgot to weep through much inhalation of salts. In such a case, there is no love which persists; the cloaca extinguishes it. Hero refuses to wash Leander's corpse. Thisbe stops her nose at sight of Pyramus, and says: 'Peugh!'

6. *The fontis*

JEAN VALJEAN found himself in presence of a *fontis*.

This kind of settling was then frequent in the subsoil of the Champs Elysées, very unfavourable for hydraulic works, and giving poor support to underground constructions, from its excessive fluidity. This fluidity surpasses even that of the sands of the Saint Georges quarter, which could only be overcome by stonework upon concrete, and the clayey beds infected with gas in the quarter of the Martyrs, so liquid that the passage could be effected under the gallery of the martyrs only by means of a metallic tube. When, in 1836, they demolished, for the purpose of rebuilding, the old stone sewer under the Faubourg Saint Honoré, in which we find Jean Valjean now entangled the quicksand, which is the subsoil from the Champs Elysées to the Seine, was such an obstacle that the work lasted nearly six months, to the great outcry of the bordering proprietors, especially the proprietors of hôtels and coaches. The work was more than difficult; it was dangerous. It is true that there were four months and a half of rain, and three risings of the Seine.

The fontis which Jean Valjean fell upon was caused by the showers of the previous day. A yielding of the pavement, imperfectly upheld by the underlying sand, had occasioned a damming of the rainwater. Infiltration having taken place, sinking had followed. The floor, broken up, had disappeared in the mire. For what distance? Impossible to say. The obscurity was deeper than anywhere else. It was a mudhole in the cavern of night.

Jean Valjean felt the pavement slipping away under him. He entered into this slime. It was water on the surface, mire at the bottom. He must surely pass through. To retrace his steps was impossible. Marius was expiring, and Jean Valjean exhausted. Where else could he go? Jean Valjean advanced. Moreover, the quagmire appeared not very deep for a few steps. But in proportion as he advanced, his feet sank in. He very soon had the mire half-knee deep, and water above his knees. He walked on, holding Marius with both arms as high above the water as he could. The mud now came up to his knees, and the water to his waist. He could no longer turn back. He sank in deeper and deeper. This mire, dense enough for one man's weight, evidently could not bear two. Marius and Jean Valjean would have had a chance of escape separately. Jean Valjean continued to advance, supporting this dying man, who was perhaps a corpse.

The water came up to his armpits; he felt that he was foundering; it was with difficulty that he could move in the depth of mire in which he was. The density, which was the support, was also the obstacle. He still held Marius up, and, with an unparalleled outlay of strength, he advanced; but he sank deeper. He now had only his head out of the water, and his arms supporting Marius. There is, in the old pictures of the deluge, a mother doing thus with her child.

He sank still deeper, he threw his face back to escape the water, and to be able to breathe; he who should have seen him in this obscurity would have thought he saw a mask floating upon the darkness; he dimly perceived Marius' drooping head and livid face above him; he made a desperate effort, and thrust his foot forward; his foot struck something solid; a support. It was time.

He rose and writhed and rooted himself upon this support with a sort of fury. It produced the effect upon him of the first step of a staircase reascending towards life.

This support, discovered in the mire at the last moment, was the beginning of the other slope of the floor, which had bent without breaking, and had curved beneath the water like a board, and in a single piece. A well-constructed paving forms an arch, and has this firmness. This fragment of the floor, partly submerged, but solid, was a real slope, and, once upon this slope, they were saved. Jean Valjean ascended this inclined plane, and reached the other side of the quagmire.

On coming out of the water, he struck against a stone, and fell upon his knees. This seemed to him fitting, and he remained thus for some time, his soul lost in unspoken prayer to God.

He rose, shivering, chilled, infected, bending beneath this dying man, whom he was dragging on, all dripping with slime, his soul filled with a strange light.

7. *Sometimes we get aground when we expect to get ashore*

He resumed his route once more.

However, if he had not left his life in the fontis, he seemed to have left his strength. This supreme effort had exhausted him. His exhaustion was so great, that every three or four steps he was obliged to take breath, and leaned against the wall. Once he had to sit down upon the curb to change Marius's position, and he thought he should stay there. But if his vigour were dead, his energy was not. He rose again.

He walked with desperation, almost with rapidity, for a hundred paces, without raising his head, almost without breathing, and suddenly struck against the wall. He had reached an angle of the sewer, and, arriving at the turn with his head down, he had encountered the wall. He raised his eyes, and at the extremity of the passage, down there before him, far, very far away, he perceived a light. This time, it was not the terrible light; it was the good and white light. It was the light of day.

Jean Valjean saw the outlet.

A condemned soul who, from the midst of the furnace, should suddenly perceive an exit from Gehenna, would feel what Jean Valjean felt. It would fly frantically with the stumps of its burned wings towards the radiant door. Jean Valjean felt exhaustion no more, he felt Marius' weight no longer, he found again his knees of steel, he ran rather than walked. As he approached, the outlet assumed more and more distinct outline. It was a circular arch, not so high as the vault which sank down by degrees, and not so wide as the gallery which narrowed as the top grew lower. The tunnel ended on the inside in the form of a funnel; a vicious contraction, copied from the wickets of houses of detention, logical in a prison, illogical in a sewer, and which has since been corrected.

Jean Valjean reached the outlet.

There he stopped.

It was indeed the outlet, but it did not let him out.

The arch was closed by a strong grating, and the grating which, according to all appearance, rarely turned upon its rusty hinges, was held in its stone frame by a stout lock which, red with rust, seemed an enormous brick. He could see the keyhole, and the strong bolt deeply plunged into the iron staple. The lock was plainly a double-lock. It was one of those Bastille locks of which the old Paris was so lavish.

Beyond the grating, the open air, the river, the daylight, the beach, very narrow, but sufficient to get away. The distant quays, Paris, that gulf in which one is so easily lost, the wide horizon, liberty. He distinguished at his right, below him, the Pont d'Iéna, and at his left, above, the Pont des Invalides; the spot would have been propitious for awaiting night and escaping. It was one of the most solitary points in Paris; the beach which fronts on the Gros Caillou. The flies came in and went out through the bars of the grating.

It might have been half-past eight o'clock in the evening. The day was declining.

Jean Valjean laid Marius along the wall on the dry part of the floor, then walked to the grating and clenched the bars with both hands; the shaking was frenzied, the shock nothing. The grating did not stir. Jean Valjean seized the bars one after another, hoping to be able to tear out the least solid one, and to make a lever of it to lift the door or break the lock. Not a bar yielded. A tiger's teeth are not more solid in their sockets. No lever; no possible purchase. The obstacle was invincible. No means of opening the door.

Must he then perish there? What should he do? what would become of them? go back; recommence the terrible road which he had already traversed; he had not the strength. Besides, how cross that quagmire again, from which he had escaped only by a miracle? And after the quagmire, was there not that police patrol from which, certainly, one would not escape twice? And then where should he go? what direction take? to follow the descent was not to reach the goal. Should he come to another outlet, he would find it obstructed by a door or a grating. All the outlets were undoubtedly closed in this way. Chance had unsealed the grating by which they had entered, but evidently all the other mouths of the sewer were fastened. He had only succeeded in escaping into a prison.

It was over. All that Jean Valjean had done was useless. Exhaustion ended in abortion.

They were both caught in the gloomy and immense web of death, and Jean Valjean felt running over those black threads trembling in the darkness, the appalling spider.

He turned his back to the grating, and dropped upon the pavement, rather prostrate than sitting, beside the yet motionless Marius, and his head sank between his knees. No exit. This was the last drop of anguish.

Of whom did he think in this overwhelming dejection? Neither of himself nor of Marius. He thought of Cosette.

8. The torn coat-tail

In the midst of this annihilation, a hand was laid upon his shoulder, and a voice which spoke low, said to him:

'Go halves.'

Somebody in that darkness? Nothing is so like a dream as despair, Jean Valjean thought he was dreaming. He had heard no steps. Was it possible? he raised his eyes.

A man was before him.

This man was dressed in a blouse; he was barefooted; he held his shoes in his left hand; he had evidently taken them off to be able to reach Jean Valjean without being heard.

Jean Valjean had not a moment's hesitation. Unforeseen as was the encounter, this man was known to him. This man was Thénardier.

Although wakened, so to speak, with a start, Jean Valjean, accustomed to be on the alert and on the watch for unexpected blows which he must quickly parry, instantly regained possession of all his presence of mind. Besides, the condition of affairs could not be worse, a certain degree of distress is no longer capable of crescendo, and Thénardier himself could not add to the blackness of this night.

There was a moment of delay.

Thénardier, lifting his right hand to the height of his forehead, shaded his eyes with it, then brought his brows together while he winked his eyes, which, with a slight pursing of the mouth, characterises the sagacious attention of a man who is seeking to recognise another. He did not succeed. Jean Valjean, we have just said, turned his back to the light, and was moreover so disfigured, so muddy and so blood-stained, that in full noon he would have been unrecognisable. On the other hand, with the light from the grating shining in his face, a cellar light, it is true, livid, but precise in its lividness, Thénardier, as the energetic, trite metaphor expresses it, struck Jean Valjean at once. This inequality of conditions was enough to ensure Jean Valjean some advantage in this mysterious duel which was about to open between the two conditions and the two men. The encounter took place between Jean Valjean veiled and Thénardier unmasked.

Jean Valjean perceived immediately that Thénardier did not recognise him.

They gazed at each other for a moment in this penumbra, as if they were taking each other's measure. Thénardier was first to break the silence.

'How are you going to manage to get out?'

Jean Valjean did not answer.

Thénardier continued:

'Impossible to pick the lock. Still you must get away from here.'

'That is true,' said Jean Valjean.

'Well, go halves.'

'What do you mean?'

'You have killed the man; very well. For my part, I have the key.'

Thénardier pointed to Marius. He went on:

'I don't know you, but I would like to help you. You must be a friend.'

Jean Valjean began to understand. Thénardier took him for an assassin.

Thénardier resumed:

'Listen, comrade. You haven't killed that man without looking to what he had in his pockets. Give me my half. I will open the door for you.'

And, drawing a big key half out from under his blouse, which was full of holes, he added:

'Would you like to see how the key of the fields is made? There it is.'

Jean Valjean 'remained stupid', the expression is the elder Corneille's, so far as to doubt whether what he saw was real. It was Providence appearing in a guise of horror, and the good angel springing out of the ground under the form of Thénardier.

Thénardier plunged his fist into a huge pocket hidden under his blouse, pulled out a rope, and handed it to Jean Valjean.

'Here,' said he, 'I'll give you the rope to boot.'

'A rope, what for?'

'You want a stone too, but you'll find one outside. There is a heap of rubbish there.'

'A stone, what for?'

'Fool, as you are going to throw the *pantre* into the river, you want a stone and a rope; without them it would float on the water.'

Jean Valjean took the rope. Everybody has accepted things thus mechanically.

Thénardier snapped his fingers as over the arrival of a sudden idea:

'Ah now, comrade, how did you manage to get out of the quagmire yonder? I haven't dared to risk myself there. Pugh! you don't smell good.'

After a pause, he added:

'I ask you questions, but you are right in not answering them. That is an apprenticeship for the examining judge's cursed quarter of an hour. And then by not speaking at all, you run no risk of speaking too loud. It is all the same, because I don't see your face, and because I don't know your name, you would do wrong to suppose that I don't know who you are and what you want. Understood. You have smashed this gentleman a little; now you want to squeeze him somewhere. You need the river, the great hide-folly. I am going to get you out of the scrape. To help a good fellow in trouble that puts my boots on.'

While approving Jean Valjean for keeping silence, he was evidently seeking to make him speak. He pushed his shoulders, so as to endeavour to see his side-face, and exclaimed, without however rising above the moderate tone in which he kept his voice:

'Speaking of the quagmire, you are a proud animal. Why didn't you throw the man in there?'

Jean Valjean preserved silence.

Thénardier resumed, raising the rag which served him as a cravat up to his Adam's apple, a gesture which completes the air of sagacity of a serious man:

'Indeed, perhaps you have acted prudently. The workmen when they come tomorrow to stop the hole, would certainly have found the *pantinois* forgotten there, and they would have been able, thread by thread, straw by straw, to *pincer* the trace, and to reach you. Something has passed through the sewer. Who? Where did he come out? Did anybody see him come out? The police has plenty of brains. The sewer is treacherous and informs against you. Such a discovery is a rarity, it attracts attention, few people use the sewer in their business while the river is at everybody's service. The river is the true grave. At the month's end, they fish you up the man at the nets of Saint Cloud. Well, what does that amount to? It is a carcase, indeed! Who killed this man? Paris. And justice don't even inquire into it. You have done right.'

The more loquacious Thénardier was, the more dumb was Jean Valjean. Thénardier pushed his shoulder anew.

'Now, let us finish the business. Let us divide. You have seen my key, show me your money.'

Thénardier was haggard, tawny, equivocal, a little threatening, nevertheless friendly.

There was one strange circumstance; Thénardier's manner was not natural; he did not appear entirely at his ease; while he did not affect an air of mystery, he talked low; from time to time he laid his finger on his mouth, and muttered: 'Hush!' It was difficult to guess why. There was nobody there but them. Jean Valjean thought that perhaps some other bandits were hidden in some recess not far off, and that Thénardier did not care to share with them.

Thénardier resumed:

'Let us finish. How much did the *pantre* have in his deeps?'

Jean Valjean felt in his pockets.

It was, as will be remembered, his custom always to have money about him. The gloomy life of expedients to which he was condemned, made this a law to him. This time, however, he was caught unprovided. On putting on his national guard's uniform, the evening before, he had forgotten, gloomily absorbed as he was, to take his pocket-book with him. He had only some coins in his waistcoat pocket. He turned out his pocket, all soaked with filth, and displayed upon the curb of the sewer a louis d'or, two five-franc pieces, and five or six big sous.

Thénardier thrust out his underlip with a significant twist of the neck.

'You didn't kill him very dear,' said he.

He began to handle, in all familiarity, the pockets of Jean Valjean and Marius. Jean Valjean, principally concerned in keeping his back to the light, did not interfere with him. While he was feeling of Marius' coat, Thénardier, with the dexterity of a juggler, found means, without attracting Jean Valjean's attention, to tear off a strip, which he hid under his blouse, probably thinking that this scrap of cloth might assist him afterwards to identify the assassinated man and the assassin. He found, however, nothing more than the thirty francs.

'It is true,' said he, 'both together, you have no more than that.'

And, forgetting his words, *go halves*, he took the whole.

He hesitated a little before the big sous. Upon reflection, he took them also, mumbling:

'No matter! this is to *suriner* people too cheap.'

This said, he took the key from under his blouse anew.

'Now, friend, you must go out. This is like the fair, you pay on going out. You have paid, go out.'

And he began to laugh.

That he had, in extending to an unknown man the help of this key, and in causing another man than himself to go out by this door, the pure and disinterested intention of saving an assassin, is something which it is permissible to doubt.

Thénardier helped Jean Valjean to replace Marius upon his shoulders; then he went towards the grating upon the points of his bare feet, beckoning to Jean Valjean to follow him, he looked outside, laid his finger on his mouth, and stood a few seconds as if in suspense; the inspection over, he put the key into the lock. The bolt slid and the door turned. There was neither snapping nor grinding. It was done very quietly. It was plain that this grating and its hinges, oiled with care, were opened oftener than would have been guessed. This quiet was ominous; you felt in it the furtive goings and comings, the silent entrances and exits of the men of the night, and the wolflike tread of crime. The sewer was evidently in complicity with some mysterious band. This taciturn grating was a receiver.

Thénardier half opened the door, left just a passage for Jean Valjean, closed the grating again, turned the key twice in the lock, and plunged back into the obscurity, without making more noise than a breath. He seemed to walk with the velvet paws of a tiger. A moment afterwards, this hideous providence had entered again into the invisible.

Jean Valjean found himself outside.

9. Marius seems to be dead to one who is a good judge

He let Marius slide down upon the beach.

They were outside!

The miasmas, the obscurity, the horror, were behind him, The balmy air, pure, living, joyful, freely respirable, flowed around him. Everywhere about him silence, but the charming silence of a sunset in a clear sky. Twilight had fallen; night was coming, the great liberatress, the friend of all those who need a mantle of darkness to escape from an anguish. The sky extended on every side like an enormous calm. The river came to his feet with the sound of a kiss. He heard the airy dialogues of the nests bidding each other good night in the elms of the Champs Elysées. A few stars, faintly piercing the pale blue of the zenith, and visible to reverie alone, produced their imperceptible little resplendencies in the immensity. Evening was unfolding over Jean Valjean's head all the caresses of the infinite.

It was the undecided and exquisite hour which says neither yes nor no. There was already night enough for one to be lost in it at a little distance, and still day enough for one to be recognised near at hand.

Jean Valjean was for a few seconds irresistibly overcome by all this august and caressing serenity; there are such moments of forgetfulness; suffering refuses to harass the wretched; all is eclipsed in thought; peace covers the dreamer like a night; and, under the twilight which is flinging forth its rays, and in imitation of the sky which is illuminating, the soul becomes starry. Jean Valjean could not but gaze at that vast clear shadow which was above him; pensive, he took in the majestic silence of the eternal heavens, a bath of ecstasy and prayer. Then, hastily, as if a feeling of duty came back to him, he bent over Marius, and, dipping up some water in the hollow of his hand, he threw a few drops gently into his face. Marius' eyelids did not part; but his half-open mouth breathed.

Jean Valjean was plunging his hand into the river again, when suddenly he felt an indescribable uneasiness, such as we feel when we have somebody behind us, without seeing him.

We have already referred elsewhere to this impression, with which everybody is acquainted.

He turned round.

As just before, somebody was indeed behind him.

A man of tall stature, wrapped in a long overcoat, with folded arms, and holding in his right hand a club, the leaden knob of which could be seen, stood erect a few steps in the rear of Jean Valjean, who was stooping over Marius.

It was, with the aid of the shadow, a sort of apparition. A simple man would have been afraid on account of the twilight, and a reflective man on account of the club.

Jean Valjean recognised Javert.

The reader has doubtless guessed that Thénardier's pursuer was none other than Javert. Javert, after his unhoped-for departure from the barricade, had gone to the prefecture of police, had given an account verbally to the prefect in person in a short audience, had then immediately returned to his duty, which implied – the note found upon him will be remembered – a certain surveillance of the shore on the right bank of the Champs Elysées, which for some time had excited the attention of the police. There he had seen Thénardier, and had followed him. The rest is known.

It is understood also that the opening of that grating so obligingly before Jean Valjean was a piece of shrewdness on the part of Thénardier. Thénardier felt that Javert was still there; the man who is watched has a scent which does not deceive him; a bone must be thrown to this hound. An assassin, what a godsend! It was the scapegoat, which must never be refused. Thénardier, by putting Jean Valjean out in his place, gave a victim to the police, threw them off his own track, caused himself to be forgotten in a larger matter, rewarded Javert for his delay, which always flatters a spy, gained thirty francs, and counted surely, as for himself, upon escaping by the aid of this diversion.

Jean Valjean had passed from one shoal to another.

These two encounters, blow on blow, to fall from Thénardier upon Javert, it was hard.

Javert did not recognise Jean Valjean, who, as we have said, no longer resembled himself. He did not unfold his arms, he secured his club in his grasp by an imperceptible movement, and said in a quick and calm voice:

'Who are you?'

'I.'

'What you?'

'Jean Valjean.'

Javert put the club between his teeth, bent his knees, inclined his body, laid his two powerful hands upon Jean Valjean's shoulders, which they clamped like two vices, examined him, and recognised him. Their faces almost touched. Javert's look was terrible.

Jean Valjean stood inert under the grasp of Javert like a lion who should submit to the claw of a lynx.

'Inspector Javert,' said he, 'you have got me. Besides, since this morning, I have considered myself your prisoner. I did not give you my address to try to escape you. Take me. Only grant me one thing.'

Javert seemed not to hear. He rested his fixed eye upon Jean Valjean. His rising chin pushed his lips towards his nose, a sign of savage reverie. At last, he let go of Jean Valjean, rose up as straight as a stick, took his club firmly in his grasp, and, as if in a dream, murmured rather than pronounced this question:

'What are you doing here? and who is this man?'

Jean Valjean answered, and the sound of his voice appeared to awaken Javert:

'It is precisely of him that I wished to speak. Dispose of me as you please; but help me first to carry him home. I only ask that of you.'

Javert's face contracted, as it happened to him whenever anybody seemed to consider him capable of a concession. Still he did not say no.

He stooped down again, took a handkerchief from his pocket, which he dipped in the water, and wiped Marius' bloodstained forehead.

'This man was in the barricade,' said he in an undertone, and as if speaking to himself. 'This is he whom they called Marius.'

A spy of the first quality, who had observed everything, listened to everything, heard everything, and recollected everything, believing he was about to die; who spied even in his death-agony, and who, leaning upon the first step of the grave, had taken notes.

He seized Marius' hand, seeking for his pulse.

'He is wounded,' said Jean Valjean.

'He is dead,' said Javert.

Jean Valjean answered:

'No. Not yet.'

'You have brought him, then, from the barricade here?' observed Javert.

His preoccupation must have been deep, as he did not dwell longer upon this perplexing escape through the sewer, and did not even notice Jean Valjean's silence after his question.

Jean Valjean, for his part, seemed to have but one idea. He resumed:

'He lives in the Marais, Rue des Filles du Calvaire, at his grandfather's – I forget the name.'

Jean Valjean felt in Marius' coat took out the pocket-book, opened it at the page pencilled by Marius, and handed it to Javert.

There was still enough light floating in the air to enable one to read. Javert, moreover, had in his eye the feline phosphorescence of the birds of the night. He deciphered the few lines written by Marius, and muttered: 'Gillenormand, Rue des Filles du Calvaire, No. 6.'

Then he cried: 'Driver?'

The reader will remember the fiacre which was waiting, in case of need.

Javert kept Marius' pocket-book.

A moment later, the carriage, descending by the slope of the watering-place, was on the beach. Marius was laid upon the back seat, and Javert sat down by the side of Jean Valjean on the front seat.

When the door was shut, the fiacre moved rapidly off, going up the quays in the direction of the Bastille.

They left the quays and entered the streets. The driver, a black silhouette upon his box, whipped up his bony horses. Icy silence in the coach. Marius, motionless, his body braced in the corner of the carriage, his head dropping down upon his breast, his arms hanging, his legs rigid, appeared to await nothing now but a coffin; Jean Valjean seemed made of shadow, and Javert of stone; and in that carriage full of night, the interior of which, whenever it passed before a lamp, appeared to turn lividly pale, as if from an intermittent flash, chance grouped together, and seemed dismally to confront the three tragic immobilities, the corpse, the spectre, and the statue.

10. Return of the Prodigal Son – of his life

AT EVERY JOLT over the pavement, a drop of blood fell from Marius' hair.

It was after nightfall when the fiacre arrived at No. 6, in the Rue des Filles du Calvaire.

Javert first set foot to the ground, verified by a glance the number above the *porte-cochère*, and, lifting the heavy wrought-iron knocker, embellished in the old fashion, with a goat and a satyr defying each other, struck a violent blow. The fold of the door partly opened, and Javert pushed it. The porter showed himself, gaping and half-awake, a candle in his hand.

Everybody in the house was asleep. People go to bed early in the Marais, especially on days of *émeute*. That good old quarter, startled by the Revolution, takes refuge in slumber, as children, when they hear Bugaboo coming, hide their heads very quickly under their coverlets.

Meanwhile Jean Valjean and the driver lifted Marius out of the coach, Jean Valjean supporting him by the armpits, and the coachman by the knees.

While he was carrying Marius in this way, Jean Valjean slipped his hand under his clothes, which were much torn, felt his breast, and assured himself that the heart still beat. It beat even a little less feebly, as if the motion of the carriage had determined a certain renewal of life.

Javert called out to the porter in the tone which befits the government, in presence of the porter of a factious man.

'Somebody whose name is Gillenormand?'

'It is here. What do you want with him?'

'His son is brought home.'

'His son?' said the porter with amazement.

'He is dead.'

Jean Valjean, who came ragged and dirty, behind Javert, and whom the porter beheld with some horror, motioned to him with his head that he was not.

The porter did not appear to understand either Javert's words, or Jean Valjean's signs.

Javert continued:

'He has been to the barricade, and here he is.'

'To the barricade!' exclaimed the porter.

'He has got himself killed. Go and wake his father.'

The porter did not stir.

'Why don't you go?' resumed Javert.

And he added:

'There will be a funeral here tomorrow.'

With Javert, the common incidents of the highways were classed categorically, which is the foundation of prudence and vigilance, and each contingency had its compartment; the possible facts were in some sort in the drawers, whence they came out, on occasion, in variable quantities; there were, in the street, riot, *émeute*, carnival, funeral.

The porter merely woke Basque. Basque woke Nicolette; Nicolette woke Aunt Gillenormand. As to the grandfather, they let him sleep, thinking that he would know it soon enough at all events.

They carried Marius up to the first storey, without anybody, moreover, perceiving it in the other portions of the house, and they laid him on an old couch in M. Gillenormand's antechamber; and, while Basque went for a doctor and Nicolette was opening the linen closets, Jean Valjean felt Javert touch him on the shoulder. He understood, and went downstairs, having behind him Javert's following steps.

The porter saw them depart as he had seen them arrive, with drowsy dismay.

They got into the fiacre again, and the driver mounted upon his box.

'Inspector Javert,' said Jean Valjean, 'grant me one thing more.'

'What?' asked Javert roughly.

'Let me go home a moment. Then you shall do with me what you will.'

Javert remained silent for a few seconds, his chin drawn back into the collar of his overcoat, then he let down the window in front.

'Driver,' said he, 'Rue de l'Homme Armé, No. 7.'

11. Commotion in the absolute

THEY DID NOT OPEN their mouths again for the whole distance.

What did Jean Valjean desire? To finish what he had begun; to inform Cosette, to tell her where Marius was, to give her perhaps some other useful information, to make, if he could, certain final dispositions. As to himself, as to what concerned him personally, it was all over; he had been seized by Javert and did not resist; another than he, in such a condition, would perhaps have thought vaguely of that rope which Thénardier had given him and of the bars of the first cell which he should enter; but, since the bishop, there had been in Jean Valjean, in view of any violent attempt, were it even upon his own life, let us repeat, a deep religious hesitation.

Suicide, that mysterious assault upon the unknown, which may contain, in a certain measure, the death of the soul, was impossible to Jean Valjean.

At the entrance of the Rue de l'Homme Armé, the fiacre stopped, this street being too narrow for carriages to enter. Javert and Jean Valjean got out.

The driver humbly represented to monsieur the inspector that the Utrecht velvet of his carriage was all stained with the blood of the assassinated man and with the mud of the assassin. That was what he had understood. He added that an indemnity was due him. At the same time, taking his little book from his pocket, he begged monsieur the inspector to have the goodness to write him 'a little scrap of certificate as to what'.

Javert pushed back the little book which the driver handed him, and said:

'How much must you have, including your stop and your trip?'

'It is seven hours and a quarter,' answered the driver, 'and my velvet was brand new. Eighty francs, monsieur the inspector.'

Javert took four napoleons from his pocket and dismissed the fiacre.

Jean Valjean thought that Javert's intention was to take him on foot to the post of the Blancs-Manteaux or to the post of the Archives which are quite near by.

They entered the street. It was, as usual, empty. Javert followed Jean Valjean. They reached No. 7. Jean Valjean rapped. The door opened.

'Very well,' said Javert. 'Go up.'

He added with a strange expression and as if he were making an effort in speaking in such a way:

'I will wait here for you.'

Jean Valjean looked at Javert. This manner of proceeding was little in accordance with Javert's habits. Still, that Javert should now have a sort of haughty confidence in him, the confidence of the cat which grants the mouse the liberty of the length of her claw, resolved as Jean Valjean was to deliver himself up and make an end of it, could not surprise him very much. He opened the door, went into the house, cried to the porter who was in bed and who had drawn the cord without getting up: 'It is I!' and mounted the stairs.

On reaching the first storey, he paused. All painful paths have their halting-places. The window on the landing, which was a sliding window, was open. As in many old houses, the stairway admitted the light, and had a view upon the street. The street lamp, which stood exactly opposite, threw some rays upon the stairs, which produced an economy in light.

Jean Valjean, either to take breath or mechanically, looked out of this window. He leaned over the street. It is short, and the lamp lighted it from one end to the other. Jean Valjean was bewildered with amazement; there was nobody there.

Javert was gone.

12. The grandfather

Basque and the porter had carried Marius into the parlour, still stretched motionless upon the couch on which he had been first laid. The doctor, who had been sent for, had arrived. Aunt Gillenormand had got up.

Aunt Gillenormand went to and fro, in terror, clasping her hands, and incapable of doing anything but to say: 'My God, is it possible?' She added at intervals: 'Everything will be covered with blood!' When the first horror was over, a certain philosophy of the situation dawned upon her mind, and expressed itself by this exclamation: 'it must have turned out this way!' She did not attain to: '*I always said just so!*' which is customary on occasions of this kind.

On the doctor's order, a cot-bed had been set up near the couch. The doctor examined Marius, and, after having determined that the pulse still beat, that the sufferer had no wound penetrating his breast, and that the blood at the corners of his mouth came from the nasal cavities, he had him laid flat upon the bed, without a pillow, his head on a level with his body, and even a little lower, with his chest bare, in order to facilitate respiration. Mademoiselle Gillenormand, seeing that they were taking off Marius' clothes, withdrew. She began to tell her beads in her room.

The body had not received any interior lesion; a ball, deadened by the pocket-book, had turned aside, and made the tour of the ribs with a hideous gash, but not deep, and consequently not dangerous. The long walk underground had completed the dislocation of the broken shoulder-blade, and there were serious difficulties there. There were sword cuts on the arms. No scar disfigured his face; the head, however, was as it were covered with hacks; what would be the result of these wounds on the head? did they stop at the scalp? did they affect the skull? That could not yet be told. A serious symptom was, that they had caused the fainting, and men do not always wake from such faintings. The haemorrhage, moreover, had exhausted the wounded man. From the waist, the lower part of the body had been protected by the barricade.

Basque and Nicolette tore up linen and made bandages; Nicolette sewed them, Basque folded them. There being no lint, the doctor stopped the flow of blood from the wounds temporarily with rolls of wadding. By the side of the bed, three candles were burning on a table upon which the surgical instruments were spread out. The doctor washed Marius' face and hair with cold water. A bucketful was red in a moment. The porter, candle in hand, stood by.

The physician seemed reflecting sadly. From time to time he shook his head, as if he were answering some question which he had put to himself internally. A bad sign for the patient, these mysterious dialogues of the physician with himself.

At the moment the doctor was wiping the face and touching the still closed eyelids lightly with his finger, a door opened at the rear end of the parlour, and a long, pale figure approached.

It was the grandfather.

The *émeute*, for two days, had very much agitated, exasperated, and absorbed M. Gillenormand. He had not slept during the preceding night, and he had had a fever all day. At night, he had gone to bed very early, recommending that everything in the house be bolted, and, from fatigue, he had fallen asleep.

The slumbers of old men are easily broken; M. Gillenormand's room was next the parlour, and, in spite of the precautions they had taken, the noise had awakened him. Surprised by the light which he saw at the crack of his door, he had got out of bed, and groped his way along.

He was on the threshold, one hand on the knob of the half-opened door, his head bent a little forward and shaking, his body wrapped in a white nightgown, straight and without folds like a shroud; he was astounded; and he had the appearance of a phantom who is looking into a tomb.

He perceived the bed, and on the mattress that bleeding young man, white with a waxy whiteness, his eyes closed, his mouth open, his lips pallid, naked to the waist, gashed everywhere with red wounds, motionless, brightly lighted.

The grandfather had, from head to foot, as much of a shiver as ossified limbs can have; his eyes, the cornea of which had become yellow from his great age, were veiled with a sort of glassy haze; his whole face assumed in an instant the cadaverous angles of a skeleton head, his arms fell pendent as if a spring were broken in them, and his stupefied astonishment was expressed by the separation of the fingers of his aged tremulous hands; his knees bent forward, showing through the opening of his nightgown his poor naked legs bristling with white hairs, and he murmured:

'Marius!'

'Monsieur,' said Basque, 'monsieur has just been brought home. He has been to the barricade, and – '

'He is dead!' cried the old man in a terrible voice. 'Oh! the brigand.'

Then a sort of sepulchral, transfiguration made this centenarian as straight as a young man.

'Monsieur,' said he, 'you are the doctor. Come, tell me one thing. He is dead, isn't he?'

The physician, in the height of anxiety, kept silence.

M. Gillenormand wrung his hands with a terrific burst of laughter.

'He is dead! he is dead! He has got killed at the barricades! in hatred of me! It is against me that he did this! Ah, the blood-drinker! This is the way he comes back to me! Misery of my life, he is dead!'

He went to a window, opened it wide as if he were stifling, and, standing before the shadow, he began to talk into the street to the night:

'Pierced, sabred, slaughtered, exterminated, slashed, cut in pieces! do you see that, the vagabond! He knew very well that I was waiting for him, and that I had had his room arranged for him, and that I had had his portrait of the time when he was a little boy hung at the head of my bed! He knew very well that he had only to come back, and that for years I had been calling him, and that I sat at night in my chimney corner, with my hands on my knees, not knowing what to do, and that I was a fool for his sake! You knew it very well, that you had only to come in and say: "It is I," and that you would be the master of the house, and that I would obey you, and that you would do whatever you liked with your old booby of a grandfather. You knew it very well, and you said: "No, he is a royalist; I won't go!" And you went to the barricades, and you got yourself killed, out of spite! to revenge yourself for what I said to you about Monsieur the Duke de Berry! That is infamous! Go to bed, then, and sleep quietly! He is dead! That is my waking.'

The physician, who began to be anxious on two accounts, left Marius a moment, and went to M. Gillenormand and took his arm. The grandfather turned round, looked at him with eyes which seemed swollen and bloody, and said quietly:

'Monsieur, I thank you. I am calm, I am a man, I saw the death of Louis XVI, I know how to bear up under events. There is one thing which is terrible, to think that it is your newspapers that do all the harm. You will have scribblers, talkers, lawyers, orators, tribunes, discussions, progress, lights, rights of man, freedom of the press, and this is the way they bring home your children for you. Oh! Marius! it is abominable! Killed! dead before me! A barricade! Oh! the bandit! Doctor, you live in the quarter, I believe? Oh! I know you well. I see your carriage pass from my window. I am going to tell you. You would be wrong to think I am angry. We don't get angry with a dead man; that would be stupid. That is a child I brought up. I was an old man when he was yet quite small. He played at the Tuileries with his little spade and his little chair, and, so that the keeper should not scold, with my cane I filled up the holes in the ground that he made with his spade. One day he cried: "Down with Louis XVIII!" and went away. It is not my fault. He was all rosy and fair. His mother is dead. Have you noticed that all little children are fair? What is the reason of it? He is the son of one of those brigands of the Loire; but children are innocent of the crimes of their fathers. I remember when he was as high as this. He could not pronounce the *d's*. His talk was so soft and so obscure that you would have thought it was a bird. I recollect that once, before the Farnese Hercules, they made a circle to admire and wonder at him, that child was so beautiful! It was such a head as you see in pictures. I spoke to him in my gruff voice, I frightened him with my cane, but he knew very well it was for fun. In the morning, when he came into my room, I scolded, but it seemed like sunshine to me. You can't defend yourself against these brats. They take you, they hold on to you, they never let go of you. The truth is, that there was never any amour like that child. Now, what do you say of your Lafayette, your Benjamin Constant, and of your Tirecuir de Corcelles, who kill him for me! It can't go on like this.'

He approached Marius, who was still livid and motionless, and to whom the physician had returned, and he began to wring his hands. The old man's white lips moved as if mechanically, and made way for almost indistinct words, like whispers in a death-rattle, which could scarcely be heard: 'Oh! heartless! Oh! clubbist! Oh! scoundrel! Oh! Septembrist!' Reproaches whispered by a dying man to a corpse.

Little by little, as internal eruptions must always make their way out, the connection of his words returned, but the grandfather appeared to have lost the strength to utter them, his voice was so dull and faint that it seemed to come from the other side of an abyss:

'It is all the same to me, I am going to die too, myself. And to say that there is no little creature in Paris who would have been glad to make the wretch happy! A rascal who, instead of amusing himself and enjoying life, went to fight and got himself riddled like a brute! And for whom? for what? For the republic! Instead of going to dance at the Chaumière, as young people should! It is well worth being twenty years old. The republic, a deuced fine folly! Poor mothers, raise your pretty boys then. Come, he is dead. That will make two funerals under the *porte-cochère*. Then you fixed yourself out like that for the fine eyes of General Lamarque! What had he done for you, this General Lamarque? A sabrer! a babbler! To get killed for a dead man! If it isn't enough to make a man crazy! Think of it! At twenty! And without turning his head to see if he was not leaving somebody behind him! Here now are the poor old goodmen who must die alone. Perish in your corner, owl! Well, indeed, so much the better, it is what I was hoping, it is going to kill me dead. I am too old, I am a hundred, I am a hundred thousand; it is a long time since I have had a right to be dead. With this blow, it is done. It is all over then, how lucky! What is the use of making him breathe hartshorn and all this heap of drugs? You are losing your pains, dolt of a doctor! Go along, he is dead, stone dead. I understand it, I, who am dead also. He hasn't done the thing halfway. Yes, these times are infamous, infamous, infamous, and that is what I think of you, of your ideas, of your systems, of your masters, of your oracles, of your doctors, of your scamps of writers, of your beggars of philosophers, and of all the revolutions which for sixty years have frightened the flocks of crows in the Tuileries! And as you had no pity in getting yourself killed like that, I shall not have even any grief for your death, do you understand, assassin?'

At this moment, Marius slowly raised his lids, and his gaze, still veiled in the astonishment of lethargy, rested upon M. Gillenormand.

'Marius!' cried the old man. 'Marius! my darling Marius! my child! my dear son! You are opening your eyes, you are looking at me, you are alive, thanks!'

And he fell fainting.

BOOK 4: JAVERT OFF THE TRACK

1. Javert off the track

JAVERT MADE HIS WAY with slow steps from the Rue de l'Homme Armé.

He walked with his head down, for the first time in his life, and, for the first time in his life as well, with his hands behind his back.

Until that day, Javert had taken, of the two attitudes of Napoleon, only that which expresses resolution, the arms folded upon the breast; that which expresses uncertainty, the hands behind the back, was unknown to him. Now, a change had taken place; his whole person, slow and gloomy, bore the impress of anxiety.

He plunged into the silent streets.

Still he followed one direction

He took the shortest route towards the Seine, reached the Quai des Ormes, went along the quay, passed the Grève, and stopped, at a little distance from the post of the Place du Châtelet, at the corner of the Pont Notre Dame. The Seine there forms between the Pont Notre Dame and the Pont au Change in one direction, and in the other between the Quai de la Mégisserie and the Quai aux Fleurs, a sort of square lake crossed by a rapid.

This point of the Seine is dreaded by mariners. Nothing is more dangerous than this rapid, narrowed at that period and vexed by the piles of the mill of the bridge, since removed. The two bridges, so near each other, increase the danger, the water hurrying fearfully under the arches. It rolls on with broad, terrible folds; it gathers and heaps up; the flood strains at the piles of the bridge as if to tear them out with huge liquid ropes. Men who fall in there, one never sees again; the best swimmers are drowned.

Javert leaned both elbows on the parapet, with his chin in his hands, and while his fingers were clenched mechanically in the thickest of his whiskers, he reflected.

There had been a new thing, a revolution, a catastrophe in the depths of his being; and there was matter for self-examination.

Javert was suffering frightfully.

For some hours Javert had ceased to be natural. He was troubled; this brain, so limpid in its blindness, had lost its transparency; there was a cloud in this crystal. Javert felt that duty was growing weaker in his conscience, and he could not hide it from himself. When he had so unexpectedly met Jean Valjean upon the beach of the Seine, there had been in him something of the wolf, which seizes his prey again, and of the dog which again finds his master.

He saw before him two roads, both equally straight; but he saw two; and that terrified him – him, who had never in his life known but one straight line. And, bitter anguish, these two roads were contradictory. One of these two straight lines excluded the other. Which of the two was the true one?

His condition was inexpressible.

To owe life to a malefactor, to accept that debt and to pay it, to be, in spite of himself, on a level with a fugitive from justice, and to pay him for one service with another service; to allow him to say: 'Go away,' and to say to him in turn: 'Be free;' to sacrifice duty, that general obligation, to personal motives, and to feel in these personal motives something general also, and perhaps superior; to betray society in order to be true to his own conscience; that all these absurdities should be realised and that they should be accumulated upon himself, this it was by which he was prostrated.

One thing had astonished him, that Jean Valjean had spared him, and one thing had petrified him, that he, Javert, had spared Jean Valjean.

Where was he? He sought himself and found himself no longer.

What should he do now? Give up Jean Valjean, that was wrong; leave Jean Valjean free, that was wrong. In the first case, the man of authority would fall lower than the man of the galley; in the second, a convict rose higher than the law and set his foot upon it. In both cases, dishonour to him, Javert. In every course which was open to him, there was a fall. Destiny has certain extremities precipitous upon the impossible, and beyond which life is no more than an abyss. Javert was at one of these extremities.

One of his causes of anxiety was, that he was compelled to think. The very violence of all these contradictory emotions forced him to it. Thought, an unaccustomed thing to him, and singularly painful.

There is always a certain amount of internal rebellion in thought; and he was irritated at having it within him.

Thought, upon any subject, no matter what, outside of the narrow circle of his functions, had been to him, in all cases, a folly and a fatigue; but thought upon the day which had just gone by, was torture. He must absolutely, however, look into his conscience after such shocks, and render an account of himself to himself.

What he had just done made him shudder. He had, he, Javert, thought good to decide, against all the regulations of the police, against the whole social and judicial organisation, against the entire code, in favour of a release; that had pleased him; he had substituted his own affairs for the public affairs; could this be characterised? Every time that he set himself face to face with this nameless act which he had committed, he trembled from head to foot. Upon what should he resolve? A single resource remained: to return immediately to the Rue de l'Homme Armé, and have Jean Valjean arrested. It was clear that that was what he must do. He could not.

Something barred the way to him on that side.

Something? What? Is there anything else in the world besides tribunals, sentences, police, and authority? Javert's ideas were overturned.

A galley-slave sacred! a convict not to be taken by justice! and that by the act of Javert!

That Javert and Jean Valjean, the man made to be severe, the man made to be submissive, that these two men, who were each the thing of the law, should have come to this point of setting themselves both above the law, was not this terrible?

What then! such enormities should happen and nobody should be punished? Jean Valjean, stronger than the entire social order, should be free and he, Javert, continue to eat the bread of the government!

His reflections gradually became terrible.

He might also through these reflections have reproached himself a little in regard to the insurgent carried to the Rue des Filles du Calvaire; but he did not think of it. The lesser fault was lost in the greater. Besides, that insurgent was clearly a dead man, and legally, death extinguishes pursuit.

Jean Valjean then was the weight he had on his mind.

Jean Valjean confounded him. All the axioms which had been the supports of his whole life crumbled away before this man. Jean Valjean's generosity towards him, Javert, overwhelmed him. Other acts, which he remembered and which he had hitherto treated as lies and follies, returned to him now as realities. M. Madeleine reappeared behind Jean Valjean, and the two figures overlaid each other so as to make but one, which was venerable. Javert felt that something horrible was penetrating his soul, admiration for a convict. Respect for a galley-slave, can that be possible? He shuddered at it, yet could not shake it off. It was useless to struggle, he was reduced to confess before his own inner tribunal the sublimity of this wretch. That was hateful.

A beneficent malefactor, a compassionate convict, kind, helpful, clement, returning good for evil, returning pardon for hatred, loving pity rather than vengeance, preferring to destroy himself rather than to destroy his enemy, saving him who had stricken him, kneeling upon the height of virtue, nearer the angels than men. Javert was compelled to acknowledge that this monster existed.

This could not last.

Certainly, and we repeat it, he had not given himself up without resistance to this monster, this infamous angel, this hideous hero, at whom he was almost as indignant as he was astounded. Twenty times, while he was in that carriage face to face with Jean Valjean, the legal tiger had roared within him. Twenty times he had been tempted to throw himself upon Jean Valjean, to seize him and to devour him, that is to say, to arrest him. What more simple, indeed? To cry at the first post in front of which they passed: 'Here is a fugitive from justice in breach of his ban!' to call the gendarmes and say to them: 'This man is yours!' then to go away, to leave this condemned man there, to ignore the rest, and to have nothing more to do with it. This man is for ever the prisoner of the law; the law will do what it will with him. What more just? Javert had said all this to himself; he had desired to go further, to act, to apprehend the man, and, then as now, he had not been able; and every time that his hand had been raised convulsively towards Jean Valjean's collar, his hand, as if under an enormous weight, had fallen back, and in the depths of his mind he had heard a voice, a strange voice crying to him: 'Very well. Give up your saviour. Then have Pontius Pilate's basin brought; and wash your claws.'

Then his reflections fell back upon himself, and by the side of Jean Valjean exalted, he beheld himself, him, Javert, degraded.

A convict was his benefactor!

But also why had he permitted this man to let him live? He had, in that barricade, the right to be killed. He should have availed himself of that right. To have called the other insurgents to his aid against Jean Valjean, to have secured a shot by force, that would have been better.

His supreme anguish was the loss of all certainty. He felt that he was uprooted. The code was now but a stump in his hand. He had to do with scruples of an unknown species. There was in him a revelation of feeling entirely distinct from the declarations of the law, his only standard hitherto. To retain his old virtue, that no longer sufficed. An entire order of unexpected facts arose and subjugated him. An entire new world appeared to his soul; favour accepted and returned, devotion, compassion, indulgence, acts of violence committed by pity upon austerity, respect of persons, no more final condemnation, no more damnation, the possibility of a tear in the eye of the law, a mysterious justice according to God going counter to justice according to men. He perceived in the darkness the fearful rising of an unknown moral sun, he was horrified and blinded by it. An owl compelled to an eagle's gaze.

He said to himself that it was true then, that there were exceptions, that authority might be put out of countenance, that rule might stop short before a fact, that everything was not framed in the text of the code, that the unforeseen would be obeyed, that the virtue of a convict might spread a snare for the virtue of a functionary, that the monstrous might be divine, that destiny had such ambuscades as these, and he thought with despair that even he had not been proof against a surprise.

He was compelled to recognise the existence of kindness. This convict had been kind. And he himself, wonderful to tell, he had just been kind. Therefore he had become depraved.

He thought himself base. He was a horror to himself.

Javert's ideal was not to be humane, not to be great, not to be sublime; it was to be irreproachable. Now he had just failed.

How had he reached that point? How had all this happened? He could not have told himself. He took his head in his hands, but it was in vain; he could not explain it to himself.

He had certainly always had the intention of returning Jean Valjean to the law, of which Jean Valjean was the captive, and of which he, Javert, was the slave. He had not confessed to himself for a single moment while he held him, that he had a thought of letting him go. It was in some sort without his knowledge that his hand had opened and released him.

All manner of interrogation points flashed before his eyes. He put questions to himself, and he made answers, and his answers frightened him. He asked himself: 'This convict, this desperate man, whom I have pursued even to persecution, and who has had me beneath his feet, and could have avenged himself, and who ought to have done so as well for his revenge as for his security, in granting me life, in sparing me, what has he done? His duty? No. Something more. And I, in sparing him in my turn, what have I done? My duty? No. Something more. There is then something more than duty.' Here he was startled; his balances were disturbed; one of the scales fell into the abyss, the other flew into the sky, and Javert felt no less dismay from the one which was above than from the one which was below. Without being the least in the world what is called a Voltairean, or a philosopher, or a sceptic, respectful on the contrary, by instinct, towards the established church, he knew it only as an august fragment of the social whole; order was his dogma and was enough for him; since he had been of the age of a man, and an official, he had put almost all his religion in the police. Being, and we employ the words here without the slightest irony and in their most serious acceptation, being, we have said, a spy as men are priests. He had a superior, M. Gisquet; he had scarcely thought, until today, of that other superior, God.

This new chief, God, he felt unawares, and was perplexed thereat.

He had lost his bearings in this unexpected presence; he did not know what to do with this superior; he who was not ignorant that the subordinate is bound always to yield, that he ought neither to disobey, nor to blame, nor to discuss, and that, in presence of a superior who astonishes him too much, the inferior has no resource but resignation.

But how manage to send in his resignation to God?

However this might be, and it was always to this that he returned, one thing overruled all else for him, that was, that he had just committed an appalling infraction. He had closed his eyes upon a convicted second offender in breach of his ban. He had set a galley-slave at large. He had robbed the laws of a man who belonged to them. He had done that. He could not understand himself. He was not sure of being himself. The very reasons of his action escaped him; he caught only the whirl of them. He had lived up to this moment by that blind faith which a dark probity engenders. This faith was leaving him, this probity was failing him. All that he had believed was dissipated. Truths which he had no wish for inexorably besieged him. He must henceforth be another man. He suffered the strange pangs of a conscience suddenly operated upon for the cataract. He saw what he revolted at seeing. He felt that he was emptied, useless, broken off from his past life, destitute, dissolved. Authority was dead in him. He had no further reason for existence.

Terrible situation! to be moved.

To be granite, and to doubt! to be the statue of penalty cast in a single piece in the mould of the law, and to suddenly perceive that you have under your breast of bronze something preposterous and disobedient which almost resembles a heart. To be led by it to render good for good, although you may have said until today that this good was evil! to be the watchdog, and to fawn! to be ice, and to melt! to be a vice, and to become a hand! to feel your fingers suddenly open! to lose your hold, appalling thing!

The projectile man no longer knowing his road, and recoiling!

To be obliged to acknowledge this: infallibility is not infallible, there may be an error in the dogma, all is not said when a code has spoken, society is not perfect, authority is complicate with vacillation, a cracking is possible in the immutable, judges are men, the law may be deceived, the tribunals may be mistaken! to see a flaw in the immense blue crystal of the firmament!

What was passing in Javert was the Fampoux of a rectilinear conscience, the throwing of a soul out of its path, the crushing of a probity irresistibly hurled in a straight line and breaking itself against God. Certainly, it was strange, that the fireman of order, the engineer of authority, mounted upon the blind iron-horse of the rigid path, could be thrown off by a ray of light! that the incommutable, the direct, the correct, the geometrical, the passive, the perfect, could bend! that there should be a road to Damascus for the locomotive!

God, always interior to man, and unyielding, he the true conscience, to the false; a prohibition to the spark to extinguish itself; an order to the ray to remember the sun; an injunction to the soul to recognise the real absolute when it is confronted with the fictitious absolute; humanity imperishable; the human heart inadmissible; that splendid phenomenon, the most beautiful perhaps of our interior wonders, did Javert comprehend it? did Javert penetrate it? did Javert form any idea of it? Evidently not. But under the pressure of this incontestable incomprehensible, he felt that his head was bursting.

He was less the transfigured than the victim of this miracle. He bore it, exasperated. He saw in it only an immense difficulty of existence. It seemed to him that henceforth his breathing would be oppressed for ever.

To have the unknown over his head, he was not accustomed to that.

Until now all that he had above him had been in his sight a smooth, simple, limpid surface; nothing there unknown, nothing obscure; nothing which was not definite, co-ordinated, concatenated, precise, exact, circumscribed, limited, shut in, all foreseen; authority was a plane; no fall in it, no dizziness before it. Javert had never seen the unknown except below. The irregular, the unexpected, the disorderly opening of chaos, the possible slipping into an abyss; that belonged to inferior regions, to the rebellious, the wicked, the miserable. Now Javert was thrown over backward, and he was abruptly startled by this monstrous apparition: a gulf on high.

What then! he was dismantled completely! he was disconcerted, absolutely! In what should he trust? That of which he had been convinced gave way!

What! the flaw in the cuirass of society could be found by a magnanimous wretch! what! an honest servant of the law could find himself suddenly caught between two crimes, the crime of letting a man escape, and the crime of arresting him! all was not certain in the order given by the state to the official! There might be blind alleys in duty! What then! was all that real! was it true that an old bandit, weighed down by condemnations, could rise up and be right at last? was this credible? were there cases then when the law ought, before a transfigured crime, to retire, stammering excuses?

Yes, there were! and Javert saw it! and Javert touched it! and not only could he not deny it, but he took part in it. They were realities. It was abominable that real facts could reach such deformity.

If facts did their duty, they would be contented with being the proofs of the law; facts, it is God who sends them. Was anarchy then about to descend from on high?

So – and beneath the magnifying power of anguish, and in the optical illusion of consternation, all that might have restrained and corrected his impression vanished, and society, and the human race, and the universe, were summed up henceforth in his eyes in one simple and terrible feature – so punishment, the thing judged, the force due to legislation, the decrees of the sovereign courts, the magistracy, the government, prevention and repression, official wisdom, legal infallibility, the principle of authority, all the dogmas upon which repose political and civil security, sovereignty, justice, the logic flowing from the code, the social absolute, the public truth, all that, confusion, jumble, chaos; himself, Javert, the spy of order, incorruptibility in the service of the police, the mastiff-providence of society, vanquished and prostrated; and upon all this ruin a man standing, with a green cap on his head and a halo about his brow; such was the overturn to which he had come; such was the frightful vision which he had in his soul.

Could that be endurable? No.

Unnatural state, if ever there was one. There were only two ways to get out of it. One, to go resolutely to Jean Valjean, and to return the man of the galleys to the dungeon. The other –

Javert left the parapet, and, his head erect this time, made his way with a firm step towards the post indicated by a lamp at one of the corners of the Place du Châtelet.

On reaching it, he saw a *sergent de ville* through the window, and he entered.

Merely from the manner in which they push open the door of a guardhouse, policemen recognise each other. Javert gave his name, showed his card to the sergent, and sat down at the table of the post, on which a candle was burning. There was a pen on the table, a leaden inkstand, and some paper in readiness for chance reports and the orders of the night patrol.

This table, always accompanied by its straw chair, is an institution; it exists in all the police posts; it is invariably adorned with a boxwood saucer, full of saw-dust, and a pasteboard box, full of red wafers, and it is the lower stage of the official style. On it the literature of the state begins.

Javert took the pen and a sheet of paper, and began to write. This is what he wrote:

SOME OBSERVATIONS FOR THE BENEFIT OF THE SERVICE

First: I beg monsieur the prefect to glance at this.

Secondly: the prisoners, on their return from examination, take off their shoes and remain barefooted upon the pavement while they are searched. Many cough on returning to the prison. This involves hospital expenses.

Thirdly: spinning is good, with relays of officers at intervals; but there should be, on important occasions, two officers at least who do not lose sight of each other, so that, if, for any cause whatever, one officer becomes weak in the service, the other is watching him, and supplies his place.

Fourthly: it is difficult to explain why the special regulation of the prison of the Madelonnettes forbids a prisoner having a chair, even on paying for it.

Fifthly: at the Madelonnettes, there are only two bars to the sutler's window, which enables the sutler to let the prisoners touch her hand.

Sixthly: the prisoners, called barkers, who call the other prisoners to the parlour, make the prisoner pay them two sous for calling his name distinctly. This is a theft.

Seventhly: for a dropped thread, they retain ten sous from the prisoner in the weaving shop; this is an abuse on the part of the contractor, since the cloth is just as good.

Eighthly: it is annoying that the visitors of La Force have to cross the Cour des Mômes to reach the parlour of Sainte Marie l'Egyptienne.

Ninthly: it is certain that gendarmes are every day heard relating, in the yard of the prefecture, the examinations of those brought before the magistrates. For a gendarme, who should hold such things sacred, to repeat what he has heard in the examining chamber, is a serious disorder.

Tenthly: Mme Henry is an honest woman; her sutler's window is very neat; but it is wrong for a woman to keep the wicket of the trap-door of the secret cells. It is not worthy the Conciergerie of a great civilisation.

Javert wrote these lines in his calmest and most correct handwriting, not omitting a dot, and making the paper squeak resolutely under his pen. Beneath the last line he signed:

Javert
Inspector of the 1st class.
At the Post of the Place du Châtelet.
June 7, 1832, about one o'clock in the morning.'

Javert dried the fresh ink of the paper, folded it like a letter, sealed it, wrote on the back: *Note for the administration,* left it on the table, and went out of the post.

The glazed and grated door closed behind him.

He again crossed the Place du Châtelet diagonally, regained the quay, and returned with automatic precision to the very point which he had left a quarter of an hour before, he leaned over there, and found himself again in the same attitude, on the same stone of the parapet. It seemed as if he had not stirred.

The darkness was complete. It was the sepulchral moment which follows midnight. A ceiling of clouds concealed the stars. The sky was only an ominous depth. The houses in the city no longer showed a single light; nobody was passing; all that he could see of the streets and the quays was deserted; Notre Dame and the towers of the Palais de Justice seemed like features of the night. A lamp reddened the curb of the quay. The silhouettes of the bridges were distorted in the mist, one behind the other. The rains had swelled the river.

The place where Javert was leaning was, it will be remembered, situated exactly over the rapids of the Seine, perpendicularly over that formidable whirlpool which knots and unknots itself like an endless screw.

Javert bent his head and looked. All was black. He could distinguish nothing. He heard a frothing sound; but he did not see the river. At intervals, in that giddy depth, a gleam appeared in dim serpentine contortions, the water having this power, in the most complete night, of taking light, nobody knows whence, and changing it into an adder. The gleam vanished, and all became again indistinct. Immensity seemed open there. What was beneath was not water, it was chasm. The wall of the quay, abrupt, confused, mingled with vapour, suddenly lost to sight, seemed like an escarpment of the infinite.

He saw nothing, but he perceived the hostile chill of the water, and the insipid odour of the moist stones. A fierce breath rose from that abyss. The swollen river guessed at rather than perceived, the tragical whispering of the flood, the dismal vastness of the arches of the bridge, the imaginable fall into that gloomy void, all that shadow was full of horror.

Javert remained for some minutes motionless, gazing into that opening of darkness; he contemplated the invisible with a fixedness which resembled attention. The water gurgled. Suddenly he took off his hat and laid it on the edge of the quay. A moment afterwards, a tall and black form, which from the distance some belated passer might have taken for a phantom, appeared standing on the parapet, bent towards the Seine, then sprang up, and fell straight into the darkness; there was a dull splash; and the shadow alone was in the secret of the convulsions of that obscure form which had disappeared under the water.

BOOK 5: THE GRANDSON AND THE GRANDFATHER

1. *In which we see the tree with the plate of zinc once more*

SOMETIME AFTER the events which we have just related, the Sieur Boulatruelle had a vivid emotion.

The Sieur Boulatruelle is that road-labourer of Montfermeil of whom we have already had a glimpse in the dark portions of this book.

Boulatruelle, it will perhaps be remembered, was a man occupied with troublous and various things. He broke stones and damaged travellers on the highway. Digger and robber, he had a dream; he believed in treasures buried in the forest of Montfermeil. He hoped one day to find money in the ground at the foot of a tree; in the meantime, he was willing to search for it in the pockets of the passers-by.

Nevertheless, for the moment, he was prudent. He had just had a narrow escape. He had been, as we know, picked up in the Jondrette garret with the other bandits. Utility of a vice: his drunkenness had saved him. It could never be clearly made out whether he was there as robber or as robbed. An order of *nol. pros.*, founded upon his clearly proved state of drunkenness on the evening of the ambuscade, had set him at liberty. He regained the freedom of the woods. He returned to his road from Gagny to Lagny to break stones for the use of the state, under administrative surveillance, with downcast mien, very thoughtful, a little cooled towards robbery, which had nearly ruined him, but only turning with the more affection towards wine, which had just saved him.

As to the vivid emotion which he had a little while after his return beneath the thatched roof of his road-labourer's hut, it was this:

One morning a little before the break of day, Boulatruelle, while on the way to his work according to his habit, and upon the watch, perhaps, perceived a man among the branches, whose back only he could see, but whose form, as it seemed to him, through the distance and the twilight, was not altogether unknown to him. Boulatruelle, although a drunkard, had a correct and lucid memory, an indispensable defensive arm to him who is slightly in conflict with legal order.

'Where the devil have I seen something like that man?' inquired he of himself.

But he could make himself no answer, save that it resembled somebody of whom he had a confused remembrance.

Boulatruelle, however, aside from the identity which he did not succeed in getting hold of, made some comparisons and calculations. This man was not of the country. He had come there. On foot, evidently. No public carriage passes Montfermeil at that hour. He had walked all night. Where did he come from? not far off. For he had neither bag nor bundle. From Paris, doubtless. Why was he in the wood? why was he there at such an hour? what had he come there to do?

Boulatruelle thought of the treasure. By dint of digging into his memory he dimly recollected having already had, several years before, a similar surprise in relation to a man who, it struck him, was very possibly the same man.

While he was meditating, he had, under the very weight of his meditation, bowed his head, which was natural, but not very cunning. When he raised it again there was no longer anything there. The man had vanished in the forest and the twilight.

'The deuce,' said Boulatruelle, 'I will find him again. I will discover the parish of that parishioner. This Patron-Minette prowler upon has a why, I will find it out. Nobody has a secret in my woods without I have a finger in it.'

He took his pickaxe, which was very sharp.

'Here is something,' he muttered, 'to pry into the ground or a man with.'

And, as one attaches one thread to another thread, limping along at his best in the path which the man must have followed, he took his way through the thicket.

When he had gone a hundred yards, daylight, which began to break, aided him. Footsteps printed on the sand here and there, grass matted down, heath broken off, young branches bent into the bushes and rising again with a graceful slowness, like the arms of a pretty woman who stretches herself on awaking, indicated to him a sort of track. He followed it, then he lost it. Time was passing. He pushed further forward into the wood and reached a kind of eminence. A morning hunter who passed along a path in the distance, whistling the air of Guillery, inspired him with the idea of climbing a tree. Although old, he was agile. There was near by a beech tree of great height, worthy of Tityrus and Boulatruelle. Boulatruelle climbed the beech as high as he could.

The idea was good. In exploring the solitude on the side where the wood was entirely wild and tangled, Boulatruelle suddenly perceived the man.

Hardly had he perceived him when he lost sight of him.

The man entered, or rather glided, into a distant glade, masked by tall trees, but which Boulatruelle knew very well from having noticed there, near a great heap of burrstone, a wounded chestnut tree bandaged with a plate of zinc nailed upon the bark. This glade is the one which was formerly called the Blaru ground. The heap of stones, intended for nobody knows what use, which could be seen there thirty years ago, is doubtless there still. Nothing equals the longevity of a heap of stones, unless it be that of a palisade fence. It is there provisionally. What a reason for enduring!

Boulatruelle, with the rapidity of joy, let himself fall from the tree rather than descended. The lair was found, the problem was to catch the game. That famous treasure of his dreams was probably there.

It was no easy matter to reach that glade. By the beaten paths, which make a thousand provoking zigzags, it required a good quarter of an hour. In a straight line, through the underbrush, which is there singularly thick, very thorny, and very aggressive, it required a long half-hour. There was Boulatruelle's mistake. He believed in the straight line; an optical illusion which is respectable, but which ruins many men. The underbrush, bristling as it was, appeared to him the best road.

'Let us take the wolves' Rue de Rivoli,' said he.

Boulatruelle, accustomed to going astray, this time made the blunder of going straight.

He threw himself resolutely into the thickest of the bushes.

He had to deal with hollies, with nettles, with hawthorns, with sweetbriers, with thistles, with exceedingly irascible brambles. He was very much scratched.

At the bottom of the ravine he found a stream which must be crossed.

He finally reached the Blaru glade, at the end of forty minutes, sweating, soaked, breathless, torn, ferocious.

Nobody in the glade.

Boulatruelle ran to the heap of stones. It was in its place. Nobody had carried it away.

As for the man, he had vanished into the forest. He had escaped. Where? on which side? in what thicket? Impossible to guess.

And, a bitter thing, there was behind the heap of stones, before the tree with the plate of zinc, some fresh earth, a pick, forgotten or abandoned, and a hole.

This hole was empty.

'Robber!' cried Boulatruelle, showing both fists to the horizon.

2. *Marius escaping from civil war, prepares for domestic war*

MARIUS was for a long time neither dead nor alive. He had for several weeks a fever accompanied with delirium, and serious cerebral symptoms resulting rather from the concussion produced by the wounds in the head than from the wounds themselves.

He repeated the name of Cosette during entire nights in the dismal loquacity of fever and with the gloomy obstinacy of agony. The size of certain gashes was a serious danger, the suppuration of large wounds always being liable to reabsorption, and consequently to kill the patient, under certain atmospheric influences; at every change in the weather, at the slightest storm, the physician was anxious, 'Above all, let the wounded man have no excitement,' he repeated. The dressings were complicated and difficult, the fastening of cloths and bandages with sparadrap not being invented at that period. Nicolette used for lint a sheet 'as big as a ceiling', said she. It was not without difficulty that the chloruretted lotions and the nitrate of silver brought the gangrene to an end. As long as there was danger, M. Gillenormand, in despair at the bedside of his grandson, was, like Marius, neither dead nor alive.

Every day, and sometimes twice a day, a very well dressed gentleman with white hair, such was the description given by the porter, came to inquire after the wounded man, and left a large package of lint for the dressings.

At last, on the 7th of September, four months, to a day, after the sorrowful night when they had brought him home dying to his grandfather, the physician declared him out of danger. Convalescence began. Marius was, however, obliged still to remain for more than two months stretched on a long chair, on account of the accidents resulting from the fracture of the shoulder-blade. There is always a last wound like this which will not close, and which prolongs the dressings, to the great disgust of the patient.

However, this long sickness and this long convalescence saved him from pursuit. In France, there is no anger, even governmental, which six months does not extinguish. *Émeutes*, in the present state of society, are so much the fault of everybody that they are followed by a certain necessity of closing the eyes.

Let us add that the infamous Gisquet order, which enjoined physicians to inform against the wounded, having outraged public opinion, and not only public opinion, but the king first of all, the wounded were shielded and protected by this indignation; and, with the exception of those who had been taken prisoners in actual combat, the courts-martial dared not disturb any. Marius was therefore left in peace.

M. Gillenormand passed first through every anguish, and then every ecstasy. They had great difficulty in preventing him from passing every night with the wounded man; he had his large armchair brought to the side of Marius' bed; he insisted that his daughter should take the finest linen in the house for compresses and bandages. Mademoiselle Gillenormand, like a prudent and elder person, found means to spare the fine linen, while she left the grandfather to suppose that he was obeyed. M. Gillenormand did not permit anybody to explain to him that for making lint cambric is not so good as coarse linen, nor new linen so good as old. He superintended all the dressings, from which

Mademoiselle Gillenormand modestly absented herself. When the dead flesh was cut with scissors, he would say: '*aïe! aïe!*' Nothing was so touching as to see him hand a cup of gruel to the wounded man with his gentle senile trembling. He overwhelmed the doctor with questions. He did not perceive that he always asked the same.

On the day the physician announced to him that Marius was out of danger, the goodman was in delirium. He gave his porter three louis as a gratuity. In the evening, on going to his room, he danced a gavot, making castanets of his thumb and forefinger, and he sang a song which follows:

Jeanne est née à Fougère,
Vrai nid d'une bergère;
J'adore son jupon,
    Fripon.

Amour, tu vis en elle;
Car c'est dans sa prunelle
Que tu mets ton carquois,
    Narquois!

Moi, je la chante, et j'aime,
Plus que Diane même,
Jeanne et ses durs tétons
    Bretons.

Then he knelt upon a chair, and Basque, who watched him through the half-open door, was certain that he was praying.

Hitherto, he had hardly believed in God.

At each new phase of improvement, which continued to grow more and more visible, the grandfather raved. He did a thousand mirthful things mechanically; he ran up and downstairs without knowing why. A neighbour, a pretty woman withal, was amazed at receiving a large bouquet one morning; it was M. Gillenormand who sent it to her. The husband made a scene. M. Gillenormand attempted to take Nicolette upon his knees. He called Marius Monsieur the Baron.

He cried, '*Vive la République!*'

At every moment, he asked the physician: 'There is no more danger, is there!' He looked at Marius with a grandmother's eyes. He brooded him when he ate. He no longer knew himself, he no longer counted on himself. Marius was the master of the house, there was abdication in his joy, he was the grandson of his grandson.

In this lightness of heart which possessed him, he was the most venerable of children. For fear of fatiguing or of annoying the convalescent, he got behind him to smile upon him. He was contented, joyous, enraptured, delightful, young. His white hairs added a sweet majesty to the cheerful light upon his face. When grace is joined with wrinkles, it is adorable. There is an unspeakable dawn in happy old age.

As for Marius, while he let them dress his wounds and care for him, he had one fixed idea: Cosette.

Since the fever and the delirium had left him, he had not uttered that name, and they might have supposed that he no longer thought of it. He held his peace, precisely because his soul was in it.

He did not know what had become of Cosette; the whole affair of the Rue de la Chanvrerie was like a cloud in his memory; shadows, almost indistinct, were floating in his mind, Eponine, Gavroche, Mabeuf, the Thénardiers, all his friends mingled drearily with the smoke of the barricade; the strange passage of M. Fauchelevent in that bloody drama produced upon him the effect of an enigma in a tempest; he understood nothing in regard to his own life; he neither knew how, nor by whom, he had been saved, and nobody about him knew; all that they could tell him was that he had been brought to the Rue des Filles du Calvaire in a fiacre by night; past, present, future, all was now to him but the mist of a vague idea; but there was within this mist an immovable point, one clear and precise feature, something which was granite, a resolution, a will: to find Cosette again. To him the idea of life was not distinct from the idea of Cosette; he had decreed in his heart that he would not accept the one without the other, and he was unalterably determined to demand from anybody, no matter whom, who should wish to compel him to live, from his grandfather, from Fate, from Hell, the restitution of his vanished Eden.

He did not hide the obstacles from himself.

Let us emphasise one point here: he was not won over, and was little softened by all the solicitude and all the tenderness of his grandfather. In the first place, he was not in the secret of it all; then, in his sick man's reveries, still feverish perhaps, he distrusted this gentleness as a new and strange thing, the object of which was to subdue him. He remained cold. The grandfather expended his poor old smile for nothing. Marius said to himself it was well so long as he, Marius, did not speak and offered no resistance; but that, when the question of Cosette was raised, he would find another face, and his grandfather's real attitude would be unmasked. Then it would be harsh recrudescence of family questions, every sarcasm and every objection at once: Fauchelevent, Coupelevent, fortune, poverty, misery, the stone at the neck, the future. Violent opposition; conclusion, refusal. Marius was bracing himself in advance.

And then, in proportion as he took new hold of life, his former griefs reappeared, the old ulcers of his memory reopened, he thought once more of the past. Colonel Pontmercy appeared again between M. Gillenormand and him, Marius; he said to himself that there was no real goodness to be hoped for from him who had been so unjust and so hard to his father. And with health, there returned to him a sort of harshness towards his grandfather. The old man bore it with gentleness.

M. Gillenormand, without manifesting it in any way, noticed that Marius, since he had been brought home and restored to consciousness, had not once said to him 'father'. He did not say monsieur, it is true; but he found means to say neither the one nor the other, by a certain manner of turning his sentences.

A crisis was evidently approaching.

As it almost always happens in similar cases, Marius, in order to try himself, skirmished before offering battle. This is called feeling the ground. One morning it happened that M. Gillenormand, over a newspaper which had fallen into his hands, spoke lightly of the Convention and discharged a royalist epiphonema upon Danton, Saint Just, and Robespierre. 'The men of '93 were giants,' said Marius, sternly. The old man was silent, and did not whisper for the rest of the day.

Marius, who had always present to his mind the inflexible grandfather of his early years, saw in this silence an intense concentration of anger, augured from it a sharp conflict, and increased his preparations for combat in the inner recesses of his thought.

He determined that in case of refusal he would tear off his bandages, dislocate his shoulder, lay bare and open his remaining wounds, and refuse all nourishment. His wounds were his ammunition. To have Cosette or to die.

He waited for the favourable moment with the crafty patience of the sick.

That moment came.

3. Marius attacks

One day M. Gillenormand, while his daughter was putting in order the vials and the cups upon the marble top of the bureau, bent over Marius and said to him in his most tender tone:

'Do you see, my darling Marius, in your place I would eat meat now rather than fish. A fried sole is excellent to begin a convalescence, but, to put the sick man on his legs, it takes a good cutlet.'

Marius, nearly all whose strength had returned, gathered it together, sat up in bed, rested his clenched hands on the sheets, looked his grandfather in the face, assumed a terrible air, and said: 'This leads me to say something to you.'

'What is it?'

'It is that I wish to marry.'

'Foreseen,' said the grandfather. And he burst out laughing.

'How foreseen?'

'Yes, foreseen. You shall have her, your lassie.'

Marius, astounded, and overwhelmed by the dazzling burst of happiness, trembled in every limb.

M. Gillenormand continued:

'Yes, you shall have her, your handsome, pretty little girl. She comes every day in the shape of an old gentleman to inquire after you. Since you were wounded, she has passed her time in weeping and making lint. I have made inquiry. She lives in the Rue de l'Homme Armé, Number Seven. Ah, we are ready! Ah! you want her! Well, you shall have her. That catches you. You had arranged your little plot; you said to yourself: I am going to make it known bluntly to that grandfather, to that mummy of the Regency and of the Directory, to that old beau, to that Dorante become a Géronte; he has had his levities too, himself, and his amours, and his grisettes, and his Cosettes; he has made his display, he has had his wings, he has eaten his spring bread; he must remember it well. We shall see. Battle. Ah! you take the bug by the horns. That is good. I propose a cutlet, and you answer: "A propos, I wish to marry." That is what I call a transition. Ah! you had reckoned upon some bickering. You didn't know that I was an old coward. What do you say to that? You are spited. To find your grandfather still more stupid than yourself, you didn't expect that, you lose the argument which you were to have made to me, monsieur advocate; it is provoking. Well, it is all the same, rage. I do what you wish, that cuts you out of it, idiot. Listen. I have made inquiries, I am sly too; she is charming, she is modest, the lancer is not true, she has made heaps of lint, she is a jewel, she worships you; if you had died, there would have been three of us; her bier would have accompanied mine. I had a strong notion, as soon as you were better, to plant her square at your bedside, but it is only in romances that they introduce young girls unceremoniously to the side of the couch of the pretty wounded men who interest them. That does not do. What would your aunt have said? You have been quite naked three-quarters of the time, my goodman. Ask Nicolette, who has not left you a minute, if it was possible for a woman to be here. And then what would the doctor have said? That doesn't cure a fever, a pretty girl. Finally, it is all right; don't let us talk any more about it, it is said, it is done, it is fixed; take her. Such is my ferocity. Do you see, I saw that you did not love me; I said: What is there that I can do, then, to make this animal love me? I said: Hold on! I have my little Cosette under my hand; I will give her to him, he must surely love a little then, or let him tell why. Ah! you thought that the old fellow was going to storm, to make a gruff voice, to cry No, and to lift his cane upon all this dawn. Not at all. Cosette, so be it; love, so be it; I ask nothing better. Monsieur, take the trouble to marry. Be happy, my dear child.'

This said, the old man burst into sobs.

And he took Marius' head, and he hugged it in both arms against his old breast, and they both began to weep. That is one of the forms of supreme happiness.

'Father!' exclaimed Marius.

'Ah! you love me then!' said the old man.

There was an ineffable moment. They choked and could not speak.

At last the old man stammered:

'Come! the ice is broken. He has called me, "Father".'

Marius released his head from his grandfather's arms, and said softly:

'But, father, now that I am well, it seems to me that I could see her.'

'Foreseen again, you shall see her tomorrow.'

'Father!'

'What?'

'Why not today?'

'Well, today. Here goes for today. You have called me "Father", three times, it is well worth that. I will see to it. She shall be brought to you. Foreseen, I tell you. This has already been put into verse. It is the conclusion of André Chénier's elegy of the *Jeune malade*, André Chénier who was murdered by the scound – , by the giants of '93.'

M. Gillenormand thought he perceived a slight frown on Marius' brow, although, in truth, we should say, he was no longer listening to him, flown off as he had into ecstasy, and thinking far more of Cosette than of 1793. The grandfather, trembling at having introduced André Chénier so inopportunely, resumed precipitately:

'Murdered is not the word. The fact is that the great revolutionary geniuses, who were not evil disposed, that is incontestable, who were heroes, egad! found that André Chénier embarrassed them a little, and they had him guillot – That is to say that those great men, on the seventh of Thermidor, in the interest of the public safety, begged André Chénier to have the kindness to go – '

M. Gillenormand, choked by his own sentence, could not continue; being able neither to finish it nor to retract it, while his daughter was arranging the pillow behind Marius, the old man, overwhelmed by so many emotions, threw himself, as quickly as his age permitted, out of the bedroom, pushed the door to behind him, and, purple, strangling, foaming, his eyes starting from his head, found himself face to face with honest Basque who was polishing boots in the antechamber. He seized Basque by the collar and cried full in his face with fury: 'By the hundred thousand Javottes of the devil, those brigands assassinated him!'

'Who, monsieur?'

'André Chénier!'

'Yes, monsieur,' said Basque in dismay.

4. Mademoiselle Gillenormand at last thinks it not improper that Monsieur Fauchelevent should come in with something under his arm

Cosette and Marius saw each other again.

What the interview was, we will not attempt to tell. There are things which we should not undertake to paint; the sun is of the number.

The whole family, including Basque and Nicolette, were assembled in Marius' room when Cosette entered.

She appeared on the threshold; it seemed as if she were in a cloud.

Just at that instant the grandfather was about to blow his nose; he stopped short, holding his nose in his handkerchief and looking at Cosette above it:

'Adorable!' he exclaimed.

Then he blew his nose with a loud noise.

Cosette was intoxicated, enraptured, startled, in Heaven. She was as frightened as one can be by happiness. She stammered, quite pale, quite red, wishing to throw herself into Marius' arms, and not daring to. Ashamed to show her love before all those people. We are pitiless towards happy lovers; we stay there when they have the strongest desire to be alone. They, however, have no need at all of society.

With Cosette and behind her had entered a man with white hair, grave, smiling nevertheless, but with a vague and poignant smile. This was 'Monsieur Fauchelevent'; this was Jean Valjean.

He was *very well dressed*, as the porter had said, in a new black suit, with a white cravat.

The porter was a thousand miles from recognising in this correct bourgeois, in this probable notary, the frightful corpse-bearer who had landed at his door on the night of the 7th of June, ragged, muddy, hideous, haggard, his face masked by blood and dirt, supporting the fainting Marius in his arms; still his porter's scent was awakened. When M. Fauchelevent had arrived with Cosette, the porter could not help confiding this remark to his wife: 'I don't know why I always imagine that I have seen that face somewhere.'

Monsieur Fauchelevent, in Marius' room, stayed near the door, as if apart. He had under his arm a package similar in appearance to an octavo volume, wrapped in paper. The paper of the envelope was greenish, and seemed mouldy.

'Does this gentleman always have books under his arm like that?' asked Mademoiselle Gillenormand, who did not like books, in a low voice to Nicolette.

'Well,' answered M. Gillenormand, who had heard her, in the same tone, 'he is a scholar. What then? is it his fault? Monsieur Boulard, whom I knew, never went out without a book, he neither, and always had an old volume against his heart, like that.'

And bowing, he said, in a loud voice:

'Monsieur Tranchelevent – '

Father Gillenormand did not do this on purpose, but inattention to proper names was an aristocratic way he had.

'Monsieur Tranchelevent, I have the honour of asking of you for my grandson, Monsieur the Baron Marius Pontmercy, the hand of mademoiselle.'

Monsieur Tranchelevent bowed.

'It is done,' said the grandfather.

And, turning towards Marius and Cosette, with arms extended and blessing, he cried: 'Permission to adore each other.'

They did not make him say it twice. It was all the same! The cooing began. They talked low, Marius leaning on his long chair, Cosette standing near him. 'Oh my God!' murmured Cosette, 'I see you again! It is you! it is you! To have gone to fight like that! But why? It is horrible. For four months I have been dead. Oh, how naughty it is to have been in that battle! What had I done to you? I pardon you, but you won't do it again. Just now, when they came to tell us to come, I thought again I should die, but it was of joy. I was so sad! I did not take time to dress myself; I must look like a fright. What will your relatives say of me, to see me with a collar ragged? But speak now! You let me do all the talking. We are still in the Rue de l'Homme Armé. Your shoulder, that was terrible. They told me they could put their fist into it. And then they have cut your flesh with scissors. That is frightful. I have cried; I have no eyes left. It is strange that anybody can suffer like that. Your grandfather has a very kind appearance. Don't disturb yourself; don't rest on your elbow; take care, you will hurt yourself. Oh, how happy I am! So our trouble is all over! I am very silly. I wanted to say something to you that I have forgotten completely. Do you love me still? We live in the Rue de l'Homme Armé. There is no garden. I have been making lint all the time. Here, monsieur, look, it is your fault, my fingers are callous.'

'Angel!' said Marius.

Angel is the only word in the language which cannot be worn out. No other word would resist the pitiless use which lovers make of it.

Then, as there were spectators, they stopped, and did not say another word, contenting themselves with touching each other's hands very gently.

M. Gillenormand turned towards all those who were in the room, and cried:

'Why don't you talk loud, the rest of you? Make a noise, behind the scenes. Come, a little uproar, the devil! so that these children can chatter at their ease.'

And, approaching Marius and Cosette, he said to them very low:

'Make love. Don't be disturbed.'

Aunt Gillenormand witnessed with amazement this irruption of light into her aged interior. This amazement was not at all aggressive; it was not the least in the world the scandalised and envious look of an owl upon two ring-doves; it was the dull eye of a poor innocent girl of fifty-seven; it was incomplete life beholding that triumph, love.

'Mademoiselle Gillenormand the elder,' said her father to her, 'I told you plainly that this would happen.'

He remained silent a moment and added:

'Behold the happiness of others.'

Then he turned towards Cosette:

'How pretty she is! how pretty she is! She is a Greuze. You are going to have her all alone to yourself then, rascal! Ah! my rogue, you have a narrow escape from me, you are lucky, if I were not fifteen years too old, we would cross swords for who should have her. Stop! I am in love with you, mademoiselle. That is very natural. It is your right. Ah! the sweet pretty charming little wedding that this is going to make! Saint Denis du Saint Sacrement is our parish, but I will have a dispensation so that you may be married at Saint Paul's. The church is better. It was built by the Jesuits. It is more coquettish. It is opposite the fountain of Cardinal de Birague. The masterpiece of Jesuit architecture is at Namur. It is called Saint Loup. You must go there when you are married. It is worth the journey. Mademoiselle, I am altogether of your opinion, I want girls to marry, they are made for that. There is a certain St Catherine whom I would always like to see with her hair down. To be an old maid, that is fine, but it is cold. The Bible says: Multiply. To save the people, we need Jeanne d'Arc; but to make the people, we used Mother Gigogne. So, marry, beauties. I really don't see the good of being an old maid. I know very well that they have a chapel apart in the church, and that they talk a good deal about the sisterhood of the Virgin; but, zounds, a handsome husband, a fine fellow, and, at the end of the year, a big flaxen-haired boy who sucks you merrily, and who has good folds of fat on his legs, and who squeezes your breast by handfuls in his little rosy paws, while he laughs like the dawn, that is better after all than holding a taper at vespers and singing *Turris eburnea!*'

The grandfather executed a pirouette upon his ninety-year-old heels, and began to talk again, like a spring which flies back:

> Ainsi, bornant le cours de tes rêvasseries,
> Alcippe, il est donc vrai, dans peu tu te maries.

'By the way!'

'What, father?'

'Didn't you have an intimate friend?'

'Yes, Courfeyrac.'

'What has become of him?'

'He is dead.'

'Very well.'

He sat down near them, made Cosette sit down, and took their four hands in his old wrinkled hands:

'She is exquisite, this darling. She is a masterpiece, this Cosette! She is a very little girl and a very great lady. She will be only a baroness, that is stooping; she was born a marchioness. Hasn't she lashes for you? My children, fix it well in your noddles that you are in the right of it. Love one another. Be foolish about it. Love is the foolishness of men, and the wisdom of God. Adore each other. Only,' added he, suddenly darkening, 'what a misfortune! This is what I am thinking of! More than half of what I have is in annuity as long as I live, it's all well enough, but after my death, twenty years from now, ah! my poor children, you will not have a sou. Your beautiful white hands, Madame the Baroness, will do the devil the honour to pull him by the tail.'

Here a grave and tranquil voice was heard, which said:

'Mademoiselle Euphrasie Fauchelevent has six hundred thousand francs.'

It was Jean Valjean's voice.

He had not yet uttered a word, nobody seemed even to remember that he was there, and he stood erect and motionless behind all these happy people.

'How is Mademoiselle Euphrasie in question?' asked the grandfather, startled.

'That is me,' answered Cosette.

'Six hundred thousand francs!' resumed M. Gillenormand.

'Less fourteen or fifteen thousand francs, perhaps,' said Jean Valjean.

And he laid on the table the package which Aunt Gillenormand had taken for a book.

Jean Valjean opened the package himself; it was a bundle of banknotes. They ran through them, and they counted them. There were five hundred bills of a thousand francs, and a hundred and sixty-eight of five hundred. In all, five hundred and eighty-four thousand francs.

'That is a good book,' said M. Gillenormand.

'Five hundred and eighty-four thousand francs!' murmured the aunt.

'This arranges things very well, does it not, Mademoiselle Gillenormand the elder?' resumed the grandfather. 'This devil of a Marius, he has found you a grisette millionaire on the tree of dreams! Then trust in the love-making of young folks nowadays! Students find studentesses with six hundred thousand francs. Chérubin works better than Rothschild.'

'Five hundred and eighty-four thousand francs!' repeated Mademoiselle Gillenormand in an undertone. 'Five hundred and eighty-four! you might call it six hundred thousand, indeed!'

As for Marius and Cosette, they were looking at each other during this time; they paid little attention to this incident.

5. *Deposit your money rather in some forest than with some notary*

THE READER has doubtless understood, without it being necessary to explain at length, that Jean Valjean, after the Champmathieu affair, had been able, thanks to his first escape for a few days, to come to Paris, and to withdraw the sum made by him, under the name of Monsieur Madeleine, at M— sur M—, from Laffitte's in time; and that, in the fear of being retaken, which happened to him, in fact, a short time after, he had concealed and buried that sum in the forest of Montfermeil, in the place called the Blaru grounds. The sum, six hundred and thirty thousand francs, all in banknotes, was of small bulk, and was contained in a box; but, to preserve the box from moisture he had placed it in an oaken chest, full of chestnut shavings. In the same chest, he had put his other treasure, the bishop's candlesticks. It will be remembered that he carried away these candlesticks when he escaped from M— sur M—. The man perceived one evening, for the first time, by Boulatruelle, was Jean Valjean. Afterwards, whenever Jean Valjean was in need of money, he went to the Blaru glade for it. Hence the absences of which we have spoken. He had a pickaxe somewhere in the bushes, in a hiding-place known only to himself. When he saw Marius convalescent, feeling that the hour was approaching when this money might be useful, he had gone after it; and it was he again whom Boulatruelle saw in the wood, but this time in the morning, and not at night. Boulatruelle inherited the pickaxe.

The real sum was five hundred and eighty-four thousand five hundred francs Jean Valjean took out the five hundred francs for himself. 'We will see afterwards,' thought he.

The difference between this sum and the six hundred and thirty thousand francs withdrawn from Laffitte's represented the expenses of ten years, from 1823 to 1833. The five years spent in the convent had cost only five thousand francs.

Jean Valjean put the two silver candlesticks upon the mantel, where they shone, to Toussaint's great admiration.

Moreover, Jean Valjean knew that he was delivered from Javert. It had been mentioned in his presence, and he had verified the fact in the *Moniteur*, which published it, that an inspector of police, named Javert, had been found drowned under a washerwoman's boat between the Pont au Change and Pont Neuf, and that a paper left by this man, otherwise irreproachable and highly esteemed by his chiefs, led to a belief that he had committed suicide during a fit of mental aberration. 'In fact,' thought Jean Valjean, 'since having me in his power, he let me go, he must already have been crazy.'

6. The two old men do everything, each in his own way, that Cosette may be happy

All the preparations were made for the marriage. The physician being consulted said that it might take place in February. This was in December. Some ravishing weeks of perfect happiness rolled away.

The least happy was not the grandfather. He would remain for a quarter of an hour at a time gazing at Cosette.

'The wonderful pretty girl!' he exclaimed. 'And her manners are so sweet and so good. It is of no use to say my love my heart, she is the most charming girl that I have seen in my life. Besides, she will have virtues for you sweet as violets. She is a grace, indeed! You can but live nobly with such a creature. Marius, my boy, you are a baron, you are rich, don't pettifog, I beg of you.'

Cosette and Marius had passed abruptly from the grave to paradise. There had been but little caution in the transition, and they would have been stunned if they had not been dazzled.

'Do you understand anything about it?' said Marius to Cosette.

'No,' answered Cosette, 'but it seems to me that the good God is caring for us.'

Jean Valjean did all, smoothed all, conciliated all, made all easy. He hastened towards Cosette's happiness with as much eagerness, and apparently as much joy, as Cosette herself.

As he had been a mayor, he knew how to solve a delicate problem, in the secret of which he was alone: Cosette's civil state. To bluntly give her origin, who knows? that might prevent the marriage. He drew Cosette out of all difficulty. He arranged a family of dead people for her, a sure means of incurring no objection. Cosette was what remained of an extinct family; Cosette was not his daughter, but the daughter of another Fauchelevent. Two brothers Fauchelevent had been gardeners at the convent of the Petit Picpus. They went to this convent, the best recommendations and the most respectable testimonials abounded; the good nuns, little apt and little inclined to fathom questions of paternity, and understanding no malice, had never known very exactly of which of the two Fauchelevents little Cosette was the daughter. They said what was wanted of them, and said it with zeal. A notary's act was drawn up. Cosette became before the law Mademoiselle Euphrasie Fauchelevent. She was declared an orphan. Jean Valjean arranged matters in such a way as to be designated, under the name of Fauchelevent, as Cosette's guardian, with M. Gillenormand as overseeing guardian.

As for the five hundred and eighty-four thousand francs, that was a legacy left to Cosette by a dead person who desired to remain unknown. The original legacy had been five hundred and ninety-four thousand francs; but ten thousand francs had been expended for Mademoiselle Euphrasie's education, of which five thousand francs were paid to the convent itself. This legacy, deposited in the hands of a third party, was to be given up to Cosette at her majority or at the time of her marriage. Altogether this was very acceptable, as we see, especially with a basis of more than half a million. There were indeed a few singularities here and there, but nobody saw them; one of those interested had his eyes bandaged by love, the other by the six hundred thousand francs.

Cosette learned that she was not the daughter of that old man whom she had so long called father. He was only relative; another Fauchelevent was her real father. At any other time, this would have broken her heart. But at this ineffable hour, it was only a little shadow, a darkening, and she had so much joy that this cloud was of short duration. She had Marius. The young man came, the goodman faded away; such is life.

And then, Cosette had been accustomed for long years to see enigmas about her: everybody who has had a mysterious childhood is always ready for certain renunciations.

She continued, however, to say 'Father' to Jean Valjean.

Cosette, in raptures, was enthusiastic about Grandfather Gillenormand. It is true that he loaded her with madrigals and with presents. While Jean Valjean was building a normal condition in society for Cosette, and a possession of an unimpeachable state, M. Gillenormand was watching over the wedding corbeille. Nothing amused him so much as being magnificent. He had given Cosette a dress of Binche guipure which descended to him from his own grandmother. 'These fashions have come round again,' said he,' old things are the rage, and the young women of my old age dress like the old women of my childhood.'

He rifled his respectable round-bellied bureaus of Coromandel lac which had not been opened for years. 'Let us put these dowagers to the confession,' said he; 'let us see what they have in them.' He noisily stripped the deep drawers full of the toilets of all his wives, of all his mistresses, and of all his ancestresses. Pekins, damasks, lampas, painted moires, dresses of gros de Tours, Indian handkerchiefs embroidered with a gold which could be washed, dauphines in the piece finished on both sides, Genoa and Alençon point, antique jewellery, comfit-boxes of ivory ornamented with microscopic battles, clothes, ribbons, he lavished all upon Cosette. Cosette, astonished, desperately in love with Marius and wild with gratitude towards M. Gillenormand, dreamed of a boundless happiness clad in satin and velvet. Her wedding corbeille appeared to her upborne by seraphim. Her soul soared into the azure on wings of Mechlin lace.

The intoxication of the lovers was only equalled, as we have said, by the ecstasy of the grandfather. It was like a flourish of trumpets in the Rue des Filles du Calvaire.

Every morning, a new offering of finery from the grandfather to Cosette. Every possible furbelow blossomed out splendidly about her.

One day Marius, who was fond of talking gravely in the midst of his happiness, said in reference to I know not what incident:

'The men of the revolution are so great that they already have the prestige of centuries, like Cato and like Phocion, and each of them seems a *mémoire antique* (antique memory).'

'Moire antique!' exclaimed the old man. 'Thank you, Marius. That is precisely the idea that I was in search of.'

And the next day a magnificent dress of tea-coloured moire antique was added to Cosette's corbeille.

The grandfather extracted a wisdom from these rags:

'Love, all very well; but it needs that with it. The useless is needed in happiness. Happiness is only the essential. Season it for me enormously with the superfluous. A palace and her heart. Her heart and the Louvre. Her heart and the grand fountains of Versailles. Give me my shepherdess, and have her a duchess if possible. Bring me Phillis crowned with bluebells, and add to her a hundred thousand francs a year. Open me a bucolic out of sight under a marble colonnade. I consent to the bucolic, and also to the fairy work in marble and gold. Dry happiness is like dry bread. We eat, but we do not dine. I wish for the superfluous, for the useless, for the extravagant, for the too much, for that which is not good for anything. I remember having seen in the cathedral of Strasbourg, a clock as high as a three-storey house, which marked the hour, which had the goodness to mark the hour, but which did not look as if it were made for that; and which, after having struck noon or midnight, noon, the hour of the sun, midnight, the hour of love, or any other hour that you please, gave you the moon and the stars, the earth and the sea, the birds and the fish, Phœbus and Phœbe, and a host of things which came out of a niche, and the twelve apostles, and the Emperor Charles V, and Eponine and Sabinus, and a crowd of little gilded goodmen who played on the trumpet, to boot. Not counting the ravishing chimes which it flung out into the air on all occasions without anybody knowing why. Is a paltry naked dial which only tells the hours, as good as that? For my part I agree with the great clock of Strasbourg, and I prefer it to the cuckoo clock of the Black Forest.'

M. Gillenormand raved especially concerning the wedding, and all the pier glasses of the eighteenth century passed pell-mell through his dithyrambs.

'You know nothing about the art of fêtes. You do not know how to get up a happy day in these times,' he exclaimed. 'Your nineteenth century is soft. It lacks excess. It ignores the rich, it ignores the noble. In everything, it is shaven close. Your third estate is tasteless, colourless, odourless, and shapeless. Dreams of your bourgeoises who set up an establishment, as they say: a pretty boudoir freshly decorated in palissandre and chintz. Room! room! the sieur Hunks espouses the lady Catchpenny. Sumptuosity and splendour. They have stuck a louis-d'or to a taper. There you have the age. I beg to flee away beyond the Sarmatians. Ah! in 1787, I predicted that all was lost, the day I saw the Duke de Rohan, Prince de Léon, Duke de Chabot, Duke de Montbazon, Marquis de

Soubise, Viscount de Thouars, peer of France, go to Longchamps in a chaise-cart. That has borne its fruits. In this century, people do business, they gamble at the Bourse, they make money, and they are disagreeable. They care for and varnish their surface; they are spruced up, washed, soaped, scraped, shaved, combed, waxed, smoothed, rubbed, brushed, cleaned on the outside, irreproachable, polished like a pebble, prudent, nice, and at the same time, by the virtue of my mistress, they have at the bottom of their conscience dung-heaps and cloacas enough to disgust a cow-girl who blows her nose with her fingers. I grant to these times this device: Nasty neatness. Marius, don't get angry; let me speak; I speak no evil of the people, you see; I have my mouth full of your people; but take it not amiss that I have my little fling at the bourgeoisie. I am one of them. Who loves well, lashes well. Upon that, I say it boldly, people marry nowadays, but they don't know how to marry. Ah! it is true, I regret the pretty ways of the old times. I regret the whole of them. That elegance, that chivalry, those courtly and dainty ways, that joyous luxury which everybody had, music making part of the wedding, symphony above, drumming below, dances, joyful faces at table, far-fetched madrigals, songs, squibs, free laughter, the devil and his train, big knots of ribbon. I regret the bride's garter. The bride's garter is cousin to the cestus of Venus. Upon what turns the war of Troy? By heavens, upon Helen's garter. Why do they fight, why does Diomede the divine shatter that great bronze helmet with ten points on Meriones' head, why do Achilles and Hector pick each other with great pike thrusts? Because Helen let Paris take her garter. With Cosette's garter, Homer would make the Iliad. He would put into his poem an old babbler like me, and he would call him Nestor. My friends, formerly, in that lovely formerly, people married scientifically; they made a good contract, then a good jollification. As soon as Cujas went out, Gamache came in. But, forsooth! the stomach is an agreeable animal which demands its due, and which wants its wedding also. They supped well, and they had a beautiful neighbour at table, without a stomacher, who hid her neck but moderately! Oh! the wide laughing mouths, and how gay they were in those times! Youth was a bouquet; every young man terminated in a branch of lilac or a bunch of roses; was one a warrior, he was a shepherd; and if, by chance, he was a captain of dragoons, he found some way to be called Florian. They thought everything of being pretty, they embroidered themselves, they empurpled themselves. A bourgeois had the appearance of a flower, a marquis had the appearance of a precious stone. They did not wear straps, they did not wear boots. They were flaunting, glossy, moire, gorgeous, fluttering, dainty, coquettish, which did not prevent them from having a sword at their side. The humming bird has beak and claws. That was the time of the *Indes galantes.* One of the sides of the century was the delicate, the other was the magnificent; and, zookers! they amused themselves. Nowadays, they are serious. The bourgeois is miserly, the bourgeoise is prudish; your century is unfortunate. People would drive away the Graces for wearing such low necks. Alas! they hide beauty as a deformity. Since the revolution, everything has trousers, even the ballet girls; a danseuse must be grave; your rigadoons are doctrinaire. We must be majestic. We should be very much shocked without our chin in our cravat. The ideal of a scapegrace of twenty who gets married, is to be like Monsieur Royer Collard. And do you know to what we are coming with this majesty? to being small. Learn this: joy is not merely joyful; it is great. So be lovers gaily then, the devil! and marry, when you do marry, with the fever and the dizziness and the uproar and the tohubohu of happiness. Gravity at the church, all right. But, as soon as mass is over, odzooks! we must make a dream whirl about the bride. A marriage ought to be royal and chimerical; it ought to walk in procession from the cathedral of Rheims to the pagoda of Chanteloup. I have a horror of a mean wedding. 'Zblews! be in Olympus, at least for that day. Be gods. Ah! you might be sylphs, Games and Laughters, Argyraspides; you are elfs! My friends, every new husband ought to be the Prince Aldobrandini. Profit by this unique moment of your life to fly away into the empyrean with the swans and the eagles, free to fall back on the morrow into the bourgeoisie of the frogs. Don't economise upon Hymen, don't strip him of his splendours; don't stint the day on which you shine. Wedding is not housekeeping. Oh! if I had my fancy, it should be gallant, you should hear violins in the trees. This is my programme: sky-blue and silver. I would join the rural divinities in the fête, I would convoke the dryads and the nereids. Nuptials of Amphitrite, a rosy cloud, nymphs with well-dressed heads and all naked, an academician offering quatrians to the goddess, a car drawn by marine monsters.

Tritton trottait devant, et tirait de sa conque
Des sons si ravissants qu'il ravissait quiconque.

There is a programme for a fête that is one, or I don't know anything about it, 'odsboddikins!'

While the grandfather, in full lyric effusion, was listening to himself, Cosette and Marius were intoxicated with seeing each other freely.

Aunt Gillenormand beheld it all with her imperturbable placidity. She had had within five or six months a certain number of emotions; Marius returned, Marius brought back bleeding, Marius brought back from a barricade, Marius dead, then alive, Marius reconciled, Marius betrothed, Marius marrying a pauper, Marius marrying a millionaire. The six hundred thousand francs had been her last surprise. Then her first communicant indifference returned to her. She went regularly to the offices, picked over her rosary, read her prayer-book, whispered *Aves* in one part of the house, while they were whispering *I Love Yous* in the other, and, vaguely, saw Marius and Cosette as two shadows. The shadow was herself.

There is a certain condition of inert asceticism in which the soul, neutralised by torpor, a stranger to what might be called the business of living, perceives, with the exception of earthquakes and catastrophes, no human impressions, neither pleasant impressions, nor painful impressions. 'This devotion,' said Grandfather Gillenormand to his daughter, 'corresponds to a cold in the head. You smell nothing of life. No bad odour, but no good one.'

Still, the six hundred thousand francs had determined the hesitation of the old maid. Her father had acquired the habit of counting her for so little, that he had not consulted her in regard to the consent to Marius' marriage. He had acted with impetuosity, according to his wont, having, a despot become a slave, but one thought, to satisfy Marius. As for the aunt, that the aunt existed, and that she might have an opinion, he had not even thought; and, perfect sheep as she was, this had ruffled her. A little rebellious inwardly, but outwardly impassible, she said to herself: 'My father settles the question of the marriage without me, I will settle the question of the inheritance without him.' She was rich, in fact, and her father was not. She had therefore reserved her decision thereupon. It is probable that, if the marriage had been poor, she would have left it poor. So much the worse for monsieur, my nephew! He marries a beggar, let him be a beggar. But Cosette's half-million pleased the aunt, and changed her feelings in regard to this pair of lovers. Some consideration is due to six hundred thousand francs, and it was clear that she could not do otherwise than leave her fortune to these young people, since they no longer needed it.

It was arranged that the couple should live with the grandfather. M. Gillenormand absolutely insisted upon giving them his room, the finest in the house. '*It will rejuvenate me,*' he declared. '*It is an old project. I always had the idea of making a wedding in my room.*' He filled this room with a profusion of gay old furniture. He hung the walls and the ceiling with an extraordinary stuff which he had in the piece, and which he believed to be from Utrecht, a satin background with golden immortelles, and velvet auriculas. 'With this stuff,' said he, 'the Duchess d'Anville's bed was draped at La Roche Guyon.' He put a little Saxony figure on the mantel, holding a muff over her naked belly.

M. Gillenormand's library became the attorney's office which Marius required; an office, it will be remembered, being rendered necessary by the rules of the order.

7. *The effects of dream mingled with happiness*

THE LOVERS saw each other every day. Cosette came with M. Fauchelevent. 'It is reversing the order of things,' said Mademoiselle Gillenormand, 'that the intended should come to the house to be courted like this.' But Marius' convalescence had led to the habit; and the armchairs in the Rue des Filles du Calvaire, better for long talks than the straw chairs of the Rue de l'Homme Armé, had rooted it. Marius and M. Fauchelevent saw one another, but did not speak to each other. That seemed to be understood. Every girl needs a chaperon. Cosette could not have come without M. Fauchelevent. To Marius, M. Fauchelevent was the condition of Cosette. He accepted it. In bringing upon the carpet, vaguely and generally, matters of policy, from the point of view of the general amelioration of the lot of all, they succeeded in saying a little more than yes and no to each other. Once, on the subject of education, which Marius wished gratuitous and obligatory, multiplied under all forms, lavished upon all like the air and the sunshine, in one word, respirable by the entire people, they fell into unison and almost into a conversation. Marius remarked on this occasion that M. Fauchelevent talked well, and even with a certain elevation of language. There was, however, something wanting. M. Fauchelevent had something less than a man of the world, and something more.

Marius, inwardly and in the depth of his thought, surrounded this M. Fauchelevent, who was to him simply benevolent and cold, with all sorts of silent questions. There came to him at intervals doubts about his own recollections. In his memory there was a hole, a black place, an abyss scooped out by four months of agony. Many things were lost in it. He was led to ask himself if it were really true that he had seen M. Fauchelevent, such a man, so serious and so calm, in the barricade.

This was not, however, the only stupor which the appearances and the disappearances of the past had left in his mind. We must not suppose that he was delivered from all those obsessions of the memory which force us, even when happy, even when satisfied, to look back with melancholy. The head which does not turn towards the horizons of the past, contains neither thought nor love. At moments, Marius covered his face with his hands, and the vague past tumultuously traversed the twilight which filled his brain. He saw Mabeuf fall again, he heard Gavroche singing beneath the grape, he felt upon his lip the chill of Eponine's forehead; Enjolras, Courfeyrac, Jean Prouvaire, Combeferre, Bossuet, Grantaire, all his friends, rose up before him, then dissipated. All these beings, dear, sorrowful, valiant, charming or tragical, were they dreams? had they really existed? The *émeute* had wrapped everything in its smoke. These great fevers have great dreams. He interrogated himself; he groped within himself; he was dizzy with all these vanished realities; Where were they all then? Was it indeed true that all were dead? A fall into the darkness had carried off all, except himself. It all seemed to him to have disappeared as if behind a curtain at a theatre. There are such curtains which drop down in life. God is passing to the next act.

And himself, was he really the same man? He, the poor, he was rich; he, the abandoned, he had a family; he, the despairing, he was marrying Cosette. It seemed to him that he had passed through a tomb, and that he had gone in black, and that he had come out white. And in this tomb, the others had remained. At certain moments, all these beings of the past, returned and present, formed a circle about him and rendered him gloomy; then he thought of Cosette, and again became serene; but it required nothing less than this felicity to efface this catastrophe.

M. Fauchelevent almost had a place among these vanished beings. Marius hesitated to believe that the Fauchelevent of the barricade was the same as this Fauchelevent in flesh and blood, so gravely seated near Cosette. The first was probably one of those nightmares coming and going with his hours of delirium. Moreover, their two natures showing a steep front to each other, no question was possible from Marius to M. Fauchelevent. The idea of it did not even occur to him. We have already indicated this characteristic circumstance.

Two men who have a common secret, and who, by a sort of tacit agreement, do not exchange a word upon the subject, such a thing is less rare than one would think.

Once only, Marius made an attempt. He brought the Rue de la Chanvrerie into the conversation, and, turning towards M. Fauchelevent, he said to him:

'You are well acquainted with that street?'

'What street?'

'The Rue de la Chanvrerie.'

'I have no idea of the name of that street,' answered M. Fauchelevent in the most natural tone in the world.

The answer, which bore upon the name of the street, and not upon the street itself, appeared to Marius more conclusive than it was.

'Decidedly,' thought he, 'I have been dreaming. I have had a hallucination. It was somebody who resembled him. M. Fauchelevent was not there.'

8. *Two men impossible to find*

THE ENCHANTMENT, great as it was, did not efface other preoccupations from Marius' mind.

During the preparations for the marriage, and while waiting for the time fixed upon, he had some difficult and careful retrospective researches made.

He owed gratitude on several sides, he owed some on his father's account, he owed some on his own.

There was Thénardier; there was the unknown man who had brought him, Marius, to M. Gillenormand's.

Marius persisted in trying to find these two men, not intending to marry, to be happy, and to forget them, and fearing lest these debts of duty unpaid might cast a shadow over his life, so luminous henceforth. It was impossible for him to leave all these arrears unsettled behind him; and he wished, before entering joyously into the future, to have a quittance from the past.

That Thénardier was a scoundrel, took away nothing from this fact that he had saved Colonel Pontmercy. Thénardier was a bandit to everybody except Marius.

And Marius, ignorant of the real scene of the battlefield of Waterloo, did not know this peculiarity, that his father was, with reference to Thénardier, in this singular situation, that he owed his life to him without owing him any thanks.

None of the various agents whom Marius employed, succeeded in finding Thénardier's track. Effacement seemed complete on that side. The Thénardiess had died in prison pending the examination on the charge. Thénardier and his daughter Azelma, the two who alone remained of that woeful group, had plunged back into the shadow. The gulf of the social Unknown had silently closed over these beings. There could no longer even be seen on the surface that quivering, that trembling, those obscure concentric circles which announce that something has fallen there, and that we may cast in the lead.

The Thénardiess being dead, Boulatruelle being put out of the case, Claquesous having disappeared, the principal accused having escaped from prison, the prosecution for the ambuscade at the Gorbeau house was almost abortive. The affair was left in deep obscurity. The Court of Assizes was obliged to content itself with two subalterns, Panchaud, alias Printanier, alias Bigrenaille, and Demi-Liard, alias Deux Milliards, who were tried and condemned to ten years at the galleys. Hard labour for life was pronounced against their accomplices who had escaped and did not appear. Thénardier, chief and ringleader, was, also for non-appearance, condemned to death. This condemnation was the only thing which remained in regard to Thénardier, throwing over that buried name its ominous glare, like a candle beside a bier.

Moreover, by crowding Thénardier back into the lowest depths, for fear of being retaken, this condemnation added to the thick darkness which covered this man.

As for the other, as for the unknown man who had saved Marius, the researches at first had some result, then stopped short. They succeeded in finding the fiacre which had brought Marius to the Rue des Filles du Calvaire on the evening of the 6th of June. The driver declared that on the 6th of June, by order of a police officer, he had been 'stationed', from three o'clock in the afternoon until night, on the quay of the Champs Elysées, above the outlet of the Grand Sewer; that, about nine o'clock in the evening, the grating of the sewer, which overlooks the river beach, was opened; that a man came out, carrying another man on his shoulders, who seemed to be dead; that the officer, who was watching at that point, arrested the living man, and seized the dead man; that, on the order of the officer, he, the driver, received 'all those people' into the fiacre; that they went first to the Rue des Filles du Calvaire; that they left the dead man there; that the dead man was Monsieur Marius, and that he, the driver, recognised him plainly, although he was alive 'this time'; that they then got into his carriage again; that he whipped up his horses; that, within a few steps of the door of the Archives, he had been called to stop; that there, in the street, he had been paid and left, and that the officer took away the other man; that he knew nothing more, that the night was very dark.

Marius, we have said, recollected nothing. He merely remembered having been seized from behind by a vigorous hand at the moment he fell backwards into the barricades, then all became a blank to him. He had recovered consciousness only at M. Gillenormand's.

He was lost in conjectures.

He could not doubt his own identity. How did it come about, however, that, falling in the Rue de la Chanvrerie, he had been picked up by the police officer on the banks of the Seine, near the Pont des Invalides? Somebody had carried him from the quarter of the markets to the Champs Elysées. And how? By the sewer. Unparalleled devotion!

Somebody? who?

It was this man whom Marius sought.

Of this man, who was his saviour, nothing; no trace; not the least indication.

Marius, although compelled to great reserve in this respect pushed his researches as far as the prefecture of police. There, no more than elsewhere, did the information obtained lead to any eclaircissement. The prefecture knew less than the driver of the fiacre. They had no knowledge of any arrest made on the 6th of June at the grating of the Grand Sewer; they had received no officer's report upon that fact, which, at the prefecture, was regarded as a fable. They attributed the invention of this fable to the driver. A driver who wants drink-money is capable of anything, even of imagination. The thing was certain, for all that, and Marius could not doubt it, unless by doubting his own identity, as we have just said.

Everything, in this strange enigma, was inexplicable.

This man, this mysterious man, whom the driver had seen come out of the grating of the Grand Sewer bearing Marius senseless upon his back, and whom the police officer on the watch had arrested in the very act of saving an insurgent, what had become of him? what had become of the officer himself? Why had this officer kept silence? had the man succeeded in escaping? had he bribed the officer? Why did this man give no sign of life to Marius, who owed everything to him? His disinterestedness was not less wonderful than his devotion. Why did not this man reappear? Perhaps he was above recompense, but nobody is above gratitude. Was he dead? what kind of a man was this? how did he look? Nobody could tell. The driver answered: 'The night was very dark.' Basque and Nicolette, in their amazement, had only looked at their young master covered with blood. The porter, whose candle had lighted the tragic arrival of Marius, alone had noticed the man in question, and this is the description which he gave of him: 'This man was horrible.'

In the hope of deriving aid in his researches from them, Marius had had preserved the bloody clothes which he wore when he was brought back to his grandfather's. On examining the coat, it was noticed that one skirt was oddly torn. A piece was missing.

One evening, Marius spoke, before Cosette and Jean Valjean, of all this singular adventure, of the numberless inquiries which he had made, and of the uselessness of his efforts. The cold countenance of 'Monsieur Fauchelevent' made him impatient. He exclaimed with a vivacity which had almost the vibration of anger:

'Yes, that man, whoever he may be, was sublime. Do you know what he did, monsieur? He intervened like the archangel. He must have thrown himself into the midst of the combat, have snatched me out of it, have opened the sewer, have drawn me into it, have borne me through it! He must have made his way for more than four miles through hideous subterranean galleries, bent, stooping, in the darkness, in the cloaca, more than four miles, monsieur, with a corpse upon his back! And with what object? With the single object of saving that corpse. And that corpse was I. He said to himself: "There is perhaps a glimmer of life still there; I will risk my own life for that miserable spark!" And his life, he did not risk it once, but twenty times! And each step was a danger. The proof is, that on coming out of the sewer he was arrested. Do you know, monsieur, that that man did all that? And he could expect no recompense. What was I? An insurgent. What was I? A vanquished man. Oh! if Cosette's six hundred thousand francs were mine – '

'They are yours,' interrupted Jean Valjean.

'Well,' resumed Marius, 'I would give them to find that man!'

Jean Valjean kept silence.

BOOK 6: THE WHITE NIGHT

1. The 16th of February 1833

THE NIGHT of the 16th of February 1833, was a blessed night. Above its shade the heavens were opened. It was the wedding night of Marius and Cosette.

The day had been adorable.

It had not been the sky-blue festival dreamed by the grandfather, a fairy scene with a confusion of cherubs and cupids above the heads of the married pair, a marriage worthy a frieze panel; but it had been sweet and mirthful.

The fashion of marriage was not in 1833 what it is today. France had not yet borrowed from England that supreme delicacy of eloping with one's wife, of making one's escape on leaving the church, of hiding oneself ashamed of one's happiness, and of combining the behaviour of a bankrupt with the transports of Solomon's Song. They had not yet learned all that there is chaste, exquisite, and decent, in jolting one's paradise in a post-chaise, in intersecting one's mystery with click-clacks, in taking a tavern bed for a nuptial bed, and in leaving behind, in the common alcove at so much a night, the most sacred of life's memories pell-mell with the interviews between the diligence conductor and the servant girl of the tavern.

In this second half of the nineteenth century in which we live, the mayor and his scarf, the priest and his chasuble, the law and God, are not enough; we must complete them with the Longjumeau postilion; blue waistcoat with red facings and bell-buttons, a plate for a vambrace, breeches of green leather, oaths at Norman horses with knotted tails, imitation galloon, tarpaulin hat, coarse powdered hair, enormous whip, and heavy boots. France does not yet push elegance so far as to have, like the English nobility, a hailstorm of slippers down at the heel and old shoes, beating upon the bridal post-chaise, in memory of Churchill, afterwards Marlborough, or Malbrouck, who was assailed on the day of his marriage by the anger of an aunt who brought him good luck. The old shoes and the slippers do not yet form a part of our nuptial celebrations; but patience, good taste continuing to spread, we shall come to it.

In 1833, a hundred years ago, marriage was not performed at a full trot.

It was still imagined at that day, strange to tell, that a marriage is an intimate and social festival, that a patriarchal banquet does not spoil a domestic solemnity, that gaiety, even excessive, provided it be seemly, does no harm to happiness, and finally that it is venerable and good that the fusion of these two destinies whence a family is to arise, should commence in the house, and that the household should have the nuptial chamber for a witness henceforth.

And they had the shamelessness to be married at home.

The marriage took place, therefore, according to that now obsolete fashion, at M. Gillenormand's.

Natural and ordinary as this matter of marriage may be, the banns to be published, the deeds to be drawn up, the mairie, the church, always render it somewhat complex. They could not be ready before the 16th of February.

Now, we mention this circumstance for the pure satisfaction of being exact, it happened that the 16th was Mardi Gras. Hesitations, scruples, particularly from Aunt Gillenormand.

'Mardi Gras!' exclaimed the grandfather. 'So much the better. There is a proverb:

> Mariage un Mardi Gras,
> N'aura point d'enfants ingrats.

Let us go on. Here goes for the 16th! Do you want to put it off, you, Marius?'

'Certainly not!' answered the lover.

'Let us get married,' said the grandfather.

So the marriage took place on the 16th, notwithstanding the public gaiety. It rained that day, but there is always a little patch of blue in the sky at the service of happiness, which lovers see, even though the rest of creation be under an umbrella.

On the previous evening, Jean Valjean had handed to Marius, in presence of M. Gillenormand, the five hundred and eighty-four thousand francs.

The marriage being performed under the law of community, the deeds were simple.

Toussaint was henceforth useless to Jean Valjean; Cosette had inherited her and had promoted her to the rank of waiting-maid.

As for Jean Valjean, there was a beautiful room in the Gillenormand house furnished expressly for him, and Cosette had said to him so irresistibly: 'Father, I pray you,' that she had made him almost promise that he would come and occupy it.

A few days before the day fixed for the marriage, an accident happened to Jean Valjean; he slightly bruised the thumb of his right hand. It was not serious; and he had allowed nobody to take any trouble about it, nor to dress it, nor even to see his hurt, not even Cosette. It compelled him, however, to muffle his hand in a bandage, and to carry his arm in a sling, and prevented his signing anything. M. Gillenormand, as Cosette's overseeing guardian, took his place.

We shall take the reader neither to the mairie nor to the church. We hardly follow two lovers as far as that, and we generally turn our backs upon the drama as soon as it puts its bridegroom's bouquet into its buttonhole. We shall merely mention an incident which, although unnoticed by the wedding party, marked its progress from the Rue des Filles du Calvaire to Saint Paul's.

They were repaving, at that time, the northern extremity of the Rue Saint Louis. It was fenced off where it leaves the Rue du Parc Royal. It was impossible for the wedding carriages to go directly to Saint Paul's. It was necessary to change the route, and the shortest way was to turn off by the boulevard. One of the guests observed that it was Mardi Gras, and that the boulevard would be encumbered with carriages. 'Why?' asked M. Gillenormand. 'On account of the masks.' 'Capital!' said the grandfather; 'let us go that way. These young folks are marrying; they are going to enter upon the serious things of life. It will prepare them for it to see a bit of masquerade.'

They went by the boulevard. The first of the wedding carriages contained Cosette and Aunt Gillenormand, M. Gillenormand, and Jean Valjean. Marius, still separated from his betrothed, according to the custom, did not come till the second. The nuptial cortège, on leaving the Rue des Filles du Calvaire, was involved in the long procession of carriages which made an endless chain from the Madeleine to the Bastille and from the Bastille to the Madeleine.

Masks abounded on the boulevard. It was of no avail that it rained at intervals; Pantaloon and Harlequin were obstinate. In the good-humour of that winter of 1833, Paris had disguised herself as Venice. We see no such Mardi Gras nowadays. Everything being an expanded carnival, there is no longer any carnival.

The cross-alleys were choked with passengers, and the windows with the curious. The terraces which crown the peristyles of the theatres were lined with spectators. Besides the masks, they beheld that row, peculiar to Mardi Gras as well as to Longchamps, of vehicles of all sorts, hackney coaches, spring carts, carrioles, cabriolets, moving in order, rigorously riveted to one another by the regulations of the police, and, as it were, running in grooves. Whoever is in one of these vehicles is, at the same time, spectator and spectacle. *Sergents de ville* kept those two interminable parallel files on the lower sides of the boulevard Moving with a contrary motion, and watched, so that nothing should hinder their double current, over those two streams of carriages flowing, the one down, the other up, the one towards the Chaussée d'Antin, the other towards the Faubourg Saint Antoine. The emblazoned carriages of the peers of France, and the ambassadors, kept the middle of the roadway, going and coming freely.

Certain magnificent and joyous cortèges, especially the Fat Ox, had the same privilege. In this gaiety of Paris, England cracked her whip; the postchaise of Lord Seymour, teased with a nickname by the populace, passed along with a great noise.

In the double file, along which galloped some Municipal Guards like shepherds' dogs, honest family carry-alls, loaded down with great-aunts and grandmothers, exhibited at their doors fresh groups of disguised children, clowns of seven, clownesses of six, charming little creatures, feeling that they were officially a portion of the public mirth, penetrated with the dignity of their harlequinade, and displaying the gravity of functionaries.

From time to time, there was a block somewhere in the procession of vehicles; one or the other of the two lateral files stopped until the knot was disentangled; one carriage obstructed was enough to paralyse the whole line. Then they resumed their course.

The wedding carriages were in the file going towards the Bastille, and moving along the right side of the boulevard. At the Rue du Pont aux Choux, there was a stop for a time. Almost at the same instant, on the other side, the other file, which was going towards the Madeleine, also stopped. There was at this point of that file, a carriage-load of masks.

These carriages, or, to speak more correctly, these cart-loads of masks, are well known to the Parisians. If they failed on a Mardi Gras, or a Mid-Lent, people suspected something, and would they say: '*There is something at the bottom of that. Probably the ministry is going to change.*' A heaping up of Cassandras, Harlequins, and Columbines, jolted above the passers-by, every possible grotesqueness from the Turk to the savage, Hercules supporting marchionesses, jades who would make Rabelais stop his ears even as the Bacchantes made Aristophanes cast down his eyes; flax wigs, rosy swaddling-bands, coxcombs' hats, cross-eyed spectacles, Janot cocked hats, teased by a butterfly, shouts thrown to the foot-passengers, arms akimbo, bold postures, naked shoulders, masked faces, unmuzzled shamelessness; a chaos of effrontery marshalled by a driver crowned with flowers; such is this institution.

Greece required the chariot of Thespis, France requires the fiacre of Vadé.

Everything may be parodied, even parody. The saturnalia, that grimace of the ancient beauty, has gradually grown to Mardi Gras, and the bacchanal, formerly crowned with vine branches, inundated with sunlight, showing bosoms of marble in a divine half-nudity, today grown flabby under the soaking rags of the north, has ended by calling herself the *chie-en-lit.*

The tradition of the carriages of masks goes back to the oldest times of the monarchy. The accounts of Louis XI allow to the bailiff of the palace 'twenty sous tournois for three masquerade coaches at the street corners.' In our days, these noisy crowds of creatures are commonly carted by some ancient van, the top of which they load down, or overwhelm with their tumultuous group an excise cart whose cover is broken in. There are twenty of them in a carriage for six. They are on the seat, on the stool, on the bows of the cover, on the pole. They even got astride of the carriage lanterns. They are standing, lying, sitting, feet curled up, legs hanging. The women occupy the knees of the men. Their mad pyramid can be seen from a distance above the swarming heads. These carriage-loads make mountains of mirth in the midst of the mob. Collé, Panard, and Piron, flow from them, enriched with argot. They spit the Billingsgate catechism down upon the people. This fiacre, become measureless by its load, has an air of conquest. Uproar is in front, Tohubohu is in the rear. They vociferate, they vocalise, they howl, they burst, they writhe with happiness; gaiety bellows, sarcasm flames, joviality spreads itself as if it were purple; two harridans lead on the farce which expands into apotheosis; it is the triumphal car of Laughter.

Laughter too cynical to be free. And, in fact, this laughter is suspicious. This laughter has a mission. Its business is to prove the carnival to the Parisians.

These Billingsgate wagons, in which we feel an indefinable darkness, make the philosopher think. There is something of government therein. In them we lay our finger upon a mysterious affinity between public men and public women.

That turpitudes heaped up should give a total of gaiety, that by piling ignominy upon opprobrium, a people is decoyed; that espionage serving as a caryatide to prostitution, amuses the crowds while insulting them; that the mob loves to see pass along on the four wheels of a fiacre, this monstrous living heap, rag-tinsel, half ordure and half light, barking and singing; that people should clap their hands at this glory made up of every shame; that there should be no festival for the multitudes unless the police exhibit among them this sort of twenty-headed hydra of joy, certainly it is sad! But what is to be done? These tumbrils of beribboned and beflowered slime are insulted and forgiven by the public laughter. The laughter of all is the accomplice of the universal degradation. Certain unwholesome festivals disintegrate the people, and make it a populace. And for populaces as well as for tyrants, buffoons are needed. The king has Roquelaure, the people has Harlequin. Paris is the great foolish town, whenever she is not the great sublime city. The carnival is a part of her politics. Paris, we must admit, willingly supplies herself with comedy through infamy. She demands of her masters – when she has masters – but one thing: 'Varnish me the mud!' Rome was of the same humour. She loved Nero. Nero was a titanic lighterman.

Chance determined, as we have just said, that one of these shapeless bunches of masked women and men, drawn along in a huge calash, stopped on the left of the boulevard while the wedding cortège was stopping on the right. From one side of the boulevard to the other, the carriage in which the masks were, looked into the carriage opposite, in which was the bride.

'Hullo!' said a mask, 'a wedding.'

'A sham wedding,' replied another. 'We are the genuine.'

And, too far off to be able to accost the wedding party, fearing moreover the call of the *sergents de ville*, the two masks looked elsewhere.

The whole carriage-load of masks had enough to do a moment afterwards, the multitude began to hoot at it, which is the caress of the populace to the maskers, and the two masks which had just spoken were obliged to make front to the street with their comrades, and had none too many of all the weapons from the storehouse of the markets, to answer the enormous jaw of the people. A frightful exchange of metaphors was carried on between the masks and the crowd.

Meanwhile, two other masks in the same carriage, a huge-nosed Spaniard with an oldish air and enormous black moustaches, and a puny jade, a very young girl, with a black velvet mask, had also noticed the wedding party, and, while their companions and the passers-by were lampooning one another, carried on a dialogue in a low tone.

Their aside was covered by the tumult and lost in it. The gusts of rain had soaked the carriage, which was thrown wide open; the February wind is not warm; even while answering the Spaniard, the girl, with her low-necked dress, shivered, laughed, and coughed.

This was the dialogue:

'Say, now.'

'What, *daron?*'*

'Do you see that old fellow?'

'What old fellow?'

'There, in the first *roulotte* † of the wedding party by our side.'

'Who has his arm hooked into a black cravat?'

'Yes.'

'Well?'

'I am sure I know him.'

'Ah!'

'I wish that somebody may *faucher* my *colabre* and have never in my *vioc* said *vousaille*, *tonorgue*, nor *mézig*, if I don't know that *pantinois*.' ‡

'Today Paris is Pantin.'

'Can you see the bride by stooping over?'

'No.'

'And the groom?'

'There is no groom in that *roulotte*.'

'Pshaw!'

'Unless it may be the other old fellow.'

'Bend forward well and try to see the bride.'

'I can't.'

'It's all the same, that old fellow who has something the matter with his paw, I am sure I know him.'

'And what good does it do you to know him?'

'Nobody knows. Sometimes!'

'I don't get much amusement out of old men, for my part.'

'I know him.'

'Know him to your heart's content.'

'How the devil is he at the wedding?'

'We are at it, too, ourselves.'

'Where does this wedding party come from?'

'How do I know?'

'Listen.'

'What?'

'You must do something.'

'What?'

'Get out of our *roulotte* and *filer* ** that wedding party.'

'What for?'

'To know where it goes and what it is. Make haste to get out, run, my *fée*, †† you are young.'

* *Daron*, father † *Roulotte*, carriage ‡ I wish that somebody may cut my throat and have never in my life said you, thee, nor me, if I don't know that Parisian.

** *Filer*, follow †† *Fée*, daughter

'I can't leave the carriage.'

'Why not?'

'I am rented.'

'Ah, the deuce!'

'I owe my day to the prefecture.'

'That is true.'

'If I leave the carriage, the first officer who sees me arrests me. You know very well.'

'Yes, I know.'

'Today I am bought by *Pharos.*' *

'It is all the same. That old fellow worries me.'

'Old men worry you. You are not a young girl, however.'

'He is in the first carriage.'

'Well?'

'In the bride's *roulotte.*'

'What then?'

'Then he is the father.'

'What is that to me?'

'I tell you that he is the father.'

'There isn't any other father.'

'Listen.'

'What?'

'For my part, I can hardly go out unless I am masked. Here, I am hidden, nobody knows that I am here. But tomorrow, there are no more masks. It is Ash-Wednesday. I risk falling.† I must get back to my hole. You are free.'

'Not too much so.'

'More than I, still.'

'Well, what then?'

'You must try to find out where this wedding party have gone.'

'Where it is going?'

'Yes.'

'I know that.'

'Where is it going, then?'

'To the Cadran Bleu.'

'In the first place, it is not in that direction.'

'Well! to the Râpée.'

'Or somewhere else.'

'It is free. Weddings are free.'

'That isn't all. I tell you that you must try to let me know what that wedding party is, that this old fellow belongs to, and where that wedding party lives.'

'Not often! that will be funny. It is convenient to find, a week afterwards, a wedding party which passed by in Paris on Mardi Gras. A *tiquante*‡ in a haystack! Is it possible!'

'No matter, you must try. Do you understand, Azelma?'

The two files resumed their movement in opposite directions on the two sides of the boulevard, and the carriage of the masks lost sight of the bride's 'roulotte'.

* *Pharos*, the government † *Falling*, being arrested ‡ *Tiquante*, pin

2. *Jean Valjean still has his arm in a sling*

To realise his dream. To whom is that given? There must be elections for that in heaven; we are all unconscious candidates; the angels vote. Cosette and Marius had been elected.

Cosette, at the mairie and in the church, was brilliant and touching. Toussaint, aided by Nicolette, had dressed her.

Cosette wore her dress of Binche guipure over a skirt of white taffetas, a veil of English point, a necklace of fine pearls, a crown of orange flowers; all this was white, and, in this whiteness, she was radiant. It was an exquisite candour, dilating and transfiguring itself into luminousness. One would have said she was a virgin in process of becoming a goddess.

Marius' beautiful hair was perfumed and lustrous; here and there might be discerned, under the thickness of the locks, pallid lines, which were the scars of the barricade.

The grandfather, superb, his head held high, uniting more than ever in his toilet and manners all the elegances of the time of Barras, conducted Cosette. He took the place of Jean Valjean, who, as his arm was in a sling, could not give his hand to the bride.

Jean Valjean, in black, followed and smiled.

'Monsieur Fauchelevent,' said the grandfather to him, 'this is a happy day. I vote for the end of afflictions and sorrows. There must no longer be any sadness anywhere henceforth. By Jove! I decree joy! Evil has no right to be. That there should be unfortunate men – in truth, it is a shame to the blue sky. Evil does not come from man, who, in reality, is good. All human miseries have for their chief seat and central government Hell, otherwise called the Tuileries of the devil. Good, here am I saying demagogical words now! As for me, I no longer have any political opinions; that all men may be rich, that is to say, happy, that is all I ask for.'

When, at the completion of all the ceremonies, after having pronounced before the mayor and the priest every possible yes, after having signed the registers at the municipality and at the sacristy, after having exchanged their rings, after having been on their knees elbow to elbow under the canopy of white moire in the smoke of the censer, hand in hand, admired and envied by all, Marius in black, she in white, preceded by the usher in colonel's epaulettes, striking the pavement with his halberd, between two hedges of marvelling spectators, they arrived under the portal of the church where the folding-doors were both open, ready to get into the carriage again, and all was over, Cosette could not yet believe it. She looked at Marius, she looked at the throng, she looked at the sky; it seemed as if she were afraid of awaking. Her astonished and bewildered air rendered her unspeakably bewitching. To return, they got into the same carriage, Marius by Cosette's side; M. Gillenormand and Jean Valjean sat opposite. Aunt Gillenormand had drawn back one degree, and was in the second carriage. 'My children,' said the grandfather, 'here you are Monsieur the Baron and Madame the Baroness, with thirty thousand francs a year.' And Cosette, leaning close up to Marius, caressed his ear with this angelic whisper: 'It is true, then. My name is Marius. I am Madame You.'

These two beings were resplendent. They were at the irrevocable and undiscoverable hour, at the dazzling point of intersection of all youth and of all joy. They realised Jean Prouvaire's rhymes; together they could not count forty years. It was marriage sublimated; these two children were two lilies. They did not see each other, they contemplated each other. Cosette beheld Marius in a glory; Marius beheld Cosette upon an altar. And upon that altar and in that glory, the two apotheoses mingling, in the background, mysteriously, behind a cloud to Cosette, in flashing flame to Marius, there was the ideal, the real, the rendezvous of the kiss and the dream, the nuptial pillow.

Every torment which they had experienced was returned by them in intoxication. It seemed to them that the griefs, the sleeplessness, the tears, the anguish, the dismay, the despair, become caresses and radiance, rendered still more enchanting the enchanting hour which was approaching; and that their sorrows were so many servants making the toilet of their joy. To have suffered, how good it is! Their grief made a halo about their happiness. The long agony of their love terminated in an ascension.

There was in these two souls the same enchantment, shaded with anticipation in Marius and with modesty in Cosette. They said to each other in a whisper: 'We will go and see our little garden in the Rue Plumet again.' The folds of Cosette's dress were over Marius.

Such a day is an ineffable mixture of dream and of certainty. You possess and you suppose. You still have some time before you for imagination. It is an unspeakable emotion on that day to be at noon and to think of midnight. The delight of these two hearts overflowed upon the throng and gave joy to the passers-by.

People stopped in the Rue Saint Antoine in front of Saint Paul's, to see, through the carriage window, the orange flowers trembling upon Cosette's head.

Then they returned to the Rue des Filles du Calvaire, to their home. Marius, side by side with Cosette, ascended, triumphant and radiant, that staircase up which he had been carried dying. The poor gathered before the door, and, sharing their purses, they blessed them. There were flowers everywhere. The house was not less perfumed than the church; after incense, roses. They thought they heard voices singing in the infinite; they had God in their hearts; destiny appeared to them like a ceiling of stars; they saw above their heads a gleam of sunrise. Suddenly the clock struck. Marius looked at Cosette's bewitching bare arm and the rosy things which he dimly perceived through the lace of her corsage, and Cosette, seeing Marius look, began to blush even to the tips of her ears.

A good number of the old friends of the Gillenormand family had been invited; they pressed eagerly about Cosette. They vied with each other in calling her Madame the Baroness

The officer Théodule Gillenormand, now a captain, had come from Chartres, where he was now in garrison, to attend the wedding of his cousin Pontmercy. Cosette did not recognise him.

He, for his part, accustomed to being thought handsome by the women, remembered Cosette no more than any other.

'I was right in not believing that lancer's story!' said Grandfather Gillenormand to himself.

Cosette had never been more tender towards Jean Valjean. She was in unison with Grandfather Gillenormand; while he embodied joy in aphorisms and in maxims, she exhaled love and kindness like a perfume. Happiness wishes everybody happy.

She went back, in speaking to Jean Valjean, to the tones of voice of the time when she was a little girl. She caressed him with smiles.

A banquet had been prepared in the dining-room.

An illumination à giorno is the necessary attendant of a great joy. Dusk and obscurity are not accepted by the happy. They do not consent to be dark. Night, yes; darkness, no. If there is no sun, one must be made.

The dining-room was a furnace of cheerful things. In the centre, above the white and glittering table, a Venetian lustre with flat drops, with all sorts of coloured birds, blue, violet, red, green, perched in the midst of the candles; about the lustre girandoles, upon the wall reflectors with triple and quintuple branches; glasses, crystals, glassware, vessels, porcelains, Faënza-ware, pottery, gold and silver ware, all sparkled and rejoiced. The spaces between the candelabra were filled with bouquets, so that, wherever there was not a light, there was a flower.

In the antechamber three violins and a flute played some of Haydn's quartettes in softened strains.

Jean Valjean sat in a chair in the parlour, behind the door, which shut back upon him in such a way as almost to hide him. A few moments before they took their seats at the table, Cosette came, as if from a sudden impulse, and made him a low courtesy, spreading out her bridal dress with both hands, and, with a tenderly frolicsome look, she asked him:

'Father, are you pleased?'

'Yes,' said Jean Valjean, 'I am pleased.'

'Well, then, laugh.'

Jean Valjean began to laugh.

A few moments afterwards, Basque announced dinner.

The guests, preceded by M. Gillenormand giving his arm to Cosette, entered the dining-room, and took their places, according to the appointed order, about the table.

Two large armchairs were placed, on the right and on the left of the bride, the first for M. Gillenormand, the second for Jean Valjean. M. Gillenormand took his seat. The other armchair remained empty.

All eyes sought 'Monsieur Fauchelevent'.

He was not there.

M. Gillenormand called Basque.

'Do you know where Monsieur Fauchelevent is?'

'Monsieur,' answered Basque. 'Exactly. Monsieur Fauchelevent told me to say to monsieur that he was suffering a little from his sore hand, and could not dine with Monsieur the Baron and Madame the Baroness. That he begged they would excuse him, that he would come tomorrow morning. He has just gone away.'

This empty armchair chilled for a moment the effusion of the nuptial repast. But, M. Fauchelevent absent, M. Gillenormand was there, and the grandfather was brilliant enough for two. He declared that M. Fauchelevent did well to go to bed early, if he was suffering, but that it was only a 'scratch'. This declaration was enough. Besides, what is one dark corner in such a deluge of joy? Cosette and Marius were in one of those selfish and blessed moments when we have no faculty save for the perception of happiness. And then, M. Gillenormand had an idea. 'By Jove, this armchair is empty. Come here, Marius. Your aunt, although she has a right to you, will allow it. This armchair is for you. It is legal, and it is proper. "Fortunatus beside Fortunata." ' Applause from the whole table. Marius took Jean Valjean's place at Cosette's side; and things arranged themselves in such a way that Cosette, at first saddened by Jean Valjean's absence, was finally satisfied with it. From the moment that Marius was the substitute, Cosette would not have regretted God. She put her soft little foot encased in white satin upon Marius' foot.

The armchair occupied, M. Fauchelevent was effaced; and nothing was missed. And, five minutes later, the whole table was laughing from one end to the other with all the spirit of forgetfulness.

At the dessert, M. Gillenormand standing, a glass of champagne in his hand, filled half full so that the trembling of his ninety-two years should not spill it, gave the health of the married pair.

'You shall not escape two sermons,' exclaimed he. 'This morning you had the curé's, tonight you shall have the grandfather's. Listen to me; I am going to give you a piece of advice: Adore one another. I don't make a heap of flourishes. I go to the end, be happy. The only sages in creation are the turtledoves. The philosophers say: Moderate your joys. I say: Give them the rein. Be enamoured like devils. Be rabid. The philosophers dote. I would like to cram their philosophy back into their throats. Can there be too many perfumes, too many open rosebuds, too many nightingales singing, too many green leaves, too much aurora in life? can you love each other too much? can you please each other too much? Take care, Estelle, you are too pretty! Take care, Némorin, you are too handsome! The rare absurdity! Can you enchant each other too much, pet each other too much, charm each other too much? can you be too much alive? can you be too happy? Moderate your joys. Ah, pshaw! Down with the philosophers! Wisdom is jubilation. Jubilate, jubilate. Are we happy because we are good: or are we good because we are happy? Is the Sancy called the Sancy because it belonged to Harlay de Sancy, or because it weighs *cent-six* [a hundred and six] carats? I know nothing about it; life is full of such problems; the important thing is to have the Sancy, and happiness. Be happy without quibbling. Obey the sun blindly. What is the sun? It is love. Who says love, says woman. Ah, ha! There is an omnipotence; it is woman. Ask this demagogue of a Marius if he be not the slave of this little tyrant of a Cosette, and with his full consent, the coward. Woman! There is no Robespierre who holds out, woman reigns. I am no longer a royalist except for that royalty. What is Adam? He is the realm of Eve. No '89 for Eve. There was the royal sceptre surmounted by a fleur-de-lis; there was the imperial sceptre surmounted by a globe; there was the sceptre of Charlemagne, which was of iron; there was the sceptre of Louis XIV, which was of gold, the revolution twisted them between his thumb and finger like half-penny wisps of straw; they are finished, they are broken, they are on the ground, there is no longer a sceptre; but get me up some revolutions now against this little embroidered handkerchief which smells of patchouly! I would like to see you at it. Try. Why is it immovable? Because it is a rag. Ah! you are the nineteenth century! Well, what then? We were the eighteenth! and we were as stupid as you. Don't imagine that you have changed any great thing in the universe because your stoop-galant is called the cholera morbus, and because your boree is called the cachucha. At heart you must always love women. I defy you to get away from that. These devilesses are our angels. Yes, love, woman, the kiss, that is a circle which I defy you to get out of; and, as for myself, I would like very well to get back into it. Which of you has seen rising into the infinite, calming all beneath her, gazing upon the waves like a woman, the star Venus, the great coquette of the abyss, the Celimene of the ocean? The ocean is a rude Alceste. Well, he scolds in vain; Venus appears, he is obliged to smile. That brute beast submits. We are all so. Wrath, tempest, thunderbolts, foam to the sky. A woman enters on the scene, a star rises; flat on your face! Marius was fighting six months ago; he is marrying today. Well done. Yes, Marius, yes, Cosette, you are right. Live boldly for one another, love one another, make us die with rage that we cannot do as much, idolatrise each other. Take in your two beaks all the little straws of felicity on earth, and build yourselves a nest for life. By Jove, to love, to be loved, the admirable miracle when one is young! Don't imagine that you have invented it. I, too, I have had my dream, my vision, my sighs; I, too, have had a moonlight soul. Love is a child six thousand years old. Love has a right to a long white beard. Methuselah is a *gamin* beside Cupid. For sixty centuries, man and woman have got out of the scrape by loving. The devil, who is malicious, took to hating man; man, who is more malicious, took to loving woman. In this way he has done himself more good than the devil has done him harm. This trick was discovered at the time of the earthly paradise. My friends, the invention is old, but it is quite new. Profit by it. Be Daphnis and Chloe, while you are waiting to be Philemon and Baucis. So act that, when you are with each other, there shall be nothing wanting, and that Cosette may be the sun to Marius, and that Marius may be the universe to Cosette. Cosette, let your fine weather be the smile of your husband: Marius, let your rain be the tears of your wife. And may it never rain in your household. You have filched the good number in the lottery, a love-match; you have the highest prize, take good care of it, put it under lock and key, don't squander it, worship each other, and snap your fingers at the rest. Believe what I tell you. It is good sense. Good sense cannot lie. Be a religion to each other. Everyone has his own way of worshipping God. Zounds! the best way to worship God is to love your wife. I love you! that is my catechism. Whoever loves is orthodox. Henry IV's oath puts sanctity between gluttony and drunkenness. *Ventre-saint-gris!* I am not of the religion of that oath. Woman is forgotten in it. That astonishes me on the part of Henry IV's oath. My friends, long live woman! I am old, they say; it is astonishing how I feel myself growing young again. I would like to go and listen to the bagpipes in the woods. These children who are so fortunate as to be beautiful and happy, that fuddles me. I would get married myself if anybody wished. It is impossible to imagine that God has made us for anything but this: to idolise, to coo, to plume, to be pigeons, to be cocks, to bill with our loves from morning to night, to take pride in our little wives, to be vain, to be triumphant, to put on airs; that is the aim of life. That is, without offence to you, what we thought, we old fellows, in our times when we were the young folks. Ah! odswinkers! what charming women there were in those days, and pretty faces, and lasses! There's where I made my ravages. Then love each other. If people did not love one another, I really don't see what use there would be in having any spring; and, for my part, I should pray the good God to pack up all the pretty things which he shows us, and take them away from us, and to put the flowers, the birds, and the pretty girls, back into his box. My children, receive the benediction of the old goodman.'

The evening was lively, gay, delightful. The sovereign good-humour of the grandfather gave the keynote to the whole festival, and everybody regulated himself by this almost centenarian cordiality. They danced a little, they laughed much; it was a good childlike wedding. They might have invited the goodman Formerly. Indeed, he was there in the person of Grandfather Gillenormand.

There was tumult, then silence.

The bride and groom disappeared.

A little after midnight the Gillenormand house became a temple.

Here we stop. Upon the threshold of wedding-nights stands an angel smiling, his finger on his lip.

The soul enters into contemplation before this sanctuary, in which is held the celebration of love.

There must be gleams of light above those houses. The joy which they contain must escape in light through the stones of the walls, and shine dimly into the darkness. It is impossible that this sacred festival of destiny should not send a celestial radiation to the infinite. Love is the sublime crucible in which is consummated the fusion of man and woman; the one being, the triple being, the final being, the human trinity springs from it. This birth of two souls into one must be an emotion for space. The lover is priest; the rapt maiden is affrighted. Something of this joy goes to God. Where there is really marriage, that is where there is love, the ideal is mingled with it. A nuptial bed makes a halo in the darkness. Were it given to the eye of flesh to perceive the fearful and enchanting sights of the superior life, it is probable that we should see the forms of night, the winged strangers, the blue travellers of the invisible, bending, a throng of shadowy heads, over the luminous house, pleased, blessing, showing to one another the sweetly startled maiden bride, and wearing the reflection of the human felicity upon their divine countenances. If, at that supreme hour, the wedded pair, bewildered with pleasure, and believing themselves alone, were to listen, they would hear in their chamber a rustling of confused wings. Perfect happiness implies the solidarity of the angels. That little obscure alcove has for its ceiling the whole heavens. When two mouths, made sacred by love, draw near each other to create, it is impossible that above that ineffable kiss there should not be a thrill in the immense mystery of the stars.

These are the true felicities. No joy beyond these joys. Love is the only ecstasy, everything else weeps.

To love or to have loved, that is enough. Ask nothing further. There is no other pearl to be found in the dark folds of life. To love is a consummation.

3. The inseparable

WHAT HAD BECOME of Jean Valjean?

Immediately after having laughed, upon Cosette's playful injunction, nobody observing him, Jean Valjean had left his seat, got up, and, unperceived, had reached the antechamber. It was that same room which eight months before he had entered, black with mire, blood, and powder, bringing the grandson home to the grandfather. The old woodwork was garlanded with leaves and flowers; the musicians were seated on the couch upon which they had placed Marius. Basque, in a black coat, short breeches, white stockings, and white gloves, was arranging crowns of roses about each of the dishes which was to be served up Jean Valjean had shown him his arm in a sling, charged him to explain his absence, and gone away.

The windows of the dining-room looked upon the street. Jean Valjean stood for some minutes motionless in the obscurity under those radiant windows. He listened. The confused sounds of the banquet reached him. He heard the loud and authoritative words of the grandfather, the violins, the clatter of the plates and glasses, the bursts of laughter, and through all that gay uproar he distinguished Cosette's sweet joyous voice.

He left the Rue des Filles du Calvaire and returned to the Rue de l'Homme Armé.

To return, he went by the Rue Saint Louis, the Rue Culture Sainte Catherine, and the Blancs Manteaux; it was a little longer, but it was the way by which, for three months, to avoid the obstructions and the mud of the Rue Vieille du Temple, he had been accustomed to come every day, from the Rue de l'Homme Armé to the Rue des Filles du Calvaire, with Cosette.

This way over which Cosette had passed excluded for him every other road.

Jean Valjean returned home. He lighted his candle and went upstairs. The apartment was empty. Toussaint herself was no longer there. Jean Valjean's step made more noise than usual in the rooms. All the closets were open. He went into Cosette's room. There were no sheets on the bed. The pillow, without a pillow-case and without laces, was laid upon the coverlets folded at the foot of the mattress of which the ticking was to be seen and on which nobody should sleep henceforth. All the little feminine objects to which Cosette clung had been carried away; there remained only the heavy furniture and the four walls. Toussaint's bed was also stripped. A single bed was made and seemed waiting for somebody, that was Jean Valjean's.

Jean Valjean looked at the walls, shut some closet doors, went and came from one room to the other.

Then he found himself again in his own room, and he put his candle on a table.

He had released his arm from the sling, and he helped himself with his right hand as if he did not suffer from it.

He approached his bed, and his eye fell, was it by chance? was it with intention? upon the *inseparable*, of which Cosette had been jealous, upon the little trunk which never left him. On the 4th of June, on arriving in the Rue de l'Homme Armé, he had placed it upon a candle-stand at the head of his bed. He went to this stand with a sort of vivacity, took a key from his pocket, and opened the valise.

He took out slowly the garments in which, ten years before, Cosette had left Montfermeil; first the little dress, then the black scarf, then the great heavy child's shoes which Cosette could have almost put on still, so small a foot she had, then the bodice of very thick fustian, then the knit-skirt, then the apron with pockets, then the woollen stockings. Those stockings, on which the shape of a little leg was still gracefully marked, were hardly longer than Jean Valjean's hand. These were all black. He had carried these garments for her to Montfermeil. As he took them out of the valise, he laid them on the bed. He was thinking. He remembered. It was in winter, a very cold December, she shivered half-naked in rags, her poor little feet all red in her wooden shoes. He, Jean Valjean, he had taken her away from those rags to clothe her in this mourning garb. The mother must have been pleased in her tomb to see her daughter wear mourning for her, and especially to see that she was clad, and that she was warm. He thought of that forest of Montfermeil; they had crossed it together, Cosette and he; he thought of the weather, of the trees without leaves, of the forest without birds, of the sky without sun; it is all the same, it was charming. He arranged the little things upon the bed, the scarf next the skirt, the stockings beside the shoes, the bodice beside the dress, and he looked at them one after another. She was no higher than that, she had her great doll in her arms, she had put her louis d'or in the pocket of this apron, she laughed, they walked holding each other by the hand, she had nobody but him in the world.

Then his venerable white head fell upon the bed, this old stoical heart broke, his face was swallowed up, so to speak, in Cosette's garments, and anybody who had passed along the staircase at that moment, would have heard fearful sobs.

4. *Immortale Jecur*

THE FORMIDABLE OLD STRUGGLE, several phases of which we have already seen, recommenced.

Jacob wrestled with the angel but one night. Alas! how many times have we seen Jean Valjean clenched, body to body, in the darkness with his conscience, and wrestling desperately against it.

Unparalleled struggle! At certain moments, the foot slips; at others, the ground gives way. How many times had that conscience, furious for the right, grasped and overwhelmed him! How many times had truth, inexorable, planted her knee upon his breast! How many times, thrown to the ground by the light, had he cried to it for mercy! How many times had that implacable light, kindled in him and over him by the bishop, irresistibly dazzled him when he desired to be blinded! How many times had he risen up in the combat, bound to the rock, supported by sophism, dragged in the dust, sometimes bearing down his conscience beneath him, sometimes borne down by it! How many times, after an equivocation, after a treacherous and specious reasoning of selfishness, had he heard his outraged conscience cry in his ear: 'A trip! wretch!' How many times had his refractory thought writhed convulsively under the evidence of duty. Resistance to God. Agonising sweats. How many secret wounds, which he alone felt bleed! How many chafings of his miserable existence! How many times had he risen up bleeding, bruised, lacerated, illuminated, despair in his heart, serenity in his soul! and, conquered, felt himself conqueror. And, after having racked, torn, and broken him, his conscience, standing above him, formidable, luminous, tranquil, said to him: 'Now, go in peace!'

But, on coming out of so gloomy a struggle, what dreary peace, alas!

That night, however, Jean Valjean felt that he was giving his last battle.

A poignant question presented itself.

Predestinations are not all straight; they do not develop themselves in a rectilinear avenue before the predestinated; they are blind alleys, cœcums, obscure windings, embarrassing crossroads offering several paths. Jean Valjean was halting at this moment at the most perilous of these crossroads.

He had reached the last crossing of good and evil. He had that dark intersection before his eyes. This time again, as it had already happened to him in other sorrowful crises, two roads opened before him; the one tempting, the other terrible. Which should he take?

The one which terrified him was advised by the mysterious indicating finger which we all perceive whenever we fix our eyes upon the shadow.

Jean Valjean had, once again, the choice between the terrible haven and the smiling ambush.

It is true, then? the soul may be cured, but not the lot. Fearful thing! an incurable destiny!

The question which presented itself was this:

In what manner should Jean Valjean comport himself in regard to the happiness of Cosette and Marius? This happiness, it was he who had willed it, it was he who had made it; he had thrust it into his own heart, and at this hour, looking upon it, he might have the same satisfaction that an armourer would have, who should recognise his own mark upon a blade, on withdrawing it all reeking from his breast.

Cosette had Marius, Marius possessed Cosette. They had everything, even riches. And it was his work.

But this happiness, now that it existed, now that it was here, what was he to do with it, he, Jean Valjean? Should he impose himself upon this happiness? Should he treat it as belonging to him? Unquestionably, Cosette was another's; but should he, Jean Valjean, retain all of Cosette that he could retain? Should he remain the kind of father, scarcely seen, but respected, which he had been hitherto? Should he introduce himself quietly into Cosette's house? Should he bring, without saying a word, his past to this future? Should he present himself there as having a right, and should he come and take his seat, veiled, at that luminous hearth? Should he take, smiling upon them, the hands of those innocent beings into his two tragical hands? Should he place upon the peaceful andirons of the Gillenormand parlour, his feet which dragged after them the infamous shadow of the law? Should he enter upon a participation of chances with Cosette and Marius? Should he thicken the obscurity upon his head and the cloud upon theirs? Should he put in his catastrophe as a companion for their two felicities? Should he continue to keep silence? In a word, should he be, by the side of these two happy beings, the ominous mute of destiny?

We must be accustomed to fatality and its encounter, to dare to raise our eyes when certain questions appear to us in their horrible nakedness. Good or evil are behind this severe interrogation point. 'What are you going to do?' demands the sphynx.

This familiarity with trial Jean Valjean had. He looked fixedly upon the sphynx.

He examined the pitiless problem under all its phases.

Cosette, that charming existence, was the raft of this shipwreck. What was he to do? Cling on, or let go his hold?

If he clung to it, he escaped disaster, he rose again into the sunshine, he let the bitter water drip from his garments and his hair, he was saved, he lived.

If he loosed his hold?

Then, the abyss.

Thus bitterly he held counsel with his thoughts, or, to speak more truthfully, he struggled; he rushed, furious, within himself, sometimes against his will, sometimes against his conviction.

It was a good thing for Jean Valjean that he had been able to weep. It gave him light, perhaps. For all that, the beginning was wild. A tempest, more furious than that which had formerly driven him towards Arras, broke loose within him. The past came back to him face to face with the present; he compared and he sobbed. The sluice of tears once opened, the despairing man writhed.

He felt that he was stopped.

Alas! in this unrelenting pugilism between our selfishness and our duty, when we thus recoil step by step before our immutable ideal, bewildered, enraged, exasperated at yielding, disputing the ground, hoping for possible flight, seeking some outlet, how abrupt and ominous is the resistance of the wall behind us!

To feel the sacred shadow which bars the way,

The inexorable invisible, what an obsession!

We are never done with conscience. Choose your course by it, Brutus; choose your course by it, Cato. It is bottomless, being God. We cast into this pit the labour of our whole life, we cast in our fortune, we cast in our riches, we cast in our success, we cast in our liberty or our country, we cast in our well-being, we cast in our repose, we cast in our happiness. More! more! more! Empty the vase! turn out the urn! We must at last cast in our heart.

There is somewhere in the mist of the old hells a vessel like that.

Is it not pardonable to refuse at last? Can the inexhaustible have a claim? Are not endless chains above human strength? Who then would blame Sisyphus and Jean Valjean for saying: 'It is enough!'

The obedience of matter is limited by friction; is there no limit to the obedience of the soul? If perpetual motion is impossible, is perpetual devotion demandable?

The first step is nothing; it is the last which is difficult. What was the Champmathieu affair compared with Cosette's marriage and all that it involved? What is this: to return to the galleys, compared with this: to enter into nothingness?

Oh, first step of descent, how gloomy thou art! Oh, second step, how black thou art!

How should he not turn away his head this time?

Martyrdom is a sublimation, a corrosive sublimation. It is a torture of consecration. You consent to it the first hour; you sit upon the throne of red-hot iron, you put upon your brow the crown of red-hot iron, you receive the globe of red-hot iron, you take the sceptre of red-hot iron, but you have yet to put on the mantle of flame, and is there no moment when the wretched flesh revolts, and when you abdicate the torture?

At last Jean Valjean entered the calmness of despair.

He weighed, he thought, he considered the alternatives of the mysterious balance of light and shade.

To impose his galleys upon these two dazzling children, or to consummate by himself his irremediable engulfment. On the one side the sacrifice of Cosette, on the other of himself.

At what solution did he stop?

What determination did he take? What was, within himself, his final answer to the incorruptible demand of fatality? What door did he decide to open? Which side of his life did he resolve to close and to condemn? Between all these unfathomable precipices which surrounded him, what was his choice? What extremity did he accept? To which of these gulfs did he bow his head?

His giddy reverie lasted all night.

He remained there until dawn, in the same attitude, doubled over on the bed, prostrated under the enormity of fate, crushed perhaps, alas! his fists clenched, his arms extended at a right angle, like one taken from the cross and thrown down with his face to the ground. He remained twelve hours, the twelve hours of a long winter night, chilled, without lifting his head, and without uttering a word. He was as motionless as a corpse, while his thought writhed upon the ground and flew away, now like the hydra, now like the eagle. To see him thus without motion, one would have said he was dead; suddenly he thrilled convulsively, and his mouth, fixed upon Cosette's garments, kissed them; then one saw that he was alive.

What one? since Jean Valjean was alone, and there was nobody there?

The One who is in the darkness.

BOOK 7: THE LAST DROP IN THE CHALICE

1. The seventh circle and the eighth heaven

THE DAY AFTER A WEDDING is solitary. The privacy of the happy is respected. And thus their slumber is a little belated. The tumult of visits and felicitations does not commence until later. On the morning of the 17th of February, it was a little after noon, when Basque, his napkin and duster under his arm, busy 'doing his antechamber', heard a light rap at the door. There was no ring, which is considerate on such a day. Basque opened and saw M. Fauchelevent. He introduced him into the parlour, still cumbered and topsy-turvy, and which had the appearance of the battlefield of the evening's festivities.

'Faith, monsieur,' observed Basque, 'we are waking up late.'

'Has your master risen?' inquired Jean Valjean.

'How is monsieur's arm?' answered Basque.

'Better. Has your master risen?'

'Which? the old or the new one?'

'Monsieur Pontmercy.'

'Monsieur the Baron?' said Basque, drawing himself up.

One is baron to his domestics above all. Something of it is reflected upon them; they have what a philosopher would call the spattering of the title, and it flatters them. Marius, to speak of it in passing, a republican militant, and he had proved it, was now a baron in spite of himself. A slight revolution had taken place in the family in regard to this title. At present it was M. Gillenormand who clung to it and Marius who made light of it. But Colonel Pontmercy had written: *My son will bear my title.* Marius obeyed. And then Cosette, in whom the woman was beginning to dawn, was in raptures at being a baroness.

'Monsieur the Baron?' repeated Basque. 'I will go and see. I will tell him that Monsieur Fauchelevent is here.'

'No. Do not tell him that it is I. Tell him that somebody asks to speak with him in private, and do not give him any name.'

'Ah!' said Basque.

'I wish to give him a surprise.'

'Ah!' resumed Basque, giving himself his second ah! as an explanation of the first.

And he went out.

Jean Valjean remained alone.

The parlour, as we have just said, was all in disorder. It seemed that by lending the ear the vague rumour of the wedding might still have been heard. There were all sorts of flowers, which had fallen from garlands and head-dresses, upon the floor. The candles, burned to the socket, added stalactites of wax to the pendants of the lustres. Not a piece of furniture was in its place. In the corners, three or four armchairs drawn up and forming a circle, had the appearance of continuing a conversation. Altogether it was joyous. There is still a certain grace in a dead festival. It has been happy. Upon those chairs in disarray, among those flowers which are withering, under those extinguished lights, there have been thoughts of joy. The sun succeeded to the chandelier, and entered cheerfully into the parlour.

A few minutes elapsed. Jean Valjean was motionless in the spot where Basque had left him. He was very pale. His eyes were hollow, and so sunken in their sockets from want of sleep that they could hardly be seen. His black coat had the weary folds of a garment which has passed the night. The elbows were whitened with that down which is left upon cloth by the chafing of linen. Jean Valjean was looking at the window marked out by the sun upon the floor at his feet.

There was a noise at the door, he raised his eyes.

Marius entered, his head erect, his mouth smiling, an indescribable light upon his face, his forehead radiant, his eye triumphant. He also had not slept.

'It is you, father!' exclaimed he on perceiving Jean Valjean; 'that idiot of a Basque with his mysterious air! But you come too early. It is only half an hour after noon yet. Cosette is asleep.'

That word: Father, said to M. Fauchelevent by Marius, signified: Supreme felicity. There had always been, as we know, barrier, coldness, and constraint between them; ice to break or to melt. Marius had reached that degree of intoxication where the barrier was falling, the ice was dissolving, and M. Fauchelevent was to him, as to Cosette, a father.

He continued; words overflowed from him, which is characteristic of these divine paroxysms of joy:

'How glad I am to see you! If you knew how we missed you yesterday! Good morning, father. How is your hand? Better, is it not?'

And, satisfied with the good answer which he made to himself, he went on:

'We have both of us talked much about you. Cosette loves you so much! You will not forget that your room is here. We will have no more of the Rue de l'Homme Armé. We will have no more of it at all. How could you go to live in a street like that, which is sickly, which is scowling, which is ugly, which has a barrier at one end, where you are cold, and where you cannot get in? you will come and install yourself here. And that today. Or you will have a bone to pick with Cosette. She intends to lead us all by the nose, I warn you. You have seen your room, it is close by ours, it looks upon the gardens; the lock has been fixed, the bed is made, it is all ready, you have nothing to do but to come. Cosette has put a great old easy chair of Utrecht velvet beside your bed, to which she said: stretch out your arms for him. Every spring, in the clump of acacias which is in front of your windows, there comes a nightingale, you will have her in two months. You will have her nest at your left and ours at your right. By night she will sing, and by day Cosette will talk. Your room is full in the south. Cosette will arrange your books there for you, your voyage of Captain Cook, and the other, Vancouver's, all your things. There is, I believe, a little valise which you treasure, I have selected a place of honour for it. You have conquered my grandfather, you suit him. We will live together. Do you know whist? you will overjoy my grandfather, if you know whist. You will take Cosette to walk on my court-days, you will give her your arm, you know, as at the Luxembourg, formerly. We have absolutely decided to be very happy. And you are part of our happiness, do you understand, father? Come now, you breakfast with us today?'

'Monsieur,' said Jean Valjean, 'I have one thing to tell you. I am an old convict.'

The limit of perceptible acute sounds may be passed quite as easily for the mind as for the ear. Those words: *I am an old convict*, coming from M. Fauchelevent's mouth and entering Marius' ear, went beyond the possible. Marius did not hear. It seemed to him that something had just been said to him; but he knew not what. He stood aghast.

He then perceived that the man who was talking to him was terrible. Excited as he was, he had not until this moment noticed that frightful pallor.

Jean Valjean untied the black cravat which sustained his right arm, took off the cloth wound about his hand, laid his thumb bare, and showed it to Marius.

'There is nothing the matter with my hand,' said he.

Marius looked at the thumb.

'There has never been anything the matter with it,' continued Jean Valjean.

There was, in fact, no trace of a wound.

Jean Valjean pursued:

'It was best that I should be absent from your marriage. I absented myself as much as I could. I feigned this wound so as not to commit a forgery, not to introduce a nullity into the marriage acts, to be excused from signing.'

Marius stammered out:

'What does this mean?'

'It means,' answered Jean Valjean, 'that I have been in the galleys.'

'You drive me mad!' exclaimed Marius in dismay.

'Monsieur Pontmercy,' said Jean Valjean, 'I was nineteen years in the galleys. For robbery. Then I was sentenced for life. For robbery. For a second offence. At this hour I am in breach of ban.'

It was useless for Marius to recoil before the reality, to refuse the fact, to resist the evidence; he was compelled to yield. He began to comprehend, and as always happens in such a case, he comprehended beyond the truth. He felt the shiver of a horrible interior flash; an idea which made him shudder, crossed his mind. He caught a glimpse in the future of a hideous destiny for himself.

'Tell all, tell all!' cried he. 'You are Cosette's father!'

And he took two steps backward with an expression of unspeakable horror.

Jean Valjean raised his head with such a majesty of attitude that he seemed to rise to the ceiling.

'It is necessary that you believe me in this, monsieur; although the oath of such as I be not received.'

Here he made a pause; then, with a sort of sovereign and sepulchral authority, he added, articulating slowly and emphasising his syllables:

'– You will believe me. I, the father of Cosette! before God, no. Monsieur Baron Pontmercy, I am a peasant of Faverolles. I earned my living by pruning trees. My name is not Fauchelevent, my name is Jean Valjean. I am nothing to Cosette. Compose yourself.'

Marius faltered:

'Who proves it to me? –'

'I. Since I say so.'

Marius looked at this man. He was mournful, yet self-possessed. No lie could come out of such a calmness. That which is frozen is sincere. We feel the truth in that sepulchral coldness.

'I believe you,' said Marius.

Jean Valjean inclined his head as if making oath, and continued:

'What am I to Cosette? a passer. Ten years ago, I did not know that she existed. I love her, it is true. A child whom one has seen when little, being himself already old, he loves. When a man is old, he feels like a grandfather towards all little children. You can, it seems to me, suppose that I have something which resembles a heart. She was an orphan. Without father or mother. She had need of me. That is why I began to love her. Children are so weak, that anybody, even a man like me, may be their protector. I performed that duty with regard to Cosette. I do not think that one could truly call so little a thing a good deed; but if it is a good deed, well, set it down that I have done it. Record that mitigating circumstance. Today Cosette leaves my life; our two roads separate. Henceforth I can do nothing more for her. She is Madame Pontmercy. Her protector is changed. And Cosette gains by the change. All is well. As for the six hundred thousand francs, you have not spoken of them to me, but I anticipate your thought; that is a trust. How did this trust come into my hands? What matters it? I make over the trust. Nothing more can be asked of me. I complete the restitution by telling my real name. This again concerns me. I desire, myself, that you should know who I am.'

And Jean Valjean looked Marius in the face.

All that Marius felt was tumultuous and incoherent. Certain blasts of destiny make such waves in our soul.

We have all had such moments of trouble, in which everything within us is dispersed; we say the first things that come to mind, which are not always precisely those that we should say. There are sudden revelations which we cannot bear, and which intoxicate like a noxious wine. Marius was so stupefied at the new condition of affairs which opened before him that he spoke to this man almost as though he were angry with him for his avowal.

'But after all,' exclaimed he, 'why do you tell me all this? What compels you to do so? You could have kept the secret to yourself. You are neither denounced, nor pursued, nor hunted. You have some reason for making, from mere wantonness, such a revelation. Finish it. There is something else. In connection with what do you make this avowal? From what motive?'

'From what motive?' answered Jean Valjean, in a voice so low and so hollow that one would have said it was to himself he was speaking rather than to Marius. 'From what motive, indeed, does this convict come and say: I am a convict? Well, yes! the motive is strange. It is from honour. Yes, my misfortune is a cord which I have here in my heart and which holds me fast. When one is old these cords are strong. The whole life wastes away about them; they hold fast. If I had been able to tear out this cord, to break it, to untie the knot, or to cut it, to go far away, I had been saved, I had only to depart; there are diligences in the Rue du Bouloy; you are happy, I go away. I have tried to break this cord, I have pulled upon it, it held firmly, it did not snap, I was tearing my heart out with it. Then I said I cannot live away from here. I must stay. Well, yes; but you are right, I am a fool, why not just simply stay? You offer me a room in the house, Madame Pontmercy loves me well, she says to that armchair: Stretch out your arms for him, your grandfather asks nothing better than to have me, I suit him, we shall all live together, eat in common, I will give my arm to Cosette – to Madame Pontmercy, pardon me, it is from habit – we will have but one roof, but one table, but one fire, the same chimney corner in winter, the same promenade in summer, that is joy, that is happiness, that, it is everything. We will live as one family, one family!'

At this word Jean Valjean grew wild. He folded his arms, gazed at the floor at his feet as if he wished to hollow out an abyss in it, and his voice suddenly became piercing.

'One family! no. I am of no family. I am not of yours. I am not of the family of men. In houses where people are at home I am an incumbrance. There are families, but they are not for me. I am the unfortunate; I am outside. Had I a father and a mother? I almost doubt it. The day that I married that child it was all over, I saw that she was happy, and that she was with the man whom she loved, and that there was a good old man here, a household of two angels, all joys in this house, and that it was well, I said to myself: Enter thou not. I could have lied, it is true, have deceived you all, have remained Monsieur Fauchelevent. As long as it was for her, I could lie; but now it would be for myself, I must not do it. It was enough to remain silent, it is true, and everything would continue. You ask me what forces me to speak? a strange thing; my conscience. To remain silent was, however, very easy. I have passed the night in trying to persuade myself to do so; you are confessing me, and what I come to tell you is so strange that you have a right to do so; well, yes, I have passed the night in giving myself reasons, I have given myself very good reasons, I have done what I could, it was of no use. But there are two things in which I did not succeed; neither in breaking the cord which holds me by the heart fixed, riveted, and sealed here, nor in silencing someone who speaks low to me when I am alone. That is why I have come to confess all to you this morning. All, or almost all. It is useless to tell what concerns only myself; I keep it for myself. The essential you know. So I have taken my mystery, and brought it to you. And I have ripped open my secret under your eyes. It was not an easy resolution to form. All night I have struggled with myself. Ah! you think I have not said to myself that this is not the Champmathieu affair, that in concealing my name I do no harm to anybody, that the name of Fauchelevent was given to me by Fauchelevent himself in gratitude for a service rendered, and I could very well keep it, and that I should be happy in this room which you offer me, that I should interfere with nothing, that I should be in my little corner, and that, while you would have Cosette, I should have the idea of being in the same house with her. Each one would have had his due share of happiness. To continue to be Monsieur Fauchelevent, smoothed the way for everything. Yes, except for my soul. There was joy everywhere about me, the depths of my soul were still black. It is not enough to be happy, we must be satisfied with ourselves. Thus I should have remained

Monsieur Fauchelevent, thus I should have concealed my real face, thus, in presence of your cheerfulness, I should have borne an enigma, thus, in the midst of your broad day, I should have been darkness, thus, without openly crying beware, I should have introduced the galleys at your hearth, I should have sat down at your table with the thought that, if you knew who I was, you would drive me away, I should have let myself be served by domestics who, if they had known, would have said: How horrible! I should have touched you with my elbow which you have a right to shrink from, I should have filched the grasp of your hand! There would have been in your house a division of respect between venerable white hairs and dishonoured white hairs; at your most intimate hours, when all hearts would have thought themselves open to each other to the bottom, when we should have been all four together, your grandfather, you two, and myself; there would have been a stranger there! I should have been side by side with you in your existence, having but one care, never to displace the covering of my terrible pit. Thus I, a dead man, should have imposed myself upon you, who are alive. Her I should have condemned to myself for ever. You, Cosette, and I, we should have been three heads in the green cap! Do you not shudder? I am only the most depressed of men, I should have been the most monstrous. And this crime I should have committed every day! And this lie I should have acted every day! And this face of night I should have worn every day! And of my disgrace, I should have given to you your part every day! every day! to you, my loved ones, you, my children, you, my innocents! To be quiet is nothing? to keep silence is simple? No, it is not simple. There is a silence which lies. And my lie, and my fraud, and my unworthiness, and my cowardice, and my treachery, and my crime, I should have drunk drop by drop, I should have spat it out, then drunk again, I should have finished at midnight and recommenced at noon, and my good-morning would have lied, and my good-night would have lied, and I should have slept upon it, and I should have eaten it with my bread, and I should have looked Cosette in the face, and I should have answered the smile of the angel with the smile of the damned, and I should have been a detestable impostor! What for? to be happy. To be happy, I! Have I the right to be happy? I am outside of life, monsieur.'

Jean Valjean stopped. Marius listened. Such a chain of ideas and of pangs cannot be interrupted. Jean Valjean lowered his voice anew, but it was no longer a hollow voice, it was an ominous voice.

'You ask why I speak? I am neither informed against, nor pursued, nor hunted, say you. Yes! I am informed against! yes! I am pursued! yes! I am hunted! By whom? by myself. It is I myself who bar the way before myself, and I drag myself, and I urge myself, and I check myself, and I exert myself, and when one holds himself he is well held.'

And seizing his own coat in his clenched hand and drawing it towards Marius:

'Look at this hand, now,' continued he. 'Don't you think that it holds this collar in such a way as not to let go? Well! conscience has quite another grasp! If we wish to be happy, monsieur, we must never comprehend duty; for, as soon as we comprehend it, it is implacable. One would say that it punishes you for comprehending it; but no, it rewards you for it; for it puts you into a hell where you feel God at your side. Your heart is not so soon lacerated when you are at peace with yourself.'

And, with a bitter emphasis, he added:

'Monsieur Pontmercy, this is not common sense, but I am an honest man. It is by degrading myself in your eyes that I elevate myself in my own. This has already happened to me once, but it was less grievous then; it was nothing. Yes, an honest man. I should not be one if you had, by my fault, continued to esteem me; now that you despise me, I am one. I have this fatality upon me that, being forever unable to have any but stolen consideration, that consideration humiliates me and depresses me inwardly, and in order that I may respect myself, I must be despised. Then I hold myself erect. I am a galley slave who obeys his conscience. I know well that is improbable. But what would you have me do? it is so. I have assumed engagements towards myself; I keep them. There are accidents which bind us, there are chances which drag us into duties. You see, Monsieur Pontmercy, some things have happened to me in my life?'

Jean Valjean paused again, swallowing his saliva with effort, as if his words had a bitter after-taste, and resumed:

'When one has such a horror over him, he has no right to make others share it without their knowledge, he has no right to communicate his pestilence to them, he has no right to make them slip down his precipice without warning of it, he has no right to let his red cap be drawn upon them, he has no right craftily to encumber the happiness of others with his own misery. To approach those who are well, and to touch them in the shadow with his invisible ulcer, that is horrible. Fauchelevent lent me his name in vain. I had no right to make use of it; he could give it to me, I could not take it. A name is a Me. You see, monsieur, I have thought a little, I have read a little, although I am a peasant; and you see that I express myself tolerably. I form my own idea of things. I have given myself an education of my own. Well, yes, to purloin a name, and to put yourself under it, is dishonest. The letters of the alphabet may be stolen as well as a purse or a watch. To be a false signature in flesh and blood, to be a living false key, to enter the houses of honest people by picking their locks, never to look again, always to squint, to be infamous within myself, no! no! no! no! It is better to suffer, to bleed, to weep, to tear the skin from the flesh with the nails, to pass the nights in writhing, in anguish, to gnaw away body and soul. That is why I come to tell you all this. In mere wantonness, as you say.'

He breathed with difficulty, and forced out these final words: 'To live, once I stole a loaf of bread; today, to live, I will not steal a name.'

'To live!' interrupted Marius. 'You have no need of that name to live!'

'Ah! I understand,' answered Jean Valjean, raising and lowering his head several times in succession.

There was a pause. Both were silent, each sunk in an abyss of thought. Marius had seated himself beside a table, and was resting the corner of his mouth on one of his bent fingers. Jean Valjean was walking back and forth. He stopped before a glass and stood motionless. Then, as if answering some inward reasoning, he said, looking at that glass in which he did not see himself:

'While at present, I am relieved!'

He resumed his walk and went to the other end of the parlour. Just as he began to turn, he perceived that Marius was noticing his walk. He said to him with an inexpressible accent:

'I drag one leg a little. You understand why now.'

Then he turned quite round towards Marius:

'And now, monsieur, picture this to yourself: I have said nothing, I have remained Monsieur Fauchelevent, I have taken my place in your house, I am one of you, I am in my room, I come to breakfast in the morning in slippers, at night we all three go to the theatre, I accompany Madame Pontmercy to the Tuileries and to the Place Royale, we are together, you suppose me your equal; some fine day I am there, you are there, we are chatting, we are laughing, suddenly you hear a voice shout this name: Jean Valjean! and you see that appalling hand, the police, spring out of the shadow and abruptly tear off my mask!'

He ceased again; Marius had risen with a shudder. Valjean resumed:

'What say you?'

Marius' silence answered.

Jean Valjean continued:

'You see very well that I am right in not keeping quiet. Go on, be happy, be in heaven, be an angel of an angel, be in the sunshine, and be contented with it, and do not trouble yourself about the way which a poor condemned man takes to open his heart and do his duty; you have a wretched man before you, monsieur.'

Marius crossed the parlour slowly, and, when he was near Jean Valjean, extended him his hand.

But Marius had to take that hand which did not offer itself, Jean Valjean was passive, and it seemed to Marius that he was grasping a hand of marble.

'My grandfather has friends,' said Marius. 'I will procure your pardon.'

'It is useless,' answered Jean Valjean. 'They think me dead, that is enough. The dead are not subjected to surveillance. They are supposed to moulder tranquilly. Death is the same thing as pardon.'

And, disengaging his hand, which Marius held, he added with a sort of inexorable dignity:

'Besides, to do my duty, that is the friend to which I have recourse; and I need pardon of but one, that is my conscience.'

Just then, at the other end of the parlour, the door was softly opened a little way, and Cosette's head made its appearance. They saw only her sweet face, her hair was in charming disorder, her eyelids were still swollen with sleep. She made the movement of a bird passing its head out of its nest, looked first at her husband, then at Jean Valjean, and called to them with a laugh, you would have thought you saw a smile at the bottom of a rose:

'I'll wager that you're talking politics. How stupid that is, instead of being with me!'

Jean Valjean shuddered.

'Cosette,' faltered Marius – And he stopped. One would have said that they were two culprits.

Cosette, radiant, continued to look at them both. The frolic of paradise was in her eyes.

'I catch you in the very act,' said Cosette. 'I just heard my father Fauchelevent say, through the door: "Conscience – Do his duty." – It is politics, that is. I will not have it. You ought not to talk politics the very next day. It is not right.'

'You are mistaken, Cosette,' answered Marius. 'We were talking business. We are talking of the best investment for your six hundred thousand francs – '

'It is not all that,' interrupted Cosette. 'I am coming. Do you want me here?'

And, passing resolutely through the door, she came into the parlour. She was dressed in a full white morning gown, with a thousand folds and with wide sleeves which, starting from the neck, fell to her feet. There are in the golden skies of old Gothic pictures such charming robes for angels to wear.

She viewed herself from head to foot in a large glass, then exclaimed with an explosion of ineffable ecstasy:

'Once there was a king and a queen. Oh! how happy I am!'

So saying, she made a reverence to Marius and to Jean Valjean.

'There,' said she, 'I am going to install myself by you in an armchair; we breakfast in half an hour, you shall say all you wish to; I know very well that men must talk, I shall be very good.'

Marius took her arm, and said to her lovingly:

'We are talking business.'

'By the way,' answered Cosette, 'I have opened my window, a flock of *pierrots* [sparrows or masks] have just arrived in the garden. Birds, not masks. It is Ash Wednesday today; but not for the birds.'

'I tell you that we are talking business; go, my darling Cosette, leave us a moment. We are talking figures. It will tire you.'

'You have put on a charming cravat this morning, Marius. You are very coquettish, monseigneur. It will not tire me.'

'I assure you that it will tire you.'

'No. Because it is you. I shall not understand you, but I will listen to you. When we hear voices that we love, we need not understand the words they say. To be here together is all that I want. I shall stay with you; pshaw!'

'You are my darling Cosette! Impossible.'

'Impossible!'

'Yes.'

'Very well,' replied Cosette. 'I would have told you the news. I would have told you that grandfather is still asleep, that your aunt is at mass, that the chimney in my father Fauchelevent's room smokes, that Nicolette has sent for the sweep, that Toussaint and Nicolette have had a quarrel already, that Nicolette makes fun of Toussaint's stuttering. Well, you shall know nothing. Ah! it is impossible! I too, in my turn, you shall see, monsieur, I will say: it is impossible. Then who will be caught? I pray you, my darling Marius, let me stay here with you two.'

'I swear to you that we must be alone.'

'Well, am I anybody?'

Jean Valjean did not utter a word. Cosette turned towards him.

'In the first place, father, I want you to come and kiss me. What are you doing there, saying nothing, instead of taking my part? who gave me such a father as that? You see plainly that I am very unfortunate in my domestic affairs. My husband beats me. Come, kiss me this instant.'

Jean Valjean approached.

Cosette turned towards Marius.

'You, sir, I make faces at you.'

Then she offered her forehead to Jean Valjean.

Jean Valjean took a step towards her.

Cosette drew back.

'Father, you are pale. Does your arm hurt you?'

'It is well,' said Jean Valjean.

'Have you slept badly?'

'No.'

'Are you sad?'

'No.'

'Kiss me. If you are well, if you sleep well, if you are happy, I will not scold you.'

And again she offered him her forehead.

Jean Valjean kissed that forehead, upon which there was a celestial reflection.

'Smile.'

Jean Valjean obeyed. It was the smile of a spectre.

'Now defend me against my husband.'

'Cosette! – ' said Marius.

'Get angry, father. Tell him that I must stay. You can surely talk before me. So you think me very silly. It is very astonishing then what you are saying! business, putting money in a bank, that is a great affair. Men play the mysterious for nothing. I want to stay. I am very pretty this morning. Look at me, Marius.'

And with an adorable shrug of the shoulders and an inexpressibly exquisite pout, she looked at Marius. It was like a flash between these two beings. That somebody was there mattered little.

'I love you!' said Marius.

'I adore you!' said Cosette.

And they fell irresistibly into each other's arms.

'Now,' resumed Cosette, readjusting a fold of her gown with a little triumphant pout, 'I shall stay.'

'What, no,' answered Marius, in a tone of entreaty, 'we have something to finish.'

'No, still?'

Marius assumed a grave tone of voice:

'I assure you, Cosette, that it is impossible.'

'Ah! you put on your man's voice, monsieur. Very well, I'll go. You, father, you have not sustained me. Monsieur my husband, monsieur my papa, you are tyrants. I am going to tell grandfather of you. If you think that I shall come back and talk nonsense to you, you are mistaken. I am proud. I wait for you now, you will see that it is you who will get tired without me. I am going away, very well.'

And she went out.

Two seconds later, the door opened again, her fresh rosy face passed once more between the two folding doors, and she cried to them:

'I am very angry.'

The door closed again and the darkness returned.

It was like a stray sunbeam which, without suspecting it, should have suddenly traversed the night.

Marius made sure that the door was well closed.

'Poor Cosette!' murmured he, 'when she knows '

At these words, Jean Valjean trembled in every limb. He fixed upon Marius a bewildered eye.

'Cosette! Oh yes, it is true, you will tell this to Cosette. That is right. Stop, I had not thought of that. People have the strength for some things, but not for others. Monsieur, I beseech you, I entreat you, Monsieur, give me your most sacred word, do not tell her. Is it not enough that you know it yourself? I could have told it of myself without being forced to it, I would have told it to the universe, to all the world, that would be nothing to me. But she, she doesn't know what it is, it would appal her. A convict, why! you would have to explain it to her, to tell her: It is a man who has been in the galleys. She saw the Chain pass by one day. Oh, my God!'

He sank into an armchair and hid his face in both hands. He could not be heard, but by the shaking of his shoulders it could be seen that he was weeping. Silent tears, terrible tears.

There is a stifling in the sob. A sort of convulsion seized him, he bent over upon the back of the armchair as if to breathe, letting his arms hang down and allowing Marius to see his face bathed in tears, and Marius heard him murmur so low that his voice seemed to come from a bottomless depth: 'Oh! would that I could die!'

'Be calm,' said Marius, 'I will keep your secret for myself alone.'

And, less softened perhaps than he should have been, but obliged for an hour past to familiarise himself with a fearful surprise, seeing by degrees a convict superimposed before his eyes upon M. Fauchelevent, possessed little by little of this dismal reality, and led by the natural tendency of the position to determine the distance which had just been put between this man and himself, Marius added:

'It is impossible that I should not say a word to you of the trust which you have so faithfully and so honestly restored. That is an act of probity. It is just that a recompense should be given you. Fix the sum yourself, it shall be counted out to you. Do not be afraid to fix it very high.'

'I thank you, monsieur,' answered Jean Valjean gently.

He remained thoughtful a moment, passing the end of his forefinger over his thumb-nail mechanically, then he raised his voice:

'It is all nearly finished. There is one thing left – '

'What?'

Jean Valjean had as it were a supreme hesitation, and, voiceless, almost breathless, he faltered out rather than said:

'Now that you know, do you think, monsieur, you who are the master, that I ought not to see Cosette again?'

'I think that would be best,' answered Marius coldly.

'I shall not see her again,' murmured Jean Valjean.

And he walked towards the door.

He placed his hand upon the knob, the latch yielded, the door started, Jean Valjean opened it wide enough to enable him to pass out, stopped a second motionless, then shut the door, and turned towards Marius.

He was no longer pale, he was livid. There were no longer tears in his eyes, but a sort of tragical flame. His voice had again become strangely calm.

'But, monsieur,' said he, 'if you are willing, I will come and see her. I assure you that I desire it very much. If I had not clung to seeing Cosette, I should not have made the avowal which I have made, I should have gone away; but wishing to stay in the place where Cosette is and to continue to see her, I was compelled in honour to tell you all. You follow my reasoning, do you not? that is a thing which explains itself. You see, for nine years past, I have had her near me. We lived first in that ruin on the boulevard, then in the convent, then near the Luxembourg. It was there that you saw her for the first time. You remember her blue plush hat. We were afterwards in the quarter of the Invalides where there was a grating and a garden. Rue Plumet. I lived in a little back-yard where I heard her piano. That was my life. We never left each other. That lasted nine years and some months. I was like her father, and she was my child. I don't know whether you understand me, Monsieur Pontmercy, but from the present time, to see her no more, to speak to her no more, to have nothing more, that would be hard. If you do not think it wrong, I will come from time to time to see Cosette. I should not come often. I would not stay long. You might say I should be received in the little low room. On the ground floor. I would willingly come in by the back-door, which is for the servants, but that would excite wonder, perhaps. It is better, I suppose, that I should enter by the usual door. Monsieur, indeed, I would really like to see Cosette a little still. As rarely as you please. Put your self in my place, it is all that I have. And then, we must take care. If I should not come at all, it would have a bad effect, it would be thought singular. For instance, what I can do, is to come in the evening, at nightfall.'

'You will come every evening,' said Marius, 'and Cosette will expect you.'

'You are kind, monsieur,' said Jean Valjean.

Marius bowed to Jean Valjean, happiness conducted despair to the door, and these two men separated.

2. *The obscurities which a revelation may contain*

MARIUS WAS COMPLETELY unhinged.

The kind of repulsion which he had always felt for the man with whom he saw Cosette was now explained. There was something strangely enigmatic in this person, of which his instinct had warned him. This enigma was the most hideous of disgraces, the galleys. This M. Fauchelevent was the convict Jean Valjean.

To suddenly find such a secret in the midst of one's happiness is like the discovery of a scorpion in a nest of turtle-doves.

Was the happiness of Marius and Cosette condemned henceforth to this fellowship? Was that a foregone conclusion? Did the acceptance of this man form a part of the marriage which had been consummated? Was there nothing more to be done?

Had Marius espoused the convict also?

It is of no avail to be crowned with light and with joy; it is of no avail to be revelling in the royal purple hour of life, happy love; such shocks would compel even the archangel in his ecstasy, even the demi-god in his glory, to shudder.

As always happens in changes of view of this kind, Marius questioned himself whether he had not some fault to find with himself? Had he been wanting in perception? Had he been wanting in prudence? Had he been involuntarily stupefied? A little, perhaps. Had he entered, without enough precaution in clearing up its surroundings, upon this love adventure which had ended in his marriage with Cosette? He determined – it is thus, by a succession of determinations by ourselves in regard to ourselves, that life improves us little by little – he determined the chimerical and visionary side of his nature, a sort of interior cloud peculiar to many organisations, and which, in paroxysms of passion and grief, dilates, the temperature of the soul changing, and pervades the entire man, to such an extent as to make him nothing more than a consciousness steeped in a fog. We have more than once indicated this characteristic element of Marius' individuality. He recollected that, in the infatuation of his love, in the Rue Plumet, during those six or seven ecstatic weeks, he had not even spoken to Cosette of that drama of the Gorbeau den in which the victim had taken the very strange course of silence during the struggle, and of escape after it. How had he managed not to speak of it to Cosette? Yet it was so near and so frightful? How had he managed not even to name the Thénardiers to her, and, particularly, the day that he met Eponine? He had great difficulty now in explaining to himself his former silence. He did account for it, however. He recalled his stupor, his intoxication for Cosette, love absorbing everything, that uplifting of one by the other into the ideal, and perhaps also, as the imperceptible quantity of reason mingled with this violent and charming state of the soul, a vague and dull instinct to hide and to abolish in his memory that terrible affair with which he dreaded contact, in which he wished to play no part, which he shunned, and in regard to which he could be neither narrator nor witness without being accuser. Besides, those few weeks had been but a flash; they had had time for nothing, except to love. Finally, everything being weighed, turned over, and examined, if he had told the story of the Gorbeau ambuscade to Cosette, if he had named the Thénardiers to her, what would have been the consequences, if he had even discovered that Jean Valjean was a convict, would that have changed him, Marius? Would that have changed her, Cosette? Would he have shrunk back? Would he have adored her less? Would he the less have married her? No. Would it have changed anything in what had taken place? No. Nothing then to regret, nothing to reproach himself with. All was well. There is a God for these drunkards who are called lovers. Blind, Marius had followed the route which he would have chosen had he seen clearly. Love had bandaged his eyes, to lead him where? To Paradise.

But this paradise was henceforth complicated with an infernal accompaniment.

The former repulsion of Marius towards this man, towards this Fauchelevent become Jean Valjean, was now mingled with horror.

In this horror, we must say, there was some pity, and also a certain astonishment.

This robber, this twice-convicted robber, had restored a trust. And what a trust? Six hundred thousand francs. He was alone in the secret of the trust. He might have kept all, he had given up all.

Moreover, he had revealed his condition of his own accord. Nothing obliged him to do so. If it were known who he was, it was through himself. There was more in that avowal than the acceptance of humiliation, there was the acceptance of peril. To a condemned man, a mask is not a mask, but a shelter. He had renounced that shelter. A false name is security; he had thrown away this false name. He could, he, a galley-slave, have hidden himself for ever in an honourable family; he had resisted this temptation. And from what motive? from conscientious scruples. He had explained it himself with the irresistible accent of reality. In short, whatever this Jean Valjean might be, he had incontestably an awakened conscience. There was in him some mysterious regeneration begun; and, according to all appearance, for a long time already the scruple had been master of the man. Such paroxysms of justice and goodness do not belong to vulgar natures. An awakening of conscience is greatness of soul.

Jean Valjean was sincere. This sincerity, visible, palpable, unquestionable, evident even by the grief which it caused him, rendered investigation useless and gave authority to all that this man said. Here, for Marius, a strange inversion of situations. What came from M. Fauchelevent? distrust. What flowed from Jean Valjean? confidence.

In the mysterious account which Marius thoughtfully drew up concerning this

Jean Valjean, he verified the credit, he verified the debit, he attempted to arrive at a balance. But it was all as it were in a storm. Marius, endeavouring to get a clear idea of this man, and pursuing, so to speak, Jean Valjean in the depths of his thought, lost him and found him again in a fatal mist.

The trust honestly surrendered, the probity of the avowal, that was good. It was like a break in the cloud, but the cloud again became black.

Confused as Marius' recollections were, some shadow of them returned to him.

What was the exact nature of that affair in the Jondrette garret? Why, on the arrival of the police, did this man, instead of making his complaint, make his escape? Here Marius found the answer. Because this man was a fugitive from justice in breach of ban.

Another question: Why had this man come into the barricade? For now Marius saw that reminiscence again distinctly, reappearing in these emotions like sympathetic ink before the fire. This man was in the barricade. He did not fight there. What did he come there for? Before this question a spectre arose, and made response. Javert. Marius recalled perfectly to mind at this hour the fatal sight of Jean Valjean dragging Javert bound outside the barricade, and he again heard the frightful pistol-shot behind the corner of the little Rue Mondétour. There was, probably, hatred between the spy and this galley-slave. The one cramped the other. Jean Valjean had gone to the barricade to avenge himself. He had arrived late. He knew probably that Javert was a prisoner there. The Corsican vendetta has penetrated into certain lower depths and is their law; it is so natural that it does not astonish souls half turned back towards the good; and these hearts are so constituted that a criminal, in the path of repentance, may be scrupulous in regard to robbery and not be so in regard to vengeance. Jean Valjean had killed Javert. At least, that seemed evident.

Finally, a last question: but to this no answer. This question Marius felt like a sting. How did it happen that Jean Valjean's existence had touched Cosette's so long? What was this gloomy game of providence which had placed this child in contact with this man? Are coupling chains then forged on high also, and does it please God to pair the angel with the demon? Can then a crime and an innocence be room-mates in the mysterious galleys of misery? In this strait of the condemned, which is called human destiny, can two foreheads pass close to one another, the one childlike, the other terrible, the one all bathed in the divine whiteness of the dawn, the other for ever pallid with the glare of an eternal lightning? Who could have determined this inexplicable fellowship? In what manner, through what prodigy, could community of life have been established between this celestial child and this old wretch? Who had been able to bind the lamb to the wolf, and, a thing still more incomprehensible, attach the wolf to the lamb? For the wolf loved the lamb, for the savage being adored the frail being, for, during nine years, the angel had had the monster for a support. Cosette's childhood and youth, her coming to the day, her maidenly growth towards life and light, had been protected by this monstrous devotion. Here, the questions exfoliated, so to speak, into innumerable enigmas, abyss opened at the bottom of abysm, and Marius could no longer bend over Jean Valjean without dizziness. What then was this man precipice?

The old Genesiac symbols are eternal; in human society, such as it is and will be, until the day when a greater light shall change it, there are always two men, one superior, the other subterranean; he who follows good is Abel; he who follows evil is Cain. What was this remorseful Cain? What was this bandit religiously absorbed in the adoration of a virgin, watching over her, bringing her up, guarding her, dignifying her, and enveloping her, himself impure, with purity? What was this cloaca which had venerated this innocence to such an extent as to leave it immaculate? What was this Jean Valjean watching over the education of Cosette? What was this figure of darkness, whose only care was to preserve from all shadow and from all cloud the rising of a star?

In this was the secret of Jean Valjean; in this was also the secret of God.

Before this double secret, Marius recoiled. The one in some sort reassured him in regard to the other. God was as visible in this as Jean Valjean. God has his instruments. He uses what tool He pleases. He is not responsible to man. Do we know the ways of God? Jean Valjean had laboured upon Cosette. He had, to some extent, formed that soul. That was incontestable. Well, what then? The workman was horrible; but the work admirable. God performs His miracles as seems good to Himself. He had constructed this enchanting Cosette, and he had employed Jean Valjean on the work. It had pleased Him to choose this strange co-worker. What reckoning have we to ask of Him? Is it the first time that the dunghill has aided the spring to make the rose?

Marius made these answers to himself, and declared that they were good. On all the points which we have just indicated, he had not dared to press Jean Valjean, without avowing to himself that he dared not. He adored Cosette, he possessed Cosette. Cosette was resplendently pure. That was enough for him. What explanation did he need? Cosette was a light. Does light need to be explained? He had all; what could he desire? All, is not that enough. The personal affairs of Jean Valjean did not concern him. In bending over the fatal shade of this man, he clung to this solemn declaration of the miserable being: '*I am nothing to Cosette. Ten years ago, I did not know of her existence.*'

Jean Valjean was a passer. He had said so, himself. Well, he was passing away. Whatever he might be, his part was finished. Henceforth Marius was to perform the functions of Providence for Cosette. Cosette had come forth to find in the azure her mate, her lover, her husband, her celestial male. In taking flight, Cosette, winged and transfigured, left behind her on the ground, empty and hideous, her chrysalis, Jean Valjean.

In whatever circle of ideas Marius turned, he always came back from it to a certain horror of Jean Valjean. A sacred horror, perhaps, for, as we have just indicated, he felt a *quid divinum* in this man. But, whatever he did, and whatever mitigation he sought, he was always obliged to fall back upon this: he was a convict; that is, the creature who, on the social ladder, has no place, being below the lowest round. After the lowest of men, comes the convict. The convict is no longer, so to speak, the fellow of the living. The law has deprived him of all the humanity which it can take from a man. Marius, upon penal questions, although a democrat, still adhered to the inexorable system, and he had, in regard to those whom the law smites, all the ideas of the law. He had not yet, let us say, adopted all the ideas of progress. He had not yet come to distinguish between what is written by man and what is written by God, between law and right. He had not examined and weighed the right which man assumes to dispose of the irrevocable and the irreparable. He had not revolted from the word *vengeance*. He thought it natural that certain infractions of the written law should be followed by eternal penalties, and he accepted social damnation as growing out of civilisation. He was still at that point, infallibly to advance in time, his nature being good, and in reality entirely composed of latent progress.

Through the medium of these ideas, Jean Valjean appeared to him deformed and repulsive. He was the outcast. He was the convict. This word was for him like a sound of the last trumpet; and, after having considered Jean Valjean long, his final action was to turn away his head. *Vade retro.*

Marius, we must remember, and even insist upon it, though he had questioned Jean Valjean to such an extent, that Jean Valjean had said to him: *You are confessing me;* had not, however, put to him two or three decisive questions. Not that they had not presented themselves to his mind, but he was afraid of them. The Jondrette garret? The barricade? Javert? Who knows where the revelations would have stopped? Jean Valjean did not seem the man to shrink, and who knows whether Marius, after having urged him on, would not have desired to restrain him? In certain supreme conjunctures, has it not happened to all of us, after having put a question, to stop our ears that we might not hear the response? We have this cowardice especially when we love. It is not prudent to question untoward situations to the last degree, especially when the indissoluble portion of our own life is fatally interwoven with them. From Jean Valjean's despairing explanations, some appalling light might have sprung, and who knows but that hideous brilliancy might have been thrown even upon Cosette? Who knows but a sort of infernal glare would have remained upon the brow of this angel? The spatterings of a flash are still lightning. Fatality has such solidarities, whereby innocence itself is impressed with crime by the gloomy law of colouring reflections. The purest faces may preserve for ever the reverberation of a horrible surrounding. Wrongly or rightly Marius had been afraid. He knew too much already. He sought rather to blind than to enlighten himself. In desperation, he carried off Cosette in his arms, closing his eyes upon Jean Valjean.

This man was of the night, of the living and terrible night. How should he dare to probe it to the bottom? It is appalling to question the shadow. Who knows what answer it will make? The dawn might be blackened by it for ever.

In this frame of mind it was a bitter perplexity to Marius to think that this man should have henceforth any contact whatever with Cosette. These fearful questions, before which he had shrunk, and from which an implacable and definitive decision might have sprung, he now reproached himself almost, for not having put. He thought himself too good, too mild, let us say the word, too weak. This weakness had led him to an imprudent concession. He had allowed himself to be moved. He had done wrong. He should have merely and simply cast off Jean Valjean. Jean Valjean was the Jonah, he should have done it, and relieved his house of this man. He was vexed with himself he was vexed with the abruptness of that whirl of emotions which had deafened, blinded, and drawn him on. He was displeased with himself.

What should be done now? Jean Valjean's visits were very repugnant to him. Of what use was this man in his house? What should he do? Here he shook off his thoughts; he was unwilling to probe, he was unwilling to go deeper; he was unwilling to fathom himself. He had promised, he had allowed himself to be led into a promise; Jean Valjean had his promise; even to a convict, especially to a convict, a man should keep his word. Still, his first duty was towards Cosette. In short a repulsion, which predominated over all else, possessed him.

Marius turned all this assemblage of ideas over in his mind confusedly, passing from one to another, and excited by all. Hence a deep commotion. It was not easy for him to hide this commotion from Cosette, but love is a talent, and Marius succeeded.

Besides, he put without apparent object, some questions to Cosette, who, as candid as a dove is white, suspected nothing; he talked with her of her childhood and her youth, and he convinced himself more and more that all a man can be that is good, paternal, and venerable, this convict had been to Cosette. All that Marius had dimly seen and conjectured was real. This darkly mysterious nettle had loved and protected this lily.

BOOK 8: THE TWILIGHT WANE

1. The basement room

THE NEXT DAY, at nightfall, Jean Valjean knocked at the M. Gillenormand *porte-cochère*. Basque received him. Basque happened to be in the courtyard very conveniently, and as if he had had orders. It sometimes happens that one says to a servant: 'You will be on the watch for Monsieur So-and-so, when he comes.'

Basque, without waiting for Jean Valjean to come up to him, addressed him as follows:

'Monsieur the Baron told me to ask monsieur whether he desires to go upstairs or to remain below?'

'To remain below,' answered Jean Valjean.

Basque, who was moreover absolutely respectful, opened the door of the basement room and said: 'I will inform madame.'

The room which Jean Valjean entered was an arched and damp basement, used as a cellar when necessary, looking upon the street, paved with red tiles, and dimly lighted by a window with an iron grating.

The room was not of those which are harassed by the brush, the duster, and the broom. In it the dust was tranquil. There the persecution of the spiders had not been organised. A fine web, broadly spread out, very black, adorned with dead flies, ornamented one of the window-panes. The room, small and low, was furnished with a pile of empty bottles heaped up in one corner. The wall had been washed with a wash of yellow ochre, which was scaling off in large flakes. At the end was a wooden mantel, painted black, with a narrow shelf. A fire was kindled, which indicated that somebody had anticipated Jean Valjean's answer: *To remain below.*

Two armchairs were placed at the corners of the fireplace. Between the chairs was spread, in guise of a carpet, an old bedside rug, showing more warp than wool.

The room was lighted by the fire in the fireplace and the twilight from the window.

Jean Valjean was fatigued. For some days he had neither eaten nor slept. He let himself fall into one of the armchairs.

Basque returned, set a lighted candle upon the mantel, and retired. Jean Valjean, his head bent down and his chin upon his breast, noticed neither Basque nor the candle.

Suddenly he started up. Cosette was behind him.

He had not seen her come in, but he had felt that she was coming.

He turned. He gazed at her. She was adorably beautiful. But what he looked upon with that deep look, was not her beauty but her soul.

'Ah well!' exclaimed Cosette, 'father, I knew that you were singular, but I should never have thought this. What an idea! Marius tells me that it is you who wish me to receive you here.'

'Yes, it is I.'

'I expected the answer. Well, I warn you that I am going to make a scene. Let us begin at the beginning. Father, kiss me.'

And she offered her cheek.

Jean Valjean remained motionless.

'You do not stir. I see it. You act guilty. But it is all the same, I forgive you. Jesus Christ said: "Offer the other cheek." Here it is.'

And she offered the other cheek.

Jean Valjean did not move. It seemed as if his feet were nailed to the floor.

'This is getting serious,' said Cosette. 'What have I done to you? I declare I am confounded. You owe me amends. You will dine with us.'

'I have dined.'

'That is not true. I will have Monsieur Gillenormand scold you. Grandfathers are made to scold fathers. Come. Go up to the parlour with me. Immediately.'

'Impossible.'

Cosette here lost ground a little. She ceased to order and passed to questions.

'But why not? and you choose the ugliest room in the house to see me in. It is horrible here.'

'You know, madame, I am peculiar, I have my whims.'

Cosette clapped her little hands together.

'Madame! Still again! What does this mean?'

Jean Valjean fixed upon her that distressing smile to which he sometimes had recourse:

'You have wished to be madame. You are so.'

'Not to you, father.'

'Don't call me father any more.'

'What?'

'Call me Monsieur Jean. Jean, if you will.'

'You are no longer father? I am no longer Cosette? Monsieur Jean? What does this mean? but these are revolutions, these are! what then has happened? look me in the face now. And you will not live with us! And you will not have my room! What have I done to you? what have I done to you? Is there anything the matter?'

'Nothing.'

'Well then?'

'All is as usual.'

'Why do you change your name?'

'You have certainly changed yours.'

He smiled again with that same smile and added:

'Since you are Madame Pontmercy I can surely be Monsieur Jean.'

'I don't understand anything about it. It is all nonsense; I shall ask my husband's permission for you to be Monsieur Jean. I hope that he will not consent to it. You make me a great deal of trouble. You may have whims, but you must not grieve your darling Cosette. It is wrong. You have no right to be naughty, you are too good.'

He made no answer.

She seized both his hands hastily and, with an irresistible impulse, raising them towards her face, she pressed them against her neck under her chin, which is a deep token of affection.

'Oh!' said she to him, 'be good!'

And she continued:

'This is what I call being good: being nice, coming to stay here, there are birds here as well as in the Rue Plumet, living with us, leaving that hole in the Rue de l'Homme Armé, not giving us riddles to guess, being like other people, dining with us, breakfasting with us, being my father.'

He disengaged his hands.

'You have no more need of a father, you have a husband.'

Cosette could not contain herself.

'I no more need of a father! To things like that which have no common sense, one really doesn't know what to say!'

'If Toussaint was here,' replied Jean Valjean, like one who is in search of authorities and who catches at every straw, 'she would be the first to acknowledge that it is true that I always had my peculiar ways. There is nothing new in this. I have always liked my dark corner.'

'But it is cold here. We can't see clearly. It is horrid, too, to want to be Monsieur Jean. I don't want you to talk so to me.'

'Just now, on my way here,' answered Jean Valjean, 'I saw a piece of furniture in the Rue Saint Louis. At a cabinet maker's. If I were a pretty woman, I should make myself a present of that piece of furniture. A very fine toilet table; in the present style. What you call rosewood, I think. It is inlaid. A pretty large glass. There are drawers in it. It is handsome.'

'Oh! the ugly bear!' replied Cosette.

And with a bewitching sauciness, pressing her teeth together and separating her lips, she blew upon Jean Valjean. It was a Grace copying a kitten.

'I am furious,' she said. 'Since yesterday, you all make me rage. Everybody spites me. I don't understand. You don't defend me against Marius. Marius doesn't uphold me against you, I am all alone. I arrange a room handsomely. If I could have put the good God into it, I would have done it. You leave me my room upon my hands. My tenant bankrupts me. I order Nicolette to have a nice little dinner. Nobody wants your dinner, madame. And my father Fauchelevent, wishes me to call him Monsieur Jean, and to receive him in a hideous, old, ugly, mouldy cellar, where the walls have a beard, and where there are empty bottles for vases, and spiders' webs for curtains. You are singular, I admit, that is your way, but a truce is granted to people who get married. You should not have gone back to being singular immediately. So you are going to be well satisfied with your horrid Rue de l'Homme Armé. I was very forlorn there, myself! What have you against me? You give me a great deal of trouble. Fie!'

And, growing suddenly serious, she looked fixedly at Jean Valjean, and added:

'So you don't like it that I am happy?'

Artlessness, unconsciously, sometimes penetrates very deep. This question, simple to Cosette, was severe to Jean Valjean. Cosette wished to scratch; she tore.

Jean Valjean grew pale. For a moment he did not answer, then, with an indescribable accent and talking to himself, he murmured:

'Her happiness was the aim of my life. Now, God may beckon me away. Cosette, you are happy; my time is full.'

'Ah, you have called me Cosette!' exclaimed she.

And she sprang upon his neck.

Jean Valjean, in desperation, clasped her to his breast wildly. It seemed to him almost as if he were taking her back.

'Thank you, father!' said Cosette to him.

The transport was becoming poignant to Jean Valjean. He gently put away Cosette's arms, and took his hat.

'Well?' said Cosette.

Jean Valjean answered:

'I will leave you madame; they are waiting for you.'

And, from the door, he added:

'I called you Cosette. Tell your husband that that shall not happen again. Pardon me.'

Jean Valjean went out, leaving Cosette astounded at that enigmatic farewell.

2. *Other steps backward*

THE FOLLOWING DAY, at the same hour, Jean Valjean came.

Cosette put no questions to him, was no longer astonished, no longer exclaimed that she was cold, no longer talked of the parlour; she avoided saying either father or Monsieur Jean. She let him speak as he would. She allowed herself to be called madame. Only she betrayed a certain diminution of joy. She would have been sad, if sadness had been possible for her.

It is probable that she had had one of those conversations with Marius, in which the beloved man says what he pleases, explains nothing, and satisfies the beloved woman. The curiosity of lovers does not go very far beyond their love.

The basement room had made its toilet a little. Basque had suppressed the bottles, and Nicolette the spiders.

Every succeeding morrow brought Jean Valjean at the same hour. He came every day, not having the strength to take Marius' words otherwise than to the letter. Marius made his arrangements, so as to be absent at the hours when Jean Valjean came. The house became accustomed to M. Fauchelevent's new mode of life. Toussaint aided: '*Monsieur always was just so,*' she repeated. The grandfather issued this decree: 'He is an original!' and all was said. Besides, at ninety, no further tie is possible; all is juxtaposition; a newcomer is an annoyance. There is no more room; all the habits are formed. M. Fauchelevent, M. Tranchelevent, Grandfather Gillenormand asked nothing better than to be relieved of 'that gentleman.' He added: 'Nothing is more common than these originals. They do all sorts of odd things. No motive. The Marquis de Canaples was worse. He bought a palace to live in the barn. They are fantastic appearances which people put on.'

Nobody caught a glimpse of the nether gloom. Who could have guessed such a thing, moreover? There are such marshes in India; the water seems strange, inexplicable, quivering when there is no wind; agitated where it should be calm.

You see upon the surface this causeless boiling; you do not perceive the Hydra crawling at the bottom.

Many men have thus a secret monster, a disease which they feed, a dragon which gnaws them, a despair which inhabits their night. Such a man resembles other people, goes, comes. Nobody knows that he has within him a fearful parasitic pain, with a thousand teeth, which lives in the miserable man, who is dying of it. Nobody knows that this man is a gulf. It is stagnant, but deep. From time to time, a troubling, of which we understand nothing, shows itself on its surface. A mysterious wrinkle comes along, then vanishes, then reappears; a bubble of air rises and bursts. It is a little thing, it is terrible. It is the breathing of the unknown monster.

Certain strange habits, coming at the time when others are gone, shrinking away while others make a display, wearing on all occasions what might be called the wall-coloured mantle, seeking the solitary path, preferring the deserted street, not mingling in conversations, avoiding gatherings and festivals, seeming at one's ease and living poorly, having, though rich, one's key in his pocket and his candle at the porter's, coming in by the side door, going up the back stairs, all these insignificant peculiarities, wrinkles, air bubbles, fugitive folds on the surface, often come from a formidable deep.

Several weeks passed thus. A new life gradually took possession of Cosette; the relations which marriage creates, the visits, the care of the house, the pleasures, those grand affairs. Cosette's pleasures were not costly; they consisted in a single one: being with Marius. Going out with him, staying at home with him, this was the great occupation of her life. It was a joy to them for ever new, to go out arm in arm, in the face of the sun, in the open street, without hiding, in sight of everybody, all alone with each other. Cosette had one vexation. Toussaint could not agree with Nicolette, the wedding of two old maids being impossible, and went away. The grandfather was in good health; Marius argued a few cases now and then; Aunt Gillenormand peacefully led by the side of the new household, that lateral life which was enough for her. Jean Valjean came every day.

The disappearance of familiarity, the madame, the Monsieur Jean, all this made him different to Cosette. The care which he had taken to detach her from him, succeeded with her. She became more and more cheerful, and less and less affectionate. However, she still loved him very much, and he felt it. One day she suddenly said to him, 'You were my father, you are no longer my father, you were my uncle, you are no longer my uncle, you were Monsieur Fauchelevent, you are Jean. Who are you then? I don't like all that. If I did not know you were so good, I should be afraid of you.'

He still lived in the Rue de l'Homme Armé, unable to resolve to move further from the quarter in which Cosette dwelt.

At first he stayed with Cosette only a few minutes, then went away.

Little by little he got into the habit of making his visits longer. One would have said that he took advantage of the example of the days which were growing longer: he came earlier and went away later.

One day Cosette inadvertently said to him: 'Father'. A flash of joy illuminated Jean Valjean's gloomy old face. He replied to her: 'Say Jean.' 'Ah! true,' she answered with a burst of laughter, 'Monsieur Jean.' 'That is right,' said he, and he turned away that she might not see him wipe his eyes.

3. They remember the garden in the Rue Plumet

THAT WAS THE LAST TIME. From that last gleam onward, there was complete extinction. No more familiarity, no more good-day with a kiss, never again that word so intensely sweet: Father! he was, upon his own demand and through his own complicity, driven in succession from every happiness; and he had this misery, that after having lost Cosette wholly in one day, he had been obliged afterwards to lose her again little by little.

The eye at last becomes accustomed to the light of a cellar. In short, to have a vision of Cosette every day sufficed him. His whole life was concentrated in that hour. He sat by her side, he looked at her in silence, or rather he talked to her of the years long gone, of her childhood, of the convent, of her friends of those days.

One afternoon – it was one of the early days of April, already warm, still fresh, the season of the great cheerfulness of the sunshine, the gardens which lay about Marius' and Cosette's windows felt the emotion of awakening, the hawthorn was beginning to peep, a jewelled array of gilliflowers displayed themselves upon the old walls, the rosy wolf-mouths gaped in the cracks of the stones, there was a charming beginning of daisies and buttercups in the grass, the white butterflies of the year made their first appearance, the wind, that minstrel of the eternal wedding, essayed in the trees the first notes of that grand auroral symphony which the old poets called the *renouveau* – Marius said to Cosette: 'We have said that we would go to see our garden in the Rue Plumet again. Let us go. We must not be ungrateful.' And they flew away like two swallows towards the spring. This garden in the Rue Plumet had the effect of the dawn upon them. They had behind them in life already something which was like the springtime of their love. The house in the Rue Plumet being taken on a lease, still belonged to Cosette. They went to this garden and this house. In it they found themselves again; they forgot themselves. At night, at the usual hour, Jean Valjean came to the Rue des Filles du Calvaire. 'Madame has gone out with monsieur, and has not returned yet,' said Basque to him. He sat down in silence, and waited an hour. Cosette did not return. He bowed his head and went away.

Cosette was so intoxicated with her walk to 'the garden', and so happy over having 'lived a whole day in her past', that she did not speak of anything else the next day. It did not occur to her that she had not seen Jean Valjean.

'How did you go there?' Jean Valjean asked her.

'We walked.'

'And how did you return?'

'In a fiacre.'

For some time Jean Valjean had noticed the frugal life which the young couple led. He was annoyed at it. Marius' economy was severe, and the word to Jean Valjean had its absolute sense. He ventured a question:

'Why have you no carriage of your own? A pretty brougham would cost you only five hundred francs a month. You are rich.'

'I don't know,' answered Cosette.

'So with Toussaint,' continued Jean Valjean. 'She has gone away. You have not replaced her. Why not?'

'Nicolette is enough.'

'But you must have a waiting maid.'

'Have not I Marius?'

'You ought to have a house of your own, servants of your own, a carriage, a box at the theatre. There is nothing too good for you. Why not have the advantages of being rich? Riches add to happiness.'

Cosette made no answer.

Jean Valjean's visits did not grow shorter. Far from it. When the heart is slipping we do not stop on the descent.

When Jean Valjean desired to prolong his visit, and to make the hours pass unnoticed, he eulogised Marius; he thought him beautiful, noble, courageous, intellectual, eloquent, good. Cosette surpassed him. Jean Valjean began again. They were never silent. Marius, this word was inexhaustible; there were volumes in these six letters. In this way Jean Valjean succeeded in staying a long time. To see Cosette, to forget at her side, it was so sweet to him. It was the staunching of his wound. It happened several times that Basque came down twice to say: 'Monsieur Gillenormand sends me to remind Madame the Baroness that dinner is served.'

On those days, Jean Valjean returned home very thoughtful.

Was there, then, some truth in that comparison of the chrysalis which had presented itself to Marius' mind? Was Jean Valjean indeed a chrysalis who was obstinate, and who came to make visits to his butterfly.

One day he stayed longer than usual. The next day, he noticed that there was no fire in the fireplace. 'What!' thought he. 'No fire.' And he made the explanation to himself: 'It is a matter of course. We are in April. The cold weather is over.'

'Goodness! how cold it is here!' exclaimed Cosette as she came in.

'Why no,' said Jean Valjean.

'So it is you who told Basque not to make a fire?'

'Yes. We are close upon May.'

'But we have fire until the month of June. In this cellar, it is needed the year round.'

'I thought that the fire was unnecessary.'

'That is just one of your ideas!' replied Cosette.

The next day there was a fire. But the two armchairs were placed at the other end of the room, near the door. 'What does that mean?' thought Jean Valjean.

He went for the armchairs, and put them back in their usual place near the chimney.

This fire being kindled again encouraged him, however. He continued the conversation still longer than usual. As he was getting up to go away, Cosette said to him:

'My husband said a funny thing to me yesterday.'

'What was it?'

'He said: "Cosette, we have an income of thirty thousand francs. Twenty-seven that you have, three that my grandfather allows me." I answered: "That makes thirty." "Would you have the courage to live on three thousand?" I answered: "Yes, on nothing. Provided it be with you." And then I asked: "Why do you say this?" He answered: "To know." '

Jean Valjean did not say a word. Cosette probably expected some explanation from him; he listened to her in a mournful silence. He went back to the Rue de l'Homme Armé; he was so deeply absorbed that he mistook the door, and instead of entering his own house, he entered the next one. Not until he had gone up almost to the second storey did he perceive his mistake, and go down again.

His mind was racked with conjectures. It was evident that Marius had doubts in regard to the origin of these six hundred thousand francs, that he feared some impure source, who knows? that he had perhaps discovered that this money came from him, Jean Valjean, that he hesitated before this suspicious fortune and disliked to take it as his own, preferring to remain poor, himself and Cosette, than to be rich with a doubtful wealth.

Besides, vaguely, Jean Valjean began to feel that the door was shown him.

The next day, he received, on entering the basement room, something like a shock. The armchairs had disappeared. There was not even a chair of any kind.

'Ah now,' exclaimed Cosette as she came in, 'no chairs! Where are the armchairs, then?'

'They are gone,' answered Jean Valjean.

'That is a pretty business!'

Jean Valjean stammered:

I told Basque to take them away.'

'And what for?'

'I shall stay only a few minutes today.'

'Staying a little while is no reason for standing while you do stay.'

'I believe that Basque needed some armchairs for the parlour.'

'What for?'

'You doubtless have company this evening.'

'We have nobody.'

Jean Valjean could not say a word more.

Cosette shrugged her shoulders.

'To have the chairs carried away! The other day you had the fire put out. How singular you are!'

'Goodbye,' murmured Jean Valjean.

He did not say: 'Goodbye, Cosette.' But he had not the strength to say: 'Goodbye, madame.'

He went away overwhelmed.

This time he had understood.

The next day he did not come. Cosette did not notice it until night.

'Why,' said she, 'Monsieur Jean has not come today.'

She felt something like a slight oppression of the heart, but she hardly perceived it, being immediately diverted by a kiss from Marius.

The next day he did not come.

Cosette paid no attention to it, passed the evening and slept as usual, and thought of it only on awaking. She was so happy! She sent Nicolette very quickly to Monsieur Jean's to know if he were sick, and why he had not come the day before. Nicolette brought back Monsieur Jean's answer. He was not sick. He was busy. He would come very soon. As soon as he could. However, he was going to make a little journey. Madame must remember that he was in the habit of making journeys from time to time. Let there be no anxiety. Let them not be troubled about him.

Nicolette, on entering Monsieur Jean's house, had repeated to him the very words of her mistress. That madame sent to know 'why Monsieur Jean had not come the day before'. 'It is two days that I have not been there,' said Jean Valjean mildly.

But the remark escaped the notice of Nicolette, who reported nothing of it to Cosette.

4. Attraction and extinction

DURING THE LAST MONTHS of the spring and the first months of the summer of 1833, the scattered wayfarers in the Marais, the storekeepers, the idlers upon the doorsteps, noticed an old man neatly dressed in black, every day, about the same hour, at nightfall, come out of the Rue de l'Homme Armé, in the direction of the Rue Sainte Croix de la Bretonnerie, pass by the Blancs Manteaux, to the Rue Culture Sainte Catherine, and, reaching the Rue de l'Echarpe, turn to the left, and enter the Rue Saint Louis.

There he walked with slow steps, his head bent forward, seeing nothing, hearing nothing, his eye immovably fixed upon one point, always the same, which seemed studded with stars to him, and which was nothing more nor less than the corner of the Rue des Filles du Calvaire. As he approached the corner of that street, his face lighted up; a kind of joy illuminated his eye like an interior halo, he had a fascinated and softened expression, his lips moved vaguely, as if he were speaking to someone whom he did not see, he smiled faintly, and he advanced as slowly as he could. You would have said that even while wishing to reach some destination, he dreaded the moment when he should be near it. When there were but a few houses left between him and that street which appeared to attract him, his pace became so slow, that at times you might have supposed he had ceased to move. The vacillation of his head and the fixedness of his eye reminded you of the needle seeking the pole. However long he succeeded in deferring it, he must arrive at last; he reached the Rue des Filles du Calvaire; then he stopped, he trembled, he put his head with a kind of gloomy timidity beyond the corner of the last house, and he looked into that street, and there was in that tragical look something which resembled the bewilderment of the impossible, and the reflection of a forbidden paradise. Then a tear, which had gradually gathered in the corner of his eye, grown large enough to fall, glided over his cheek, and sometimes stopped at his mouth. The old man tasted its bitterness. He remained thus a few minutes, as if he had been stone; then he returned by the same route and at the same pace; and, in proportion as he receded, that look was extinguished.

Little by little, this old man ceased to go as far as the corner of the Rue des Filles du Calvaire; he stopped half way down the Rue Saint Louis; sometimes a little further, sometimes a little nearer. One day, he stopped at the corner of the Rue Culture Sainte Catherine, and looked at the Rue des Filles du Calvaire from the distance. Then he silently moved his head from right to left as if he were refusing himself something, and retraced his steps.

Very soon he no longer came even as far as the Rue Saint Louis. He reached the Rue Pavée, shook his head, and went back; then he no longer went beyond the Rue des Trois Pavillons; then he no longer passed the Blancs Manteaux. You would have said a pendulum which has not been wound up, and the oscillations of which are growing shorter ere they stop.

Every day, he came out of his house at the same hour, he commenced the same walk, but he did not finish it, and, perhaps unconsciously, he continually shortened it. His whole countenance expressed this single idea; What is the use? The eye was dull; no more radiance. The tear also was gone; it no longer gathered at the corner of the lids; that thoughtful eye was dry. The old man's head was still bent forward; his chin quivered at times; the wrinkles of his thin neck were painful to behold. Sometimes, when the weather was bad, he carried an umbrella under his arm, which he never opened. The good women of the quarter said: 'He is a natural.' The children followed him laughing.

BOOK 9: SUPREME SHADOW, SUPREME DAWN

1. Pity for the unhappy, but indulgence for the happy

It is a terrible thing to be happy! How pleased we are with it! How all-sufficient we think it! How, being in possession of the false aim of life, happiness, we forget the true aim, duty!

We must say, however, that it would be unjust to blame Marius.

Marius as we have explained, before his marriage, had put no questions to M. Fauchelevent, and, since, he had feared to put any to Jean Valjean. He had regretted the promise into which he had allowed himself to be led. He had reiterated to himself many times that he had done wrong in making that concession to despair. He did nothing more than gradually to banish Jean Valjean from his house, and to obliterate him as much as possible from Cosette's mind. He had in some sort constantly placed himself between Cosette and Jean Valjean, sure that in that way she would not notice him, and would never think of him. It was more than obliteration, it was eclipse.

Marius did what he deemed necessary and just. He supposed he had, for discarding Jean Valjean, without harshness, but without weakness, serious reasons, which we have already seen, and still others which we shall see further on. Having chanced to meet, in a cause in which he was engaged, an old clerk of the house of Laffitte, he had obtained, without seeking it, some mysterious information which he could not, in truth, probe to the bottom, from respect for the secret which he had promised to keep, and from care for Jean Valjean's perilous situation. He believed, at that very time, that he had a solemn duty to perform, the restitution of the six hundred thousand francs to somebody whom he was seeking as cautiously as possible. In the meantime, he abstained from using that money.

As for Cosette, she was in none of these secrets; but it would be hard to condemn her also.

There was an all-powerful magnetism flowing from Marius to her, which compelled her to do, instinctively and almost mechanically, what Marius wished. She felt, in regard to 'Monsieur Jean', a will from Marius; she conformed to it. Her husband had had nothing to say to her; she experienced the vague, but clear pressure of his unspoken wishes, and obeyed blindly. Her obedience in this consisted in not remembering what Marius forgot. She had to make no effort for that. Without knowing why herself, and without affording any grounds for censure, her soul had so thoroughly become her husband's soul, that whatever was covered with shadow in Marius' thought, was obscured in hers.

We must not go too far, however; in what concerns Jean Valjean, this forgetfulness and this obliteration were only superficial. She was rather thoughtless than forgetful. At heart, she really loved him whom she had so long called father. But she loved her husband still more. It was that which had somewhat swayed the balance of this heart, inclined in a single direction.

It sometimes happened that Cosette spoke of Jean Valjean, and wondered. Then Marius calmed her: 'He is absent, I think. Didn't he say that he was going away on a journey?' 'That is true,' thought Cosette. 'He was in the habit of disappearing in this way. But not for so long.' Two or three times she sent Nicolette to inquire in the Rue de l'Homme Armé if Monsieur Jean had returned from his journey. Jean Valjean had the answer returned that he had not.

Cosette did not inquire further, having but one need on earth, Marius.

We must also say that, on their part, Marius and Cosette had been absent. They had been to Vernon. Marius had taken Cosette to his father's grave.

Marius had little by little withdrawn Cosette from Jean Valjean. Cosette was passive.

Moreover, what is called much too harshly, in certain cases, the ingratitude of children, is not always as blameworthy a thing as is supposed. It is the ingratitude of nature. Nature, as we have said elsewhere, 'looks forward'. Nature divides living beings into the coming and the going. The going are turned towards the shadow, the coming towards the light. Hence a separation, which, on the part of the old, is a fatality, and, on the part of the young, involuntary. This separation, at first insensible, gradually increases, like every separation of branches. The limbs, without parting from the trunk, recede from it. It is not their fault. Youth goes where joy is, to festivals, to brilliant lights, to loves. Old age goes to its end. They do not lose sight of each other, but the ties are loosened. The affection of the young is chilled by life; that of the old by the grave. We must not blame these poor children.

2. *The last flickerings of the exhausted lamp*

One day Jean Valjean went downstairs, took three steps into the street, sat down upon a stone block, upon that same block where Gavroche, on the night of the 5th of June, had found him musing; he remained there a few minutes, then went upstairs again. This was the last oscillation of the pendulum. The next day, he did not leave his room. The day after he did not leave his bed.

His portress, who prepared his frugal meal, some cabbage, a few potatoes with a little pork, looked into the brown earthen plate, and exclaimed:

'Why, you didn't eat anything yesterday, poor dear man!'

'Yes, I did,' answered Jean Valjean.

'The plate is all full.'

'Look at the water-pitcher. That is empty.'

'That shows that you have drunk; it don't show that you have eaten.'

'Well,' said Jean Valjean, 'suppose I have only been hungry for water?'

'That is called thirst, and, when people don't eat at the same time, it is called fever.'

'I will eat tomorrow.'

'Or at Christmas. Why not eat today? Do people say: I will eat tomorrow! To leave me my whole plateful without touching it! My coleslaw, which was so good!'

Jean Valjean took the old woman's hand:

'I promise to eat it,' said he to her in his benevolent voice.

'I am not satisfied with you,' answered the portress.

Jean Valjean scarcely ever saw any other human being than this good woman. There are streets in Paris in which nobody walks, and houses into which nobody comes. He was in one of those streets, and in one of those houses.

While he still went out, he had bought of a brazier for a few sous a little copper crucifix, which he had hung upon a nail before his bed. The cross is always good to look upon.

A week elapsed, and Jean Valjean had not taken a step in his room. He was still in bed. The portress said to her husband: 'The goodman upstairs does not get up any more, he does not eat any more, he won't last long. He has trouble, he has. Nobody can get it out of my head that his daughter has made a bad match.'

The porter replied, with the accent of the marital sovereignty:

'If he is rich, let him have a doctor. If he is not rich, let him not have any. If he doesn't have a doctor, he will die.'

'And if he does have one?'

'He will die,' said the porter.

The portress began to dig up with an old knife some grass which was sprouting in what she called her pavement, and, while she was pulling up the grass, she muttered:

'It is a pity. An old man who is so nice! He is white as a chicken.'

She saw a physician of the quarter passing at the end of the street; she took it upon herself to beg him to go up.

'It is on the second floor,' said she to him. 'You will have nothing to do but go in. As the goodman does not stir from his bed now, the key is in the door all the time.'

The physician saw Jean Valjean, and spoke with him.

When he came down, the portress questioned him:

'Well, doctor?'

'Your sick man is very sick.'

'What is the matter with him?'

'Everything and nothing. He is a man who, to all appearance, has lost some dear friend. People die of that.'

'What did he tell you?'

'He told me that he was well.'

'Will you come again, doctor.'

'Yes,' answered the physician. 'But another than I must come again.'

3. A pen is heavy to him who lifted Fauchelevent's cart

ONE EVENING JEAN VALJEAN had difficulty in raising himself upon his elbow; he felt his wrist and found no pulse; his breathing was short, and stopped at intervals; he realised that he was weaker than he had been before. Then, undoubtedly under the pressure of some supreme desire, he made an effort, sat up in bed, and dressed himself. He put on his old working-man's garb. As he went out no longer, he had returned to it, and he preferred it. He was obliged to stop several times while dressing; the mere effort of putting on his waistcoat, made the sweat roll down his forehead.

Since he had been alone, he had made his bed in the ante-room, so as to occupy this desolate tenement as little as possible.

He opened the valise and took out Cosette's suit.

He spread it out upon his bed.

The bishop's candlesticks were in their place, on the mantel. He took two wax tapers from a drawer, and put them into the candlesticks. Then, although it was still broad daylight, it was in summer, he lighted them. We sometimes see torches lighted thus in broad day, in rooms where the dead lie.

Each step that he took in going from one piece of furniture to another, exhausted him, and he was obliged to sit down. It was not ordinary fatigue which spends the strength that it may be renewed; it was the remnant of possible motion; it was exhausted life pressed out drop by drop in overwhelming efforts, never to be made again.

One of the chairs upon which he sank, was standing before that mirror, so fatal for him, so providential for Marius, in which he had read Cosette's note, reversed on the blotter. He saw himself in this mirror, and did not recognise himself. He was eighty years old; before Marius' marriage, one would hardly have thought him fifty; this year had counted thirty. What was now upon his forehead was not the wrinkle of age, it was the mysterious mark of death. You perceived on it the impress of the relentless talon. His cheeks were sunken; the skin of his face was of that colour which suggests the idea of earth already above it; the corners of his mouth were depressed as in that mask which the ancients sculptured upon tombs; he looked at the hollowness with a look of reproach; you would have said it was one of those grand tragic beings who rise in judgement.

He was in that condition, the last phase of dejection, in which sorrow no longer flows; it is, so to speak, coagulated; the soul is covered as if with a clot of despair.

Night had come. With much labour he drew a table and an old armchair near the fireplace, and put upon the table pen, ink, and paper.

Then, he fainted. When he regained consciousness, he was thirsty. Being unable to lift the water-pitcher, with great effort he tipped it towards his mouth, and drank a swallow.

Then he turned to the bed, and, still sitting, for he could stand but a moment, he looked at the little black dress, and all those dear objects.

Such contemplations last for hours which seem minutes. Suddenly he shivered, he felt that the chill was coming; he leaned upon the table which was lighted by the bishop's candlesticks, and took the pen.

As neither the pen nor the ink had been used for a long time, the tip of the pen was bent back, the ink was dried, he was obliged to get up and put a few drops of water into the ink, which he could not do without stopping and sitting down two or three times, and he was compelled to write with the back of the pen. He wiped his forehead from time to time.

His hand trembled. He slowly wrote the few lines which follow:

'Cosette, I bless you. I am going to make an explanation to you. Your husband was quite right in giving me to understand that I ought to leave; still there is some mistake in what he believed, but he was right. He is very good. Always love him well when I am dead. Monsieur Pontmercy, always love my darling child. Cosette, this paper will be found, this is what I want to tell you, you shall see the figures, if I have the strength to recall them, listen well, this money is really your own. This is the whole story: The white jet comes from Norway, the black jet comes from England, the black glass imitation comes from Germany. The jet is lighter, more precious, more costly. We can make imitations in France as well as in Germany. It requires a little anvil two inches square, and a spirit-lamp to soften the wax. The wax was formerly made with resin and lamp-black, and cost four francs a pound. I hit upon making it with gum lac and turpentine. This costs only thirty sous, and it is much better. The buckles are made of a violet glass, which is fastened by means of this wax to a narrow rim of black iron. The glass should be violet for iron trinkets, and the black for gold trinkets. Spain purchases many of them. That is the country of jet – '

Here he stopped, the pen fell from his fingers, he gave way to one of those despairing sobs which rose at times from the depths of his being, the poor man clasped his head with both hands, and reflected.

'Oh!' exclaimed he within himself (pitiful cries, heard by God alone), 'it is all over. I shall never see her more. She is a smile which has passed over me. I am going to enter into the night without even seeing her again. Oh! a minute, an instant, to hear her voice, to touch her dress, to look at her, the angel! and then to die! It is nothing to die, but it is dreadful to die without seeing her. She would smile upon me, she would say a word to me. Would that harm anybody? No, it is over, morever. Here I am, all alone. My God! my God! I shall never see her again.'

At this moment there was a rap at his door.

4. A bottle of ink which serves only to whiten

THAT VERY DAY, or rather that very evening, just as Marius had left the table and retired into his office, having a bundle of papers to study over, Basque had handed him a letter, saying: 'the person who wrote the letter is in the antechamber'.

Cosette had taken grandfather's arm, and was walking in the garden.

A letter, as well as a man, may have a forbidding appearance. Coarse paper, clumsy fold, the mere sight of certain missives displeases. The letter which Basque brought was of this kind.

Marius took it. It smelt of tobacco. Nothing awakens a reminiscence like an odour. Marius recognised this tobacco. He looked at the address: *To Monsieur, Monsieur the Baron Pommerci. In his hôtel.* The recognition of the tobacco made him recognise the handwriting. We might say that astonishment has its flashes. Marius was, as it were, illuminated by one of those flashes.

The scent, the mysterious *aide-memoire*, revived a whole world within him. Here was the very paper, the manner of folding, the paleness of the ink; here was, indeed, the well-known handwriting; above all, here was the tobacco. The Jondrette garret appeared before him.

Thus, strange freak of chance! one of the two traces which he had sought so long, the one which he had again recently made so many efforts to gain, and which he believed forever lost, came of itself to him.

He broke the seal eagerly, and read:

> MONSIEUR BARON – If the Supreme Being had given me the talents for it, I could have been Baron Thénard, member of the Institute (Academy of Ciences), but I am not so. I merely bear the same name that he does, happy if this remembrance commends me to the excellence of your bounties. The benefit with which you honour me will be reciprocal. I am in possession of a secret conserning an individual. This individual conserns you. I hold the secret at your disposition, desiring to have the honour of being yuseful to you. I will give you the simple means of drivving from your honourable family this individual who has no right in it, Madame the Baronness being of high birth. The sanctuary of virtue could not coabit longer with crime without abdicating.
>
> I atend in the entichamber the orders of Monsieur the Baron. – With respect.

The letter was signed 'THÉNARD'.

This signature was not a false one. It was only a little abridged.

Besides the rigmarole and the orthography completed the revelation. The certificate of origin was perfect. There was no doubt possible.

The emotion of Marius was deep. After the feeling of surprise, he had a feeling of happiness. Let him now find the other man whom he sought, the man who had saved him, Marius, and he would have nothing more to wish.

He opened one of his secretary drawers, took out some banknotes, put them in his pockets, closed the secretary, and rang. Basque appeared.

'Show him in,' said Marius.

Basque announced:

'Monsieur Thénard.'

A man entered.

A new surprise for Marius. The man who came in was perfectly unknown to him.

This man, old withal, had a large nose, his chin in his cravat, green spectacles, with double shade of green silk over his eyes, his hair polished and smoothed down his forehead close to the eyebrows, like the wigs of English coachmen in high life. His hair was grey. He was dressed in black from head to foot, in a well worn but tidy black; a bunch of trinkets, hanging from his fob, suggested a watch. He held an old hat in his hand. He walked with a stoop, and the crook of his back increased the lowliness of his bow.

What was striking at first sight was, that this person's coat, too full, although carefully buttoned, did not seem to have been made for him. Here a short digression is necessary.

There was in Paris, at that period, in an old shanty, in the Rue Beautreillis, near the Arsenal, an ingenious Jew, whose business it was to change a rascal into an honest man. Not for too long a time, which might have been uncomfortable for the rascal. The change was made at sight, for a day or two, at the rate of thirty sous a day, by means of a costume, resembling, as closely as possible, that of honest people generally. This renter of costumes was called the Changer; the

Parisian thieves had given him this name, and knew him by no other. He had a tolerably complete wardrobe. The rags with which he tricked out his people were almost respectable. He had specialties and categories; upon each nail in his shop, hung, worn and rumpled, a social condition; here the magistrate's dress, there the curé's dress, there the banker's dress, in one corner the retired soldier's dress, in another the literary man's dress, further on the statesman's dress. This man was the costumer of the immense drama which knavery plays in Paris. His hut was the green-room whence robbery came forth, and whither swindling returned. A ragged rogue came to this wardrobe, laid down thirty sous, and chose, according to the part which he wished to play that day, the dress which suited him, and, when he returned to the street, the rogue was somebody. The next day the clothes were faithfully brought back, and the Changer, who trusted everything to the robbers, was never robbed. These garments had one inconvenience, they 'were not a fit'; not having been made for those who wore them, they were tight for this man, baggy for that, and fitted nobody. Every thief who exceeded the human average in smallness or in bigness, was ill at ease in the costumes of the Changer. He must be neither too fat nor too lean. The Changer had provided only for ordinary men. He had taken the measure of the species in the person of the first chance vagabond, who was neither thick nor thin, neither tall nor short. Hence adaptations, sometimes difficult, with which the Changer's customers got along as well as they could. So much the worse for the exceptions! The Statesman's dress, for instance, black from top to toe, and consequently suitable, would have been too large for Pitt and too small for Castelcicala. The Statesman's suit was described as follows in the Changer's catalogue; we copy: 'A black cloth coat, pantaloons of black double-milled cassimere, a silk waistcoat, boots, and linen'. There was in the margin: '*Ancient ambassador*', and a note which we also transcribe; 'In a separate box, a wig neatly frizzled, green spectacles, trinkets, and two little quill tubes an inch in length wrapped in cotton'. This all went with the Statesman, ancient ambassador. This entire costume was, if we may use the word, emaciated; the seams were turning white, an undefined buttonhole was appearing at one of the elbows; moreover, a button was missing on the breast of the coat; but this was a slight matter; as the Statesman's hand ought always to be within the coat and upon the heart, its function was to conceal the absent button.

If Marius had been familiar with the occult institutions of Paris, he would have recognised immediately, on the back of the visitor whom Basque had just introduced, the Statesman's coat borrowed from the Unhook-me-that of the Changer.

Marius' disappointment, on seeing another man enter than the one he was expecting, turned into dislike towards the new comer. He examined him from head to foot, while the personage bowed without measure, and asked him in a sharp tone:

'What do you want?'

The man answered with an amiable grin of which the caressing smile of a crocodile would give some idea:

'It seems to me impossible that I have not already had the honour of seeing Monsieur the Baron in society. I really think that I met him privately some years ago, at Madame the Princess Bagration's and in the salons of his lordship the Viscount Dambray, peer of France.'

It is always good tactics in rascality to pretend to recognise one whom you do not know.

Marius listened attentively to the voice of this man. He watched for the tone and gesture eagerly, but his disappointment increased; it was a whining pronunciation, entirely different from the sharp and dry sound of voice which he expected. He was completely bewildered.

'I don't know,' said he, 'either Madame Bagration or M. Dambray. I have never in my life set foot in the house of either the one or the other.'

The answer was testy. The person, gracious notwithstanding, persisted:

'Then it must be at Chateaubriand's that I have seen monsieur? I know Chateaubriand well. He is very affable. He says to me sometimes: "Thénard, my friend, won't you drink a glass of wine with me?" '

Marius' brow grew more and more severe:

'I have never had the honour of being received at Monsieur de Chateaubriand's. Come to the point. What is it you wish?'

The man, in view of the harsher voice, made a lower bow.

'Monsieur Baron, deign to listen to me. There is in America, in a region which is near Panama, a village called La Joya. This village is composed of a single house. A large, square, three-storey adobe house, each side of the square five hundred feet long, each storey set back twelve feet from the storey below, so as to leave in front a terrace which runs round the building, in the centre an interior court in which are provisions and ammunition, no windows, loopholes, no door, ladders, ladders to mount from the ground to the first terrace, and from the first to the second, and from the second to the third, ladders to descend into the interior court, no doors to the rooms, hatchways, no stairs to the rooms, ladders; at night the hatchways are closed, the ladders drawn in: swivels and carbines are aimed through the port-holes; no means of entering; a house by day, a citadel by night, eight hundred inhabitants, such is this village. Why so much precaution? because the country is dangerous; it is full of anthropophagi. Then why do people go there? because that country is wonderful; gold is found there.'

'What are you coming to?' Marius interrupted, who from disappointment was passing to impatience.

'To this, Monsieur Baron. I am an old weary diplomatist. The old civilisation has used me up. I wish to try the savages.'

'What then?'

'Monsieur Baron, selfishness is the law of the world. The proletarian country-woman who works by the day, turns round when the diligence passes, the proprietary country-woman who works in her own field, does not turn round. The poor man's dog barks at the rich man, the rich man's dog barks at the poor man. Everyone for himself. Interest is the motive of men. Gold is the loadstone.'

'What then? Conclude.'

'I would like to go and establish myself at La Joya. There are three of us. I have my spouse and my young lady; a girl who is very beautiful. The voyage is long and dear. I must have a little money.'

'How does that concern me?' inquired Marius.

The stranger stretched his neck out of his cravat, a movement characteristic of the vulture, and replied, with redoubled smiles:

'Then Monsieur the Baron has not read my letter?'

That was not far from true. The fact is, that the contents of the epistle had glanced off from Marius. He had seen the handwriting rather than read the letter. He scarcely remembered it. Within a moment a new clue had been given him. He had noticed this remark: My spouse and my young lady. He fixed a searching eye upon the stranger. An examining judge could not have done better. He seemed to be lying in ambush for him. He answered:

'Explain.'

The stranger thrust his hands into his fobs, raised his head without straightening his backbone, but scrutinising Marius in his turn with the green gaze of his spectacles.

'Certainly, Monsieur the Baron. I will explain. I have a secret to sell you.'

'A secret?'

'A secret.'

'Which concerns me?'

'Somewhat.'

'What is this secret?'

Marius examined the man more and more closely, while listening to him.

'I commence gratis,' said the stranger. 'You will see that I am interesting.'

'Go on.'

'Monsieur Baron, you have in your house a robber and an assassin.'

Marius shuddered.

'In my house? no,' said he.

The stranger, imperturbable, brushed his hat with his sleeve, and continued:

'Assassin and robber. Observe, Monsieur Baron, that I do not speak here of acts, old, bygone, and withered, which may be cancelled by prescription in the eye of the law, and by repentance in the eye of God. I speak of recent acts, present acts, acts yet unknown to justice at this hour. I will proceed. This man has glided into your confidence, and almost into your family, under a false name. I am going to tell you his true name. And to tell it to you for nothing.'

'I am listening.'

'His name is Jean Valjean.'

'I know it.'

'I am going to tell you, also for nothing, who he is.'

'Say on.'

'He is an old convict.'

'I know it.'

'You know it since I have had the honour of telling you.'

'No. I knew it before.'

Marius' cool tone, that double reply, *I know it,* his laconic method of speech, embarrassing to conversation, excited some suppressed anger in the stranger. He shot furtively at Marius a furious look, which was immediately extinguished. Quick as it was, this look was one of those which are recognised after they have once been seen; it did not escape Marius. Certain flames can only come from certain souls; the eye, that window of the thought, blazes with it; spectacles hide nothing; you might as well put a glass over hell.

The stranger resumed with a smile:

'I do not permit myself to contradict Monsieur the Baron. At all events, you must see that I am informed. Now, what I have to acquaint you with, is known to myself alone. It concerns the fortune of Madame the Baroness. It is an extraordinary secret. It is for sale. I offer it to you first. Cheap. Twenty thousand francs.'

'I know that secret as well as the others,' said Marius.

The person felt the necessity of lowering his price a little.

'Monsieur Baron, say ten thousand francs, and I will go on.'

'I repeat, that you have nothing to acquaint me with. I know what you wish to tell me.'

There was a new flash in the man's eye. He exclaimed:

'Still I must dine today. It is an extraordinary secret, I tell you. Monsieur the Baron, I am going to speak. I will speak. Give me twenty francs.'

Marius looked at him steadily:

'I know your extraordinary secret; just as I knew Jean Valjean's name: just as I know your name.'

'My name?'

'Yes.'

'That is not difficult, Monsieur Baron. I have had the honour of writing it to you and telling it to you. Thénard.'

'Dier.'

'Eh?'

'Thénardier.'

'Who is that?'

In danger the porcupine bristles, the beetle feigns death, the Old Guard forms a square; this man began to laugh.

Then, with a fillip, he brushed a speck of dust from his coat-sleeve.

Marius continued:

'You are also the working-man Jondrette, the comedian Fabantou, the poet Genflot, the Spaniard Don Alvarès, and the woman Balizard.'

'The woman what?'

'And you have kept a chop-house at Montfermeil.'

'A chop-house! never.'

'And I tell you that you are Thénardier.'

'I deny it.'

'And that you are a scoundrel. Here.'

And Marius, taking a banknote from his pocket, threw it in his face.

'Thanks! pardon! five hundred francs! Monsieur Baron!'

And the man, bewildered, bowing, catching the note, examined it.

'Five hundred francs!' he repeated in astonishment. And he stammered out in an undertone: 'A serious *fafiot!*'

Then bluntly:

'Well, so be it,' exclaimed he. 'Let us make ourselves comfortable.'

And, with the agility of a monkey, throwing his hair off backwards, pulling off his spectacles, taking out of his nose and pocketing the two quill tubes of which we have just spoken, and which we have already seen elsewhere on another page of this book, he took off his countenance as one takes off his hat.

His eye kindled; his forehead, uneven, ravined, humped in spots, hideously wrinkled at the top, emerged; his nose became as sharp as a beak; the fierce and cunning profile of the man of prey appeared again.

'Monsieur the Baron is infallible,' said he in a clear voice from which all nasality had disappeared, 'I am Thénardier.'

And he straightened his bent back.

Thénardier, for it was indeed he, was strangely surprised; he would have been disconcerted if he could have been. He had come to bring astonishment, and he himself received it. This humiliation had been compensated by five hundred francs, and, all things considered, he accepted it; but he was none the less astounded.

He saw this Baron Pontmercy for the first time, and, in spite of his disguise, this Baron Pontmercy recognised him, and recognised him thoroughly. And not only was this baron fully informed, in regard to Thénardier, but he seemed fully informed in regard to Jean Valjean. Who was this almost beardless young man, so icy and so generous, who knew people's names, who knew all their names, and who opened his purse to them, who abused rogues like a judge and who paid them like a dupe?

Thénardier, it will be remembered, although he had been a neighbour of Marius, had never seen him, which is frequent in Paris; he had once heard some talk of his daughters about a very poor young man named Marius who lived in the house. He had written to him, without knowing him, the letter which we have seen. No connection was possible in his mind between that Marius and M. the Baron Pontmercy.

Through his daughter Azelma, however, whom he had put upon the track of the couple married on the 16th of February, and through his own researches, he had succeeded in finding out many things, and, from the depth of his darkness, he had been able to seize more than one mysterious clue. He had, by dint of industry, discovered, or, at least, by dint of induction, guessed who the man was whom he had met on a certain day in the Grand Sewer. From the man, he had easily arrived at the name. He knew that Madame the Baroness Pontmercy was Cosette. But, in that respect, he intended to be prudent. Who was Cosette? He did not know exactly himself. He suspected indeed some illegitimacy. Fantine's story had always seemed to him ambiguous; but why speak of it? to get paid for his silence? He had, or thought he had, something better to sell than that. And to all appearance, to come and make, without any proof, this revelation to Baron Pontmercy: *Your wife is a bastard*, would only have attracted the husband's boot towards the revelator's back.

In Thénardier's opinion, the conversation with Marius had not yet commenced. He had been obliged to retreat, to modify his strategy, to abandon a position, to change his base; but nothing essential was yet lost, and he had five hundred francs in his pocket. Moreover, he had something decisive to say, and even against this Baron Pontmercy, so well informed and so well armed, he felt himself strong. To men of Thénardier's nature, every dialogue is a battle. In that which was about to be commenced what was his situation? He did not know to whom he was speaking, but he knew about what he was speaking. He rapidly made this interior review of his forces, and after saying: '*I am Thénardier*,' he waited.

Marius remained absorbed in thought. At last, then, he had caught Thénardier; this man, whom he had so much desired to find again, was before him: so he would be able to do honour to Colonel Pontmercy's injunction. He was humiliated that that hero should owe anything to this bandit, and that the bill of exchange drawn by his father from the depth of the grave upon him, Marius, should have been protested until this day. It appeared to him, also, in the complex position of his mind with regard to Thénardier, that here was an opportunity to avenge the colonel for the misfortune of having been saved by such a rascal. However that might be, he was pleased. He was about to deliver the colonel's shade at last from this unworthy creditor, and it seemed to him that he was about to release his father's memory from imprisonment for debt.

Besides this duty, he had another, to clear up, if he could, the source of Cosette's fortune. The opportunity seemed to present itself. Thénardier knew something, perhaps. It might be useful to probe this man to the bottom. He began with that.

Thénardier had slipped the 'serious *fafiot*' into his fob, and was looking at Marius with an almost affectionate humility.

Marius interrupted the silence.

'Thénardier, I have told you your name. Now your secret, what you came to make known to me, do you want me to tell you that? I too have my means of information. You shall see that I know more about it than you do. Jean Valjean, as you have said, is an assassin and a robber. A robber, because he robbed a rich manufacturer, M. Madeleine, whose ruin he caused. An assassin, because he assassinated the police-officer, Javert.'

'I don't understand, Monsieur Baron,' said Thénardier.

'I will make myself understood. Listen. There was, in an arrondissement of the Pas-de-Calais, about 1822, a man who had had some old difficulty with justice, and who, under the name of M. Madeleine, had reformed and re-established himself. He had become in the full force of the term an upright man. By means of a manufacture, that of black glass trinkets, he had made the fortune of an entire city. As for his own personal fortune, he had made it also, but secondarily, and, in some sort, incidentally. He was the foster-father of the poor. He founded hospitals, opened schools, visited the sick, endowed daughters, supported widows, adopted orphans; he was, as it were, the guardian of the country. He had refused the Cross, he had been appointed mayor. A liberated convict knew the secret of a penalty once incurred by this man; he informed against him and had him arrested, and took advantage of the arrest to come to Paris and draw from the banker, Laffitte – I have the fact from the cashier himself – by means of a false signature, a sum of more than half a million which belonged to M. Madeleine. This convict who robbed M. Madeleine is Jean Valjean. As to the other act, you have just as little to tell me. Jean Valjean killed the officer Javert; he killed him with a pistol. I, who am now speaking to you, I was present.'

Thénardier cast upon Marius the sovereign glance of a beaten man, who lays hold on victory again, and who has just recovered in one minute all the ground which he had lost. But the smile returned immediately; the inferior before the superior can only have a skulking triumph, and Thénardier merely said to Marius:

'Monsieur Baron, we are on the wrong track.'

And he emphasised this phrase by giving his bunch of trinkets an expressive twirl.

'What!' replied Marius, 'do you deny that? These are facts.'

'They are chimeras. The confidence with which Monsieur the Baron honours me makes it my duty to tell him so. Before all things, truth and justice. I do not like to see people accused unjustly. Monsieur Baron, Jean Valjean never robbed Monsieur Madeleine, and Jean Valjean never killed Javert.'

'You speak strongly! how is that?'

'For two reasons.'

'What are they? tell me.'

'The first is this: he did not rob Monsieur Madeleine, since it is Jean Valjean himself who was Monsieur Madeleine.'

'What is that you are telling me?'

'And the second is this: he did not assassinate Javert, since Javert himself killed Javert.'

'What do you mean?'

'That Javert committed suicide.'

'Prove it! prove it!' cried Marius, beside himself.

Thénardier resumed, scanning his phrase in the fashion of an ancient Alexandrine:

'The – police – of – ficer – Ja–vert – was – found – drowned – under – a – boat – by – the – Pont – au – Change .'

'But prove it now!'

Thénardier took from his pocket a large envelope of grey paper, which seemed to contain folded sheets of different sizes.

'I have my documents,' said he, with calmness.

And he added:

'Monsieur Baron, in your interest, I wished to find out Jean Valjean to the bottom. I say that Jean Valjean and Madeleine are the same man; and I say that Javert had no other assassin than Javert; and when I speak I have the proofs. Not manuscript proofs; writing is suspicious; writing is complaisant, but proofs in print.

While speaking, Thénardier took out of the envelope two newspapers, yellow, faded, and strongly saturated with tobacco. One of these two news–papers, broken at all the folds, and falling in square pieces, seemed much older than the other.

'Two facts, two proofs,' said Thénardier. And unfolding the two papers, he handed them to Marius.

With these two newspapers the reader is acquainted. One, the oldest, a copy of the *Drapeau Blanc*, of the 25th of July 1823, the text of which can be found on page 244 of the first volume of this book, established the identity of M. Madeleine and Jean Valjean. The other, a *Moniteur* of the 15th of June 1832, verified the suicide of Javert, adding that it appeared from a verbal report made by Javert to the prefect that, taken prisoner in the barricade of the Rue de la Chanvrerie, he had owed his life to the magnanimity of an insurgent who, though he had him at the muzzle of his pistol, instead of blowing out his brains, had fired into the air.

Marius read. There was evidence, certain date, unquestionable proof; these two newspapers had not been printed expressly to support Thénardier's words. The note published in the *Moniteur* was an official communication from the prefecture of police. Marius could not doubt. The information derived from the cashier was false, and he himself was mistaken. Jean Valjean, suddenly growing grand, arose from the cloud. Marius could not restrain a cry of joy:

'Well, then, this unhappy man is a wonderful man! all that fortune was really his own! he is Madeleine, the providence of a whole region! he is Jean Valjean, the saviour of Javert! he is a hero! he is a saint!'

'He is not a saint, and he is not a hero,' said Thénardier. 'He is an assassin and a robber.'

And he added with the tone of a man who begins to feel some authority in himself: 'Let us be calm.'

Robber, assassin; these words, which Marius supposed were gone, yet which came back, fell upon him like a shower of ice.

'Again,' said he.

'Still,' said Thénardier. 'Jean Valjean did not rob Madeleine, but he is a robber. He did not kill Javert, but he is a murderer.'

'Will you speak,' resumed Marius, 'of that petty theft of forty years ago, expiated, as appears from your newspapers themselves, by a whole life of repentance, abnegation, and virtue?'

'I said assassination and robbery, Monsieur Baron. And I repeat that I speak of recent facts. What I have to reveal to you is absolutely unknown. It belongs to the unpublished. And perhaps you will find in it the source of the fortune adroitly presented by Jean Valjean to Madame the Baroness. I say adroitly, for, by a donation of this kind, to glide into an honourable house, the comforts of which he will share, and, by the same stroke, to conceal his crime, to enjoy his robbery, to bury his name, and to create himself a family, that would not be very unskilful.'

'I might interrupt you here,' observed Marius; 'but continue.'

'Monsieur Baron, I will tell you all, leaving the recompense to your generosity. This secret is worth a pile of gold. You will say to me: why have you not gone to Jean Valjean? For a very simple reason: I know that he has dispossessed himself, and dispossessed in your favour, and I think the contrivance ingenious; but he has not a sou left, he would show me his empty hands, and, since I need some money for my voyage to La Joya, I prefer you, who have all, to him who has nothing. I am somewhat fatigued; allow me to take a chair.'

Marius sat down, and made sign to him to sit down.

Thénardier installed himself in a cappadine chair, took up the two newspapers, thrust them back into the envelope, and muttered, striking the *Drapeau Blanc* with his nail: 'It cost me some hard work to get this one.' This done, he crossed his legs and lay back in his chair, an attitude characteristic of people who are sure of what they are saying, then entered into the subject seriously, and emphasising his words:

'Monsieur Baron, on the 6th of June 1832, about a year ago, the day of the *émeute*, a man was in the Grand Sewer of Paris, near where the sewer empties into the Seine, between the Pont des Invalides and the Pont d'Iéna.'

Marius suddenly drew his chair near Thénardier's. Thénardier noticed this movement, and continued with the deliberation of a speaker who holds his interlocutor fast, and who feels the palpitation of his adversary beneath his words:

'This man, compelled to conceal himself, for reasons foreign to politics, however, had taken the sewer for his dwelling, and had a key to it. It was, I repeat it, the 6th of June; it might have been eight o'clock in the evening. The man heard a noise in the sewer. Very much surprised, he hid himself, and watched. It was a sound of steps, somebody was walking in the darkness; somebody was coming in his direction. Strange to say, there was another man in the sewer beside him. The grating of the outlet of the sewer was not far off. A little light which came from it enabled him to recognise the newcomer, and to see that this man was carrying something on his back. He walked bent over. The man who was walking bent over was an old convict, and what he was carrying upon his shoulders was a corpse. Assassination in *flagrante delicto*, if ever there was such a thing. As for the robbery, it follows of course; nobody kills a man for nothing. This convict was going to throw this corpse into the river. It is a noteworthy fact, that before reaching the grating of the outlet, this convict, who came from a distance in the sewer, had been compelled to pass through a horrible quagmire in which it would seem that he might have left the corpse; but, the sewer-men working upon the quagmire might, the very next day, have found the assassinated man, and that was not the assassin's game. He preferred to go through the quagmire with his load, and his efforts must have been terrible; it is impossible to put one's life in greater peril; I do not understand how he came out of it alive.'

Marius' chair drew still nearer. Thénardier took advantage of it to draw a long breath. He continued:

'Monsieur Baron, a sewer is not the Champ de Mars. One lacks everything there, even room. When two men are in a sewer, they must meet each other. That is what happened. The resident and the traveller were compelled to say good-day to each other, to their mutual regret. The traveller said to the resident: "*You see what I have on my back, I must get out, you have the key, give it to me.*" This convict was a man of terrible strength. There was no refusing him. Still he who had the key parleyed, merely to gain time. He examined the dead man, but he could see nothing, except that he was young, well dressed, apparently a rich man, and all disfigured with blood. While he was talking, he found means to cut and tear off from behind, without the assassin perceiving it, a piece of the assassinated man's coat. A piece of evidence, you understand; means of getting trace of the affair, and proving the crime upon the criminal. He put this piece of evidence in his pocket. After which he opened the grating, let the man out with his incumbrance on his back, shut the grating again and escaped, little caring to be mixed up with the remainder of the adventure, and especially desiring not to be present when the assassin should throw the assassinated man into the river. You understand now. He who was carrying the corpse was Jean Valjean; he who had the key is now speaking to you, and the piece of the coat – '

Thénardier finished the phrase by drawing from his pocket and holding up, on a level with his eyes, between his thumbs and his forefingers, a strip of ragged black cloth, covered with dark stains.

Marius had risen, pale, hardly breathing, his eye fixed upon the scrap of black cloth, and, without uttering a word, without losing sight of this rag, he retreated to the wall, and, with his right hand stretched behind him, groped about for a key which was in the lock of a closet near the chimney. He found this key, opened the closet, and thrust his arm into it without looking, and without removing his startled eyes from the fragment that Thénardier held up.

Meanwhile Thénardier continued:

'Monsieur Baron, I have the strongest reasons to believe that the assassinated young man was an opulent stranger drawn into a snare by Jean Valjean, and the bearer of an enormous sum.'

'The young man was myself, and there is the coat!' cried Marius, and he threw an old black coat covered with blood upon the carpet.

Then, snatching the fragment from Thénardier's hands, he bent down over the coat, and applied the piece to the cut skirt. The edges fitted exactly, and the strip completed the coat.

Thénardier was petrified. He thought this: 'I am floored.'

Marius rose up, quivering, desperate, flashing.

He felt in his pocket, and walked, furious, towards Thénardier, offering him and almost pushing into his face his fist full of five hundred and a thousand franc notes.

'You are a wretch! you are a liar, a slanderer, a scoundrel. You came to accuse this man, you have justified him; you wanted to destroy him, you have succeeded only in glorifying him. And it is you who are a robber! and it is you who are an assassin! I saw you, Thénardier, Jondrette, in that den on the Boulevard de l'Hôpital. I know enough about you to send you to the galleys, and further even, if I wished. Here, there are a thousand francs, braggart that you are!'

And he threw a bill for a thousand francs to Thénardier.

'Ah! Jondrette, Thénardier, vile knave! let this be a lesson to you, pedlar of secrets, trader in mysteries, fumbler in the dark, wretch! Take these five hundred francs, and leave this place! Waterloo protects you.'

'Waterloo!' muttered Thénardier, pocketing the five hundred francs with the thousand francs.

'Yes, assassin! you saved the life of a colonel there – '

'Of a general,' said Thénardier, raising his head.

'Of a colonel!' replied Marius with a burst of passion. 'I would not give a farthing for a general. And you came here to act out your infamy! I tell you that you have committed every crime. Go! out of my sight! Be happy only, that is all that I desire. Ah! monster! there are three thousand francs more. Take them. You will start tomorrow for America, with your daughter, for your wife is dead, abominable liar. I will see to your departure, bandit, and I will count out to you then twenty thousand francs. Go and get hung elsewhere!'

'Monsieur Baron,' answered Thénardier, bowing to the ground, 'eternal gratitude.'

And Thénardier went out, comprehending nothing, astounded and transported with this sweet crushing under sacks of gold and with this thunderbolt bursting upon his head in banknotes.

Thunderstruck he was, but happy also; and he would have been very sorry to have had a lightning rod against that thunderbolt.

Let us finish with this man at once. Two days after the events which we are now relating, he left, through Marius' care, for America, under a false name, with his daughter Azelma, provided with a draft upon New York for twenty thousand francs. Thénardier, the moral misery of Thénardier, the broken-down bourgeois, was irremediable; he was in America what he had been in Europe. The touch of a wicked man is often enough to corrupt a good deed and to make an evil result spring from it. With Marius' money, Thénardier became a slaver.

As soon as Thénardier was out of doors, Marius ran to the garden where Cosette was still walking:

'Cosette! Cosette!' cried he. 'Come! come quick! Let us go. Basque, a fiacre! Cosette, come. Oh! my God! It was he who saved my life! Let us not lose a minute! Put on your shawl.'

Cosette thought him mad, and obeyed.

He did not breathe, he put his hand upon his heart to repress its beating. He walked to and fro with rapid strides, he embraced Cosette: 'Oh! Cosette! I am an unhappy man!' said he.

Marius was in amaze. He began to see in this Jean Valjean a strangely lofty and saddened form. An unparalleled virtue appeared before him, supreme and mild, humble in its immensity. The convict was transfigured into Christ. Marius was bewildered by this marvel. He did not know exactly what he saw, but it was grand.

In a moment, a fiacre was at the door.

Marius helped Cosette in and sprang in himself.

'Driver,' said he, 'Rue de l'Homme Armé, Number 7.'

The fiacre started.

'Oh! what happiness!' said Cosette. 'Rue de l'Homme Armé! I dared not speak to you of it again. We are going to see Monsieur Jean.'

'Your father! Cosette, your father more than ever. Cosette, I see it. You told me that you never received the letter which I sent you by Gavroche. It must have fallen into his hands. Cosette, he went to the barricade to save me. As it is a necessity for him to be an angel, on the way, he saved others; he saved Javert. He snatched me out of that gulf to give me to you. He carried me on his back in that frightful sewer. Oh! I am an unnatural ingrate. Cosette, after having been your providence, he was mine. Only think that there was a horrible quagmire, enough to drown him a hundred times, to drown him in the mire, Cosette! he carried me through that. I had fainted; I saw nothing, I heard nothing, I could know nothing of my own fate. We are going to bring him back, take him with us, whether he will or no, he shall never leave us again. If he is only at home! If we only find him! I will pass the rest of my life in venerating him. Yes, that must be it, do you see. Cosette? Gavroche must have handed my letter to him. It is all explained. You understand.'

Cosette did not understand a word.

'You are right,' said she to him.

Meanwhile the fiacre rolled on.

5. *Night behind which is dawn*

AT THE KNOCK which he heard at his door, Jean Valjean turned his head.

'Come in,' said he feebly.

The door opened. Cosette and Marius appeared.

Cosette rushed into the room.

Marius remained upon the threshold, leaning against the casing of the door.

'Cosette!' said Jean Valjean, and he rose in his chair, his arms stretched out and trembling, haggard, livid, terrible, with immense joy in his eyes.

Cosette, stifled with emotion, fell upon Jean Valjean's breast.

'Father!' said she.

Jean Valjean, beside himself, stammered:

'Cosette! she? you, madame? it is you, Cosette? Oh, my God!'

And, clasped in Cosette's arms, he exclaimed:

'It is you, Cosette? you are here? You forgive me then!'

Marius, dropping his eyelids that the tears might not fall, stepped forward and murmured between his lips which were contracted convulsively to check the sobs:

'Father!'

'And you too, you forgive me!' said Jean Valjean.

Marius could not utter a word, and Jean Valjean added: 'Thanks.'

Cosette took off her shawl and threw her hat upon the bed.

'They are in my way,' said she.

And, seating herself upon the old man's knees, she stroked away his white hair with an adorable grace, and kissed his forehead.

Jean Valjean, bewildered, offered no resistance.

Cosette, who had but a very confused understanding of all this, redoubled her caresses, as if she would pay Marius' debt.

Jean Valjean faltered:

'How foolish we are! I thought I should never see her again. Only think, Monsieur Pontmercy, that at the moment you came in, I was saying to myself: It is over. There is her little dress, I am a miserable man, I shall never see Cosette again, I was saying that at the very moment you were coming up the stairs. Was not I silly? I was as silly as that! But we reckon without God. God said: You think that you are going to be abandoned, dolt? No. No, it shall not come to pass like that. Come, here is a poor goodman who has need of an angel. And the angel comes; and I see my Cosette again! and I see my darling Cosette again! Oh! I was very miserable!'

For a moment he could not speak, then he continued:

'I really needed to see Cosette a little while from time to time. A heart does want a bone to gnaw. Still I felt plainly that I was in the way. I gave myself reasons: they have no need of you, stay in your corner, you have no right to continue for ever. Oh! bless God, I see her again! Do you know, Cosette, that your husband is very handsome? Ah, you have a pretty embroidered collar, yes, yes. I like that pattern. Your husband chose it, did not he? And then, Cosette, you must have cashmeres. Monsieur Pontmercy, let me call her Cosette. It will not be very long.'

And Cosette continued again:

'How naughty to have left us in this way! Where have you been? why were you away so long? Your journeys did not use to last more than three or four days. I sent Nicolette, the answer always was: He is absent. How long since you returned? Why did not you let us know? Do you know that you are very much changed. Oh! the naughty father! he has been sick, and we did not know it! Here, Marius feel his hand, how cold it is!'

'So you are here, Monsieur Pontmercy, you forgive me!' repeated Jean Valjean.

At these words, which Jean Valjean now said for the second time, all that was swelling in Marius' heart found an outlet, he broke forth:

'Cosette, do you hear? that is the way with him! he begs my pardon, and do you know what he has done for me, Cosette? he has saved my life. He has done more. He has given you to me. And, after having saved me, and after having given you to me, Cosette, what did he do with himself? he sacrificed himself. There is the man. And, to me the ungrateful, to me the forgetful, to me the pitiless, to me the guilty, he says: Thanks! Cosette, my whole life passed at the feet of this man would be too little. That barricade, that sewer, that furnace, that cloaca, he went through everything for me, for you. Cosette! He bore me through death in every form which he put aside from me, and which he accepted for himself. All courage, all virtue, all heroism, all sanctity, he has it all, Cosette, that man is an angel!'

'Hush! hush!' said Jean Valjean in a whisper. 'Why tell all that?'

'But you!' exclaimed Marius, with a passion in which veneration was mingled, 'why have not you told it? It is your fault, too. You save people's lives, and you hide it from them! You do more, under pretence of unmasking yourself, you calumniate yourself. It is frightful.'

'I told the truth,' answered Jean Valjean.

'No,' replied Marius, 'the truth is the whole truth; and you did not tell it. You were Monsieur Madeleine, why not have said so? You had saved Javert, why not have said so? I owe my life to you, why not have said so?'

'Because I thought as you did. I felt that you were right. It was necessary that I should go away. If you had known that affair of the sewer, you would have made me stay with you. I should then have had to keep silent. If I had spoken, it would have embarrassed all.'

'Embarrassed what? embarrassed whom?' replied Marius. 'Do you suppose you are going to stay here? We are going to carry you back. Oh! my God! when I think it was by accident that I learned it all! We are going to carry you back. You are a part of us. You are her father and mine. You shall not spend another day in this horrid house. Do not imagine that you will be here tomorrow.'

'Tomorrow,' said Jean Valjean, 'I shall not be here, but I shall not be at your house.'

'What do you mean?' replied Marius. 'Ah now, we shall allow no more journeys. You shall never leave us again. You belong to us. We will not let you go.'

'This time, it is for good,' added Cosette. 'We have a carriage below. I am going to carry you off. If necessary, I shall use force.'

And laughing, she made as if she would lift the old man in her arms.

'Your room is still in our house,' she continued. 'If you knew how pretty the garden is now. The azaleas are growing finely. The paths are sanded with river sand: there are some little violet shells. You shall eat some of my strawberries. I water them myself. And no more madame, and no more Monsieur Jean, we are a republic, are we not, Marius? The programme is changed. If you knew, father, I have had some trouble, there was a red-breast which had made her nest in a hole in the wall, a horrid cat ate her up for me. My poor pretty little red-breast who put her head out at her window and looked at me! I cried over it. I would have killed the cat! But now, nobody cries any more. Everybody laughs, everybody is happy. You are coming with us. How glad grandfather will be! You shall have your bed in the garden, you shall tend it, and we will see if your strawberries are as fine as mine. And then, I will do whatever you wish, and then, you will obey me.'

Jean Valjean listened to her without hearing her. He heard the music of her voice rather than the meaning of her words; one of those big tears which are the gloomy pearls of the soul, gathered slowly in his eye. He murmured:

'The proof that God is good is that she is here.'

'Father!' said Cosette.

Jean Valjean continued:

'It is very true that it would be charming to live together. They have their trees full of birds. I would walk with Cosette. To be with people who live, who bid each other good morning, who call each other into the garden, would be sweet. We would see each other as soon as it was morning. We would each cultivate our little corner. She would have me eat her strawberries. I would have her pick my roses. It would be charming. Only – '

He paused and said mildly:

'It is a pity.'

The tear did not fall, it went back, and Jean Valjean replaced it with a smile.

Cosette took both the old man's hands in her own

'My God!' said she, 'your hands are colder yet. Are you sick? Are you suffering?'

'No,' answered Jean Valjean. 'I am very well. Only – '

He stopped.

'Only what?'

'I shall die in a few minutes.'

Cosette and Marius shuddered.

'Die!' exclaimed Marius.

'Yes, but that is nothing,' said Jean Valjean.

He breathed, smiled, and continued:

'Cosette, you were speaking to me, go on, speak again, your little red-breast is dead then, speak, let me hear your voice!'

Marius, petrified, gazed upon the old man, Cosette uttered a piercing cry:

'Father! my father! you shall live. You are going to live. I will have you live, do you hear!'

Jean Valjean raised his head towards her with adoration.

'Oh yes, forbid me to die. Who knows? I shall obey perhaps. I was just dying when you came. That stopped me, it seemed to me that I was born again.'

'You are full of strength and life,' exclaimed Marius. 'Do you think people die like that? You have had trouble, you shall have no more. I ask your pardon now, and that on my knees! You shall live, and live with us, and live long. We will take you back. Both of us here will have but one thought henceforth, your happiness!'

'You see,' added Cosette in tears, 'that Marius says you will not die.'

Jean Valjean continued to smile.

'If you should take me back, Monsieur Pontmercy, would that make me different from what I am? No; God thought as you and I did, and he has not changed his mind; it is best that I should go away. Death is a good arrangement. God knows better than we do what we need. That you are happy, that Monsieur Pontmercy has Cosette, that youth espouses morning, that there are about you, my children, lilacs and nightingales, that your life is a beautiful lawn in the sunshine, that all the enchantments of heaven fill your souls, and now, that I who am good for nothing, that I die; surely all this is well. Look you, be reasonable, there is nothing else possible now, I am sure that it is all over. An hour ago I had a fainting fit. And then, last night, I drank that pitcher full of water. How good your husband is, Cosette! You are much better off than with me.'

There was a noise at the door. It was the physician coming in.

'Good day and goodbye, doctor,' said Jean Valjean. 'Here are my poor children.'

Marius approached the physician. He addressed this single word to him: 'Monsieur?' but in the manner of pronouncing it, there was a complete question.

The physician answered the question by an expressive glance.

'Because things are unpleasant,' said Jean Valjean, 'that is no reason for being unjust towards God.'

There was a silence. All hearts were oppressed.

Jean Valjean turned towards Cosette. He began to gaze at her as if he would take a look which should endure through eternity. At the depth of shadow to which he had already descended, ecstasy was still possible to him while beholding Cosette. The reflection of that sweet countenance illumined his pale face. The sepulchre may have its enchantments.

The physician felt his pulse.

'Ah! it was you he needed!' murmured he, looking at Cosette and Marius.

And, bending towards Marius' ear he added very low:

'Too late.'

Jean Valjean, almost without ceasing to gaze upon Cosette, turned upon Marius and the physician a look of serenity. They heard these almost inarticulate words come from his lips:

'It is nothing to die; it is frightful not to live.'

Suddenly he arose. These returns of strength are sometimes a sign also of the death-struggle. He walked with a firm step to the wall, put aside Marius and the physician, who offered to assist him, took down from the wall the little copper crucifix which hung there, came back, and sat down with all the freedom of motion of perfect health, and said in a loud voice, laying the crucifix on the table:

'Behold the great martyr.'

Then his breast sank in, his head wavered, as if the dizziness of the tomb seized him, and his hands resting upon his knees, began to clutch at his pantaloons.

Cosette supported his shoulders, and sobbed, and attempted to speak to him, but could not. There could be distinguished, among the words mingled with that mournful saliva which accompanies tears, sentences like this: 'Father! do not leave us. Is it possible that we have found you again only to lose you?'

The agony of death may be said to meander. It goes, comes, advances towards the grave, and returns towards life. There is some groping in the act of dying.

Jean Valjean, after this semi-syncope, gathered strength, shook his forehead as if to throw off the darkness, and became almost completely lucid once more. He took a fold of Cosette's sleeve, and kissed it.

'He is reviving! Doctor, he is reviving!' cried Marius.

'You are both kind,' said Jean Valjean. 'I will tell you what has given me pain. What has given me pain, Monsieur Pontmercy, was that you have been unwilling to touch that money. That money really belongs to your wife. I will explain it to you, my children, on that account I am glad to see you. The black jet comes from England, the white jet comes from Norway. All this is in the paper you see there, which you will read. For bracelets, I invented the substitution of clasps made by bending the metal, for clasps made by soldering the metal. They are handsomer, better, and cheaper. You understand how much money can be made. So Cosette's fortune is really her own. I give you these particulars so that your minds may be at rest.'

The portress had come up, and was looking through the half-open door. The physician motioned her away, but he could not prevent that good, zealous woman from crying to the dying man before she went:

'Do you want a priest?'

'I have one,' answered Jean Valjean.

And, with his finger, he seemed to designate a point above his head, where, you would have said, he saw someone.

It is probable that the Bishop was indeed a witness of this death-agony.

Cosette slipped a pillow under his back gently.

Jean Valjean resumed:

'Monsieur Pontmercy, have no fear, I conjure you. The six hundred thousand francs are really Cosette's. I shall have lost my life if you do not enjoy it! We succeeded very well in making glasswork. We rivalled what is called Berlin jewellery. Indeed, the German black glass cannot be compared with it. A gross, which contains twelve hundred grains very well cut, costs only three francs.'

When a being who is dear to us is about to die, we look at him with a look which clings to him, and which would hold him back. Both, dumb with anguish, knowing not what to say to death, despairing and trembling, they stood before him, Marius holding Cosette's hand.

From moment to moment, Jean Valjean grew weaker. He was sinking; he was approaching the dark horizon. His breath had become intermittent; it was interrupted by a slight rattle. He had difficulty in moving his wrist, his feet had lost all motion, and, at the same time that the distress of the limbs and the exhaustion of the body increased, all the majesty of the soul rose and displayed itself upon his forehead. The light of the unknown world was already visible in his eye.

His face grew pale, and at the same time smiled. Life was no longer present, there was something else. His breath died away, his look grew grand. It was a corpse on which you felt wings.

He motioned to Cosette to approach, then to Marius; it was evidently the last minute of the last hour, and he began to speak to them in a voice so faint it seemed to come from afar, and you would have said that there was already a wall between them and him.

'Come closer, come closer, both of you. I love you dearly. Oh! it is good to die so! You too, you love me, my Cosette. I knew very well that you still had some affection for your old goodman. How kind you are to put this cushion under my back! You will weep for me a little, will you not? Not too much. I do not wish you to have any deep grief. You must amuse yourselves a great deal, my children. I forgot to tell you that on buckles without tongues still more is made than on anything else. A gross, twelve dozen, costs ten francs, and sells for sixty. That is really a good business. So you need not be astonished at the six hundred thousand francs, Monsieur Pontmercy it is honest money. You can be rich without concern. You must have a carriage, from time to time a box at the theatres, beautiful ball dresses, my Cosette, and then give good dinners to your friends, be very happy. I was writing just now to Cosette. She will find my letter. To her I bequeathe the two candlesticks which are on the mantel. They are silver; but to me they are gold, they are diamond; they change the candles which are put into them, into consecrated tapers. I do not know whether he who gave them to me is satisfied with me in heaven. I have done what I could. My children, you will not forget that I am a poor man, you will have me buried in the most convenient piece of ground under a stone to mark the spot. That is my wish. No name on the stone. If Cosette will come for a little while sometimes, it will give me a pleasure. You too, Monsieur Pontmercy. I must confess to you that I have not always loved you; I ask your pardon. Now, she and you are but one to me. I am very grateful to you. I feel that you make Cosette happy. If you knew, Monsieur Pontmercy, her beautiful rosy cheeks were my joy; when I saw her a little pale, I was sad. There is a five-hundred-franc bill in the bureau. I have not touched it. It is for the poor. Cosette, do you see your little dress, there on the bed? do you recognise it? Yet it was only ten years ago. How time passes! We have been very happy. It is over. My children, do not weep, I am not going very far, I shall see you from there. You will only have to look when it is night, you will see me smile. Cosette, do you remember Montfermeil? You were in the wood, you were very much frightened; do you remember when I took the handle of the water-bucket? That was the first time I touched your poor little hand. It was so cold! Ah! you had red hands in those days, mademoiselle, your hands are very white now. And the great doll! do you remember? you called her Catharine. You regretted that you did not carry her to the convent. How you made me laugh sometimes, my sweet angel! When it had rained you launched spears of straw in the gutters, and you watched them. One day, I gave you a willow battledore, and a shuttlecock with yellow, blue, and green feathers. You have forgotten it. You were so cunning when you were little! You played. You put cherries in your ears. Those are things of the past. The forests through which we have passed with our child, the trees under which we have walked, the convents in which we have hidden, the games, the free laughter of childhood, all is in shadow. I imagined that all that belonged to me. There was my folly. Those Thénardiers were wicked. We must forgive them. Cosette, the time has come to tell you the name of your mother. Her name was Fantine. Remember that name: Fantine. Fall on your knees whenever you pronounce it. She suffered much. And loved you much. Her measure of unhappiness was as full as yours of happiness. Such are the distributions of God. He is on high, he sees us all, and he knows what he does in the midst of his great stars. So I am going away, my children. Love each other dearly always. There is scarcely anything else in the world but that: to love one another. You will think sometimes of the poor old man who died here. O my Cosette! it is not my fault, indeed, if I have not seen you all this time, it broke my heart; I went as far as the corner of the street, I must have seemed strange to the people who saw me pass, I looked like a crazy man, once I went out with no hat. My children, I do not see very clearly now, I had some things more to say, but it makes no difference. Think of me a little. You are blessed creatures. I do not know what is the matter with me, I see a light. Come nearer. I die happy. Let me put my hands upon your dear beloved heads.'

Cosette and Marius fell on their knees, overwhelmed, choked with tears, each grasping one of Jean Valjean's hands. Those august hands moved no more.

He had fallen backwards, the light from the candlesticks fell upon him; his white face looked up towards heaven, he let Cosette and Marius cover his hands with kisses; he was dead.

The night was starless and very dark. Without doubt, in the gloom some mighty angel was standing, with outstretched wings, awaiting the soul.

6. Grass hides and rain blots out

There is, in the cemetery of Père Lachaise, in the neighbourhood of the Potter's Field, far from the elegant quarter of that city of sepulchres, far from all those fantastic tombs which display in presence of eternity the hideous fashions of death, in a deserted corner, beside an old wall, beneath a great yew on which the bindweed climbs, among the dog-grass and the mosses, a stone. This stone is exempt no more than the rest from the leprosy of time, from the mould, the lichen, and the droppings of the birds. The air turns it black, the water green. It is near no path, and people do not like to go in that direction, because the grass is high, and they would wet their feet. When there is a little sunshine, the lizards come out. There is, all about, a rustling of wild oats. In the spring, the linnets sing in the tree.

This stone is entirely blank. The only thought in cutting it was of the essentials of the grave, and there was no other care than to make this stone long enough and narrow enough to cover a man.

No name can be read there.

Only many years ago, a hand wrote upon it in pencil these four lines which have become gradually illegible under the rain and the dust, and which are probably effaced:

Il dort. Quoique le sort fût pour lui bien étrange,
Il vivait. Il mourut quand il n'eut plus son ange.
La chose simplement d'elle-même arriva,
*Comme la nuit se fait lorsque le jour s'en va.**

* He sleeps. Although his fate was very strange, he lived. He died when he had no longer his angel. The thing came to pass simply, of itself, as the night comes when the day is gone.

WORDSWORTH CLASSICS

REQUESTS FOR INSPECTION COPIES Lecturers wishing to obtain copies of Wordsworth Classics, Wordsworth Poetry Library or Wordsworth Classics of World Literature titles on inspection are invited to contact: Dennis Hart, Wordsworth Editions Ltd, Crib Street, Ware, Herts SG12 9ET; E-mail: dennis.hart@wordsworth-editions.com. Please quote the author, title and ISBN of the titles in which you are interested; together with your name, academic address, E-mail address, the course on which the books will be used and the expected enrolment.

Teachers wishing to inspect specific core titles for GCSE or A level courses are also invited to contact Wordsworth Editions at the above address.

Inspection copies are sent solely at the discretion of Wordsworth Editions Ltd.

JANE AUSTEN
Emma
Mansfield Park
Northanger Abbey
Persuasion
Pride and Prejudice
Sense and Sensibility

ARNOLD BENNETT
Anna of the Five Towns
The Old Wives' Tale

R. D. BLACKMORE
Lorna Doone

M. E. BRADDON
Lady Audley's Secret

ANNE BRONTË
Agnes Grey
The Tenant of Wildfell Hall

CHARLOTTE BRONTË
Jane Eyre
The Professor
Shirley
Villette

EMILY BRONTË
Wuthering Heights

JOHN BUCHAN
Greenmantle
The Island of Sheep
John Macnab
Mr Standfast
The Thirty-Nine Steps
The Three Hostages

SAMUEL BUTLER
Erewhon
The Way of All Flesh

LEWIS CARROLL
Alice in Wonderland

M. CERVANTES
Don Quixote

ANTON CHEKHOV
Selected Stories

G. K. CHESTERTON
The Club of Queer Trades
Father Brown: Selected Stories
The Man Who Was Thursday
The Napoleon of Notting Hill

ERSKINE CHILDERS
The Riddle of the Sands

JOHN CLELAND
Fanny Hill – Memoirs of a Woman of Pleasure

WILKIE COLLINS
The Moonstone
The Woman in White

JOSEPH CONRAD
Almayer's Folly
Heart of Darkness
Lord Jim
Nostromo
Sea Stories
The Secret Agent
Selected Short Stories
Victory

J. FENIMORE COOPER
The Last of the Mohicans

STEPHEN CRANE
The Red Badge of Courage

THOMAS DE QUINCEY
Confessions of an English Opium Eater

DANIEL DEFOE
Moll Flanders
Robinson Crusoe

CHARLES DICKENS
Barnaby Rudge
Bleak House
Christmas Books
David Copperfield
Dombey and Son
Ghost Stories
Great Expectations
Hard Times
Little Dorrit
Martin Chuzzlewit
The Mystery of Edwin Drood
Nicholas Nickleby
The Old Curiosity Shop
Oliver Twist
Our Mutual Friend
Pickwick Papers
Sketches by Boz
A Tale of Two Cities

BENJAMIN DISRAELI
Sybil

FYODOR DOSTOEVSKY
Crime and Punishment
The Idiot

ARTHUR CONAN DOYLE
The Adventures of Sherlock Holmes
The Case-Book of Sherlock Holmes
The Return of Sherlock Holmes
The Best of Sherlock Holmes
The Hound of the Baskervilles
The Lost World & Other Stories
Sir Nigel
A Study in Scarlet & The Sign of Four
The Valley of Fear
The White Company

GEORGE DU MAURIER
Trilby

ALEXANDRE DUMAS
The Count of Monte Cristo
The Three Musketeers

MARIA EDGEWORTH
Castle Rackrent

GEORGE ELIOT
Adam Bede
Daniel Deronda
Felix Holt the Radical
Middlemarch
The Mill on the Floss
Silas Marner

HENRY FIELDING
Tom Jones

RONALD FIRBANK
Valmouth & Other Stories

F. SCOTT FITZGERALD
The Diamond as Big as the Ritz & Other Stories
The Great Gatsby
Tender is the Night

GUSTAVE FLAUBERT
Madame Bovary

JOHN GALSWORTHY
In Chancery
The Man of Property
To Let

ELIZABETH GASKELL
Cranford
North and South
Wives and Daughters

GEORGE GISSING
New Grub Street

OLIVER GOLDSMITH
The Vicar of Wakefield

KENNETH GRAHAME
The Wind in the Willows

G. & W. GROSSMITH
Diary of a Nobody

H. RIDER HAGGARD
She

THOMAS HARDY
Far from the Madding Crowd
Jude the Obscure
The Mayor of Casterbridge
A Pair of Blue Eyes
The Return of the Native
Selected Short Stories
Tess of the D'Urbervilles
The Trumpet Major
Under the Greenwood Tree
The Well-Beloved
Wessex Tales
The Woodlanders

NATHANIEL HAWTHORNE
The Scarlet Letter

O. HENRY
Selected Stories

JAMES HOGG
The Private Memoirs and Confessions of a Justified Sinner

HOMER
The Iliad
The Odyssey

E. W. HORNUNG
Raffles: The Amateur Cracksman

VICTOR HUGO
The Hunchback of Notre Dame
Les Misérables
IN TWO VOLUMES

HENRY JAMES
The Ambassadors
Daisy Miller & Other Stories
The Europeans
The Golden Bowl
The Portrait of a Lady
The Turn of the Screw & The Aspern Papers
What Maisie Knew

M. R. JAMES
Ghost Stories
Ghosts and Marvels

JEROME K. JEROME
Three Men in a Boat

JAMES JOYCE
Dubliners
A Portrait of the Artist as a Young Man

OMAR KHAYYAM
The Rubaiyat
TRANSLATED BY E. FITZGERALD

RUDYARD KIPLING
The Best Short Stories
Captains Courageous
Kim
The Man Who Would Be King & Other Stories
Plain Tales from the Hills

D. H. LAWRENCE
The Plumed Serpent
The Rainbow
Sons and Lovers
Women in Love

SHERIDAN LE FANU
In a Glass Darkly
Madam Crowl's Ghost & Other Stories

GASTON LEROUX
The Phantom of the Opera

JACK LONDON
Call of the Wild & White Fang

KATHERINE MANSFIELD
Bliss & Other Stories

GUY DE MAUPASSANT
The Best Short Stories

HERMAN MELVILLE
Billy Budd & Other Stories
Moby Dick
Typee

GEORGE MEREDITH
The Egoist

H. H. MUNRO
The Collected Stories of Saki

SHIKH NEFZAOUI
The Perfumed Garden
TRANSLATED BY SIR RICHARD BURTON

THOMAS LOVE PEACOCK
Headlong Hall & Nightmare Abbey

EDGAR ALLAN POE
Tales of Mystery and Imagination

FREDERICK ROLFE
Hadrian VII

SIR WALTER SCOTT
Ivanhoe
Rob Roy

WILLIAM SHAKESPEARE
All's Well that Ends Well
Antony and Cleopatra
As You Like It
The Comedy of Errors
Coriolanus
Hamlet
Henry IV Part 1
Henry IV Part 2
Henry V
Julius Caesar
King John
King Lear
Love's Labours Lost
Macbeth
Measure for Measure
The Merchant of Venice
The Merry Wives of Windsor
A Midsummer Night's Dream
Much Ado About Nothing
Othello
Pericles
Richard II
Richard III
Romeo and Juliet
The Taming of the Shrew
The Tempest
Titus Andronicus
Troilus and Cressida
Twelfth Night
Two Gentlemen of Verona
A Winter's Tale

MARY SHELLEY
Frankenstein
The Last Man

TOBIAS SMOLLETT
Humphry Clinker

LAURENCE STERNE
A Sentimental Journey
Tristram Shandy

ROBERT LOUIS STEVENSON
Dr Jekyll and Mr Hyde
The Master of Ballantrae & Weir of Hermiston
Travels with a Donkey & Other Writings

BRAM STOKER
Dracula

HARRIET BEECHER STOWE
Uncle Tom's Cabin

R. S. SURTEES
Mr Sponge's Sporting Tour

JONATHAN SWIFT
Gulliver's Travels

W. M. THACKERAY
Vanity Fair

LEO TOLSTOY
Anna Karenina
War and Peace

ANTHONY TROLLOPE
Barchester Towers
Can You Forgive Her?
Dr Thorne
The Eustace Diamonds
Framley Parsonage
The Last Chronicle of Barset
Phineas Finn
The Small House at Allington
The Warden
The Way We Live Now

IVAN SERGEYEVICH TURGENEV
Fathers and Sons

MARK TWAIN
Tom Sawyer & Huckleberry Finn

JULES VERNE
Around the World in Eighty Days & Five Weeks in a Balloon
Journey to the Centre of the Earth
Twenty Thousand Leagues Under the Sea

VIRGIL
The Aeneid

VOLTAIRE
Candide

LEW WALLACE
Ben Hur

ISAAC WALTON
The Compleat Angler

EDITH WHARTON
The Age of Innocence
Ethan Frome

GILBERT WHITE
The Natural History of Selborne

OSCAR WILDE
De Profundis, The Ballad of Reading Gaol, etc.
Lord Arthur Savile's Crime & Other Stories
The Picture of Dorian Gray
The Plays
IN TWO VOLUMES

VIRGINIA WOOLF
Mrs Dalloway
Orlando
To the Lighthouse
The Waves

P. C. WREN
Beau Geste

CHARLOTTE M. YONGE
The Heir of Redclyffe

TRANSLATED BY VRINDA NABAR & SHANTA TUMKUR
Bhagavadgita

EDITED BY CHRISTINE BAKER
The Book of Classic Horror Stories

SELECTED BY REX COLLINGS
Classic Victorian and Edwardian Ghost Stories

EDITED BY DAVID STUART DAVIES
Shadows of Sherlock Holmes
Tales of Unease
Selected Stories of the Nineteenth Century

Distribution

AUSTRALIA & PAPUA NEW GUINEA
Peribo Pty Ltd
58 Beaumont Road, Mount Kuring-Gai
NSW 2080, Australia
Tel: (02) 457 0011 Fax: (02) 457 0022

CZECH REPUBLIC
Bohemian Ventures s r. o.,
Delnicka 13, 170 00 Prague 7
Tel: 042 2 877837 Fax: 042 2 801498

FRANCE
Copernicus Diffusion
81 Rue des Entrepreneurs, Paris 75015
Tel: 01 53 95 38 00 Fax: 01 53 95 38 01

GERMANY & AUSTRIA
Taschenbuch-Vertrieb
Ingeborg Blank GmbH
Lager und Buro Rohrmooser Str 1
85256 Vierkirchen/Pasenbach
Tel: 08139-8130/8184 Fax: 08139-8140

GHANA, THE GAMBIA, LIBERIA,
CAMEROON & SIERRA LEONE
Readwide Bookshop Ltd
1st Floor, Kingsway Business
Kingsway Building, Adabraka
P O Box 0600, Osu – Accra, Ghana
Tel: 00233 21663347 Fax: 00233 21663725

GREAT BRITAIN & EIRE
Wordsworth Editions Ltd
Cumberland House, Crib Street
Ware, Hertfordshire SG12 9ET
Tel: 01920 465167 Fax: 01920 462267
E-mail: enquiries@wordsworth-editions.com

INDIA
Om Books International
4379/4B, Prakash House, Ansari Road
Darya Ganj, New Delhi – 110002
Tel: 3263363/3265303 Fax: 3278091
E-mail: sales@ombooks.com

INDONESIA
Sulcor
P.T.Sulcor Investindo
Plaza Pasifik Blok A3/63
JL. Raya bulevar Barat, Kelapa Gading,
Jakarta 14241, Indonesia
Tel: (62-21) 45844883 Fax: (62-21) 45844886
E-mail: sulcor@cbn.net.id

ISRAEL
Sole Agent —**Timmy Marketing Limited**
55 Rehov HaDekel, Lapid, Hevel Modi'in
Tel: 972-8-9765874 Fax: 972-8-9766552
e-mail: timmy@bezeqint.net

ITALY
Tarab Edizioni S R L
Via S. Zanobi No 37
50129 Firenze, Italy
Tel: 0039 055 490209
Fax: 0039 055 473515

NEW ZEALAND & FIJI
Allphy Book Distributors Ltd
4-6 Charles Street, Eden Terrace, Auckland,
Tel: (09) 3773096 Fax: (09) 3022770
MALAYSIA & BRUNEI
Vintrade SDN BHD
5 & 7 Lorong
Datuk Sulaiman 7
Taman Tun Dr Ismail
60000 Kuala Lumpur,
Malaysia
Tel: (603) 717 3333 Fax: (603) 719 2942

MALTA & GOZO
Agius & Agius Ltd
42A South Street, Valletta VLT 11
Tel: 234038 - 220347 Fax: 241175

PHILIPPINES
I J Sagun Enterprises
P O Box 4322 CPO Manila, 2 Topaz Road,
Greenheights Village, Taytay, Rizal
Tel: 631 80 61 TO 66

POLAND
Top Mark Centre
Urbanistow 1 M 51
02397 Warszawa, Poland
Tel: 004822 319439 Fax: 004822 6582676

SOUTH AFRICA
Chapter Book Agencies
Postnet Private bag X10016
Edenvale, 1610 Gauteng, South Africa
Tel: (++27) 11 425 5990
Fax: (++27) 11 425 5997

SLOVAK REPUBLIC
Slovak Ventures s r. o.,
Stefanikova 128, 949 01 Nitra
Tel/Fax: 042 87 525105/6/7

SPAIN
Ribera Libros, S.L.
Poligono Martiartu, Calle 1 - no 6
48480 Arrigorriaga, Vizcaya
Tel: 34 4 6713607 (Almacen)
34 4 4418787 (Libreria)
Fax: 34 4 6713608 (Almacen)
34 4 4418029 (Libreria)

UNITED STATES OF AMERICA
(Education only)
NTC/Contemporary
Publishing Company
4225 West Touhy Avenue
Lincolnwood (Chicago)
Illinois 60646-4622, USA
Tel: (847) 679 5500 Fax: (847) 679 2494

DIRECT MAIL
Bibliophile Books
5 Thomas Road, London E14 7BN,
Tel: 020 7515 9222 Fax: 020 7538 4115
E-mail: orders@bibliophilebooks.com
Order hotline 24 hours Tel: 020 7515 9555
Cash with order + £2.50 p&p (UK)